ANGEL IN RED

Recent Titles by Christopher Nicole from Severn House

The Jessica Jones series

THE FOLLOWERS
A FEARFUL THING

The Russian Sagas

THE SEEDS OF POWER
THE MASTERS
THE RED TIDE
THE RED GODS
THE SCARLET GENERATION
DEATH OF A TYRANT

The Arms of War Series

THE TRADE
SHADOWS IN THE SUN
GUNS IN THE DESERT
PRELUDE TO WAR

TO ALL ETERNITY
THE QUEST
BE NOT AFRAID
THE SEARCH
RANSOM ISLAND
POOR DARLING
THE PURSUIT
THE VOYAGE
DEMON
THE FALLS OF DEATH

The Secret Service Series

ANGEL FROM HELL
ANGEL IN RED

ANGEL IN RED

Christopher Nicole

This first world edition published in Great Britain 2006 by
SEVERN HOUSE PUBLISHERS LTD of
9–15 High Street, Sutton, Surrey SM1 1DF.
This first world edition published in the USA 2006 by
SEVERN HOUSE PUBLISHERS INC of
595 Madison Avenue, New York, N.Y. 10022.

British Library Cataloguing in Publication Data

Nicole, Christopher
Angel in red
1. World War, 1939-1945 - Secret Service - Germany - Fiction
2. Suspense fiction
I. Title
823.9'14 [F]

ISBN-13: 978-0-7278-6394-2
ISBN-10: 0-7278-6394-0

All Severn House titles are printed on acid-free paper.

Typeset by Palimpsest Book Production Ltd.,
Grangemouth, Stirlingshire, Scotland.
Printed and bound in Great Britain by
MPG Books Ltd., Bodmin, Cornwall.

'Oh, wherefore come ye forth in triumph from the north,
With your hands, and your feet, and your raiment all red?'

Lord Macaulay

Contents

Prologue

Visiting the Countess always induced in me mixed feelings of apprehension and anticipation. It was difficult not to be apprehensive of a woman who had rubbed shoulders with many of the most famous, and infamous, people of her time; who had cut her way through them and lived to tell the tale, while nearly all of them were dead. She had told me that her survival had been due largely to her speed of thought and decision, comparable perhaps to that of a great batsman at cricket, who has the ability to determine the length and direction of the ball, and thus the stroke to be played, a split second faster than ordinary mortals.

At the same time it was impossible not to anticipate being in the intimate presence of a woman known for her numerous love affairs who, when well into her eighties, retained sufficient evidence of her former beauty to quicken the blood. I had searched for this woman, or any trace of her, for some forty years. I had always believed that she was still alive, and at last I had found her and been granted an interview. That had been the most thrilling experience of my life. And now I had been invited back again!

The villa was several hundred feet up the mountain known as Montgo, overlooking the Jalon Valley on the Spanish Costa Blanca. The narrow road twisted its way up the hillside until one reached the villa's wrought-iron gates. A wire fence extended to either side, and indeed round the entire property. There was no evidence of any serious deterrent to intruders besides the locked gates, but as the Countess had illustrated to me on my previous visit, she was not only capable of protecting herself, but was also prepared to go out in a blaze of glory, taking as many of her surviving enemies with her as she could. She had always been prepared to do that. I got out of the car and rang the bell.

'Si?' asked the familiar voice of the Spanish maid.

I preferred to stick to English, which I knew she understood. 'It is Mr Nicole, Encarna.'

'Ah! Señor Nicole! The Countess is expecting you.'

The electrically controlled gates swung open and I drove up the hill to park behind the house. Encarna was waiting for me. She was a plumply pretty young woman. I had no idea if she knew anything of her mistress's background.

'The Countess is on the naya,' she said, and led me through the house to the glass double doors that led on to the veranda.

Anna Fehrbach sat in her favourite cane armchair looking down at the swimming pool below, one hand resting on the glass-topped table beside her. Even sitting her height was obvious. She remained slim – perhaps too slim for her age – but the swell of her loose shirt hinted that little had changed since the days when she had turned heads in every drawing room in Europe. Her bone structure was perfection, providing her face with the most flawless features, even if the suntanned flesh was perhaps a little thin. She had long since cut the magnificent straight golden hair I had admired in her early photographs, and now wore it just below her ears; it was quite white.

Her exposed earrings were tiny gold bars dangling from a gold setting, and she wore a single ring on the third finger of her right hand; the size of the ruby solitaire suggested that it could well pay for the entire villa. A solitary indication of her essentially innocent Catholic girlhood was the gold crucifix on a chain round her neck. I could not stop myself from looking to see if I could spot the automatic pistol she apparently always kept handy and could produce with such startling rapidity. But to me it was invisible.

'Mr Nicole. I have decided to call you Christopher, since you have returned to see me again.' Her voice, low but still resonant, retained just a hint of the Irish brogue she had inherited from her mother.

'After what you told me the last time, no human power could have kept me away,' I replied.

'Then you must call me Anna. Sit down. Encarna!'

Encarna hurried forward with the tray on which rested an

ice bucket containing an open bottle of Bollinger and two flutes. Anna now raised hers.

'Here is to . . . story-telling. So, now you know one of my secrets, or perhaps two. Have you told anyone what I said the last time?'

'I have it on my computer, ready for publication when you give your permission. I shall, of course, submit it to you first for your approval.'

'Thank you. And what do you think of Anna Fehrbach, Countess von Widerstand, the Honourable Mrs Ballantine Bordman? What a mouthful. And that was all before I was twenty!'

'As I said when last we met, Anna, the biggest regret of my life is that I wasn't around to meet you then.'

She gave one of her entrancing smiles. 'But then you would not be sitting here now. It is always better to be alive than dead.'

'Do you glory in the number of people you have killed? You have confessed to seven . . . ah . . .'

'Murders?' she asked gently. 'And those too were by the time I had celebrated my twentieth birthday. But only two were actually murders. Or, as my employers would have it, "executions". The other five were in self-defence. As were most of the others,' she added reminiscently.

'Were there very many others?'

Another smile. 'That is what you are here to find out, isn't it? But is that all you wish to know of me?'

'I wish to know everything about you. I know you were forced to do what you did. Will you tell me about your family, and about the hold Himmler and Heydrich had on you?'

Now the smile faded. 'It was a very sad period of my life. Where would you like me to begin?'

'After you escaped England, in May 1940, you returned to Germany as a double agent. Were you welcomed?'

'Oh, indeed, thanks to the British press trumpeting about the beautiful German spy who had escaped capture. My Nazi masters were very pleased with me.'

'And they allowed you to see your parents.'

'After a while. Heydrich decided to take a month to debrief me.' Her mouth twisted. 'You may take that literally if you wish.'

'That must have made it difficult for MI6 to contact you.'

'It did.'

'And then Russia,' I mused. 'Is it true that you are the only person ever to escape the Lubianka? How did you manage that?'

Anna Fehrbach smiled.

One

Memories

The Mercedes Tourer proceeded slowly through the trees. The road was hardly more than a track and very uneven. Tall pines clustered to either side and turned the bright June morning gloomy. Captain Wilhelm Evers glanced at the woman seated beside him. He was a slim young man, handsome in the black uniform of the SS and, unusually for an officer in that elite corps, he was nervous. When the woman returned his glance, he gulped anxiously.

He had been told that Anna Fehrbach was not yet twenty-one. Certainly her face, shaded by a huge picture hat with its blue ribbon fluttering in the faint breeze, suggested the most utter innocence. But, from what he had been told, her beauty alone would have affected any man. Her slightly aquiline features were flawlessly carved and enhanced by the shroud of her long, straight, pale-golden hair. She was several inches taller than himself, and the calf-length blue dress she was wearing indicated that her figure would almost certainly match her beautiful face.

She looked utterly calm, even relaxed, her blue eyes hidden behind her dark glasses.. But, according to Colonel Glauber, she was the most treasured agent of the SD – the *Sicherheitsdienst*, the most secret of the German secret services. And today he was to be her minder. He licked his lips. 'You do understand, Fraulein, that there are certain things you may not say?'

'I understand.' Her voice was low, soft, caressing.

'And I am to allow you only half an hour in there.'

'Half an hour. After two years. It is not very long.'

'The visit has been arranged at *your* request, Fraulein. Not theirs. It is for your reassurance. We have arrived.'

* * *

Before them stood a pair of large wooden gates. To each side an equally high barbed-wire fence extended out of sight. There could be no doubt that they were entering a prison. A guard-house stood immediately within the gates and from this two uniformed men now emerged.

'Herr Captain!' shouted one of the men. 'This is a restricted area.'

Evers took a folded sheet of stiff paper from his breast pocket. 'The order is signed by General Heydrich.' He passed it through the bars.

The sergeant read it and then saluted. 'Heil Hitler!' He signalled to the private, who opened the gates. Evers got back into the car and drove through. By this time the two soldiers had noticed his companion, and now three more men emerged from the hut to stare at the young woman. Perhaps, Anna thought, they are hoping I am a new inmate, with the promise of future unimaginable pleasures. She smiled at them, and the car drove on.

Within seconds the tall gates and barbed-wire fence were out of sight as they rounded a bend. Several rustic buildings with thatched roofs came into view. The setting was idyllic, save for the armed guards standing outside the largest of the buildings – and the two Alsatian dogs that now advanced, fur bristling and teeth bared.

An officer emerged from the building. 'Do not get out,' he called. 'I will have the dogs chained.'

Anna Fehrbach ignored him, released her door catch, and stepped down.

'My God, no!' Evers shouted.

The dogs emitted low growls and ran at her. Anna stood absolutely still and, taking off her glasses, stared at them. They halted within a few feet of her, returning her stare for a few seconds before sitting down, clearly uncertain as to what to do next.

'Holy shit!' the officer exclaimed, coming up beside her. 'They are trained to kill!'

'So am I,' Anna said, as softly as ever.

The officer looked at Evers. 'Fraulein Fehrbach is here by order of the SD,' Evers explained.

'To . . .' The officer now looked at Anna, and swallowed.

'To see my parents, Herr Major,' Anna said. 'And my sister.'

'Ah.' The major nodded. 'Of course. Please come inside, Fraulein.'

Anna walked past him to the open door. The two dogs padded along behind her. The three guards stood to attention, clearly petrified. Anna heard the major giving instructions and a moment later he joined her.

'In here, Fraulein,' he invited, opening an inner door.

'I am to see them alone,' Anna reminded him.

He looked at Evers who had followed them into the office. 'General Heydrich has agreed to this?'

Evers nodded. 'The Fraulein understands where her duty lies.'

The door was opened and Anna stepped into what seemed like a large games room. There were straight chairs arranged around the walls and a ping-pong table in the centre of the floor. Her practised eye immediately picked out wall fittings that might contain microphones or hidden cameras. The door behind her closed. She took off her hat and walked slowly across the room, her high heels clicking on the wood. She faced another door, which now opened to allow two women to enter the room.

'Annaliese?' cried the older of the pair, taking a couple of steps forward. 'Is it really you?'

Anna placed her hat and glasses on the table. 'Mama!'

They hugged each other tightly for a long time, and then Jane Fehrbach held her daughter at arms' length.

'How well you look, Anna.' She spoke English, her mother tongue, as she had always spoken English to her daughters.

'And you, Mama,' Anna replied in turn, although she had no doubt that at least one of the listening Germans would be able to understand English, and she knew that she could neither risk any confidences nor change her pre-determined plan.

Anna's reply was not as truthful as she would have liked. No one could have had any doubt that they were mother and daughter. Jane Fehrbach was in her early fifties. She was tall, with the same golden hair as her daughter, hers worn short and now streaked with grey, and the same chiselled features, but these were lined with stress and worry. Her figure was somewhat fuller, but she moved gracefully enough.

Many people had been astonished when in 1919 Jane

Haggerty, correspondent for a top English newspaper, after being sent on assignment to Vienna, had elected to remain there and marry a Viennese journalist. As far as Anna knew, it had been a genuine love match, resulting in her appearance a year later. She had been raised in a liberal background which had, inevitably, taught her to oppose Fascism and the dictators it spawned. Johann Fehrbach had been constantly in trouble with the Dollfuss government, but the real crisis had arisen when, following the dictator's assassination and the relatively relaxed rule of Schusnigg, Hitler had decided to quell further opposition by making Austria part of the Reich.

Anna now recalled the day, just over two years ago, when the Wehrmacht had triumphantly marched into Vienna. Johann and his entire family had been arrested. Anna had not known at the time why she had been separated from her parents and sister. She had been handed over to the SS because, with her beauty and intelligence, she was obviously too valuable to be merely brutalised and then thrown aside.

From the start it had been made clear that if she worked with and for her captors then her family would remain unharmed, albeit in confinement. Should she decide to defy them, she was left in no doubt that her parents would die in a concentration camp while she would be sent to a brothel. And so she had submitted to them, learning how to seduce men when commanded to do so – and to kill them when commanded to do so. Her quick thinking and sharp concentration, regardless of the possible consequences, had made her what she was today: the most valuable agent in the SD.

That she hated them and all they stood for – for their treatment of her as much as for what they had required her to do – was her secret. That she was fighting them in her own quiet way was shared with half a dozen men, but was an even more deadly secret. None of which could possibly be revealed even to her mother, even if she did not know that their conversation was being taped. And so now, jolting herself out of her reverie, she peered at the tormented face in front of her.

'You *are* all right, aren't you, Mama?'

'We are in a prison. But we have a cottage of our own, and your father is given certain writing tasks.' Jane's mouth twisted. 'It is simply that he must write what he is told to write, and that we are not allowed to leave this place.'

'But you are adequately fed? And you are not ill treated?'

'No.'

Anna turned to the girl beside her. Katherine was eighteen and was in many ways a younger version of her sister, but the slight coarseness of her features, and the thickness of her body, indicated that she would never match Anna for looks. Now she in turn came forward for an embrace.

'And Papa?' Anna asked.

Jane sighed, and sat down. 'He would not come. He believes what the guards tell us, that you are working for the Nazis.' She gazed at Anna. 'Will you reassure me so that I can re-assure him? He is very distressed.'

Anna returned her mother's gaze for some seconds. Then she drew a deep breath. 'I am doing what I have to do, Mama, for all of our sakes.'

Slowly a frown gathered between Jane's eyes. She looked Anna up and down, as if for the first time, taking in the obviously expensive frock, the silk stockings, the court shoes, and the many items of valuable jewellery. 'My God! Your father is right. You have become a German whore!'

Even before the interview had been arranged, Anna had realized this was the easiest, and safest, conclusion for her mother to draw, and so had dressed the part. 'As I said, Mama, I do what I have to do to survive. We all need to survive.'

'You unutterable wretch!' Jane stood up. 'I despise you.'

Would you rather be dead? Anna thought. But that was not something she could risk saying to the listening Germans. 'I am sorry, Mama. It will all come right one day, I promise.'

'Not for you,' Jane snapped. 'Not for any of us.' She went to the door, opened it and left the room.

The sisters looked at each other. 'Do you feel the same way?' Anna asked.

'It . . . it's all so confusing,' Katherine said. 'Major Luther tells me that if I cooperate I could leave this place. He says that I could become like you.' Her eyes were enormous.

'Would you like to become like me?' Anna asked.

'That dress, that ring . . . Would I have things like that to wear?'

'Perhaps.'

'And would I have to sleep with men?'

'Perhaps,' Anna repeated. 'But it can be a difficult life, and it would destroy Mama and Papa. It would be better for you to remain here for the time being.'

'But for how long?' Katherine almost wailed.

'I do not think it will be for very long,' Anna said. 'The war is virtually over. Then things will be different. Be patient and keep your health. Now you had better go.'

'Will I see you again?'

'I am sure of it. One day.'

'An uncooperative woman, your mother,' Captain Evers remarked as the car made its way back along the track to the highway. 'It makes one wonder why such a long journey was necessary for such a brief and unsatisfactory interview.'

'It was necessary to me,' Anna said quietly. 'Where are we going now?'

'To the airport. There is a plane waiting to take you back to Berlin.'

He was looking at her, she knew, but she continued to stare straight ahead. The visit had not lightened her mood, but had she really expected anything better? She knew she would be forgiven everything if her mother knew her true situation. But despite her optimistic words of farewell, she had to wonder if that would ever happen. For eighteen months she had been the Honourable Mrs Ballantine Bordman, to the satisfaction of both her husband and her German masters, thanks to Bordman's position as an under-secretary at the Foreign Office, and his gullible weakness for sharing his professional secrets with the wife he had adored. But she had fled England – and her husband – in the first week of May, when the Allies and Germany had been poised for battle. Both sides had been confident of victory; now, only five weeks later, the Allies were utterly defeated. So where did that leave her, and by extension, her parents? Her value to the Reich lay in her ability to bewitch men as much as to carry out her orders with ruthless efficiency. Were the war to end in an overwhelming German victory, where would her value then lie? There would then surely be no one to seduce and no one to assassinate. Heydrich would have no more use for her, and she knew him well enough to know that he would discard her like a piece of unwanted paper. Her family would undoubtedly follow. As for Clive Bartley, the man for whose love she had agreed to work for the English, while she felt that he personally would do everything he could to extricate her, he was in turn at the mercy of his superiors in MI6. Nor could she ever openly accept his help without destroying her parents. When last they had been together he had been full of confident promises, because soon the British Government would control events in Europe. But as it seemed Germany was not going to be defeated . . .

'On the other hand,' Evers ventured, interrupting her train of thought, 'I do not suppose there is any great urgency. Would you like to spend a night in Warsaw, Fraulein?' He hurried on, terrified by his own audacity. 'The city has been rather knocked about, but it is still a beautiful place. And there is at least one good hotel still standing.'

He waited, anxiously, until Anna at last turned her head. 'I can think of nothing I would like less, Herr Captain. So please take me to the airport and speak a little less.'

His flush deepened. 'You are a very arrogant woman, Fraulein. I have heard that you do not like men. I can provide a woman, if you wish.'

'Then do so, Herr Captain. For yourself. You are correctly informed. I do not like most men, but that is probably because I have met so few men worth liking.'

The door was opened by a secretary. 'Fraulein Fehrbach, Herr Colonel.'

'Anna!' Colonel Glauber rose from behind his desk and hurried forward.

Before he could reach her, Anna came to attention and saluted, arm out flung. 'Heil Hitler!'

'Ah. Heil Hitler. Come and sit down. You are satisfied?'

Anna sat before his desk and crossed her knees. 'I am satisfied, Herr Colonel, that my parents and my sister are alive and appear to be in good health.'

'Well then . . .' Glauber's manner was habitually genial; this went with his somewhat overweight figure, bulging against his uniform, and his round red features. Anna knew he was capable of paroxysms of violent rage, but he had seldom inflicted them on her, and she was in a mood to prick him a little.

'But they are depressed and unhappy.'

'Well, they opposed the Reich. They should be in a concentration camp. They *would* be in a concentration camp but for you, my dear girl. However, it will not be for much longer.'

'Can I really believe that, Herr Colonel?'

'You can. The war is over.'

Anna sat straight. 'Sir?'

'France surrendered yesterday.'

'My God!' If this was the news she had been anticipating, it was also the news she had most feared. 'And the British?'

'They are still making bellicose and absurd statements of defiance, or at least that lunatic Churchill is. But as we have destroyed more than half of their air force – and all of their army, to all intents and purposes – this can only be a temporary phase. The Fuehrer is about to make a speech pointing out their situation and calling upon them to accept a negotiated peace. He is the most reasonable of men, you know.'

Anna drew a deep breath. 'Then I am redundant, Herr Colonel.'

Glauber chuckled. 'As regards the British, you were redundant the moment you boarded that ship out of Southampton.' Anna felt a sudden, physical pain in her chest. 'But do you suppose a girl like you could ever be truly redundant? I remember the first time I saw you in Vienna two years ago. A seventeen-year-old schoolgirl sitting on a chair in the middle of that cell. What were you thinking of at that moment, Anna?'

'I was wondering how soon I would be raped or tortured or shot, Herr Colonel.'

'What terrible thoughts for a young girl to think. But do you know Hallbrun – you remember Hallbrun?'

'He arrested me, and my family.'

'Yes,' Glauber agreed. 'But did you know the lout actually offered you to me as a mistress?'

Anna's head jerked.

Glauber smiled. 'And I thought to myself, such beauty, such intelligence, such sheer charisma – in a seventeen-year-old girl! What will she be like when she is a woman? And you suppose you could be redundant? We may have defeated the Western Allies, but that does not mean that the task of Nazi Germany is completed. I told you two years ago what that task was, did I not?'

'To combat Soviet Russia,' she said hesitantly.

'And to *destroy* it,' Glauber insisted. 'I don't suppose you include Russian among your many accomplishments?'

'No, sir.'

'Next week you will begin a course. I wish you to be fluent in the language in one month. Can you do this?'

'If I am doing nothing else, Herr Colonel.'

'That will be your principal concern. However, I do not suppose you had a great many opportunities for training in London. And then there was that business of falling down the stairs. You spent several weeks in hospital, did you not?'

Anna kept her face immobile; she still felt the occasional twinge where Hannah Gehrig's bullet had slammed into her ribs. There was, in fact, still a blue mark on her flesh, which meant she had to be careful about who she let see her exposed body. Heydrich had certainly been curious but she had told him it was a birthmark. 'Yes, Herr Colonel.'

'And when last did you have to undertake executive action?' Glauber asked jovially. 'That unhappy woman, Mayers, was it not?'

How little you know, Anna thought. 'Am I required to execute a Russian, Herr Colonel?' Her voice could be like the cooing of a dove.

'One would hope not. But you never know. I also want you to spend a week with Doctor Cleiner. You will do this first.'

Oh, Lord, Anna thought. The week she had spent in that training camp had been the most horrendous of her life. 'I am perfectly fit, sir, and I have forgotten none of my skills.'

'No one can ever be too highly trained, Anna, not even you. But you do not like the idea of going back to the doctor? He was very fond of you.'

'I know. He will wish to strip me naked and paw me about.' And see the blue mark, she thought.

'The perks of being a doctor. I envy him. You will go to the training camp tomorrow. A car will pick you up at ten. After your spell at the camp, you will undertake concentrated lessons in Russian language, manners, mores and history. That is your programme for the next five weeks. Then you will be given your instructions.' He beamed at her. 'I want you to know – and always be sure – that I, and all of us in the SD, are proud of you. Proud to have you working with us. Now go home, have a good night's rest, and be prepared to start work tomorrow.'

Anna took a taxi to the apartment block situated in a street just off the Unter den Linden. Berlin sparkled in the summer sunshine. It was, in fact, one of the best summers in living memory, and the Berliners, always eager to enjoy sunshine, had been drinking beer at the pavement cafes. But this year, having achieved the most outstanding military success in their nation's history – the more euphoric for being so largely unexpected – there were nothing but smiles to be seen. Indeed, as the news of the French surrender had only recently been released, today there were cheers and dancing on the pavements, giving lie to the fact that there was a war on. But apparently the war was over. Anna was in limbo. From everything she had ever read or heard, Russia was not an attractive prospect. True, what she had been told was largely Nazi propaganda. But the British attitude, including that of Clive Bartley, had not been so very different. Oh, Clive! How she wanted to be in touch with him. But her orders, given her on the night she had fled England, had been to wait. He would get to her. But could she afford to wait, now that she was about to receive new orders from the SD?

When she had left England, she had been given a set of written instructions, to be memorised and then destroyed. They had been simple enough, but the essential words remained burning in her brain: Antoinette's Boutique. Antoinette's Boutique. Did she dare? She had been so occupied with Heydrich over the preceding month, and with the anticipation of seeing her family again after so long, but now . . .

She leaned forward and tapped on the glass. The driver slid it aside. 'Do you know of a dress shop called Antoinette's Boutique?'

'Oh yes, Fraulein. It has quite a reputation, amongst the . . .' He looked in the rear-view mirror and judged that Anna had to be an aristocrat. 'It is very expensive. Run by an Italian gentleman.' Now his tone was disparaging.

'Is it far?'

'Three blocks, Fraulein.'

'Take me there.'

He chose his moment and turned across the stream of traffic without further comment.

As the taxi stopped, Anna realized that his remarks had been entirely appropriate: the only word for Antoinette's Boutique was extravagant, from the richly dressed mannequins in the window to the garishly large letters over the glass swing doors.

'Wait for me,' she said before crossing the pavement and entering the large, airy display room.

A well-dressed woman hurried forward. 'Fraulein? May we be of assistance?'

The emporium might be Italian-owned, but this woman was definitely German.

'I am the Countess von Widerstand,' Anna announced. 'I am seeking an outfit for a party, and I was told by my friend Belinda that this would be a good place to look.'

The woman showed no response to either name. 'I am sure we will have what you require, Countess. If we do not, we shall create it for you.'

Anna had been surveying the visible stock. 'You have your own dressmakers?'

'Certainly, Countess.'

'What I am looking for,' Anna said, having ascertained just what was *not* present, 'is a calf-length, pale-blue sheath, with a scarlet hem and belt.'

The woman clearly had to make an effort not to wrinkle her nose at such appalling taste.

'With scarlet shoes,' Anna added.

'Yes, Countess. I am sure we will be able to manage that. Unfortunately, two of our seamstresses are off sick, so it may take a week or two.'

'That will be acceptable. The party is in a fortnight. But I must have a fitting by the end of next week. I shall be out of town until then, anyway.'

'Of course, Countess. There should be . . . ah . . .'

Anna opened her handbag and sorted out a hundred marks. 'Will that be sufficient?'

'Of course, Countess. If you will just step inside so that we may take your measurements. And we will require a telephone number.'

Anna took a card from her bag and followed her into one of the fitting rooms.

Later, Anna entered the lobby of her apartment building.

'Good afternoon, Fraulein,' said the concierge. Like most men he was always pleased to see his most glamorous tenant. 'Did you have a good trip?'

'Yes, thank you.' Anna smiled at him and went across to the elevator. Her apartment was on the sixth floor. Every time she entered this apartment she had a sense of disbelief. Her parents' home in Vienna had been comfortably middle class; there had been no money for elegance or excessive luxury. When she had been swept into the clutches of the Gestapo training school she had assumed that even such comforts as she had known would be lost forever. Now she lived in this absolutely sumptuous place, with its soft carpets, deep-upholstered furniture, valuable prints on the walls and a bedroom and bathroom of the very latest and most expensive fashion.

Birgit emerged from the kitchen. Although older than Anna, she was a young, vivacious woman, dark-haired and slender, excitedly enthusiastic at working for who she supposed to be a member of the aristocracy. Anna liked her at least partly because, unlike her previous maids, she was not a superior member of the SD, sent to monitor her every movement and every thought. Did the fact that she had been allowed to find her own maid since returning from England mean that her employers now accepted her as one of them? She had to doubt that.

'Oh, Countess, I did not expect you back until tomorrow.'

'There was nothing to stay for,' Anna said. 'But I am going away again tomorrow for a week.' She looked at her watch; it was just coming up to five. 'So I would like the evening to start now. I will have a glass of champagne, dinner at seven, and then I will go to bed.'

'Yes, Countess.'

Anna undressed and peered at herself in the full-length mirror. There was no ignoring the blue mark some four inches below her right breast. She could remember that afternoon as if it were yesterday, even if at the time she had rapidly fainted from shock and loss of blood. But in those few minutes she had broken Hannah Gehrig's neck, and in doing so all but destroyed her cover. She would have been lost but for Clive. MI6 had acted with a speed and precision not even equalled by the SD disposal squads. The British had let it become known that Frau Gehrig had been uncovered as a German spy, but had managed to flee the country before she could be arrested. The SD were still mystified by her disappearance – still, in fact, expected her to turn up some day, perhaps soon. But that was no longer her concern, except that her story might now have to be revised, and utterly convincingly.

Anna lay in bed that night and stared at the darkened ceiling. In the early days of her career as a spy and seductress – and executioner when required – her then minder, Elsa Mayers, had put her to bed every night with a sleeping pill. Since her marriage to the Honourable Ballantine Bordman she had abandoned the sedatives. Life had not really been any less traumatic, but the knowledge that Clive Bartley was in the shadows behind her had been totally reassuring. Of course she'd also had to endure the attentions of Bally. To him she had been like a toy; he had been unable to keep his hands off her. His constant pawing, his constant desire for sex, had done nothing to better her low opinion of men in general.

She knew there were some people who believed her to be a closet lesbian. Others, mainly her employers, thought that she was simply devoid of any emotion, erotic or otherwise. This pleased them. They liked the way she went about her duties with cold and calculated ruthlessness. They had no idea of the mental anguish she suffered every time a job was completed – the screaming, mind-consuming desire to get out, the utter despair at the knowledge that she could never do that without sacrificing her parents and sister.

She had, not for the first time, an urgent desire to go to church. She had not confessed for more than two years, since the day before the German invasion of Austria in 1938. But how could she confess now? *Forgive me, Father, for I have sinned. Tell me of these sins, my child. I have killed men and women, over and over and over again. Forgive me, Father, for I have sinned. How have you sinned, my child? I have betrayed people who thought they were my friends, I have betrayed my country, I have betrayed my religion, I have betrayed myself. Forgive me, Father, for I have sinned. How have you sinned, my child? I have lived a lie, I am living a lie, I will go on living a lie for the foreseeable future.*

Only Clive stood between her and perdition. He was the rock to which she must cling, surrounded as she was by a maelstrom of political, emotional and distressing situations. Did she love him? If she did not, it was because she knew she could not allow herself to love anyone while living in these circumstances. Besides, she could not be sure if he – for all his obvious desire for her when they were alone together – loved her, or wished to do so. She was a prize, who had dropped unexpectedly into his arms, and into the arms of his superiors, a lethal weapon thrust into the heart of Nazi Germany to be used, twisted, as they thought best for the Allied cause. She wondered when the first twist would be made and what it would entail.

And now she was required to return to the clutches of the man who, of all the dislikeable men with whom she had been forced to associate over the past two years, was the most loathsome.

'May I say, Countess, that it is a great privilege to meet you and to know that we shall be working together.'

Another nervous young captain was now sitting beside her in the back of a car. His name was Gutemann, and like Evers he kept casting her surreptitious glances, half admiring and half anticipatory, although today she wore a somewhat severe dress. She was on her way to work. He was some years younger than Evers was, and not as good looking. He seemed anxious at once to please her and to avoid being overwhelmed by her.

'I am sure that it will be a privilege for me as well, Herr Captain,' she agreed.

They were out of Berlin and following the road she remembered so well.

'Then, as we are to be, shall I say, intimate, shall we not be more friendly? My name is Gunther.'

'Gunther Gutemann,' Anna mused. 'I do not think your parents liked you, Herr Captain. I also do not think that our intimacy should extend beyond, shall *I* say, office hours. We have not yet reached the office, have we?'

He flushed, with a mixture of embarrassment and anger. 'They told me that you were an unnatural creature,' he remarked. 'So beautiful, but so cold.'

‘Well,’ she said, ‘would you not agree that I am engaged in an unnatural pursuit?’

He digested this for some moments, then ventured, ‘And if you were instructed by our superiors to have sex with me, would you still be as cold as ice?’

‘By no means. I am a professional. I would make you the happiest man in the world.’

‘Then . . .’

‘Equally,’ she added, ‘if immediately afterwards I was instructed by our superiors to kill you, I would do so without hesitation. But it would be as quick and painless as possible.’ At last she looked at him and smiled. ‘As I said, I am a professional.’

He moved across the seat, as far away from her as possible.

The camp seemed exactly as she had left it two years before; it could have been yesterday. She was not even sure that it wasn’t the same sergeant at the desk of the female barracks.

‘Fraulein Fehrbach, it is good to see you again. Doctor Cleiner wished to see you the moment you arrived.’

‘I shall just place my valise in my quarters,’ Anna said.

‘I will do that for you, Fraulein.’

‘Thank you. Are there any other ladies in residence?’

‘There are two, Fraulein. They will be overwhelmed to meet you. But Doctor Cleiner comes first.’

‘Of course.’ Anna went to the outer door, where Gutemann had waited for her. He fell into step beside her as she walked along the gravelled path towards the doctor’s offices.

‘I see you know your way about this place,’ he suggested.

‘Why, yes. Did you not know that?’

Once again he fell silent. But she had a fairly good idea of what he was thinking – how much he would like to have this arrogant bitch in his power for even a few minutes. She found that amusing. She was in the mood, as she had been since that terrible meeting with her mother, to indulge her dislike for the entire human race.

Their walk took them past the parade grounds, filled with sweating, panting recruits being introduced to the weapons they would use in combat. All were under the imperious eyes of their drill sergeants but none could resist the temptation to look at the beautiful young woman in their midst.

Anna reached the command house, went up the short flight of steps, and tapped on the door.

'Enter.'

She opened the door into an outer office where a hard-faced woman sat behind a desk and a typewriter. 'Ah!' the woman said, 'you will be Fehrbach. The doctor is waiting for you.'

Anna crossed the room to the inner door. She knew Gutemann was immediately behind her. She stopped and turned. 'I am sure the doctor will wish to see me alone.'

He gazed at her uncertainly, but she opened the door, stepped through, and closed it behind her before he could react.

'Anna!' Doctor Cleiner hurried round his huge desk and took her in his arms for a bear hug. He was overweight, bald, wore horn-rimmed glasses on a pudgy nose, and sweated. It was several seconds before he released her, his fingers running up and down her spine as if he was looking for a dislocated disc. Then he stepped back, now holding her arms, allowing his hands to slide down her short sleeves and then her forearms to hold her hands. 'It is so good to see you again. And looking so well. Do you know, I would swear that you have not changed a bit in the last two years.'

'Neither have you, Herr Doctor.'

'Ha ha! And I am to make sure that you are as fit, mentally and physically, as when last we met. That is good.'

Cleiner returned behind his desk, sat down and picked up the sheet of paper lying there. 'You are to undergo the complete course, as if you were a novice. But this time I am sure you will find it very easy. And I am sure there are some aspects in which you no longer need instruction. You have enjoyed the experience of being a married woman, have you not?'

There was no other chair in the room, so Anna remained standing before the desk. 'As you say, Herr Doctor.'

'Did you enjoy it, Anna?'

'I was doing a job of work, Herr Doctor.' She wanted to change the subject. 'I understand you have two trainees in residence.'

'Ah, yes. They came in this morning. They are very excited at the prospect of working with you.'

'So, it seems, is Captain Gutemann. Is he necessary?'

'Well, you know he is. But you also know he is not allowed to touch you – or any of the others – unless so commanded by me.' He looked at his watch. 'It is an hour until lunch. There is time for me to give you a physical examination. Undress.'

'I do assure you, Herr Doctor, that I am as fit as, or perhaps even fitter than, I was two years ago.'

'And even more modest? I cannot believe that, Anna, as you are a married woman.'

'I *was* a married woman, Herr Doctor.'

'You still are, my dear girl. Your husband may be suing for divorce, but these things take time. You are likely to remain married for another year.' He chuckled. 'Unless, of course, you were to fall into the hands of the British, when they would terminate matters by hanging you. You are still an English citizen, are you not?'

'You say the most encouraging things, Herr Doctor.'

'But it is not our intention to let that happen. Now come along, Anna. I wish to look at you. I do enjoy looking at you.'

Anna sighed. She had formed a plan as to how to deal with the coming crisis; it was a matter of whether or not he would believe her – and how soon he would divulge what she told him to her superiors. She took off her bandanna, shook out her hair and removed her dress.

'Lay it on that table,' he suggested.

This she did, carefully spreading the material so as to avoid crushing it. Then, with her back to him, she took off her cami-knickers.

'Everything,' he said.

Anna sighed again, although she had known he would require this. She stepped out of her shoes, released her suspender belt and, bending over, rolled down her stockings. She heard him come across the room, and a moment later his hands closed on her buttocks. Instantly she straightened. 'Are you examining me, Herr Doctor?' she asked innocently.

'Why, yes. Turn around.' Anna did so and he looked her up and down. 'As you say, perfection. There can be no more delightful vision than a beautiful naked woman. Even if he discovered you were a spy, that man Bordman must have been out of his mind to divorce you. But do you know, Anna, after what I have read in your file, I almost expected to find a pistol strapped somewhere.'

'I do not need a pistol, Herr Doctor. You taught me not to need a pistol.'

'I did indeed. Although you may remember that I also taught you how to use one. Tell me, how many people have you killed since you shot that fellow here in this camp?'

'At your command, Herr Doctor,' Anna reminded him. 'As for how many others, is it not in my file?'

'Two are listed. Elsa Mayers and Gottfried Friedemann. Both are recorded as enemies of the Reich; one was killed with a bullet, the other with a single blow to the carotid. I taught you that blow, Anna. I am proud of that.'

'May I get dressed, Herr Doctor?'

'Oh, no. I have not yet examined you.'

She waited while he peered at her, keeping her breathing under control. The moment of truth was approaching. Needless to say, he found it necessary to finger her breasts before slowly moving down her ribcage and suddenly bending forward. 'What is this?'

'A bruise, Herr Doctor.'

Cleiner looked more closely, taking off his spectacles as his nose almost touched her flesh. 'I never thought you would lie to me, Anna. I never thought you would dare. You may have become a valuable member of the SD, but in this camp I retain the power of life and death over any one of my pupils.'

'Herr Doctor . . .'

Cleiner touched the blue mark with his finger. 'This was a bullet wound.' He straightened. 'There is no record in your file of you having been shot. Why is this?'

Anna licked her lips. 'It was a private matter, Herr Doctor.'

'How can being shot be a private matter?'

'Because it had nothing to do with my mission. My husband shot me.'

'As I suggested, he must have been mad. Why did he shoot you?'

'He thought he had found out that I was having an affair.'

'I see. When did this happen?'

'In August last year.'

Cleiner sat down at his desk to look at her file, replacing his spectacles. 'It says here that in August last year you fell down a flight of stairs and broke several ribs. You were in hospital for over a month.'

'That was the story given to the press, Herr Doctor. Bordman was an important man. We were prominent in London society. If it had come out that he had shot me, the scandal would have been tremendous.'

'I see. So, tell me, had you had an affair?'

'Certainly not.'

'Because you basically do not like men. Or sex.'

'That is correct, Herr Doctor.'

'That must have been very frustrating for him. Had I been your husband, I would probably have shot you without the excuse of adultery. Tell me why this incident was never reported to your superiors?'

'As I said, sir, it had nothing to do with my assignment. I did not report it because it would have unnecessarily complicated things.'

'But you went on living with Bordman for another nine months.'

'When he realized his mistake, he was utterly contrite. Besides, I still had my work to do. Being the Honourable Mrs Ballantine Bordman was the very core of my work as an agent. The information I was able to gather in that position was invaluable.'

'And he had nothing to do with the eventual betrayal which caused you to flee England?'

'No,' Anna insisted.

'Well, you understand that I must enter this in your file. It is possible that General Heydrich may wish you to explain it further. Now get yourself dressed and join your fellow pupils.'

Gutemann was waiting for her outside. 'I trust all went well, Fraulein?'

'Why, yes, Herr Captain. Did you suppose it would not? I can find my own way back to the barracks.'

She stepped past him and walked along the path. She carried her bandanna in her hand and let her hair float behind her. Her heart was pounding. Cleiner had been simple because, like so many of her adversaries, he suffered from the handicap of being more than a little in love with her, but she did not feel that Reinhard Heydrich was capable of being in love with anyone – save perhaps Reinhard Heydrich. But having adopted that cover story she now had to stick with it.

The problem was that the date of her 'accident' was recorded as 25 August 1939. This was the same date as Hannah Gehrig was recorded as having disappeared, just as it was also the day before news had been released of the Nazi–Soviet Pact, which had created the favourable conditions for this war to be started in the first place. She knew that Gehrig had been ordered to flee England, as *she* had not taken out British citizenship, and would almost certainly have been arrested when the news broke. That she had successfully escaped had always been accepted. That her charge and accomplice had fallen down a flight of stairs, while no doubt in an agitated state of mind, had also been accepted. But that that accomplice should have been shot by her husband on the same day that Gehrig had disappeared was perhaps moving into the realms of extreme coincidence.

At the barracks she smiled at the sergeant, went along the corridor and opened the door to the dormitory, which had not changed in two years. There was the same row of neatly made beds along one wall, the same lockers beside each bed, the same shower and toilet facilities at the far end, and the same high, barred windows.

There were also two young women sitting on adjacent beds, engaged in animated conversation, both of whom sprang to their feet as she entered. She smiled at them in turn. 'I am Anna,' she said.

'Anna Fehrbach!' gasped one of the girls; they were both younger than she.

Anna frowned. 'You know my name?'

'We were told it at training school,' the other girl said. 'Do well, they told us, and you could be another Anna Fehrbach.'

Anna looked from one to the other. 'Well then, I think you should introduce yourselves.'

'I am Lena Postitz,' said the first girl. She was a short, dark-haired young woman, with small, somewhat tight features.

'Lena,' Anna said, and turned to the other girl. She was taller, also dark-haired, but with much stronger, handsome features. There was something vaguely familiar about her. 'And you?'

'I am Marlene Gehrig,' the girl replied.

Two

The Boutique

For a moment Anna could not think.

'My mother told me of you,' Marlene Gehrig said. 'She was very proud of you. She often told me that you were the best agent she knew.' She smiled. 'I think she wanted me to be like you. And then she became your Controller.' The features puckered. 'But I have not seen her for nearly a year. Can you tell me where she is now?'

Anna had been making some very rapid calculations. As this girl's name was also Gehrig, Hannah had clearly not married the father. That she had spared the time to get pregnant by any man was a surprise in itself. Having been forced to live with her for several months, Anna had had no doubt that she was a lesbian, and not of the closet variety. As she knew that the SD recruited at least as many volunteers as those they conscripted, the fact that Hannah should have offered her daughter to the services of the Reich was not the least improbable: she had been the most dedicated of Nazis.

'I'm afraid I have no idea where your mother is now,' she said with her usual convincing innocence. Save, she thought, that I am pretty sure she is somewhere in hell.

'But . . . was she not in England with you?'

'Of course. But she received orders to leave England the day it became certain there was going to be a war. This she did. Is she not here in Germany?'

'She never came home,' Marlene said sombrely. 'Nothing has been heard since she left England. What can have happened to her?'

'Oh, my dear girl,' Anna said. 'She was a most capable officer in the SD. I am sure she must be somewhere.'

To her great relief a bugle call rang through the camp. 'Lunch! It is not something you wish to miss.'

As Anna remembered, while they ate in the communal mess hall, the three girls were segregated from the men, and while they attracted interested glances, no one dared speak to them. The large room was entirely overlooked by several NCOs, and all conversation was necessarily in hushed whispers.

'What is going to happen to us?' Lena asked.

'You will begin by learning about men,' Anna told her. 'How to seduce them, and how to allow yourself to be seduced by them.'

'Gosh!' Lena exclaimed. 'Do they . . . well . . .?'

'Oh, yes. You have to touch them, and they have to touch you.'

'But . . .'

Anna smiled at her. 'You will have to make them very happy.' She gazed at the girl. 'You know what I mean?'

'Oh, good Lord! I have never, well, seen a man. Well, I have, of course, but never, well . . .'

'Had sex with one? Neither had I, when I first came here,' Anna assured her. 'You will get used to it. You may even enjoy it. It helps if you do.'

'And you enjoyed it?' Marlene spoke for the first time.

Anna met her gaze, sensing hostility that could not be more than instinctive. 'No. I did not enjoy it.'

'But you passed out with honour?'

'Honour? There is no such thing in our profession.'

There was little further conversation over the meal. Lena was lost in a private world; whether it was a world of dreams or nightmares Anna could not be sure. Marlene stared at her between mouthfuls. Anna would have given a great deal to know what was going on inside that brain – what things her mother might have told her.

Well, she thought, we are only going to spend this week together, and then hopefully we may never meet again. And as only she and a handful of British MI6 agents knew the truth of what had happened, any dislike Marlene felt for her must be instinctive, and would remain so. Then she frowned. There were five others in the know: Belinda Hoskin, Clive

Bartley's fashion editor mistress; Bowen, Ballantine's valet; and Ballantine himself, who had walked in on the scene, plus the police inspector and his sergeant who had been summoned. Clive had assured her they had all been sworn to secrecy, and she had to believe that. But the very presence of this rather intense young woman made her uneasy.

She was relieved when the bell went to end the meal.

Anna was even more relieved to find that she was not required to attend the initial classes. She had always found it distasteful to fondle a man and even more to be fondled by him, unless his name happened to be Clive Bartley. Gutemann instead took her off to the gymnasium for a severe workout.

She was also required to attend the hospital for an X-ray of her ribs. Cleiner joined her here. 'It was a long time ago,' she reminded him. 'I am perfectly all right.'

'We must be absolutely sure,' he insisted, and without warning drove his fingers into the scar. Anna gave a squeal and sat up. 'There. You see?'

Anna glared at him. 'I would have reacted the same, Herr Doctor, had you done that on my other side.'

'But I have never seen you react like that. I thought for a moment you were going to hit me.'

'If I had hit you, Herr Doctor, the course would be over. Unless you have a replacement waiting.'

He chuckled. 'You are a treasure. One day you and I must get together.'

Over my dead body, Anna thought. But she would prefer it to be his.

Needless to say, the other girls were in a twitter in the barracks that evening. Or at least Lena was. Marlene continued to say little and stare at Anna.

'She worships you,' Lena whispered when Marlene went to the bathroom.

'I do not believe that,' Anna said, brushing her hair. 'She is just finding it a bit overwhelming. That is not surprising. I know I was completely overwhelmed on my first day here. Don't tell me you are not affected?'

'Oooh! He was so big. Are all men that big?'

'Thankfully, no,' Anna said, remembering her husband.

‘What does it feel like to have a man inside you?’

‘It can feel very nice, if it’s the right man. Unfortunately, we do not select our partners. Have you never had a boyfriend?’

‘Well, I was in the Youth, you know. We had some fun when camping in the woods.’

‘But you’re still a virgin. Or you wouldn’t be here.’

‘Well, yes. But isn’t it strange, that they want only virgins, when they are training us to seduce men?’

Anna shrugged. ‘It is part of their determination to be in total control. You will lose your virginity when it is considered best for the Reich. Not for you.’

‘You speak so badly of the Reich. Yet you work for them. They say there is no more dedicated female agent in the service.’

Anna’s mouth twisted. ‘I do what has to be done. That is the only way to survive.’

By this time Marlene had returned and had overheard the end of the conversation. ‘My mother told me you do not like sex at all, either with men or with women. She said that you first came to her attention when you nearly killed a girl who made advances to you at the training school.’

‘I broke her arm in two places,’ Anna said quietly, wondering just what else Hannah had confided to her daughter. That was something she certainly needed to find out.

‘What do we have to do tomorrow?’ Lena asked, anxious to defuse the incipient conflict.

‘Tomorrow,’ Anna said, ‘you will be taught how to hurt a man.’

For this lesson Anna was required to remain with the girls. Cleiner beamed at them. ‘Yesterday was amusing, was it not?’

Lena and Marlene stared at him, uncertain what response he was seeking.

‘What did you enjoy more – playing with him or having him play with you? Come along now.’

Lena licked her lips. ‘Playing with him, Herr Doctor.’

‘You would like to have one of your very own, eh? Perhaps even if it was not attached to a body. Ha! And you, Marlene?’

‘I did not like him at all, Herr Doctor.’ She drew a sharp breath, as if wondering if she had said the wrong thing, and cast a quick glance at Anna, seeking support.

Cleiner gave one of his chuckles. 'Oh, Anna would agree with you. But she has the ability, which you must learn, to make any man feel she desires him more than anything else in the world. This is the secret of her success. As it must become your secret as well. Do you not agree, Anna?'

'As you say, Herr Doctor.'

'But at the same time you must always remember that the man you are told to deal with will be an enemy of the Reich, and therefore an enemy of you. And thus there will be occasions when you must be, shall I say, *rid* of him, perhaps immediately. This means that while learning to love the man, you must also learn how to destroy him, when required.' He smiled at Anna. 'Anna is an expert at this.'

Anna's feelings of discontent were growing all the time. She did not like being depicted as a monster when it was men like Cleiner who had created that monster, just as it was a man like Clive Bartley who had reminded her of both her humanity and her femininity. But the act had to be maintained, whatever her own simmering anger at her position, until exactly the right moment. So she merely smiled.

Cleiner rang the bell on his desk, and immediately the two guards opened the door to admit a man who had been standing outside, also with a guard. A push had him stumbling into the room, trying to maintain his balance; his hands were cuffed behind his back. He seemed just like the man Anna had been given to work on two years before – of medium height but burly, unshaven, and shabbily dressed in shirt and pants and rope-soled shoes. Having got his balance back he blinked at the doctor and then at the three young women, who were as usual wearing only singlets and shorts.

'This is Boris,' Cleiner announced. 'He is a Polish Jew and speaks no German. So he will not interrupt our conversation, eh? Ha ha.'

The girls looked petrified; Anna presumed that the man they had been introduced to the previous day had been young and reasonably attractive. This man was not.

The guard pushed Boris forward to stand in the open space beside the desks at which the girls were seated.

'Now,' Cleiner said. 'This fellow is at least twice the weight of any of you, and I can assure you he is very strong. But there is no man who can withstand an educated and determined attack. The question is to get in your delivery before he gets in his. Now, Lena, supposing you had to completely disable this man, what would you do?'

Lena again licked her lips and glanced at Anna, who remained impassive as usual. 'Well,' she said, 'I suppose I should kick him there.' She pointed at Boris's crotch.

'Anna?' Cleiner asked.

'That would hurt him but not disable him,' Anna said quietly. 'Assuming he did not catch your leg before you could reach him. It would certainly make him very angry.'

'Exactly. When you hit it must be to disable, if only for a few seconds. You go for the pressure points, from which emanate the vital functions of the human body.' He went up to Boris and began touching him with his wand. 'Here. And here. And here. A blow to any one of these places will at least momentarily paralyse his ability to function. Of course, in most cases – certainly with a man like Boris – he will recover quickly enough, so the destruction must be completed during the short time he is incapacitated. Then, for example, if he is down, you may stamp on his neck, or on his genitals. But you must be absolutely certain that he is unable to use his hands, as if he manages to catch hold of you it could turn out very badly. So come along, Marlene. We will start with you.' He stood behind Boris. 'These are the kidneys. A properly delivered blow here will cause the most severe agony. Hit him. Remember that it must be with all the strength you can command.'

Marlene also looked at Anna for a moment, then got up and stepped behind the man and swung her arm. Anna knew that the girl would already have learned the rudiments of unarmed combat and the correct way to deliver a blow, but she did not seem to have any great effect upon Boris. Clearly he was hurt. He grunted and staggered but did not fall, while he looked from one to the other of the people around him with aggrieved eyes.

'No, no!' Cleiner said. 'That was no good at all. You must hit with your full strength. You must get every ounce of your weight into the blow.'

Marlene was massaging her arm and breathing heavily, while Boris, having somewhat recovered, looked around himself in angry bewilderment.

'Anna,' Cleiner said, 'show them how it should be done.'

Anna sighed, but she had known it would come to this. She

stood up and took a couple of deep breaths. When something had to be done, it had to be done to the exclusion of everything else. Every thought, every emotion, every hope, every fear, every memory, and any pity had to be entirely excluded. She stepped forward behind Boris and in the same movement swung her arm, delivering all her weight into the edge of her palm. Boris uttered a shriek, fell to his knees, and then over on to his side, moaning and writhing.

'Gosh!' Lena gasped.

Marlene stared at the stricken man.

Cleiner smiled. 'There, you see? I do not expect you to be as good as Anna right away, but you must become so. Get him up,' he told the guards.

It took two of them to set Boris on his feet and he remained unsteady while panting, but the pain was wearing off.

'He may well have suffered permanent damage,' Cleiner pointed out. 'Anna has killed with that right hand. Not with a kidney punch, of course. But there are certain places where a properly delivered blow can be fatal. Illustrate, Anna.'

Anna turned her head sharply.

'Oh,' Cleiner said, 'he is of no more use to us now. Show these young ladies how you disposed of Fraulein Mayers, Anna. I know that General Heydrich was most impressed.'

Anna realized that this was the opportunity she had been waiting for. It was a very high-risk strategy, but if it reduced the later risk of condemnation by Heydrich it would be worth it. 'I did not kill Fraulein Mayers in cold blood, Herr Doctor,' she said in a low voice.

'Come now, Anna. Your blood is always cold, is it not?' He turned to the girls. 'The blow is delivered here.' He touched where Boris's neck joined his shoulder. 'Under there is the carotid artery. It conveys the blood to the brain, and as I am sure you know, when the brain is robbed of blood it cannot function. For how long it cannot function depends on how long the artery is closed, but a blow of sufficient strength will stop the blood flow long enough for death to follow. Anna!'

Anna looked at him, then at the two girls, then acted with tremendous speed, hitting Boris at the indicated place, but pulling the blow at the last moment. It was still completely effective. Boris went down without a sound.

'There, you see? It is really very simple. Take him out.'

The two soldiers stooped to grasp Boris's body, and one looked up. 'You wish him brought back, Herr Doctor?'

'What are we supposed to do with a corpse?' Cleiner enquired.

'But he is alive, Herr Doctor.'

'What?' Cleiner stooped and took Boris's pulse. Then he looked up at Anna. 'What happened?'

'You wished a demonstration of what could be accomplished with that blow, Herr Doctor. I have given that demonstration. You know I could have killed him had I wished, but I did not see the necessity for it.'

Cleiner slowly stood up. His face was red. 'Come into my office,' he snapped.

Anna glanced at the two girls, who were even more petrified than before. Then she followed the doctor from the room.

Anna sat on her bed, for the moment alone. She could not prevent herself being frightened; she remembered too well that session in the SD's torture chamber. It was not so much the caning or even the electrodes being thrust into her body that got to her, but the utter humiliation of being at the mercy of so many unpleasant human beings, one of whom had been Hannah Gehrig. She wondered if Hannah had told her daughter about that incident, and had a sudden disturbing thought: was Marlene Hannah's only daughter?

How simple it would have been to avoid this new crisis by simply killing that man. Could his death, which was certain to happen in this camp anyway, be of the least importance beside the other seven people she had on her conscience? Even her dear Clive Bartley would probably have advised her to do as Cleiner commanded and avoid the confrontation. But I am not a monster, she told herself savagely. So now I must face the consequences. And what she had done had been a deliberate stratagem; it was too late to change her plans now.

The door opened and the two girls came in. 'Anna!' Lena cried. 'What has happened to you?'

'Nothing has happened to me.' *Yet*, she thought.

'But when you did not come back . . .'

'The doctor seemed to be very angry,' Marlene suggested.

'Oh, he is always very angry about something or other. Listen, I do not know what is going to happen to me, or whether I will be here for the rest of the course. But if you wish to survive, do not fail him. He will ask you to shoot at a living target. Do so, and kill, and live.'

Despite everything, she knew she had an ace up her sleeve. When she had returned from England, a master spy fleeing one step ahead of the British police, General Heydrich had welcomed her with open arms. Although he had lost a beautifully placed agent, the publicity given to her escape – and to her activities in England, a ploy devised by Clive to save her reputation with the Nazis – had been such valuable propaganda as to be sufficient compensation. It was as if he had seen her as a woman, rather than a *thing*, for the first time.

She had in fact been afraid that he was going to appropriate her entirely as his mistress. But they had only slept together a few times. To Reinhard Heydrich sex, even with a beautiful and compliant woman, was secondary to his desire for power, for the manipulation of other human beings.

Clive was not aware of that relationship as it had only occurred after her return from England, and he had not been in contact with her since. She thought it possible that he would have liked the situation to continue. Heydrich was as potent a source of secret information as anyone in Germany, save perhaps Hitler himself. But she had been happy not to be called upon over the past few weeks. Of all the men she had ever met she hated her commanding officer the most. But now she had to carry out the seduction of her life.

'General Heydrich is waiting for you,' the secretary said.

She did not get up from her desk to open the doors. Anna drew a deep breath, opened the doors herself and stood to attention, staring at the huge painting of Adolf Hitler that hung on the wall behind the desk. 'Heil Hitler!'

She was wearing one of her most flattering, form-hugging dresses, in pale green, with sufficient décolletage to be interesting, high heels, and her principal jewellery, but had left her head bare, her silky hair a golden mat below her shoulders. This was make or break.

'Heil Hitler.' Reinhard Heydrich was a tall, slim, very blond man, his pale colouring exaggerated by his black uniform. His features should have been handsome, but were spoiled by an utter coldness that particularly seemed to affect his mouth and eyes. And she had slept with this man, who held her life in the palm of his hand. 'Close the doors.' His voice was as lacking in warmth as his gaze, although she did not doubt that he liked what he now saw.

Anna closed the doors and advanced to his desk. To her relief there was no one else in the large room, and very little furniture; Heydrich liked to be surrounded by space. There was however a chair before the desk. She sat down and waited, as usual in these circumstances, forcing herself to breathe normally, and to look at his face and nowhere else.

Heydrich flicked the papers on his desk. 'Sometimes I despair of you, Anna. This report is quite damning. You know the rules under which you – we – must operate: instant and unquestioning obedience to any command given by a superior officer.'

'Instant and unreasoning obedience to any command given me in the name of the Reich or in the furtherance of the Nazi Party, Herr General. Surely not to gratify the desires of a lecher.'

'Did he . . . interfere with you?'

'In the pretended process of giving me a physical examination, sir. When I first attended the camp two years ago there was no physical examination. It was accepted that if I had been selected for special training as an agent for the SD, I was by definition both physically and mentally fit. On this occasion, after I think I can say two years of some success in the field, the first thing he did was command me to strip, so that he could look at me. He was quite open about this.'

She paused, not having been able to control her breathing as she would have liked. Heydrich studied her. 'I agree that was uncalled for, although you must admit, Anna, you are a temptation to any man. That is why we employ you. And it appears that this uncalled-for examination turned up something of interest. Why did you tell me the mark was a birthmark instead of reporting this incident with your husband?'

Anna had known this was coming. 'I was too embarrassed, sir. And when Bordman shot me, Herr General, I fainted from loss of blood. I was in an intensive-care ward for several days, and then, as you know, had to remain in hospital some weeks longer. I had no means of communicating with any of our people until Celestina came to see me. By then the police and the government, in their determination to avoid a scandal which would involve Lord Bordman's son and heir, had put out the story of my having fallen down the stairs. It seemed pointless to tell the truth at that stage, especially as it might have jeopardized my mission. I am sorry, but it was a decision I had to take on my own.'

'And you did not feel you could tell Celestina? She was your superior officer.'

'I am sorry, Herr General. I could not bring myself entirely to trust her when first we met.'

'I take your point. Poor Celestina. She died for the Reich.'

'I know,' Anna said sadly. *She died when I put two bullets into her chest.*

'But there is also the matter of your public disobedience of the doctor's orders.'

'Again I am sorry, Herr General. I believe you know that if you commanded me to kill someone, anyone, for the protection of the Reich, I would do so without hesitation. But I think that for me to start killing people for the amusement of others would have a derogatory influence upon both my ability and my powers of decision. Killing can never be a sport, Herr General.'

Again Heydrich considered her for several minutes. 'Your intellectual powers are considerable. I think, when your value as a field agent has ended, we should train you as a departmental lawyer. You would probably become a judge. But hopefully that is still some distance in the future. Very good, Anna. No more will be said of this. You know that on Monday you are to commence a crash course in Russian. I do not expect even you to become fluent in a month. But you must be able to understand what is being said around you.'

'I think I can manage that, Herr General. Am I being sent to Russia?'

'You will become Personal Assistant to Herr Meissenbach, who is currently Chief Secretary to the Governor General of Czechoslovakia, but who will shortly be taking up a new post as Chief Secretary at the Moscow Embassy. You will accompany him and I have no doubt you will rapidly become an important part of the social scene.' He gave a brief smile. 'I am informed that there *is* a social scene, even in Moscow, amongst the commissars and the diplomatic corps at any rate.'

'And you think they will divulge important information to a member of the German Embassy?'

'Probably not. But you have a target.' He opened a drawer, took out a photograph and held it out.

Anna studied it. The man was in his forties, she estimated. As it was head and shoulders only, she could not deduce his height, but he was clearly well built. His features were heavy but by no means ugly, and he had lively eyes. His thick black hair was brushed straight back from his high forehead. He wore what appeared to be a military tunic, but with no trace of insignia or medal ribbons.

'What do you think of him?' Heydrich asked.

'He looks quite pleasant.'

'Let us hope he is. You are to become his mistress.'

Anna raised her head sharply. 'Sir?'

'I think he will prove a far superior lover to Bordman. He has a great reputation for virility.'

Oh Lord, Anna thought. 'And he is an important man?'

'Very. His name is Ewfim Chalyapov, and he is one of Marshal Stalin's closest associates. A sort of trouble-shooter. As such he has access to the innermost workings of Stalin's mind. Your business will be to gain access to *his* mind, and what he knows.'

'But are the Russians not our friends, Herr General?'

'I never thought of you as naïve, Anna. The Russians are above all our enemies. We needed their alliance, or at least their acceptance of our wish for peace between our two nations, to give us a free hand in the west. Now that we have won the war, we must look east. The Bear cannot have expected us to win so quickly and so completely. He now finds himself facing a Europe that is united under the Swastika. He will undoubtedly be disturbed by this development. We need to know *how* disturbed, and if he has any plans for doing anything about it.'

Anna could not resist the temptation. 'Is England now a part of this united Europe?'

'England is no longer of any importance. It will either have been invaded and forced to surrender or have made peace by the end of this year.'

'And you think that this man Chalyapov will go for me?'

Heydrich smiled. 'My dear Anna, you are too modest. We have done our homework on Herr Chalyapov. He is unmarried, but goes for women rather than men. He changes his mistress roughly once a year. He likes them young, well built, intelligent, and blonde. Do you think he will not regard you as a gift from the gods? He also likes them to be able to match his virility, and I at least can vouch for that. In fact, I would like to test you again for myself. We will go down to my country house in Bavaria for this weekend. Does that please you?'

Shit, Anna thought; she had hoped for a couple of days at home just in case Antoinette's Boutique wished to get in touch with her. 'That would please me very much, Herr General. There is just one point: under what name will I be going to Moscow? Surely the Russians have heard of the infamous Mrs Bordman, the German spy?'

'They may have heard of you in that capacity, Anna. They may even have obtained a photograph of Mrs Bordman. But I doubt it will be a very good one. In any event you are going as the Countess von Widerstand. They may be Bolsheviks and claim to be classless, but they remain fascinated by titles.'

'And you think this man will pick me up and then cast me down again. Within a year?'

'Do I detect a touch of feminine pride? I have no doubt that he will "pick you up", as you put it. How you handle that is up to you, but perhaps you could be a little hard to get, in the beginning. Above all be patient. Be at your vibrant best when in his company, but he must make the first move. There must be no risk of his suspecting that you are anything more than an innocent, if perhaps amoral, young woman. As to whether he will throw you out after a year or so, I would say that also will be up to you. But if by then you have milked him for all the information you can, would that not be the perfect solution? Then you would return to Berlin in a huff and no one would be any the wiser. I will have additional instructions for you before you leave. For the time being concentrate on your Russian. My car will pick you up tomorrow afternoon at five.'

'I look forward to it, Herr General. May I ask a question?'

'Certainly.'

'How much does Herr Meissenbach know of me?'

'Good point. Obviously, in view of the publicity we have given to your escape from England, he knows that you have been a spy, and may still be. But he knows nothing of your' – he smiled – 'special skills or accomplishments. To him you will be Anna, Countess von Widerstand, a very lovely and compliant young woman, who works for the SD. It would be better if you did nothing to enlighten him as to your secrets. Unless, of course' – he smiled again – 'it should become a matter of life and death.'

'But will he know I am going to Moscow to seduce this man Chalyapov? I mean, I have to have some reason for being there at all.'

'Herr Meissenbach is to know nothing of your mission. He will be told only that he has to find some employment for you during office hours, but that he is not to interfere with or restrict your social activities.'

'But if I am officially in his employ, isn't it possible he may disapprove of my taking up with a Russian commissar? What happens if he attempts to prevent this?'

'You will remind him that your social life is no concern of his.'

'And if he wishes to dismiss me? Or at least report me to the Ambassador?'

'The Ambassador can do nothing without the approval of the SD. And he will be told to keep his hands off. Does that satisfy you?'

'If it satisfies you, Herr General, it satisfies me. I look forward to tomorrow afternoon.'

'What do you think of the Gehrig girl?' Heydrich asked, running his fingers up and down Anna's spine.

She had actually nodded off, enjoying the warm sunlight on her naked body. In a life as filled with tension as hers, she had had to cultivate the ability to empty her mind and relax whenever possible, and this was certainly the most delightfully relaxing of places, at least in the summer, with the distant snow caps of the Alps providing such a scenic background. But it had been less easy to relax than usual, not only because being with Heydrich was a stressful business, but because she had so much on her mind.

It was now coming up to two months since she had fled England, and there had not been a word from Clive; there had been no message waiting for her from the Boutique. She kept telling herself it was pointless to expect it so soon, but if she was being sent off to Moscow, MI6 simply had to be informed immediately.

And now, just as she had managed to drift away, this damned man had brought her back into her problems with a bump. 'I did not know you knew of her,' she said.

'Didn't you? I thought Hannah was a close friend of yours. I know she was forced to punish you for that breach of discipline last year, but she was only doing her duty.'

'I understand that, Herr General. And I do not hold it against her.' One should never hold grudges against people when one has broken their necks.

'And you were very close when you served together in London, were you not? She never mentioned her family to you?'

'No, sir. She was always very conscious of her superior rank.'

'Well, answer my question about the girl.'

'She seemed very enthusiastic,' Anna ventured. 'And she certainly knew a lot about me.'

'You resent this?'

Anna rolled over and allowed him to have a go at her breasts and stomach; there was no harm in causing his mind to wander. 'I did not resent it, Herr General. But it is an uneasy position to be in, meeting someone who knows so much about you, while you never knew she existed.'

'That is a good point. She is a problem.'

'Sir? She did not fail the course?'

Heydrich sat up. 'As you say, she was very enthusiastic, very eager. But she was just not up to it. Do you know, she emptied three magazines against her target in the final lesson, and did not succeed in killing him?'

Anna sat up in turn, memory flooding back to two years before, when the helpless condemned prisoner had been forced to run across the firing range so that they could prove their proficiency with the pistol. Her fellow pupil, Karen, had been unable to shoot him, for which lapse she had been condemned to an SS brothel. That Anna had obeyed her orders with deadly proficiency had earned her the position she now held. But Marlene . . . 'She has not been degraded?'

'Cleiner wished to do so, certainly. But the fact is that the girl really tried. She hit the target several times, but could not do so fatally. And being Hannah Gehrig's daughter . . . Well, he referred the matter to me.'

'And what was your decision, Herr General?'

'I have not yet made a decision. It is difficult, you see. Once a girl has been accepted for the training camp and has been subject to our training methods, she cannot be returned to what might be called a normal civilian life. Women do talk to each other and seem to have a compulsion to share their experiences and seek a sympathetic ear. But as I say, to condemn Hannah's daughter to a military brothel, or worse, is really not something I wish to contemplate.'

Anna was surprised. She had no idea he possessed that much humanity. 'I would not like to see her degraded either, Herr General, but I cannot offer an answer to the problem.'

'You can provide the answer, Anna.'

Anna turned her head.

'You are going to Moscow as PA to Herr Meissenbach, which is an important and senior position. No one could question your possessing a PA of your own.'

Anna gulped.

'That way she would be employed within the SD, understanding the secrecy that is required, and you would be able both to guide her and teach her, and at the same time assess her. If she failed you, you would inform me and her position would be terminated. While under your guidance it is entirely probable she may turn out to be a valuable servant of the Reich. Just like yourself. I think that would be an ideal solution to our problem. Don't you?'

'Yes, Herr General. Has she received complete training?'

'What do you mean?'

'After I had completed my initial training, Herr General, you may remember that I spent a month under the tutelage of Frau Mayers, being schooled not only in the Party philosophy, but also in how to behave and dress in the highest circles, and how to hold my liquor. Only when Frau Mayers was satisfied did I attend Doctor Cleiner's course.'

'Ah. Marlene Gehrig needs no schooling in the Party philosophy. She is, after all, Hannah's daughter. But she has not been educated in the social graces. You will attend to that. It may amuse you.'

I am sure it will, Anna thought. 'And will she speak Russian?'

'She will attend your course with you. You will be friends.'

Anna reflected that having disobeyed so many orders given

her by her German superiors, one more was unlikely to make much difference.

What a foul-up, Anna thought as she got into a taxi at the station.

She really had no time for Marlene Gehrig, but she *had* killed the girl's mother. So did that mean she owed the girl anything? She might like to feel that she was not a monster, but she was entirely alone in an ocean filled with sharks, not one of whom would hesitate for a moment to take a bite out of her if they felt it necessary.

The temptation to stop at the boutique and see if there was anything for her was overwhelming. She needed a shoulder to cry on. But again she reminded herself that she had been instructed to wait for them to contact her. So she let the taxi drive by.

'Oh, Countess!' Birgit's greeting was as enthusiastic as ever. 'Did you have a pleasant weekend?'

'I was sharing a bed,' Anna told her, and left her to make what she could of the reply.

She went into the bedroom and began undressing. Then she discovered that Birgit was hovering in the doorway. 'Herr Toler called. He wished to know if you would be joining the class tomorrow?'

'And you told him yes, I hope.'

'Yes, Countess. And the secretary of a man called Herr Meissenbach called. She made him sound terribly grand.'

'I suppose he is terribly grand,' Anna agreed as she began running a bath.

'She said that Herr Meissenbach wished to take you out to dinner.'

So soon? Anna thought. And she had not been ordered to seduce *him*.

'I told her I could not agree a date until you returned, and she said she would call back.'

'Excellent.' Anna added bath foam and sank into the suds. 'I must try to be out then, too. Anything else?'

'Yes, Countess. The Antoinette's Boutique telephoned. They said the gown you ordered is ready for a fitting, and wished you to come in at your convenience.'

Bath water scattered as Anna leapt from the tub.

Three

Incident in Prague

Anna telephoned the boutique, but it was closed. She had had to wait until nine the next morning. Toler's Russian class began at nine, but he would have to wait too.

'Countess von Widerstand,' the woman said. 'When would suit you?'

'As soon as possible. I look forward to seeing the dress.'

'Ah, yes. Would eleven o'clock be satisfactory?'

'Eleven o'clock. Yes. That would be quite convenient.' She replaced the receiver and immediately telephoned the SS school to inform the tutor that something important had cropped up and she would not be able to attend class until after lunch. He sounded somewhat disgruntled, but had to accept the decision of so important an agent.

'Will you be in for lunch, Countess?' Birgit asked.

'Probably not.' Anna picked up her handbag, went to the door, and the telephone jangled. 'I'll take it,' she said as Birgit hurried into the hall. She was surprised at how anxious she was; if this was the boutique calling back . . . 'Yes?'

'Would I be speaking with the Countess von Widerstand?' the man asked.

Anna drew a deep breath. 'This is she.'

'Countess! I am so pleased to make your acquaintance, even at a distance. My name is Heinz Meissenbach. Perhaps you have heard of me?'

Released breath rushed through Anna's nostrils. 'Of course, Herr Meissenbach. I am told we are to work together. I am looking forward to that. Are you calling from Prague?'

Meissenbach also seemed to be taking deep breaths. 'No, no. I am in Berlin for only a few days, and I also am looking forward to our . . . working relationship. I think it is necessary for us to get to know each other, if we are to adventure together.'

'I understood you – we – would not be going to Moscow until next month, Herr Meissenbach?'

'That is so, my dear lady. But it is essential that when we do go to Moscow, we are totally au fait with each other. I suggest we begin by having dinner tonight.'

'Tonight? Ah . . .' That was the very last thing she wanted.

'It is a convenient date for me,' Meissenbach said. 'My wife is joining me tomorrow.'

'Your wife,' Anna said thoughtfully. The situation was growing more fraught by the second. If in addition to seducing Chalyapov she was going to have to fight off the advances of this lout, she suspected it was going to be a rather busy year ahead. But she had to continue acting her role as an SD agent who, at least until the crunch, was totally obedient to her superiors. 'In that case, Herr Meissenbach, I shall be delighted.'

'Then I shall pick you up at seven.'

Anna thought that if the boutique had indeed prepared that absurd dress for her, she might well wear it.

'Ah, Countess, how nice to see you,' the woman said. Her tone was far warmer than on the occasion of their first meeting. 'Signor Bartoli is waiting for you.'

Anna followed her through a door at the rear of the showroom, and down a corridor into a surprisingly large room that contained several dummies and a variety of clothes and uncut cloth scattered about various trestle tables. There were also three sewing-machine tables, but currently no seamstresses. The only occupant was a small, dapper man, with a long nose and even longer hair. He was in his shirtsleeves, and appropriately had a tape measure draped around his neck. He looked Anna up and down appreciatively: she was wearing her best, with a picture hat.

'Countess von Widerstand! How nice to meet you.' His German was very heavily accented.

'My pleasure, Signor Bartoli. You have something for me?'

'Indeed. That will be all, thank you, Edda.'

The woman hesitated, as if reluctant to leave Anna alone with him. Then she left, closing the door.

Bartoli held up the blue dress with the red trim. 'One would almost suppose, Countess, that you are trying to fly some sort of flag.' His voice had dropped several octaves.

'I wanted to be quite sure I was brought to your attention, Signor.'

'You should not have come here at all, Anna. You do not mind if I call you Anna, I hope?'

'So what do I call you?' Anna asked.

'I think sir would be appropriate. I am your Controller in Germany.'

Anna sat down and crossed her knees; this war was growing longer by the minute. 'I do not even call my London Controller "sir".'

Bartoli regarded her for some moments. 'I was told you were a spirited young lady. You may call me Luigi.'

'Luigi,' Anna repeated without enthusiasm. 'So I am to place my life in your hands.'

'Is not mine in yours, Anna? Now come along. We cannot be here for too long. Undress.'

Anna gave him an old-fashioned look. If this was becoming the initial advance of every man with whom she came professionally into contact, it was also becoming rather tiresome.

Bartoli understood her expression. 'It is necessary, my dear girl, for me to be fitting you and measuring you should anyone walk in. It would be quite inappropriate for me to lock the door.'

Anna sighed, but she knew he was right. She removed her hat, got up and took off her dress.

'I think the petticoat as well, if you don't mind.'

Anna removed this garment also and instinctively stepped out of her shoes.

'No no. Keep the shoes. The dress must hang absolutely correctly.'

Anna replaced the shoes.

'You are exquisite, Fraulein. Has anyone ever told you that?'

'Everyone I meet,' Anna said.

'And it is Fraulein?'

'Here in Germany. It is Frau in England. You said we should not waste time.'

'Then will you stand here.' He indicated the position immediately in front of him, and took the tape measure from round his neck. 'Now, I am going to take your measurements again, just to be certain, you understand.' He stepped closer to her and began arranging the tape round the bodice of her cami-knickers, taking great care to place it exactly over the nipples. 'What is on your mind that makes you so impatient?'

'I have been here for eight weeks and have not been contacted. Have you instructions for me?'

He released the tape reluctantly and made a note on the pad on his desk. 'London has been waiting for you to settle down and to be given a position commensurate with your talents.' He chuckled. 'And your measurements.' He draped the tape round her waist. 'Are you so anxious to get back to work? As far as I have been able to ascertain, you have been enjoying yourself.'

'You mean you have been keeping me under surveillance?'

'We are in business together, Anna . . . Your hips are perfection.' He released her to write the figures on his pad. 'And your legs. Are they perfection too?'

'It is for you to tell me.'

'But I am just getting to know you.'

'Before you do that, I need a confirming name,' Anna said.

'Ah, yes. Should you not have asked for that immediately?'

'I take my time, Luigi. So?'

'I was told Belinda would register.'

'Thank you. It does.'

'Tell me, Anna, if I had not had a name for you, or the name had not registered, what would you have done?'

'I would have broken your neck, Luigi.' Anna continued to speak as softly as ever. 'Then I would have opened the door and screamed that you were trying to rape me.'

'And you think the police would believe you?'

'I have nothing to do with the police. My German employers accept that I am inclined to react violently when insulted, and they would never let anything happen to me.'

'But I could betray you.'

'My dear Luigi, you would be dead.'

'Ah.' Luigi put down the tape measure.

'Now listen. I am about to take up a position as Personal Assistant to the First Secretary at the German Embassy in Moscow. I have been told this posting may be for a year. I have also been told I am to see what I can learn about current Russian attitudes towards the Reich, in view of the recent dramatic changes in the political situation. You should inform London of this immediately. If they have any instructions for me to follow in Russia, I have to receive them within the next three weeks. As they also have an Embassy in Moscow, it should be possible for them to contact me once I get there but it will have to be handled with the utmost discretion.'

Bartoli had been staring at her while she spoke. 'You speak so calmly. You act so calmly. Does nothing ever frighten or upset you?'

If you only knew, Anna thought. 'No, Signor Bartoli. I am made of ice. Were you not told?' She put on her slip and then her dress. 'I do not think I will have a fitting now. Complete the dress as it is, and then call me back. Remember, it must be within three weeks. Ciao.'

Having decided against being outrageous, Anna wore her favourite pale blue sheath evening gown, and was very glad to have done so: Meissenbach turned out to be far better than she had dared hope. He was taller than her, which was a pleasant change. His features, if rounded, were by no means soft, and his eyes were incisive. His hair was black with grey wings and he had a strong body. To top it all, his manner was an intriguing mixture of charm and hesitancy. She supposed this was a result of his diplomatic training. But she sensed, from his occasional directness, that there could be a layer of steel beneath.

'Countess!' He bent over her hand. 'I am enchanted. They told me you were an attractive woman, but that was clearly an understatement.'

'Thank you, Herr Meissenbach.'

'My car is waiting.'

He made no effort to touch her, even when assisting her into her cape, and although they sat beside each other in the back of the chauffeur-driven car, he scrupulously left a space between them. She felt herself warming to him, which had not been her intention.

The restaurant was up-market. She had been here before with Heydrich, and Meissenbach was clearly impressed when the maitre d' greeted her obsequiously.

'So,' he said as they sipped their aperitifs after ordering, 'the Countess von Widerstand. Would you care to explain that to me, Fraulein?'

'You would have to ask General Himmler about that,' Anna

said. Heydrich had told her to admit nothing of her background that was not already public knowledge.

'But you do have a real name?'

'Anna.'

'That is delightful. If I had been asked to choose a name for you I would have selected Anna. And I gather you have been living an exciting life?'

'It has been interesting. What should I call you, Herr Meissenbach?'

'When we are in public, it should be sir or Herr Meissenbach. When we are in private I should like you to call me Heinz.'

Anna nibbled her lobster salad. 'Are we going to be in private, sir?'

'We are in private now.'

Anna looked around the crowded dining room.

Meissenbach smiled. 'I should have said when we are off duty. Now, tell me why they are sending you to Moscow.'

'To be your PA, Heinz.'

He regarded her for several moments while they finished their first course and the meat was served. Then he raised his glass. 'I will drink to that. Do you have, shall I say, a man? A protector? Any young woman in this day and age needs a protector. Especially if she is as handsome as you.'

'You are absolutely right,' Anna agreed.

'Ah! I think we are going to have a very good relationship.'

'I sincerely hope so,' Anna said. 'I should tell you now that I do have a protector. His name is Reinhard Heydrich. Perhaps you know him?'

Meissenbach spilt some wine.

Anna sat up in bed to drink her coffee. 'This is not very strong.' She had not really noticed the previous morning, having had a slight head; Meissenbach had plied her with wine, but after her snub, he had not attempted to follow it up.

'We are nearly out, Countess,' Birgit protested.

'And you have not ordered more?'

'We are only allowed one kilogram a month, Countess. It has been rationed.'

'Good Lord! Well, no doubt they will have ample supplies of coffee in Moscow.'

'I am so excited, Countess.'

'So am I. Oh, what can that be?'

Birgit hurried from the bedroom to open the front door in response to the bell. Anna could not distinctly hear what was being said, but a few minutes later the maid returned carrying a bouquet of twelve red roses. 'Ooh, Countess! Aren't these lovely?'

Anna took the card. *I must see you again. Expect me at noon. Heinz.*

Anna looked at Birgit, who flushed; she had clearly read the note before bringing in the flowers. 'Put these in water and make sure the vase is conspicuous in the drawing room. You may have to entertain the gentleman for a little while before I get home.' Her morning session with the Russian tutor did not end until twelve.

She soaked in her bath and considered the situation. She was surprised. If he had been going to follow up the evening she would have supposed he would have done it the day after. Now Meissenbach seemed to have recovered his nerve, but he had given no indication that this might happen when he had brought her home. He had, in fact, been in a great hurry to get away. He had not even kissed her hand.

But now he was coming on very strong. She actually thought he might be very congenial company. Obviously he wanted to get her into bed. It was a question of whether it was better to antagonize him now, or to go along with him and risk a much greater antagonism when she 'fell in love' with the Russian. But if she went along with him now, he might have exhausted his passion before the Russian business came to a head. But she still needed to be careful, at least until she discovered how Heydrich might view the situation.

Yet she hurried home from her lesson with pleasant anticipation, and there he was, sitting in an armchair drinking schnapps. He stood up, and this time kissed her hand. 'You have a most attentive maid.'

'I am sorry I am late.'

'You are taking Russian lessons. I know this.'

'It is rather boring.'

'But necessary. I understand. May I give you lunch?'

'I thought perhaps we would lunch here. Birgit is also a very good cook.'

'And afterwards?'

'We could talk, if you wished.'

'Talk?'

Anna gave a wry smile. 'There is not much else we can do at this moment. I am in a woman's situation.'

'Oh. Ah. But you would still like me to stay for lunch?'

'It does not affect my appetite, Heinz, or my appetite for entertaining attractive men.'

'You are delightful. Anna, I would like you to visit me in Prague. Will you do that? When this unfortunate situation has ended.' He gazed at her.

'Are you sure this is wise?' Anna asked.

Meissenbach flushed. 'I will confess something to you. I was so taken with you when we dined that I took the liberty of discussing the matter with General Heydrich yesterday. He assured me that while he is very fond of you, and regards himself as your protector, he lays no claim to your private life, except in so far as it might need that protection. He is sure I will take good care of you.'

The bastard, Anna thought, *he doesn't just regard me as a thing, he regards me as a whore.* But she was not going to be a total pushover. 'I am sure that greatly relieves you.'

'And you?'

Anna got up and refilled their glasses. 'If I come to Prague, will I have the pleasure of meeting Frau Meissenbach?'

'The weekend after next – which, incidentally, will be my last in Prague – she will be visiting her mother in Hanover.'

'Does she spend any time at all at home with you?'

Meissenbach smiled. 'We have an understanding.'

'But she is coming to Moscow with us?'

'Oh, indeed. And she will enjoy meeting you, I know, at the appropriate moment. There is nothing for you to be concerned about. So . . .'

'I think lunch is ready,' Anna said.

'I have a message from Anna,' Clive Bartley announced, standing in the office doorway.

Billy Baxter raised his head somewhat suspiciously, but then he was inclined to do everything suspiciously. The two men could not have offered a stronger contrast. Clive Bartley, if by no means handsome, was over six feet tall and built to match; his rather lank black hair tended to droop across features which were of the hatchet variety but could be relieved by his ready smile. He looked as if he was close to smiling now. Baxter, with his somewhat diminutive body, usually hunched over the papers he was reading, his thinning pale brown hair, his tobacco-stained tweed jacket and loosely knotted tie, suggested a down at heel retired academic. He could look gloomy even on a bright July morning, but this, Clive suspected, might be because of the news, which was not getting any better, even if, this far, the War had had very little effect on London's way of life.

Despite their character differences, each man knew the other's worth. For all his appearance, Billy Baxter had possibly the most acute brain in MI6. This, and his willingness to accept the most difficult tasks, led to his having those tasks dumped on his desk with great regularity. Clive knew that he was not actually as cold-blooded as he sometimes appeared. He genuinely worried about the agents he had scattered all over Nazi-occupied Europe, genuinely grieved when one of them was picked up by the Gestapo to suffer a horrendous death. But that did not stop him immediately seeking a replacement.

Baxter, for his part, knew that Clive, for all his slightly raffish appearance and debonair attitude, was one of the most dedicated and, when necessary, deadly agents he possessed. But he also knew that Clive had gone overboard about the glamorous German spy he had managed to turn. Baxter was still not entirely convinced that Anna Fehrbach was to be trusted. Now he snorted. 'Are you saying she is bending the rules again?'

'She has sent it through the channel we gave her.'

'That channel was only to be used in response to a communication from us. I am not aware that we have sent any such communication.'

'Yes,' Clive said. 'And in my opinion that was a mistake. We have left this important agent in limbo for eight weeks. I don't blame her in the least for wondering what is going on.'

'Do we know what she has been doing in that time? What job she has been given which could be of value to us? The name of this game, as you well know, Clive, is patience. When she is posted somewhere important we will call on her for information. Until then—'

'She has been posted, Billy. That is why she needed to be in touch. She is going to Moscow as Personal Assistant to the Chief Secretary at the German Embassy.'

'Shit! Then we have lost her.'

'I don't think she would have hurried to give us that information if she wanted to be lost. Think of this, Billy. She is just about the most highly trained and dangerous operative the SD possess. I know we took a risk in sending her back, but she insisted on taking that risk for the sake of her family. And it would appear that her story has been totally accepted. That being so, would the SD send such a woman to Moscow just to be a PA?'

Baxter began to fill his pipe, a sure sign that he was thinking. 'She did not say why she was going?'

'Yes. She is to learn all she can about Russia's feelings towards Germany in view of the hegemony the Reich appears to have established over Europe.'

'That seems straightforward enough.'

'Billy, if we had Anna here in London under our sole jurisdiction, would we send her to Russia to tell us the Soviets feelings towards us? There has to be another reason. Perhaps she has not yet received specific instructions. But there has to be a reason, and it certainly isn't her proficiency as a typist.'

Baxter was busily dropping tobacco on his jacket and his desk. 'Who do we have in Moscow?'

'Commander Sprague. He is officially a naval attaché.'

'A good man?'

'Very. But Anna will not know him, or recognize him.'

Baxter struck a match and puffed. 'Can't he use the Belinda code?'

'I still think it would be risky. We should never forget Anna's little ways.'

Baxter leaned back in his chair. 'Are you saying . . .?'

'I am saying that if Anna got the impression she was at risk of exposure or betrayal, we would have to find a new naval attaché.'

'And you have actually slept with this creature.'

'As I have told you before, Billy, don't knock it if you have never known it.'

'What about Operation Tomorrow?'

'Done and dusted.'

'It's your baby.'

'Not any more. You know what the Czechs are like. They want our backing, they want our expertise, they want our weaponry. Then they want to be on their own. No interference. I don't even know their plans, save that it is scheduled for next weekend.'

'But you do know they're going after this character Meissenbach instead of the Governor-General. Have they told you why?'

'Yes. It seems that Tropa is an amiable old goat. Meissenbach has been virtually running the country for the past year. He's the man who actually signed the death warrant for those two lads who pulled down the Swastika flag. Now it seems they have learned that he is about to complete his term of office and be transferred to other duties. They both want to make an example of him, and let the Nazis know they're still fighting.'

'And they realize there are liable to be some pretty fearsome repercussions?'

'They do, and they seem prepared to accept that. The point is that my part is done, and our prime agent needs looking after. Billy, think. Anna is going to Moscow. She could be going to commit murder; she could be going as a spy. You tell me why Germany, publicly holding hands with the Reds, would send their most lethal weapon into their midst. We have to find out what she is doing and whether or not it can be turned to our advantage. You can have me seconded to the Embassy as an attaché or something. Or I could go as a businessman. Just a visit, to make contact and arrange future liaisons.'

'And you would eagerly get between the sheets with the young lady.'

Clive flushed. 'Only if it could be done safely.'

'I don't think the word safely comes into it where Anna Fehrbach is concerned. But I agree it is necessary to contact her, and if you're hell-bent on committing suicide, so be it. What about Belinda? I am speaking of the lady, not the password.'

'She won't like it. She never likes it when I am sent away for any lengthy period. But she's got used to it.'

'I meant does she know about Anna?'

'Well of course she does. She was there when the woman Gehrig started shooting.'

'And Anna snapped Gehrig's neck. You never did tell me how Belinda reacted to that.'

'Well, she was shocked, of course.'

'Does she know that you and Anna had an affair?'

'Yes. She found out.'

'And forgave you?'

'Circumstances were unusual.'

'Oh, indeed. And does she have any idea what Anna does when she becomes agitated?'

'Well, it's difficult to watch a woman calmly break another woman's neck and not get the impression that she has her bad moods.'

'So how do you think she will react to your charging off after your glamorous viper again?'

'There is no need for her to know anything more than that I am being posted abroad for a few weeks.'

'Didn't you once tell me that you intended to marry her? Belinda, I mean.'

'I did, and I asked her, four years ago. She didn't like the idea of being an MI6 wife. She thought it was too close to being a widow. She is also not a hundred per cent domesticated, in the housewife sense.'

'I thought she was an excellent cook.'

'She is. Because she enjoys it. She does not enjoy, and has no interest in, such chores as washing a man's socks, or making his bed.'

Baxter stuck to the point. 'But four years ago was before any of us knew that Anna existed, and the world was a comparatively peaceful place. I think you should force the issue and marry her as soon as possible.'

'But then,' Clive pointed out, 'you would be asking me to commit adultery and deceive my wife.'

Baxter put down his pipe. 'You are an unmitigated scoundrel, Clive. You will receive your posting as soon as it can be arranged.'

'What's this?' Belinda Hoskin inquired in that deceptively quiet voice she used when displeased. A small, dark-haired woman with prettily sharp features, she presented the greatest possible contrast to Anna Fehrbach, not least in the intensity of her personality. Clive knew very well that Anna's personality was just as intense, but she kept it securely hidden behind that glacial exterior, even in moments of enormous stress.

Now he smiled as disarmingly as he could and held out the glass of scotch he had just poured. 'It's a suitcase, darling. I had no idea you were coming round tonight.'

'You mean you were planning a moonlight flit?'

He took her in his arms to kiss her, having to raise her from the floor to get her mouth level with his. But he knew she enjoyed this, especially as he had grasped her buttocks to hold her in position. 'I was going to tell you.'

She wriggled down his body, disengaged herself, took a sip of the drink, and carried it into the kitchen. It was her nature to take immediate control of every situation that presented itself, and even if she was in Clive's flat she intended to prepare dinner herself. Her system was perhaps necessary for the fashion editor of a leading London magazine. And he had no objection to her practising it around him; he knew she found him very frustrating because he was so often carried in an alternate direction by the requirements of his job. As he had told Baxter, although she claimed she was not into washing socks and preparing regular meals, he had no doubt that the real reason she had always declined to marry him was that lack of total control.

And recently she had been more adrift than usual. To walk in, as she had done the previous year, on her lover entertaining a stunningly beautiful woman in a compromising situation, had led to an immediate decision to deal with the situation. She had followed Anna Bordman back to her Mayfair apartment. She had never told him exactly what she had had in mind, or even what the two women had said to each other when she had gained access: she certainly had had no idea just who and what she was preparing to engage. But she had still been there when Anna's apparent 'servant' had appeared and sought to kill them both. Clive had never been sure which had upset Belinda more: the fact that she had looked death in the face, or that Anna had reacted with such consuming and lethal force.

If Anna had saved her life by that prompt action, Belinda had in turn saved Anna's life by immediately calling him to the rescue, while her rival lay on the floor, apparently bleeding to death. He supposed these things made a bond. In any event it had been necessary both to put Belinda as much into the picture as was required, and make her swear secrecy under the Official Secrets Act.

From that moment she had treated him with a new respect, and quite forgiven him for his brief fling. If she had always known he worked, and travelled, for MI6, this had been her first intimation of just how dangerous that work could be.

'So where are you going?' she asked now.

'Away for a couple of days. Company business.'

She started breaking eggs with more force than was actually necessary. 'That's a big suitcase, for a couple of days.'

'Well, it could be a couple of weeks. Shall I open a bottle of wine?'

'I hate you,' she announced. 'I loathe and despise you. Do you have any of that Bollinger left?'

'Always happy to oblige, ma'am.'

He laid the table while she completed scrambling the eggs and making toast. They touched glasses as they sat facing each other. 'You're not going to get shot or something stupid, are you?'

'I shall be moving strictly amongst friends. Or at least neutrals.'

She brooded while drinking champagne. 'Do you think she got away?'

'Who?'

'Your inamorata. It's been all of two months.'

'Well, we didn't really expect her to telephone and say hello.'

'But she is working for us now, isn't she?'

'She worked for us, darling, to help us destroy that German spy ring here in London. So we sent her home. She wanted to go. She's done her bit as far as we're concerned.'

'And if the Nazis ever found out what she did?'

'That is not something to consider while eating scrambled eggs.'

Belinda shivered. Clive felt like doing the same.

'You may have next weekend off,' Anna said. 'I am going down to Prague.'

'Am I not to come with you?' Birgit asked.

'No. It is a private visit. Spend the days with your family;

when we go to Moscow at the end of the month you will be away from Berlin for perhaps a year.'

She dressed and went to her Russian class. She reckoned she was about as proficient as she was going to get in the limited time she'd been allowed. Obviously, even with spending an hour or so on homework every night, there was no possibility of her developing a Moscovite accent, but with her memory and her ear for words she had mastered the fundamentals of grammar and developed quite a vocabulary. She felt she was perfectly capable of carrying out the task of picking up what was being said around her. In any event, she had no doubt that Chalyapov would wish to speak German with her. However . . .

'There was another young lady supposed to join me for these lessons,' she remarked to Herr Toler after class.

He was an eager young man who wore a goatee beard and regarded her with longing eyes. He clearly enjoyed their one-to-one sessions, sitting beside her at the big desk, shoulders often touching as they parsed sentences and delved into what passed for Communist literature. 'Fraulein Gehrig. Yes, I have been expecting her, but she has not turned up as yet.'

'I see,' Anna said grimly. The wretched girl was going to be even more difficult than she had supposed. 'Well, let us hope she appears on Monday. I will see you then, Herr Toler.'

She took herself home to the apartment; she had not yet had any further communication from Antoinette's Boutique, and therefore intended to spend the afternoon in the gym.

Birgit rolled her eyes as she opened the door. 'There is someone here to see you, Countess.'

'Oh Lord!' She was not in the mood to fend off either amorous men or officious clerks. She opened the drawing-room door and gazed at Marlene Gehrig, who was on her feet and looking anxious.

'I have been told I am to go to Russia with you,' Marlene said in her husky voice.

Anna surveyed her. She wore a dress of no great style and low-heeled shoes. Her hair was in a bun and her face, although it could never be unattractive, wore an apprehensive expression. 'You were supposed to be here two weeks ago.'

'Well . . .' Marlene looked sulky. 'When that ghastly Doctor Cleiner dismissed me, he just told me to leave. I was taken to the SS female barracks and given a room, but as no one seemed to have any orders for me, I took a break.'

'One does not take a break unless specifically instructed to do so,' Anna pointed out. 'Where did you go?'

'Bonn.'

'What on earth did you have to do in Bonn?'

'I went to see my sister.'

Just what she had feared. The situation was becoming impossible. 'You have a sister living in Bonn.'

'Yes. Her husband works there.'

'I see. Tell me, how many other sisters do you have?'

'Only Elena. Then when I returned to Berlin, I was told I had to start taking Russian lessons. Do you know what is to happen to me?'

Anna supposed that one more Gehrig was tolerable. 'Yes,' she said. 'As you are coming with me to Russia you are required to speak Russian. You are supposed to have been learning the language for the past fortnight. Now you have just two more weeks. You will attend classes morning, afternoon and evening for those two weeks, commencing today.'

Marlene's lips were trembling. 'You're angry with me.'

'Well of course I'm angry with you. I should punish you.'

Tears rolled down Marlene's cheeks. 'Please don't be angry with me, Anna. I so want to work with you. I'll do anything you wish.'

'I have told you what I wish.' The girl looked so pitiable. Anna went to the sideboard and poured two glasses of schnapps, gave her one. 'Welcome. So you could not bring yourself to kill a living target?'

Marlene sat down, knees pressed together, holding the glass in both hands as she sipped. 'I tried. But my hand would not stop shaking.'

'Did you want to?'

'I don't know. I kept remembering what you told me, that when a thing has to be done it has to be done. But then I also remembered that you refused to kill that man in the schoolroom.'

'As you have just reminded yourself, the essential aspect of being able to survive in our profession is to be able to do what has to be done when it has to be done. I have proved my ability to do this on several previous occasions. I do not enjoy killing people. So I saw no necessity to prove my ability again for Cleiner's amusement. You have not yet proved your ability – at anything. And I think you should know that I can be every bit as brutal as Cleiner, if I have to. You have been seconded to me by General Heydrich for the sake of your mother's memory. So I am now your commanding officer, and if I give you an order it must be obeyed instantly and without question. Our lives may depend on it.'

'But what exactly are we – am I – going to do?'

'We are going to spy for the Reich. I will do most of this, but I will require you to act as my back-up, as and when I need you, regardless of the consequences. Do you understand this?'

Marlene licked her lips and then swallowed the rest of her schnapps.

'So you will have lunch with me, and this afternoon you will come with me to the gym before going to your Russian class. I will inform Herr Toler that you are coming, and that you are required to work evenings as well for the next fortnight.'

'Am I going to the gym to shoot somebody?'

Anna smiled. 'To do whatever I tell you to do.'

Anna was aware of a most peculiar sensation. Although she knew that most people with whom she came into contact considered her to be a dominant personality, and she knew that she could be, she had spent her entire life thus far as a subordinate. Even when head girl in the Vienna convent, she had been strictly controlled by the nuns. Since being conscripted into the SD she had been entirely at the mercy of her superiors, and indeed had suffered a terrible punishment for trying to assert herself. This young woman's mother had been one of the punishers. She understood that she would never be free of the control of men like Reinhard Heydrich or Billy Baxter, although she often reflected with some satisfaction that if she played her cards right she could survive while one of them went to the wall at the end of the war.

But she remained totally vulnerable until that end came. And here she was being given total control of another woman for the first time in her life. To complicate the situation she also knew that this girl was a potential deadly enemy who might have to be destroyed if she ever gleaned the slightest inkling of how her mother had died.

But Marlene herself broached the subject over lunch, again raising the question she had asked at their first meeting. 'Do you really have no idea of what could have happened to my mother?' she asked.

'I have not really had the time to think about it,' Anna confessed. 'As I told you, I only know that she was ordered to flee England because of the imminence of war. But shortly after she left I had an accident and was in hospital for several weeks. Then I was betrayed to the British and had to flee.' This was telescoping events but she did not think Marlene could possibly know that.

'But you fled back to Germany. Mother didn't. You don't think she could have been the one who betrayed you?'

'Is that something you really want to think about your mother?'

'Well, of course not. But has the thought never crossed your mind? After the way she just disappeared?'

Anna appeared to consider this. 'The first thing you want always to remember is that your mother is a dedicated Nazi and believer in the Third Reich. I do not believe it possible for her to have been a traitor. I'm afraid we must consider the possibility, perhaps the probability, that something went wrong with the escape route.'

'You mean she might have been captured by the British?'

'She cannot possibly have been taken alive or I would almost certainly have been arrested long before they actually got around to suspecting me. But when on assignment, we are all issued with cyanide capsules to be used in the last resort.'

Marlene stared at her with enormous eyes. 'You think . . .? Oh my God!'

'Your mother trained me,' Anna reminded her. 'So when I say that what has to be done has to be done, I am quoting her.'

'You admired her?'

I hated, loathed, and despised her, Anna thought. But she said, 'How could anyone not admire so strong and dedicated a character?'

Marlene burst into tears.

That did not encourage Anna to make her training any easier. If she still felt that the girl had to be a potential danger, she also felt that she might just need her, and over the next week she made her undertake an exhausting regime of both physical training and firearms practice in addition to her concentrated Russian lessons.

But this, as she knew, was but an aspect of her own uncertainty. However distasteful it had been to have to marry Ballantine Bordman and allow him the use of her body, it had been possible to approach the business with the single-mindedness that was her greatest strength. Even when Clive had entered her life to complicate matters, he had been both a back-up and the promise of an eventual haven. Now she felt utterly adrift. It was more than two months since she had left England, and not a word. She was committed to another love affair, no doubt as distasteful as the last. And now, to top it all, she had acquired Heinz Meissenbach. Her guilt and uncertainty was compounded by the fact that she was actually looking forward to her weekend in Prague. At the very least he seemed to be both an educated and a cultivated man. But she knew she was taking him on in anger at being ignored by London as much as anything.

And then on the Friday morning before she left for Prague, the telephone rang and Birgit appeared in the doorway. 'It is that boutique place, Countess.'

'Oh!' Anna knew colour had rushed into her cheeks. She brushed past the maid and grasped the phone. 'Yes?'

'Countess? Signor Bartoli here. I have made the alterations you wanted in that dress and it is ready for another fitting.'

'Oh!' Anna said again. The train left at four. 'I am going out of town for a few days, but I would like to take the dress with me if it is suitable. Shall I come in this morning?'

'Certainly, Countess. Shall we say ten?'

As if she did not have enough on her mind. But this had to be more important than anything else. She felt quite breathless.

Marlene turned up at nine to say goodbye. 'Do I continue training while you are away?'

Anna gave her a bright smile. 'You may take the weekend off, Marlene. Go somewhere and have a good time and I will see you on Monday evening.'

'A good time?'

'Don't you have any family left, apart from your sister?'

'No.'

Oh Lord, Anna thought, she's going to start crying again! 'You must have a boyfriend?'

'No. Do you have a boyfriend, Anna?'

'I think I am about to acquire one,' Anna said. 'What about friends? You must have some friends. What about the other SS girls in your barracks?'

'They have all heard of my mother and they seem afraid of me. And now they know that I'm working for you . . .'

Anna wondered if Heydrich had deliberately set this up to make her life more difficult. 'Well, you will have to go to a couple of movies or something. I will see you on Monday.'

She hurried her downstairs, watched her walk away along the street, and proceeded to call a taxi.

Bartoli beamed at her. 'Seeing you always makes the day brighter, Countess.'

Anna reflected that he had made a good recovery from the snubbing she had administered the last time they had met. 'As you always bring me back to reality, Signor Bartoli.'

He gave one of his gulps and ushered her into the fitting room, dismissing various females and closing the door. 'If you would be so kind . . .'

Anna removed her dress and petticoat and waited. The new dress was actually complete, and was even more garish than she remembered. But it fitted very well, although Bartoli found it necessary to bob about with pins and a piece of chalk. 'Yes,' he said, 'this will do very nicely.' His face was close to her breasts. 'When do you leave for Moscow?'

'A week today.'

'London is interested in anything you may be able to tell them about either current Nazi–Soviet relations, or current Soviet thinking. From what you said, this last is your prime objective, is it not?'

'Yes. You realize that I am being posted for what may be a year. I do not think I shall be allowed to return to Berlin during that time. After a year my information may be out of date.'

'You will be contacted in Moscow.'

'By someone discreet, I hope.'

'I understand so. Your contact will be known to you as you both are known to Belinda.'

Anna stared at him, feeling the blood rushing into her cheeks from her suddenly pounding heart. Could it be true?

Bartoli had been so close he might well have heard the quickened heartbeat. Now he stepped back and studied her. 'You are upset. Is the news reassuring, or alarming?'

It is both, Anna thought. To see Clive again! But they would have to be so terribly discreet. 'It is reassuring, Signor Bartoli. You may inform London that I understand the message and anticipate a profitable relationship with my contact.'

'Of course. And the dress?'

'I am sure it needs something else doing to it. If you can complete the work by next Friday, I would like to hear from you. If you cannot, I would burn it.'

'It is an expensive dress, Countess. My women have put in a lot of work on it.'

'So send the bill to my apartment. Ciao.'

The rest of the day passed in a dream. They had not only contacted her, but they were sending Clive!

But before then she had to accommodate Meissenbach. Almost she felt like telephoning to tell the secretary she had a stomach upset and would have to cancel their assignation. In fact both her mind and her body were in such an agitated state that that would not be such a lie. But she had to control herself.

It was a three-hour journey to Prague, and she shared the first-class compartment with two officers, who naturally wanted to flirt. She put them off by telling them she was going to spend the weekend with her uncle, who was Chief Secretary to the Governor-General. But it was all change in Dresden, and when she joined the Prague train they had disappeared. She was alone in her compartment, while people filed up and down the corridor, but the train had already pulled out of the station before anyone came in. She recognized him as a man who had actually passed her door three times while going to and fro looking for a seat. Now he raised his hat as he entered the compartment. 'Am I permitted, Fraulein?'

'Certainly, sir.'

He was an elderly gentleman, at least to her – certainly over fifty. His hair was grey, he wore horn-rimmed spectacles and a short beard. His three-piece suit was excellently cut, his shoes polished. He wore a gold watch chain across his ample stomach. His expression was benign. She put him down as a senior civil servant, a prosperous businessman or, most likely of all, a university professor. But incongruously, over his left arm was draped a topcoat, on a blazing-hot late July afternoon. Nor did he have any luggage. And her instincts warned her that he had actually been looking for her, and making sure that she was alone, before joining her.

But, whatever he was after, she was content to let him make the first move; it was in any event less than an hour to Prague. So, having given him a polite smile, she resumed looking out of her window.

He carefully placed his topcoat on the seat beside him and, having seated himself opposite her, he addressed her in an incomprehensible language.

'I am so sorry,' she said. 'I do not speak Bohemian.'

'That was Moravian,' he pointed out, reverting to German. 'You are not Czech?'

'I was born in Vienna, sir.'

'Ah. You are very young, and very attractive, to be travelling alone.'

Anna sighed. 'I am going to spend the weekend with my uncle. He is meeting the train.'

'Of course. He is with the . . .' He was clearly choosing his words with care. 'The German government?'

'I believe so,' Anna said carelessly.

He realized she was not going to answer any of his questions, at least in that direction, and lapsed into silence for the next fifteen minutes. Then he asked, 'You have been to Prague before?'

'This is my first visit.'

'Ah! It is the most beautiful city in Europe.'

'I am looking forward to seeing it,' Anna acknowledged. She had no extensive acquaintance with any European cities save Vienna, Berlin, London and, briefly, Rome during her flight from England. But she did not think she was being unduly patriotic when she still placed Vienna at the top of the list.

'It will be in sight when we top that hill. Did you know that, like Rome, Prague is built on seven hills? On either side of a river. There!' He pointed out of the window into the still-bright evening; it was just coming up to half past seven. 'The Vltava! Do you see all the bridges? And the spires? Prague is known as the city of a hundred spires, but actually there are many more than that.'

Anna smiled. He was so obviously a proudly patriotic Czech that she murmured, 'It is stupendous.'

The train was slowing. The man got up and picked up his topcoat with the same care as he had placed it. Anna also rose, smoothed her dress, straightened her hat, and lifted her small weekend valise down from the rack. Then, as he appeared to be waiting for her to lead the way, she opened the compartment door and stepped into the corridor, aware that he was immediately behind her. As they moved towards the exit, where several other people were already waiting, he suddenly held her arm, and she felt the steel ring of a gun muzzle being pressed into her ribs. 'I am truly sorry, Fraulein,' he said into her ear very softly. 'Just do as I wish, and I will endeavour not to hurt you.'

'What *do* you wish?' she asked without turning her head. She could not undertake immediate action because of the risk to the lives of the other passengers.

'Just to meet your "uncle". I am sure he is not alone.'

The train had stopped. The passengers disembarked one by one. Anna and her captor were last off, and there, some twenty feet away, stood Meissenbach alongside two other men, in plain clothes but with Gestapo virtually written all over them.

'Introduce me,' the man said, still holding her close.

The people who had disembarked in front of them had moved to either side, greeting friends or relations, casting anxious glances at the clearly important trio who were waiting; presumably the Chief Secretary was known by sight to a good many people. The immediate vicinity was clear. 'I do not know your name,' Anna said.

'You may call me Herr Reiffel.'

'Herr Reiffel,' Anna said, and stepped to one side. As she did so, she dropped her valise and stamped down with the high heel of her shoe, at the same time swinging right round, delivering a back-handed blow with the edge of her hand to Reiffel's neck.

Four

A Necessary Tragedy

Reiffel fired, even as he gasped. The angle was not right for a killing blow, but he lost consciousness and fell to his knees. Anna, now standing over him, kicked him in the ribs and, as his body went flaccid, stooped to take the pistol from his hand.

There were several shots, and she stayed on her knees while she watched one of the Gestapo agents go down, and saw two men standing at the far end of the platform, both carrying pistols. They were surrounded by people, but she never doubted her skills. She levelled the automatic she had taken from Reiffel's hand and fired four times. Each of the two men received two bullets in the chest before they could determine that it was the woman firing at them. They both went down.

People were screaming and running in every direction, and the station was rapidly filling with both uniformed police and German soldiers. Anna looked down at the man at her knees. He was groaning and gasping for breath, his hands clutching his stomach. He was, as she had surmised, a Czech patriot. As, no doubt, were his two accomplices. So they were all basically on the same side. But she had destroyed them. Because she could not risk anyone ever learning the truth of her? Or in self-defence? Or had it been to save Meissenbach and her mission to Moscow? Or simply because she was so trained to kill she had reacted instinctively?

Meissenbach crouched to put his arm round her shoulders. 'Anna!' he said, gasping. 'My God, Anna! You saved my life. How . . .?'

Anna had already decided that the best way to avoid over-exposure was to revert to the innocent-girl act, if that were possible. 'Please, Heinz, take me away from here.'

'Of course, my darling.' His arm tightened and he raised her to her feet.

'Ahem!' said a uniformed officer standing in front of them. 'If you will permit me, Herr Meissenbach.' Very gently he removed the pistol from Anna's hand.

'This man . . .' Anna began.

'Oh, he will tell us what he was about, Fraulein,' the officer said. 'His accomplices are unfortunately dead. That was remarkable shooting.'

'I closed my eyes,' Anna murmured, 'and just kept firing.' The officer looked as if he wanted to scratch his head, but he resisted the urge. 'And that man,' Anna hurried on, looking at the fallen Gestapo agent. 'Is he . . .?'

There were several people round him as well. His partner looked up. 'He is hit, but he will survive. You saved our lives as well, Fraulein.'

'I just closed my eyes,' Anna protested again.

'I would like to have a word with you, Fraulein,' the officer requested.

'When the Countess has recovered,' Meissenbach said severely. 'Stand aside.'

The crowd parted and he picked up the valise and assisted Anna to the back of the platform, several of the policemen falling in around them. They emerged on to the street, which was also crowded with excited people. The car door was opened, and Anna collapsed on to the seat, Meissenbach beside her.

'Did I really kill two men?' she whispered.

'Yes,' he said, too thoughtfully, in her opinion.

'We were leaving the train and this man suddenly pushed his pistol into my back and told me to walk him past your guards. I knew he was planning something terrible. So I just, well . . .'

'Closed your eyes and went berserk,' Meissenbach suggested. 'But in a most professional way. Do you do this often?'

'Well of course I do not. I have never had a gun thrust into my back before.' Which was not absolutely true; she had dealt with the Gestapo agent attempting to arrest her in London in exactly the same way.

'And if this news gets around,' Meissenbach said, 'as it certainly will, I very much doubt that anyone will ever push a pistol into your back again. There is a great deal about you, young lady, that I feel I should know.'

'Is that not why I am here?'

'I was not thinking sexually.'

His tone suggested that he might have some difficulty in thinking of her sexually ever again. But that might not be a bad thing . . .

The car swung into the grounds of Prague's Hradcany Castle, where several men and women were waiting for them; obviously the police at the station had telephoned ahead. 'Are you all right, Herr Secretary?' someone asked.

'Yes,' Meissenbach replied. 'Thanks to the Countess von Widerstand.'

Anna gave them a shy smile. 'Do you think I could change my clothes?' she asked softly.

'Of course. Frieda, take the Countess to the apartment we prepared for her.' He looked at his watch. 'Eight o'clock. Will you join me for dinner at nine?'

'Yes. I would like that.'

She followed Frieda, who had taken charge of the valise. The woman was somewhat angular, her yellow hair secured in a tight bun, and had sombre features. She wore skirt and blouse and low-heeled shoes. 'I am sorry your arrival in Prague was so distressing, Countess.'

'So am I. Do things like this happen often?'

'I'm afraid the Reich is much hated here.' They had climbed a flight of stairs and proceeded along a wide corridor. Now she opened a door. 'But to attempt to assassinate the First Secretary . . . well, that is outrageous. There will be repercussions. Can I get you anything, Countess?'

'I should like a bath.'

'The bathroom is beyond that door. Shall I draw it for you?'

'Thank you, but I can manage.'

Frieda peered at her. 'Are you all right, Countess? Such an experience.'

'I will be all right,' Anna said bravely.

The woman did not look convinced, but she nodded and left the room. Anna ran the water; the bathroom was clearly shared with another bedroom, but she locked the intervening door. Then she undressed. *There will be repercussions*, she thought. How little that woman knew. But however much she regretted what she had had to do, she could have no doubt that it was the only thing she could have done while remaining Anna Fehrbach in the eyes of her German masters. How they would react was another matter.

She soaked in the bath and nearly nodded off; she was far more exhausted than she had realized, and now that the flow of adrenaline was starting to slow she felt absolutely drained.

'Anna?'

She sat up. Shit! She had not locked the outer door. 'I am in the bath. I will be out in a moment.' There was a short towelling gown hanging on the door. She wrapped herself in this, released her hair, and returned to the bedroom.

Meissenbach was standing at the window, looking out. Now he turned to face her. 'Forgive me, Anna. I did not mean to intrude.'

'I did not realize you were so . . .'

'I have General Heydrich on the line.'

'So quickly?'

'The news of what happened was wired straight through to Berlin. He wishes to speak with you.'

Anna looked left and right.

'There is no telephone up here. You must come down.'

'Just give me a few moments to get dressed.'

'Anna, General Heydrich is on the line. Now.'

Anna sighed, and allowed herself to be escorted down the stairs and into an office, causing every head they passed to turn and look at her exposed legs and bare feet; they could tell that she was naked under the robe. She picked up the phone on the desk and held the receiver in the other hand. 'Herr General?'

'Anna! What has happened?'

'I had to shoot a man. Well, actually two men. To stop them killing Herr Meissenbach.'

'I was told a third man was involved.'

'Yes. But I didn't have to shoot him.'

'Anna, was not Meissenbach guarded? Were there no police on the platform? Did they not shoot anybody?'

'Well, no, Herr General. There were only three assassins.'

'And with all those policemen present as well as his guards, you were left to do the shooting?'

'Well . . . I suppose I reacted the quickest.'

'As you always do. But Anna, we do not wish the Russians to get the idea that we are sending them a professional assassin. It might just put this fellow Chalyapov off.'

Anna looked over the phone at Meissenbach, who, while clearly enjoying the view, was also clearly listening: Heydrich had a penetrating voice.

'I will do my best to hush the business up,' the general went on. 'But as it happened in front of a few hundred people that may be difficult. However, I would be much obliged if you would refrain from shooting anybody else without orders from me. Now tell me this: I understand you left the train in the company of the third man, with a pistol held to your back. How did this happen?'

'He joined me in my compartment.'

'And?'

'Nothing. He made polite conversation. But there was something suspicious about him. I am sure he had been looking for me before joining me. And when the train stopped he pulled this gun and made me escort him towards Herr Meissenbach. I then realized his intention, and stopped him.'

'And his two accomplices. You say he was looking for you? How did he know who you were?'

'I do not know, sir.'

'Well, I wish you to find out. As of now you are in charge of the investigation as an officer in the SD. I will inform the local Gestapo. But remember, no more shooting.'

Anna continued to look at Meissenbach, whose face was expressionless, but whose brain was clearly working very fast. 'And as regards anyone who might have been there, sir, and wishes to know more about it? Or me?'

'Whoever that may be, from the Governor-General down, refer him to me.'

The phone went dead.

Meissenbach was now looking decidedly apprehensive. 'I think you heard what he said,' Anna suggested.

'What do you want me to do?'

'I need to know everyone you told that I was coming. Everyone, please. I will go and dress and join you for dinner.'

* * *

Dinner was set in a small private room. A single waiter served champagne and was then dismissed; it was a cold table.

'You look enchanting,' Meissenbach said, bending over Anna's hand. 'You *are* enchanting. Will you . . .?'

Anna moved her finger to and fro. 'You heard the General, Heinz.' She served cold meat on to her plate, added salad and sat down.

Meissenbach did the same, sitting opposite her and pouring them each a glass of wine. 'But you are not coming to Moscow as my assistant.'

'Did you ever really suppose that I was?'

'And you are a professional assassin,' he said thoughtfully.

'I have been trained to kill,' Anna said carefully. 'When it is necessary to do so. It is not my prime function. But I am not prepared to continue this conversation in this direction. I am sorry, but as you have gathered, I am controlled by the head of the Secret Service.'

'I do understand, my dear Anna. But you must forgive me for wondering . . . What is the purpose of your visit to Prague?'

'Why, Heinz, I came here to sleep with you. Is that not what you had in mind?'

Meissenbach drank some wine. 'Well, I did have that in mind.'

'But?'

'Well, let me put it this way. You are not exactly the young woman whom I thought I was . . . How shall I put it?'

'Attempting to seduce? I suppose older men often misjudge the character of young women they attempt to pick up. Would you like me to return to Berlin?'

'Well, no, of course not. It's just that . . .'

Now that she had had a bath and a glass of wine, the adrenaline was racing through her arteries once again. 'Would you like *me* to seduce you, Heinz? A lot of men find this a good idea.'

'Did you make up that list?' Anna asked. The room was still dark, but there were chinks of light beyond the curtains.

Meissenbach rolled on to his side to nuzzle her. 'Will you answer a question?'

'Another one? If it is not to do with my job.'

'Did you feel any passion at all? I almost thought you had an orgasm.'

'I did.'

'But you were thinking of other things.'

'When I am making love, Heinz, I am making love. Nothing else matters. Were you not satisfied?'

'I have never had an experience like that in my life.' He reached for her, rolling her on to her side to hold her against him. 'Will you do it again?'

Anna kissed him. 'Of course. But we must not be long; we have work to do.'

'And when you are working, you are working. Just as when you are killing someone, you are killing someone. I am beginning to understand certain things about you. But I doubt I could ever understand what is your driving force.'

Anna threw a leg across his and studied him. 'I think you probably could. But I am not going to tell you.' She felt beneath her. 'Let us love some more and then leave it for the day.'

He was like a very young man, at that moment, although she knew she was exhausting him and it took a long time. Then she lay on his chest and allowed her hair to trickle across his face. 'You are supreme,' he muttered, his hands caressing her buttocks. 'An absolute goddess.'

'You say the sweetest things.'

'I have fallen in love with you.'

She swung her legs off the bed and sat up. 'That would be very unwise of you, Heinz. It would also be very dangerous. You have me, for the next few months. Enjoy them. Love my body. But my mind is not a lovable place.'

She went into the bathroom, ran the water. He joined her a moment later. 'May I watch you?'

'There is room for two.' She sank into the foam. 'Then we must prepare that list. General Heydrich will expect to hear from us by lunchtime.'

He sat in the tub opposite her. 'There is no list. I told no one you were coming. The staff here only knew that I was expecting a guest for the weekend. They had no idea who the guest was.' He smiled at her. 'Neither did I.'

Anna soaked. 'But you sent me the tickets. Did you get the tickets and write the envelope yourself?'

'Well, no. My secretary did that.'

'Just as she also telephoned my apartment to set up our first date.'

'But she has been with me for the past year.'

'Which is probably at least eleven months too long,' Anna remarked. 'Will she come in today?'

'She does not come in on Saturdays, no. She will be in on Monday.'

'And that is forty-eight hours too late. You know where she lives?'

'Yes,' he muttered. 'You wish her picked up? Gabriella! I cannot believe it. What will you do to her?'

Anna got out of the bath and wrapped herself in a towel. 'Believe me, Heinz, I dislike the idea of doing anything to her. I would like to think she will be cooperative. But it would seem that she is a member of some resistance organization. She will have to be very cooperative if she is to save herself a lot of unpleasantness.'

Heinz also got out of the bath. 'But at the end of it . . .'

'She will either die or be sent to a concentration camp. I would say death is the preferable alternative. But she may think differently.'

'I am glad we did not have this conversation before . . . well . . .'

Anna went into the bedroom and put on a flowered summer dress and high heels, added her ring and earrings and also her crucifix, then strapped on her watch. 'We do what we have to do to survive. I do, anyway. She must be picked up right away. But I wish her brought to me first.'

Anna was given a small office of her own, and was promptly visited by a little man in plain clothes who made her think of a ferret. 'I am Herr Feutlanger,' he announced importantly. 'Gestapo Commander in Prague.'

'Then do sit down,' Anna invited.

He did so, peering at her. '*You* are Anna Fehrbach?'

'I am afraid so.'

He stared at her dress and jewellery. 'You are not what I expected.'

'The story of my life,' Anna said sadly.

'I have been told that I am to treat you as a senior officer in the SD.' His tone suggested that he could not believe what he was saying.

'I am a senior officer in the SD.'

'But you are a young girl.'

'I began early. Is this a social call, or do you have something for me? I would like to know how the business is being handled.'

Feutlanger gazed at her for several seconds. 'It is reported in the press as an assassination attempt which was handled by Herr Meissenbach's bodyguards. I gather quite a few people saw you with a gun in your hand but it all happened so very quickly that no one can be certain who fired the shots. In any event, you will be kept anonymous. Those are my instructions from Berlin.'

'Thank you, that is very satisfactory. But I did not kill the third man.'

'That is what I wish to speak to you about. We would, under normal circumstances, expect to obtain vital information from this man, as regards his principals and other members of his group. Unfortunately, these are not normal circumstances.'

'What do you mean?'

'His neck is broken.'

'Surely not. I did not—'

'Hit him that hard? In that case, Fraulein, he is probably fortunate that his head is still on his shoulders. The fact remains that three vertebrae in his neck are shattered, he is breathing with great difficulty, and he cannot articulate at all. The doctor tells me he may regain some speech in the future, although he is likely to be paralysed from the neck down. However, the future is of no use to us.'

'I am sorry. I acted instinctively.' Feutlanger looked sceptical, so she continued. 'However, we have another lead, a woman called Gabriella Hosek.'

'You are speaking of Herr Meissenbach's secretary? We have no information that she is involved in any subversive activity.'

'Nevertheless, she is the only person, apart from Herr Meissenbach himself, who knew that I was coming to Prague. I do not mean that she knew anything about me, apart from my address, which presumably allowed me to be placed under surveillance, and my description given to the assassination squad so that I could be picked up and used as a shield for Reiffel to get close to Herr Meissenbach.'

'Which was unlucky for him,' Feutlanger observed. 'I had an uncle who worked in West Africa. One day he thrust his hand into a laundry basket to find something he thought he had left in the pocket of a dirty shirt, and pulled it out attached to a very large scorpion. He nearly died from the sting.'

Anna regarded him in turn for some seconds, then she said, 'You say the sweetest things. We must hope that Herr Reiffel is as fortunate as your uncle. Herr Meissenbach has sent some of his people to tell Fraulein Hosek that she is needed. I will interview her when she is brought in, but perhaps you would like to be present.'

'If she has a radio or reads a newspaper, she will know what has happened, and has probably already left Prague.'

'In which case I expect you to find her and bring her to me. But I would like her to be in one piece and able to speak.'

Feutlanger nodded, and stood up. 'She will be found and brought to you. I will do this personally. But tell me, Fraulein, are there many women like you employed by the SD?'

'No,' Anna said. 'I am unique.'

Feutlanger closed the door, and she remained gazing at it for some seconds. Again she was aware of some most peculiar sensations. She supposed she could be developing a split personality. Her reactions to what had happened yesterday afternoon had been absolutely instantaneous. She had acted as a dedicated SD agent to the great gratification of her superiors, however much Heydrich might feel she had been overzealous.

But she was not a dedicated SD agent. She was working for MI6. And there was every possibility that the assassination attempt on Meissenbach had been set up by MI6. Why London should wish to eliminate Meissenbach, who did not appear to be a vital cog in the Nazi war machine, she could not imagine. The important point was that she had foiled the plot. There had, of course, been no reason whatsoever for London to inform her that there was a plot; they had no idea she had ever met Meissenbach, quite apart from the possibility that she might be setting off to spend this particular weekend with him. She had to wonder what Billy Baxter's reaction would be when the news of what had happened filtered back, as it certainly would.

And now she was committed to torturing some unfortunate female to find out, for the benefit of her Nazi superiors, just where, and from whom, the plot had emanated. Having herself suffered the sort of treatment she knew the Gestapo could inflict, the thought gave her goose-pimples.

There was a way to avoid that, but that was horrifyingly distasteful as well. On the other hand, whether or not Gabriella Hosek was a fellow MI6 employee, she could be quite sure that the woman would not be able to withstand the treatment, and would therefore reveal everything she knew, which might well jeopardize a much larger network than appeared on the surface.

Shit, shit, shit! she thought. She remembered her Shakespeare, how Richard III had been tormented by the shades of all the people he had sent to their deaths, innocent or guilty. Just how many shades would surround her when this was over?

Her head jerked as the door opened. But it was Meissenbach. 'We have lost her.'

'Obviously she heard or was informed. Feutlanger is after her.' Pray to God, she thought, she either uses her capsule or is killed trying to avoid arrest.

'So you also give orders to the Gestapo.'

She shrugged. 'Essentially they work for the SD, and I am the only SD representative in Prague at this moment.'

'So do you intend to spend the entire day sitting here? I had hoped we would be able to do things together. I mean,' he hastily added, 'like riding together, or going to the museum. Or the cathedral; it is only just up the hill.'

'I think I should stay here, Heinz, until at least lunchtime. We can go sightseeing this afternoon. Unless you think someone else may be waiting to take a pot shot at you?'

'You find all this amusing,' he suggested.

'It is interesting. I try to find all aspects of life interesting.'

'But it is always work before play.'

'Yes. It has to be.'

The telephone on the desk jangled and she picked up the receiver. 'Yes?'

'Who is this speaking?' a woman asked.

'Who do you wish to speak to?' Anna countered.

'Why, my husband of course, you silly girl.'

'Ah!' Anna said, and held out the telephone. 'Your wife.'

Meissenbach gulped as he took it. 'My dear!'

'Are you all right? I have just heard the news.'

'I am quite all right, my dear.'

'People were shooting at you, the radio said.'

'But they all missed.'

'Good heavens!' Frau Meissenbach's voice was every bit as penetrating as Heydrich's. Anna couldn't decide whether she was pleased or sorry at the turn in events. 'I shall of course return immediately. Expect me for lunch.'

'Ah . . . Yes, my dear. It is good of you to cut short your holiday.'

'You are my husband. My place is at your side in this hour of need. By the way, who answered the telephone? It did not sound like Fraulein Hosek.'

'It was one of the maids.'

'Well, she deserves a good caning. Her tone was quite brusque.'

'Ah. Yes, my dear.'

'Have a car meet me at the station.'

The telephone went dead and Meissenbach gazed at Anna. 'That seems rather to spoil your plans for the weekend,' she said. 'Unless you propose to attempt to carry out her suggestion?'

'My dear Anna, it is just her manner.'

'I was sure of it.'

'But, I suppose you should leave here before lunch.'

Anna smiled at him. 'I am not in a position to do that, sir. I have been ordered by General Heydrich to carry out an investigation into the attempted assassination of a German official. And, as I am sure you understand, I do not propose to disobey my master. If Feutlanger is at all efficient, he will bring in Fraulein Hosek sometime today, so I should be able to leave either tonight or tomorrow morning. However, I agree that I should lunch alone. Perhaps you could have a sandwich and a glass of wine sent in to me?'

'Yes, yes, of course. Anna . . .'

'*Nil desperandum!* We shall be in Moscow together. But I do suggest you learn how to cope with your wife by then.'

She smiled at him. 'I am sure you appreciate that it would be most unfortunate were she and I to, shall I say, come to blows.'

Left alone, Anna paced the room. The mood she had known in Berlin was back. She had again been catapulted into a position of supreme power, only this time she was not going to be able to side-step it, to let events take their course. That course was already delineated. And it was attracting her, that was the terrifying thought. I am a monster, she told herself. I am not yet twenty-one, and I am a monster. Then she told herself, I am doing what has to be done. As long as I remember that, and do not use it for personal gratification, I surely can still, one day, become a human being again.

The telephone jangled. 'Feutlanger here, Fraulein. We have found the woman.'

Breath rushed through Anna's nostrils. 'Where is she?'

'She is here, in our downstairs department.'

'Is she badly hurt?'

'She is not hurt at all. Well, a few bruises.'

'Have you interrogated her?'

'Not as yet. I was under the impression that you wished to do that, personally.'

'Yes,' Anna said. 'I will be right down.'

She replaced the phone, remained sitting absolutely still for several minutes. She felt vaguely sick. There could be no doubt about what she had to do; even Gabriella Hosek would know she was being saved hours of agony and a horrible death. But that did not relieve her of the guilt. She had to kill in the coldest of blood. She had only ever done that twice before; all her other victims had been in immediate and dynamic response to a certain situation which could only be resolved by force. The two men she had executed had been on direct orders from her superiors. But if Clive could somehow be here, would he not command her to prevent this woman from revealing the names of her accomplices? She had to believe that. Hosek should have attended to the matter herself. But as she had not . . .

She opened her handbag and took out the cyanide capsule she always kept secreted in a special little pocket. Then she closed the handbag and slung it on her arm. The capsule she palmed inside her closed left hand, got up and went down the stairs.

She had reached the ground floor when she was suddenly joined by Meissenbach.

'Anna! I am told they have brought in Gabriella.'

'Yes. I am going to see her now.'

'When you say "see" . . .'

'Yes, Heinz. I am going to ask her to give us the names of her associates in this plot.'

'Do you think she will tell you?'

Anna gazed at him. 'They always do.'

'You are a devil from hell.'

'I am a servant of the Reich, who has been taught to do her duty.'

He licked his lips. 'I should like to be present.'

'It gives you pleasure to see a woman tortured?'

'I wish to see you at work.'

Anna considered. But his presence might just provide the distraction she needed for Feutlanger and his people. She did not suppose a man so essentially uncertain in his relations with women would be unable at least to comment, if not actually interfere. 'If you wish,' she agreed. But she could not resist adding, 'And if you are sure your wife will not object.'

'She need not know of it.'

Anna shrugged and led him down the next flight of stairs as indicated by the Gestapo agent who was waiting for them. At the bottom there was a corridor and several closed doors. But one of these was guarded by another agent, who opened it for her.

'Fraulein!' Feutlanger beamed at her, then looked past her at Meissenbach. 'Herr Secretary?'

'Fraulein Hosek happens to be my secretary,' Meissenbach said.

'Yes, sir. Well . . .'

He stepped aside and Anna led Meissenbach into the room. Having been in a Gestapo interrogation chamber before, she was not affected by the rows of unpleasant-looking instruments on the walls, or hanging from the ceiling. But she was interested in the woman who was sitting in a straight chair before the desk, her hands cuffed behind her back. She wore a skirt and blouse, both somewhat dishevelled, and had lost her shoes. She was quite an attractive woman, with short fair hair and good features. Her eyes lit up as she saw her employer. 'Herr Meissenbach! Heinz!'

Meissenbach gave Anna an embarrassed glance. She waggled her eyebrows at him.

'Please help me,' Gabriella begged. 'These men . . .'

'Your people tried to kill me,' Meissenbach pointed out. 'And you were involved. Why did you do this, Gabriella?'

Gabriella bit her lip, and Feutlanger looked at Anna; it was his turn to raise his eyebrows.

'Yes,' Anna said. 'With respect, Herr Meissenbach, we are wasting time. Every moment is important if this woman's accomplices are not to get away.'

'Yes,' Meissenbach agreed. 'Yes. What will you do to her?'

'We will begin with a flogging. This often is all that is required, with a woman.'

'Absolutely,' Feutlanger said enthusiastically. 'Strip the bitch.'

'I will do it,' Anna said. The men all looked at her, and she smiled at them. 'I have my rights.'

Feutlanger and Meissenbach exchanged glances. As they did so Anna gave a little cough and put her hand to her mouth, slipping the capsule under her tongue. 'Excuse me,' she said and then bent over the woman. 'What a pretty blouse,' she said softly. 'It goes with your pretty face, Gabriella. Do you think your face will still be pretty when we have finished with you? I should like to kiss you.'

Gabriella stared at her in a mixture of horror and consternation, as Anna took her face between her hands and kissed her very firmly. Gabriella's lips parted, and Anna used her tongue to push the capsule into the woman's mouth. With her right hand she appeared to be stroking Gabriella's chin, but was actually holding her mouth closed, while with her left hand she stroked Gabriella's cheek, following the fingers with her lips to reach her ear. 'Bite,' she whispered. 'For God's sake, bite.'

She straightened and stepped back. 'Now then.' She dug her fingers into Gabriella's blouse and pulled, to tear the buttons open. 'I will need a knife for the underclothes,' she said.

'Fraulein!' shouted one of the agents. 'Fraulein!'

Anna again straightened and watched Gabriella's head droop.

'What the . . .?' Feutlanger pushed her out of the way, thrust his hand into Gabriella's hair to pull her head up and looked into the staring eyes.

'That is cyanide!' Anna cried, apparently distraught. 'My God, and I kissed her!' Her knees gave way and Meissenbach had to hold her up.

'How did this happen?' the Secretary demanded.

Anna was recovering. 'Was she not searched?'

'Of course she was searched,' Feutlanger snapped. But he was looking at his men for confirmation.

'Yes, Herr Feutlanger,' one of them said. 'I searched her myself.'

'You searched her mouth?' Anna demanded.

'Yes, Fraulein.'

'Well, you were obviously not very efficient. This is a shitting awful mess. She was our only lead.' She looked at Meissenbach. 'Will you kindly arrange for me to return to Berlin immediately? This whole sorry business must be reported to General Heydrich.'

'Fraulein,' Feutlanger protested.

'You will no doubt hear from General Heydrich in due course,' Anna told him, and left the room.

Although it was late Saturday afternoon before Anna regained Berlin, Heydrich was still in his office. 'There's a pity,' he remarked. 'There can be no doubt it was a conspiracy. Now we shall never know who else was involved. I am not blaming you, Anna. I have no doubt that you have saved Meissenbach's neck. Do you think Feutlanger will get any further?'

Anna's nerves had settled down during the train journey, although her mind was still a mass of jumbled emotions. But her voice was as calmly composed as always. 'I very much doubt it, after the mess he and his men made over the Hosek arrest. What I would like to know is what the conspirators had in mind. Surely if they were going to murder anybody, it should have been General von Tropa, not his First Secretary.'

'Ah, but you see, von Tropa is an indecisive imbecile, and

the Czechs know this. That they are kept in subjection is because of the ruthlessness of Heinz Meissenbach.'

Anna raised her eyebrows. 'Herr Meissenbach is ruthless?' She thought of the rather diffident Lothario who was apparently terrified of his wife.

'You did not know this, eh? Tell me, did you sleep with him?'

'Well . . .' Anna could feel her cheeks burning. 'He wanted to, and he is to be my boss. And he said you had given permission.'

'I did, but I assumed he would not seek to use the permission until after you had got to Moscow. You must have turned his head completely. Was his lovemaking gentle or brutal?'

'He actually found it difficult to get going at all. He had no idea, well . . .'

'That you could be more deadly than a black mamba? That too is a pity. As you remember, I did not want him to know so much about you. I will have to have a chat with him when he arrives on Monday. However, I would not like you to underestimate him. He may have been temporarily overcome by your special skills, especially as he appears to have been entirely overcome by your looks, and he may also be somewhat afraid of his wife – she has the family money – but his record for quite savage behaviour towards those he regards as his enemies, or as enemies of the Reich, is unquestionable.'

'You told me that he would not be able to touch me – I mean in a disciplinary manner.'

'He has no powers to do so, certainly. But he is a man, as I have said, of rather deep instability. Just keep that in mind.'

'May I ask, Herr General, why you did not warn me of this when giving me this assignment? And would you have warned me of it now, but for that incident on the platform?'

Heydrich shrugged. 'What I do, or do not do, is not something I expect you to enquire into. Your job is to carry out your assignment and please me. However, I did not warn you because I did not suppose it would be necessary. You made it so. Now listen. General Himmler feels that it would be improper for us to leave Count von Schulenburg entirely in the dark, and that to do so may make your task more difficult than is necessary. The Count will not be informed of your exact mission, but he is being told that you are an SD agent who is carrying out a special and top-secret assignment.'

'Yes sir.'

'General Himmler also feels that, again to ease your position, it is necessary to put the head Gestapo agent in the Embassy into the picture. He will be told to lend you all assistance, and you are, of course, his senior. His name is Groener.'

'Yes sir. I feel I should point out that Herr Feutlanger was not very happy at having to take orders from me. Will Herr Groener be more amenable?'

'Whether he is or not, he is an agent of the Reich, and will obey his orders. As will you, Anna. Now, it may be necessary from time to time to give you additional information or instructions. These will come through Groener. However, he is not to be informed of your overall objective at any time. I expect great things of you. Now, off you go and get me some results.'

'I am sorry, Fraulein,' Bartoli said. 'I have received nothing further from London. When do you leave for Moscow?'

'Next week.'

'Then we must assume that your orders stand. I will wish you good fortune. Will I be seeing you again?'

'When I return to Berlin. But that may not be for a few months. I will wish *you* good fortune.'

She went to her apartment. She had gone straight to the boutique from Gestapo Headquarters knowing that as it was Saturday it would be open late. It had been one of the longest days of her life, and there had been quite a few of those.

She thought she could still taste Gabriella's lips, and she was sure she could taste the capsule, although she knew that had to be impossible, or she would also be dead. But it would have to be replaced. Not that she supposed there was the least risk of her being arrested by the NKVD; she would be a fully accredited German Embassy official, and even if they found cause to be suspicious of any of her activities, they could only deport her back to Germany.

She paid off the taxi and entered the lobby. 'Countess?' The concierge was agitated. 'I did not expect you until Monday.'

'Prague was rather boring,' Anna said.

'Ah. Yes. Shall I inform Fraulein Gessner?'

'I gave her the weekend off; you mean she is there?'

'Oh, yes, Countess.'

'Well I am going straight up, so there is nothing for you to do.' She frowned as she saw his eyes dilate. She rode up in the elevator, as was her custom whenever her suspicions were aroused, running over in her mind all the various possibilities. But there was only one. Was Birgit entertaining someone? The young woman had always appeared totally sexless. She thought it might be rather amusing.

She unlocked the apartment door, crossed the lobby and entered the drawing room. She gazed at the coffee table on which there were two empty schnapps glasses. She could hear voices coming from the kitchen, and again frowned, because both of them were female. Birgit and . . .?

She walked along the corridor. The kitchen door was open. She stood in the doorway, gazing at Birgit, who was in the midst of cooking, and Marlene, both of whom were naked. *When the cat's away*, she thought.

They seemed to notice her at the same time.

'Countess?' Birgit gasped.

'Anna!' Marlene cried.

'We . . .' Birgit began.

'Did not expect me back until Monday? When did you move in, Marlene?'

'Well . . . I was so lonely . . .' Marlene was blushing.

Anna's heart was pounding. Coming on top of the Gabriella Hosek incident, seeing the two attractively naked young women in front of her, knowing what they must have been doing, had her emotions seething again. At the same time she was furious. The fury was mainly directed at herself for being turned on, but it still made her want to hurt, to destroy. And did this creature not deserve to be destroyed? It could be done now. All she had to do was pick up the telephone and tell Heydrich that the girl was again not measuring up, and she would be gone forever. In fact, she could execute her here and now, and explain to Heydrich afterwards.

Emotions apart, she had so many problems to be attended to that the removal of even a potential one would be a great relief. And what was she concerned about? Just twenty-four hours ago she had killed two men and destroyed a third. And nine hours ago she had executed Gabriella Hosek. Executing Marlene would certainly be protecting herself, and possibly other MI6 agents such as Bartoli.

And the girl was an SD operative, however much she might be on probation. But she knew she was not going to do it. The fact was that she was desperate to prove, if only to herself, that she was not an indiscriminate murderess.

Birgit and Marlene had insensibly moved towards each other and were now holding hands; if one was going to be punished, so would the other. Anna surveyed them, and realized that they both smelt faintly of her very expensive perfume. 'Do I understand that you have been having sex in my bedroom?'

'I . . . we . . . it is such a lovely bedroom,' Marlene stammered.

Again Anna had a powerful desire to punish her, at least physically, to stretch her across the bed and whip her insensible. But she knew herself too well. If she once allowed that destructive urge to control her, she would do the girl a serious injury. And in fact her violent emotions were beginning to calm. But at the same time, she would need to keep a very close eye on her.

'You were sent to me on probation. I wish you to remember that your very existence hangs by a thread. Now return to the barracks, collect your things and come back here. I will allow you an hour. You will remain here until we leave Berlin. I think the dinner is burning, Birgit. Turn off the stove, and then strip my bed and remake it with clean sheets. When Marlene returns she will clean the bathroom. When you have finished making the bed you will prepare a fresh meal. Remember that, as of now, you are also on probation.'

She went into the drawing room to pour herself a glass of schnapps. Then she sat on the settee. She had sat here for her first embrace with Clive Bartley. She had also sat here with her arm round Gottfreid Friedemann's shoulders, her pistol resting on the nape of his neck, before executing him.

That had been just under two years ago. She wondered if she had advanced or declined since that day. She also wondered if she had just made a mistake. Only time would tell.

* * *

'I just dropped in to say cheerio,' Clive said. 'They have at last got their act together, and I am off tomorrow. Gibraltar then Cairo.'

'How is Belinda?' Baxter asked.

'Browned off.'

'While you are like a dog with two tails. Before you push off, something has come in which I thought might interest you.'

Clive sat down and waited.

'We heard this morning that Operation Tomorrow has collapsed.'

'Just like that?'

'There seems to have been some kind of battle at Prague central railway station. Janos and Petar were shot dead, Reiffel was taken prisoner and somehow the Gestapo got on to Hosek.'

'Shit! Did they take her?'

'Apparently not, thank God, but she's also dead. She committed suicide when she was arrested.'

'What a waste. Was it worth it? For Meissenbach?'

'The Czechs thought it was. But that is not really what concerns me. The matter has been rather blanked out by the German news media, which means of course the Czech news media as well. But Razzak was at the station. He was not involved in Tomorrow, he was there as an observer. And naturally he made himself as scarce as possible. But he saw what happened. The shoot-out was a trifle one-sided. Janos and Petar did get off a shot each and one of Meissenbach's bodyguards was hit, but before they could fire again they were both cut down by four shots, each of which hit. Those shots were fired by a young woman who had just got off the train from Dresden.'

Clive frowned.

'She left the train,' Baxter went on, 'in the company of Reiffel. And then suddenly demolished him with a couple of highly sophisticated blows, took his pistol, and opened fire with, as I said, consummate speed and accuracy. Razzak says that Reiffel is not dead, but was paralysed by a blow to the neck, which has left him unable to articulate. Obviously the Gestapo are going to do their damnedest to fix him up, but at least that gives us time to pull the others out. I wonder if anything in this pattern of events is familiar to you?'

'Shit!' Clive muttered.

'Just in case it isn't,' Baxter went on, 'Razzak was able to give a description of the young lady who committed the mayhem: tall, slender, long golden hair, and strikingly handsome features.' He stared at Clive.

'What the devil was she doing in Prague?'

'Killing our agents. You won't believe how it happened. According to Razzak, Hosek learned that Meissenbach was planning to entertain a young woman he had met in Berlin, and told Hosek to arrange her train passage for the weekend. Razzak and his people immediately realized that this was their chance to get right up to the target. So Reiffel picked her up on the train. Can you believe it? I mean, if you were going duck-shooting in a swamp, would you take a crocodile as company?'

'Hold on. You are not suggesting she was sent by the SD? There is no possible way they, or she, could have known of Tomorrow. She was protecting Meissenbach.'

'Well there must be some kind of link. And I suggest you find out. All I can say is thank God she is going to Russia. That should at least keep her from bumping off any more of our people in Central Europe, however inadvertently. You know how the boffins are always chattering about how one day they will be able to create the ultimate weapon of mass destruction. They don't realize that we already possess it, and that it is quite out of control. Anna is your baby, Clive. You virtually created her. Now it is up to you to sort her out. You had better get to Moscow before she does, just in case she takes a dislike to any of our people there. I am thinking especially of poor Sprague. Have a good flight.'

Five

Moscow

'Mr Bartley!' The Flying Officer ticked Clive's name off a list on his desk. 'Welcome to Gibraltar. You're for Cairo.'

'That is correct. ASAP.'

'Everyone wants everything ASAP. The problem letter is the P. However, you're in luck. Your flight leaves at 1800.'

Clive looked at his watch: it was just after eleven, or as this bloke would have it, 2300. 'That is nineteen hours away,' he pointed out. 'I really am in a hurry.'

'Everyone is in a hurry. You really don't want to go flying the length of the Mediterranean in daylight, old man. Musso may not be up to much, but he does have an air force, and you won't have any fighter protection. Have a good night's sleep and a restful day. I am sure Cairo can exist for another twenty-four hours without you.'

It's not Cairo that bothers me, Clive thought. 'And where do you recommend I have this good night's sleep?'

'Accommodation . . . Ah, Parkyn!' he called.

'Sir?' A young woman, trim in her WAAF uniform, appeared in the doorway. She had pleasant features, a solid figure, and short yellow hair. Everyone's concept of the girl next door, Clive supposed.

'Would you attend to this gentleman, Mr . . .' He checked his list again. 'Mr Bartley. He needs accommodation until 1700. Perhaps you could also arrange to have him picked up at that time and brought back to the station.'

'Of course, sir.' Miss Parkyn smiled at Clive and then at her superior. 'Will that be all for tonight, sir?'

'Oh, indeed. You may go off then.'

'If you'd come with me, sir.'

Clive picked up his suitcase and followed her into another

office presently unoccupied. 'Do sit down.' She sat herself behind the desk.

Clive took a chair, glancing out of the open window. It was a brilliantly starry night, and so delightfully warm. He had a sudden feeling of relaxation. The flight over Biscay had been tensing because of the possibility of German planes coming out from the French coast. They had seen none, but he had still been very pleased to land. The airstrip lay across the neck of land between the fortress and the Spanish mainland, and to their left the lights of Algeciras had glowed with all the brightness of a typical Spanish evening.

'Are you a VIP?' Miss Parkyn asked.

'Not really.'

'You're not in uniform. And yet you have the use of RAF transport. Or am I being too inquisitive?'

'I'm afraid the answer has to be yes.'

'Ah. Hush hush. But I need to have some idea of where to put you. *If* I can put you anywhere.'

'Somewhere inconspicuous. Not the Rock.'

She began telephoning while he studied her, although he really wanted to think about Anna. Anna was a huge question mark. He knew that she had turned to him entirely by chance. He had happened to reappear in her life at the very moment when she had been 'disciplined' by her German employers, and had been a bundle of angry and humiliated nerves. Contrary to Baxter's supposition he had not created Anna: Anna had created him for her own purposes. She had loved him, physically, with all the intensity that made her at once the most desirable, and equally the most deadly woman in the world. How much, and how honestly, she had accepted his tutelage and then his leadership, he did not know. Perhaps he would never know. Baxter certainly was not yet convinced that she was genuinely committed to the Allied cause. *He* believed in her, but was that because he so desperately *wanted* to believe in her?

Yet the questions continued to cluster about her. What had she been doing in Prague? He did not really believe she had been a bodyguard for Heinz Meissenbach. There was nothing in his knowledge of her to indicate that she had ever been employed in that capacity by the SD, or that she had ever met Meissenbach – yet she had apparently been intending to spend the weekend with him. He simply could not afford to be jealous of a woman like Anna, but it was difficult. And why was she going to Russia? He knew it could not be for so simplistic a reason as to obtain current Russian opinion. No doubt that mystery at least would be resolved when he finally saw her.

Which could be within the next couple of days. Cairo, Athens, probably some town in southern Russia, and then Moscow – not more than a week, depending upon how many officious flight controllers he encountered. And how soon after that would he hold her in his arms? It was one of those thoughts that could leave a man breathless, but which had to be resisted. He could not argue with Baxter's opinion that he was an utter scoundrel. But his excellence at his job was based upon an often ruthless single-mindedness which he liked to think was almost, if not quite, in the class of Anna herself. Spending the next week dreaming of Anna would be extremely distracting, and could even be dangerous. But here was this rather appealing, if alarmingly normal, young woman, who wore no rings, and was now smiling at him.

'I'm afraid the situation looks a bit grim, Mr Bartley. You see, since Italy entered the war, the garrison here has been more than doubled, and in addition, it is the staging post for everyone trying to get to Malta or the Middle East. So . . .'

'I sleep on a park bench, is that it? Is there a park in Gibraltar?'

'There's the beach front. But it would be a little uncomfortable.' She gazed at him, as if considering the situation, but he had an idea that she had already reached a decision. She was a serving soldier, and had to be circumspect in her relations with all other servicemen – or women – and that apparently now comprised ninety per cent of the Rock's population. But he was not in the services, at least as far as she knew. 'I could find you a bed . . .'

He waited.

'I share a room with another girl, but she has a furlough and has gone up into Spain. She apparently wants to see a bullfight.'

'One room?'

'I'm afraid so. If sharing isn't really your sort of thing, well . . .' She gave a pretty little blush.

'My dear Miss Parkyn, I don't seem to have much alternative. But I don't think I'd want to take the alternative, even if it was offered. Are you quite sure you want to put up with me for the next twelve hours or so?'

'I'm sure that you are a gentleman, Mr Bartley,' she said enigmatically.

'Well then, at least tell me your Christian name.'

'Thistleton-Brown,' announced the handle-bar moustache, who wore the insignia of a Wing-Commander.

'Bartley.'

Thistleton-Brown looked him up and down as best he could in the gathering gloom. 'Diplomatic wallah?'

'That's one way of putting it,' Clive agreed.

'And you're for Cairo?'

'If that's where this plane is going.'

'Been here long?'

'Overnight.'

'Did you have any sleep? Not a bed in the place.'

'I managed to find one,' Clive said modestly. He had in fact slept very well, and as Alice Parkyn had told him to make himself at home when she had left for the station that morning, he had had a very comfortable and relaxing day. Then she had returned for him as arranged, and had just dropped him off in the small car she had the use of. 'I really am grateful,' he had said, 'for your generosity.'

'I am grateful too.'

'For having me hanging around?'

'For your being a gentleman,' she had said a trifle wistfully.

Perhaps he had missed something there. But it had not been the time, and he already had at least one woman too many on his mind.

'Gentlemen,' said the Flying Officer. 'All set? Malta in two hours, for fuel. Cairo by dawn.'

It was a very small aircraft and Clive and the Wing-Commander were the only passengers, sitting one in front of the other. 'Not nervous, I hope?' Thistleton-Brown asked over his shoulder.

'Should I be?' Clive asked innocently.

The noise of the engine precluded further conversation, and

they climbed into another disturbingly bright night, with the lights of Spain blazing away behind them. Clive tried not to think about anything, and especially not Anna. She was there, and he was going to her.

'Gentlemen,' said the pilot over the Tannoy, 'I'm sorry to say that we have company. I am going down. We stand our best chance of avoiding interference close to the sea.'

The plane dropped sharply. Clive looked out of his window but could see nothing. They descended for several seconds, then straightened out again. 'I think we've lost the buggers,' the pilot said.

But just then there was a tearing sound. Clive twisted his head and saw a large rent in the fuselage behind him. The plane swerved violently and began to climb again. Another tearing sound and he felt a sudden jolt. *My God!* he thought. *I've been hit!* The night suddenly became very dark.

Anna gazed out of the window at the seemingly endless Polish plain. The soil was black; the harvest had recently been gathered, before the onset of the autumnal rains.

She was glad to have put Warsaw behind her. The pinewoods the train had passed through on its way to the capital had brought back her visit to her mother and sister too vividly. She turned her thoughts to what lay ahead: the Soviet Union – and Chalyapov. If it had been amusing to hear Heydrich say that the Russian wanted a totally uninhibited woman, and that she was clearly such a woman, she wondered for how long she could maintain that façade. She had been required to do it on a day by day basis for nearly a year with Ballantine Bordman, but he, being a totally inhibited Englishman, had been easy to satisfy. Heydrich had indicated that Chalyapov might just fall into the satyr variety.

And then there was Meissenbach. And his wife. She had met the lady when boarding the train, and had been formally introduced. Frau Meissenbach was a rather plump woman of slightly above average height, though several inches shorter than Anna herself. She wore her hair bobbed, perhaps to make her rather severe features more severe yet. As Heydrich had indicated, Meissenbach could only have married her in the first place for her money, so it was simple to understand why he could not keep his hands off any available woman. She had regarded Anna with the deepest suspicion. 'This lady is your assistant?' she had enquired coldly. 'Have we met, Countess?'

'I do not think so.'

'Your voice is familiar.'

Anna had glanced at Meissenbach, who was standing behind his wife, waggling his eyebrows in desperation. 'I am afraid you are mistaken, Frau,' she had said.

'I am never mistaken, you have a very distinctive accent,' Frau Meissenbach announced, and boarded the train.

'Here's to a jolly journey,' Anna remarked.

'It will be all right,' Meissenbach assured her. 'She really does not like travelling.'

Anna raised her eyebrows.

'I will try to see you on the train.'

'I'm sure you will, Heinz; there is only one dining car. I think that if you do not join your wife now, she may come back to look for you.'

He had hurried off, and she had made sure that Marlene and Birgit were settled in their second-class compartment. They seemed to have become inseparable in a couple of days. There was also the extreme intimacy of lovers between them, the occasional secret glance or touch of hands. Should that be cause for concern? She had actually considered calling on Heydrich, or at least Glauber, to supply her with an additional agent to keep an eye on them, but had decided against it. It would inevitably have led to questions, and the agent would necessarily have had to be a woman if she was to share a railway couchette compartment for three days. In any event, both had been totally subservient and anxious to please during the week before their departure from Berlin. Now they were both highly excited.

'This is a Russian train, Countess,' Birgit said in a stage whisper.

'Well of course it is. It is going to Moscow.'

'Will we be all right?' Marlene had asked.

'If there is any trouble, report to me. I shall expect you both in my compartment at six o'clock this evening.'

If she had to deal with a crisis, she was prepared to do so, ruthlessly. She had given them their second chance, to obey her in all things without question, which was more than they would have received from any other SD agent.

*　*　*

She nodded off, found herself dreaming of Clive. She wondered if he would be in Moscow before her. But as she did not see how he could get there except via the Mediterranean and the Black Sea, that was unlikely.

She was startled by a knock on the door. She had lowered the corridor blind to ensure complete privacy, but had not locked the door. It now slid back without invitation and a shaggy head looked in.

'Tea, Fraulein?' the guard asked in German. Like all Russian trains, at least in the first-class carriages, there was a huge samovar always bubbling away at the end of the corridor.

'That would be very nice, thank you.'

He returned in five minutes carrying a large pewter container with a handle, inside of which was a pint glass of steaming tea. He did not offer either sugar or milk.

'Thank you,' Anna said faintly. 'Will you tell me who makes up my bed?' She gestured at the bunk opposite; the pillow and blankets were on the net tray above it. Presumably the sheets were already in place.

'I do, Fraulein. I will do it while you are having dinner.'

'Ah. Thank you.'

She assumed he would now leave, but he hesitated. 'You are the Countess,' he proclaimed.

'That is correct.' She wondered if she was to be handed over to the nearest NKVD agent.

'I have a message for the Countess,' he announced.

But perhaps he was only seeking some form of identification, or a tip, before delivering his missive. 'How nice,' she said. 'Will you not tell me what it is?'

'It is from Herr Meissenbach. He invites you to dine with him. At eight o'clock. We will be in Brest-Litovsk by then.'

'Is that important?'

He regarded her with some contempt. 'It is where the change takes place.'

'You mean we change to another train?'

'No, no, Countess. You stay on this train all the way to Moscow.' His tone indicated that in Soviet Russia such wonders of modern science were commonplace. 'But it is necessary to change the gauge, you see.'

Anna did not see at all, but she said, 'You may tell Herr Meissenbach that I shall be pleased to join him for dinner.'

Again he hesitated, now definitely expecting something.

'Is it not illegal either to offer or receive tips in Russia?' she asked innocently.

'Everything in Russia is illegal, Countess.'

'Or immoral, or it makes you fat,' Anna suggested. The guard looked bewildered, so she tipped him anyway, and he left.

The main part of Anna's luggage was in the guard's van, but in the two suitcases she had had delivered to her compartment she had packed three evening gowns. Punctually at six Birgit and Marlene arrived to help her dress. There was no possibility of a bath, and even topping and tailing from the tiny washbasin was a lengthy process. But the two girls worked enthusiastically and were just drying her when the train clanked to a halt.

They had of course drawn the blinds over both the windows and the door, but from the virtually incomprehensible shouts on the platform, she gathered that they were in Brest-Litovsk. It was disconcerting that she recognized so little of what was being said, but she reminded herself that a country as vast as Russia would obviously have a vast number of local dialects.

They heard stamping feet in the corridor and a succession of thunderous raps that now arrived at her door. Anna had only got as far as putting on her cami-knickers. Birgit hastily wrapped the towel around her mistress's torso, just before the door opened to reveal the conductor backed by a man in a green uniform and side cap, armed with a rifle.

Marlene gave a shriek of alarm. Birgit goggled at him, still trying to hold the towel in place. Anna assumed her most imperious expression. 'What is the meaning of this?'

'Passports,' the conductor said. 'You must show your passports.'

'In that bag, Marlene,' Anna said. Marlene delved into the handbag and handed the passport to the conductor who passed it to the soldier. He gave it no more than a perfunctory glance, preferring to gaze at Anna, whose legs were totally exposed. As he seemed speechless, the conductor spoke for him. 'And the other ladies?'

'Their passports will be in their compartments, as you well know,' Anna said severely.

'Then they will have to come with us.'

Anna nodded and took control of the towel herself. 'Go along then. May I have my passport back?'

The conductor returned the passport. The soldier had not taken his gaze from Anna.

'I assume your friend has seen a woman before?' Anna enquired, speaking Russian for the first time.

The soldier's head jerked. He flushed and saluted, then moved along the corridor followed by the conductor.

'My God!' Marlene remarked. 'Will this sort of thing happen often?'

'Very probably,' Anna said. 'Now off you go before they place you under arrest. Just remember to come back as quickly as you can.'

In what Anna had to suppose was a remarkable feat of engineering, the entire train was now shunted on to a huge turntable and in some incomprehensible manner moved from the narrow gauge of the European railway system to the broad gauge of the Russian. The shunting process took an hour, with a succession of jerks and thuds and sudden stops. With some difficulty she finished dressing, and with even more difficulty completed her make-up. Birgit and Marlene, still outraged, returned to help her do her hair. Then at eight o'clock she made her way to the dining car.

The car was little more than half full, and only a few of the people present, all men with the exception of Greta Meissenbach, were wearing dinner suits. Anna estimated that this minority was the German passengers, the men in lounge suits being Russian. But all their heads turned to watch Anna make her way up the centre aisle, having to pause every few steps to place a gloved hand on the back of a seat; the train was now moving again.

Meissenbach was on his feet to greet her. 'My dear Anna, how charming you look.'

'Thank you, sir.' Anna took the indicated banquette seat beside his wife. 'What a lovely dress,' she lied convincingly. Actually, Greta was wearing a most attractive dress, but it did very little for her rather heavy figure.

'Thank you, Fraulein.' Anna raised her eyebrows and Greta smiled at her. 'Heinz has no secrets from me.'

'Really,' Anna said. 'What a remarkable man.'

Meissenbach sat opposite them, looking apprehensive. 'I felt I should put my wife into the picture. As far as possible,' he hastily added, and signalled the waiter for menus.

'Which is not actually very far,' Greta remarked. 'What exactly is it you do, Fraulein?'

Meissenbach coughed.

'What exactly does your husband do?' Anna asked. 'I mean, what is he going to Moscow to do?'

'Why, he is going to Moscow to take charge of the personnel and organization of the Embassy.'

'Then that is what I am also going to do. Under his supervision, of course.' As Meissenbach did not appear to be ordering aperitifs, she filled her water glass from the carafe on the table, drank and all but choked. 'My God!'

The waiter was now standing beside them, pad and pencil poised. 'Fraulein?'

'What in the name of God is that?'

'It is vodka, Fraulein.' He spoke excellent German.

Greta snorted.

'The Russians drink vodka with everything,' Meissenbach explained.

And you never warned me, Anna thought. 'Well, I would like a jug of water.'

The waiter looked sceptical and then at Meissenbach, who nodded. 'They are an uncouth lot,' he remarked, as the waiter departed. 'But we will have to put up with their little ways.'

'Apparently. Were you visited by the border guards?'

'Indeed. Outrageous. I intend to raise the matter with Count von Schulenburg. But I don't suppose it'll change their detestable habits.'

It was one of the least enjoyable meals of Anna's recent life. But at last Greta needed to powder her nose. Having made this announcement, she waited for Anna to accompany her, but as Anna made no move to do so, she set off by herself, steam emanating from the back of her head.

'I think we are in for a difficult time,' Anna said, stirring her coffee. She had had several glasses of vodka, and now had to contemplate some extremely poor brandy. With her training it took a good deal of alcohol to make her tight, but it could easily make her irritable.

'Please do not let her upset you.' Meissenbach's hand slid across the table to hold hers. 'Anna, I adore you. I must see you again.'

'Aren't you seeing me now?'

'You know what I mean. Listen, I will come to you tonight.'

'Are you out of your mind?'

'There is nothing to be afraid of.' He flushed. 'I don't suppose you would be afraid, no matter what happened. But Greta takes a sleeping pill every night when travelling; any motion, either from a train or a boat, keeps her awake. Midnight.'

Anna looked past him at Greta, just entering the car, and withdrew her hand. But Greta had enjoyed her discomfort over the vodka, not to mention her obvious distaste for caviar. She had it coming. 'I shall look forward to that,' she said softly.

Thanks to the alcohol she fell into a deep sleep, and awoke with a start at the knock on her door. This time she had locked it and had to get out of her couchette. It was a double compartment, and Birgit had thoughtfully laid a dressing gown on the other seat. She put this on, opened the door, and was immediately in his arms. He was certainly anxious; Anna had to reach past him to close and lock the door, and switch on the light.

While she was doing this, he got inside the dressing gown to caress her naked flesh. 'How I have dreamed of this,' he said into her ear. 'You and I on a train together, making love.'

Having sex, she thought. 'Why, Heinz, I thought you had gone off me.'

He sat beside her on the bed, continuing to caress her, moving the dressing gown from her shoulders so that it slipped down her back. 'I was overcome. I admit it. And then Gabriella . . . The way you kissed her.' He gazed at her with wide eyes.

'It is my way,' Anna smiled. She had anticipated this question at some stage. 'She was a pretty woman. I like pretty things.'

'But you also like destroying them?'

'Sometimes.'

'You are a woman to fear. But then, to be loved by you . . . Anna, will you hold him, as you did in Prague?'

That seemed a quick solution to his problem. She slipped her hand inside his pyjamas, and only a few seconds later was washing it in the basin, while he lay back with a sigh. 'Anna, you are a goddess! Anna, if I were to divorce Greta . . .'

Anna dried her hands and sat beside him. 'Dear Heinz, we are going to Moscow to work. I am, anyhow.'

His eyes, which had been closed, now opened. 'No one has ever told me what that work is. When I think of what you can do . . . You do realize that if you were to shoot someone in Russia, it could lead to an international incident?'

'I told you, I am not being sent to Russia to shoot anybody. I am assuming that there is no one in Russia who is going to try to shoot *you*.'

'I should hope not. But you are not going to pretend you are really coming as my aide. Can you type? Can you file? Can you handle public relations? Make appointments, refuse appointments without giving offence, which is often the more important?'

Anna squeezed in beside him on the narrow bunk. 'I have not been trained to do any of those things, but you must pretend that I am indispensable. I am going to Russia to observe and report. General Heydrich, which means the Secret Services, which means the highest level of the Reich Government, wishes to know how the Russians are thinking. He also wishes,' she added thoughtfully, 'to learn whatever he can of the relations between the Russians and the British and the French. So you see, I need to mingle with the diplomats of all of these countries.'

'How do you propose to do that?'

She kissed him. 'You are going to arrange that, Heinz. I wish to be included in all receptions thrown at the Embassy. I wish to be found invitations to all receptions thrown by other embassies, or by Russian diplomats and politicians, to which any Germans are invited.'

'That is a tall order.'

'If it proves at all difficult, I wish you – and your wife, of course – to throw a succession of parties. Dinner parties would be best, to which you will invite anyone of the least importance. I am sure you agree that I will be an attractive guest.'

'I don't know that Schulenburg will be pleased with that. As for Greta . . .'

Anna again slid her hand inside his pyjamas. 'You will be doing it for the Reich. And for me, of course.'

Belinda Hoskin opened her door to the knock, and gazed at her visitor in astonishment. She had met Billy Baxter before, and she knew that he was Clive's boss, but he had never attempted to contact her before. Now she immediately knew he was the bearer of bad news. 'Mr Baxter?'

'May I come in?'

'Of course, do forgive me.' She stepped back, and closed the door behind him. 'It's about Clive.'

Baxter advanced into the room, looked at the sideboard. 'Shall we have a drink?'

Belinda poured two scotches. 'Tell me.' Baxter sat down and took a long sip. Belinda also sat, the glass held in both hands. 'He's dead.'

'He's in hospital. His plane was shot down, and he is suffering from extreme exposure, as well as various other injuries. I am informed that his condition is not life-threatening, but it may be a little while before he is fit again.'

Belinda had an instinctive feeling that he was lying. 'Shot down? Where was he shot down?'

'Now, Miss Hoskin – Belinda – you know I cannot tell you that. I can tell you that he was on a mission for the Department.'

'And shot down. Am I allowed to see him?'

'Ah . . . I'm afraid that is not practical.'

'Why not? You mean . . . My God, he's burned!'

Baxter took his pipe from his pocket, regarded it for a few seconds as a drowning man might regard a lifebelt that had suddenly been thrown to him, and then replaced it in his pocket. 'Clive has not been burned, to my knowledge.'

'You mean you have not seen him either? He's in intensive care?'

'I understand that he was in intensive care, yes. But as I have said, he is now off the danger list.'

'But he was on it. And I'm not allowed to see him.'

'It is simply not practical.'

'So when will he be coming home?'

'As I told you, not for some time.' Baxter finished his drink and stood up. 'I just felt that you should understand the situation.'

'I do *not* understand the situation. Who was with him on this plane?'

Baxter could tell where her thoughts were heading. 'I am not in a position to give you that information. But I can tell you that there was no one on the plane that you know, or have ever known. I will be in touch when I have some more information.' He closed the front door behind himself.

Belinda stared at it for several seconds then hurled the still full glass of whisky at it.

'This place is a dump,' Marlene complained.

Anna had to agree with her. The Kremlin was starkly dramatic, but lacked any suggestion of architectural beauty. At the top end of Red Square were the magnificent, multi-coloured onion domes of St Basil's Cathedral, but they seemed an ornament stuck on the front of a very plain face: the church was no longer used for any religious purpose, and in any event, she had been educated at the Vienna convent to regard Russian Orthodoxy as even more obnoxious than Protestantism.

Surrounding the square were some substantial buildings, such as the GUM department store, open only to non-Russians as long as they spent their own currency, and the Historical Museum, but neither of these was the least attractive to look at. On the west bank of the Moscow River were several other large buildings that could almost be called palaces; these were, in the main, the foreign embassies. For the rest, there were endless streets of very ordinary houses, and worse, on the outskirts of the city were a mass of drab high-rise apartment blocks.

'It is utterly soulless,' Marlene continued.

'Sssh!' Anna recommended, for their Intourist guide was approaching them; it had been decided that their first duty was to be shown the sights of the city.

He was a nervous young man named Dmitri who spoke German with a pronounced accent. 'Now here, Frauleins, is Red Square, the centre of the city.'

'Why is it called Red Square?' Birgit asked. 'There is nothing red in it.'

'Red does not refer to the colour,' Dmitri said severely. 'In Russian red means brave, courageous, bold. Now, I am going to take you on a tour of the Kremlin. You will see all the art treasures, as well as the great bell and the huge cannon with which our ancestors repelled the Mongols.'

Anna reflected that they were going to get a very one-sided view of history: to her knowledge the Russians had never succeeded in repelling the Mongols.

'But first,' Dmitri went on, 'we will visit the tomb of our great leader.'

'Herr Stalin is dead?' Marlene asked.

Dmitri raised his eyes to heaven. 'I am referring to Vladimir Lenin, the founder of the Communist State. Over here.'

He led them across the cobbles to the Kremlin wall towering some forty feet above them. Let into the wall were a series of niches, each fronted by a portrait. 'In those,' he explained, 'are the ashes of all our great leaders, who have sadly departed from this world.'

Anna could not resist the temptation. 'You mean men like Marshal Tukhachevski and Nicolai Bukharin?' They were two of the Bolshevik leaders executed by Stalin three years before.

'I was speaking of our great leaders, not criminal deviationists,' Dmitri said stiffly.

'Oh, I am sorry. I always thought that Marshal Tukhachevski was the greatest of all Soviet soldiers.'

'A criminal deviationist,' Dmitri insisted firmly. 'Come along, Frauleins.'

'This is going to take all day,' Marlene muttered as they approached the wall and the end of a long line of people.

Anna had to suppose she was right. But Dmitri merely led them up the line to the front, repeating in a loud voice, 'Intourist! Intourist!' and everyone immediately stepped aside.

'Pays to have friends in high places,' she murmured.

There were two armed soldiers slowly goose-stepping up and down outside the entrance to the tomb. Inside the darkened chamber there were more armed guards. The three young women were escorted to the railing to look down past the glass casket at the dead hero reclining on his back with his hands on his chest. He wore a three-piece grey suit and black shoes, and his goatee beard reminded Anna of Reiffel.

'Gosh!' Birgit said. 'When did he die?'

'Sixteen years ago,' Dmitri told her.

'But . . .'

'He's embalmed, silly,' Marlene said.

As they left the tomb it began to rain. 'This is going to be a long winter,' Anna commented.

Weather-wise she was absolutely correct. At the beginning of September it started to rain seriously; at the beginning of October it started to snow and by the beginning of November the temperatures were well below zero.

'How long does this last?' Marlene enquired of one of the Embassy staff.

'It may start to thaw in April,' he told her.

'Jesus!' she muttered.

Yet they were not uncomfortable, certainly within the Embassy. Anna was given a spacious apartment, to which she was shown by Countess von Schulenburg herself, who explained that this was a wing of the building which had been recently modernised. It contained three bedrooms, the master bedroom being en suite, while the other two had a bathroom between them, a sitting room with a dining table at the far end, and its own small kitchen, so that they did not have to attend meals in the mess hall unless they wished. The original heavy furniture and tasselled brocade curtains remained.

Nor were they bored, at least for a while. In keeping with the role Anna was required to play, Meissenbach allotted her an office of her own where she and Marlene could be surrounded by typewriters and filing cabinets, and even found them work to do, handling various internal affairs of the Embassy. In the evenings they were often escorted to the Puppet Theatre, or the Bolshoi ballet, or concerts at the Moscow Conservatoire, which sometimes included performances by Shostakovich.

To Anna, brought up in Vienna, the work of even the Russian genius was heavy and unexciting, probably due to the fact that everything he wrote had to be approved by a Party official. This applied even more to the film industry, which produced an endless succession of bowdlerised and turgid romances about young women falling in love with young men who were heroes of the Soviet Union for having dug five tons of coal more than their comrades.

The overall word for the society in which she found herself was grey. Even the cocktail parties to which Meissenbach saw that she was regularly invited were grey affairs in her opinion. The liquor consisted mainly of vodka and Russian 'champagne', which was hardly more than fizzy water. The conversation was so carefully non-committal as to be puerile. Nor did the various commissars appear terribly responsive to her charms. In fact she got the strong impression that the average Russian did not like the average German. Or even the exceptional German.

The atmosphere was slightly better, overall, at the small parties Meissenbach threw in his own quarters, but from Anna's point of view they were rendered less than attractive by the presence of the hostess, whose dislike for her became more evident every day.

But the most important, and disappointing, aspect of her situation was that she was not getting any real work done, on either front. She thought her big moment had come at a party in early October when almost as soon as she entered the room she recognized Chalyapov, standing some distance away, smoking a cigarette and talking to several men. As the young Embassy official who was escorting her obviously did not know who Chalyapov was, and therefore could not be asked to provide an introduction – and as Heydrich had warned her not to be forward, but to let events take their course – she could do nothing more than slowly work her way closer to her target and wait to be noticed. But suddenly, when she was still some ten feet away from him, with quite a few people between them, Chalyapov left the room, apparently without seeing her at all. She scanned the guest lists for every Embassy party, but his name was never on it, while on the one occasion she managed to get hold of a list of staff at the British Embassy, Clive Bartley was also not to be seen. Nor was any attempt made to contact her.

Which was not to say that she lacked male attention. Count von Schulenburg himself clearly enjoyed the view, although equally clearly he was far too much of an old-fashioned gentleman ever to consider taking off after an employee, however attractive. The Count was also disturbed by her very presence. 'This is most unusual and irregular, Countess,' he had remarked when he received her in his office. 'We have never had an SD agent here before, and these instructions that you are to have carte blanche, as it were . . .' He peered at her. 'I mean, you are really very young to be given such responsibility, and, well . . .'

'I am also a woman, sir,' Anna said softly.

'Isn't the SD a counter-espionage department? I had no idea they employed women at all.'

'That is one of their secrets, Your Excellency, and we are, after all, a secret department. As regards both my gender and my age, I am merely carrying out my orders. As we are all required to do.'

He frowned at the implied rebuke. 'And I am not to know what those orders are. That is most unsatisfactory.'

'I am sorry, sir. You are of course quite entitled to take the matter up with Herr von Ribbentrop, or indeed with General Himmler, if you so wish.'

'I may take that under consideration, Countess. But I will say this: I will allow you carte blanche to pursue your allotted task, but I will not have the workings of this Embassy – and even more the good relations I have established with Monsieur Molotov and the Soviet Government – in any way disrupted. Please remember that. Good morning.'

If that was ominous, what was even more disturbing was the fact that she definitely did attract Hans Groener. Even if he had no idea what her mission was, there could be no doubt that he had a predatory eye for beauty. Sadly, with his tall, lanky frame, his moon face, and his bristly Prussian hair cut, he was not the least attractive as a man.

He made his move early on, summoning her to his office only a week after her arrival. 'You understand, Fraulein, that I am in charge of Embassy security. And in this regard I require absolute compliance from every member of the staff.'

'That must be very interesting,' Anna said agreeably, sitting before his desk with her knees crossed.

Groener opened the file in front of him. 'There are a few things I need to verify.'

'One of them should be that I am the Countess von Widerstand,' Anna said.

He regarded her for several seconds. 'You are Anna Fehrbach. You are a secretary in the Gestapo. It says so here.

Thus you are my junior. But I am informed that you are here in a special capacity, which places you outside my jurisdiction. I wish to know what this is.'

'I am here as Personal Assistant to Herr Meissenbach in whatever capacity he requires of me.'

Another long stare. 'What possible assistance could he expect from a Gestapo secretary?'

Anna smiled at him. 'You will have to ask him that, Herr Groener.' She decided to drop Heinz into it, as that was the easiest solution for her. 'He arranged for the posting.'

Groener's nostrils twitched. 'You have known Herr Meissenbach a long time?'

'It seems that I have known him a very long time,' Anna replied, being absolutely truthful.

'I see. Well, I shall keep an eye on you, and Herr Meissenbach. We do not wish any scandal. I assume Frau Meissenbach is also an old friend?'

Anna smiled again. 'Wives are never close friends with their husband's female aides, Herr Groener.'

It was disconcerting to feel that she was regarded with such suspicion by her own people, but she could do nothing more than ignore them, especially as she had not yet found herself in a position to commence her mission. But it was Groener who came to her at the beginning of December and placed an envelope on her desk. It was addressed to the Countess von Widerstand and marked Top Secret. 'From Berlin,' he announced.

Anna turned the envelope over to look at the seal, which appeared unbroken.

'I have not opened it, Countess. But I am entitled to ask you to inform me of the contents.'

Anna broke the seal and took out the single sheet of paper; it bore Heydrich's personal crest.

> I am disappointed not to have heard from you. The situation changes every day, and while I recommended patience, that is now no longer possible. You must make contact with your quarry by Christmas. Inform me the moment this is done. Heydrich.

‘Well?’ Groener inquired.

Anna struck a match and carefully burned the letter.

‘What the hell . . .?’

‘This is a personal message from General Heydrich to me. If you feel entitled to know what was in it, I suggest you contact the General and ask for a transcript.’

He glared at her for several seconds, then turned and left the room.

Clearly Heydrich was growing impatient. So was she, but her impatience was more to discover why Clive had not turned up – and, if his visit had been cancelled, why no one from the British Embassy had attempted to make contact. However, satisfying Heydrich had to take priority, only she did not see what she could do about it.

It was Meissenbach who inadvertently provided the answer. He had not been making life any easier for her. As Greta was now firmly on dry land, as it were, she no longer took sleeping pills, and thus he found it impossible to get away at night. It was obviously even more difficult for them to get together during the day. He came to her office regularly, which was reasonable, but here again he always found Marlene in situ. It was only a few days after Heydrich’s letter that he paid one of his calls.

‘Apparently Count von Schulenburg is very proud of the Embassy’s Christmas parties. I would like you to handle the invitations for this year’s. It’s very simple. It seems we invite exactly who we invited last year.’

Alarm bells immediately started jangling in Anna’s brain.

Meissenbach was now bending over her shoulder, as if continuing his instructions. ‘Can’t you get rid of her?’ he whispered. ‘I don’t understand what she is doing here in the first place. Do you need an assistant?’

‘My superiors feel that it is necessary.’

‘For what purpose? Don’t tell me she is also a professional assassin?’

‘I would not call her a professional anything. Neither would I call myself an assassin. You should think of me as a bodyguard.’

‘I only wish to think of you as the most desirable woman in the world. Anna, I’ve got to have you. I am going mad.’

For the time being he had to be humoured. She squeezed his hand. 'Let us see what can be done.' The idea was crystallising; everything she sought, on both fronts, could be dropping into her lap. All that was required was to keep this lovesick oaf happy. 'Marlene, would you go down to the Records Office and find me the guest list for last year's Christmas party?'

'Of course, Countess.' Marlene hurried from the room.

'I cannot offer you more than fifteen minutes,' she said.

'I can prolong it,' Meissenbach said, and picked up her telephone to dial the Records Office. 'Ah, Bluther? Will you come up to my office, please? There is something I wish to discuss with you. Thank you.' He replaced the phone. 'It will take Bluther ten minutes to get up to the office, where Frau Estner will tell him that I am not there. She does not know where I have gone. He will probably wait for at least five minutes to see if I return, and then he will go back to Records. By that time Fraulein Gehrig will be waiting to access the document she requires. Then they will have to find it before she can return here. I would say we have half an hour.'

'You are an organisational genius. But . . .' Anna looked around her. In addition to the filing cabinets, and two tables with typewriters on them, the office contained two desks, each with a reasonably comfortable but not very large chair, as well as two straight chairs. 'I do not have much to offer you.'

'You have everything I wish,' he declared, sweeping blotting paper and pens from her desk. Then she was stretched across it, her dress around her waist, her cami-knickers pulled aside, and he was inside her. *The things I do for Germany*, she reflected. Or was it for England? But it enhanced her image as a woman who could not resist the offer of sex, and she felt that might come in very handy later on.

They were again fully dressed, and her desk restored, before Marlene returned, even if Heinz was still breathing somewhat heavily.

Anna glanced down the invitation list. 'These are all Russians and Americans.'

'Well, we are in Russia. And the Americans are neutral.'

'They are such boring people. So are the Yanks. Don't you

think it might be rather amusing to invite a few people from the British Embassy?'

Meissenbach raised his eyebrows. 'You wish to invite British Embassy officials to come here?'

'Why not? They are not likely to arrive with guns in hand, shooting at us.'

'But we are still at war.'

'Isn't the war just about over? What military activity has there been, except at sea or in the air, since July?'

'They are certainly shooting at the Italians in Libya.'

'The Italians.' Anna got all the Aryan contempt she could into her voice.

'I know. As allies they are not worth a damn. And they are making a complete mess of their so-called invasion of Greece. But I imagine the British lump them together with us.'

'I still think it may be amusing, and it could well be informative to entertain them.'

'And you will be present?'

'Well, I would hope so.'

'Anna, to the British you are a traitor.'

'And do you suppose they will endeavour to arrest me? They have no jurisdiction anywhere in Russia, outside of their own embassy. In any event, I should not think any member of the British Embassy has any idea who the Countess von Widerstand is. The famous spy who escaped from England in May was the Honourable Mrs Ballantine Bordman.'

He stroked his chin.

Anna pressed home her advantage. 'Do you know, I could even try vamping one of them . . .'

'Anna, you are incorrigible. But I adore you. Invite who you like. Just let me have the list before you send the invitations. You do understand that I will have to submit both the idea and the guest list to the Ambassador?'

Anna kissed him. 'Tell him it is my idea.'

'This place is impossible,' Marlene complained when Meissenbach left. 'Herr Bluther was not there, and no one knew where he was. So I had to wait. Then when he returned he told me that he had been summoned to Herr Meissenbach's office. But when he got there, Herr Meissenbach was not there, and no one knew where *he* was. Well, I could have told him that. But he hung around Herr Meissenbach's office for ten minutes before coming back down to Records! How we won the war defeats me.'

Anna sat behind her desk. 'Well, I have another job for you. I wish a complete list of everyone who is employed by, or at, the British embassy.'

Marlene's eyes became as large as saucers. 'You mean we are . . .'

Anna rested her finger on her lips. 'We are going to invite them to the party. Some of them, at any rate.'

Marlene bustled off. Anna glanced at the previous year's list and frowned. There was no Chalyapov! But Meissenbach had told her to invite whichever of the Russians she chose. On the other hand, if Clive *was* in Moscow, she did not really want them both meeting her at the same time.

Marlene returned fifteen minutes later with another list. 'Do you think any of them will come?'

'I am sure of it.' Anna hoped the girl could not hear the pounding of her heart as she scanned the names. None of them meant anything to her. Damnation! Of course he might not be risking his own name. But as far as she knew he had never previously operated in Russia, nor was he even widely known in the Gestapo. Certainly she did not think that Groener, who had been in Moscow for some years, would ever have heard of him.

But on the fairly safe assumption that, for whatever reason, Clive had not yet arrived, or might not be coming at all – she had only the code word Belinda to work on – she owed it to both her employers to get on with her mission.

'Well then,' she said. 'Let's see. We'll start with the ambassador and his wife, with this chap . . .' She ticked each name. 'And this chap and his wife. And this chap: a Commander Sprague; he sounds interesting.'

Marlene took the list, looking increasingly sceptical.

'Now for the Russian guests.' Anna spread the previous year's list in front of her and again began ticking names. 'I think we'll just add one: Ewfim Chalyapov.'

'You haven't ticked Marshal Stalin,' Marlene pointed out.

Stalin's name was certainly on the previous list. 'Well, of course we shall invite Marshal Stalin,' Anna agreed, although she saw from the cross beside his name that he had declined last year's invitation. Molotov had come, though.

As Anna had anticipated, a summons to the Ambassador's office soon arrived.

'You are a very enterprising young woman, Countess,' Count von Schulenburg remarked. A copy of the guest list lay on his desk. 'Herr Meissenbach tells me you are hoping to obtain some information from these people. I know, of course, that you are carrying out an instruction given to you by General Himmler. I just wish to repeat that I will permit nothing that may jeopardize the standing or the reputation of the Reich here in Moscow. I am sure, having spent three months here, you appreciate that the Soviet Regime is confoundedly suspicious of everything that does not seem to them to be above board. The point I am making is that there is almost as much hostility and mistrust between Moscow and London as there is between London and Berlin. Were the Soviets to become suspicious that the Wilhelmstrasse was attempting any kind of negotiation with Whitehall, the repercussions could be serious.'

He was entirely missing the point, for which she was grateful. 'I do understand that, Your Excellency. But throughout all history has it not been the accepted custom for warring states to maintain diplomatic contact in neutral capitals?'

'It is hard to regard the Soviets as neutral in any form. I will ask you this: were you sent here to open any such negotiations?'

Not in any sense that you might appreciate, Anna thought. 'No sir. I was sent here to obtain the general feel of the Soviet Government not only as regards us, but as regards Great Britain. I consider that to bring British and Russian diplomats together under our roof and in our presence, in a strictly social environment, may be interesting.'

'You are a singularly precocious young woman. Is it true that you are not yet twenty-one?'

'Yes sir.'

'And you have this much confidence placed in you by General Himmler?'

'I was trained by General Himmler,' Anna said reverently, reflecting that it was no lie, as Heydrich, Glauber – and even Hannah Gehrig – were all Himmler's creations.

'Well then, I must be content to leave the business in your hands. But I will also hold you responsible should anything unfortunate result from this scheme of yours.'

Anna was content, although again she saw some very large storm clouds on the horizon when she misbehaved herself, as it would certainly be interpreted by the scandal-conscious old gentleman.

But first the party. The invitations went out and she awaited the replies with some anxiety. The British Ambassador declined but the other invited members of his staff accepted, no doubt on his instructions. The Americans all accepted, as did the Russians, with the exception of Stalin. This was clearly a disappointment to Meissenbach, but Anna reckoned he would only get in the way.

'Am I coming too?' Marlene asked.

'You are not invited,' Anna pointed out.

'I am just a dogsbody,' she grumbled.

'This party is for diplomats and senior officials. Your time will come,' Anna assured her.

Commander John Sprague looked up from his desk at the figure standing before him. 'My God!' he remarked. 'I had given you up for lost. I was advised by London that you had been put out of action for the foreseeable future.'

Clive Bartley sat before the desk. 'I thought I had been put out of action as well. You wouldn't believe it, but the plane I was travelling on was shot down by Italian fighters off Malta. Spent two days in a rubber dinghy drifting about the place with a bullet in my back and a chap dying on either side of me.'

'Sounds rough,' Sprague agreed. 'But you were all right?'

'Unfortunately not. I spent six weeks in a hospital, being bombed almost daily. It was worse than the Blitz.'

'May I assume that you are now again fit?'

'Entirely.'

'Well, I will wish you better fortune going back.'

'My dear fellow, I am not going back until I have done what I was sent here to do.'

Sprague gave him an old-fashioned look. 'Whatever you were sent here to do, it was four months ago. It cannot possibly still have any relevance.'

'It is just as relevant now as it was then. Perhaps more so. I am to make contact with one of our people serving in the German Embassy.'

Now Sprague was frowning. 'We have an agent in the German Embassy? Why was I not informed of this?'

'Because it is the most closely guarded secret MI6 currently possesses. This . . . ah . . . agent is one of our very best people and is carrying out a mission of the utmost importance.'

'And how do you propose to contact him?'

'Is there no liaison between the embassies at all?'

'Not so you'd notice. Although, oddly enough, half a dozen of us have been invited to their Christmas party. His nibs isn't happy, but he's agreed that we can go, providing we keep our noses clean.'

'Brilliant,' Clive said. 'I'll come with you.'

'My dear fellow, you haven't been invited.'

'Do you think they will turn me away?'

'It could happen. They have a new Chief Secretary, a chap named Meissenbach. He used to be in Prague. Earned himself a reputation as a hard man. The Czechs even tried to bump him off. You must know about that.'

'We set it up,' Clive said, his brain spinning. 'And you say Meissenbach is now in Moscow?'

'Running the embassy. He sent the invitations, or at least his sidekick did. Some Countess or other. Supposed to be quite a dish. I haven't seen her myself. I suppose she is one of these big-titted Valkyrie types. I say, old man, are you all right?'

'John,' Clive said, having got his breathing back under control. 'I am going to attend this party and take my chances.'

Six

The Party

Anna found herself becoming increasingly agitated as the date of the party approached. She had no real expectation of making any progress with the British, unless they used the opportunity to arrange contact. But Chalyapov . . . She told herself that he was only a man, surely more interesting than Bordman had ever been. But possibly far more intelligent, and therefore more difficult to hoodwink on a continual basis.

And suppose he did not, after all, find her sufficiently attractive to seduce her? Heydrich had refused to contemplate that possibility. She wore her favourite pale blue sheath, with its deep décolletage, her gold earrings and crucifix, which sat so entrancingly in the valley between her breasts. The ruby ring was unnecessary as she was wearing elbow-length white gloves. 'I think you would look even better with your hair up,' Marlene suggested.

Anna stood before her full-length mirror and scooped her hair away from her neck. 'Do you know, you could be right.'

'Nothing should be allowed to detract from your face,' Birgit said enthusiastically.

They consider me some kind of gigantic doll, Anna thought, merely to be played with. But she had to agree that it was a good idea; she could always let her hair down when the opportunity arose.

Her coiffure completed, she hurried to the ballroom to make sure everything was going according to plan: the white-gloved waiters, the champagne already opened and waiting on ice, the silver trays of canapés arranged in mouth-watering expectation in the pantry.

'Anna! You look superb.' Meissenbach kissed her gloved hand. 'I have never seen you with your hair up.'

'Then perhaps you have never seen me at my best. Frau Meissenbach.' She bestowed a gracious smile upon Greta, who was looking more out of sorts than ever, in high-necked brown velvet, dripping with what Anna considered vulgar jewellery. 'Excuse me.' She hurried across the room to greet Count von Schulenburg and his wife, who had just entered. 'Your Excellency! Countess! I hope everything is in order.'

Schulenburg kissed her glove. 'I have no doubt of it.'

'And you look absolutely charming, my dear,' Countess von Schulenburg said. She was a tall, gracious woman who must have been a beauty twenty years before, Anna estimated. She did not know if the Count had confided any of his disquiet at her presence in Moscow to his wife, but the Countess had always been unfailingly pleasant to her.

Then she found herself facing Groener. 'Did I invite you?' she asked. 'I don't remember doing so.'

'I do not require an invitation. I am on duty.'

'I do not think a Christmas party is a suitable place for a policeman to be on duty.'

'But my dear Countess, you are a policewoman. Are you not also on duty?'

Anna glared at him, but the room was starting to fill with senior embassy staff members and their wives; it was time to form the reception line. Anna had not supposed she should be involved in this, but Schulenburg insisted. 'This is your party, Countess. You organized it.'

So she found herself number five, next to Greta Meissenbach, who produced a monumental sniff.

The Americans arrived first, and came slowly down the line. Anna was not very interested in them, until one man, who was not accompanied by a wife, bent over her glove. 'I have waited a long time for this privilege, Countess.'

Anna stared at him. He was tall, quite handsome in a somewhat cynical manner, and very well dressed, but she could not remember having seen him before. 'Have we met, sir?' she asked.

He was still holding her hand. 'Sadly, no. But I saw you at the Cheltenham race meeting, two years ago.' He smiled. 'Your name, as I recall, was the Honourable Mrs Ballantine Bordman.'

Anna felt vaguely sick. 'Are you sure you are not mistaken, Mr . . .?' His name had been announced, but she had not been listening.

'Andrews, Countess. Joseph Andrews. And I do assure you that no man could possibly mistake your face once he has seen you.'

Anna withdrew her hand. 'I look forward to having a talk with you, Mr Andrews. Later on.'

'I am looking forward to that, too.'

He went on to join the other guests, and Anna let her breath go in a vast sigh. She supposed something like this had always been bound to happen. But what repercussions might there be? If he had known about Anna Bordman, he would know that she was a German spy. That would only matter here in Moscow if he felt obliged to pass the information on to a local contact. But why should he do that? As far as she knew there was no great love lost between Russia and the United States at this moment.

Her reverie was interrupted by the arrival of the Russians, and a few minutes later she was gazing at Ewfim Chalyapov, who was in turn gazing at her.

'Countess von Widerstand.' His voice was quiet, his German faultless. 'They told me the most beautiful woman in Europe was working at the German Embassy, and I did not believe them.'

'Because you possess sufficient beautiful women of your own, Herr Chalyapov?'

He looked into her eyes. Perhaps, she thought, he does not like women who can riposte. But then he squeezed her fingers. 'No man could ever possess a beauty to equal yours, Countess. Will I see you later?'

'I shall be circulating, Herr Chalyapov.'

'And I shall be waiting, Countess.'

He moved off. Once again she was breathless. But it had seemed almost too easy.

The English guests were arriving. She glanced along the line before they reached her, and this time felt quite paralysed.

'Commander John Sprague, Countess,' the Commander explained. 'And this is an associate who has just arrived in Moscow, Mr Clive Bartley. I know he was not invited, but the Ambassador seems to feel he is acceptable.'

'Of course.' Anna kept her voice at its normal pitch with some effort. She could hardly believe this was happening, and her usual quickness of thought and decision had for the moment deserted her. 'Welcome to Moscow, Mr Bartley.'

'I had intended to visit the city some time ago,' Clive said. 'But I was delayed. Now I feel it was almost worthwhile.'

Sprague had moved on. Clive opened his mouth again, and she said softly, 'Wait.'

He followed Sprague into the throng. There were still more guests to be greeted and it was fifteen minutes before the reception line broke up and she was able to move away. She took a glass of champagne from a passing tray and went into the crowd of people, having to stop and chat with most of them, while she took her bearings, acutely aware that Groener was watching her. Chalyapov was standing, as she remembered from the previous occasion she had seen him, against the far wall, smoking, as usual surrounded by several people. They were talking animatedly, and he appeared to be listening, but like Groener he was watching the room and she knew he was looking for her. Their eyes met, and he gave a little inclination of his head. She responded and began to move towards him only to find herself joined by both Clive and Andrews, who seemed to know each other.

'Small world, Countess,' Andrews remarked.

'And growing smaller by the moment, Mr Andrews,' she agreed. 'Do I gather you are acquainted with this gentleman?'

'You could say we're in the same line of business,' Andrews acknowledged. 'But of course you and Mr Bartley know each other.'

Anna raised her eyebrows.

'There, you see, Clive old boy, she's forgotten you.'

'We met in Berlin in 1938,' Clive said. 'When I was there with your husband. He is still your husband, is he not?'

'Perhaps, just about,' Anna said. 'I know he sued for divorce, after I left England. But as that was only seven months ago, I do not know if the matter has been concluded as yet.'

'Bit tiresome if nobody troubles to inform you,' Andrews suggested.

Anna shrugged. 'It is of no matter. In Germany, and here in Russia, I have reverted to my maiden name, the Countess von Widerstand.'

'But surely, even in Germany, you cannot marry again until your divorce is finalized?'

'I have not considered the matter, Mr Andrews, as at this moment I have no desire to marry again.'

'Point taken. Did you ever get close to catching the Countess, Clive?'

'That is a state secret. And definitely not cocktail party conversation,' Clive said with a smile. 'Countess, I hate to be gauche, but I am not used to this cold weather. Would I be arrested if I went looking for a bathroom?'

Anna smiled back. 'Very probably. We could not have an English Secret Service agent wandering about the corridors of the German Embassy, now could we? If you will excuse us, Mr Andrews, I will just indicate to Mr Bartley where he should go, and find him an escort. Mr Bartley?'

Clive followed her to one of the exit doors. 'God, it's been too long. When?'

'I will walk in Gorky Park tomorrow at eleven.'

'It's twenty below.'

'I'm sure you can borrow a fur coat. We meet by accident. Ah, Gustav . . .' She summoned a footman. 'This gentleman needs to use the bathroom. Will you accompany him please? And bring him back to the ballroom.'

Gustav gave a brief bow.

'You have been very kind,' Clive said. 'I would hope to see you again, Countess.'

'I'm sure you shall, Mr Bartley.'

Anna waited for a few seconds before re-entering the ballroom. She was not used to having her emotions in such a jangled state, at least when she had not recently engaged in any extreme action. She had almost given up hope of seeing him again. Apart from the emotional loss she had been growing increasingly anxious about the way she had apparently been dropped by MI6. But he was here, and she would see him tomorrow, even if in the middle of a snowstorm. What might happen after that she was prepared to leave up to him. She had no doubt that he wanted to get together with her as much as she wanted to get together with him. Love? Or lust? Or just a desperate need to know that somewhere in the world there was someone who actually cared about her? That was her need, certainly; the problem was she did not know if it was his.

But meanwhile, back to work. She arranged her features

and entered the room, paused, looked around her, and had a sudden spasm of sheer panic. Chalyapov was nowhere to be seen. If he had made one of his sudden departures, she was in deep trouble: there was no saying when she could arrange for them to meet again.

Then she saw him. He had moved to the far side of the room and had his back to her. She hurried towards him, smiling at people and resisting as politely as possible their desire to have her stop and talk with them. Groener was in turn moving towards her, but she neatly side-stepped him. 'Herr Chalyapov.'

He turned, frowned, and then raised his eyebrows; as always, he had a cigarette in his fingers.

'I just wanted to make sure you were being looked after.'

Now his face relaxed. 'And I thought you had forgotten all about me, Countess. When I saw you leave the room with that fellow . . . He was with the English party, was he not?'

'I think so. Believe it or not, he wished to relieve himself.' She chose her words with care: according to Heydrich, this man wanted earthy women. 'And I could not merely direct him. He is an enemy of the Reich.'

'So did you accompany him, and hold his . . . hand?'

'I handed him over to one of our people. You have not told me whether you are enjoying yourself.'

'Frankly, no – up to this moment. Do you think things will change for the better?'

'I would like to think so, Herr Chalyapov. It is my business to see that our guests have all they require.'

He put the cigarette to his lips and inhaled deeply. 'What I require may not be acceptable to you.'

Anna lowered her eyes. 'Tell me, and I will do my best to find it for you.'

'Your company, Countess. Shall we say supper?'

'Tonight, sir?'

'Why not? You have surely done everything that you possibly can to ensure the success of the party. Now you must enjoy yourself.'

'But not here?'

'A man and a woman can only truly appreciate each other's company when they are *tête à tête*.'

'I take your point. But you will have to be patient. I cannot possibly leave the party until it is over.'

He smiled and stubbed out his cigarette on an adjacent ashtray. 'But you will be leaving with me. I do assure you that no one will attempt to stop us.'

Anna hesitated briefly. But she had already deduced that he was not a man to take no for an answer, without at the same time taking offence, and she was under orders. If a crisis with either Schulenburg or Meissenbach would therefore happen sooner rather than later, it would just have to happen.

'It is snowing outside,' he said. 'You will need a coat and heavier shoes.'

'Give me ten minutes.' She hurried from the room, praying that she would not encounter Clive. She ran upstairs to her apartment where Birgit and Marlene were playing chess.

'Oh, Countess!' Marlene cried. 'Is it going well?'

'I think so.' Anna took her mink and matching hat from the wardrobe, slung the coat over her arm and tucked the hat under it, added a silk scarf, and smiled at them, 'Don't wait up.'

As the party was still bubbling, few people actually observed Chalyapov and Anna leave the ballroom for the lobby. Clive was back in the room, and endeavoured to catch her eye, but she merely smiled at him and went on. Chalyapov helped her into her coat, watched while she wrapped her scarf round her neck, adjusted her hat in the mirror and then stooped to slide her feet into the boots she kept in the porter's office. The two guards on duty pretended not to notice them. She slipped her dainty shoes into the mink pockets.

'Is the rest of you as elegant as your clothes, Countess?'

'Perhaps one day you may be able to form a judgement on that.'

'In Russia,' he said, 'we learn to live for today.'

Anna was still digesting this as they approached the waiting limousine. She slipped on the icy ground as she reached the car and would have fallen had Chalyapov not grabbed her round the waist with one hand, opened the door with the other, and then placed the same hand on her buttocks to thrust her in. She gave a little shriek as she landed on her knees, half on the seat. The door slammed and the car moved away, but Chalyapov's hand remained grasping her bottom to push her up on to the seat, still on her knees. While she gasped for breath, face pressed into the back cushions, he slid his hand under the coat and the gown to feel her calves. 'You are frozen,' he said solicitously.

'All over,' she panted.

This was a mistake, as he now turned her round, released the belt of the coat, opened it and was inside her décolletage before she could do anything to stop him. Although he was not at that moment smoking, she was enveloped in an aroma of stale tobacco. As she had never smoked herself, she found this extremely off-putting.

His hands were also cold, but not as cold as her frozen nipples. 'You are enchanting,' he murmured, and kissed her, not brutally, but with extreme passion..

She pushed him away, drawing great breaths. She could see his frown even in the darkness. 'You do not like me,' he protested.

'Of course I like you, Herr Chalyapov. But you must give me time to breathe.' *And to understand what is going to happen to me.* But whatever it was, it had to be accepted, endured, and if possible enjoyed. Certainly it was an experience outside anything she had previously known. Quite apart from never having had sex in the back of a car before, she had never been quite so manhandled. Again, there was no brutality in what he did, but his hands seemed to be everywhere at the same time, moving with irresistible purpose. He did not bother to remove her coat, but had her long skirt up to her thighs in a moment. She was wearing nothing under her gown, and she got a brief glimpse of the driver adjusting his rear-view mirror before Chalyapov had released his pants, and had her sitting astride him, surging to and fro while he nuzzled her breasts, fondled her buttocks, and kissed her mouth.

It was all rather quick. As she felt him spend, she kissed him and removed herself.

'The moment I saw you,' he said, 'I knew I must have you.'

'And you do everything immediately,' she suggested.

'If I can. Now, we shall go to my home, and make love all night.'

Oh Lord, she thought. It was only eight o'clock. 'You said something about supper.'

'Oh, there will be food. But I would rather make love.'

'I will be better after I have eaten.'

'You could not be better. But I want you naked. Do you know what I am going to do to you?'

She wasn't sure she wanted to find out. 'You will have to tell me.'

'I wish to lick you, from head to toe.'

It was three in the morning before Anna got home. The embassy was in darkness, save for the lobby, where two different night guards were on duty.

'Countess?' They peered at her. She knew she must look a sight. Chalyapov had released her hair and had proceeded to play with it, leaving it a tangled mess. She had no make-up left, her cheeks were still flushed, and although her mink hid the ruination of her dress, they could have no doubt that she had spent a thoroughly tousling evening.

She smiled at them and went up to her apartment. The debris of the party had already been cleared away, and she encountered no one. She had taken off her boots in the lobby and entered the suite on tiptoe, so as not to disturb the girls, and locked her bedroom door. Then she threw her clothes on the floor and stood beneath the hot shower for several minutes. This was necessary because she had again become very chilled on the drive home, but it was also important if she was ever going to feel clean again. As he had soon resumed smoking, her hair stank of it.

The disturbing fact was that she had enjoyed most of what had been done to her. When Chalyapov had said he wanted to lick her all over, he had meant it. He had revealed a remarkable knowledge of the female anatomy, and of its requirements, and had brought her to orgasm with his tongue, before resuming what she might consider normal sex. She supposed he must have entered her about six times, and in between had never stopped playing with her. And he wanted to see her again, and again and again. As she must want to see him. But if indeed he liked to maintain a mistress for a year, she supposed this might be considered some sort of punishment for her sins.

And in the meantime, crisis. On several fronts.

She could only take each one as it came. The girls were in a state of high excitement, which increased as they sorted out her discarded clothing and examined the torn dress. 'Burn that,' Anna told them. 'And I shall need a dressmaker. Have you anything to report?'

'Oh, Countess . . .' They both started speaking together. Apparently Meissenbach had visited the suite when the party ended, looking for her, and they had felt obliged to tell him that she had gone out. 'He seemed awfully put out,' Marlene said.

'He is always put out about something or other,' Anna remarked. She breakfasted, dressed and went down to her office. The Embassy was just waking up, and those people she passed on the stairs or in the corridors gave her nervous smiles. She sat at her desk, took out a sheet of her personal notepaper, and wrote two words: *Contact! Wow!* As she addressed and sealed the envelope, marking it Private and Confidential, she wondered if Heydrich had any sense of humour.

She took the envelope along to the Gestapo offices, received another anxious smile from the woman secretary at the outer desk, and entered Groener's office after a brief knock.

'Countess? I am told you left the Embassy without permission or notifying anyone last night, and that you did not return until three o'clock this morning. I wish an explanation.'

'I left the Embassy on official business for the Reich,' Anna said coldly. 'Business which, as you are aware, is known only to the SD. I have a message here for General Heydrich which I wish to go off in today's pouch.' She laid the envelope on his desk.

He gazed at it. 'I do not think I can permit this.'

'Herr Groener, I am giving you an order as an officer in the SD. If you wish to disobey that order, I will have to report the matter to General Heydrich.'

'I intend to report the matter to the Ambassador,' Groener snapped.

'That, Herr Groener, is your prerogative. But if General Heydrich does not receive that letter tomorrow, I will not answer for your future.'

She returned to her office and found Meissenbach waiting, a terrified Marlene cowering behind her desk. 'Where were you last night?' he demanded.

'Out.'

'You walked out in the middle of the party with one of those Russian louts. I saw you go. I could not believe my eyes. And you had not returned three hours later.'

'You know this because you checked. I will not be spied on, Heinz. Spying is my business, not yours. Nor will I be treated like some schoolgirl Cinderella. What I do, and whom I do it with, is my business. If it will reassure you, it is also the business of the Reich.'

Meissenbach stared at her with his mouth open, his cheeks turning red. 'And you expect me to continue the charade of having you work for me?'

'Of course. That also is for the Reich.'

The telephone jangled. Marlene hurried across the room to pick it up. 'Countess von Widerstand's office . . . Oh. Ah . . . Yes of course. Immediately.' She replaced the receiver and looked at Anna. 'That was Count von Schulenburg's secretary. The Ambassador wishes to see you immediately, Countess.'

'I would say your days are numbered,' Meissenbach said smugly. 'Or are you going to attempt to tell the Ambassador to mind his own business?'

'If I have to,' Anna said.

'Sit down, Countess,' Schulenburg invited.

Anna did so and crossed her knees.

'I have received a most serious complaint from Herr Groener. Would you like to explain it to me?'

'I had to go out last night, for a prolonged period, sir.'

'With a senior Russian official?'

'Yes sir.'

Schulenburg looked down at the paper on his desk. 'Groener states here that his security people reported that you did not return until three o'clock this morning, and that you were . . .' He hesitated. '. . . in a dishevelled state.'

'I'm afraid I was. Yes sir.'

'And you do not feel able to give me an explanation?'

'I cannot, sir.'

Schulenburg leaned back in his chair. 'That you absented yourself for some seven hours, at night, in the company of a commissar, is apparently known throughout the Embassy. Which means, I have no doubt, that it is rapidly becoming well known throughout Moscow. I warned you that I would not tolerate any scandal that could bring this Embassy into disrepute. I regard your behaviour as being unacceptable.'

'Are you placing me under arrest, Your Excellency?' Anna asked in her most dulcet tone.

'I am today going to make a full report of this incident to Herr von Ribbentrop, and request that he instruct General Himmler immediately to recall you from Moscow.' He stared at her.

'You will do as you think fit, Your Excellency.' Anna looked at her watch. It was ten o'clock. 'Now, sir, if you will excuse me, I must leave the Embassy again.'

'And if I refuse you permission to do so?'

Anna stood up. 'I would reflect very seriously as to whether that would be a wise step to take, Your Excellency, in the absence of any instructions from Berlin.' She stood to attention. 'Heil Hitler!'

It was a great relief to get out of the Embassy, even if it was well below freezing outside. Anna was thoroughly wrapped up; apart from her furs, she wound a thick woollen scarf round her face from the nose down, and she wore dark glasses and ear-muffs. But the pleasure was more than physical. She actually disliked verbal confrontations, and to have three in rapid succession was disturbing. Nor did she truly know what the outcome would be. But she was carrying out her orders as faithfully as she could.

The park was deserted, save for the odd keeper, and she saw the unmistakable figure of Clive at a distance. 'Isn't this a terribly public place?' he asked.

'Not today. And we are meeting by accident, are we not? Did you enjoy last night?'

'No. Did you?'

She fell into step beside him. 'I was working.'

'I sincerely hope so. I understand that Russian chap you left with is quite important.'

'He is very important.'

'And you seduced him.'

'As I said, I was working. I hope you are not going to carp?'

'I wouldn't dream of it. Even if . . . Shit, Anna, the thought of you in another man's arms makes me, well . . .'

She squeezed his hand. 'Listen. Matters are a little fraught right now, but I hope they will be resolved within three days at the most. By the end of that time I shall either have been recalled to Berlin, or my position here will be unchallengeable. I am, of course, anticipating the latter. Now, that being so, I must continue and build on my relationship with Chalyapov. If it will relieve your mind, this is not a very entertaining prospect.'

'But you will carry it out to the best of your ability.'

'I do what has to be done, Clive, to the best of my ability at all times. That is my motto, and it is the key to my survival.'

'Even if it involves shooting two of our people in Prague.'

'I did not know they were your people. And in any event I was in my capacity as an SD agent. I hope you did not come here to quarrel.'

'I came here officially to find out just what you are at. And to see you. And . . .'

'You will, and I will give you a complete account of what I have been, and am, doing. But there is no need for me to see Chalyapov every night. What you must do is take a hotel room somewhere in Moscow, and I will come to you whenever I can.'

'You will be able to do this?'

'I've told you. In three days' time I shall either be back in Berlin, or my own mistress.' She squeezed his fingers. 'I would rather be your mistress. If you will walk here again in four days' time, I will be here, if I am still in Moscow. If I am not here, you will know that I have been recalled. If I am here, you will give me the address to go to, and I will come to you whenever I can.'

'Four days' time is Christmas Day.'

'Well then, we shall be a Christmas present to each other.'

He stopped walking and gazed at her. 'If the Russians . . .'

'All they can do is expel me.' Another smile. 'And you, perhaps.'

'You know, I am supposed to be controlling you.'

'Try it from the other side, just for once. You may enjoy it.'

'Anna, I adore you.'

'And I look forward to adoring you.' She released him and walked away.

'Dicey,' Sprague commented. 'She could be setting you up.'

'She isn't.'

Sprague regarded Clive for several seconds. 'It is highly

irregular for one of our people to live in a hotel instead of the Embassy. You do understand that the Reds have almost every hotel room bugged, and also make irregular checks.'

Clive grinned. 'The mysterious midnight phone call. I know a bit about bugs.'

'Well, I will have to inform the Ambassador. He may not like it.'

'I am travelling as an ordinary businessman,' Clive pointed out. 'If anything happens to me, you simply deny all knowledge of me.'

'Even if we know you are on your way to a gulag via the Lubianka. These chaps play pretty rough.'

'So do I,' Clive said. 'When I have to.'

Groener entered Anna's office, and without a word placed the envelope on her desk. Then he stared at her for several seconds, turned and left the room again.

'Ooh!' Marlene said. 'I thought he was going to arrest you.'

'In which case he would have arrested you as well,' Anna told her, and broke the seal on the envelope.

> Congratulations! I have cleared the air for you. These instructions are not to be confided to anyone, even your assistant. Circumstances continue to change every day, and your position must change with them. The political attitude of the Soviets towards Germany is no longer of great importance. We wish you to obtain information about the dispositions, morale, and commanding officers of the Soviet Army, particularly those on the Western frontier. You will of course be discreet. It is also important that you gain access to Marshal Stalin, which will require a working knowledge of the interior of the Kremlin. Inform me the moment this has been achieved. Burn this immediately. Heydrich.

Anna remained gazing at the note for some time. She was aware of a peculiarly chilled sensation across her shoulders. Heydrich could have no doubt that she was an intellectual genius. Therefore he must know that she would be able to interpret what he had just told her. Therefore the matter had to be urgent.

She struck a match and carefully burned the paper. As she

did so the telephone jangled. Marlene picked it up. 'The Countess von Widerstand's office. Yes, sir,' she put her hand over the mouthpiece. 'Herr Meissenbach,' she hissed.

She took the receiver. 'Good morning, Heinz.'

'I wish to see you.'

'In your office?'

'Yes. Now.'

'Now.' She handed the phone back to Marlene.

'Is there going to be trouble?' the girl asked.

'No,' Anna said, and went to the door.

'This is an intolerable situation,' Meissenbach announced.

Anna sat before his desk and crossed her knees. 'In what way, Heinz?'

'Berlin has virtually placed you in charge of the Embassy.'

'Of course they have not. They merely wish me to be allowed to carry out my duties without interference.'

'The Ambassador is furious. He is seeking further clarification from the Foreign Minister. It is quite unacceptable that he should not have ultimate jurisdiction over every member of his staff.'

'I am sure any clarification he requires will be provided. As you know, I can only carry out my orders, and this I intend to do.'

'By seducing every commissar you can lay hands on, is that it? Do you intend to turn the German Embassy into a brothel?'

'You have my word, Heinz, that I intend to seduce no one within these walls. But I would appreciate it if your interference in my affairs ceases now. And you should also require Herr Groener to do the same.' She smiled at him. 'I am sure this new arrangement will make Greta very happy.'

Seven

The Betrayal

Clive, with his irrepressible sense of humour, had chosen the Hotel Berlin as his Moscow residence, but there was method in his madness. It was a large, bustling place, its foyer dominated by a huge stuffed brown bear. There was always a crowd of people coming and going, even after dinner. No one paid the least attention to Anna when she entered; wrapped up against the cold as she was, even her beauty could not be noticed, while her obviously expensive clothes – she was wearing her mink – precluded any suggestion that she might be a prostitute looking for business.

Clive had given her his room number when they had met on Christmas Day. She crossed the foyer to the lifts. 'Five,' she told the attendant.

'Yes, comrade.' He pressed the appropriate button and they rode up. He gazed at her, but she did not remove any of her protective clothing, not even the scarf over her nose and mouth, although it was perfectly warm inside the hotel.

She left the lift and walked along the empty corridor. She knocked on the door, and was soon in his arms. He lifted her from the floor and carried her into the room, kicked the door shut while he kissed her mouth as she pulled the scarf away. 'I think I have waited all my life for this moment.'

He released her and she unwrapped herself, took off her hat, and shook out her hair. 'What actually kept you?'

'Would you believe that I was shot down?'

She had been laying her mink across a chair, but now she turned sharply. 'Where?'

'Over the Med.'

'But you're all right?'

'Well, obviously; I'm here. But I was a bit bashed up at the time. I stopped a bullet in the back of my thigh, and as it was a couple of days before I was rescued, I needed God knows how many blood transfusions. I spent a couple of months in a Maltese hospital, which put things back a bit.'

'God, I have been so worried, not knowing if you were coming at all.'

He stood against her, to slide his hands over her dress and down her back to caress her buttocks. 'Were you worried for me or for you?'

She kissed him. 'I have never lied to you. Are we alone?'

'I've taken out two rather obvious bugs.'

'Which you were meant to find. I think we need to be up close and personal.'

'I won't say no to that.'

They undressed facing each other, and then she was again in his arms. 'The thought of you in—'

She kissed him. 'No names. Let's get into bed.' He slid in beside her, and she put her hands down to hold him. 'We should have sex first. Or this chap will get in the way. How long is it since you had a woman?'

'I told you, I've been in hospital or recuperating for the last few months.'

'Umm. That means you're going to be away in seconds.'

'But we have all night. Haven't we?'

'Most of it. So, how would you like to start?'

'Well . . . Do you know, I have no idea what you do. What turns you on?'

'Everything turns me on, when I wish to be turned on. And I do everything. And I love you. You must not be shy with me. You want something we have not done before, and perhaps you do not do with Belinda. So do it with me.'

Clive took a deep breath. 'Would you suck me?'

She raised her head. 'You do not do that with Belinda?'

'Belinda is a rather old-fashioned woman. Don't get the wrong idea. She enjoys sex, but she likes to, well, close her eyes and let events take their course.'

'I think you were sex-starved even before your swim in the Med. Of course I will fellate you. But I think you wish to watch.'

She threw back the covers, and he caught her hand. 'What I would like most is . . . ah . . . well . . .'

Anna gazed at him for several seconds, and then gave a

gurgle of laughter. 'You shall have what you wish, sir, and we will see who can get the other off first.' She rose to her knees, turned her back on him, swung her leg across his chest to straddle him, and tossed hair from her eyes before lowering her head.

He lay with his arm round her, her head on his shoulder; for the moment their passion was spent. 'Tell me about Chalyapov.'

'He is a job of work.'

'Which is also my work.'

'Of course. What do you wish to know?'

'What precisely are your instructions?'

'They have changed, but I do not know how important you will think them. I came here to gain what information I could about Soviet feelings towards the Reich.'

'You did not find this odd?'

'Why should I?'

'Well, my darling, with the greatest possible respect, you are twenty years old, you have been trained to seduce men and you have been trained to kill. I don't think any of those accomplishments can have properly prepared you for evaluating political currents.'

'Perhaps you are right. In any event my instructions have now been changed, as I told you. I am now to use my intimacy with Chalyapov to discover as much as I can about Soviet troop concentrations.'

'And?'

'Well, I have not actually started yet. I am going to work on him the next time I meet him, which is the day after tomorrow.'

'He can provide this information?'

'According to Heydrich, he is one of Stalin's closest associates, and has access to the most sensitive information.'

'And have you drawn any conclusions from this?'

'Yes. I think Hitler is preparing for a war with Russia.'

'It certainly seems like it.'

'Will that help Great Britain?'

'Well, obviously, if Germany and Russia went to war it would take the heat off us, at least for a while.' He stroked her hair.

'Would it not provide you with an ally? A very powerful ally?'

‘That’s difficult to say. As to whether the Soviets would prove a worthwhile ally, I have no idea. They lost all their top generals in 1937, and they made very little impression on the Finns last year.’

‘There are an awful lot of them.’

‘A lot of men do not automatically make a successful army. And then there is the question of whether the Government, our Government, will ever consider an alliance with Communist Russia. I think Winston hates them even more than he hates Nazi Germany. Still, that is a pretty important piece of news, and I shall certainly relay it. What happens if your friend suspects what you are after? I mean, how does he regard you?’

She laughed. ‘Ewfim Chalyapov believes that he is God’s gift to the female sex. He selects every beautiful woman who drifts into his orbit, and expects them to fall madly in love with him. I am just following fashion. He knows absolutely nothing about me except that I am an employee of the Embassy.’

Clive hugged her protectively. ‘And is he God’s gift to womankind?’

‘He is very virile. But he is also very rough and ready, and totally uncouth in his personal habits. And he smokes like a chimney and stinks of tobacco. Every time I have been with him, I stink too.’

She sat bolt upright as there was a knock on the door. Clive squeezed her hand as he got out of bed and put on a dressing gown. ‘It’s only the night porter.’

‘What? Checking up?’

Clive grinned. ‘No. I told him to bring up a bottle of champagne at midnight.’

‘Suppose I hadn’t come?’

‘Then I’d have drunk myself insensible. But you did come. Now we are going to toast the future. Our future. You just snuggle down beneath the covers and keep out of sight.’

He went to the door.

It was three in the morning when she sat up again. ‘I think I should be getting back.’

He put his arms round her waist to nuzzle her. ‘I am going to see you again?’

'Next Tuesday.'

He sighed. 'That seems a hell of a long time away.'

'Six days.'

'During which—'

'It is a *job*! Are you not pleased with what I have told you? Who knows what I may have for you next week?'

He released her and lay back. 'I am being very schoolboyish. Seriously, it's what Heydrich wants you to do that seems more important than what you get out of Chalyapov. How often do you hear from him?'

Anna got up and started to dress, but continued to speak in a whisper. 'Whenever he wants something specific. Unless the situation changes again, I do not expect to hear from him for a while. He may have something he wants from Stalin.'

Clive sat up. 'Stalin? What has he told you about Stalin?' he hissed.

Anna peered into the mirror to freshen her make-up. 'Only that he wants me to persuade Chalyapov to introduce me, and that I should obtain a working knowledge of the Kremlin.'

Clive swung his legs out of bed. 'Holy Jesus Christ!'

Anna turned. 'Sssh! What is wrong with that?'

He came over to stand against her. 'My darling, how can a working knowledge of the Kremlin and access to Marshal Stalin be of any value to the Reich, unless we put that alongside the fact that the person obtaining this knowledge and this access is a trained assassin?'

Anna slowly sat down on the dressing stool.

'Just as Heydrich commanded you to assassinate Churchill last May, which is why we had to get you out of England, remember? This is a death sentence. We can't manipulate things here in Russia.'

Anna got up again, put on her hat and her mink.

'What are you going to do?' he asked.

'I cannot disobey Heydrich.'

He took her in his arms. 'And I cannot let you die.'

She kissed him. 'It may not come to that. Chalyapov apparently tires of women as enthusiastically as he takes them up. I must make him tire of me as rapidly as possible, after I have discovered those military dispositions. Once he does that I will no longer have access to the Kremlin, and then there will be no reason for me to remain in Russia.' They gazed at each other, and kissed again. 'That is what we must believe. I will see you on Tuesday.'

For the first time since that terrible March day in 1938, she was frightened. She lay in bed, unable to sleep, staring into the darkness. It was snowing outside, and for all her warm clothing she had become chilled on the walk home. Now she found herself shivering. She could not doubt that Clive's analysis was correct; she should have worked it out for herself. But up till now her Russian adventure had been no more than an enjoyable caper, in which she had been able to use her authority to its utmost. But no one was ever given such authority without being expected to earn it.

The situation was very similar to that in England the previous year. When she had received the dreadful command from Berlin, she had felt in an impossible position. To kill Churchill would have meant her execution, and once she had been executed there would be no more reason for the SD to keep her family alive. The same applied now. But not to carry out her instructions, and save her own life, would equally have condemned her family to death. So, as the outcome was inevitable in either case, why should she not save her own life? And live with those deaths on her conscience for the rest of that life?

She remembered thinking back then that at least the English were gentlemen. She would not have been tortured, and even the act of placing the noose over her head would be carried out with the utmost courtesy. She could expect no courtesy in Russia.

She finally fell asleep just before dawn, and awoke with a start to find Marlene sitting on her bed and peering at her.

'Countess! Anna! Is something the matter?'

Anna blinked. For the past hour she had been sleeping so heavily that she was unsure where she was. The curtains had been drawn back and the room was filled with bright winter sunshine.

'Anna!' To Anna's consternation, Marlene threw both arms round her to hug her and began nuzzling and kissing her neck. Then one of the hands closed on her breast. 'Oh, Anna, I adore you so. I admire you so. I *love* you so. Anna—'

Anna threw her off violently. Marlene gave a little shriek

and collapsed on the floor. Anna sat up. 'Do not do that again. What time is it?'

'Nine o'clock,' Marlene gasped, her cheeks crimson.

'Oh my God!' Anna threw back the covers and leapt out of bed. Marlene stared at her; she slept in the nude. 'Has anyone asked for me?'

'There is a message from that man Chalyapov.'

Anna went into the bathroom to shower. 'I will be down in five minutes.'

Marlene stood in the doorway to watch her. 'Anna! Please! Do not be angry with me. Mother told me . . .'

Anna stepped out of the stall and towelled herself. 'Whatever your mother told you about me was a lie. And my name is the Countess von Widerstand. Only my friends may call me Anna. And if you ever touch me again I will break your neck.'

She was more upset than she had supposed she would be. But the girl was definitely proving a nuisance. At the same time she had no wish further to upset the internal working of the Embassy by asking Heydrich to recall her.

Anyway, she had more than enough on her plate to get on with. The situation was actually easier than she had dared hope. Chalyapov was certainly overboard. He wanted to see her as often as possible, which was a bore, but his adoration was also productive.

'Our army?' he asked, holding her on top of him as he liked best, so that he could wrap his legs around hers. 'What does a pretty girl want with an army?'

'I adore armies,' Anna said, shaking her head gently to and fro so that her hair trailed across his face. 'My grandfather was a famous soldier. And I have heard so much about the great Red Army. I should love to see some of it.'

He kissed her. 'And so you shall. But the Red Army is everywhere, and getting about in this weather is very difficult.'

'Don't you have some units on the border?'

'Well, of course. We have three fronts situated on the border.'

'What is a front?' Anna asked innocently.

'It is what you would call an Army Corps.'

'And you have them on the border? Who are you going to fight?'

He grinned. 'As you said, every country needs to have units on its borders. We have no desire to fight anyone in Europe.'

'And outside of Europe?'

'Ah, well, the Japanese are a threat. Do you not know that we have been fighting an undeclared war with Japan along the border with Manchuria for the past three years?'

'I did not know that,' Anna said more innocently yet.

'Well, we don't publicize it. But we generally win the battles. On the other hand it is something we have to sort out eventually. Those little yellow men seem to wish to take over all of Asia. We could never allow that.'

'I wish I were a Russian,' Anna said dreamily, wriggling her hips as she felt him hardening beneath her.

'I have never heard a German say that before.'

'But you are so immense, so strong, so unbeatable.'

He chuckled. 'Are you speaking of me or the country?'

'You are the country,' Anna assured him and spread her legs.

'Now that is very interesting,' Clive said. 'If Russia and Japan were to start a real war, that would change quite a few things.'

'Is England not friendly with Japan?'

'God, no! We were once, but since 1922, when we went along with the USA in reducing the strength of all navies at the expense of Japan, they have been increasingly hostile. And since this war started they have been flexing their muscles more and more contemptuously. They feel that we cannot fight Germany and Japan at the same time. And the damned thing is they are right. They are even giving us orders, like telling us to close the Burma Road through which Chiang Kai-Shek's army obtains most of its supplies. And we have felt obliged to do that to avoid any risk of a clash. That really is a bitter pill.'

Anna kissed him. 'You will work it out. Does not Great Britain always win the last battle?'

He ruffled her hair. 'So they say. I assume you are reporting all of this to Heydrich?'

'I have done so, certainly. But I have not heard anything further from him.'

'And what about the Kremlin, and Stalin?'

'I am about to start working on that.'

'I wish to God you wouldn't.'

Anna got out of bed and began to dress. 'You know I must,' she whispered. 'I will see you next week.'

'Well?' Groener demanded. 'What do you want?'

Marlene stood in front of the door. 'To speak with you, Herr Groener.'

'You? What do you have to say to me? You work for the Countess von Widerstand.'

'I am required to do so, yes, Herr Groener. But my loyalty must be to the Reich.'

Groener stared at her for several seconds. 'You have something to tell me about the Countess?'

'There is something I think you should know.'

'Is she not your friend?'

'She is not my friend, Herr Groener. She is nobody's friend. She is an utterly selfish person, as cold as ice.'

Groener stroked his chin. 'I see. So what would you like to say about her? I know that she has been away these past few weeks. I understood that she had gone to the country with Herr Chalyapov."

'Yes sir. But now that she has returned, she has begun leaving the Embassy just about every night and staying out till three in the morning.'

Groener snorted. 'Do you think I don't know that, you silly girl?'

'Do you also know where she goes?'

'She meets Herr Chalyapov, of course. He appears to be totally infatuated with her. Count von Schulenburg seems prepared to accept this relationship. He and I have received instructions from Berlin that she is not to be interfered with, so I assume they think she is obtaining information from this lout. Perhaps she is. But surely you know all this as you are her assistant? Even if,' he added, 'you seem to have fallen out with her.'

Marlene ignored the implied criticism. 'Suppose I was to tell you that she does not always go to Chalyapov?'

Groener raised his eyebrows. 'Where else does she go?'

'I do not know.'

'Then what are you saying?'

Marlene advanced right up to the desk. 'Herr Chalyapov is

a heavy smoker. When the Countess returns from him, her clothes stink of cigarette smoke, but at least once a week when she comes in, there is no smell.'

'And that is proof that she has been with someone else? Perhaps Chalyapov does not smoke every night.'

'He is a chain-smoker, Herr Groener.'

Groener considered. 'Then she is no doubt servicing some other Russian as well. One who does not smoke.'

'Perhaps. But don't you think it is something you should know about?'

'I have told you that I have been given specific instructions, from General Heydrich himself, that under no circumstances am I to interfere with Fraulein Fehrbach's activities. That includes interrogating her as to those activities.'

Marlene looked as if she was about to stamp her foot. But she kept her temper. 'Not even if she is betraying the Reich?'

'You have given me no proof of that. Provide me with proof that she is engaged in some subversive activity, and I will act.'

Marlene regarded him for several seconds, then she said, 'You are asking me to risk my life.'

'Now you are being melodramatic.'

'I do not think you know this woman, Anna Fehrbach.'

'I know all I need to know: that she is a glamorous little bitch who enjoys the patronage of the head of the Gestapo. That is not difficult to understand, in view of her looks. That he chooses to employ her as a whore is his business, just as the fact that she appears to enjoy it is hers.'

'Then you are unaware that she is a trained killer.'

Groener leaned back in his chair. 'You are starting to irritate me, Fraulein. How can a twenty-year-old-girl be a trained killer?'

'Are you aware that my mother was Commandant Hannah Gehrig of the SD?'

'Which is no doubt why you have been given a position in the service. Yes, I know of your mother, Fraulein. I also know that she is presumed dead.'

Marlene nodded. 'I believe that she is dead, too. But perhaps you do not know that when she disappeared she was Fraulein Fehrbach's controller, and that before then she had personally supervised Fraulein Fehrbach's training, both as an agent and as an assassin. She told me that Fraulein Fehrbach had killed several times, before she was even twenty.'

'And she was never arrested for these crimes?'

'They were carried out on the instructions of the SD, of General Heydrich himself. All except one, which she claimed was in self-defence.'

'I will say again: if you feel that Fraulein Fehrbach is doing something, anything, that could harm the Reich, prove it. Unless you can do that, do not trouble me again.'

Marlene stared at him. 'I would like a weapon.'

'What?'

'I have told you, if I am to secure the proof you wish, I will have to endanger my life. I need to be able to protect myself.'

'You mean to shoot Fraulein Fehrbach.'

'If I have to.'

'And you understand that should you kill her without providing proof of what you claim, you will hang.'

'If I have to shoot her, it will be because I have secured that proof.'

Groener considered for a last few moments, then opened a drawer in his desk, took out a Walther PPK, and held it out. Marlene gazed at it. 'That is only a five millimetre shot.'

Groener shrugged. 'It will kill, if accurately aimed and fired at not more than twenty-five metres.'

Marlene remembered shooting at the man in the training camp, with a pistol exactly like this, and being unable to hit a vital part. But she did not think she would be unable to kill the bitch who had so arrogantly rejected her. She took the pistol, and tucked it out of sight beneath her blouse. 'I shall also need permission to leave the Embassy as I choose at any hour of the day or night. Written permission.'

Once again Groener considered for several seconds. Then he pulled a block of headed notepaper towards him and began to write.

'So where have you been the past month?' Clive asked. 'Last Tuesday was the loneliest night of my life.'

'Except, surely, when drifting around the Mediterranean with a bullet in your backside,' Anna suggested. She kissed him. 'I have been working.'

'I am sure. On exactly which part of Chalyapov's anatomy?'

'You are in a grouch. I have been with Ewfim to inspect the troops.'

'Say again?'

'He took me to Brest-Litovsk, and then up and down the border. They have an awful lot of troops concentrated there. He even introduced me to the various generals and showed me over some of their units.'

'And you have relayed this information to Heydrich?'

'That is my job, just as I am now relaying it to you.'

'I don't imagine even a vast Russian army perched along the Polish border is about to invade Great Britain. Do you think they are planning a war with Germany?'

'Ewfim says definitely not.'

'Then why are they there?'

'He says because they have to be somewhere, and because Stalin is paranoid about his borders.'

'You believe him?'

'Well, the troops I saw did not look as if they were preparing to go to war. Mind you, it is still ten below.'

'And in another month or so it may be up to zero. What do you think Heydrich will make of this information?'

'I have no idea. It may even put his, or Hitler's, plans back a bit. Which can't be a bad thing. But I am sure I will receive follow-up instructions in due course.'

'And what progress have you made in that other direction?'

'Two days ago I took tea with Marshal Stalin.'

'You what?'

'Fact. I have virtually the run of the Kremlin. Everyone adores me. I told Ewfim that I would like to become a Russian citizen and he is working on it. He told Stalin about me and I was invited to tea. Have you ever met him? Stalin, I mean.'

'You are operating out of my class.'

'He is a charmer. He speaks through that huge moustache and makes me think of my grandfather. My real grandfather, not the invented one.'

'And because of this "charm", you are going to commit suicide?'

'I would rather not. I am working on it. Now, let us make love. We have talked business long enough.'

* * *

'Oh, my darling girl.' Clive held her close, kissed her forehead, her chin, her cheek, her eyes, her nose, and then her mouth. 'To have you here, and know—'

'You know nothing,' Anna said fiercely. 'I have received no instructions as yet, except that I should become acceptable in the Kremlin. This I have done. When I receive further instructions, I will tell you, and we will discuss it.' She looked at her watch. 'Now I must go. I will see you next Tuesday.'

She got out of bed, and he caught her hand. 'I won't be here next Tuesday.'

Anna paused in the act of pulling on her cami-knickers. 'Where will you be?'

'I have been recalled to England.'

'Why?'

'Presumably they are happy with the way things are going here.'

'So who will be my contact?'

'Commander Sprague.'

Anna smoothed her dress. 'He's not really my type.'

Clive got out of bed to take her in his arms. 'You don't have to go to bed with him. In fact, I would prefer it if you didn't. But he'll be here on Tuesday nights. All you have to do is bring him up to date, have a drink, and then push off.'

'Does he know about you and me?'

'I haven't given him chapter and verse, but he's not a fool. On the other hand, he is a gentleman. He won't bring it up unless you do.'

'Um.' She put on her mink and held him close. 'When do you leave?'

'Tomorrow morning.'

'And you're telling me now?'

'My instructions only arrived on Friday, and there was no way of getting in touch.'

'I wish you weren't going. Your being here gives me a sense of security, a feeling that I'm not entirely alone.'

'Is that all I give you?'

'You know it isn't.'

'Well, your being here gives me the heebie-jeebies. I want you to start work on irritating Chalyapov just as soon as you can, as we agreed. If he drops you, you'll be no more use to the Nazis here, so they'll have to recall you, and you'll be off the hook.'

She nodded, released him, and put on her hat.

'Promise?' he asked.

'Promise.'

She kissed him and left the room. It was just after two, and the hotel was quiet. She was in a hurry to get back to the Embassy and into the privacy of her room. She felt quite shattered. It was absurd, of course. She had existed in Moscow for four months without Clive, without even knowing whether he was going to appear or not. It was illogical now to feel that she was being abandoned, just as it was illogical ever to feel that his presence in any way protected her. She had to be her own salvation, as she had always been in the past. But how often in the past had she felt no less lonely?

She stepped from the elevator, wrapped her scarf round her face, and crossed the now empty foyer towards the swing doors.

'A word, comrade.'

Anna turned her head. The night porter had left the reception counter to approach her.

'You have been in Room 507.'

'Is that important?'

'To me, no. But to others, who knows?'

'You mean the NKVD?'

'I do not think so, as yet.'

'Would you explain that?'

'Well, I am required to report to the police anything that I consider may be of importance.'

'And you have reported me. But you do not know who I am.'

'I know that you are not a resident in the hotel, and I know that you regularly visit the Englishman in 507.'

'I see. And you have reported this to the NKVD.'

'No, comrade. I have reported it to the Moscow police, as I am required to do. Whether they have considered it necessary to inform the State Police I do not know. But I doubt it. I told them that a foreign lady comes to the hotel every Tuesday night, and spends several hours with an English resident, and then leaves again. The NKVD are usually only interested when a foreigner has an assignation with a Russian.'

'I see,' Anna said again, sizing him up. He was a pleasant-looking man, in early middle age, chunkily built as were so many Russians, and had somewhat sleepy – but also sly – eyes. Presumably he also had a wife, and perhaps children. But he had suddenly become a threat. 'I still do not understand why you are telling me this, but I am grateful. Would it be possible to reward you?'

'That would be very nice, comrade. But I have something else to tell you. Something more important, perhaps.' He gazed at her.

'Then I shall certainly reward you.' Anna opened her handbag.

'I do not wish money, comrade.'

'Ah. Well then, tell me what this more important matter is, and I will decide just how great a reward you will have.'

The man hesitated, as if wondering whether he should claim the reward first. Then he said, 'There was someone asking after you tonight.'

Anna frowned. 'The police?'

'No. A foreign lady like yourself. In fact, she had an accent exactly like yours.'

Anna felt a slow tensing of both her mind and her stomach muscles. 'What exactly did she ask you?'

'She said she was looking for a tall, very beautiful, yellow-haired woman who came regularly to the hotel. She wished to know if I remembered such a lady, and if I could tell her why she came here.'

'What time was this?'

'Before midnight.'

'I see. And what did you tell her?'

'Well, she had obviously been watching your movements for some time. So I said you were a visitor to one of our guests.'

'You did not tell her who?'

'No, comrade.'

'Thank you. And you do not feel that this lady was a member of the NKVD or the police.'

'No, no. The lady was definitely a foreigner. As I told you, she spoke very like you. But you are more fluent in Russian,' he added ingratiatingly.

That narrowed it down to a field of one: Marlene. The Berlin was a hotel for foreign visitors to Moscow, not Russians. That eliminated the possibility that she had been visiting another Russian commissar. Much would depend on who Marlene told of her investigation, and how soon. But in any event, that she should be spied upon by her own assistant was unacceptable. And in the circumstances there could be no question of merely writing Heydrich and requesting him to recall the girl for being no good; Heydrich might just be prepared to listen to what Hannah Gehrig's daughter had to say.

As for this poor fellow . . . 'You say that you have known of my visits to the gentleman in 507 for some time.' She was using her most innocent, but anxious, voice. 'Who else knows of these visits, apart from the police?'

'Well, comrade, I may have mentioned it to my assistant, who comes in on my nights off.'

'Was he interested?'

'Not very, as I remember.'

'And no one else? When I arrive the foyer is always crowded.'

'That is exactly it, comrade. No one else has noted your entry, because there are so many people coming in and out. But I am always here when you leave.'

'And how do you know which room I have been to?'

The porter winked. 'You come every Tuesday night. And every Tuesday night the gentleman in 507 orders a bottle of champagne. A gentleman never orders a bottle of champagne to drink all by himself. He is entertaining a visitor. And every Tuesday night you are a visitor to the hotel. Am I not a detective?'

'You are brilliant,' Anna smiled. 'Well then, what would you like your reward to be?'

'I would like to know if you are as beautiful as that woman said.'

'I think we should go into your office if I am to take anything off.'

'Oh, yes.' He was positively panting. He raised the flap and she went behind the reception counter. As she did so his hands closed on her buttocks, massaging them through the mink. Her feelings of sorrow for what she was about to do evaporated.

She went into the little office, turned and unwound the scarf from round her face. 'Oh, yes,' he said. 'The woman's right. You are superb.'

'You say the sweetest things,' Anna said, and hit him on the side of the neck. He saw the blow coming, but it was delivered at such a speed and with such force that he could do no more than get his hands half up before he lost consciousness. He hit the floor with a thump. Anna knelt on his chest to hold his body in place, grasped his head in both hands and gave it a violent twist with all her strength. She heard the snap. She stood up and made the sign of the cross. Then she closed the office door behind her and left the hotel.

She regained the Embassy at three. The guards by now regarded her with a mixture of embarrassment and apprehension. She smiled at them and went upstairs to her apartment. There was no sound but the light was on in Marlene's bedroom. She went to her bedroom and undressed. Then she opened the bag in which she kept various essential supplies, and took out a bottle of strong sleeping pills. Carrying this she returned to Marlene's room and opened the door, immediately closing it again behind her.

Marlene had been sitting at her table writing on several sheets of paper. She looked up and gave a little gasp; it was not Anna's normal practice to wander around the apartment in the nude. 'Countess?'

Anna stood next to her. 'Are you writing your autobiography? Or a confession? Or merely an observation?'

Marlene opened her mouth and closed it again.

'No matter,' Anna said. 'You are not looking well. You have spent too much time out in the cold night air. I think you need a very good night's sleep. What is left of it. Here. I have brought you these. They are very good.' She held out the bottle invitingly.

Marlene stared at it as a rabbit might have stared at a snake. 'I do not like to take pills.'

'But I insist. I know what is best for you.'

Marlene licked her lips, and glanced at her bureau.

'Ah.' Anna stepped to the chest and opened the top drawer. Marlene stood up, and then sat down again; she knew better than to take on Anna at unarmed combat.

Anna took out the Beretta. 'How nice,' she remarked. 'Where did you find this? Under a bush?'

Marlene was trembling.

'Or was it given to you by a friend? So tell me, if you had had it handy, would you have shot me?'

'I . . .'

'Of course. You would have claimed that it was self-defence. But why should I attack you physically when I can destroy you with a few words? Who gave you the gun?' Her voice was suddenly crisp and harsh.

'Herr Groener.'

'I see. You have been a busy little bee. But it is very obvious that you are distraught. Now, take these pills and go to bed. I will have the doctor examine you in the morning.'

'I . . . I . . .'

'If you do not obey me,' Anna said, 'I will be forced to write to General Heydrich and have him recall you to Berlin, where you will be sent to an SS brothel. I do assure you it will be better for you to do as I ask. Go into the bathroom and pour a mug of water.'

Slowly Marlene got up and went to the bathroom. Anna went with her to watch. Marlene poured the water, and Anna again held out the bottle. This time Marlene took it. 'I think four should do it,' Anna told her.

Marlene unscrewed the cap, dropped four of the tablets into the palm of her hand, cupped them into her mouth and drank the water. She made a face and put down the mug beside the bottle.

'There,' Anna said. 'Now undress and go to bed.'

'I am undressed,' Marlene protested.

'You will feel better for sleeping in the nude like I do,' Anna assured her.

Another hesitation, and then Marlene took off the night-dress and got into bed. Anna pulled the sheet to her throat. 'Now close your eyes and have a good long sleep.'

She stood above the girl and watched her eyes droop shut. Then she sat at the table and read what Marlene had written. It was, as she had supposed, a long, somewhat rambling denunciation of her, listing all the suspicions Marlene claimed to have felt since their first association, relating how she had tracked her to the hotel on several occasions, and how this very night she had discovered that her quarry always visited the same room and that there could be no question of her meeting another Russian commissar. There was no indication as to whether the wretched girl had confided her suspicions to anyone else, but obviously she must have done so to Groener. But as she was only now compiling her report, which would now never be read, Anna did not feel that was relevant.

She collected the sheets together neatly and turned to look at the bed. Marlene was breathing slowly and evenly. She was certainly in a deep sleep. Anna went into the bathroom and listened at the other door; there was no sound from Birgit's room, and she remembered that the maid was a heavy sleeper. She turned on the bath water, then she returned to the bedroom, took the sheets of paper into her own room and carefully burned them, collected the ashes and flushed them down the toilet.

Next she returned to Marlene's room, stood above the sleeping girl for some moments, then threw back the covers, and with an effort lifted the inert body. Her brain was as always ice-cold and entirely concentrated on what she was doing, on what she had to do. But she felt that self-horror was lurking. Killing an armed man, or woman, or in self-defence she could accept. Cold-blooded execution left her very nearly a nervous wreck, and this was the second this night.

But it *was* again self-defence, and the defence of her family. That single essential dominated her life. She carried Marlene along the corridor into the bathroom, carefully lowered her into the water and very gently pressed on her shoulders. Marlene went under. For more than a minute there was no reaction, then her eyes suddenly opened, as did her mouth. Anna retained her grip, still gently, but sufficient to keep the head from rising, now up to her elbows in very cold water. Marlene tried to lift her hands to strike but her arms were held in place by Anna's grip. Then she kicked several times, and water splashed about the room and over Anna's body. But very quickly the kicks subsided. It was over inside three minutes.

Anna held her there for another few minutes then stood up and dried herself. She left the lights on and the open bottle of pills, which now had Marlene's fingerprints on it over hers. Then she carefully wiped the pistol free of prints and restored it to the drawer, returned to her bedroom and got beneath the covers. She was shivering and tears rolled down her cheeks.

Eight
The Plot

Surprisingly, Anna slept heavily, but she knew she was emotionally exhausted by the events of the evening. She wished she could have warned Clive of what had happened, but it would have been too risky to linger in the hotel, and she believed the porter's claim that he had told no one of his deductions; he had been too anxious to see what profit he could achieve for himself. There would of course be a great fuss when the body was found, but there would be no immediate reason for any of the guests to be implicated, and Clive would surely be back in England before the investigation could get very far.

She awoke to a piercing scream, sat up and pushed hair from her eyes just as Birgit burst into her room, still wearing her nightgown, her face white and her hair dishevelled.

'Countess! Countess! Oh, Countess!'

'What in the name of God . . .?'

Birgit panted, 'Marlene! In the bath . . .'

Anna threw back the covers and got out of bed, reaching for her robe. 'There has been an accident?'

'Yes. No. I don't know.'

Anna grasped her shoulders and shook her. 'Pull yourself together. You are saying that Marlene has fallen in the bathroom?'

'No, Countess! I do not think so. She's dead.'

'What?' Anna ran from the room, Birgit behind her. She stood above the bath and looked at Marlene. The body was almost blue from its prolonged immersion in the near-freezing water. The eyes and mouth were still open, and there were also deeper blue marks on her upper arms. These had to be accounted for immediately. 'What are those marks? They look as if someone held her there.'

'I tried to lift her up,' Birgit wailed. 'When I saw her . . .

I could not believe she was dead. I tied to lift her up. I thought I held her wrists, but I must have held her arms as well. I don't remember. I was so horrified . . .'

'Of course you were,' Anna said sympathetically. 'And you did entirely the right thing in trying to help her. Just tell Herr Groener, when he asks you, exactly what happened. I will support you. Now, I think you should go back to bed; you do not look very well.'

'But . . .'

'I will deal with this.'

'Your breakfast . . .'

'I will get my own breakfast. Off you go.'

Birgit stumbled from the bathroom. Anna closed the door and returned to her bedroom, picked up the telephone. 'Herr Meissenbach's apartment, please,' she told the switchboard operator.

Anna decided against dressing; when confronting a room full of men she knew she was at her best wearing only a dressing gown. And the room very rapidly became filled with men, and even some women. Anna sat in a corner and sipped coffee.

'When did it happen?' Meissenbach asked.

'I have no idea. Can't the doctor tell us that?'

'No, he cannot. How long a body has been dead can usually be ascertained by taking the rectal temperature, because all bodies cool at a fixed rate after death. But this system is useless when the body has been immersed in cold water since death.'

'My people say that you came in at three o'clock,' Groener said.

'That would be about right.'

'What did you do after coming in?'

'I was both tired and cold. I came straight upstairs and went to bed.'

'And you noticed nothing out of the ordinary?'

'I noticed that Marlene's light was on. But that was not out of the ordinary. She often sat up late, reading.'

'But the bathroom light was also on.'

'Apparently. I cannot see that bathroom door from my room.'

'Did you know,' Meissenbach asked, 'that Fraulein Gehrig possessed a pistol?'

Anna frowned. 'I did not know that. Anyway, it is not possible. We were not issued with firearms for this assignment.'

'Nevertheless . . .'

Groener cleared his throat. 'I do not think her possession of a weapon is relevant: she did not shoot herself. The doctor thinks that she took a dose of strong pills from the bottle on the table beside her bed.'

'Oh, my God!' Anna cried, and leapt to her feet, scattering her dressing gown and revealing a great deal of flawless leg.

'Countess?'

Anna crossed the room and opened her medical bag. 'Those are my pills. She must have taken them while I was out.'

'And having taken the pills she got into a cold bath to drown herself?' Meissenbach asked.

'The bath must have been hot when she got in.'

'The important point,' Groener said, 'is why should Fraulein Gehrig commit suicide in the first place?' He looked at Anna, who sat on her bed.

'Well?'

'It is very embarrassing,' Anna said in a low voice, hunching her shoulders.

'You mean you know why she did this thing?' Meissenbach demanded.

'Well . . . Marlene had a lover. Or at least, she was in love. But the person she loved did not respond. Could not respond.'

'You mean he was a married man? Someone here in the Embassy?'

'It was not a man.'

The two men stared at her.

'Marlene was in love with me,' Anna said.

'What?'

'I feel so bad about it,' Anna said. 'But . . .' She gazed at Meissenbach. 'I am not . . . well . . . when she made advances, I rejected her. Perhaps I was too brutal about it. I told her that if she ever attempted to come to my bed again I would inform General Heydrich and have her recalled to Berlin. She was in any event on probation. She failed her training course, and was due to be degraded. But because her mother and I had been friends I interceded for her, and begged for her to be given a second chance. But she knew that if she was returned from here in disgrace she would be dismissed from the service and sent to an SS brothel. In view of her . . . well, sexual interests, this would have been a virtual death sentence. I did not mean it, of course; I was just very angry at the time. But she must have taken me seriously. I feel so very unhappy about it. I mean, I may as well have shot her myself.'

The two men exchanged glances. 'Well,' Meissenbach said, 'I must compliment you on your frankness, Countess. No doubt you will inform your superiors of what has happened.'

'Would you stop by my office, Herr Meissenbach?' Groener requested.

'Certainly.' Meissenbach accompanied the policeman to the Gestapo office. 'Are you not satisfied?'

'Have a seat.' Groener sat behind his desk. 'May I ask how long you have known this so-called Countess?'

'Not very long. I met her for the first time last July.'

'But you know something of her background?'

'I'm afraid I know nothing of her background. I was merely told that she was to accompany me to Moscow as my aide.'

'You did not find her absurd name suspicious? Countess of Resistance?'

'Well, yes I did. And I was told that it was not my business to ask questions. That the Countess was being sent to Moscow to carry out a mission for the Reich, and her position as my aide was to provide her with a cover.'

'Hmm. You were not informed that she was a Government assassin?'

'What?' Meissenbach cried, as convincingly as he could. 'A twenty-year-old girl? How do you know this?'

'I was informed . . . by Fraulein Gehrig.'

This time Meissenbach's consternation was genuine. 'And you believed her? Who is she supposed to assassinate? Or, indeed, who *has* she assassinated?' Groener stared at him, and he gulped. 'You cannot be serious. I mean . . .'

'Oh, it was a totally professional job, and we will never be able to prove that it was not a suicide. But that is what I would expect from a professional killer.'

'But, if Gehrig made advances . . . I can tell you that the Countess is not a lesbian.'

Groener raised his eyebrows, and Meissenbach flushed. 'Well, I have been fairly close to her for several months.' Then he frowned as he recalled the loving way Anna had kissed Gabriella Hosek just before beginning to torture her – and just before Hosek had bitten the cyanide capsule. But he felt it might be unwise to confide any of the events in Prague to this man. Groener was regarding him with interest, and he hurried on. 'What I mean is, even if they were lovers who had quarrelled, that was surely no reason for her to murder the girl.'

'It is my opinion,' Groener said, 'that Fehrbach – you know her real name is Anna Fehrbach?'

Meissenbach nodded.

'Well, Gehrig became suspicious of her activities, and confided her suspicions to me. She was convinced that Fehrbach was seeing somebody else in addition to Chalyapov when on her midnight jaunts. I'm afraid I was sceptical about the importance of this, but I gave her permission to see what she could find out. I also gave her that pistol to use in case she needed it; if she had been able to shoot Fehrbach it would have solved all of our problems. However, as I was saying, I believe Fehrbach found out about her suspicions and killed her. Sadly, she does not appear to have been able to use the weapon.'

'My God! What are we to do?'

'As I have said, Herr Meissenbach, there is nothing we can do. This woman is a creature of the SD, and they will not permit anything to happen to her, certainly not until she has completed her mission. I just wished you to understand the situation, so that, if the opportunity arises, we can work together.'

'Of course. But we must inform the Ambassador.'

'That is what we must *not* do. He has been sufficiently shocked at the news that Gehrig killed herself. He is an old-fashioned Junker, whose gods are honour and duty. If he knew we suspected Fehrbach of murder he would feel compelled to take the matter to the highest level, which could well bring the SD into our midst in force, and God knows what would happen then.'

Meissenbach considered, then nodded. 'I understand. But to think that we have a cold-blooded murderess right here in the Embassy . . .'

'Patience, Herr Meissenbach. Patience is a policeman's most effective weapon. All criminals make a mistake, eventually. Fehrbach may be a cold-blooded killer, but she is still only a girl of twenty. She will make a mistake, sooner rather than later.

And then we will have her. I –' he added with thoughtful anticipation – 'will have her. But you may watch, Herr Meissenbach.'

'I hope you are glad to be home,' Baxter commented.

'No, I am not,' Clive said. 'I hate leaving unfinished business.'

'Well, I'm sure Belinda is pleased to have you back in one piece.'

'I'm not too sure about that either. She seems to feel that I was away unnecessarily long.'

'An opinion with which I entirely concur. However, I'm sure you'll be interested to hear the latest despatch from Sprague.'

'I'm not sure that I will be.'

'You mean you don't want to know about his cavortings with your beautiful protégée? Well, I can put your mind at rest in that direction. Sprague has seen neither hair nor hide of the young lady since your departure.'

'Good Lord! She did say that he wasn't her type . . .'

'Clive, we are running a secret service department, not a knocking shop. I find her reluctance to communicate with Sprague both annoying and disturbing. However, there may just be a logical if not excusable reason. I presume you are aware that there was a murder in the Hotel Berlin the night before you left?'

'Oh, yes. There was the devil of a flap. Someone mugged the night porter.'

'As you say, someone mugged the night porter. Sprague has been able to get some detail on the crime. Time of death 0230.'

Clive frowned.

'Quite. I assume, as it was your last night in Moscow, you had company between the sheets?'

'Well . . .'

'And what time did the lady leave you?'

'Jesus,' Clive muttered. 'But that can't be right. Why on earth should Anna kill the night porter? The time has to be a coincidence.'

'If it's a coincidence, she must certainly have seen the killer. But it wasn't a coincidence.'

'You mean she's been arrested? Oh, Christ!'

'Relax. The Moscow police have no idea who the assassin was, although they apparently feel fairly sure that it was a man.

Apparently the porter had a reputation as a lady killer, and they are working on the theory that the crime was committed by an outraged husband or boyfriend. There was absolutely no one around at the time. Only we know differently.'

'Oh, come now, Billy. Simply because Anna *may* have passed through the lobby at about the time the murder was committed? Isn't it most likely that she saw two men together, perhaps quarrelling, perhaps even fighting, and decided to get out of there before the noise attracted attention?'

'That would be a valid point, except for one thing: the reason the police are certain it was a man. The porter died as a result of two acts of supreme power and violence.'

'Eh?'

'He was laid out by a karate blow to the neck, and then was killed by having his head twisted until his vertebrae snapped. According to the police, only a man would – or indeed could – have done something like that. But again, we know better, don't we?'

Clive stared at him. 'Hannah Gehrig died like that!'

'Go to the head of the class.'

'But why?'

'I would say that he found out about Anna's midnight trysts with you and decided to capitalize on it, by requesting either money or favours as the price of keeping his mouth shut. The world is full of sex-hungry men who believe that innocent-looking, pretty young girls are there for the taking. Sadly, in most cases, they are absolutely right. This unfortunate character, exactly like poor Reiffel, had no idea he was snuggling up to a hungry lioness who was also engaged in secret and highly dangerous business.'

Clive sighed. 'That poor girl.'

Baxter raised his eyebrows.

'All right,' Clive conceded. 'So she reacts violently when she considers herself in danger. You know that. What you don't know is how vulnerable she is.'

Baxter snorted.

'How desperately lonely,' Clive went on. 'And she was upset at my leaving.'

'You'll have me crying my eyes out in a minute. What you are saying is we should be grateful that Moscow is still standing.'

'Anyway,' Clive said. 'Let's look on the bright side. The

only person in the world who can possibly relate Anna to that murder, apart from you and me, is Anna herself.'

'I haven't finished reading Sprague's despatch.'

'Oh my God! What now?'

'There has been a suicide at the German Embassy.'

Clive stared at him. 'No,' he muttered. 'No!' he shouted. 'It cannot be!'

'Simmer down. It's not Anna.'

'Then . . .'

'It was a young woman. However, she is listed as being secretary to the Countess von Widerstand. And this suicide apparently took place on the same night the porter was murdered. You'll never guess what the girl's name was. Marlene Gehrig.'

Once again Clive stared at him.

'As I recall,' Baxter said, 'Hannah Gehrig was in her forties when Anna broke *her* neck. This girl is reported as being in her late teens. I would suppose she must have been a daughter. I mean, it would be too much of a coincidence to suppose that Anna would employ as a secretary someone with the same name as her old enemy who was not actually a relative.'

'But would she employ a relative of the woman she killed?'

'She never mentioned this girl to you?'

'No, she did not.'

'Hmm. She certainly does like to keep her secrets. The point is that she seems to be discovering too many people who appear to be finding out, or are on the verge of finding out, too much about her. Which leads us to the question: is she becoming too vulnerable for us to continue employing her?'

'You think that again, and my resignation will be on your desk in one hour,' Clive told him. 'And when I retire I am going to write my memoirs – fuck the Official Secrets Act. We have just touched the tip of the iceberg as to what this girl can deliver. Don't we now know that Germany intends to invade Russia? Probably as soon as the thaw sets in. I presume you have passed this information on?'

'It went to the Boss, and thence to the War Cabinet, and thence to the PM himself.'

'Who no doubt chose to disbelieve it.'

'He did believe it, Clive. He took it very seriously, and conveyed it to Marshal Stalin in a personal letter. Unfortunately, Stalin did *not* believe it. Or at least, he chose not to do so. We shall just have to wait and see what evolves.'

'But it was Anna who gave us that information, and who will give us a great deal more. Obviously right now she's lying low because of what happened at the Berlin Hotel and what happened to that girl. Are you supposing that she killed her as well?'

'It would seem logical. The girl was apparently found drowned in her bath, the bath having been taken in the middle of the night. Do young girls normally take baths in the middle of the night? In mid-winter? I know that my daughter doesn't.'

'I should get back there.'

'Forget that. The last thing we want is for one of our people to get involved in whatever shenanigans are taking place in the German Embassy. I'll go along – at least for the time being – with the idea that she'll surface when she feels it's safe to do so.'

'If only,' Clive mused, 'we could have some idea of just what she's doing now.'

'Tea,' Josef Stalin remarked, beaming through his moustache. 'It is the greatest of drinks, the ultimate solace of mankind. And womankind, of course. Do you not agree, Countess?'

'Absolutely,' Anna purred.

'But it should never be adulterated with such things as milk, or lemon, or sugar, as they do in the West.'

'I couldn't agree with you more, Your Excellency.'

'You are a woman of taste. So you know, here, in the privacy of this office, I would like to call you Anna. May I call you Anna?'

'Of course, Your Excellency.'

'And you must call me Josef, when we are in this office. Anna is a good old Russian name. We had an empress once named Anna. She was very successful.'

'Were not the tsars, and the tsarinas, terrible people?' Anna asked, at her most innocent.

'Of course. But rulers need to be terrible. One of our tsars rejoiced in being *known* as the Terrible.'

As you are terrible, Anna thought. She knew that this charming old man had ruthlessly executed everyone he distrusted during the past ten years. But then, had she not done the same in a much shorter time?

'The tsars,' Stalin went on, 'were a necessary part of Russian history. They created the nation. They declined, of course, as time went by, and became corrupt and had to be eliminated, but without them none of us would be here. But you know, I did not invite you here to talk politics. You have now experienced a Russian winter. And you are about to experience a Russian spring. Already the ice is breaking. In a week or two there will be green shoots everywhere, and soon after that the entire country will erupt in colour and song. A Russian spring is the greatest natural event in the world. It truly fulfills the criteria of the old gods, that in winter the earth dies, but in spring it is reborn again.'

And it may be the last you will ever see, Anna thought. And it may be my last too. She had received no further communication from Heydrich. Not even a comment on the death of Marlene. She had been cast entirely adrift, by both her employers.

Her position in the Embassy was more equivocal than ever. All pretence of finding her something to do had been dropped; Marlene had not been replaced as an assistant, and the senior staff did their best to pretend that she wasn't there. Whether they suspected that she might have been involved in Marlene's death she had no idea, but even Meissenbach never came near her, and she was no longer invited to any dinners or cocktails parties. This was no longer important, as she remained Chalyapov's mistress, but the only company she enjoyed inside the Embassy was Birgit, and enjoyed was hardly an appropriate word in this context. Birgit seemed more terrified of her than ever, and she also clearly mourned Marlene, and also clearly kept worrying if she had, inadvertently, by word or deed, contributed to her lover's decision to take her own life.

That left Chalyapov, who remained as enthusiastic as ever. But now she was embarking upon the plan she had agreed with Clive – that of becoming an increasingly demanding, querulous and generally irritating little woman, in the hopes that he would decide to drop her so that she could be returned to Germany . . .

There was a knock on the door, which then opened.

Stalin did not turn his head, but he said quietly, 'I gave instructions that I was not to be interrupted when I was entertaining the Countess von Widerstand.'

'Comrade Molotov said that you would wish to be informed

immediately, Comrade Stalin. He has received an urgent despatch from our minister in Belgrade.'

'What can be happening in Belgrade that is so urgent?'

'It is under attack, Comrade.'

'What?' Now Stalin did turn, while Anna put down her tea cup with a clatter. 'Attack by whom?'

The secretary gave Anna an anxious glance 'It is being bombed by the Luftwaffe, and it is reported that an army corps of the Wehrmacht has crossed the frontier and is advancing on the city.'

'What steps is Comrade Molotov taking?'

'He has summoned Count von Schulenberg to a meeting and will ask for an explanation.'

'Very good. Thank Comrade Molotov for informing me so promptly, and tell him that I would like to see him at the conclusion of his meeting with the ambassador.'

The secretary withdrew, and Stalin looked at Anna. 'You did not know of this?'

'Me? I do not think anyone at the Embassy can have known of it. It does not make sense. Prince Paul, the regent for the boy king, is a supporter of the Reich.'

'So I have always understood. Well, clearly he has either changed his point of view, or more likely, he has been replaced as regent.'

'But why? And why should the Fuehrer wish to invade Yugoslavia? They have never been our enemies.'

He regarded her for some seconds, but he could have no doubt that she was as bemused by what had happened as anyone. 'And the country has little of value,' he remarked at last. 'Except . . .' He got up and went to the huge map of Europe pinned to the wall, studied it. 'It provides the only practical route for a large armed force to take through the Balkan mountains to the Aegean Sea. To Greece, in fact. I think we will find that your Fuehrer will say that he wishes to send an army to help his friend Mussolini beat the Greeks, which they are not doing, especially now that there is a British army fighting on the Greek side.'

'But you do not believe that is the true reason?'

'The true reason, my dear Anna, is that Herr Hitler intends to complete the conquest of all Europe, apart from Spain and Sweden, by occupying the entire Balkan Peninsula. Only then will he feel able to bring his full might to bear upon Great Britain. Yes. That is excellent.'

Anna felt like scratching her head. 'This does not concern you, Comrade Stalin?'

'Josef,' he reminded her. 'Concern me? It pleases me very much.'

'But . . . if Germany controls all of mainland Europe, her borders will be contiguous with yours.'

'We already have a contiguous border with the Reich. In Poland. There is no difficulty on that. Soviet Russia and Nazi Germany have a twenty-five-year non-aggression pact, with which we are both totally content. You require our oil and coal and iron ore; we require your expertise. We share the future. Now I will tell you why I am pleased. A state secret, eh? I actually received a communication from the British Prime Minister, Mr Churchill, to the effect that he had positive proof that Germany is planning an attack on Russia.'

Anna drank the last of her tea, which was by now cold.

'I did not believe what he said, of course. The British have been trying to embroil us with Germany for years. Since before the war even started. But at the same time, our agents reported to us considerable German troop movements to the East. You do not mind my admitting to you that we have agents inside your country?'

'I am sure that we have our agents inside Russia,' Anna said faintly.

'Of course. It is all part of the game, eh? But now it is all explained. Your troop movements to the east were to facilitate your takeover of the Balkans. As I have said, it is always good to have a conundrum resolved, especially when it is resolved in such a satisfactory manner. Do you know, I feel like a holiday. I should be able to get out of Moscow for a week or so, next month.' Stalin poured more tea. 'Then I generally go down to my dacha in the south, where I can relax. I would be delighted if you were to accompany me.'

Anna turned her head sharply. Although she had known from their first meeting that he had been very taken with her, he had remained entirely avuncular in their relations. She found it difficult to imagine having sex with any man over fifty. And this man . . . She wondered what Chalyapov would make of that. Or Clive? Or Heydrich?

'I am sure that you would enjoy it there,' Stalin continued. 'You would be able to meet my children. My son Jacob is in the army, but my daughter Svetlana is still a girl. I am a widower, you see,' he added ingenuously.

My God! she thought. He can't be serious! But he very evidently was, at least at this moment. She drank tea, and spoke absently. 'I have a birthday next month.'

'What is the date?'

'The twenty-first.'

'And how old will you be?'

'Twenty-one.'

'Twenty-one. Ah, to be twenty-one again. But, twenty-one on the twenty-first. That is capital. You will spend your twenty-first birthday with me.'

Time for a decision. 'I'm sure that would be most enjoyable, Your Excellency.'

'Josef,' he reminded her.

Was he living in never-never land, or could he possibly be right? Anna wondered. But he was the master of a great country, and had been that master for more than a dozen years. He had to be used to evaluating, correctly, the acts and indeed the words of other governments. But if Germany had only ever been intent on occupying the entire Balkans, what of Heydrich's orders to her, to find out all she could about Russian attitudes towards Germany, and her troop dispositions along the border? But, she realized, they too could be explained, if one was determined to do so: clearly Hitler had been concerned about Russian reaction to his projected move to the south-east.

In which case the information she had given Clive, and the inference the British had drawn from it, had been entirely erroneous. And Churchill had gone for it! He would now be hopping mad. So, where did that leave her as regards MI6?

For that matter, where did she stand in any direction? Her sole desire was to get out of Moscow. Before her week with Stalin? She just could not imagine what that might be like. But she could not refuse him now, although there could be no doubt that Heydrich had to be informed. She could not imagine *his* reaction either, save that if Stalin's judgement was accurate, there was simply no reason for her to remain in Moscow.

'I think your mind is elsewhere.' Chalyapov threw her off him with some violence, so that she rolled across the bed and lay on her back.

'I am sorry, Ewfim. Would you like me to leave?'

'You are becoming bored with me. You are seeing another man.'

'Of course I am not.'

He got out of bed. 'I do not like women who cheat on me. Or who lie to me. Give me his name.'

'There is no other man.'

'Very good. Roll over.'

Anna sighed, but obeyed. When he entered her from behind it was always painful. She spread her legs, closed her eyes, and waited for him to raise her thighs from the mattress. Instead she heard a swishing sound. She opened her eyes again and turned her head. Chalyapov had drawn the heavy leather belt from his pants. 'What are you doing?' she asked.

'I am going to beat you. I am going to make that delightful little ass of yours bleed.'

Anna rolled over and sat up. 'Please do not do that, Ewfim. I do not like to be beaten.' The last person who had flogged her was Hannah Gehrig, and she had had the assistance of three men.

'If you liked being beaten,' Chalyapov pointed out, very reasonably, 'there would be no point in doing it. Lie down!'

'Ewfim,' she said, also speaking very reasonably, 'if you attempt to hit me, I shall break your arm.'

'You?' He gave a bark of laughter. 'Very well. If you wish me to mark your tits . . .' He swung the belt.

Anna caught the flailing leather in both hands. The shock of pain only increased her anger, but her brain remained ice cold. As she caught the belt she rose to her knees and threw herself sideways. The combined jerk on the belt and her roll pulled Chalyapov off balance; his knees struck the bed and he fell across it. Anna leapt off the bed and got behind him. The temptation to hit him was enormous, but she felt that to kill him might be a mistake. While he was trying to push himself up she knelt on his back, grasped his right arm, which still held the belt, and pulled it behind him and across while shifting her knee to his shoulder. Chalyapov uttered a scream of pain as the arm was dislocated, then Anna released him and stepped away.

He rolled to and fro, groaning and holding his arm. 'Bitch!' he moaned.

'I did warn you,' Anna pointed out, dressing herself.

'I am going to have you—'

'Before you get carried away,' Anna said, 'I should tell you that you are quite right in supposing that I am seeing another man. His name is Josef Stalin.'

She closed the door behind herself.

It was only when she regained the Embassy that she realized she had wanted to hurt Chalyapov, as much as possible, ever since that first evening in his car, when he had, to all intents and purposes, raped her. Why had she not done it before? Because she had needed an excuse. Now that it was done, she could surely ask to be relieved. She sat at her desk and wrote to Heydrich.

> I deeply regret that this should have happened, but the fact is that his treatment of me has grown increasingly brutal, and indeed, sadistic, over the past weeks. I have accepted this in order to carry out my mission, but when he threatened to beat me until I bled, I am afraid something snapped. I do not think I have done him any permanent injury, but I would say that he is unlikely to wish to see me again. I may also say, and it is an opinion in which I hope you will concur, that he has exhausted his potential as a source of information.

She considered for some moments before continuing. It was very necessary to remind her boss of her continuing value.

> However, Herr Chalyapov has now become entirely irrelevant. I have become very close to Marshal Stalin himself, and have tea with him every Friday afternoon, in complete privacy; I come and go in the Kremlin as if I belonged there. I have also been invited to visit with him at his dacha in the Crimea. I will admit that he has not yet divulged any information of much value, other than that he is confident of maintaining good and friendly relations with Germany, but as we grow more intimate I am sure I will obtain results. I can in any event assure you that he is perfectly content with our moves in the Balkans and sees no reason why these should drive a

rift between our two nations. I would be very happy if you would confirm your approval of my present activities, although I am sure you understand that should you feel I have served my purpose here I am ready to return to Berlin. Anna.

She realized her heart was pounding. If Clive were right, and her German employers had designs upon Stalin's life, she was virtually inviting them to use her. But if Stalin were right . . . and Stalin had to be right.

She sealed the envelope and took it to Groener for inclusion in the Diplomatic Pouch. He regarded it for several moments. 'It is some time since you heard from General Heydrich, is it not?'

Sharks, she thought, waiting for me to fall into their pool. 'My orders from the SD, Herr Groener, are ongoing. However, I am sure you will be pleased to know that my mission here is all but completed, and that I shall shortly be recalled to Berlin.'

She prayed that it might be so.

Over the next few weeks Anna continued to be invited to tea; she had become such a regular visitor that she was no longer even searched before being admitted to the inner sanctum. Not that it would have mattered as she never carried a weapon. On the other hand, the invitation to accompany the dictator to the Crimea was not repeated. Either Stalin had been upset by what she had done to Chalyapov – although he remained unfailingly pleasant to her – or his invitation had not been serious in the first place, or events in the Balkans were not turning out quite as favourably for Russia as he had anticipated. On the whole she was relieved, although there was just a hint of disappointment: it would have been quite an experience, she had no doubt. More disturbing was the absence of any reply from Heydrich. So she celebrated her twenty-first birthday alone in her apartment with Birgit.

But Stalin was certainly right about the weather. June was a delight, the more so because of the tremendous contrast provided by warmth and sunshine to the grey skies and biting winds of only a few weeks previously. Anna took up going for a daily walk in the park; it was such a pleasure to be able to wear a summer frock and a big hat and feel the gentle breeze caressing her legs, even if she now found herself awakening each day with increasing apprehension. She had no doubt that something was going to happen this summer; her sole ambition was to get back to Germany before it happened.

'Countess! What a pleasant surprise.'

The man was speaking English! But the American accent was unmistakable. Anna turned her head. 'Mr Andrews? I did not know you were still in Moscow.'

'Like you, I guess, I go – and stay – where I'm put. But I sure thought you had gone, seeing as how you haven't been at any parties recently. And here you are, prettier than any picture I have ever seen. As always. May I walk with you?'

'Certainly, after such a nice remark.'

He fell in at her side. 'You know that fellow Bartley has returned to England? A couple of months ago.'

'I had heard. I thought Mr Bartley was a friend of yours?'

'Like I said, we're in the same line of business.'

'Military intelligence.'

'Well, intelligence. Spy-spotting.'

Anna was happy to take the bait. 'And catching?'

'Sure. When it's possible. And convenient. May I ask you a question?'

'I don't have to answer it.'

'Are you really a Nazi spy?'

'As I said, Mr Andrews, I don't have to answer your question. When I lived in England, I was married to Ballantine Bordman. Sadly, it didn't work out.'

'And when it didn't work out, you returned to Germany.'

'What else would you have me do? Germany is my home. Or at least, Austria is. My family now lives in Germany.'

'But you had become a British citizen.'

'Bally wished me to. But I retained German nationality.'

'Which I guess has put you in rather a spot regarding the British.'

'That may well be so. But as I am not in England, their feelings towards me are hardly relevant.'

'I heard someplace that your mother is actually English. Is she happy with this?'

'My mother is Irish.'

'You never did answer my question. Were you a spy? The Brits sure thought you were.'

'I never said I would answer that question, Mr Andrews.'

'But you're here, at the Embassy . . .'

'I have a living to earn. Thus I work for the German Government. I suppose in your eyes that makes me a Nazi. I can only say that in Germany today, it is the best thing to be. I would also hope that that does not make me your enemy.'

'Not mine. At least not right now. But you're not afraid of what may happen? One day?'

How little you know, she thought. 'What do I have to be scared of, Mr Andrews?'

'You don't think it's odd, that fellow turning up in Moscow and coming to your party?'

'What fellow? Oh, you mean Mr Bartley. I am sure he had some other reason for coming here. Apart from me, I mean. He surely knows that here in Russia I am outside of his jurisdiction.'

'I guess you're right,' Andrews said thoughtfully. 'Say, Countess, would I be completely out of court if I asked you to have dinner with me? I mean, June in Moscow, with the trees blossoming and the birds singing . . .' He paused, anxiously.

'Why, Mr Andrews,' she said. 'I think that is a perfectly charming idea.'

'This has been one of the pleasantest evenings I can remember,' Anna said, with considerable truth. Her moments with Clive had always been the highs of her emotional life, but they had always been stolen. They had never shared a quiet evening at a restaurant together, never been to a dance together, never strolled in a park together, except as conspirators. Now she sat on a terrace overlooking the river, dining on carp, drinking white wine and discussing sweet nothings.

She had no doubt that he was dying to ask more questions, but so far he had restrained himself, preferring to talk about the United States, about his home in Virginia, the more so as she had confessed that she had never been to America, and knew very little about it. 'You'd love it,' he promised. 'And America would love you.'

'Even if I work for the Nazis?' she asked in an unguarded moment.

'You have convinced me that it is just a job of work, a means of earning a living. Not that you truly believe the ideology. Heck, I work for a Democratic administration, even if I've always voted Republican.'

She made a moue. 'I still cannot believe that I would be very welcome in your country.'

'You would be. One thing about us, we adore beautiful things. And you would be just about the most beautiful thing any of them would ever have seen. I do apologize. I did not mean that you are a thing.'

'But I am a spy, am I not? The British say so.'

'Well, you know, the Brits aren't always right in their judgements. I find it very difficult to accept that you are anything other than what you seem: a very beautiful and very charming young lady.'

Anna stared at him with her mouth open, and he flushed.

'Again I apologize. Heck, no. I don't. I . . . well, I'd sure like to get to know you better.'

'If you did that, you might not like me at all.'

'I'll take my chances on that. May I be extremely rude, and ask a personal question?'

'That depends on how personal the question is.'

'Someone at our Embassy has the idea that you are still in your early twenties. Can that possibly be true?'

Anna sipped cognac. 'My twenty-first birthday was a fortnight ago.'

'You're putting me on.'

'Do I look that much older?'

'Heck, no. I mean . . .' He was flushing. 'Didn't you marry that fellow Bordman three years ago?'

'I was eighteen when I married Bally, yes.'

'Wow! Well, I guess that puts the kybosh on the crazy idea that you could have been a spy.'

'You say the sweetest things,' Anna commented.

'Listen! I would like you to know that if things ever turn out bad, you can count on me. I mean . . .' One of his flushes. 'If you ever feel you have to get out of Germany, you can call on my help, and I'll see you find a home in the States.'

Anna smiled. 'In Virginia?'

'I'd like that.'

Anna squeezed his hand.

* * *

'Do you have something to tell me?' Heinz Meissenbach asked. However much they had briefly been thrown together by the death of Marlene Gehrig, he had, like most Germans, an instinctive dislike and distrust of the Gestapo.

Groener closed the office door, pulled a chair in front of the desk, and sat down. 'I would like an update on your current relationship with Anna Fehrbach.'

Meissenbach raised his eyebrows. 'We greet each other when we meet.'

'But she works for you. You must see her every day.'

'I see her as little as possible, Herr Groener. She no longer works for me. What she does with her days I do not know; I assume she is following some agenda dictated by the SD. What she does with her nights . . .Well, I think we all know that.'

'And there is still nothing you can do about her.'

'You know that as well as I. If you have a solution, tell me of it.'

'I think she is a menace. I think we need to do something about her before she gets us – gets the Reich – into serious trouble. If she has not already done so.'

'And I have just reminded you that there is nothing we can do. Or have you found some proof to link her to the death of the girl Gehrig?'

'I do not suppose we shall ever know the truth of that. Unless . . .' He gave a sigh of hopeless anticipation. 'Unless I were to be given the right to interrogate her. However, as I have told you, I am always prepared to watch, and wait, and listen, and gather straws . . .'

'I am a busy man, Herr Groener.'

'I have a contact in the Kremlin.'

Meissenbach frowned.

'He is a menial, of no importance whatsoever. But he is there. And yesterday he reported that Herr Chalyapov, who has not been seen for a month, has just returned from hospital. Where, Herr Meissenbach, he was being treated for a badly dislocated shoulder. There is a rumour that he suffered this injury in the course of one of his amours.'

'He probably deserved it. I never did like that fellow.'

Groener gave another sigh, this time of impatience. 'The point I am making, Herr Meissenbach, is that we know that Chalyapov, if certainly a womaniser, only ever has one mistress at a time, and for the past six months that woman has been Anna Fehrbach. We also know that Chalyapov is very high in the Soviet Government, and a protégé of Marshal Stalin himself. And thirdly, I also know, because Marlene Gehrig told me, that Anna Fehrbach is as deadly with her bare hands as with a gun. Lastly, we know that she is Heydrich's creature, who carries out his orders without question or hesitation.'

Meissenbach scratched his head. 'What are you trying to say? That Fehrbach was sent to Moscow to assassinate Chalyapov? She has taken a very long time about it. And he isn't dead. I can tell you that when Fehrbach decides someone should be dead, he or she dies, not left merely with a broken arm.' He flushed. 'I did actually know something of her background before we came to Moscow.'

'What? It is essential that I know everything about her.'

Meissenbach sighed. 'Did you hear about that incident in Prague, last year, when an attempt was made on my life?'

'Indeed. You were saved by the prompt action of your bodyguards. I congratulate you, and them.'

'My guards had nothing to do with it. I was saved by Anna Fehrbach, who shot and killed two of my assassins, after disabling their leader with a single blow, all in a matter of ten seconds.'

'You mean Gehrig was right? She is that good?'

'Why do you suppose she is so highly valued by the SD – by Heydrich himself?'

'I see. And you did not think it worth your while to tell me this before?'

'Well . . . I was told the whole thing was top secret.'

'And of course you owe her your life. But now you have turned against her. Why?'

'It would be more correct to say that she has turned against me, cast me aside like a worn-out glove.'

Groener stared at him. 'Hell hath no fury, eh? I always thought that applied only to women. However, perhaps you will now agree that we simply have to do something about the fair Fraulein.'

The man was starting to sound like a cracked record. 'I would entirely agree with you, Herr Groener, but for the simple fact that she is protected by General Heydrich.'

'I think it is worth the risk. I am saying this to you because

I believe you are a man to be trusted, a man who has the good of the Reich at heart. Are you such a man?'

'Well . . . what exactly are you getting at?'

'I believe that General Heydrich may be following an agenda of his own, one which is not necessarily in the best interests of the Reich, and that he is employing his creature, Fraulein Fehrbach, to carry out that agenda. I believe that it is our bounden duty to the Fuehrer to find out just what that agenda is.'

'And how do you propose to do that?'

'Fehrbach uses the Diplomatic Pouch to communicate with her employer. Her letters are always carefully sealed, but I assume they contain whatever information she has obtained at the time. And he of course replies, his letters also being sealed. Now, it so happens that the last time she gave me a letter for inclusion in the pouch was a month ago, May sixteenth. That is the day after Chalyapov was taken to hospital. If we accept my hypothesis, that Fehrbach was responsible for his misfortune, then it is reasonable to assume that the letter she rushed off to Berlin the next day was to inform Heydrich of what had happened. Do you agree?'

'It would seem likely.'

'He did not reply immediately. But then, he never does. His reply arrived this morning.'

'Ah! Did Fehrbach seem concerned by its contents?'

Groener took the envelope from an inside pocket. 'She has not yet received it.'

Meissenbach gazed at him. 'You would be taking an enormous risk. Once that seal is broken . . .'

'I have been practicing for some time, and I believe I can reproduce this seal, at least sufficiently to stand up to a cursory inspection. I have never dared take the risk of doing this before. But I have observed that Fehrbach never does more than turn the envelope over to check the seal has not been broken, before herself breaking it. On this occasion, after a four-week wait and on a matter she will have to be apprehensive about, I believe she will be in such a hurry to see what her master has to say that she will hardly even check the seal.'

'If you are wrong, it will mean a concentration camp. At the very least.'

'And if I am right, and the letter proves that Heydrich is

carrying on some clandestine negotiation with the Soviet Government . . .'

'Why have you told me all this?'

'Because, as I have said, I believe that you are a patriot, who wishes to protect the Reich, and the Fuehrer, from traitors.'

'You mean, because you are afraid to act on your own.'

'Because I wish you, the most senior member of the Embassy staff after the Ambassador, to know what I am doing, and why. And because I know that your feelings about Fehrbach are the same as mine.'

Meissenbach decided not to comment on the ambiguity of that statement. He knew that Groener dreamed of nothing more pleasurable in life than to have Anna strapped naked to a table in front of him, with the right to torment her as much as he chose.

Groener was studying him. He knew he had his man. 'It must be done very carefully,' he said. 'The seal must have only one break. Give me that paper knife.'

A last hesitation, then Meissenbach slid the knife across the table. Groener inserted the narrow blade beneath the seal, and exerted just enough pressure to break it. Then with equal care he slowly prized open the flap and took out the sheet of paper within. Meissenbach found he was holding his breath as he watched Groener's expression. 'Jesus,' the policeman muttered.

'What is it?'

Groener handed him the paper, and Meissenbach scanned the words. 'My God! This must go to the Ambassador immediately.'

'That would be suicide.'

'But . . .'

'To show the Ambassador would be to reveal that we had opened General Heydrich's secret correspondence. Anyway, would you not suppose that he already knows?'

'Count von Schulenberg? He would never be a party to something like this.'

'That is as may be. But to show him this letter would be to sign our own death warrants.'

'We have to do something.'

'I will tell you what we are going to do, Heinz. We are going to reseal this letter, and then we are going to deliver it to the young lady . . . And then we will take certain steps.'

Nine

The Lubianka

'Good morning, Fraulein,' Groener said jovially, closing the office door behind himself before advancing to Anna's desk.

Anna raised her eyebrows; Groener looking pleased was neither a usual nor a pretty sight. 'Good morning, Herr Groener. May I help you?'

'No, no. It is I who am going to help you. I have a letter for you. From Berlin.'

'Ah!' Anna could not prevent her relief from showing, although the relief was also tinged with apprehension.

'Came in today.' Groener placed the envelope on the desk in front of her.

'Thank you.' She resisted the temptation immediately to pick it up.

'I think you have been waiting for this message, Fraulein.'

'I am always waiting for orders from Berlin, Herr Groener.'

She gazed at him, and he realized that she was not going to open the envelope in his presence. 'Well, then, I will leave you to it.'

He left the room, and Anna remained gazing at the closed door for some seconds. Something was up. But whatever it was, it could not be half as important as discovering what Heydrich had to say.

She broke the seal, opened the envelope, took out the single sheet of paper and unfolded it, heart pounding.

My Dear Anna. Anna frowned. Heydrich had never begun a letter so affectionately in the past.

> I most heartily congratulate you on what you have achieved, and I entirely agree that Chalyapov has become redundant in view of your progress. It now but remains for you to render

the Reich the ultimate service. I wish to make it perfectly clear that while I most fervently hope to see you back in Berlin in the near future, should you find yourself unable to return, then once your mission is completed you will occupy an honoured, immortal place in Germany history, so long as there is a Germany.

Anna was suddenly aware of feeling cold.

I also wish you to know that once the news of the successful completion of the mission is received in Berlin, your parents, and your sister, will be immediately set free, to pursue their lives as and where they choose.

Now, your Friday meetings with Premier Stalin are the key, together of course with the free access to his presence, plus the fact that you say you are alone during these meetings. Friday 20 June is the decisive day. On that afternoon it is necessary for Stalin to die. I do not anticipate that someone with your skills will find any difficulty in this. It should also be possible for you to complete the task and leave the Kremlin well before his body is found. You will proceed immediately to the address on the separate piece of paper that accompanies this letter. It is situated in the Kotay Gorod, which as you know is the busiest and most crowded part of Moscow. Memorize the address and then burn it together with this letter. You will be concealed there until it is possible to smuggle you out of the country. This has been arranged but may take a day or two to implement. It only remains for me, on behalf of General Himmler, and indeed the Fuehrer himself, to wish you Godspeed and every success. Heil Hitler. Your always admiring, Reinhard.

Anna remained gazing at the letter for some time. Just like that, she thought. Just like that. Next Friday, you will die. Just like that. So much for her dreams of escaping.

The problem with people like Heydrich was that they could never believe there were other people in the world with an intelligence equal to or greater than their own. The plan outlined was perfectly plausible. She did not doubt that she could kill Stalin and escape from the Kremlin before any alarm was raised; the Premier had made it very clear to his staff that he did not wish his sessions with the glamorous Countess von Widerstand to be interrupted. She knew she would even be able to gain the security of this apparent bookshop in the market centre. But that would be as far as she could go. It had apparently not occurred to Heydrich that she would realize there could be only one possible reason for wishing Stalin dead: as Clive had recognized so long ago, Hitler meant to go to war with Soviet Russia. There could be no doubt that Stalin's sudden death would throw the Soviet government into disorder for some time, if only because, due to his paranoia, there was no truly designated successor, and a power struggle would inevitably ensue, during which the Soviet military would also be paralysed.

And as the dictator's death had been fixed for a particular day, any German invasion, to gain most advantage from the ensuing chaos, would have to take place within at most forty-eight hours. Which would make it impossible for anyone to be smuggled out of the country. Or would it? It might just make it simpler.

She had to believe that. Because, as always, she had no choice but to carry out her orders, even if she was now realizing that this had to have been the true point of her mission from the beginning, from last June when she had first been appointed as Meissenbach's assistant. Stalin had always been her goal, and she had been planted, with infinite care and patience, to work towards that goal. And now she was there.

She felt cold and hot at the same time, while a million thoughts raced through her mind. She had known this moment had to arrive sometime, but the realization that it *had* arrived was still a shock to the system. She knew she had no right to indulge in any recriminations, even to herself. She had been taught to kill, and she had preserved herself by doing so, on too many occasions. To be called upon to die herself was perfectly fair. But there suddenly seemed so much to be done, and so little time in which to do it. But some things were more important than others.

Today was Tuesday. It was therefore her only chance to contact MI6. She did not wish to disappear entirely anonymously. She pulled her block of private notepaper towards her and wrote, quickly and concisely. The note she placed in a thick manila envelope, and then added to it her gold earrings, her crucifix, her ruby ring, and her watch; these were all of her that would remain, all that he would have to remember her by in the days to come.

She sealed the envelope, took it up to her apartment. She lunched with Birgit. They spoke little, but then they seldom spoke much nowadays; she did not imagine that Birgit noticed anything different in her demeanour.

After lunch she went to bed for several hours; she did not feel like taking the risk of encountering anyone she might have to engage in conversation. Then she had a hot bath, dressed, and ate a light supper. Again, Birgit showed no great interest in this rather unusual behaviour. The meal over, she waited until nine thirty, then she placed the manila envelope in her handbag and left the Embassy, the guards as always carefully showing no concern at her movements.

She walked to the Berlin Hotel, enjoying the brilliant June evening, and arrived at ten. It was the first time she had entered the hotel since Clive had left. She could not resist the temptation to glance at the reception desk, but the man who was now standing there was unknown to her, and he did not seem the least interested in her; the foyer was as always crowded.

She took the lift to the fifth floor, and walked along the hall, so many memories crowding upon her. What a happy miracle it would be if Clive were to open the door.

She reached 507 and knocked. It was some seconds before the door opened, and she stared at the man in his shirt sleeves who stood there. He stared back, clearly as astonished as she was. 'Señorita?' he asked.

Anna recovered. 'I am sorry. I have the wrong room. Please excuse me.'

She turned, and he stepped into the hall. 'There is no need to be sorry, señorita. It is my pleasure to be disturbed by a beautiful woman. Will you not come in? I can offer you some wine.'

'Thank you, but no. I am looking for someone, and sadly you are not he. Good night, señor.'

She walked back to the lift, leaving the Spaniard staring after her in disappointment. She felt like screaming. But again, the fault was entirely hers. It was nearly three months since she had kept the rendezvous; she certainly could not blame

Sprague for having given up waiting for her. But it seemed as if all the accumulated disasters and errors of her life were coming together in one climactic catastrophe. Now she would indeed disappear without trace, only the slightest twitch across the face of history.

She realized she was crying, and hastily patted her cheeks with a tissue from her bag. Her fingers brushed the envelope. Her last will and testament. It would now have to be thrown into the river.

'Countess! What a pleasure!'

Anna all but fainted as she turned. He wore black tie and had clearly been dining. 'Oh,' she said. 'Hello.'

'I have to be the luckiest man alive,' Andrews declared. 'I have just endured one of the most boring dinner parties of my life, and suddenly – *voila*! The night has come alive.' Then he frowned. 'You're not with someone?'

'No. I was supposed to meet someone, but he didn't turn up.'

'In that case he's a bounder, but am I glad he didn't show.' His forehead had cleared, but now the frown returned as he peered at her. 'This guy was important, huh?'

'Why, no. Not really.'

'Then why have you been crying?'

'Well, I . . . should you ask a question like that?'

'I guess not. That was damned inquisitive of me. Would you let me make it up to you? A drink in the bar?'

Anna hesitated only a moment. This man's company was incredibly soothing. Presumably it came from being an American. 'A drink would be very acceptable.'

Andrews escorted her into the bar, which was uncrowded. 'The counter or a table?'

'I'd prefer a table.'

He seated her in a corner of the room. 'What do you drink after dinner? You have had dinner?'

'Yes. I think I'd like a glass of champagne.'

'Brilliant. Bring a bottle,' he told the waiter. 'And I want the real stuff. What do you have?'

'There is Taittinger, sir. But it is very expensive.'

'You worry about the liquor, and I'll worry about the cost.' He sat beside Anna. 'I have a strong suspicion that you have had some bad news.' He raised a finger. 'Don't remind me; I'm being darned inquisitive again. But you know what they say: a trouble shared is a trouble cured.'

'And you once said that if I was ever in trouble you would help me, no matter what,' Anna remembered, more thoughtfully than she had intended. Did she dare trust this man? Of course she could not, in real terms. But if he was prepared to do her a favour . . .

'And I meant it.' The ice bucket arrived and he inspected the label before pouring. 'Let's hope this isn't a fake.' He brushed his glass against hers. 'Here's to us. I have a positive notion that one of these days you and I may be able to get together. Don't take offence. If a guy doesn't dream from time to time he becomes a bore.'

'I don't think you could ever be a bore, Mr Andrews.'

'Don't press your luck. And how about calling me Joseph, if we're to share a secret? Although,' he went on, 'I prefer Joe.'

'Are we going to share a secret?'

'I sure hope so.'

'It would have to *be* a secret. My life could be involved.' There was a sick joke.

He gazed at her for several seconds. Then he said, now serious, 'That bad?'

'I want you to do something for me. But before I tell you what it is, I want you to promise that you will ask no questions, just tell me whether you'll do it or not. And that if you can't do it, you'll forget this conversation ever took place.'

'I promise.'

'How well do you know Clive Bartley?'

Now she had really surprised him. 'I don't really know him at all. No, that's not true. We worked together, once. We were both after the same thing, and as we were outnumbered by the bad guys, it seemed sensible to pool our resources.'

'And?'

Andrews drank some champagne. 'Hell, Anna, I thought he was one hell of a guy. You could say that without him I wouldn't be here now. On the other hand, I guess without me he wouldn't be here either. Don't tell me he's getting too close?'

Anna took the envelope from her bag. 'Can you have this

sent to England in your Diplomatic Pouch, and delivered to Clive at MI6?'

Andrews did not move for several seconds. Then he said, 'You'll have to forgive me while I try to get my brain in gear. You want me to send this envelope to Clive Bartley? You?'

'You promised to ask no questions. Just tell me you can do it. Or not.'

'Of course I can do it. But Anna . . .'

'You promised.'

'So I did. I have got to be a nerd. But I'll keep my promise. I'd just like to get my facts straight. The British suspect that you are a German spy. In fact they have gone so far as to describe you as a reincarnation of Mata Hari. Right?'

'They flatter me.'

'I would dispute that. However, Clive Bartley is the MI6 officer who just failed to get you before you left England. Right?'

'So I believe.'

'And you are sending him something, but you cannot do it through the British Embassy.'

'Of course I cannot. As you say, I am a German, and the British think I am a spy.'

'But you brought this envelope here tonight, to give to someone, who didn't show.'

'You're very close to breaking your promise, Joe.'

'Yeah. I'm sorry. I just need to be sure of one thing.' He fingered the envelope, could feel the solid objects inside. 'You wouldn't be sending him a bomb, would you?'

'There is nothing lethal in that envelope. I give you my word.' Except for the damage it just might do to his heart, she reflected.

'Okay. I'll believe you. This will go off tomorrow morning, and be in London tomorrow night. I'll have to write a covering note for our security people there, but I have a fair amount of clout. Clive should get it some time on Friday.'

And London is several hours behind Moscow, she thought. Whatever his reaction, it could not possibly take effect in time to alter the course of history. 'That would be very satisfactory. I can only say thank you.' She finished her drink. 'Now I should be getting back.'

He rested his hand on top of hers. 'Anna, I'm not looking

for any reward, I promise. But would it be possible for us to have dinner together again, say next week?'

'Next week,' Anna said thoughtfully, and chose her words with care. 'I would like to think that could be possible.'

'Shall we say, right here, at seven on Monday?'

'I would like that very much,' Anna said, again telling the absolute truth.

Andrews placed the envelope on his dressing table, where he would see it first thing in the morning; the plane carrying the Diplomatic Pouch left at eleven.

He got into bed and switched off the light. But he knew he wasn't going to sleep; the envelope might as well have been giving off a brilliant white light. In view of the fact that it obviously contained some solid objects, he would have to enclose it in a larger envelope, marked Private, Confidential and Top Secret, and hope that he carried as much clout as he supposed.

So what exactly was he doing? Getting involved with a very beautiful spy was one thing. Getting mixed up in some clandestine exchange between said spy, working for Germany, and a senior member of the British Secret Service, was another. Which one was the traitor? And having been brought into the picture, as it were, could he now just close his eyes and pretend it wasn't really happening?

That was just not possible with a girl like Anna. Oh, Anna! To get together with Anna would be a dream come true. But could he ever truly get together with her unless he knew exactly what she was? It would mean betraying his promise to her. But he was a secret service operative. He lived in a world of secrets and betrayals, which could be matters of life and death, and for one's country as much as any individual. He had never allowed personal feelings to interfere with his duty.

He switched on the light, got out of bed, and took the envelope to his desk. It was sealed, but with ordinary wax; he could not make out any design, and he had sufficient wax to replace it. He broke the seal, unstuck the flap, and emptied the contents.

Her jewellery! He had known something was off about her tonight, but had been so fascinated by her very presence that it had not immediately registered: her ears, her neck, her hands and arms had been bare. And now she was sending these very expensive personal items to the man who was supposed to be her arch enemy?

He was suddenly reluctant to open the letter; he had the strangest feeling that he was about to look into Anna's soul. He drew a deep breath and unfolded the sheet of paper.

> My dearest Clive,
>
> I have received my final orders, and they are as you thought they might be, last January. And as I have not succeeded in extricating myself you know that I must carry them out. So much for hope. It is to happen when I take tea with you-know-who on Friday afternoon. H has of course devised a plan for my safe return to Germany, but I do not think even he believes that it will work. However, should it, I will be in touch as soon as possible. If it does not work . . . I enclose these items which are very dear to me for you to remember me by. Do not weep for me, Clive. Does the Bible not say 'those that live by the sword shall die by the sword?' But I do wish you to know that throughout the horrendous events of the last three years of my life, the fact that you have been there to support me and encourage me and even, I hope, to love me, has alone kept me going. Give Billy and Belinda kisses for me, and . . . see you in the hereafter. All my love, Anna.

Andrews remained staring at the sheet of paper for several minutes. He had uncovered one of the great secrets of modern espionage. And, even more important from a personal point of view, a woman who in addition to an almost unearthly beauty also possessed a quite unearthly courage and determination.

This was, to all intents and purposes, a suicide note. Only she did not intend to kill herself; she intended to die, because she knew she must, in carrying out some special duty.

Think, God damn you, he told himself. There could no longer be any doubt that she was a double agent, with the Brits. But if the Brits had given her a suicide mission, she would hardly be writing to Clive in these terms. Therefore it had to be her German masters. Thus the H she referred to would probably be Himmler, or more likely his demonic assistant, Heydrich. But what was the mission? Someone with whom she was going to have tea on Friday afternoon. Nothing could be more innocent than that. How could it turn into an event that might involve her life?

He pulled on his dressing gown and went downstairs to the Communications Room. The rather sleepy young woman on duty was painting her fingernails, and looked up in alarm as he entered. 'Mr Andrews?!'

'Hello, Carol. I need to send a telegram.'

'Yes sir. I'll get out the book.'

'No. I'll send it in clear.'

'Yes sir,' she agreed doubtfully.

Andrews sat at the table, regarded the form for a moment, then wrote rapidly.

> mutual friend in deep trouble stop possibly terminal stop you know I don't stop Friday deadline stop letter in mail but do something now stop Joe

Carol regarded it. 'In clear,' she repeated. 'We don't have a wire address for anyone named Bartley.'

'We have one for MI6 in London, don't we?'

'Yes, we do. But . . . well . . .' She peered at the form.

'Okay, Carol. Send that, and I'll square it with the ambassador in the morning. Okay?'

'Good morning, Mr Bartley.' Amy Barstow always greeted her boss brightly, even if he did not always respond.

'Morning, Amy. Anything from Moscow?'

He had asked this question, increasingly morosely, every morning since his return three months before, and she had been finding it rather tiresome. But today she was able to wave a sheet of paper at him. 'Came in overnight. In clear, believe it or not. Unless it's some code I don't recognise. It's certainly gobbledygook.'

Clive snatched the telegram, scanned it, and frowned. 'Oh, my God! Billy in?'

'Half an hour ago. Shall I call . . .?'

But Clive was already running up the stairs. Baxter was drinking coffee and reading the *Times*. 'What the hell . . .?'

Clive thrust the telegram at him. 'I have to get to Moscow. Today.'

'Just simmer down.' Baxter studied the form. 'Who the hell is Joe?'

'Joe Andrews. You remember him, Billy. His lot co-operated with us on that African business about five years ago. He's now running security at the American Embassy in Moscow.'

'And this is his idea of security, is it? I assume your "mutual friend" is Anna?'

'Yes. And . . .'

'Just tell me how he knows she is your friend? And why she should be his?'

'Well . . . I know he met her at a reception at the German Embassy, and I could see he took a shine to her. Well, I mean, who wouldn't?'

'I can think of one at least. So are you telling me that she is now working for the Yanks, as well as the Germans, as well as us? As I have said before, this woman is a walking cataclysm waiting to happen.'

'Of course she's not working for the Americans, Billy. But somehow Joe has become involved. He'll explain it in the letter he says is on its way.'

'I hope he can. I would like to see it the moment it arrives.'

'Okay. You open it when it comes in. But I can't wait. *She* can't wait.'

'Can't wait to do what? Look, go and take a sedative and calm down, and bring me that letter when you get it. And hope that it does explain what's happening.'

Clive placed his hands on the desk and leaned forward. 'Billy, don't you remember my theory on why Heydrich should send Anna of all people to Russia just to find out what they're thinking? His most highly trained and successful assassin, just to hold a watching brief? Don't you remember my report back in January? For Christ's sake, you showed it to the PM, didn't you?'

'I did. And he was unwise enough to act on it. And got roundly snubbed by Stalin. And now we are well into the summer and there has still been no German invasion. I can tell you that the boss is not happy, because Winston is not happy.'

'I'm more interested in Stalin's reaction to the conclusion I drew from Anna's presence in Russia.'

'As to that, I have no idea. We decided not to use it.'

'For God's sake!'

'No, no, Clive. It is I who should be saying for God's sake. Did you seriously expect us to ask the PM to inform the head of another country – a country that has rejected any idea of an alliance with us, and with which, in fact, we have come close to being at war more than once in the past year – that we feel there is a chance he may be in line for assassination?'

'*May* be in line?'

'Well, I suppose someone like Stalin is in line for assassination every time he leaves the Kremlin, and is protected accordingly. But that is his business, not ours. And in any event, to attempt to explain that one of our people could be involved would be to open the biggest can of worms in history, certainly in view of Russia's paranoiac distrust of us and everything we do or say.'

'Billy, I am not talking about what may happen outside the Kremlin. Anna has gained virtually free access to Stalin.'

'And you seriously think she has been commanded to murder him? In her capacity as a Nazi agent? My dear fellow, that is madness. It would mean war between Russia and Germany.'

'That is what I have been trying to convince you is going to happen for the past six months.'

Baxter picked up his pipe and his tobacco pouch. 'And you seriously think she would carry out such a command?'

'She would have no choice. You know that. There are lives she values more than her own: those of her family.'

'But it just isn't practical. She'd never be allowed to take a gun, or a knife, into the Kremlin.'

'Billy, you know as well as I that Anna does not need a gun or a knife. Think of Hannah Gehrig, or Elsa Mayers. Or the night porter at the Hotel Berlin.'

'And you think that this assassination attempt is fairly imminent.'

'According to Andrews, it is going to happen on Friday.'

'You said that Andrews doesn't know anything about Anna.'

'He doesn't, to my knowledge. But he has discovered that something involving Anna is going to happen on Friday.

Something terminal, he says. That can only be the assassination. Billy, I have got to get to Moscow before then.'

Baxter struck a match, and puffed with great satisfaction. 'War,' he said, half to himself. 'Between Russia and Germany. Do you realize, Clive, what a help that could be to us? I mean, even if Germany wins, which I suppose will be the most likely outcome, it'll still occupy her for a year or so. Maybe longer: Russia is a big country.'

'Billy, I hope, for the sake of our friendship, that you are not suggesting what I think you are suggesting.'

'Even if I let you go to Moscow, Clive, just what are you proposing to do? What *can* you do?'

'Just get me there, Billy. I'll think of something.' With Joe Andrews, he thought. Having been in a couple of tight spots with Joe in the past, he had the highest regard for the American's guts and determination, and more important than either, his ingenuity. But he decided against mentioning this to Baxter.

'Whatever you think of, the Embassy cannot be involved.'

'I have no intention of involving the Embassy.'

Baxter thought for a few minutes. 'You understand that the only way you can get to Moscow in a hurry is by the Med? Which is a hell of a lot hotter now than it was last year.'

'Lightning never strikes twice in the same place.'

'It's a philosophy,' Baxter conceded.

'But I do need the best you can get. Fast planes and no delays. This has to be top priority all the way.'

'Hmm. And Belinda?'

'You handle this right, Billy, and I'll be there and back before she knows I've gone.'

Baxter did indeed pull out all the stops. Clive just had the time to wire Joe the words *Expect me* and then he was at Hatfield where he was met by an anxious looking Flying-Officer.

'Glad to have you aboard, sir,' he said. 'Name's Revill.'

'Bartley.'

'Yes sir. Flown before?'

'As a matter of fact, yes.'

'Of course you have, sir. I meant have you flown a Mosquito before.'

'A what?'

Revill gave him an old-fashioned glance. 'This, sir. The machine you are here to try out. The de Havilland Mosquito.' His tone was reverent.

'Ah, yes. Of course.' A few pennies were starting to drop, although not all were landing right side up. 'Nifty little thing.' He had to hope it was, because its twin engines did not suggest a great deal of speed. 'The guns are concealed, are they?'

'There are no guns, sir.'

'Say again?'

'This is a PR machine, sir.'

'Ah, yes. I get it. Public Relations, eh? But I'm trying to get to Gibraltar ASAP. Will it do it?'

'PR means Photo Reconnaissance, sir,' Revill explained with great patience. 'Not a fighter. It is also a prototype; there are only a couple in existence. I believe there are plans to build a fighter version, and a bomber, if these prove as successful as anticipated.'

'A prototype,' Clive said thoughtfully, wondering if Baxter was taking the easy route to get rid of him. 'And it'll take me to Gib? Without guns? What happens if we're attacked over the Bay?'

'We cannot be attacked, sir.'

'That is very solid reasoning, Mr Revill, but is it based on anything more solid than hope?'

'Speed, sir. Speed. The fastest Messerschmitt in the best possible condition cannot fly at much over three hundred and sixty miles an hour. This little gem will do four hundred and twenty. So if we are attacked, we simply fly away. When they get around to arming the new models, it will be the most formidable fighting aircraft in the world.'

Clive had to be impressed, but when he climbed into the cockpit – the two seats were placed side by side – he had a strange feeling. 'This is very odd material,' he remarked. 'I'll swear it's not steel. Or aluminium.'

'Well, no, sir. It's wood.'

'Hold on just one moment. You are proposing to fly a wooden machine at more than four hundred miles an hour? Won't it fall apart?'

'Good heavens no, sir. The wood is laminated and glued together under extreme pressure. There are one or two steel struts, of course. But it really is as safe as a house. And it has a range of fifteen hundred miles.'

Revill was proved right, and it was the most exhilarating flight Clive had ever made, even if his heart was in his mouth most of the way. They flew so fast he wasn't sure whether or not they saw any other aircraft; certainly nothing got close enough to be a nuisance.

And there was Section Officer Parkyn waiting to greet him, as always as bright as a button. 'Well, hello,' she remarked. 'Am I glad to see you! There was a rumour that you had bought it, last year.'

'Nearly, but not quite.'

'And now you're using one of these new secret machines. You really must have clout. May I offer you a bed for the night?'

'I'd love to, Alice. But I'm off again in an hour. As soon as we're re-fuelled.'

'Ships that pass in the night,' she said sadly. 'But please don't get shot down again: the Ministry would never forgive you if you managed to lose a Mosquito.'

They were in Cairo by dusk having seen a number aircraft, both Italian and German, none of which could get near them.

'They'll all be scratching their heads,' Revill said as they walked across the burning tarmac. 'Well, Mr Bartley, it's been fun. I hope you enjoyed your flight, and I hope you'll give the machine a good report to your firm. Maybe I'll see you again some time.'

'Wait a moment. Aren't you taking me to Moscow?'

'Good lord, no. You don't think the bosses would let me fly a Mosquito over Russian air space? As for landing there . . . we'd never get off again. No, it's back to Hatfield for me, tomorrow. Don't worry. They'll get you to Moscow in a couple of days.'

'A couple of days? I have to be there on Friday morning.'

'Well, in that case . . .' Revill pulled his nose. 'I reckon I should wish you luck.'

'Don't panic, Mr Bartley,' said the Wing-Commander. 'It's all arranged. You take off tomorrow morning, and fly to Teheran.'

'Why on earth am I going to Teheran?'

'Well, we can't over-fly Greece as it's in German hands. And the Turks won't allow us to use their air space. With a German army perched on the Aegean they are keeping to strict neutrality. Anyway, as I was saying, you'll leave Teheran on Friday morning, and should make Stalingrad that evening, with Moscow the next day. How about that?'

'Wing-Commander,' Clive said earnestly, 'I have got to be in Moscow on Friday morning.'

'I'm afraid that is simply not possible, Mr Bartley. Look, I've booked you into Shepheard's. Go and have a good meal and a good night's sleep. You'll feel better in the morning. After all, is twenty-four hours really going to make that much difference?'

'It's a gorgeous day,' Birgit commented as she served breakfast. 'It's hard to believe that only a couple of months ago it was freezing.'

'Um,' Anna commented. As it was only eight o'clock, presumably it was just dawn in London. Clive would not receive her letter for another few hours.

Did it matter? There was of course a tiny voice whispering away at the back of her brain, *maybe something will happen to save me*. But that thought had to be dismissed. Even if Clive tried to get to her immediately after reading the letter, he could not possibly reach Moscow before Tuesday, at the earliest. That was supposing there was anything he *could* do, or anything he wanted to do.

It was time to put all thoughts of Clive – of survival – from her mind. Simply go out in a blaze of glory.

'I feel lazy today, Birgit,' she said. 'I think I will stay in bed.'

'But are you not taking tea with Marshal Stalin, Countess?'

'Good heavens! I had forgotten. Yes, of course. But that is not until this afternoon. I shall have my bath after lunch.'

Lying there allowed her to relax. She could not stop herself thinking, of course. She could go through the program as outlined by Heydrich, envisage herself delivering the blows that would destroy the Soviet dictator – who had always been so nice to her – and then leaving his office, telling his staff that he did not wish to be disturbed for the next hour – would they suppose that he had had sex with her? – walking along those interminable corridors and out of the great doors, resisting the temptation to break into a run, leaving the fortress and plunging into the crowded streets of the Kotoy Gorod, only a short distance away, reaching the bookshop, perhaps just as the alarm went in the Kremlin, being welcomed and concealed while all Moscow seethed about her, and then escaping . . . It *could* happen.

She heard a familiar voice and sat up. 'No, no, Herr Meissenbach. The Countess is in bed.'

Meissenbach clearly ignored her, and a moment later the bedroom door opened. 'You *are* in bed.'

Anna held the sheet to her throat with unusual modesty. 'What do you want?'

'I went to your office, and you weren't there. It is ten o'clock!'

'I do not feel very well.'

'Oh! But is today not Friday? Do you not take tea with Marshal Stalin?'

'Is that any concern of yours?'

He glared at her, unable to stop himself looking at the body thinly protected by the sheet. 'So you are not going?'

'Of course I am going. It is not until this afternoon. I shall be better then.'

He gave little sigh. 'I am glad. I do not like to think of you unwell, Anna. I will wish you good fortune.'

He left the room, and Anna stared at Birgit. 'I am sorry, Countess. He just pushed me aside.'

'Don't worry about it, Birgit.' But what a strange thing to do, she thought, after having hardly spoken to her for two months. And suddenly to be concerned about her health? It was almost as strange as Groener's quite unusual good humour on Tuesday, when he had brought her Heydrich's letter. Her instincts told her that it was something that needed thinking about. But she was not in the mood to think about anything save what lay ahead. In any event, whatever the pair of them were about, it was no longer relevant. By this evening she would be out of their range, one way or the other.

She lunched, had a bath, and dressed for the afternoon. She wore a summer frock, in pale green with matching high heels.

In her handbag she stowed a pair of flat-heeled pumps, as she suspected she would have to travel as fast and as sure-footedly as possible when she left the Kremlin. She left her hair loose, but wore a broad-brimmed summer hat. She felt naked without her watch and jewellery, but at least she knew they were in good hands.

'Will you be in for dinner, Countess?' Birgit asked.

'Aren't I always?' She had a sudden urge to hug the girl, but resisted it; she had never shown her any great affection in the past.

She went downstairs, smiled at the various people she passed, and walked out into the bright June sunlight. It was only a short walk to the Kremlin, and she was there in fifteen minutes. The guards on the outer gate all knew her by sight, and saluted her with smiles.

She passed them, crossed the inner courtyard. There were quite a few people about, but none of them paid her much attention; if she had been admitted past the outer gate her presence had to be legitimate. On the door of the inner palace the guard presented arms. She smiled at him in turn, and stepped into the hall, waiting for a moment to allow her eyes to become accustomed to the gloom, then went towards the staircase, but checked as a door on her right opened. She turned and gazed at Chalyapov.

Alarm bells jangled in her brain, but she smiled at him as well. 'Why, Ewfim, how good to see you, and looking so well.'

'So are you, Anna, even if in your case it will be a temporary condition. You are under arrest.'

Anna heard movement behind her. Other doors had opened, and when she turned her head she discovered six men, all looking extremely apprehensive, but all considerably larger than herself. She had once destroyed three Gestapo agents sent to arrest her. But they had been carrying guns, and they had made the mistake of coming too close. These men were unarmed, and they were waiting for her to move.

'It would be very unwise of you to attempt to resist,' Chalyapov said. 'We know all about you. About your skills. But I doubt even you could cope with my people. And I do know that my men would love to get their hands on your body.'

Anna's nostrils flared as she inhaled. But for the moment she was helpless. And one of her greatest assets was patience. 'Aren't they going to do that anyway?' she asked, her voice low and controlled.

'Not if you behave yourself. Give me your handbag and place your arms behind your back.'

Anna obeyed. 'May I ask why you are doing this? What am I being arrested for?'

'You will find out.'

Anna felt the touch of steel, and listened to the click of the handcuffs. She was helpless, and at the mercy of these men – of Chalyapov, whose arm she had once dislocated. She had to protest. 'I think you need to remember that I am a German citizen, and an employee of the German Embassy. I have diplomatic immunity.'

'I do not think your Embassy is any longer interested in you, Anna.'

She stared at him, and resisted the sudden panic that was threatening to cloud her judgement. 'I think Count von Schulenberg may disagree with you. I demand the right to telephone him.'

'You have no rights, comrade.' He came close to her. 'I think this is how I like you best, Anna. I have been informed that you are not carrying weapons on this assignment. But you never know.'

Once again bells jangled in Anna's brain, so violently that she hardly felt his hands sliding over her dress, squeezing her breasts, and then raising her skirt to look between her legs. If this was the worst that was going to happen to her she had nothing to worry about.

She was shrouded in stale cigarette breath, but he was stepping away. 'I am going to see a lot more of you in the near future, Anna,' he promised. 'And hear a lot more from you, as well.' He nodded at his men. 'Take her away. Remember your instructions.'

'Yes, Comrade Commissar,' one of them said. 'You will come with us, comrade.'

Anna looked at Chalyapov. 'I assume you will be informing Marshal Stalin that I will not be joining him for tea. And why.'

Chalyapov merely smiled. 'He already knows.'

* * *

Anna was marched into the yard where a car waited. The back door was opened and she was pushed into the interior, not violently, but without the use of her hands to steady herself she stumbled, landed on her knees, and would have fallen had her shoulders not been grasped.

'We do not wish to mark that so beautiful face, do we, comrade?'

Anna got her breathing under control as she was pulled up, turned round, and made to sit, her hands crushed against the back of the seat. She was moving into an unknown situation, but one which could carry a death sentence. But the risk of death was supposed to come *after* she had killed Stalin; up till that moment she had committed no crime. She knew, of course, that the Russians believed in pre-emptive action, that one merely had to be suspected of something to be arrested and put away. But there was nothing for her even to be suspected of. What she had been about to do was known only to herself and Heydrich. And presumably to Heydrich's superiors – certainly Himmler. There was no reason for any of them to betray her; it made no sense. Yet Chalyapov had seemed to know. As, apparently, did Stalin. Indeed, Chalyapov appeared to know a great deal about her secret background.

She had not been looking where they were going, but now they swung through a gateway set in the high wall of a fortress-like building, into a courtyard, to stop before an open door. Around her were more high walls, although these contained innumerable windows.

The car door was opened, and her arms were grasped to pull her out. She stumbled, and one shoe came off. One of the men picked it up, but left her to limp lopsidedly into the hall. There were several people waiting for her, men and women, but only one seemed to matter. This was a slender young woman, trim in a green uniform; with her short black hair and crisp features she would have been attractive but for the glacial coldness of her eyes and her expression. 'You have her file?' she inquired.

The man carrying Anna's shoe was also carrying both her handbag and a briefcase. These he now offered. The woman's nose wrinkled, but she took all three items. 'Along there,' she said.

Anna debated kicking off the other shoe to restore a little

dignity to her movements, but decided against it; she did not feel this was a woman to be antagonised while her arms were bound behind her back. She limped along the hall. 'To the left,' her captor instructed.

Anna turned down the indicated corridor, and came to a door. The woman reached past her, and opened it. 'Go in.'

Anna entered the room, and waited. Behind a desk sat another woman, who also wore a green uniform. But there any resemblance to the young woman ended. This woman was middle-aged, and extremely large. Her face was broad and chubby, and was remarkably good-humoured; at this moment it was wreathed in smiles. Anna felt a surge of relief.

'The Countess von Widerstand, Comrade Colonel,' the young woman said.

'Countess!' the colonel cried. 'This is such a pleasure. Do you know how long it has been since I entertained a countess? Twenty years! I was young then, oh, so young. But you . . . you are as beautiful as they said. Welcome. Oh, welcome to Lubianka!'

Ten

Knights Without Armour

'But where are my manners?' the colonel said. 'Sit down, Your Excellency, sit down. Are those handcuffs really necessary, Olga?'

'I was told that you should read the file before making a judgement on that, comrade.'

'Hmm. We are surrounded by paranoia. But sit down anyway, Your Excellency.'

Anna sank on to the chair. Olga took up a position behind her.

'My name is Ludmilla,' the colonel said. 'And while you are here, I am your friend. Remember this.'

'I will,' Anna said.

Ludmilla smiled at her. 'But you must only speak when you are asked a question. It is a rule, you understand.'

'Yes, comrade. Oh!'

A sharp pain had entered her shoulder and raced down her arm. She twisted her head and gazed at Olga's cold face, and at the small, wand-like cattle prod she carried; she had not noticed it before.

'The rule,' Ludmilla reminded her. 'Now let us see.' She opened the briefcase and took out a file, then spread this in front of her. 'Your name is Anna. What a pretty name. May I call you Anna?'

This was definitely a question. 'Yes, comrade.' Anna's voice was low; her arm and shoulder still ached.

'And you are twenty-one years old. Oh, to be twenty-one again.' She frowned. 'This says you are highly dangerous and are to be kept under the strictest confinement.' She raised her head. 'You are twenty-one years old and you are highly dangerous? How can that be?'

A question. ‘I do not know, comrade. I do not know who compiled that file.’

‘It says here that in Prague last year you shot two men dead and crippled another with a single blow, all in ten seconds.’

‘My God!’ Anna snapped, involuntarily, as the penny dropped. Only one person in Russia, other than herself, knew the truth of what had happened in Prague.

Even as she spoke, she tensed her muscles for the electric shock, but there was none: Ludmilla had raised a finger. ‘Why did you exclaim like that? Because it is true?’

Anna bit her lip.

‘Twenty-one years old,’ Ludmilla mused. ‘And now you have tried to assassinate our glorious leader.’

‘There is no proof . . .’ Again Anna bit her lip, but too late. ‘Ooh!’ Another streak of agony raced through her body.

‘You understand,’ Ludmilla said, ignoring the interruption, ‘that there will have to be a trial. It will be a public trial.’

Hopefully that was a question. ‘Will I be allowed to defend myself?’

‘Of course. It will all be done according to law. But before the trial you have to sign a confession. This must name the people who sent you here, and who have assisted you in this dreadful plan.’

‘But if I make a confession, what is the point in having a trial?’ Anna asked the question without thinking, and again braced herself for the coming shock, but Ludmilla had again signalled Olga to leave her alone for the time being.

‘If you do *not* make a confession, how is the judge supposed to determine your guilt?’ the colonel inquired. She might have been speaking to a small child. Had Anna’s wrists not been secured she would have scratched her head. ‘Of course, whether you make a confession of your own free will is entirely up to you, and will make no difference to the procedure we have to follow. You must be interrogated to ensure that you tell us the truth. You do understand this?’

I am in a madhouse, Anna thought, surrounded by lunatics. But she nodded. ‘Yes, comrade.’

‘I am so glad,’ Ludmilla said. ‘It makes life easier for everyone. Now do remember, Anna, that I wish to be your friend. Olga wishes to be your friend.’

Again Anna started to turn her head, and again changed her mind.

'All we require is your cooperation. Now, returning to this matter of your being dangerous, it is not my business to question the judgements of my superiors. But it also says here that you have a very high IQ. You should therefore understand that both Olga and I are highly trained in unarmed combat. No doubt you are even more highly trained. But for you to attempt to beat us up and fight your way out of here would be *very* counterproductive. For two reasons. One is that if you look up at the top of that wall you will observe a little box. That is a camera that is filming your every moment in here. The moment you attempt to misbehave this room will become filled with men. They will not harm you seriously, because you have to be absolutely fit when you appear in court, but in addition to their combat skills they are also trained to hurt people severely, in places that will not show. I'm sure you would not wish that.'

Anna swallowed. 'No, comrade.'

'And the other reason, of course, is that if you attacked Olga and me, you would make us your enemies instead of your friends. And we so want to be your friends. Don't you want us to be your friends, Anna?'

'Yes, comrade.'

'That makes me so happy. Well, Olga, as the Countess understands the situation, I think you can take off the handcuffs.'

The key clicked, and the handcuffs were removed. Anna rubbed her hands together; the returning circulation was painful.

'Now,' Ludmilla said. 'I would like you to take off your clothes.' Anna's head jerked, and Ludmilla smiled at her. 'I want to look at you. I do like looking at pretty things, and you are exceptional.'

Anna could not stop herself looking up at the cameras.

'Oh, they like looking at pretty things too,' Ludmilla agreed. 'Poor dears, they get such few pleasures.'

Anna sighed, stood up, and removed her dress, then hesitated.

'Oh, everything,' Ludmilla said.

She could have been Dr Cleiner's sister. Anna removed her cami-knickers and then her stockings; she had already kicked off her remaining shoe.

'Exquisite,' Ludmilla agreed. 'Now, I wish you to go to that table over there, get on to it, and lie down. On your back to begin with, with your legs pulled up. I am going to search you,' she explained, pulling on a pair of thin rubber gloves.

Oh, my God, Anna thought. Not even Cleiner had wanted to do *that*. 'What am I supposed to be concealing?'

'I very much doubt that you are concealing anything. But it is part of the procedure, you see. And I do so enjoy putting my fingers into pretty little girls. They squeal so. But you,' she added regretfully, 'are not going to squeal, are you?'

Anna looked up at the camera, which was moving to follow her as she went to the table. 'No, comrade. I am not going to squeal.'

'There,' Ludmilla said, stripping off the gloves and throwing them into the waste basket. 'That wasn't too bad, was it?'

Anna had to concede that she was right, apart from the humiliation. 'No, comrade. May I get up?'

'Of course you must get up. We must move on.'

Anna had been lying on her stomach. Now she brought her legs together and rose to her knees. Olga, standing beside her, held her breasts as if she wanted to fluff them out; Anna stared at her and she stepped away. The wand hanging from her wrist swung to and fro as if anxious to be used again, but Ludmilla had apparently forbidden this for the time being.

'You will find,' Ludmilla said chattily, 'that the procedure we follow is not on the whole very painful, although it can be, if you prove unnecessarily recalcitrant. It is far better than in the old days.'

Anna swung her legs to the floor and stood up.

'In the old days,' Ludmilla continued, 'the way to make an inmate suffer without it showing in court – apart from beating, of course – was to stuff finely broken glass up his or her ass. This was usually very effective, of course. But it was extremely painful, so much so that in some cases the victim went out of his or her mind. This was counter-productive, as you are required to be lucid when you appear before the judges. And, naturally, it did permanent damage.'

Anna felt like lying down again. 'But this method is no longer used?' she suggested optimistically.

'No, no. We are far less primitive nowadays. Come along.'

She opened a door at the rear of the room, and stepped into a corridor. Anna glanced at Olga, received a quick nod, and followed. A short walk brought them to another door, which Ludmilla opened, to enter a large, square room, entirely devoid of furniture. There was, however, a coiled hose in one corner, beneath a tap protruding from the wall, and a wooden beam extending across the ceiling, from which was suspended a thick leather strap. And in another corner the ubiquitous camera hung from the ceiling, moving slowly to and fro while it focused on Anna. Beneath the camera, set in the wall, there was an electric control box, in which there were several buttons and levers.

'This is the bathroom,' Ludmilla explained. 'You will be spending a lot of time here. Olga.'

Olga pointed to where she wanted Anna to stand, which was exactly beneath the strap, from which she now saw there was suspended a steel hook. Anna assumed the required position, and Olga took the handcuffs from her belt, brought Anna's arms in front of her, and cuffed the wrists together. Then she raised the arms and fitted the links of the cuffs over the hook to hold them there, before going to the wall and pressing a button on the box. Instantly a motor hummed, and the strap receded into the ceiling, just far enough to raise Anna on to her tiptoes.

'There,' Ludmilla said. 'That is not too uncomfortable, is it?'

'No,' Anna muttered. It was actually by no means uncomfortable at the moment, although she knew it would become so if she was forced to endure it for any length of time. She was more concerned by the fact that she was now totally exposed to whatever these two harpies wished to inflict upon her.

She watched Olga cross the room, open a door, and step through. 'It gets very wet in here,' Ludmilla explained. She now picked up the hose by the nozzle. 'The water will be somewhat cold, although not as cold as if it were midwinter, eh? Ha ha.'

'Ha ha,' Anna agreed faintly.

The door opened again and Olga returned, now as naked as Anna herself. She stood against the far wall, next to the control box. 'Now,' Ludmilla said. She still held the nozzle of the hose, and this she directed at Anna. Olga pulled one of the levers halfway down, and the hose began to swell.

Anna took a deep breath, and was then enveloped in a stream of water, playing on her legs, splattering up over her stomach. As the water was in fact not very cold, it was by no means unpleasant. Slowly she allowed her breath out of her lungs.

'Full,' Ludmilla said.

Involuntarily Anna half turned her head, and was struck a tremendous blow between her shoulder blades. The force spun her round and she glimpsed Ludmilla fighting to keep hold of the nozzle. Then water was cascading over her face and hair, and as she was turned again it struck her between her breasts, driving the breath from her lungs. Before she could react the jet was on her face itself, slamming into her mouth and nose and eyes.

I am about to die, she thought. *I am being drowned while standing on my feet*. Then the pressure died, and she was left gasping and spitting; a good deal of the water had got down her throat and she still felt as if she were choking; it was several seconds before she could take even the shallowest of breaths.

She opened her eyes and gazed at Olga, who had come forward and now slapped her on the back, so that she gasped and choked again and vomited.

'That was such *fun,*' Ludmilla said. 'Wasn't that fun, Anna?'

Anna was still gasping too much to speak. In any event, all she wanted to do was curse at her.

'But we cannot just have fun,' Ludmilla said, without regret. 'The hose can be used for a more serious purpose. It can inflict exquisite pain. It can cause damage. It can even kill. We will show you.'

Anna opened her mouth to scream, and then changed her mind. She would not give them that much pleasure. Besides, perversely, she was curious. Olga had switched off the water before coming forward. Now she returned to the panel and lowered the lever again, but only a third of the way. Water flowed, but with none of the earlier power. Ludmilla played the flow over Anna's groin. 'That is very nice, eh? But you see, if I twist the nozzle, so . . .' She did so, and the jet narrowed. Ludmilla twisted some more, and it became as thin as a pencil, and then as a pencil lead. Now it was quite painful, feeling like a needle jab. 'Try to imagine,' Ludmilla suggested, 'what it would feel like if we were to give it full volume. Do you know, I have cut off a woman's nipple with this jet? And if I were to put it inside you . . . an instant hysterectomy.'

Anna had got her breathing back under control, and kept her voice even. 'What happens if I write you out a full confession now, and do not attempt to defend myself?'

'Why, you will be convicted.'

'And sent to prison?'

'For planning to kill Marshal Stalin?' Ludmilla gave a shout of laughter, and even Olga smiled. 'Good heavens, no. You will be shot, Countess.'

'Tell me,' Clive said.

The two men sat at a corner table of a small café just around the corner from the American Embassy. It was Saturday afternoon and he had only just reached Moscow. He had telephoned immediately on landing, before even calling at his own Embassy, where he would be staying.

Now Andrews poured them each a glass of vodka. 'I think you need to tell me.'

Clive drank. 'I need to know how you became involved. And how involved.'

Andrews considered briefly, then nodded. 'That's reasonable. I met her in the Berlin on Tuesday night, entirely by chance. She told me she was looking for someone. She didn't say who, but I have an idea it was your man Sprague, only he hadn't shown. But she had this large envelope with her, addressed to you, so I'm pretty sure that she wasn't there just for a drink. However, she accepted a drink from me. I could see she was upset about something, so I asked if I could help. She thought about it for a while, then asked if I could send the envelope in our Diplomatic Pouch, and see that it got to you.' He paused to sip his drink.

'And that's all? Doesn't tie in with your telegram, old man.'

Andrews put down his glass. 'I guess not. I'm afraid old habits die hard. I could tell she was on to something big, and frankly I was intrigued. She's a German spy, and you're a British spy-catcher, and here she is sending you a personal letter. So . . .' He flushed. 'I opened the envelope.'

'I see. And what was in it?'

'I guess some would call it a suicide note. Others might go for a love letter. Either way, it sure was a farewell, from her to you. She had even enclosed some very valuable pieces of jewellery. You didn't give them to her, by any chance?'

'That poor kid! No, I did not give her any jewellery. And on the strength of that letter you made certain deductions. One being that she is actually one of ours.'

'That seemed pretty obvious. I have to congratulate you on

that. I wish she were one of *ours*, just for the chance to get close to her.' He sighed. 'I guess you've done that.'

Clive preferred not to answer. 'What about this Friday deadline. Yesterday.'

'The letter was very discreet as to events, but she did say that her orders had to be carried out on Friday. Would those have been your orders?'

'No. She gets her German orders direct from Heydrich.'

'And he had given her orders which could involve her death? Why didn't she just go to your Embassy and get out?'

'Because she can't do that.'

'Would you like to explain that?'

Clive told him the story of Anna's life.

'Holy shit! That poor kid.'

'So what has happened?'

'As far as I know, nothing. There's been no big noise about anything.'

'Nothing from the Kremlin?'

'No. Not that there ever is anything from the Kremlin,' Andrews pointed out. 'You know what the orders were?'

'I have a pretty good idea. She was ordered to enter the Kremlin and assassinate Stalin.'

Andrews stared at him for several seconds. 'If you are as fond of that girl as she seems to think you are, I think it is God dammed bad taste to joke about it.'

'One doesn't joke about Anna. You aren't aware of it, but, again on orders from Heydrich, she has wormed her way into a position of being old Joe's favourite woman. They take tea together, in private, every Friday afternoon.'

'Holy shitting cows. And you reckon . . . You mean you knew this was going to happen, and you just sat back and did nothing? You actually sacrificed the girl just to cause trouble between Germany and Russia?'

'If we had been prepared to do that, would I be here now? We knew this was on the cards, but didn't know how soon. We've been working on a plan to get her recalled to Germany, but it hasn't worked yet. Now it's too late.'

'Oh, come now. You have to be putting me on. You reckon Heydrich would employ a twenty-one-year-old girl to carry out a high-powered political assassination? And even if he was that crazy, how was it to be done? Not even Stalin's favourite woman gets to see him without being frisked by his bodyguards. So where is she supposed to conceal her tommy-gun, or grenade, or even a small pistol. It's just not practical.'

'Joseph.' Clive spoke earnestly. 'I know you think Anna is the sweetest chick currently walking the face of this earth. And she can be that. But she is also the most deadly woman walking the face of this earth. She was trained, programmed if you like, by the SD. With a gun, she could shoot your eye out at fifty yards. I have seen her at work. But she is even more deadly with her bare hands. I have seen her at work there too.'

Andrews produced a handkerchief and wiped his brow; he could have no doubt that Clive was speaking the truth. 'Her letter gave the impression that you and she were . . . had been . . . well . . .'

'Yes,' Clive said. 'We have been lovers, and I sincerely hope we will be lovers again.'

'You mean, knowing what you do about her, you can . . .?'

'You are starting to sound like my boss. Anna does everything supremely well.'

Andrews digested this while he finished his drink. 'So you reckon Stalin is dead.'

'We have to find that out. And what Anna's present status is. If she wasn't killed outright, she'll be under arrest somewhere. We have to get her out.'

'If she wasn't killed outright, after doing Stalin, she'll be in the Lubianka. Nobody gets out of the Lubianka except to go on trial and then be shot. And by the time that happens, he or she has generally been tortured into a mental state where they cannot tell white from black, and will agree to whatever the prosecutor wants.'

There was a crack, and Clive's glass broke under the pressure of his fingers. But he spoke quietly. 'Then we'll just have to break the mould. I'm asking for your help, Joe.'

'For Anna,' Andrews said thoughtfully. 'Jesus!' He looked up. 'You shall have it, and I hope we both don't live to regret it. I have an acquaintance with Lavrenty Beria. You know him?'

'I know of him. Isn't he the boss of the NKVD?'

'That's right. He's as cold-blooded as they come, but he spends a lot of time brooding on the future, and his part in it. I'm talking about when old Joe dies, even of natural causes.

That makes him amenable to suggestion. In any event, he'll know if anything happened in the Kremlin yesterday – and, if anything did, where Anna is now.'

'Then he's our best hope. When can you see him?'

'It'll have to be by appointment. And that can't happen before tomorrow. Good thing the Soviets regard Sunday as a working day.'

'By tomorrow, Anna could have spent two days in the Lubianka.'

'So she could be having a tough time. But if everything you have told me about her is true, don't you think she'll be able to take it? Just remember that the Soviets require their accused to appear in court in apparently perfect health and unmarked.'

'Cheer me up. You do understand that no one can know that Anna is a British operative. What are you going to tell Beria?'

'If life were easy, wouldn't it be a damned bore? But I have some ideas.' He got up. 'I'll be in touch, just as soon as possible.'

'Shit!' Sprague remarked, having listened to what Clive had to say. 'What a fuck-up.'

'The fuck-up is your not being at the Berlin on Tuesday night.'

'For Christ's sake, Clive, she hadn't shown for three months. We had to determine that she wasn't going to play ball any more. Anyway, it was the Ambassador's decision. You know he never was happy about the Berlin set up. It was his decision that it should be terminated.'

'So now we may have lost her. In every way.'

'Well, old man, there does happen to be a war on. People are being done every day. Even beautiful people like your Anna.'

'Listen,' Clive said, 'shut up.'

He had been given a room at the Embassy, and to his surprise slept heavily. But then, he was exhausted, physically from the three days of endless travel, and emotionally by the thought of what might have happened to Anna, or still be happening to her.

When he awoke it was to a familiar sound, but one which belonged to London, not Moscow. He sat up, and his door opened. 'What the hell is an air-raid siren for?'

Sprague was fully dressed. 'The balloon has gone up.'

'Oh, my God! Anna?' Although what she could have to do with an air-raid siren he couldn't imagine.

'She may well have had something to do with it. The Germans have invaded. Planes are supposed to be heading this way now. You reckon they were just waiting for Stalin's death?'

Clive got out of bed and began to dress.

'You realize,' Sprague went on, 'that this puts the kybosh on any hope she may have had of claiming diplomatic immunity.'

Clive was getting his thoughts under control. 'Where is this invasion taking place?'

'Everywhere. Right along every border Russia has with Europe, the whole two thousand miles. Can you imagine the forces that must be involved?'

'But the Soviets have at least as many, haven't they?'

'Maybe. But they seem to have been taken completely by surprise. There appears to be absolute chaos out there. And there is total panic here.'

'What is London doing about it?'

'I imagine London is just waking up to it.'

'Do you think we'll chip in?'

'I doubt it. Winston regards the Soviets as thieves and murderers. He's said so, publicly. Anyway, it makes sense to let them and the Nazis slug it out. Whoever wins, if anyone actually does, will be too exhausted to come back at us for a while.'

'I have to make a phone call,' Clive said. But Andrews was unavailable.

'Mr Andrews,' Lavrenty Beria said. 'I'm afraid I can only spare you five minutes. I am sure you understand the situation.' He was a very tall man, who wore a pince-nez on the bridge of his big nose. The nose and the glasses were the only notable features in the large, bland face and the entirely bald head. But unlike all the members of staff Andrews had encountered on his way up to this office, he seemed to be entirely calm.

'I do,' Andrews said. 'Those bastards. Have they given any reason?'

'I understand Count von Schulenberg called on Comrade Molotov just before dawn this morning, and presented him with a long list of so-called Soviet outrages and broken promises, accompanied by a declaration of war.'

'What did Molotov do?'

'I believe he was as polite as diplomacy requires.'

'And the German Embassy?'

'The staff are receiving their passports now, and will be out of Russia this afternoon.'

'You are very civilised.'

Beria gave a brief smile. 'Not really. We wish the return of our Embassy staff from Berlin. Now, what did you want to see me about?'

'There are two matters, actually. Have you drawn any conclusions regarding the link between this German invasion and the assassination of Marshal Stalin on Friday afternoon?'

Beria's brows drew together, a formidable sight 'How do you know about that? No one knows about that.'

'It is my business to know about everything.'

'Well, you were misinformed. Marshal Stalin is alive and well and preparing to take command of our armed forces.'

'There's a relief,' Andrews said, not entirely truthfully. 'But there was an attempt on his life?'

'I really must discover the identity of your informant,' Beria remarked. 'Yes, Mr Andrews. There was an attempt. Fortunately, we were forewarned, and were able to prevent the assassin from gaining access to the marshal.'

'I congratulate you. What happened to the assassin?'

'She is now in the Lubianka, where she will remain until she is tried and executed. In our present circumstances, this may take a little while. However, it will be worth it, as what she will say in public will reveal the depths of perfidy to which the Hitlerite gangsters are prepared to go.'

'Absolutely. You mean she has made a full confession?'

'At the moment she is being a little stubborn. We have not even found out her true identity. She persists in calling herself by that ridiculous title, the Countess of Resistance. However, I am sure we will be able to persuade her to cooperate.' Another brief smile. 'We are good at that.'

'Oh, quite.'

'Besides, we have been provided with a dossier on her. It is not complete, and frankly, much of what it contains is simply unbelievable. Still, it is something to use in tripping her up when she starts to talk.'

'Would you like me to fill in the blanks?'

'You?'

'Her real name is Anna Fehrbach, and she is an Austrian by birth. For the past three years she has been employed by the Germans as an assassin. She has considerable skills. We know of at least seven murders she has carried out for the SD. And there have been others.'

'My God! That is what our informant claims. But I could not believe it. She is only a young girl.'

'Well, let's see. I believe that Queen Joanna I of Naples was only a teenager when she did her first husband. Not that she stopped there.'

'How do you know all this? About Fehrbach, I mean.'

'We also have a dossier on her. Far more complete than yours.'

'Why?'

'This is confidential. Just over a year ago she attempted to assassinate President Roosevelt.'

'I have never heard of this.'

'Is anyone going to hear about the attempt on Marshal Stalin, until you are ready to make it public? Fehrbach failed, but she did kill two of the President's bodyguards. She is top of the FBI's most-wanted list. But she got out of the country before she could be arrested, and disappeared. I have been tracking her for two years. We are actually in the process of preparing papers for a possible extradition. But now this has happened. We want her, Commissar Beria.'

'So do we, Mr Andrews. And we have her.'

'Her attempt on Roosevelt was before her attempt on Stalin. Don't you think we have a prior claim?'

'In a case like this, Mr Andrews, it is finders keepers. But thank you for your information. I am sure it will be most useful.'

'And that is your last word?'

'I am afraid so.'

'Is that because you are afraid of upsetting Comrade Chalyapov?'

Beria raised his eyebrows. 'Comrade Chalyapov has problems of his own. It is not overlooked by Marshal Stalin that he was responsible for introducing this woman into the Kremlin in the first place. So one could say that without a full confession from the Countess, he could well wind up in the Lubianka himself. But as I say, I regard that as his problem.'

'I have an idea that you do not like Comrade Chalyapov, Comrade Commissar.'

It was impossible to make out Beria's eyes behind the glasses, but his smile was bland. 'You are a perceptive man, Mr Andrews. But that has nothing to do with my decision to bring the Countess to trial. It is my business to uphold the law, and demonstrate the perfidy of the Nazi regime.'

'Ah, well. You win some, you lose some.' Andrews got up. 'Thanks for your time, anyway. And good luck with this war you've accumulated. Do you reckon you can win it?'

'We will defend our sacred motherland to the last drop of our blood.'

'I'm sure you will. And my information is that it may come to that. In modern wars, oil and machinery counts more than blood. Isn't it true that your air force, all nine thousand planes, is antiquated and no match for the Luftwaffe? And isn't it true that while you have a huge army you are very short of modern equipment, and especially transport?'

'This is not something I wish to discuss.'

'Pity. Ambassador Davies said to me this morning, when he heard I was seeing you this afternoon, "make it plain to Mr Beria that we want to help his country in any way we can, especially as regards materiel." Still …'

'Mr Davies said that? You mean America would be prepared to help us? As she has been helping Britain for the past year?'

'Well, of course.' Andrews took a deep breath. 'I happen to know that there is a top-level delegation leaving the States today to come here and find out what you need. Mind you, there's going to be opposition. A lot of people over there hate your guts. But if the President were able to convince Congress that you were really prepared to accept our help in the spirit in which it is intended, and that in small matters of protocol you would be prepared to play ball, you know, the odd quid pro quo . . . As for illustrating the perfidy of Nazi Germany, I don't think anyone can have any doubts about that, after this unprovoked attack.'

Beria studied him for several seconds. Then he said, 'I think that my people could probably learn a lot from yours about the art of blackmail, Mr Andrews. I feel like a schoolboy.' He picked up his telephone.

The young officer saluted. 'You are Mr Andrews.'

'Correct. And you are Captain Skorzy.'

'Yes, comrade. You have something for me?' Andrews held out the sheet of paper, and Skorzy studied it. 'You are to take possession of a prisoner in the female block.'

'Right first time.'

'This is very unusual.'

'The order is signed by Comrade Beria.'

'I am not disputing that, sir.' He pressed a bell. 'If you will come with me.'

Andrews followed him from the office into the hall. He had never liked prisons, and this was the most forbidding prison he had ever entered. They came to a door where an armed guard stood to attention, clicking his heels at the sight of the officer. Skorzy opened the door. 'This is the Women's Section,' he explained. 'Ah, Olga!' He greeted the slender, attractive, dark-haired young woman who was waiting for them.

'Comrade Captain!' Olga's eyes were hostile as she looked at Andrews.

'We have come for the woman Widerstand.'

Olga frowned. 'Come for her? You wish to take her?'

'That is correct.'

'There must be some mistake.'

'Explain.'

'You will have to see Colonel Tserchenka.'

'Then take us to her.'

Olga hesitated, then led them along a corridor. The odour was mainly disinfectant; the sounds were all feminine, if muted. Olga paused before a closed door, and knocked. 'Captain Skorzy to see you, Comrade Colonel. And . . .?' She glanced at Andrews.

'My name is Andrews, and I am from the United States Embassy.'

'Comrade Captain!' Ludmilla beamed at Skorzy. 'Isn't the news terrible? Those swine.' She looked at Andrews.

'They say they have come for the Countess,' Olga explained.

'What?' The good humour faded from Ludmilla's expression.

Skorzy presented the paper. 'The woman is to be released into the custody of Mr Andrews.'

Now Ludmilla scowled. 'Are you making a joke with me? This woman is a German spy and assassin. She is guilty of attempting to assassinate Premier Stalin.'

'Has she confessed to this?' Andrews asked.

'That is not relevant. She is not to leave this prison. I have the orders of Comrade Chalyapov himself.'

'This order is signed by Commissar Beria,' Skorzy pointed out.

'Give me that!' Ludmilla snatched the paper. 'This has to be a mistake.'

'You must take that up with Commissar Beria,' Andrews said. 'If you will look at the paper, it says "immediately".'

'I will have to telephone for confirmation.'

'Immediately,' Andrews repeated, getting a sliver of steel into his voice. 'I will see the Countess now.'

Ludmilla hesitated, looked at the paper again, then jerked her head. Olga stood by the door and the two men stepped into the corridor, following her.

'Who would you suppose has the higher authority?' Andrews asked.

'Commissar Beria commands the NKVD,' Skorzy said reverently.

'Those words are manna to my ears.'

Skorzy glanced at him, obviously not understanding what he meant.

Olga stopped before one of the several doors they had passed. 'Do you wish to look first? She is very pretty.'

'I wish the door opened,' Andrews said.

Olga shrugged and unlocked the door. It swung in, and Andrews gazed at Anna, who gazed at him. She had heard the sound and risen from the bare floor on which she had been sitting. She was naked, and for a moment he was quite entranced, but when she opened her mouth in consternation, he gave a quick shake of his head, and she closed it again.

'Countess,' he said. 'The end of a long road. These people have been good enough to find you for me.' He spoke Russian, and went closer to gaze at her. Her marvellous hair was damp as if recently washed, and despite the fact that it was a warm day she was shivering. He could see no bruises.

'What do you want?' she asked, her voice low.

'Why, you, my dear Countess. You have a date with a Federal Court.'

Anna looked at Skorzy, and then Olga, unable to believe what was happening.

'Where are her clothes?' Andrews demanded.

'We have them,' Olga said.

'Then take us to them.'

Olga bit her lip. 'It is along here.'

'Come along, Countess,' Andrews said.

Anna stepped past him and followed Olga, the two men behind.

'She is quite a beauty,' Skorzy remarked. 'Those legs . . . what will you do to her?'

'Fill her full of electricity.'

'Ah. That would be better than a firing squad.'

'Is there a difference?'

'Of course. Bullets would tear her body open. Perhaps even mark her face. Your way, her beauty will remain after death.'

'I guess you haven't seen too many people after they've been electrocuted,' Andrews suggested.

Olga opened another door and showed them into a room filled with clothes, some on hangers, some lying on tables.

'You mean everyone in this place is naked?' Andrews asked.

'It is good for prisoners to be naked,' Olga said, apparently making a serious comment. 'It places them at a psychological disadvantage, makes them less likely to rebel.'

'Interesting point.'

Olga began sifting through clothes. 'Do you remember what you were wearing, Countess?'

'Yes.' Anna's voice remained low. 'Those.'

'Oh, yes, of course. A pretty dress. And these.' She held up the cami-knickers. 'I have never seen underwear like this before. But there are no shoes.'

'We will manage without shoes,' Andrews said. 'Get dressed, Countess.'

Anna dressed herself, while Skorzy moved restlessly as he watched; it occurred to Andrews that it was actually more evocative to watch a woman dressing than undressing. 'Now,' he said. 'If you will take us out of this place, Captain, I have a car waiting.'

He looked at his watch; he had been here more than half an hour, and he had a distinct, if illogical, feeling that he and Anna were living on borrowed time. And there was Ludmilla, standing in the corridor outside the door of her office, like some latter-day Brunhilde ready for combat. 'I am instructed,' she announced, 'that you must not leave until after Comrade Chalyapov has come.' She had obviously been on the telephone.

'And we are instructed, by Commissar Beria, to leave immediately.'

'You will stay,' Ludmilla insisted, and drew her pistol.

Anna drew a sharp breath.

'Are you mad, comrade?' Skorzy asked. 'Would you defy Commissar Beria?'

'There is treachery here,' Ludmilla declared. 'Comrade Chalyapov will know what to do.'

Anna looked at Andrews, but he was looking at Skorzy, apparently having determined that the captain was the key to the situation. But Skorzy was looking totally uncertain as to what to do next. She herself had no clear idea of what was happening, or how it was happening. She was in fact only just recovering from the shock of seeing Andrews, so unexpectedly, and of being offered her freedom, equally unexpectedly. Her emotions were in a jumble, but of one thing she was quite certain: she was not going back into that cell to suffer the water torture again.

The outer door opened to admit Chalyapov, and then closed again with a clang. 'What is happening?' Chalyapov demanded.

'I told you on the phone, comrade,' Ludmilla said. 'These people are trying to take Widerstand away.'

Chalyapov looked at Andrews, who had arranged his features in a smile. 'Well, hello, comrade. Nice of you to drop by.'

Chalyapov looked at Skorzy, who had come to attention. 'I am acting on the orders of Commissar Beria, comrade.'

Chalyapov snorted, and pointed. 'This man is an American spy!'

'Is that an accusation, or a compliment?' Andrews asked.

'And clearly,' Chalyapov went on, 'he is acting for the Germans in attempting to regain possession of this bitch. Arrest him.'

'Commissar Beria . . .'

'I am in command here. Olga, take the Countess back to her cell. Ludmilla, if anyone attempts to prevent this order being carried out, shoot him.'

Andrews and Skorzy both stared at him in consternation. Olga touched Anna's arm. 'Come along, comrade.'

Anna acted with all the speed and pent-up fury that always hovered on the edge of her subconscious. Olga's hand was still on her arm. She half turned, seized Olga's arm in turn, exerting all her strength and exceptional timing, and threw the girl forward. Olga gave a shriek as she was propelled through the confined space to cannon into Chalyapov and knock him against the wall. Ludmilla brought up her pistol, but Anna had not checked her movement, and as she released Olga's arm swung her left hand into Ludmilla's neck with bone-crunching force.

Ludmilla uttered no sound as she in turn fell against the wall, and slid down it to the floor. Skorzy had regained his nerve and was drawing his own pistol, but Chalyapov was quicker, producing a gun from inside his jacket and firing in the same instant. Skorzy gave a cry and went down. Chalyapov turned his gun on Andrews, his lips drawn back in a snarl, but Anna had now taken Ludmilla's gun from her inert fingers and fired in the same movement. The bullet struck Chalyapov in the middle of the chest, and he went down with a gasp.

'Holy Jesus Christ!' Andrews shouted.

Anna stood above Chalyapov. Blood was pouring from his chest, but he was still breathing, and stared at her. 'You . . .' He gasped. 'You are . . .'

'You can wait for me in hell,' Anna told him, and fired again.

'Holy Jesus Christ!' Andrews repeated.

Anna looked at Olga, who was trying to push herself along the wall, still sitting. 'Please . . . I did not . . .'

Anna lowered the gun. 'You have a file on me,' she said. 'Fetch it.'

Olga licked her lips, then pushed herself up and went to the office. Anna followed her, still pointing the pistol.

Andrews knelt beside Ludmilla. 'My God! She's dead!'

'It will happen,' Anna said over her shoulder, watching Olga sifting through the filing cabinet.

Skorzy groaned, and Andrews knelt beside him in turn. 'How is it?'

Skorzy's hand was red where it was pressed to his tunic. 'I am hit.'

'Yeah. But you're lucky you're on our side. You'll live. Listen, these people were going to kill you, and they would have done had not the Countess intervened. Remember to tell Commissar Beria exactly what happened.' He stood up as Anna returned, the file tucked under her arm, Olga in front of her. 'We will leave now, comrade. See what you can do about the captain. Give us five minutes, and then call for help. Remember that what we have done is a result of direct orders from Commissar Beria.'

Olga looked at Anna, who smiled. 'Your life,' she said. 'My gift to Russia.'

They went outside. The wing was sound-proofed, and no one appeared to have heard the shots. The guards saluted. They went to the courtyard, where the car was waiting.

'The Embassy,' Andrews said, and sat beside Anna. His hands were shaking. He knew he was suffering from a certain amount of shock at the startling and uninhibited violence he had just witnessed, his feelings accentuated by his glimpse of the naked body of this utterly beautiful creature seated beside him, who now presented the picture of a docile and innocent, if slightly dishevelled, young woman.

But she was not entirely as cold as ice. 'Will they not send behind us?' she asked. Her voice was low, and the fingers holding the file were perfectly steady.

It was time to match her calm. 'No. For two reasons. One is that Beria, and I suspect Stalin himself, will not be sorry to see the back of Comrade Chalyapov. The other is that the last thing the Russians want to do right now is fall out with us. That file . . . is it very important?'

'It is to me,' Anna said.

The marine sentry presented arms as Clive entered the Embassy. In the hall a male secretary was waiting for him. 'Mr Andrews is expecting you, Mr Bartley. First floor, door five.'

'Thank you.' Clive took the steps two at a time, was out of breath when he opened the door. Andrews stood before his desk. 'Where the hell have you been? I've been trying to get in touch with you for the last twelve hours.'

'I've been busy. I believe you know the Countess von Widerstand?'

Clive turned, his jaw dropping. Anna had been seated on a settee against the far wall, but was now standing. She wore a dressing gown, and her feet were bare. Her hair was loose, and unusually untidy. 'My God! How did you do it?'

'I used a method recommended by, if I remember correctly, Napoleon Bonaparte, who said, "the bigger the lie, the more chance there is of it being believed". Although I am going to have to do my damndest to make sure that at least part of it turns out to be true. I imagine you two would like to be alone for a few minutes.' He went to the door. 'Oh, please don't get agitated about her appearance. She is merely waiting for some clothes to be prepared for her. Her own were rather past their best.'

He closed the door, and Anna came forward. 'He is quite a man.'

Clive took her into his arms and kissed her. 'Are you all right?'

'Yes. Although it will be a long time before I feel like taking a cold shower again.'

'My God, to have you back . . But what's this about a few minutes?'

'They have to get me out of the country immediately.'

'I'll get you out of the country.'

Anna shook her head. 'They can arrange for me to get back to Germany. You cannot.'

'But Anna, you can't go back to Germany.'

'I must. You know I must.'

'You have not carried out Heydrich's command.' He frowned. 'You didn't assassinate Stalin, did you?'

'I never got near Stalin, Clive.'

'He won't believe that. Or he'll believe that you deliberately got yourself arrested so you wouldn't have to complete the assignment.'

'He will believe what I tell him, because I will prove that it is the truth.'

'I will never see you again.'

She kissed him. 'We will be together when this is over.

Until then, there is always Antoinette's Boutique. But listen . . . I would like my jewellery back.'

'How do I do that?'

'You give it to Joe. He will have it sent to his embassy in Berlin, and I can pick it up from there.'

'Hmm. This fellow Joe . . .'

'He saved my life, Clive. He is doing that now.' She gave a little gurgle of laughter. 'And you are jealous. He has never touched me. But listen, as it may be a little while before we can get together again, and we have fifteen minutes . . . It has been so long.'

Andrews knocked and opened the door. 'The dressmaker is ready for you, Countess . . . Oh! Ah!'

Anna rolled off Clive and the settee at the same moment, stood up, and put on her dressing gown.

'I sure am sorry,' Andrews said. 'I didn't mean to interrupt . . .'

'Your timing was perfection,' Anna told him, and went to the door.

'It's the next room,' Andrews said.

She nodded, and the door closed.

Clive was still panting. Andrews sat behind his desk. 'Do you know,' he remarked, 'only a few hours ago I saw that girl kill two people, just like that.' He snapped his fingers.

Clive got up and began to dress. 'So now you know all her secrets.'

'Does anyone know *all* her secrets?'

'Good point. But you're still going to help her?'

'God, yes. Not helping Anna, not preserving Anna, is unthinkable. Just so long as she's on our side. You're sure about that?'

Clive knotted his tie. 'I'm sure. Just remember, old boy, that you are in possession of an especially important secret. It has to remain that way. At least until the war is over.'

'And you guys have won it. You sure about *that*?'

Clive grinned. 'Aren't you?' He held out his hand. 'You take good care of my little girl.'

'I'll contact you when the delivery has been made.' It was Andrews' turn to grin. 'If I'm still alive.'

* * *

'Anna?' Reinhard Heydrich got up and came round his desk.

'Heil Hitler!'

'Heil! They told me you had been arrested by the NKVD.'

'That is correct, sir.'

Heydrich embraced her 'My dear girl. My dear, dear girl. But how are you here?'

'I was freed by the intervention of an officer in the American Embassy in Moscow.'

'An American got you out of the Lubianka? But how? And why? Sit down.' Anna sat before the desk, and he returned behind it. 'So?'

'He was my lover, sir.'

'Chalyapov was supposed to be your lover.'

'Yes sir. He was. But this was a genuine attachment. I did not let it interfere with my mission.'

'I see. You are not supposed to form genuine attachments. Would this be the man you were meeting clandestinely in the Hotel Berlin?'

'You knew of that, sir?'

'Groener suspected it. He had some information which he did not specify. I dismissed it as speculation. Now it seems I owe him an apology. So, you had an illegal affair with an itinerant American . . .'

'I am sorry, sir. I have my passions. And if I had not had that affair, I would not be here now.'

'But you failed in your mission. There has been no indication that Marshal Stalin is dead.'

'No, sir. Marshal Stalin is alive. I was prevented from completing my mission.'

'Is that not the excuse of every failure? Oh, I do not suppose it is a vital matter. This war with Russia was planned six months ago. The date had to be postponed because of that Balkan imbroglio, but it was going to happen whether or not you succeeded. On the other hand, the decision that Stalin should be eliminated immediately before the commencement of hostilities was taken at the highest level. I am going to have to report your failure to the Fuehrer, and I cannot say what his reaction will be.'

He paused to stare at her, but Anna's face remained as calm as her voice. 'I can proved that I was betrayed, Herr General. And by whom.'

'Then you had better do so.'

'Yes sir.' Anna opened her handbag and laid the dossier on his desk. 'This I secured from the files of the Lubianka Prison before leaving. The information was supplied to them by Chalyapov, after he had received it from the Gestapo office in our Moscow Embassy.'

Heydrich regarded her for several moments, then looked at the sheets of paper. 'It seems to outline your intentions, and your background, very convincingly. But to say it came from the Gestapo Office . . . there is no proof of that.'

'If you will read it again, Herr General, you will see that it seeks to prove that I am an assassin by relating the facts of that incident in Prague last year. As you will recall, sir, only four people know those facts: yourself, Herr Feutlanger, myself . . . and Herr Meissenbach. At your command, the business was hushed up as regards anyone else.'

Heydrich read the paper again, then raised his head. 'You are accusing both Groener and Meissenbach of betraying you? Betraying the Reich? That is incredible. Why should they do something like that?'

'Herr Groener, because he hated and distrusted me from the moment I arrived in Moscow. Herr Meissenbach, because he wished to be my lover and became very angry when I rejected him. As you will see there, the traitor, or traitors, outlined exactly what my instructions were, and these were known only to you and me. They must have opened your last letter to me.'

Heydrich stroked his chin. 'This is a very serious matter. To think that two such men would betray the Reich to avenge themselves on a woman . . . I will report the entire incident to General Himmler.'

'And what will happen then, sir?'

'They will be tried, and on the evidence you have provided, they will be executed.'

'Ah, with respect, sir . . .'

'Don't you want them to be executed?'

Anna smiled. 'I would prefer them to be sent to a concentration camp, Herr General. That way, with your permission, I can go and visit them, from time to time.'

Epilogue

'And were they imprisoned?' I asked.

'Oh, yes,' the Countess said.

'Did you visit them?'

'Once. I did not know anything about concentration camps, then. I don't think many people in Germany did, whatever the rumours and the suspicions. It was safer not to speak of it. But I found that visit nauseating. I certainly had no desire to repeat it.'

'What happened to Greta?'

'She went to Ravensbruek. In the Nazi philosophy, the wife of a traitor was, by definition, a traitor herself.'

'Did you feel guilty about that? I mean, she never actually harmed you.'

'I felt guilty when I heard that she had been arrested. But under questioning she admitted that her husband had told her what he was going to do, and she was all in favour of it. That is no way to make friends,' Anna said, somewhat ingenuously. 'However, unfortunately, she did not stay in prison long. She had money, and she had friends in high places.'

'Don't tell me you met her again?'

'I met her again.'

I waited, but she did not elaborate. 'And so you were back in the clutches of Heydrich.'

'Yes. But not for very long. Within a year of my return from Moscow, Heydrich was dead.'

'My God, yes! I'd forgotten about that. I don't suppose you had anything to do with that?'

Anna Fehrbach stared at me, and I could feel the heat in my cheeks. 'I should have known better than to ask. Will you tell me about it?'

'As I am telling you about everything else.'

'But before then, Washington. Did you ever meet Joe again?'

'Joe was my reason for going to America, Christopher.' She smiled enchantingly. 'I think you could say that I got to know him rather well. After all, did he not save my life?'

When fishing the black heron spreads its wings over its head like an umbrella. This cuts down the reflection from the surface of the water and helps it to see under the water more clearly.
The bombadier beetle shoots a jet of boiling chemicals at any animal which attacks it. The spray is produced in short bursts at a temperature of 100°C.
The African giant swallowtail butterfly has a wing span of more than 25 cm. Each front wing has special struts to strengthen it and prevent it from becoming damaged during flight. This butterfly is also poisonous. It contains enough poison to kill six cats!
The horned-toad from North America is a lizard. When it is frightened it squirts blood from its eyes. It can squirt the blood as far as one metre. It probably uses this trick as a defence mechanism.
Flamingos probably develop their pink colour from chemicals present in the food they eat. In zoos, flamingos often lose their pink colour because they don't have the right diet.
Rhinoderma is a tiny frog from South America. Male frogs swallow the fertilized eggs and keep them in a large sac in their throat where they develop. One day, the male gulps and yawns and fully-formed froglets jump out of his mouth.
The Kalahari ground squirrel uses its bushy tail like a sun-shade.
It spreads it over its head to keep its body cool in the hot Sun.
The desert holly grows in hot, dry regions of North America. There is no shade so it reduces the amount of sunlight falling on it by growing its leaves at an angle. For most of the day the Sun strikes the edges of its leaves. It shines directly on the leaf surface only in the early morning.
Some flowers produce nasty smells to attract pollinating animals. The stapelia flower smells like rotting meat which attracts flies. The smell 'tricks' the flies into visiting the flower. Sometimes the petals look like dead animals. Female flies are 'tricked' into laying their eggs on the petals as they would on a real carcass.
The electric ray can kill its prey with a powerful electric shock. The current it produces is strong enough to light 20 light bulbs.
Bamboo plants seem to have a remarkable way of timing when they flower. Different species flower at different times. Some may wait as long as 100 years before flowering. After flowering they often die.

THE YOUNG SCIENTIST'S

GUIDE TO THE LIVING WORLD

To Sara & Suzannah

THE YOUNG SCIENTIST'S

GUIDE TO THE LIVING WORLD

TONY SEDDON & JILL BAILEY

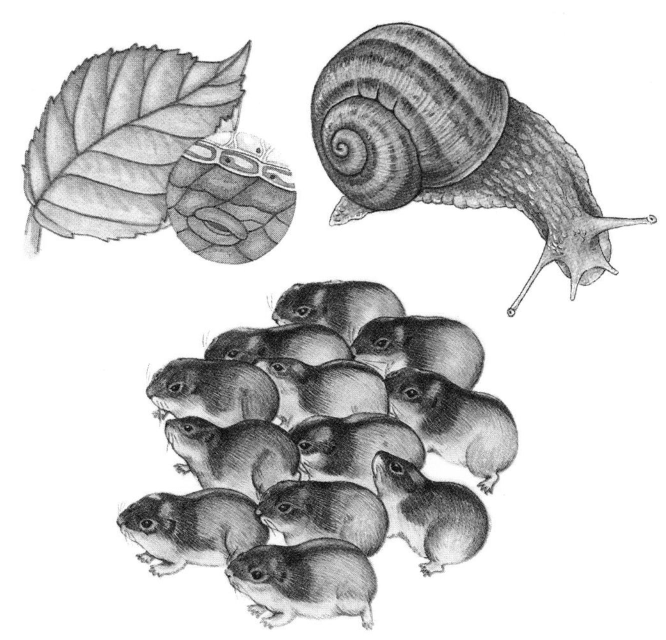

OXFORD

Published by Oxford University Press, Walton Street, Oxford OX2 6DP
Oxford New York Toronto
Delhi Bombay Calcutta Madras Karachi
Petaling Java Singapore Hong Kong Tokyo
Nairobi Dar es Salaam Cape Town
Melbourne Auckland

and associated companies in
Beirut Berlin Ibadan Nicosia

Oxford is a trade mark of Oxford University Press

First published 1986

British Library Cataloguing in Publication Data

Seddon, Tony
The young scientist's guide to the
living world.
1. Biology — Juvenile literature
I. Title II. Bailey, Jill
574 QH309.2

ISBN 0-19-918220-5

This book was designed and produced by BLA Publishing Limited,
Swan Court, London Road, East Grinstead, Sussex, England.

A member of the **Ling Kee Group**
LONDON·HONG KONG·TAIPEI·SINGAPORE·NEW YORK

Phototypeset in Britain by BLA Publishing/Composing Operations
Colour origination by Peak Litho Plates
Printed and bound in The Netherlands by Royal Smeets Offset BV, Weert

Contents

Note to the reader
On page 153 of this book you will find the glossary. This gives brief explanations of words which may be new to you.

Acknowledgements/Picture Credits

The publishers wish to thank the following people and organizations for their invaluable assistance in the preparation of this book:

Ian Redmond Paignton Zoo, Devon Flora and Fauna Preservation Society

ARTISTS:

David Anstey; Fiona Fordyce; Helen Kennett; Karen Moxon; Colin Newman/Linden Artists; David Parkins; Sallie Alane Reason; Mandy Shepherd; Rosie Vane-Wright; Phil Weare/Linden Artists; Michael Woods.

PHOTOGRAPHIC CREDITS

t = top; *b* = bottom; *c* = centre; *l* = left; *r* = right.

COVER: Stephen Dalton/NHPA. HALF-TITLE Jen and Des Bartlet/Survival Anglia. 10/11 S.Krasemann/NHPA. 10*t* Stephen Dalton/NHPA. 10*c* John and Gillian Lythgoe/Seaphot. 10*b* David Rootes/Seaphot. 11*t* John and Gillian Lythgoe/Seaphot. 11*c* Sean Morris/OSF. 11*b* J.C. Stevenson/OSF. 18 Peter Johnson/NHPA. 19 Ian Redmond. 23 Mike Price/Survival Anglia. 29 Richard Matthews/Seaphot. 32*t* Franz J.Camenzind/Seaphot. 32*b* Nick Greaves/Seaphot. 33 M.P.L. Fogden/OSF. 34*t* Barrie E. Watts/OSF. 34*b* Ken Vaughan/Seaphot. 35 Sean Avery/Seaphot. 36*t* Jonathon Scott/Seaphot. 36*c* Flip Schulke/Seaphot. 37*t* Peter David/Seaphot. 37*cl* Richard Matthews/Seaphot. 37*cr* Michael Fogden/OSF. 38*t* Ken Griffiths/NHPA. 38*c* Barrie E. Watts/OSF. 39*t* Alan Root/Survival Anglia. 39*c* Stephen Dalton/NHPA. 40*t* Anthony Bannister/NHPA. 40 *c* Dr. J.A.L. Cooke/OSF. 40*b* Anthony Bannister/NHPA. 41*t* G.I. Bernard/OSF. 41*b* Jill Bailey. 42*l* Bill Wood/NHPA. 42*r* J.H. Carmichael/NHPA. 43*t* Jill Bailey. 43*b* Bill Wood/NHPA. 44*t* J.A.L. Cooke/OSF. 44*b* N.A. Callow/NHPA. 50*l* Peri Coelho/Seaphot. 50*r* Stephen Dalton/NHPA. 51 Karl Switak/NHPA. 52*cl* Jill Bailey. 52*cr* Stephen Dalton/NHPA. 52*b* John Shaw/NHPA. 53*l*, 53*r* Philip Sharpe/OSF. 55 Anthony Bannister/NHPA. 56*tl* Stephen Dalton/NHPA. 56*tr* R.J. Erwin/NHPA. 56*bl* M.W.F. Tweedie/NHPA. 56*br* Stephen Dalton/NHPA. 57*tl* Michael Fogden/OSF. 57*tr* Geoff du Feu/Seaphot. 57*c* Michael Fogden/OSF. 58 Dr F. Köster/Survival Anglia. 59 K and K. Ammann/Seaphot. 60 Douglas Dickens. 62 Doug Allan/OSF. 63 Manfred Danegger/NHPA. 65 David C. Fritts/Animals Animals /OSF. 66 Jonathon Scott/Seaphot. 67*tl*, 67*tr* Z. Leszczynski/Animals Animals/OSF. 67*b* Peter Parks/OSF. 68 J.A.L. Cooke/OSF. 70 Sean Morris/OSF. 71*t* Karl Switak/NHPA. 71*b* David Thompson/OSF. 73 J.B. Free/NHPA. 74 R.J. Erwin. 75 Jonathon Scott/Seaphot. 76 Patrick Fagot/NHPA. 78 Massart/Jacana. 79 Jeff Foot/Survival Anglia. 80 Stephen Dalton/NHPA. 82 Richard Matthews/Seaphot. 85*t* J.B. Davidson/Survival Anglia. 85*b* Douglas Dickens/NHPA. 86 Peter Gathercole/OSF. 87 J.A.L. Cooke/OSF. 88 Stephen Dalton/NHPA. 92 Jill Bailey. 93*t* Leonard Lee Rue III/Animals Animals/OSF. 93*b* Jeff Foot/Survival Anglia. 95*tr* G.J. Cambridge/NHPA. 95*c* John Shaw/NHPA. 95*b* Stephen Dalton/NHPA. 96*t* J.A.L. Cooke/OSF. 96*b* Jill Bailey. 97*t* Avril Rawage/OSF. 97*b* Ken Lucas/Seaphot. 98 John Shaw/NHPA. 99*r* S. Krasemann/NHPA. 99*l* Peter Stephenson/Seaphot. 100*t* S. Krasemann/NHPA. 100*b* Brian Hawkes/NHPA. 101 Jack Lentfer/Survival Anglia. 102*tl* John Shaw/NHPA. 102*tr* Brian Milne/Animals Animals/OSF. 102*c* S. Krasemann/NHPA. 103 Hellio and Van Ingen/NHPA. 104*t* Jeff Foot/Survival Anglia. 104*b* Jen and Des Bartlett/Survival Anglia. 105 David and Sue Cayless/OSF. 106*t* E. Hanumantha Rao/NHPA. 106*b* Martyn F. Chillmaid/OSF. 107 Stephen Dalton/NHPA. 108*t* Michael Leach/NHPA. 108*b* Marty Stouffer Productions Ltd/Animals Animals/OSF. 109*t* Jonathon Scott/Seaphot. 109*b* John Paling/OSF. 110 D.H. Thompson/OSF. 111*t* Jack Wilburn/Animals Animals/OSF. 111*b* S. Robinson/NHPA. 114*t* Jim Standen. 114*b*, 115 Ivan Polunin/NHPA. 117*t* Peter Parks/OSF. 117*b* David Maitland/Seaphot. 118 Peter Parks/OSF. 119*t* Peter David/Seaphot. 119*b* Robert Hessler/Seaphot. 120*t* Warren Williams/Seaphot. 120*b* Hugh Jones/Seaphot. 121 Linda Pitkin/Seaphot. 123 Melvin Grey/NHPA. 124 Stephen Dalton/NHPA. 124/125 A. C. Waltham. 126*l* Peter Johnson/NHPA. 126*r* Jeff Foot/Survival Anglia. 127*l* Ralph and Daphne Keller/NHPA. 127*r* Raymond Blythe/OSF. 128 J.B. Blossom/NHPA. 129 L. Campbell/NHPA. 136 Tony Morrison/South American Pictures. 137 E. Hanumantha Rao/NHPA. 138*t* Patrick Fagot/NHPA. 138*b* Jeremy Cherfas. 139 Paignton Zoo Educational Service. 140, 141 Jill Bailey. 142*t* C.C. Lockwood/Animals Animals/OSF. 142*c* David W. Macdonald/OSF. 142*b*, 143*tl* G.I. Bernard/OSF. 143*tr* James Carmichael/NHPA. 143*b* J.A.L. Cooke/OSF.

Introduction

Did you know that humans share the Earth with more than 3 000 000 000 000 000 000 000 000 000 000 000 000 other living things. You probably have difficulty imagining how big this number is. It is a very large number indeed. If you counted once every second it would take you more than one hundred million, million, million, million years to reach the total.

This book tells you something about some of the one million or so different species of animals and plants which make up this enormous number of living things. It gives you lots of information, but it also encourages you to ask questions about the living world. Perhaps you are already well known for asking questions. In fact, your parents and teachers are probably fed up with your 'whys'. It is good to ask 'why?' especially when you look at animals and plants. So keep on asking and try to find the answers.

A famous scientist, William Beebe, once said:

> The *is-ness* of things is well worth studying but it's their *why-ness* that makes life worth living.'

By the time you get to the end of this book a lot of your 'whys?' will have been answered, but you will still have more. In fact, we hope this book makes you ask more questions than it answers. This is the way you will learn more about the one million or so different species of animals and plants who are your neighbours on planet Earth.

ROUND THE WORLD NOTEBOOK

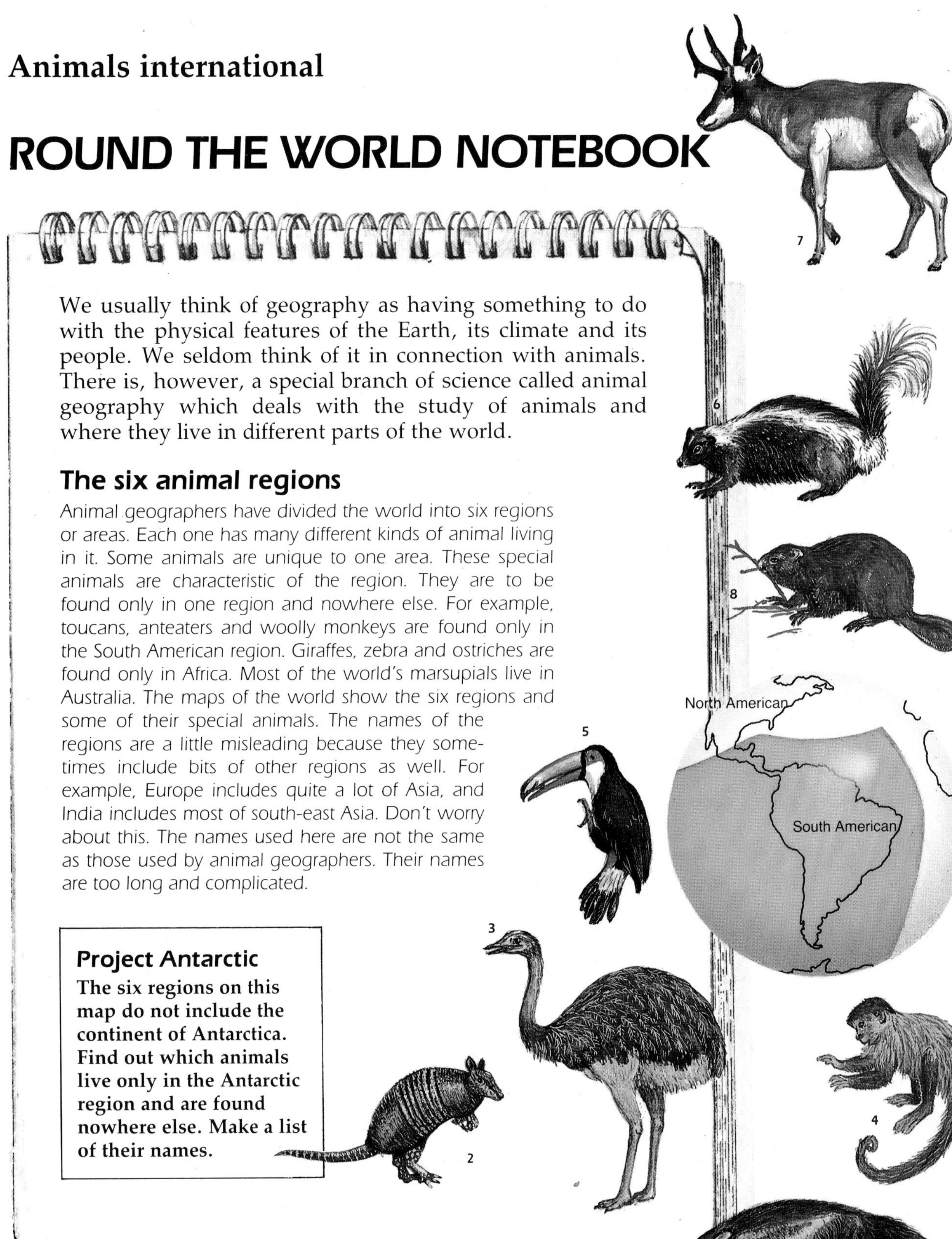

We usually think of geography as having something to do with the physical features of the Earth, its climate and its people. We seldom think of it in connection with animals. There is, however, a special branch of science called animal geography which deals with the study of animals and where they live in different parts of the world.

The six animal regions

Animal geographers have divided the world into six regions or areas. Each one has many different kinds of animal living in it. Some animals are unique to one area. These special animals are characteristic of the region. They are to be found only in one region and nowhere else. For example, toucans, anteaters and woolly monkeys are found only in the South American region. Giraffes, zebra and ostriches are found only in Africa. Most of the world's marsupials live in Australia. The maps of the world show the six regions and some of their special animals. The names of the regions are a little misleading because they sometimes include bits of other regions as well. For example, Europe includes quite a lot of Asia, and India includes most of south-east Asia. Don't worry about this. The names used here are not the same as those used by animal geographers. Their names are too long and complicated.

Project Antarctic

The six regions on this map do not include the continent of Antarctica. Find out which animals live only in the Antarctic region and are found nowhere else. Make a list of their names.

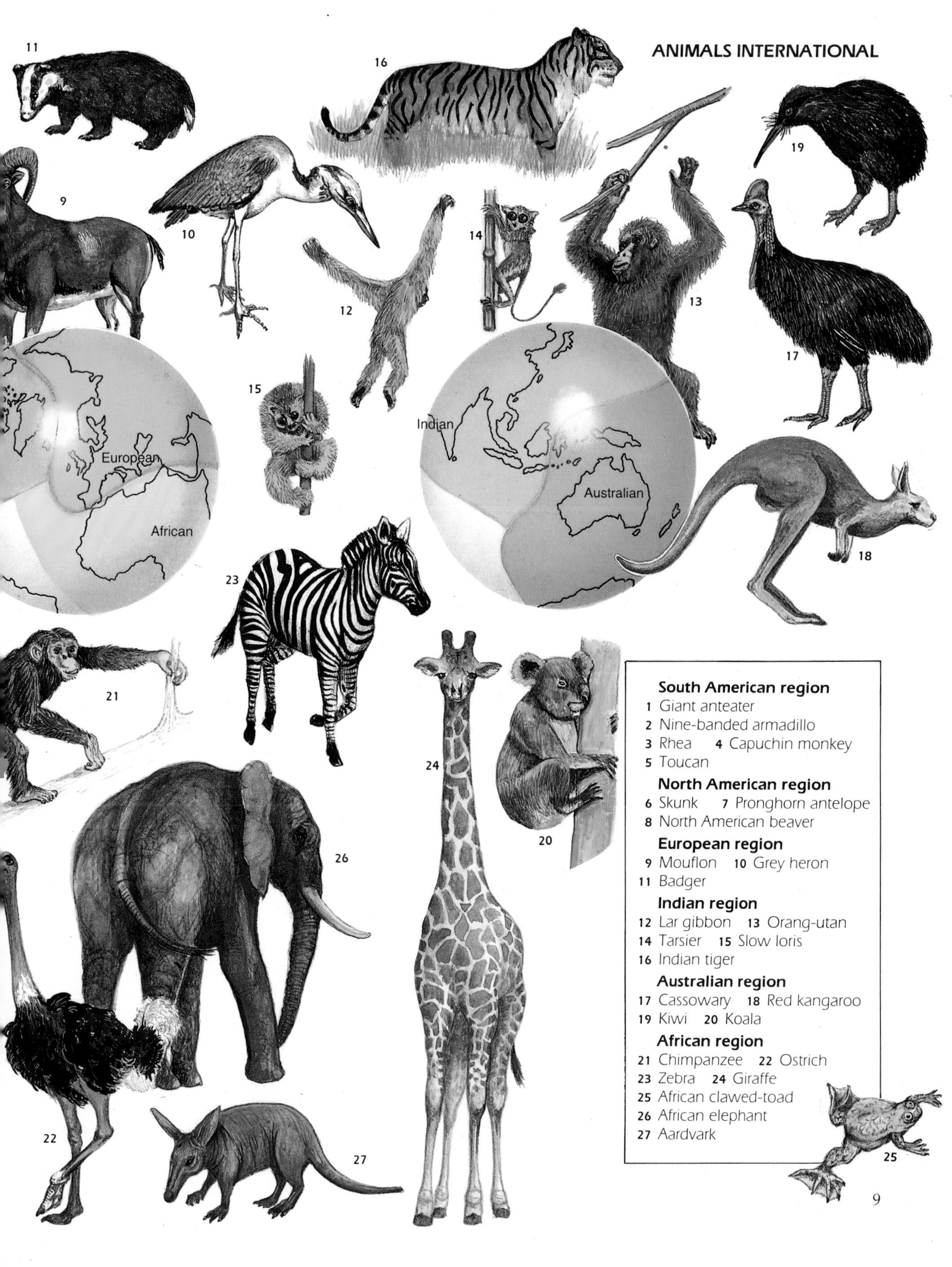

South American region
1 Giant anteater
2 Nine-banded armadillo
3 Rhea 4 Capuchin monkey
5 Toucan

North American region
6 Skunk 7 Pronghorn antelope
8 North American beaver

European region
9 Mouflon 10 Grey heron
11 Badger

Indian region
12 Lar gibbon 13 Orang-utan
14 Tarsier 15 Slow loris
16 Indian tiger

Australian region
17 Cassowary 18 Red kangaroo
19 Kiwi 20 Koala

African region
21 Chimpanzee 22 Ostrich
23 Zebra 24 Giraffe
25 African clawed-toad
26 African elephant
27 Aardvark

N

Plants around the world

Plants are found all over the world, except near the North and South Poles, on the tops of high mountains, and in very dry deserts. Every plant species has its own special needs, for temperature, light, water and mineral salts. Plants grow where the conditions suit these needs. So different plants grow in different parts of the world. If there were no farms and cities, or other kinds of human interference, certain types of wild or 'natural' vegetation would occur in particular parts of the world. Here you see the main types of natural vegetation in the northern hemisphere. Similar types of plants are found in the southern hemisphere in places where the climate and soil are suitable.

DECIDUOUS FOREST
Broad-leaved trees which lose their leaves in winter. Flowering herbs on forest floor. Shrubs, brambles and other scrambling and climbing plants.

WEST

MEDITERRANEAN FOREST
Broad-leaved trees, many of them evergreen, with waxy, shiny leaves. Many flowering herbs and shrubs, often thorny.

RAIN FOREST
Dense forest with many evergreen trees. Further from the Equator there are more trees that shed their leaves from time to time. Many vines and creepers. Epiphytic plants (plants that grow on branches and trunks of trees). Many forest herbs and ferns.

Plants from north to south

In the far north, low temperatures prevent plants growing very tall. Further south it is warmer, and there are forests. First, there are evergreen conifer forests whose trees can cope with poor soils and cold, snowy winters. As the climate gets warmer and wetter, we find forests of trees which shed their leaves in winter. Still further south, the summers are hot and dry. Here the forests are mainly of trees with shiny, waxy leaves that do not lose water easily. Finally there are the wet, warm tropical regions with their lush rain forests.

H

TUNDRA
Mosses, lichens, sedges. Slow-growing cushion plants, very short. Small evergreen dwarf shrubs.

Plenty of variety

Throughout the world there are patches of other types of vegetation, such as bogs, swamps and salt marshes, where local conditions are rather special. High mountains also create a range of different conditions for plants. Even in the tropics, the vegetation will change with altitude (height), from tropical forest to coniferous forest, and, eventually, tundra-like vegetation on the cold, exposed mountain tops.

CONIFEROUS FOREST
Mostly evergreen trees with needle-like leaves. A few broad-leaved trees like birch, willow and alder. Few flowering herbs on forest floor because of the deep shade there.

Plants from west to east

In the northern latitudes, the winds blow mainly from the west. They bring moist air from the oceans to the land. As you go further inland, there is less rainfall. The land heats up and cools down faster than the sea. So areas inland have hotter summers and colder winters than those near the coast. The forest gives way to grasslands and scrub (small bushes) and then desert.

GRASSLAND
Includes the European steppes and the American prairies. Mainly grasses, often forming tufts or clumps. Some shrubs and stunted trees. Many flowering herbs, mostly springing up from seeds or underground storage organs after rain.

DESERT
Lots of bare ground with scattered herbs, shrubs and small trees. Fleshy plants - cacti and plants with swollen leaves and stems for storing water, and spines for protection. Many plants which grow from seed after rain, flower and produce seeds in a few weeks, then die.

Animals with backbones

You have to be a detective to classify an animal. You look for clues.

Animal groups

Scientists are quite tidy people. If they can, they like to put things into groups. They do this with animals. They look for patterns which we call characteristics. Animals with similar characteristics are put in the same group. This is called classification. The backboned animals are called vertebrates and there are about 45000 different species alive today. Scientists classify vertebrates into five main groups or classes. These are fish, amphibians, reptiles, birds and mammals. Each class can be divided further into smaller groups called orders. For example, mammals which eat meat are grouped in the carnivore order. Even orders can be divided into smaller groups. You can learn about the smallest group on pages 146 and 147.

Classifying an animal can be difficult. Animals are not always what they seem to be at first sight. For example, whales and dolphins look like fish, but a closer look shows them to be mammals. The pangolin lives in Africa and Asia. Its body is covered with scales. Do you know which vertebrate class the pangolin belongs to? **Answer on page 152.**

What is a fish?

There are about 23000 different species of fish alive today.

Fish:
- are cold-blooded
- live in water
- breathe by gills
- are covered in scales.

There are three main groups. The jawless fish (hagfish and lampreys), the cartilaginous fish whose skeleton is made of cartilage (sharks and rays), and the bony fish whose skeleton is made of bone.

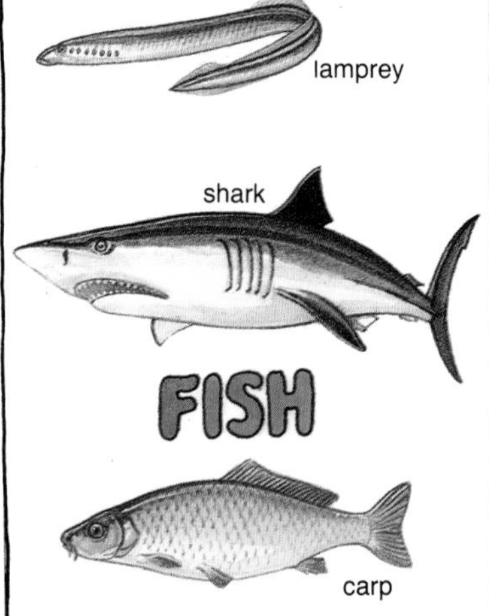

What is an amphibian?

There are more than 4000 different species of amphibians alive today.

Amphibians:
- are cold-blooded
- have smooth, wet skins
- return to water to breed
- breathe with gills when young, but as adults use their skins and lungs.

There are three main groups. These are the legless caecilians, the newts and salamanders, and the frogs and toads.

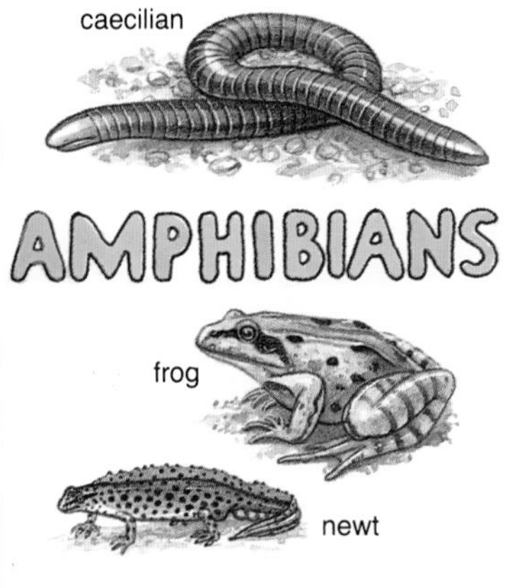

What is a reptile?

There are about 5200 different species of reptile alive today. The majority of these are snakes and lizards.

Reptiles:
- are cold-blooded
- breathe air using lungs
- have dry, scaly skins

There are four main groups. These are the turtles and tortoises, the lizards, the snakes and the crocodiles and their relatives.

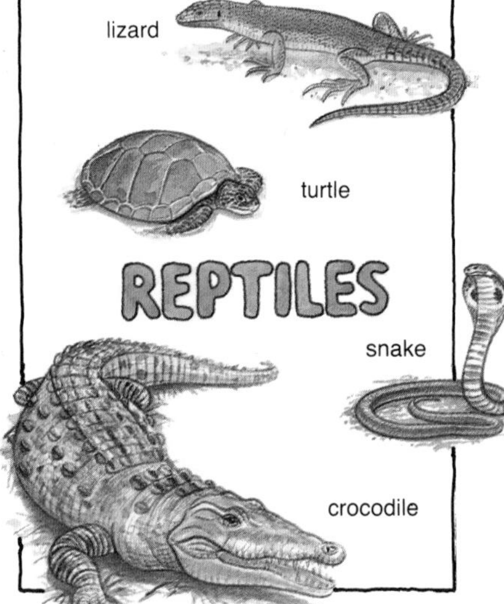

What is a bird?

There are about 8600 different species of bird alive today.

Birds:
- have wings
- are warm-blooded
- breathe air using lungs
- have feathers
- have no teeth
- lay eggs.

Not all birds fly. Some have wings which are too small for flight. Penguins have flippers instead of wings. Ostriches have long legs for fast running. There are 27 orders of birds divided into different families. Below are some examples of different birds.

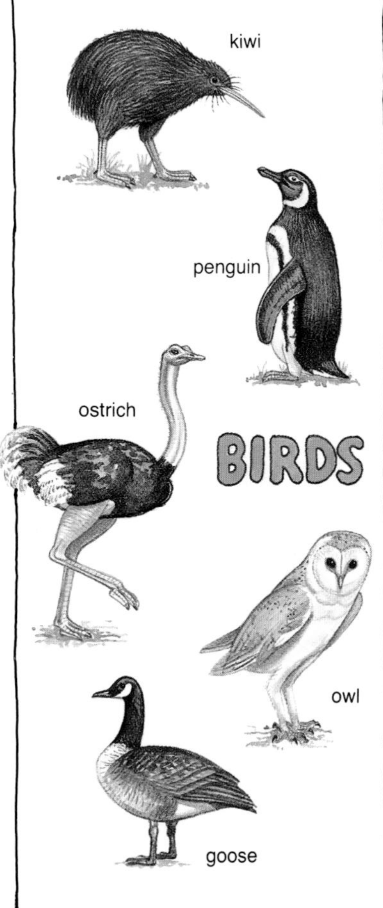

What is a mammal?

There are about 4000 different species of mammal alive today.

Mammals:
- are warm-blooded
- breathe air using lungs
- have body hair
- produce milk and suckle their young.

Altogether there are 19 orders of mammals. Below are some of these.

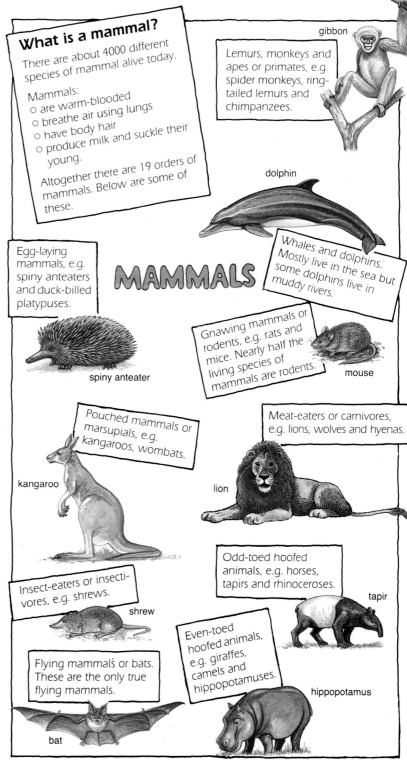

MAMMALS

Lemurs, monkeys and apes or primates, e.g. spider monkeys, ring-tailed lemurs and chimpanzees.

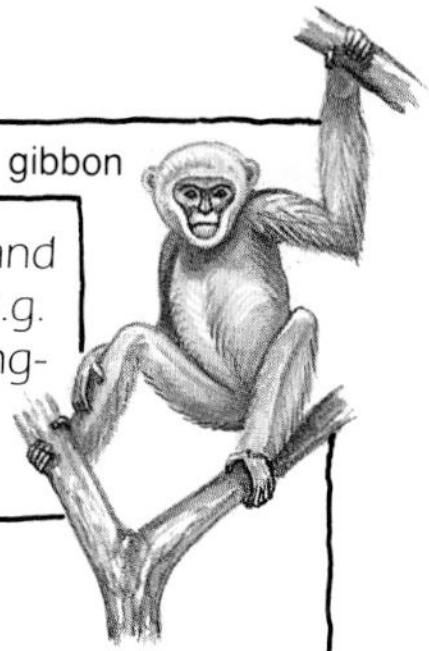

gibbon

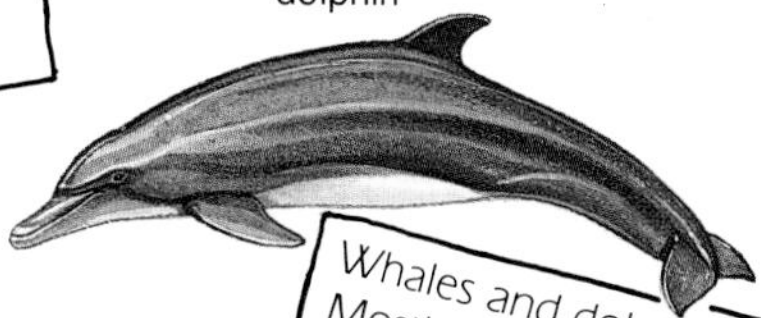

dolphin

Whales and dolphins. Mostly live in the sea but some dolphins live in muddy rivers.

Egg-laying mammals, e.g. spiny anteaters and duck-billed platypuses.

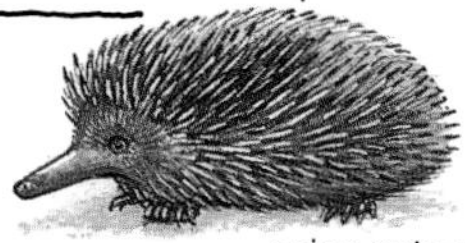

spiny anteater

Gnawing mammals or rodents, e.g. rats and mice. Nearly half the living species of mammals are rodents.

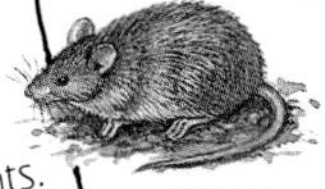

mouse

Pouched mammals or marsupials, e.g. kangaroos, wombats.

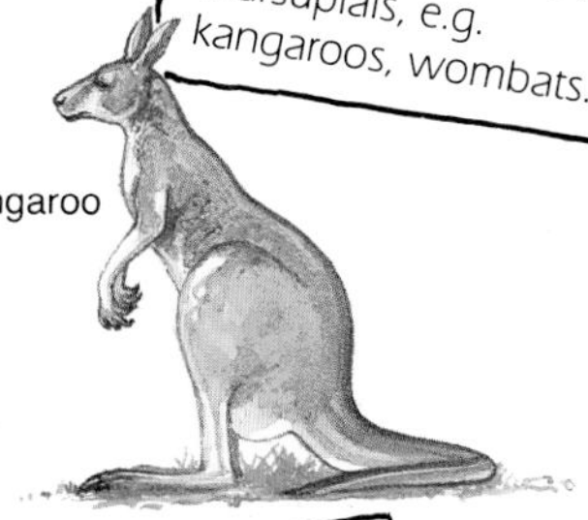

kangaroo

Meat-eaters or carnivores, e.g. lions, wolves and hyenas.

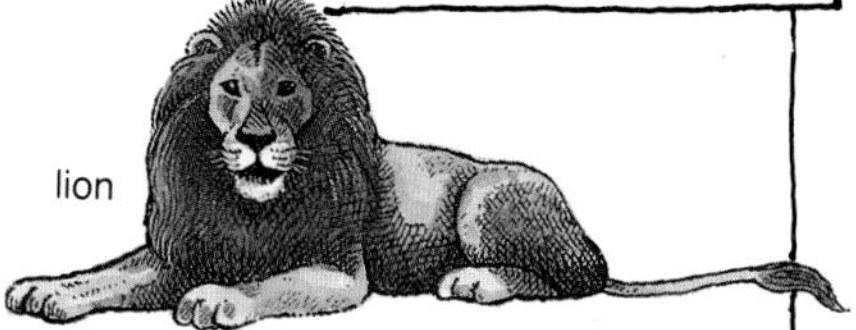

lion

Odd-toed hoofed animals, e.g. horses, tapirs and rhinoceroses.

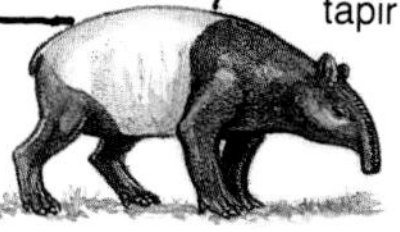

tapir

Insect-eaters or insectivores, e.g. shrews.

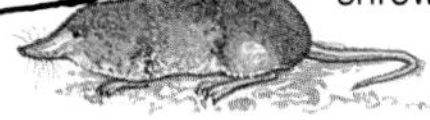

shrew

Even-toed hoofed animals, e.g. giraffes, camels and hippopotamuses.

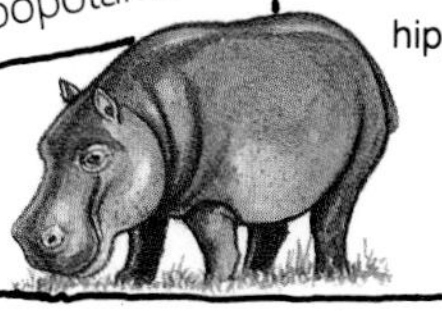

hippopotamus

Flying mammals or bats. These are the only true flying mammals.

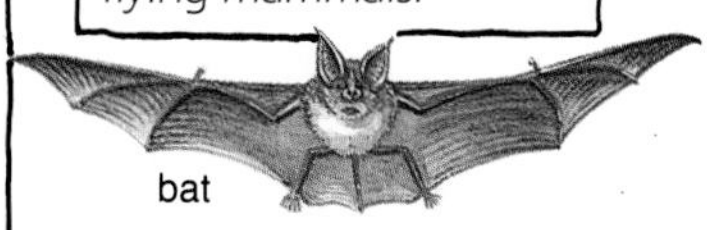

bat

Animals without backbones

ECHINODERMATA
- Animals with tough spiny skins.
- Their bodies are designed so that parts are arranged in fives or multiples of five (except sea cucumbers).

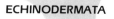

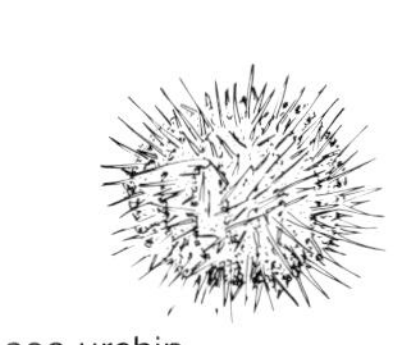
sea urchin

brittlestar

starfish

VERTEBRATES

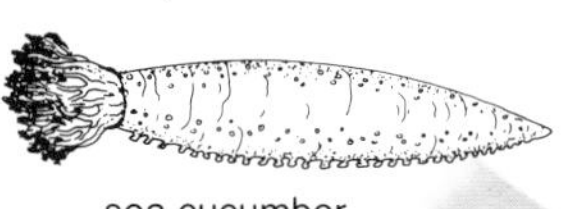
sea cucumber

CHORDATA

ECHINODERMATA

sea lily

The invertebrates

Scientists classify animals - they put animals with similar characteristics into groups. Animals without backbones are a very large and varied group. They are called the invertebrates. Ninety-five per cent of all animals are invertebrates. There are about 950 000 species of invertebrates. They range from microscopic animals, too small for the eye to see, to the giant squid, which may be up to twenty metres long. They can be found in water, on land, in the soil, in the air, and even in the snow of the polar ice-caps.

Here you can see a few of the more common groups of invertebrates and their international scientific names. Beside each group are some clues for recognising them.

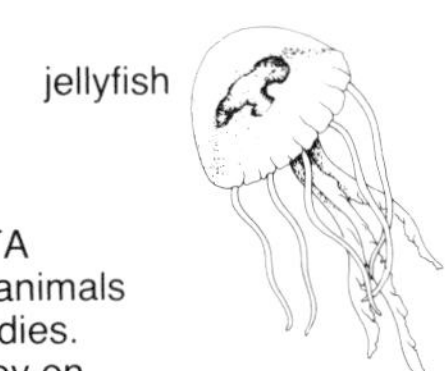
jellyfish

COELENTERATA
- Soft, jelly-like animals with hollow bodies.
- They catch prey on stinging tentacles.

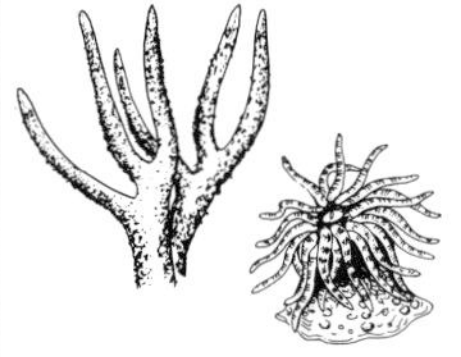
sea anemones and corals

COELENTERATA

hydra

PORIFERA
- Animals with stiff bodies.
- Sponges filter feed by passing water through their bodies.
- Water enters and leaves through a series of holes called pores.

sponge

PORIFERA

PROTOZOA
- Very simple animals made up of just one cell. Most are no bigger than 1 mm wide.

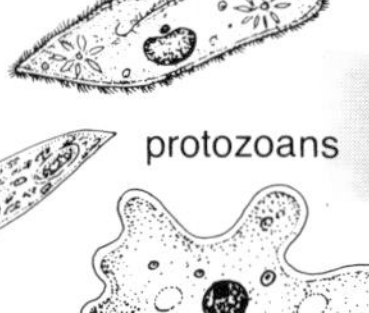
protozoans

PROTOZOA

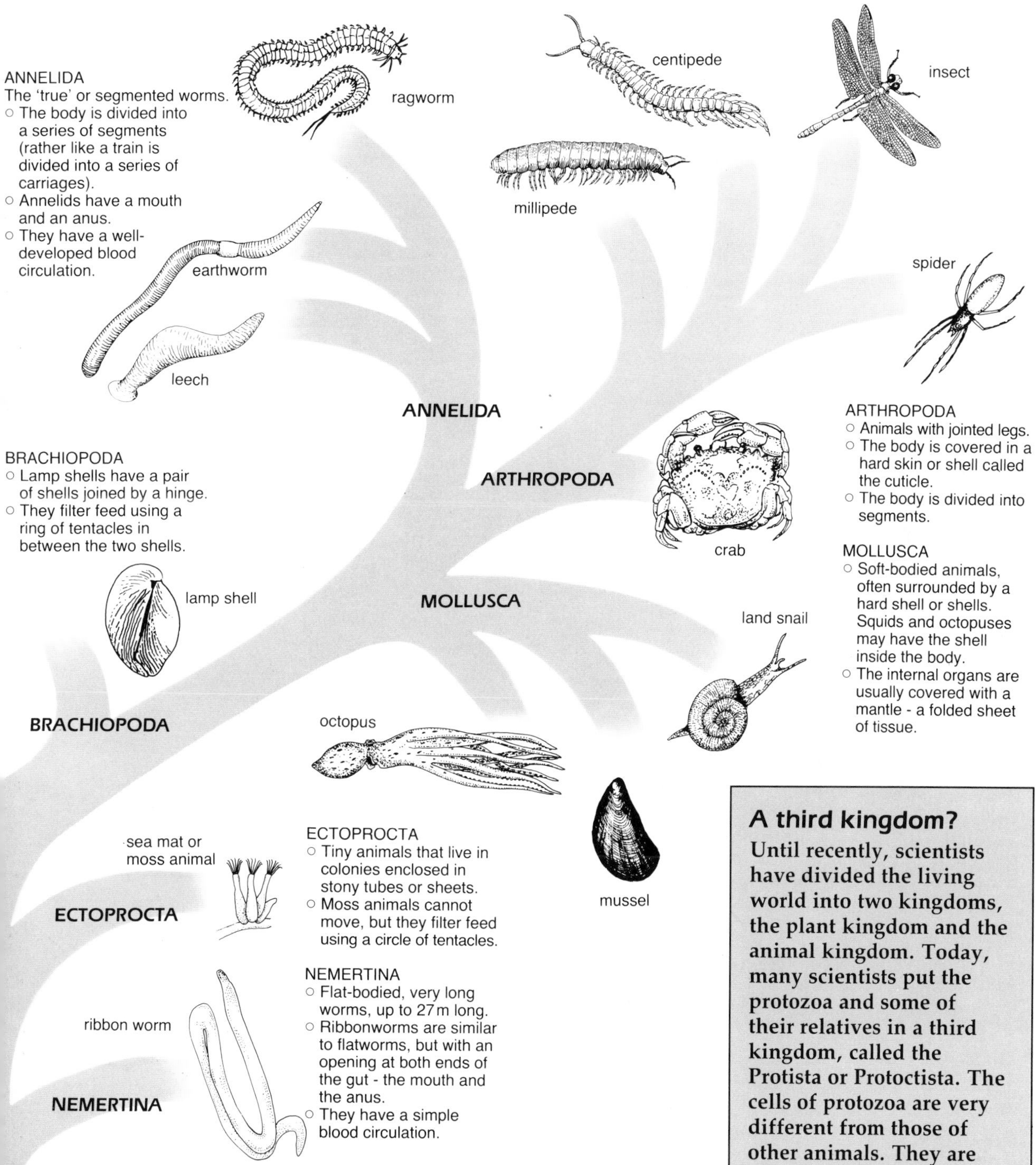

ANNELIDA
The 'true' or segmented worms.
- The body is divided into a series of segments (rather like a train is divided into a series of carriages).
- Annelids have a mouth and an anus.
- They have a well-developed blood circulation.

ARTHROPODA
- Animals with jointed legs.
- The body is covered in a hard skin or shell called the cuticle.
- The body is divided into segments.

BRACHIOPODA
- Lamp shells have a pair of shells joined by a hinge.
- They filter feed using a ring of tentacles in between the two shells.

MOLLUSCA
- Soft-bodied animals, often surrounded by a hard shell or shells. Squids and octopuses may have the shell inside the body.
- The internal organs are usually covered with a mantle - a folded sheet of tissue.

ECTOPROCTA
- Tiny animals that live in colonies enclosed in stony tubes or sheets.
- Moss animals cannot move, but they filter feed using a circle of tentacles.

NEMERTINA
- Flat-bodied, very long worms, up to 27 m long.
- Ribbonworms are similar to flatworms, but with an opening at both ends of the gut - the mouth and the anus.
- They have a simple blood circulation.

PLATYHELMINTHES
- Simple animals whose gut has only one opening - the mouth.
- Flatworms have no blood circulation.

A third kingdom?

Until recently, scientists have divided the living world into two kingdoms, the plant kingdom and the animal kingdom. Today, many scientists put the protozoa and some of their relatives in a third kingdom, called the Protista or Protoctista. The cells of protozoa are very different from those of other animals. They are much more complex, since they carry out all the activities of the animal.

Plants and other non-animals

What is a plant?

People used to think that living organisms could be divided into just two main groups - the Plant Kingdom and the Animal Kingdom. It is easy to suppose that if a living creature is not an animal, it must be a plant. But that depends on what you think a plant is.

Plants are independent

The main difference between plants and animals is that plants can use simple chemicals found in the air, water and soil to make all the materials needed to build their bodies, while animals have to eat plants or other animals.

Plants have special cells

Another feature of plants is that their cells - the smallest units of living material - are surrounded by walls made of a substance called cellulose.

Definitely plants

There are several groups of non-animals which are definitely green plants. They include the mosses and liverworts, the ferns, clubmosses and horsetails, the conifers, ginkgoes and cycads, and the flowering plants. All of them use the green substance chlorophyll to make their own food by photosynthesis.

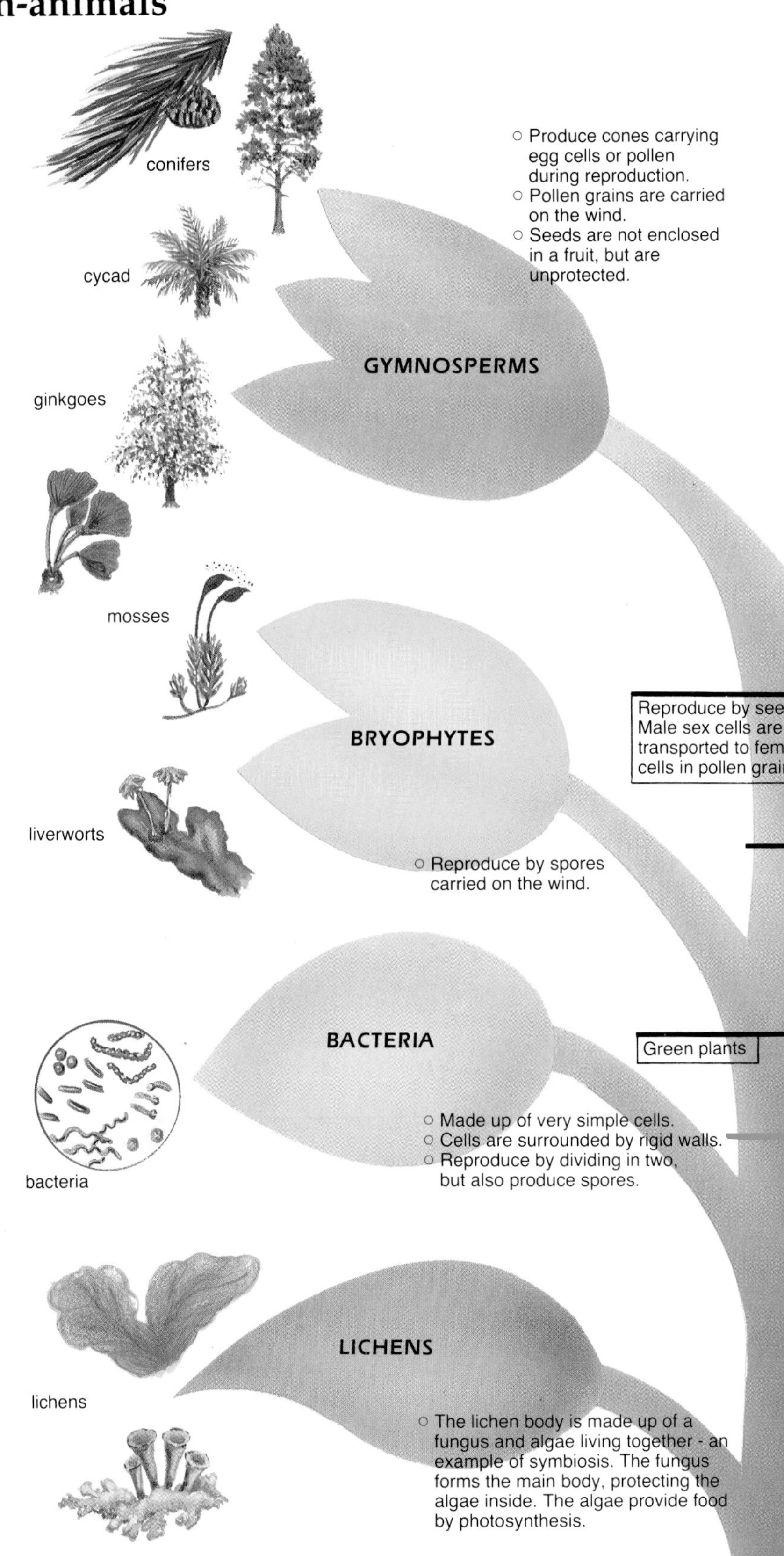

conifers
cycad
ginkgoes
○ Produce cones carrying egg cells or pollen during reproduction.
○ Pollen grains are carried on the wind.
○ Seeds are not enclosed in a fruit, but are unprotected.
GYMNOSPERMS
mosses
BRYOPHYTES
Reproduce by seeds. Male sex cells are transported to female cells in pollen grains.
liverworts
○ Reproduce by spores carried on the wind.
BACTERIA
Green plants
bacteria
○ Made up of very simple cells.
○ Cells are surrounded by rigid walls.
○ Reproduce by dividing in two, but also produce spores.
LICHENS
lichens
○ The lichen body is made up of a fungus and algae living together - an example of symbiosis. The fungus forms the main body, protecting the algae inside. The algae provide food by photosynthesis.

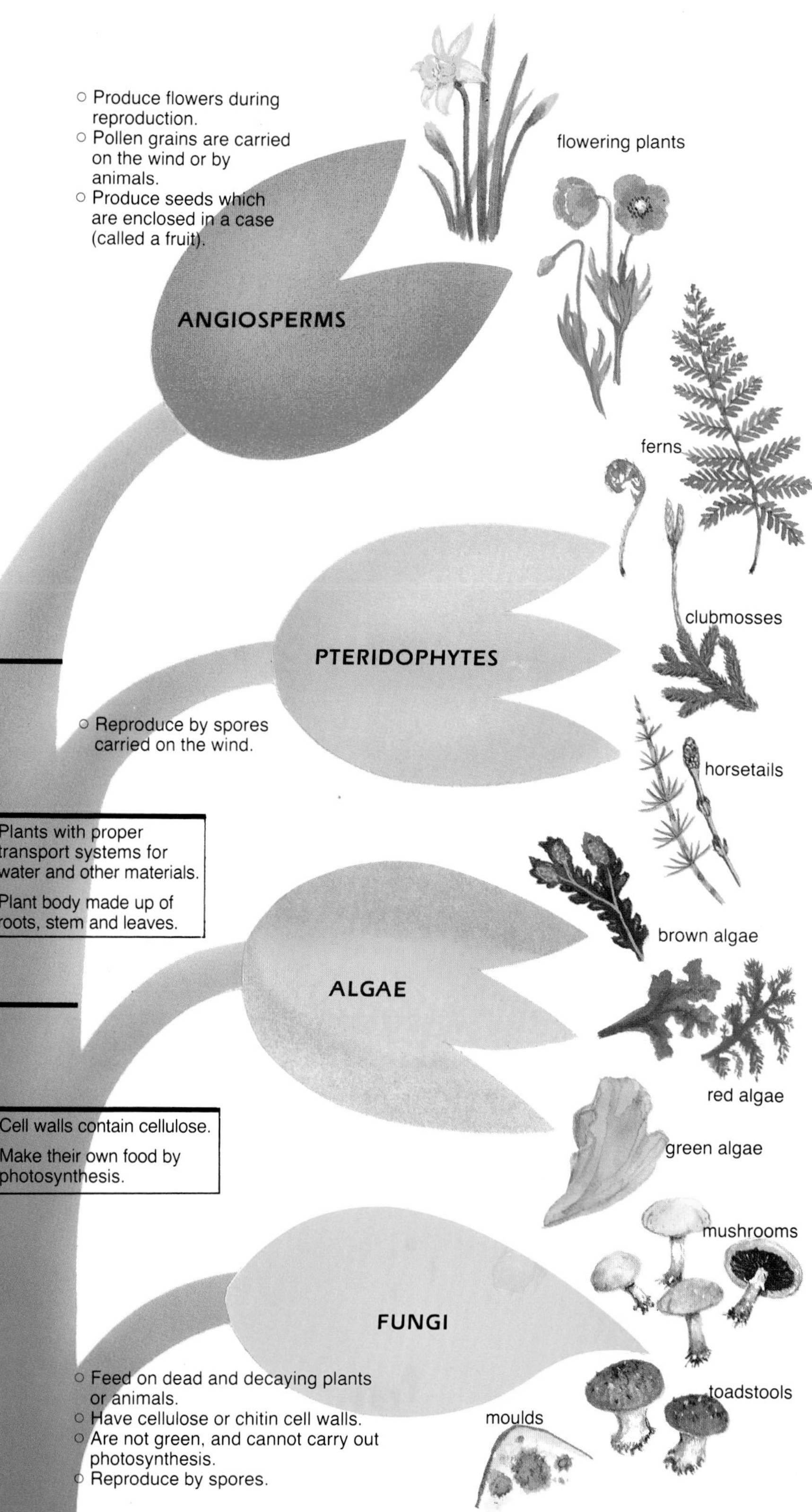

○ Produce flowers during reproduction.
○ Pollen grains are carried on the wind or by animals.
○ Produce seeds which are enclosed in a case (called a fruit).
ANGIOSPERMS
flowering plants
ferns
clubmosses
PTERIDOPHYTES
○ Reproduce by spores carried on the wind.
horsetails
Plants with proper transport systems for water and other materials.
Plant body made up of roots, stem and leaves.
brown algae
ALGAE
red algae
Cell walls contain cellulose.
Make their own food by photosynthesis.
green algae
mushrooms
FUNGI
toadstools
moulds
○ Feed on dead and decaying plants or animals.
○ Have cellulose or chitin cell walls.
○ Are not green, and cannot carry out photosynthesis.
○ Reproduce by spores.

What do you call a non-animal?

There are some living creatures that do not appear to fit in either the Plant Kingdom or the Animal Kingdom. For instance, what do you call a living organism that is rooted to the ground, has a branching body and has cellulose cell walls, but is not green, and cannot make its own food?

This is a description of a fungus. Most scientists classify the fungi as a separate group of living creatures - the Kingdom Fungi. In some fungi the cell walls are made of chitin, a substance found in insects.

Bacteria have much simpler cells than other living creatures, and may also be placed in a kingdom of their own, the Kingdom Monera.

Because plants and other non-animals have soft bodies and do not leave many fossils, we do not know how they are related to each other. Scientists have different ideas about classifying them. Here we have simply shown you the main groups, without trying to put them in a special order or giving them their special international names.

Variety is the spice of life

What is a species?

There are more than one million different types of animal and plant living on the Earth. Each type is called a species. A species is a group of animals or plants which look similar and which breed together to produce fertile offspring. So, for example, a lion is a different species from a tiger. They look very different and are easy to tell apart. But could you tell one lion from another, or could you distinguish one tiger from a group of several?

Every animal and plant is unique

Unless you are one of a pair of identical twins, there is nobody else in the world who looks exactly like you. You are a unique animal and so is every other animal. Everybody you know looks different, and you have no difficulty telling one person from another. This is true, even though all humans belong to the same species. Just as members of the human species vary, so do members of other species. No two giraffes are identical, although at first sight you might think so. Scientists call these differences variations. These variations can be big or small. Sometimes you have to look very carefully to see them.

▲ At first sight the members of this herd of zebra look identical. But are they? Look closely at the pattern of stripes on each animal. Is this pattern exactly the same on each zebra? Choose four zebra and try to draw the pattern made by their stripes. Compare your drawings. Are they all the same? Some scientists studying zebra populations become so familiar with the group that they are able to tell one zebra from another. They identify the pattern of stripes.

Each member of a population of oak trees in a wood is different from its neighbours. Trees of the same age are different in height and girth. No two trees have the same number of leaves and there is a variety of leaf shape and size. The number of acorns each tree produces varies. Even acorns from the same tree vary in size and weight. All these variations are difficult to see, but they are there. You can easily distinguish between your friends. Can you tell one oak tree from another?

There are many varieties of dog but they all belong to the same species. They vary in size and shape because they have been bred for different jobs. Humans have chosen different characteristics over hundreds of years to produce the variety of dogs we know today. Even the odd-shaped dachshund was bred for a reason. Can you guess what it was? And why do you think the bulldog looks like it does? Answers on page 152.

◀ The spectacled bear is the only species of bear living in South America. It lives in the Andes Mountains where it sometimes uses its climbing skills to find food in tall trees. Can you guess how it got its name? Look at the face markings of these bears. Do they show variations? Do you think any two bears will have identical markings?

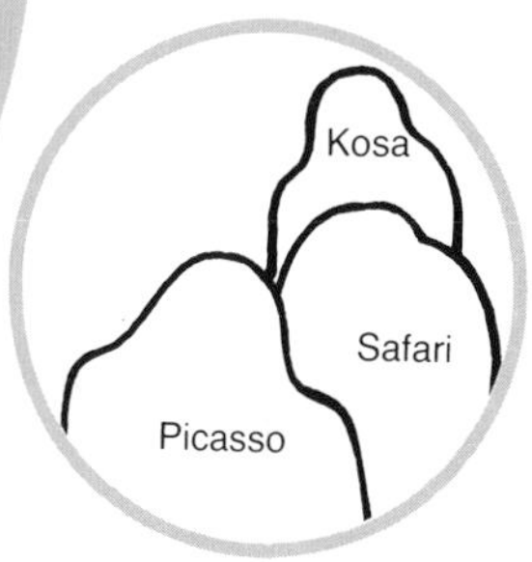

Kosa

Safari

Picasso

Noseprint identikit

Dian Fossey, an American naturalist, studied the wild mountain gorilla from tropical Africa. She got to know the population so well she was able to recognize individuals. She gave each gorilla a name. Each mountain gorilla has its own individual-shaped nose. No two gorilla noses are the same. Just as humans have unique fingerprints, gorillas have 'noseprints'. Dian Fossey was able to identify each gorilla in the population by its 'noseprint'. Can you do the same? Above is a photograph of a group of gorillas. You can find out their names by looking at the small outline drawing. Left is a drawing of one of these gorillas. Look at its 'nose-print'. Is it Picasso, Kosa or Safari? Answer on page 152.

▲ Is this the face of Picasso, Kosa, or Safari?

Evolution and change

More than enough offspring

You have already read something about variation on pages 18 and 19. There is more on this topic later on this page. But first some mathematics. A famous naturalist called Charles Darwin once worked out that, after seven hundred years, a pair of African elephants could have nineteen million descendents. The cockroach is even more remarkable. After only seven months, a pair of cockroaches could have 164 billion descendents. How can this be? Why isn't the world covered in elephants and cockroaches? To find the answer to the first question, look at the chessboard game. To answer the second, look at the pictures below. Animals are capable of increasing in numbers like the coin increases in value in the chessboard game. However, they don't. The pictures help you to understand why.

Try this on your friends

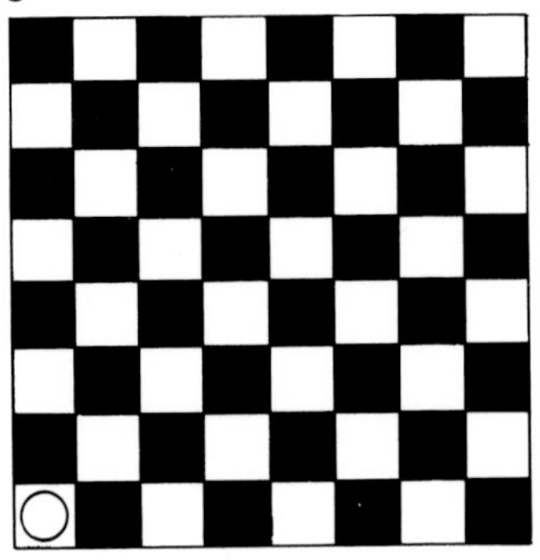

Put a 2p coin on the chessboard as shown. Move the coin from one square to the next. Imagine that the coin doubles in value every time it lands on a new square. So, for example, it is worth 2p on square 1, 4p on square 2, 8p on square 3, and so on. Ask your friends to guess how much money you have 'made' when you get to the last square at the top of the board. You might surprise them.

1

One pair of rabbits can produce a litter of babies six times a year.

2

If all the babies survived and continued to breed the world would be over-run with rabbits.

3

Scientists have found out that animal populations don't change much in size. This is because not all the offspring survive or breed.

4

Rabbits may die of disease
or be eaten by foxes
or not get enough food
or not find a mate
or not find a nesting site.

5

The rabbits in a population are not identical. They differ from each other: they vary. Some of these differences are important for survival.

6

Some rabbits might run faster to escape predators. Others might have coat colours which give camouflage from predators. They are better adapted for survival.

7

The rabbits which survive are better suited to their environment. Those which survive breed to produce offspring like themselves. The babies may inherit the characteristics of speed and coat colour. This gives them a better chance of survival. Can you now see why variation in a species is important? This survival of animals suited to the environment is called natural selection. Can you explain why the world isn't over-run by elephants or cockroaches?

What makes variation happen?

How does variation come about? How do different species develop? Both these questions worried Charles Darwin. They have worried many other scientists since Darwin. We know that animals and plants inherit characteristics from their parents. These are passed on in the sperms from the father, and eggs from the mother. Organisms don't all receive exactly the same information from their parents. It varies from one organism to another. It is this different information which offspring inherit which brings about variation. Think again about the spectacled bears on page 19. Can you now explain why they have different face markings? Answer on page 152.

But how do different species come about?

We can't go back in history, so we can never be sure how different species formed. The process usually takes place over very long periods of time. Perhaps many hundreds of thousands of years. We know it involves natural selection. However, scientists also think other things are important as well. There are three stages in species formation.

1

A population of animals or plants may become divided in two by a barrier such as a range of mountains. This stops the members of the two groups from breeding together.

2

Each of the two new groups now begins to adapt to its own local environment on either side of the mountain range. Again natural selection is at work.

The two populations gradually become different from each other. This takes a long time.

3

The two populations may become so different that they may no longer be able to breed together, even if they could meet up again. They have become different species.

Remember

Conditions on the two sides of the barrier will probably be different. The two populations have to adapt to different environments. Natural selection gradually changes the two populations to make them different. We call this evolution.

The Galapagos project

There are 13 species of finch on the Galapagos Islands in the Pacific Ocean. Each has a different shape or size of beak. Below are three examples.

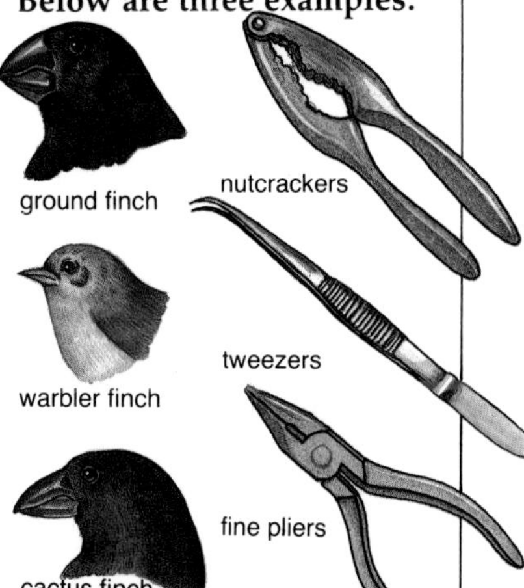

Each beak has a common tool drawn alongside to help you understand how it works. When the islands were first formed there were no animals and plants living there. Look at the map of the world and decide where the first finches came from. Find the Galapagos Islands by tracing your finger along the Equator until you come to them. Can you explain why the finches have different beaks? What is the barrier in this case. Look again at the beaks and the three foods at the top of the page. Can you match each beak with the correct food? Answers on page 152.

More about variation (pp.18, 19); reproduction (pp.66, 67)

Animals in armour

Protection and defence

Animals have many ways of protecting and defending themselves. They use colour, changes in shape and size, stings and bites, and they sometimes even pretend to be dead. Molluscs such as snails carry a hard shell around with them which protects the soft, delicate body structures inside. Other animals have evolved a rather special way to protect their bodies. They are covered in a suit of armour.

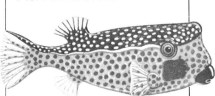

▲ Millipedes are cylindrical animals covered by a tube of armour. The joints between each piece help to make the body very flexible. A millipede can even curl up when attacked.

Animal armour

Imagine walking around all day in a suit of armour. You would probably find it very heavy, uncomfortable and difficult to move in. Animal armour is not heavy because it is made of light material. It also has lots of joints and hinges which make it flexible and easy to walk in.

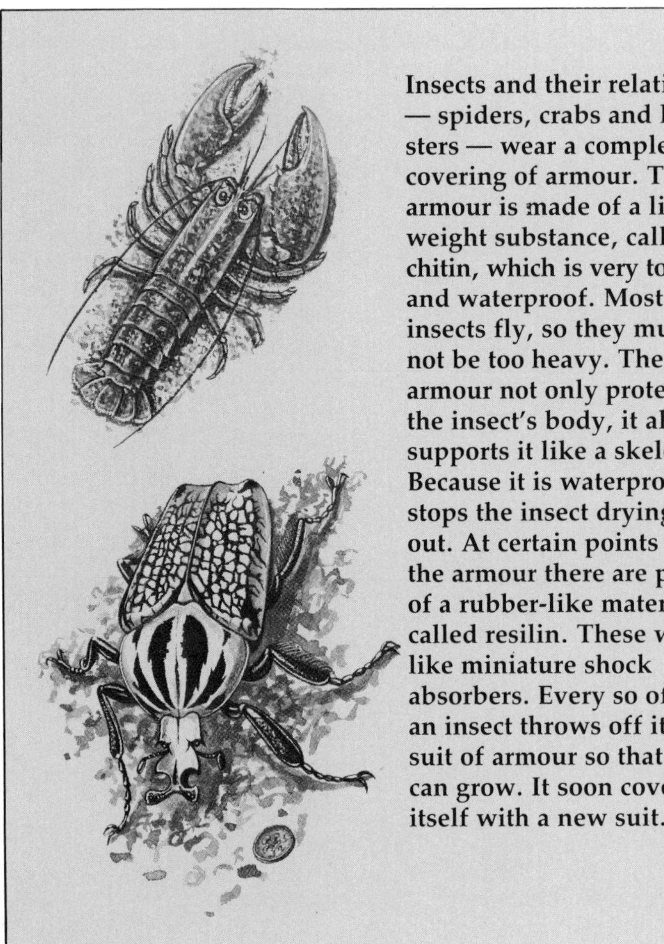

Insects and their relatives — spiders, crabs and lobsters — wear a complete covering of armour. The armour is made of a lightweight substance, called chitin, which is very tough and waterproof. Most insects fly, so they must not be too heavy. The armour not only protects the insect's body, it also supports it like a skeleton. Because it is waterproof, it stops the insect drying out. At certain points in the armour there are pads of a rubber-like material called resilin. These work like miniature shock absorbers. Every so often an insect throws off its suit of armour so that it can grow. It soon covers itself with a new suit.

Fish in armour

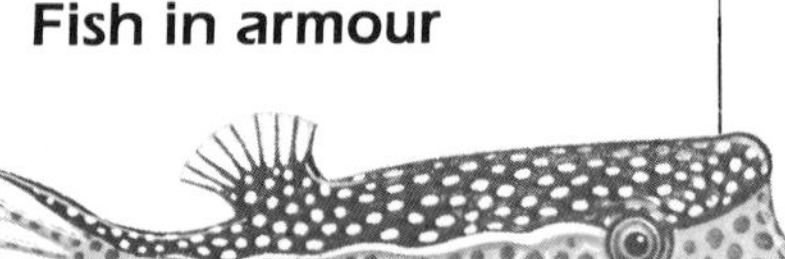

Armour-plating is not found in many fish. This is because a fish needs a flexible body for swimming. However, the trunk fish has bony pieces in its skin which fit together to form a box. It can only swim slowly and it cannot waggle its body like other fish. It has to paddle along with its fins.

The sea-horse is also covered in armour. It moves very slowly, swimming upright by means of its gently waving fins.

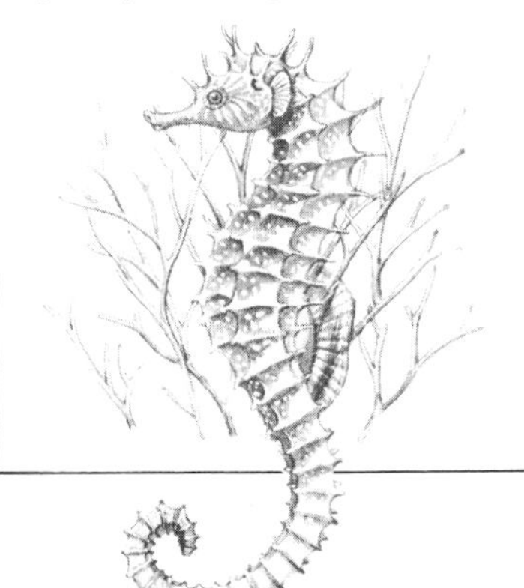

▲ Reptiles are covered in a scaly skin. In crocodiles and their relatives, the alligators, these scales become thickened, especially on the back and along the tail. They form patches of armour. Crocodiles use their tail for swimming so its covering of armour plates is jointed to make it flexible. The crocodile moves its tail to push itself through the water.

▲ Tortoises and turtles have a dome-shaped shell on their backs. It is joined to the backbone and forms a rigid covering. The legs are less heavily armoured to help in movement. Everything can be pulled under the shell for extra protection.

Pangolins live in Africa and Asia. They are nocturnal animals, and are the only mammal whose body is covered in scales. The scales are made from hair. Pangolins walk on their back legs and balance on their tails. They feed on ants and termites which they dig up with their powerful front claws. Their armour-plating gives protection from bites and stings. Pangolins curl into a ball when attacked.

Knights in armour

There are seven species of armadillo living in Central and South America. The nine-banded armadillo has even invaded North America where people think of it as a pest. The armadillos are the real armour wearers of the animal kingdom. Their protective suits are jointed just like the armour of a medieval knight. The three-banded armadillo rolls into a ball when frightened. Its head and tail fit snugly to complete the protection.

Did you know?

The female nine-banded armadillo always gives birth to identical quadruplets.

A flea has rubber pads of resilin on its back feet. They act like a catapult to shoot the animal into the air over a distance as much as 200 times its own length.

A female pangolin protects its baby by curling up round it.

More about animal defences (pp.54, 55)

Shaping up to things

Variety of shape

Animals and plants come in many different shapes and sizes. Think of the variety of shapes of living things. Some animals are shaped like a cylinder, or a slightly altered version of a cylinder. Others are very flat, and look as though they have been squashed by a heavy weight. There are animals with a thin body shape. They look as though they have been flattened from either side. Some animals are disc-shaped, some animals are spherical. Many molluscs have a spiral-shaped shell. Other animals have an even more peculiar shape. For example, starfish which, as their name suggests, are shaped like a star. Many animals have different shapes at different times in their life cycles. Others can change their shape at particular moments. Plants also come in different shapes. Some are cylindrical, some spherical, some cone-shaped, and some are flat. Often the different shapes of animals and plants reflect how they have adapted to their different habitats.

▲ Cylinder-shaped bodies are common in animals. Often animals which burrow have this shape. So do some animals which live in trees. Snakes are really just long cylinders. So are earthworms and millipedes. The cylindrical shape helps them to move in narrow tunnels underground, and also helps them wiggle between plant stems on the ground.

Adding to shape

In addition to these basic body shapes, there are structures which give variety to animal and plant shapes. Animals have wings, legs, flippers, fins, tails and flukes (a flattened tail fin). Some animals have horns or antlers. Others have flaps of loose skin such as wattles (fleshy outgrowths) and dewlaps (loose, hanging skin, like that under the throat of a turkey). Plants have a variety of leaf shapes. Some have no leaves, others have spines and thorns.

▼ This cheetah is running at full speed. When running fast, its shape becomes streamlined. By doing this its body offers less resistance to air as it moves forward. Fast-swimming aquatic animals are also streamlined or torpedo-shaped for easy movement through water. Birds take on a streamlined shape when flying. This helps reduce drag, and allows the bird to move more quickly. Many animals change the position of their limbs to become more streamlined for fast forward movement.

Thin animals

Many animals have a shape as if they have been squeezed from either side. This is a useful shape for slipping between small gaps. Fish living among coral reefs are this shape, and so are many tree-dwelling chameleons. The chameleons move easily between leaves and twigs. Fleas are also flattened from side to side so they can move between the hairs and feathers of their hosts. Some animals are shaped as though they have been flattened by a heavy weight. Animals living on rocky, exposed surfaces and on the sea-bed are like this. It makes them less likely to be knocked off by the moving water. Parasitic ticks are flat so that they stay on their host.

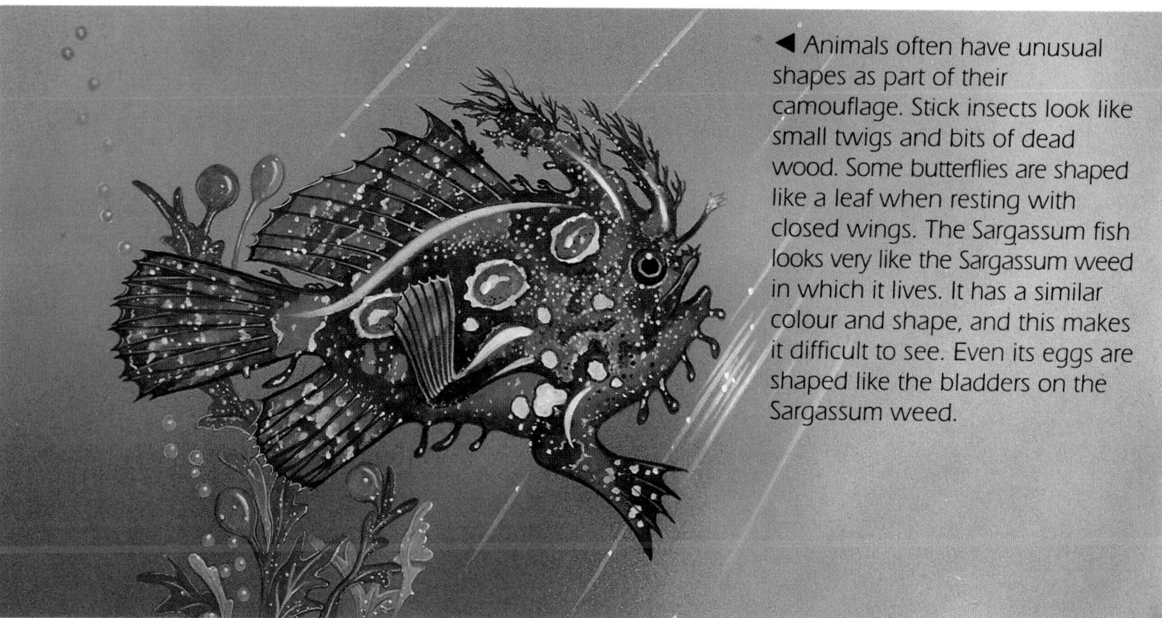

◀ Animals often have unusual shapes as part of their camouflage. Stick insects look like small twigs and bits of dead wood. Some butterflies are shaped like a leaf when resting with closed wings. The Sargassum fish looks very like the Sargassum weed in which it lives. It has a similar colour and shape, and this makes it difficult to see. Even its eggs are shaped like the bladders on the Sargassum weed.

Shape for defence

Some animals change shape when attacked. A frog swells up to look bigger. A cat makes its fur stand upright when threatened by a dog. This makes it look bigger in an attempt to frighten the dog away. Some animals curl up into a ball when defending themselves. Hedgehogs do this, and so do armadillos. Many millipedes change from a cylindrical shape to a coiled-disc shape when touched. If attacked, the frilled lizard from Australia will sometimes change its shape by unfolding a huge frill around its neck. This makes its head look bigger and fiercer.

▲ Many animals change shape during courtship, or when defending territory. The male frigate bird blows up a huge throat sac to attract its mate. This makes the front of the bird look like a large, red balloon. The male anole lizard uses a similar device. Its inflated orange throat sac makes it look bigger and more frightening to other males when defending territory, and also attracts a female.

Did you know?

Of all the shapes we know, a sphere has the smallest amount of surface compared with its volume. Some cacti living in hot, dry conditions are spherical. Plants lose water from their surface. Because these cacti are spherical, the amount of surface through which water can pass is reduced. This helps the cacti to keep water inside their tissues.

In cold conditions many animals become spherical. Sleeping dogs or cats curl up into a ball. Hibernating mammals curl up to sleep. Can you think why? Answer on page 152.

More about changing shape (pp.68, 69); camouflage (pp.52, 53); courtship (pp.64, 65)

The importance of size

What is big?

What do we mean by big? The biggest living thing is a tree, the giant sequoia. It is many million times bigger than the smallest living organism. Humans are big compared to most living things. Ninety-nine per cent of all living things are smaller than humans.

Small and big

If you play with a mouse in your hands, it may escape and fall to the ground. It won't hurt itself if it does this. But a human who fell a distance many times his or her own height would probably die. Small and large bodies of a similar shape and substance have different properties. Small animals have a very big surface compared to their volume. Big animals have a relatively small surface compared to their volume. Look at the square animals in the picture to see if this is true.

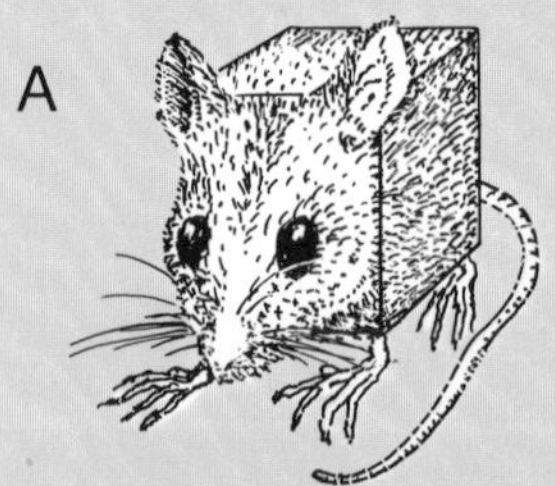

This is a cube-shaped animal. Each side of its body is 1 cm long. Its total surface is 6 cm^2. Its volume is 1 cm^3. It has 6 cm^2 of surface for every 1 cm^3 of volume.

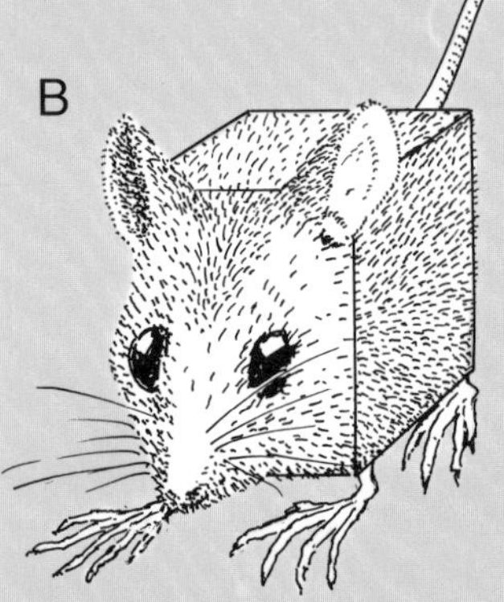

This is a bigger cube-shaped animal. Each side of its body is 6 cm long. Its total surface is 216 cm^2. Its volume is 216 cm^3. It has 1 cm^2 of surface for every 1 cm^3 of volume.

Animal A is smaller than animal B. But it has a much bigger surface compared to its volume than animal B.

Gravity

The reason we don't float off the Earth into space is because of gravity. Gravity is a force which pulls your body back to Earth. All objects are attracted to the Earth by gravity. The body of a big animal contains more material than the body of a small animal. We say it has a bigger mass. The bigger the animal, the stronger the pull of gravity on its body. This is because there is more mass to pull on. Small animals are pulled less by gravity because they have less mass to pull on. Small animals have a large surface compared to their volume. This means they are affected more by surface forces than by gravity. Forces such as wind and rain affect small animals much more than big animals. Does this help to explain the case of the falling mouse and human? Answer on page 152.

Floating in air

Tiny animals and plants have a huge surface compared to their volume. They also have very little mass. Because of this, movements of the air can keep them afloat. Tiny insects, spiders, fungal spores and pollen grains float in air because they are small.

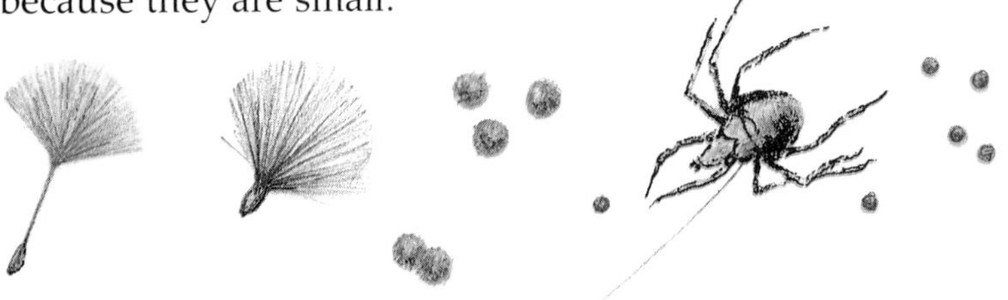

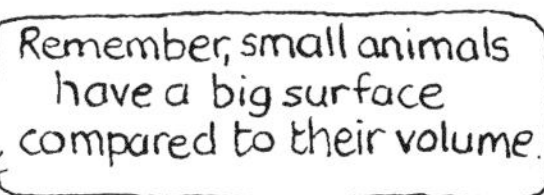

Remember, small animals have a big surface compared to their volume.

What limits size?

The size of an animal depends upon a number of things. One very important factor is how the animal breathes. Insects are quite small animals, and they get their oxygen through tiny holes in the surface of their bodies. The goliath beetle is the biggest insect, but it only weighs about 100 grams. This is about as big as an insect can grow. Any bigger and it would be unable to get all the oxygen it needed. Bigger animals need special breathing equipment like gills and lungs.

Animals grow bigger in water

Animals living in water can grow to a much bigger size than animals on land. The biggest animals in the world live in water. This is because the water supports their mass. The blue whale may have a mass of 130 tonnes. This is nearly twenty-five times the mass of an African elephant, which is the biggest land animal. Above a certain size, land animals cannot support themselves. The blue whale would not be able to support itself on land.

What is it like to be small?

We have seen that gravity has little effect on small animals. Surface forces such as wind and rain are much more important. To an animal as small as a fly, air is like water, and water is like syrup. A fly can easily be blown away or damaged by the wind. If a dog gets wet it isn't affected much. If a mouse gets wet, movement becomes very difficult. A wet fly carries an enormous amount of water on its surface. Its mass doubles when wet. It can hardly crawl.

Cool it!

An animal loses heat from its body across its surface. Small animals lose heat more quickly than big ones. Can you think why? Answer on page 152. If you were an animal living in a cold climate, would you like to be big or small?

The African elephant lives in hot conditions. Does its size give it any problems?

Did you know?

The fairy-tale giant could never exist. Imagine a man 5½ m tall, 3 times the height of an average man. The giant would be 27 times as heavy as the man but only 9 times as strong. If he were shaped like a man he wouldn't be able to walk or even stand up. Jack in 'Jack and the Beanstalk' had nothing to worry about!

More about floating in air (pp.88, 122); shapes (pp.24, 25); surface area (pp.25, 129)

The importance of light

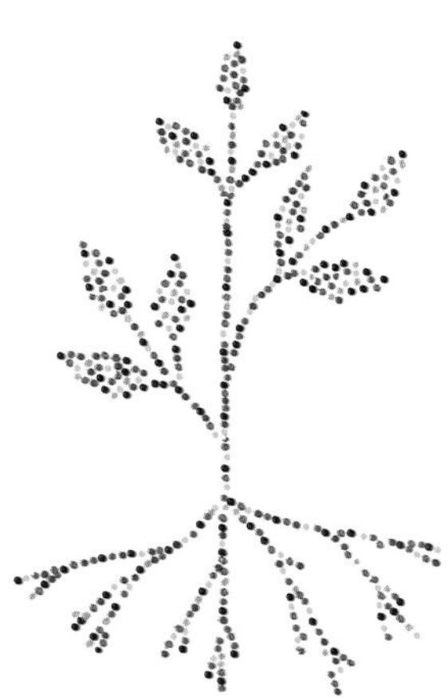

▲ A plant is made up of many different raw materials.

The importance of plants

Animals cannot live without plants. Either they eat plants, or they eat animals that eat plants. This is because animals cannot make their own body materials. Think of an animal as being made up of building blocks. The animal cannot make the building blocks, but plants can. The animal can only rearrange the building blocks to make different structures.

Photosynthesis

Green plants use a process called photosynthesis to make their own body materials from simple substances, which they take in from their surroundings. They use carbon dioxide gas from the air and water from the soil. They also use the mineral salts dissolved in water. Energy is needed to join all these simple substances together to make a complicated structure like a plant. This energy comes from sunlight.

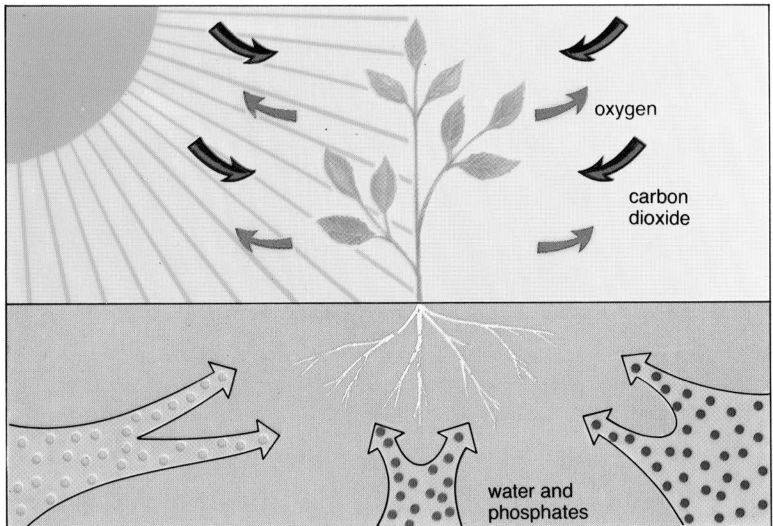

▲ This diagram shows how raw materials enter the plant. Carbon dioxide gas enters through tiny holes in the leaves, called stomata. Water and mineral salts are taken up from the soil by the roots.

Energy from light

Plants contain a green substance called chlorophyll which captures energy from light. Leaves contain a lot of chlorophyll. They are broad and flat to catch as much light as possible. In the leaves the energy from light is used to make all the materials needed by the plant body. During this process the plant produces oxygen gas. This goes off into the atmosphere, and is used by animals for breathing.

Two-way transport systems

The materials made in the leaves are carried to the rest of the plant in a series of tiny tubes. Some of these materials are used to make new plant body – they help the plant to grow. Some are stored in the roots or in special structures such as bulbs and tubers. They can be used for growth later. Another set of tiny tubes carries water and dissolved mineral salts from the roots to the leaves. These two sets of tiny tubes make up the veins of the leaf.

Sun seekers

Plants on a window-sill bend towards the light so their leaves trap light all round the shoots, instead of only on one side.

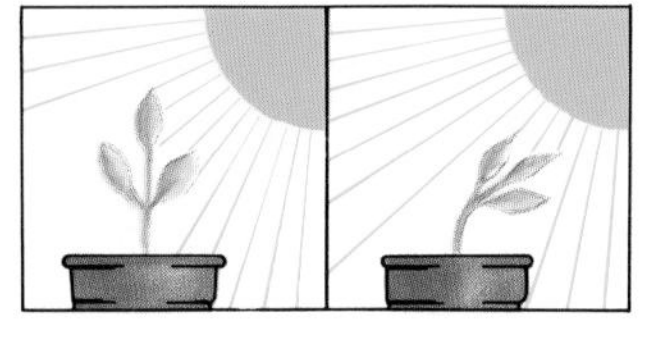

Catching sunbeams

Plants arrange their leaves so as to catch as much light as possible. If you lie on your back and look up at the leaves on a tree, you will see that hardly any of them overlap. Their stalks twist so that they do not shade each other.

Leaves have holes

Carbon dioxide gas enters the leaves through hundreds of tiny holes called stomata. Oxygen gas produced by photosynthesis goes out to the plant through these holes. Water also evaporates from the plant through the stomata, so the plant has to take up a lot of water through its roots to avoid wilting.

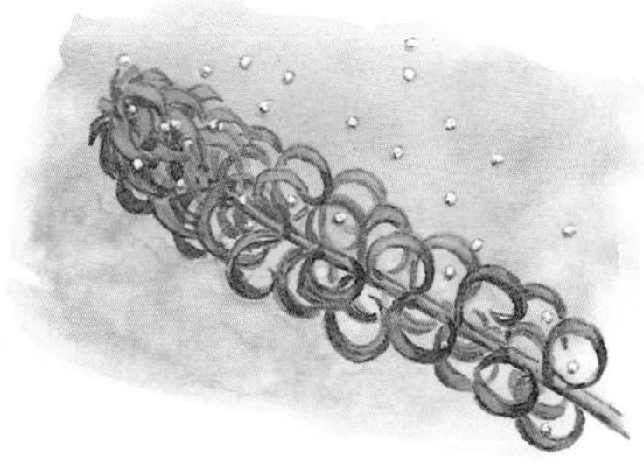

▲ Plants that live in water take in their raw materials from the water. They absorb dissolved gases and mineral salts all over their surfaces. This pondweed is giving off bubbles of oxygen as a result of photosynthesis.

Making animals from plants

You can think of living organisms as being made up of different coloured building blocks. The building blocks are really chemicals. Each colour represents a different chemical. chemical. Instead of cement, living building blocks are held together by energy. The plant acts rather like a bricklayer — it traps energy from sunlight and uses it to make complex chemicals from simpler ones.

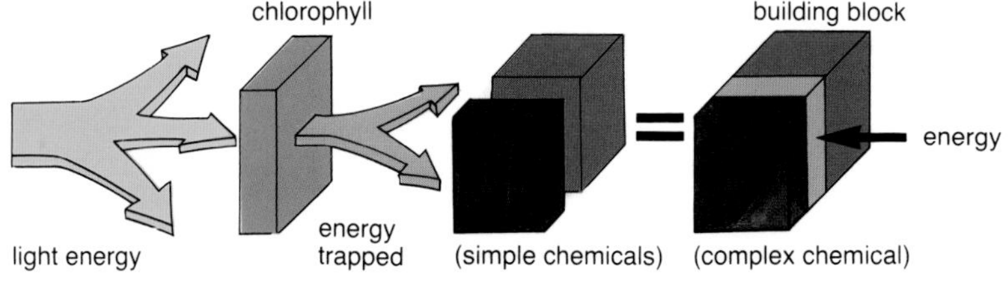

Animals cannot do this. Animals that feed on plants rearrange these building blocks to make the chemicals they need for their own bodies. Other animals get their building blocks by eating animals that feed on plants.

Animals can also break down the complex chemicals to get the energy out again. They use the energy for moving about and for keeping warm. So all the energy animals use was originally captured from sunlight by green plants. Animals are solar powered!

Did you know?

Every year plants trap nearly 25 billion tonnes of carbon from carbon dioxide gas and turn it into living material.

Most of the oxygen in the atmosphere has been produced by plants.

More about energy in plants and animals (pp.30, 31); animals that eat plants (pp.32, 33)

Energy and life

Living things

If you look at any habitat you will find many different animals and plants. There are probably more than you might think. This is because lots of living organisms are small and are not easily seen. They hide under stones and tree bark, in the soil, on other animals and plants and even inside them.

Why do living things need energy?

All living things carry out important life processes. For example, they move to find new food, or to escape danger. They feed. They sense what is going on in their surroundings. They get rid of waste materials. They breathe, and they grow and reproduce. You probably think that plants do not do some of these things, but they do. They don't move as much as animals, but they do all the other things. In order to carry out all these processes, animals and plants need energy.

Capturing energy

There are different forms of energy. Each form can be changed to another form. The Earth receives all its energy from the Sun. There is energy in sunlight. Animals can't do much with this energy, but green plants can. They capture some of the Sun's energy and use it to carry out all their life processes. This capturing of the Sun's energy by green plants is called photosynthesis. It is a very complicated process and you can read more about it on pages 28 and 29. Green plants use the Sun's energy to make their own food. For photosynthesis, they also need carbon dioxide and water. By photosynthesis, green plants make foods that are very rich in energy. They store these inside them ready for use. Animals can also use these foods.

Energy for animals

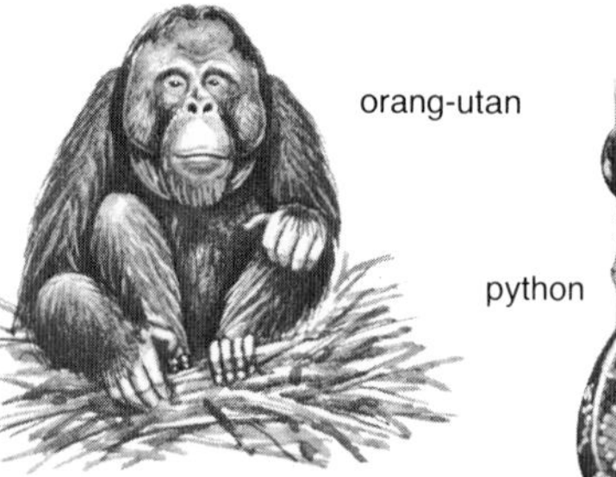

Animals get their energy by eating green plants or by eating other animals. Animals which eat plants are called herbivores. Those which eat other animals are called carnivores. Some animals eat both plants and animals and we call them omnivores. Look at the pictures of these eight animals. Can you group them based on their feeding habits? You will have to think carefully about some of them. All the answers are to be found somewhere in this book. If you get tired of looking, you will find the answers on page 152.

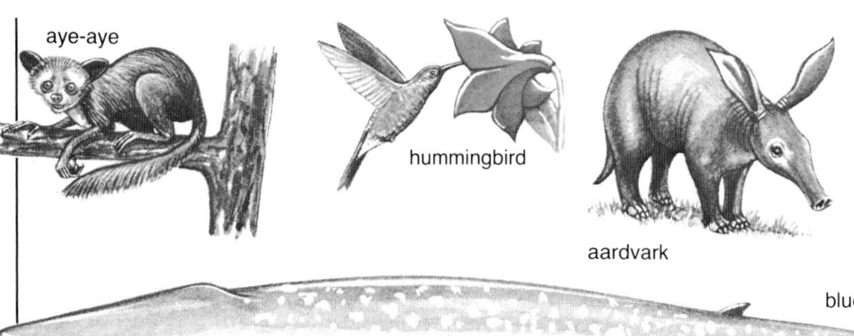

Food chains

When we think about feeding, we can imagine each plant or animal as a link in a chain. For example, a leaf can be eaten by a caterpillar, and a caterpillar can be eaten by a shrew. This is a three-link food chain. Energy is passed from one link to the other, but it moves in one direction only. Follow the arrows.

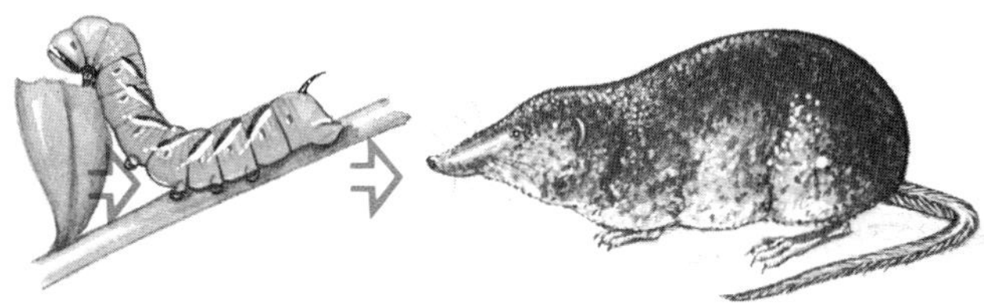

Any habitat has many three-link food chains, though they may be made up of different animals and plants. It is easy to make a four-link chain. All you have to do is add another carnivore on the right. You need an animal which eats shrews.

Why can't you turn a three-link chain into a four-link chain by adding something to the left-hand side? Try making up other food chains. Can you work out a simple food chain from an African habitat? Look at pages 130 and 131 and build a three-link chain from the information given about the wildlife in a South American rain forest.

Losing energy

Some energy is lost as it passes from one link to another along a food chain. It is a slow process. The leaf uses some of the energy captured from the Sun to carry out its life processes. It also wastes some. Therefore, there is less energy for the caterpillar. The caterpillar, in turn, uses some of the energy it got from the leaf and it also wastes some. Thus, there is even less energy to pass on to the shrew. By the time the shrew has used and wasted some of the energy it got from the caterpillar there isn't much left for the snake. Can you now see why most food chains have less than six links?

Many antelopes but few lions

There is a lot of energy at the beginning of a food chain, but not much at the end. The energy at the beginning can support many herbivores. After three or four transfers, there is only enough energy to support a few carnivores. Can you now explain why Africa has lots of antelopes but fewer lions?

Food webs

Many animals eat more than one kind of food. This means they can take food from other food chains. Imagine a food chain made up of these links: leaf → slug → toad. A lot of animals eat leaves. There are also animals which eat slugs and toads. These animals form new food chains. The food chains connect with each other to form food webs. Can you make up a food web using the animals and plants in your garden?

Remember

There is no shortage of energy from the Sun. It reaches the Earth every day. But raw materials like carbon dioxide, water and minerals are limited. They have to be recycled. The decomposers do this.

More about decomposers (pp.40, 41); how plants capture sunlight (pp.28, 29); how different animals feed (pp.32-39)

The vegetarians

▲ Bison grazing on the North American plains.

A tough diet

Unlike plants, animals cannot make their own food. Instead, they have to feed on plants or other animals. Animals which feed mainly on plants are called herbivores.

Plants contain a lot of tough fibres. Many vegetarian insects, like locusts and caterpillars, have hard horny mouthparts which help them cut up leaves. Other vegetarian animals like tortoises and turtles use sharp horny jaws, while slugs and snails use a rasping tongue covered in tiny teeth. Some birds have special bills — finches have large heavy beaks for cracking open seeds, and parrots have hooked bills for tearing into fruits.

Plant-eating mammals have large flat-topped teeth with hard ridges for grinding leaves to break down the plant fibres. The grinding motion wears the teeth down very quickly. Because of this, the teeth grow all the time. Cows and sheep move their jaws sideways as they chew, which helps them grind the food. Try moving your jaws sideways — can you hear your teeth grinding together?

Reach for it

Some animals are specially adapted for eating certain kinds of plant food. Rodents and monkeys have flexible fingers for grasping and picking at food. The giraffe has a long neck which allows it to feed on leaves that other animals cannot reach.

▲ Reach for it! The elephant uses its trunk to pull down branches.

Eating all the time

Plant cells have thick walls made of a material called cellulose, which is very difficult to digest. The plant leaves have to be chewed for a very long time. Some animals, like cows, sheep and deer, have special stomachs for storing undigested food, so they can take in a lot of food in a short time and chew it later. When they have finished feeding, they find a safe sheltered place, and bring the food back into their mouths to chew it. This is called chewing the cud. Cows sit for hours just chewing grass.

A secret army

Animals like cows have a secret army of helpers. In their stomachs are special bacteria which are good at breaking down cellulose. The cow supplies the bacteria with food, and the bacteria help the cow digest the grass.

Liquid food

A few animals feed on nectar from flowers. Butterflies and moths have long tube-like mouthparts for sucking up the nectar. The mouthparts reach deep inside the flower, and can be rolled up out of the way when not in use. Many flowers have special lines and patterns which guide insects to the nectar. Hummingbirds use brush-like tongues to lap up nectar, and so do some bats. Bees not only feed on nectar, but they also collect pollen to eat later, storing it in bristly baskets on their legs.

▲ *Squirrels, mice and chipmunks have long, sharp front teeth for breaking open nuts, and flexible fingers for holding them.*

Did you know?

An adult elephant needs to eat 136 kg of plants a day.

Beavers' teeth are so strong that they can fell trees by gnawing through the tough wood.

Leaf-cutter ants grow their own food. They cultivate fungi in special underground gardens.

More about how plants make their own food (pp.28, 29); leaf-cutter ants (p.44); hummingbirds (pp.74, 91)

Filter feeders

Food you cannot see

Floating in the water of lakes, ponds, rivers and the oceans are millions of tiny plants and animals which cannot be seen by the naked eye. There are also many small particles of dead organic material. Some of them are excreted by living organisms, others are the broken-up remains of dead plants and animals.

Many different animals, both large and small, feed on these tiny pieces of food. They are filter feeders, trapping their food by passing the water through a fine net or sieve. This lets the water through but holds back the particles.

Bristly legs

When they are feeding, barnacles open their cases and comb the water with their bristly legs. Some shrimps and water fleas also use bristle-fringed legs to filter food from the water.

Moving water

Some animals use rows of tiny beating hairs to make their own water currents to bring food in. Sponges are filter feeders — if you look closely at the surface of a sponge you will see lots of tiny holes through which water enters and leaves. Inside the sponge, food particles in the water are trapped by tiny hairs.

Mussels, oysters and clams draw water over their gills where tiny hairs filter out food particles.

Herring and their relatives also use specially adapted gills to sieve food from the water. They swim along with their mouths open so that water flows over the gills.

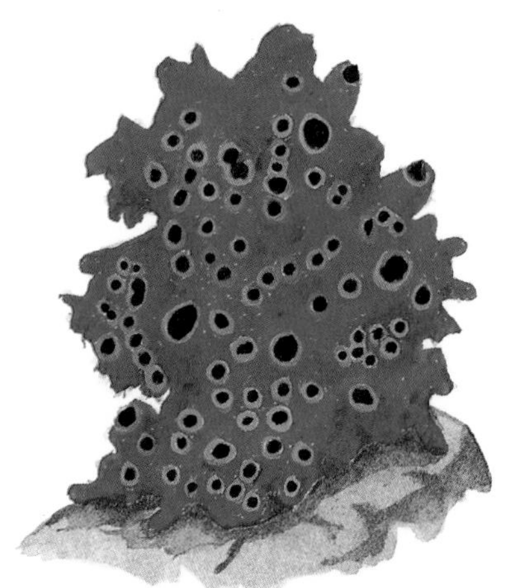

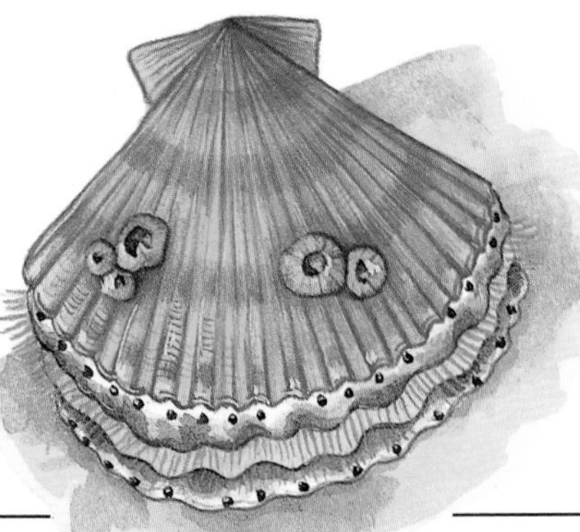

▲ Barnacles filter feeding.

▲ Fan worms live in tubes or burrows on the sea-bed, and put out a fan of feathery tentacles which sift the water for food. Tiny hairs on the tentacles sweep the food particles on to a moving sheet of sticky mucus which carries them into the worm's mouth.

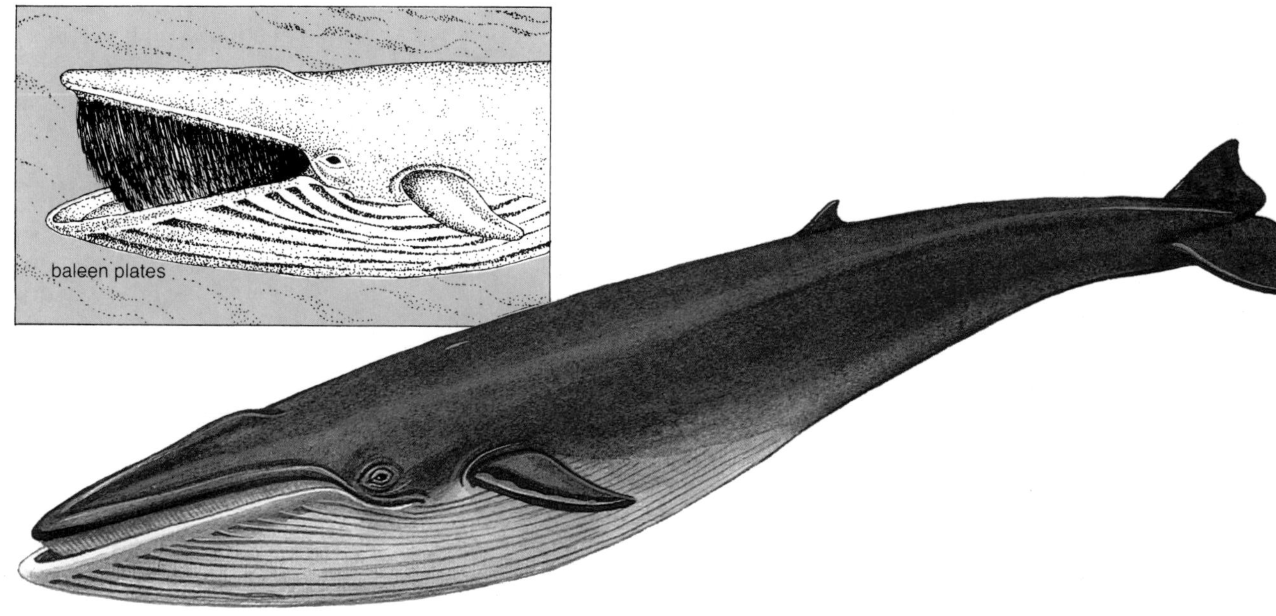

Giant filter feeders

Baleen whales have no teeth. Instead, they have about four hundred large plates of whalebone or 'baleen', which act as a strainer. The whale takes in enormous mouthfuls of water. It then forces the water out over the baleen plates and licks off the food that is left behind, mostly small creatures like plankton and shrimps. The mouth of a baleen whale may take up almost one-third of its body.

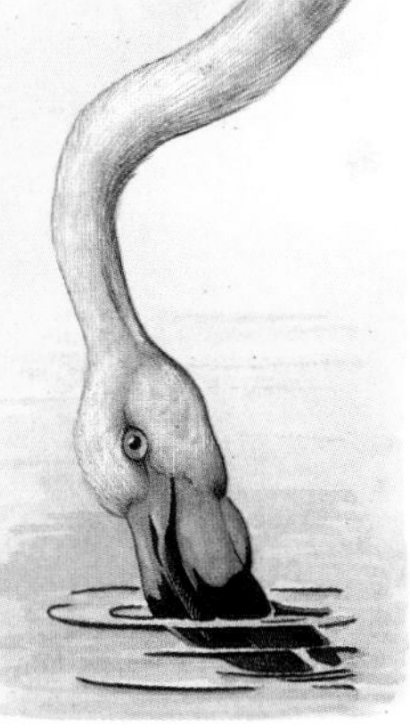

▲ Flamingoes have strange upside-down beaks which they sweep through the water. The edges of the bills are lined with rows of horny plates, forming a strainer that lets water through but traps tiny organisms.

Did you know?

The largest animal in the world, the blue whale, is a filter feeder. It is about 25 m long, and weighs about 130 tonnes, about the size of four large dinosaurs. It will eat 10 tonnes of shrimps in one meal. Each gulp filters 55 litres of water.

The largest bivalve in the world, the giant clam, is also a filter feeder. It can weigh up to 454 kg.

Water fleas have such fine filters that they can trap bacteria which are only 1/1000 mm long.

More about filter feeders in rock pools (p.113); filter-feeding fish (p.117)

Carnivores — the meat-eaters

Carnivores

Animals which eat other animals are called carnivores, which means meat-eaters. Unlike plants, animals move, so carnivores first have to catch their prey.

Ambush!

Many animals ambush their prey. The praying mantis stays very still, its colour blending with its background. When an insect comes within reach, it grabs it with its long front legs. In the lake, pike lie in wait for smaller fish, their striped bodies matching the pattern of sunlight shining through the water weeds. Crocodiles and alligators can lurk just below the water surface, with only their eyes and nostrils above the water, waiting for animals to come to drink at the water's edge.

The chase

Other animals stalk their prey, relying on a fast pounce or a quick chase to catch it. White pelicans work in a team, forming a circle round a shoal of fish and driving them into the centre. Lions also hunt in groups to cut off individual animals from a herd, while cheetahs rely on out-running their prey. Army ants use sheer weight of numbers. Hundreds of them swarm over any small creature on the forest floor, biting and stinging it until it dies.

Stingers and biters

Some animals can take quite large prey by biting or stinging it. Snakes may strike at an animal with poison fangs, then track it until it dies. When they have trapped a fly, spiders rush in and bite it, waiting for their paralysing poison to take effect before wrapping up the victim. Sea anemones and jelly-fish have stinging tentacles which shoot poisoned hooks into any small animal that touches them, paralysing and trapping it at the same time.

▲ *Portuguese man-o'-war jellyfish with trapped fish.*

Clingers

Octopuses, squids and cuttlefish have long curling tentacles armed with rows of suckers which cling to the prey and sweep it into the mouth. Constrictor snakes coil around their victims and squeeze them until they suffocate to death.

Biting and sucking

Meat-eating mammals have special teeth for dealing with their prey. In the front of the mouth are sharp incisors for cutting into meat and scraping it off the bone. Behind them is a pair of long, curved, pointed canines for piercing and stabbing the prey and holding it as it struggles. Next are the big carnassial teeth, which act like shears to slice off flesh and crack bones. Finally, there are the flatter molars for crushing bones and flesh.

The spiders handle their prey the easy way. After wrapping it safely in bands of silk, they dribble digestive juices on to it. They then suck up the dissolved remains.

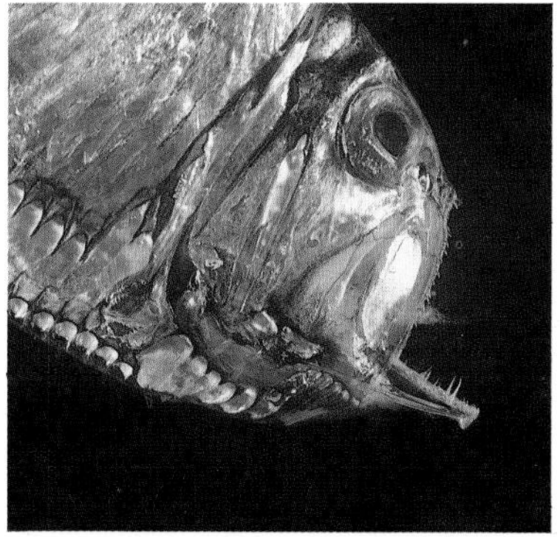

▲ Some animals just open their mouths and wait for their prey to fall in. Swallows, swifts and nightjars fly along with their mouths open to catch flying insects, while the deep-sea hatchetfish swims with its huge mouth wide open to catch fish it can hardly see in the darkness.

▲ An egg-eating snake swallowing the egg of a small bird.

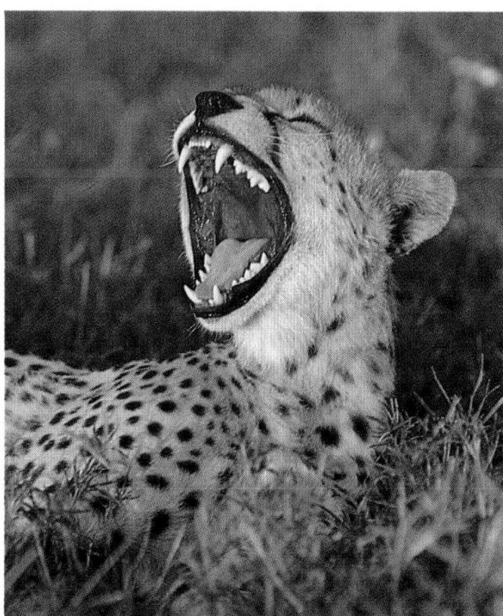

▲ The cheetah's teeth are adapted for eating meat.

Swallowing specials

Some animals swallow their prey whole. The master swallowers are the snakes. They can actually unhinge their jaws to swallow large prey, and their skin is very elastic, stretching around the prey as it moves back through the snake's body.

Stealing a living

Not all carnivores catch their own prey. Some steal the prey of others. Skuas are seabirds which attack other seabirds in the air until they drop the fish they have just caught. Bears will drive wolves off their prey, and packs of hyenas will drive other African mammals, such as lions, away from the carcass they have just killed.

Did you know?

The cheetah is the fastest animal on land. It can run at up to 96 km/h while chasing its prey.

The spine-tailed swift, from Asia, moves even faster, reaching a speed of 170 km/h when flying.

A column of army ants is like a super-animal weighing over 200 kg, with 20 million mouths and stings.

More about animal trappers (pp.48, 49); deceits and disguises (pp.52, 53); hunting in the dark (pp.118, 119, 126, 127)

The insect-eaters

▲ The insect-eating bats hunt in darkness. They find their prey by 'echolocation'. They utter high-pitched squeaks and listen for the echo to bounce back from the flying insects. Their teeth are similar to those of other insectivores, but they use their wing tips to flick insects into their mouths.

Insectivores

Animals which feed mainly on insects are usually specialists. Some have special teeth for crushing the hard shells of insects, others have special ways of catching hundreds of tiny insects at a time. Some catch insects in the air, others hunt them underground.

One group of mammals specializes in eating insects. They are called the insectivores. They include shrews, hedgehogs and moles. The teeth of an insectivore look very alike, with pointed ends for seizing and crushing their prey.

Most insectivores rely on sound and smell to find their prey. Many, like the shrew, have flexible snouts with long sensitive whiskers. Insectivores are usually nocturnal, but some tiny shrews hunt by day and by night. Moles live in the dark most of the time, tunnelling through the soil with huge scoop-shaped paws in search of insects and worms.

The star-nosed mole

The star-nosed mole has a remarkable fleshy star on its nose which is loaded with 22 sensitive feelers which it uses to help find its food.

Close your nose

In the African grasslands the aardvark, or earth pig, raids termite mounds, using its strong claws and long sticky tongue. Its pig-like snout has a fringe of bristles to keep off the termites, and it can close its nostrils for extra protection.

Sticky tongues

Some animals specialize in eating only ants and their relatives, the termites. These are such small insects that they have to eat a lot of them. The anteater is a big lumbering animal with a very good sense of smell and a very long snout. It digs termites out of their large earth mounds with its huge curved claws. Once it has made a hole in the termite mound it pushes in its long sticky tongue. As many as five hundred termites at a time stick to the tongue and are then swallowed. The anteater has a thick skin which protects it against the bites of the termites. Anteaters have no teeth, but grind up the insects using their powerful stomach muscles.

▲ The anteater uses its sticky tongue to pick up its prey. Other insect-eaters also use sticky tongues. The woodpecker drills into tree trunks to find insect grubs, then uses its tongue to get them out. Frogs and toads flick out their tongues to catch passing flies.

The most amazing tongue is that of the chameleon. When stretched out, it is about thirty centimetres long — twice its body length. When not in use, the tongue is folded like a concertina in the mouth. The chameleon can change colour to match its background, so that it is almost invisible to its prey. Its eyes are on little turrets, and can look in different directions at the same time, useful for spotting approaching insects. Once it has seen its prey, the chameleon focuses both eyes on it and very slowly gets into position to attack, holding on to its branch firmly. Then the tongue flicks out, the insect sticks to its tip, and it flicks back into the mouth, all in the space of four-hundredths of a second.

Did you know?

Savi's white-toothed pigmy shrew, an insect-eater, is the smallest mammal in the world, only 6 cm long, including its tail. It weighs 1.5 g.

The giant anteater has a tongue 60 cm long.

A toad can flick its tongue out and back in 1/10th of a second.

The aardvark is one of the fastest burrowers in the world. It can dig a hole with its claws faster than a man can with a spade.

More about ants and anteaters (p.105); animal senses (pp.50, 51)

Scavengers and decomposers

▼ Small corpses are often buried. Burying-beetles dig away the soil underneath the corpse to form a pit, into which the corpse falls. Then they lay their eggs in the dead flesh. The eggs hatch into grubs which feed on the corpse.

The great disappearing act

Plants and animals are always multiplying. If they lived forever, the Earth would soon become overcrowded. But plants and animals die of old age or disease, or are killed and eaten by other animals. This prevents their numbers from becoming too large.

Yet we do not see many dead animals and plants. The leaves that fall in autumn slowly disappear, old tree trunks rot, and animal carcasses are soon reduced to heaps of bones. Many different organisms are involved in this disappearing act. Scavengers feed off the carcasses, and decomposers break down the dead organic matter into smaller and smaller pieces. The mineral salts and other nutrients of the dead material are released into the soil or the sea, ready to become part of new living organisms.

Scavengers large and small

Some animals specialize in scavenging. Hyenas and jackals of the African plains can hunt their own prey, but usually feed on animals which are already dead — the remains of lion kills, or animals that have died of disease or old age.

Vultures eat only carrion (dead meat). They are big, powerful birds with hooked bills for stripping skin and flesh. Their heads and necks are usually bald, with no feathers to be messed up when they are feeding on the carcasses.

Along the sea-shore, seagulls scavenge for food washed ashore by the tide. They also follow ships at sea to feed on the waste that is thrown overboard.

▼ Dung beetles bury animal dung, making it into a large ball which they roll to a safe place.

Underwater scavengers

In the sea, some fish scavenge on the corpses of other fish. The hagfish has a long eel-like body which it wriggles into carcasses. Mullet feed on particles of organic matter which sink to the sea-bed, feeling for them with tentacles on their snouts. Crabs scavenge along the shore and on the sea-bed.

▲ Crab scavenging on the sea-shore.

Many different sea creatures, from shrimps and barnacles to sea fans and tube worms, filter organic particles from the water. Some tiny pond animals feed like this too.

If it were not for all the scavengers and decomposers on land and in the sea, the living world would soon run out of nutrients, and there would be no future generations of living creatures.

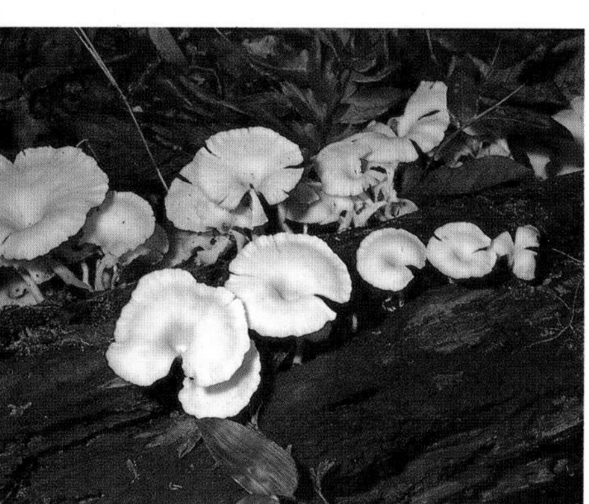

◀ The most important decomposers are the fungi and bacteria. The fungi form a hidden network of threads covering the undersides of dead leaves, rotting wood, dung, carcasses and decaying pieces of organic matter in the soil. These fungus threads pour digestive juices on the dead material and absorb it. Bacteria feed on dead material, helping it to decay. Millions of them occur in the soil, in ponds and lakes, and in the sea.

Hidden decomposers

Flies lay their eggs in corpses and dung pats. The eggs hatch into maggots which feed on the dead meat or the dung. Some moth larvae can even digest the horns of dead animals. In the tropics, termites feed on wood, and all over the world wood-boring beetles, like the death-watch beetles, and their grubs, the 'woodworms' chew tunnels in tree trunks, furniture and house timbers.

Slugs and snails, millipedes, woodlice and worms all feed on dead and decaying organic matter in the soil.

Did you know?

A pair of burying-beetles can bury a mouse in just a few minutes.

Museums use carrion beetles to clean bones for exhibits.

A dung beetle only 2 cm long can bury 100 cm^3 of dung in one night.

More about life in the soil (p.94); scavengers on the seashore (p.113)

Living together

Feeding each other

Some of the commonest partners in symbiosis are algae. These are tiny one-celled plants, small enough to live inside the cells of other organisms. Algae make their own food by a process called photosynthesis. They use water, carbon dioxide gas from the air, and energy from sunlight. During this process they produce oxygen, which animals need to breathe, and sugars and proteins, which are then used by their partners. Animals breathe out carbon dioxide, the gas which the algae need for photosynthesis.

Many algae live protected inside animal cells. The bright colours of corals, the green of hydra and the brilliant blues of the mantles of giant clams (below) are all caused by algae in their tissues.

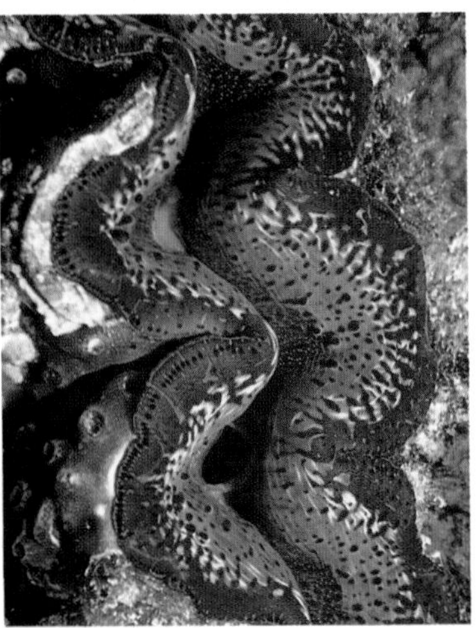

Symbiosis

Sometimes quite different animals and plants live and work together. This kind of close relationship between different living organisms is called symbiosis, which means 'living together'.

One example of symbiosis can be seen in Africa. A small bird, called a honeyguide, likes to eat wild bee grubs and wax, but the honeyguide cannot break open the bees' nest to reach them. So it attracts the attention of a honey badger (who is fond of honey) by bobbing in front of it and leading it to the bees' nest. The badger uses its sharp claws to tear open the nest, so that both of them can feed. In this case both partners are better off together than on their own. This kind of symbiosis is called mutualism.

The protection game

Some symbiotic animals can get on very well without their partners, but they usually choose to live or work together. Hermit crabs often have sea anemones riding on their shells. Some hermit crabs will actually pick up the anemones and place them on their backs. It seems likely that the anemone's stinging tentacles put off predators who might attack the crab, while the anemone gets a free ride to new feeding grounds. It also eats the crab's left-overs.

Nature's cleaners

Another protection game occurs in the sea. This time the enemies are parasites — animals that live on, or inside, other animals or plants, and get food or shelter from them. In the sea, some parasites cling to the scales of fish, and feed on their flesh. In turn, cleaner fish feed on these parasites. This cleaning activity is very important to the fish. So important, that fish that are usually enemies queue together at special 'cleaning stations'. Many fish spend as much time being cleaned as they do hunting for food. The cleaner has easy-to-recognize bright stripes. To signal that it is a cleaner, and not a tasty meal, it has very distinctive bright stripes, and does a special dance. The large fish will open their mouths, and even their gills, for the little cleaner.

On land, tick-birds and oxpeckers stand on cattle and other grazing animals, and feed on the parasites in their fur and skin. One bird, the Egyptian plover, is said to clean inside the open mouths of crocodiles.

▲ A lichen is made up of a fungus and an alga, which work together as one organism. Lichens can grow even on bare rock. They are found all over the world, from the hottest deserts to the edges of permanent snow and ice where no other plants can grow.

Mutual protection

Brightly coloured clownfish live among the stinging tentacles of coral reef anemones. These protect them from enemies. But the clownfish also protect the anemone, chasing off other fish that would like to eat the soft tentacles.

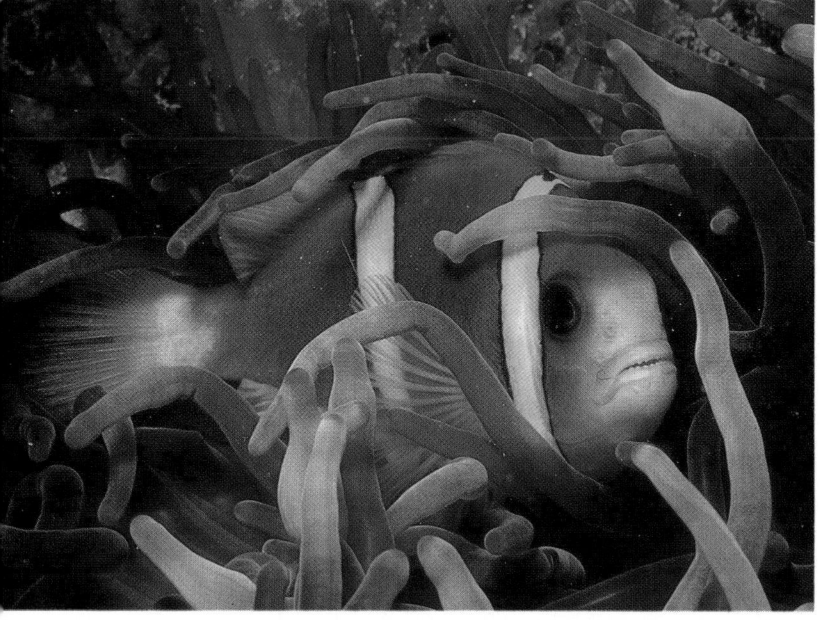

Did you know?

The smallest zoo on Earth? A termite just a few millimetres long is not a single organism, but anything from 10 to 100 different organisms, all depending upon each other. In addition, bacteria and other tiny one-celled organisms live in its gut. They break down the tough fibres of the wood it eats, and make substances the termite can use.

Many plants, especially forest trees, have a layer of fungi around their roots. These fungi absorb valuable nutrients from the soil and pass them to the plant.

More about living together (pp.44, 45); corals (pp.120,121); photosynthesis (pp.28, 29); parasites (p.45)

Living together

One-sided friendships

It is easy to see how both partners can benefit from living together. But sometimes only one partner appears to benefit. The antbirds of tropical forests use ants to flush out their prey. They fly just ahead of the marching columns of army ants, feeding on the insects fleeing before them. But the ants do not benefit. This type of association is called commensalism, which means 'eating at the same table'. The partner which benefits is called the commensal.

Fungus gardens

Ants form many symbiotic partnerships. Leaf-cutter ants cut up vast numbers of leaves and take them to a garden deep inside the ant nest. Here they grow a special fungus, which is found only in ant nests. The ants cannot digest the tough plant food, but the fungus can. It grows special knobs of fungus for the ants to eat. The ants provide the fungus with leaf pieces and a warm shelter. They also weed out any other fungi that try to grow in the garden.

▲ Leaf-cutter ants on trail.

▼ Ants with aphids.

▼ Humans are also involved in symbiosis. In our guts we have millions of bacteria, which help us break down the vegetables and fruit we eat. We farm crops and animals for food and milk. We also grow fungi — mushrooms to eat, yeast to make bread and alcohol, and microscopic fungi and bacteria to make cheese and yoghurt.

Ant farmers

Other ants farm aphids (greenfly), sheltering them in the ant nest at night and leading them up the food plants to eat by day, guarding them against predators. The aphids feed on plant sap, but they take in too much sugar. This extra sugar is squeezed out of the aphids as droplets of honeydew. The ants can make the aphids produce honeydew by stroking them. Then the ants feed on the honeydew.

Unwelcome guests

Not all partners are welcome. Many animals and plants live at the expense of others. They are called parasites. Fleas and lice cling to the skin of other animals (their 'hosts') and suck their blood. Mosquitoes are temporary visitors, stopping only for a quick drink of blood. Leeches, ticks and mites have bodies like elastic bags, which stretch as they fill up with blood. Some ticks can live for a whole year on a single meal of blood.

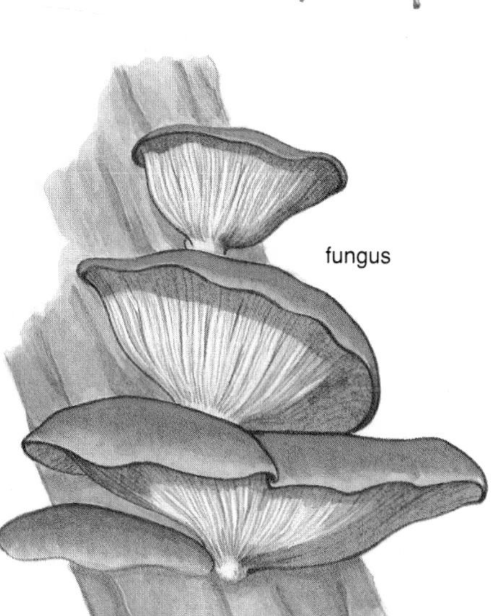

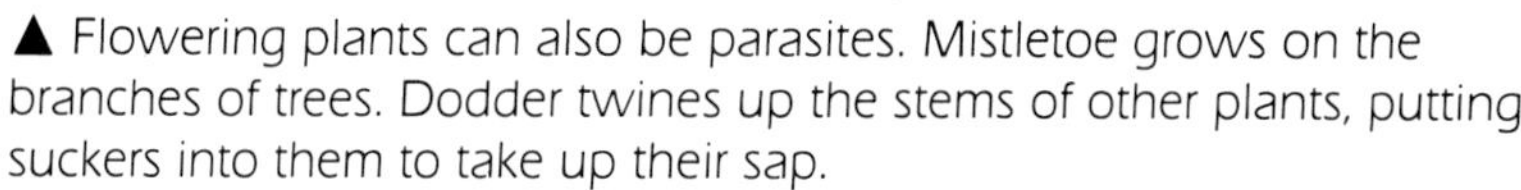

▲ Flowering plants can also be parasites. Mistletoe grows on the branches of trees. Dodder twines up the stems of other plants, putting suckers into them to take up their sap.

Some parasites live inside their hosts. Tapeworms live in the guts of other animals, absorbing the ready-digested food and enjoying warmth and protection. Many fungi live in, or on, other living organisms. Some cause lung and skin diseases, including athlete's foot. Others live in the trunks of living trees, making them rot.

Animal, vegetable or mineral?

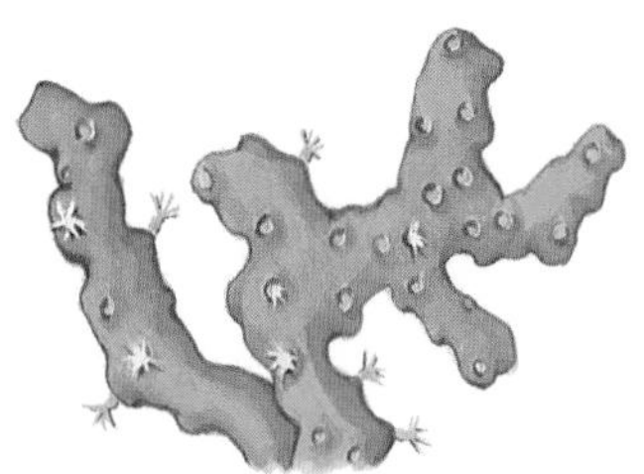

This coral is really all three. The coral is an animal which secretes a mineral skeleton around itself, and contains in its tissues colourful tiny plants (algae).

Did you know?

The bull's horn acacia tree has its own private army — colonies of ants living in its hollow thorns. These ants drive off any animal, large or small, that tries to feed on the acacia. They even weed out stray seedlings from around the base of the tree. As well as shelter, the tree provides food for the ants in the form of sugary nectar and special round knobs containing oil and protein.

The largest flower in the world, *Rafflesia,* is a parasite of tropical vines. The flower is up to 1 m wide, and weighs 7 kg.

More about living together (pp.42, 43); corals (pp.120, 121); plant-eating bacteria (p.43)

Plants of prey

▲ **Jug-of-water trap** (pitcher plant)
The leaf is shaped like a jug or pitcher. Insects landing on the rim of the jug slide down the slippery slope to the inside. They land at the bottom of the jug. Waxy scales make the slope slippery. They stick to the insect's feet like small skis, and make it slide down quickly.

Fact or fiction

A famous author, H.G. Wells, once wrote a story called *The First Men on the Moon*. It was about some plants which could capture and eat humans. Another book, by John Wyndham, called *The Day of the Triffids*, told the story of a group of plants which tried to destroy all humans. Neither of these stories was based on fact. Plants like that do not exist. However, some plants can trap very small animals, such as insects. The animal is killed, often by drowning, or simply by being digested by plant juices as it lies trapped. Sometimes the plants catch even larger animals, like baby frogs. Plants which trap animals are called carnivorous plants.

Plants and energy

All green plants make their own food. They capture the Sun's energy and use it to make sugars in their leaves. This process is called photosynthesis. Green plants also take in mineral salts from the soil. They use these salts and the sugars they make to build all the materials they need. Some plants live in poor soils which do not have all the important mineral salts. Boggy soils and marshland are like this. The plants living in them must find other sources of minerals. Carnivorous plants are sometimes found in marshy and boggy areas, although they also grow in other soils, especially in the tropics.

Different types of trap

▼ **Sticky-surface trap** (sundew)
This trap captures its prey by means of a sticky substance. Other traps have small tentacles on the surface of the leaf. These have sticky heads which catch insects.

▼ **Snap-trap** (Venus fly-trap)
This is made of a hinged leaf. When the trap is set the leaf lies flat and open. An insect landing on the leaf touches sensitive hairs. These trigger the leaf to close and the insect is trapped inside.

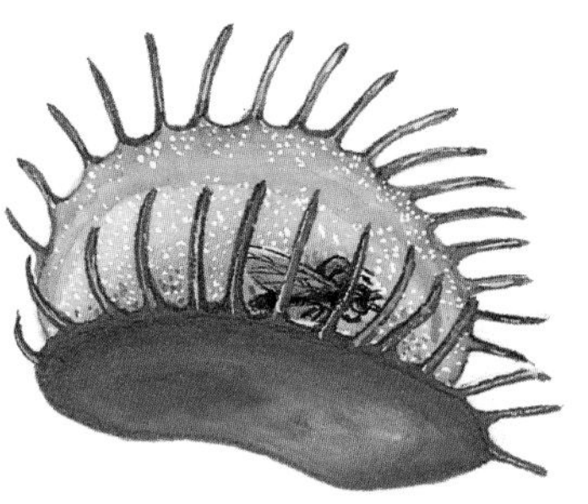

▲ **Suction trap** (bladderwort)
Suction traps are usually found in water plants. Each trap is like a tiny ball. It has a small trap-door or lid. This opens to let the animal be sucked in with a rush of water. The trap-door closes once the animal is caught.

Trapping the prey

There are many different kinds of carnivorous plant. They are found in various shapes and sizes. Even though they look different, these plants have some things in common. They have a bait to attract their prey. They also have a trap in which to catch the prey. Plants are not able to move like animals. Instead, they have to lure or attract their prey to them. They do this by means of colour, smell and a sugary liquid called nectar. If the animal takes the bait it becomes trapped. After this it is killed and digested. In some plants, the trap must be reset after the animal has been eaten. The plant can then catch another animal. Carnivorous plants have different kinds of trap and they catch their prey in different ways. The pictures opposite show the four main types of trap used by carnivorous plants.

The daredevils inside traps

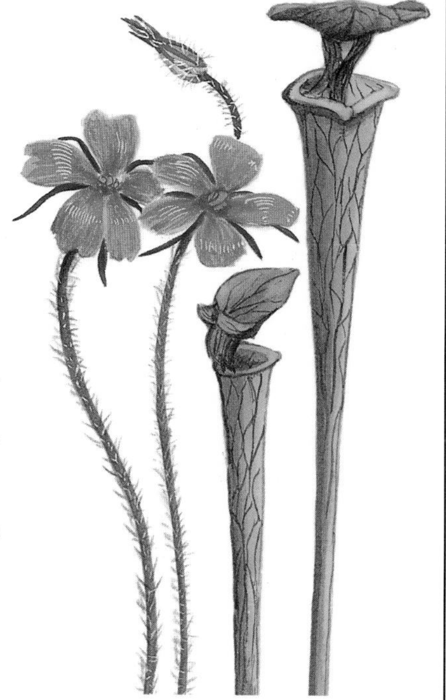

Some animals are able to live quite happily within these deadly traps. A small bug lives on the leaves of a plant called *Byblis* which grows in Australia. This plant sets a sticky-surface trap like the ones set by sundews. The small bug is able to walk on the trap without getting stuck. It avoids capture and digestion. We don't yet know how this bug escapes being caught and eaten. A species of fly has found a way of living inside the trap of the American pitcher plant, *Sarracenia*. The maggots of the fly crawl in the digestive juices at the bottom of the trap, but they are not digested. A species of mosquito also lives in the same sort of trap. It is even able to carry out its life cycle within the trap. The adult mosquito enters and leaves the trap like a tiny helicopter. Even small bladderwort traps contain animals living inside them. It is puzzling that the animals do not come to any harm.

The body-snatcher

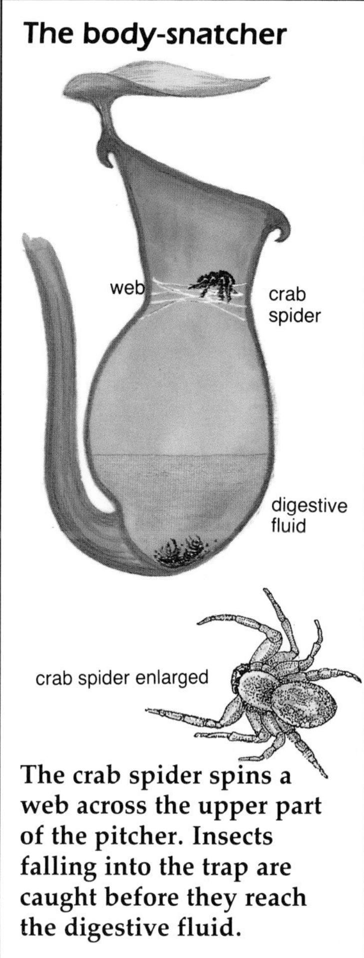

The crab spider spins a web across the upper part of the pitcher. Insects falling into the trap are caught before they reach the digestive fluid.

Did you know?

Some pitcher plants may catch thousands of insects in a few weeks.

The Portuguese sundew takes about a day to digest a small insect.

A Venus fly-trap can catch a small frog.

More about photosynthesis (pp.28, 29); trappers (pp.48, 49)

Animal trappers

Come into my parlour

Most animals find their food by moving around. Plant eaters need to move around to find new vegetation on which to feed. Carnivores rely on their senses and speed to catch their prey. Some animals have solved the problem of catching food in another way. These animals live a much less active life. Instead of looking for food, they let their prey come to them. These are the 'trappers' of the animal world.

Different kinds of trap

There are many different kinds of trap. Each one is designed to catch its victim in a different way. Some traps are simple in structure and need few building skills. Others are very complicated and take a long time to make. Most 'trappers' catch their prey by means of pits, trap-doors, snares, nets or webs. Some specialized animals use a 'fishing line' technique. Whatever type of trap is used, it has to be kept in good working order. The animal must also repair the trap if it becomes damaged. Some traps must be reset when they have been used.

A silken trap

A poisonous spider from Australia builds a trap similar to that of the ant lion. It makes a burrow lined with silk. The entrance to the burrow is woven into a funnel shape. The spider feeds on small animals which fall into the funnel.

The waiting jaws

The ant lion, found mainly in the tropics, is the larval form of an insect which looks like a damsel fly. The female lays her eggs in fine, sandy soil in a sunny place. When each egg hatches, the tiny ant lion larva digs a funnel-shaped pit. The ant lion hides at the bottom of the pit with only its head and pincer-like jaws showing. If an insect, such as an ant, falls into the pit, it slides to the bottom and into the large, powerful jaws of the ant lion.

Behind the trap-door

Trap-door spiders hunt by night. The trap-door is kept closed during the day. At night, the spider keeps the door half-open, its front legs sticking out. When an insect comes near it touches trip lines of silk which the spider has laid down. This alerts the spider which pounces on the insect and drags it into its tube. The trap-door closes automatically.

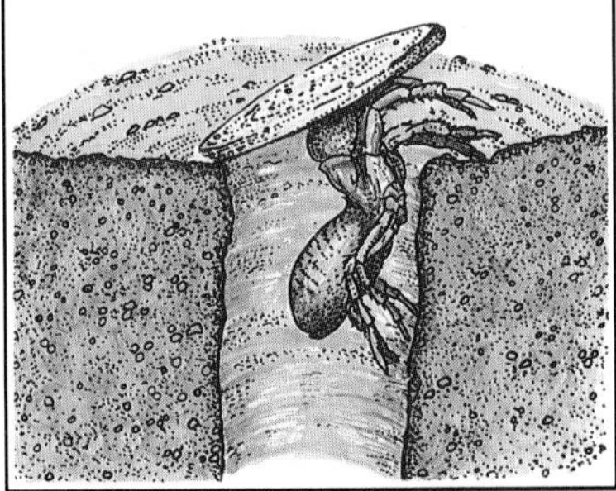

Setting a trap

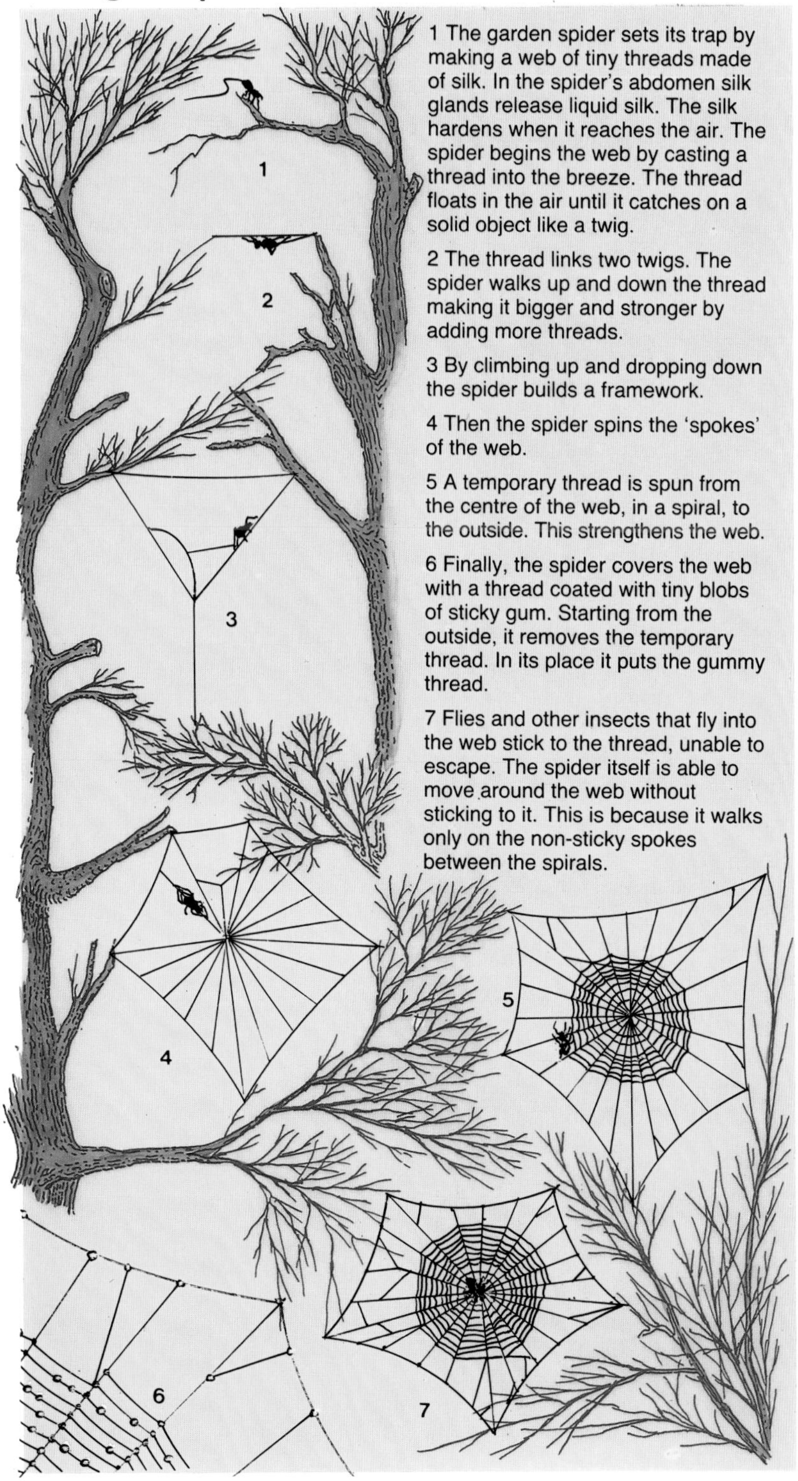

1 The garden spider sets its trap by making a web of tiny threads made of silk. In the spider's abdomen silk glands release liquid silk. The silk hardens when it reaches the air. The spider begins the web by casting a thread into the breeze. The thread floats in the air until it catches on a solid object like a twig.

2 The thread links two twigs. The spider walks up and down the thread making it bigger and stronger by adding more threads.

3 By climbing up and dropping down the spider builds a framework.

4 Then the spider spins the 'spokes' of the web.

5 A temporary thread is spun from the centre of the web, in a spiral, to the outside. This strengthens the web.

6 Finally, the spider covers the web with a thread coated with tiny blobs of sticky gum. Starting from the outside, it removes the temporary thread. In its place it puts the gummy thread.

7 Flies and other insects that fly into the web stick to the thread, unable to escape. The spider itself is able to move around the web without sticking to it. This is because it walks only on the non-sticky spokes between the spirals.

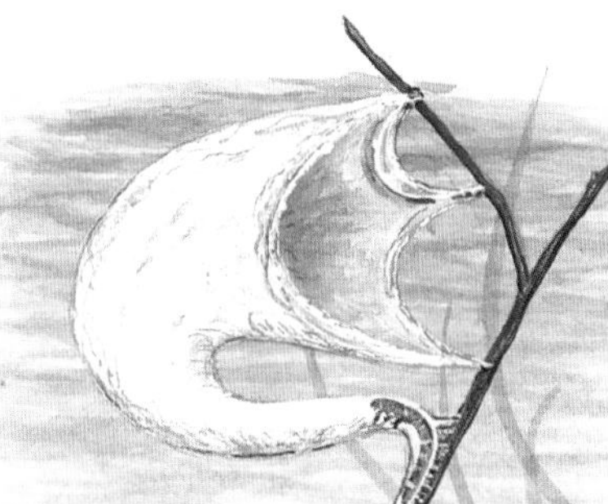

The larva of one kind of caddis fly lives in water. It builds a 'fishing net' from silk. The net is funnel-shaped. The larva stays in the narrow part of the funnel. It feeds on small animals caught in the net. The flowing water keeps the net open.

Did you know?

An Australian spider called *Dinopis* holds a sheet of sticky web in its front legs. It drops the sheet over a passing insect, like a gladiator's net.

The bolas spider, from Australia, dangles a long thread with a sticky blob on its end. It swings the thread round and round and catches insects on the sticky blob.

Glow-worms living in caves in New Zealand catch their prey on fine threads hung from the roof. The threads are covered with glowing droplets to attract the prey.

More about carnivores (pp.36, 37); animals in ambush (pp.109, 111); animal trappers (p.119)

Animal senses

Senses

We use our senses to find out about the world around us. We look, listen, smell, taste and touch. Most of all we look. Animals have the same senses, but different animals rely on different senses as their main source of information. Animals use their senses to find food, to warn them of danger, and even to attract a mate.

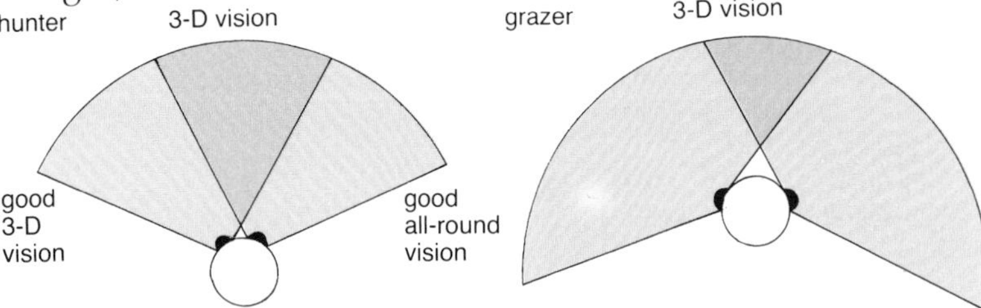

Seeing is believing

You can tell a lot about an animal's way of life by looking at its eyes. If it relies a lot on sight, its eyes will be relatively big. If it is a hunting animal, like the tiger, its eyes will be placed towards the front of its head, so that the fields of view of the two eyes overlap. This allows it to judge distance accurately for pouncing on prey. Animals with many predators, like the rabbit, usually have eyes at the sides of their heads. They can spot a predator coming from almost every angle, but they are not very good at judging distance.

Not all animals see in colour. Many see only in black-and-white. Some, like dogs and squirrels, are partly colour-blind, and cannot see reds and greens. Their world is a blue and yellow one. Bees can see colours we cannot see. They see ultraviolet light. Many flowers look dull to us, but have bright patterns on them when viewed by a bee.

▼ Insects have compound eyes made up of lots of tiny lenses.

Some unusual senses

Some animals have senses we do not have. The rattle-snake has hollows on each side of its head which contain heat-sensing cells. It can find warm-blooded prey, like mice, even in the dark, by sensing the direction from which the warmth is coming. Some fish can give off and detect electricity. They use electricity to find their prey, rather like bats use echolocation. Most animals can detect gravity, and use the information to keep themselves the right way up, and to balance. Some birds and whales can even detect the Earth's magnetism, and use it for navigation.

Feeling the vibrations

Fish and tadpoles have a sensitive line running along the side of the body which can detect movements in the water.

▼ The chameleon can look in two directions at once.

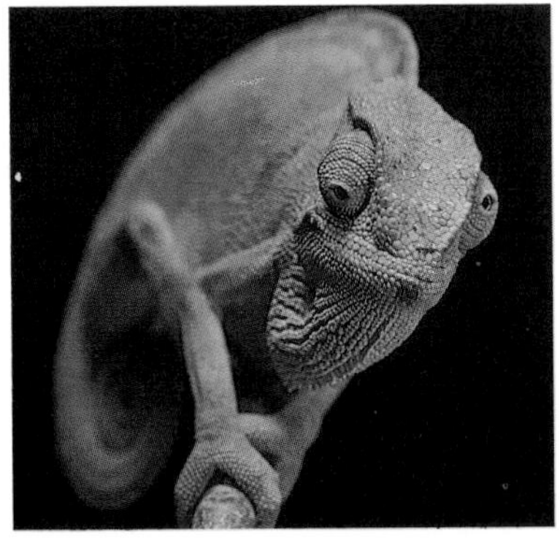

Smell and taste

Most animals have a much better sense of smell than we do. Backboned animals use their nostrils to smell. Insects have scent detectors on their feelers. Male moths have very large feelers to pick up the special scent given off by the female moth.

We taste with our tongues, but many animals, including fish, have taste sensors all over their bodies. Butterflies taste with their feet.

▲ The snake's flickering forked tongue wafts scent particles back to special smell sensors in the roof of its mouth.

Hearing without ears

Only mammals have big ear flaps. Some mammals, such as dogs and deer, can twist their ear flaps towards the source of sound. Crocodiles and seals close their ears when they are underwater. Frogs, lizards and birds have no ear flaps at all.

Hearing is particularly important for animals which hunt and feed by night. Bats find their prey by sending out high-pitched sounds (so high that we cannot hear them), and listening for the echoes. This is called echolocation.

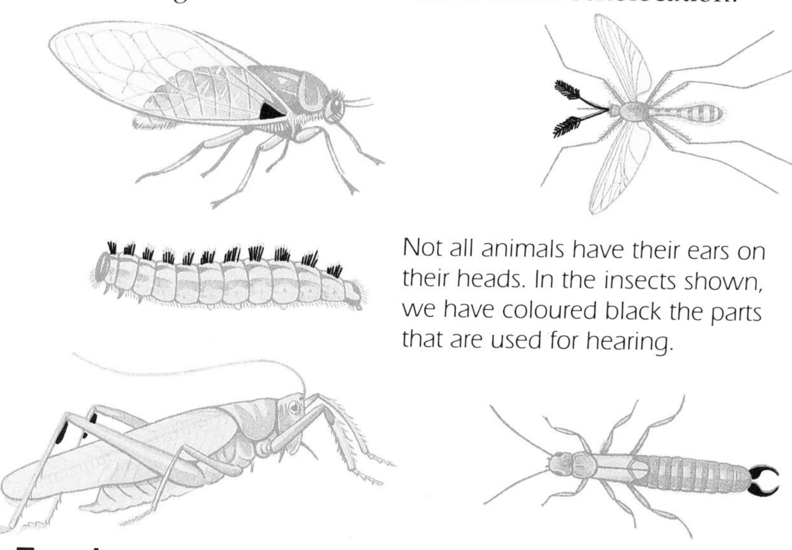

Not all animals have their ears on their heads. In the insects shown, we have coloured black the parts that are used for hearing.

Touch

Our skin is covered in tiny cells which detect pressure. This gives us the sense of touch. Our fingers are especially sensitive to touch. We use them to handle and investigate objects. Insects have touch sensors on their antennae. Watch a wasp crawling across a path. See how it waves its antennae over the ground ahead. Touch is particularly important for nocturnal animals, such as cats and mice. The long whiskers on their snouts are sensitive to touch.

Did you know?

Fish have no eyelids. They sleep with their eyes open.

The largest eye in the world belongs to the giant squid. It is 370 cm in diameter, 123 times as big as the human eye.

Sound travels faster in water than in air. Whales can hear each other's calls when they are hundreds of kilometres apart.

The tip of your tongue is more sensitive to touch than your fingertips. Why do you think that is? Answer on page 152.

More about using senses in the dark (pp.118, 125, 126, 127); attracting a mate (pp.64, 65)

Camouflage

The art of disguise

Some animals are very difficult to see. They match their backgrounds, or look like other objects. It can be useful to have such disguises. The animals may need to hide from their enemies, or they may need to ambush or sneak up on their prey without being noticed.

Many animals simply blend in to their backgrounds. Moths that rest on tree bark may be mottled grey and brown. Lions blend with the dried grasses of the African plains, and fish are often silvery-blue. Many tiny animals that float in the sunlit waters of lakes and oceans are transparent, so that their background shows through them.

Some animals look like inedible objects. Moths, grasshoppers, katydids, and even tropical toads, may look like dead leaves, with vein-like patterns. Desert mantids often look like stones.

▲ This praying mantis looks like a flower. It catches insects which fly straight into its arms.

▲ This katydid is pretending to be a dead leaf.

▲ How many moths can you see on this tree?

Acting the part

Just matching the background is not always a good enough disguise. If an animal moves, its shadow may give it away. Many camouflaged caterpillars and moths do not move at all by day, but feed at night. Stick insects and leaf-like praying mantids will stay motionless by day, or sway gently in the breeze. The potoo is a bird the colour of tree bark. When resting, it sits on top of a small tree trunk and flattens its head on its shoulders to look like the end of a branch.

Confusing colours

How many zebra can you see? Predators often recognize their prey by its shape. Patterns like the stripes of a zebra and the blotches of a giraffe break up the animal's outline.

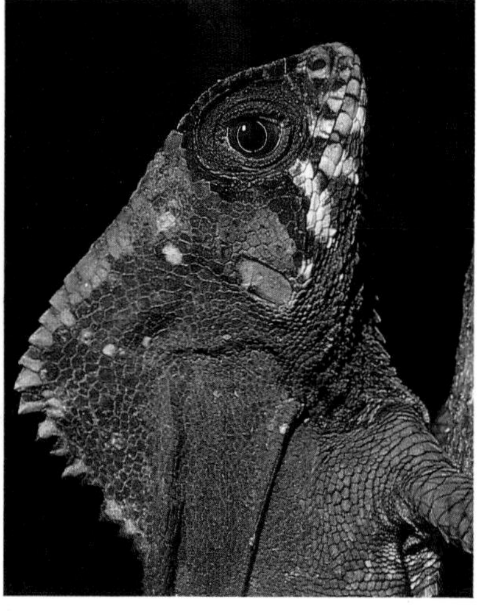

Changing colour

Some animals can change colour. The chameleon and related lizards are good at this. They can change from pale green to dark grey on different backgrounds and in different lighting conditions. The plaice, which lives on the sea-bed, can even match a chessboard put under it.

Hiding shadows

Shadows are a real give-away. In the sunshine, an animal looks paler on top and darker underneath as a result of shading. Some moths have fringes along the edges of their wings to break up their shadows when they are resting on tree trunks.

Mammals like the antelopes that graze on the African plains often have 'countershading'. They are light below and dark above, so the effect of shading is cancelled out.

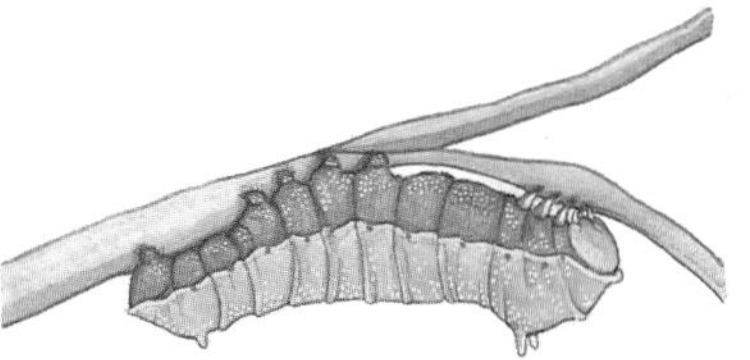

▲ Caterpillars that live upside-down on twigs have their shading the 'wrong' way up.

In the sea, fish are often dark on top so that seabirds will not see them against the dark water below, and light underneath, so that predators below them cannot see them against the bright sunlit water above. Some fish have shiny reflective sides so that they do not look like dark shapes when seen from the side.

Did you know?

Some caterpillars and spiders look just like bird droppings.

Decorator crabs attach pieces of seaweed and other materials to their backs so that they look like their surroundings.

Some plant bugs are shaped like thorns to deceive their enemies.

More about defence (pp.54, 55); camouflage (pp.102, 117, 118, 121); countershading (p.84)

On the defensive

Food for thought

With so many animals living by killing and eating other animals, it is not surprising that the victims have developed various ways of defending themselves. Plants, too, have defences against the animals that would like to eat them.

Armour-plating

Some animals, like the armadillo, have their own armour-plating. Oysters and mussels can simply shut their shells, and snails and turtles can retreat inside their shells. Horns, antlers and claws can all be useful weapons for defending yourself. Many caterpillars are covered in spines which make them unpleasant to eat. Plants also use spines to keep off browsing animals. Who wants to eat a cactus? Or a thorny rose stem?

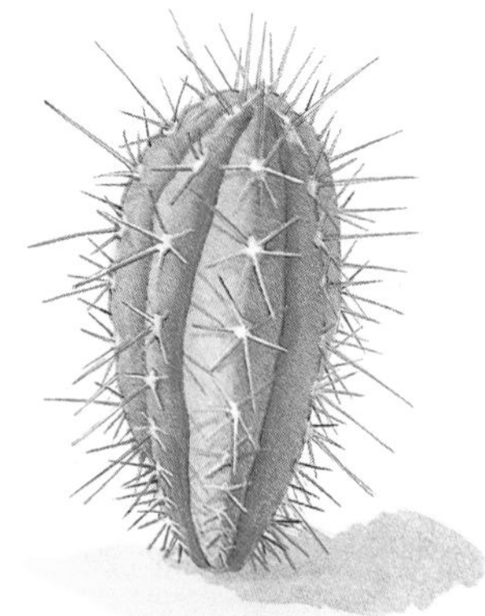

▲ Who wants to eat a cactus?

▼ Sometimes it is enough just to startle the attacker. Many insects have brilliantly coloured underwings which flash into view as they fly off. Some lizards have coloured throat pouches that can inflate very quickly. The frilled lizard can unfold a huge fan of skin all around its head, making itself look very fierce indeed. Squids and octopuses squirt out clouds of purple 'ink' which hide their escape.

Larger than life

A quick increase in size can scare off a predator. Frightened cats arch their backs, fluff out their fur and hiss. Owls will spread their wings and raise their feathers if disturbed. This pufferfish has quickly inflated itself into a round ball covered in spines, making it impossible to swallow.

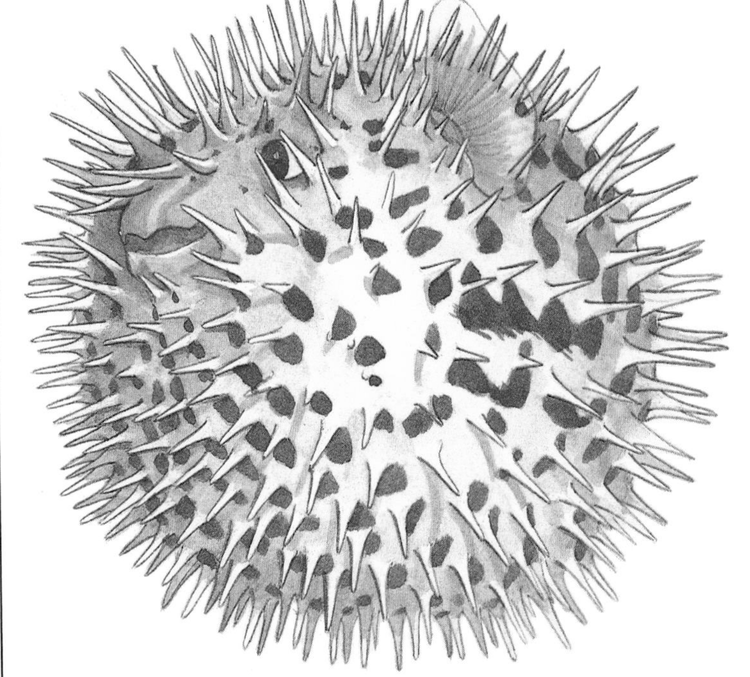

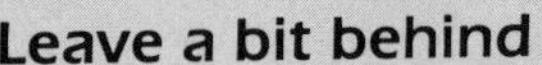

Leave a bit behind

Some lizards have tails which can break off, leaving a surprised predator holding the twitching tail. The lizard grows a new tail later. Many butterflies and moths have a loose coating of scales on their wings, which they can leave behind as they flee.

Stingers and biters

The best defence is sometimes attack. Bees, wasps and hornets have stings. Many animals, from ants to snakes, will bite if attacked. Often they are brightly coloured so that a predator will easily recognize them and soon learn to leave them alone.

A nasty taste

Warning colours are also used by animals which taste unpleasant, like some caterpillars, frogs and salamanders. Whip-scorpions or 'vinegaroons' squirt acid at their attackers, and skunks produce a foul-smelling liquid. Some plants ooze poisonous sap if injured.

Poisonous hairs and spines are also good defences. It can be fatal to step on the camouflaged spines of a stonefish. Hairy caterpillars can cause skin rashes, and poison ivy and stinging nettles are definitely not for picking.

Running away

You can always try running away. Leaf hoppers and frogs can leap great distances if threatened. Hares and antelopes are excellent long distance runners, and can soon tire out a predator that gives chase.

Dead or alive?

If all else fails, you can pretend to be dead, as many predators will only attack moving animals. Snakes and opossums and many beetles use this trick, staying perfectly still and limp until the enemy has gone away.

▼ Snake pretending to be dead.

Whose eyes are these?

Another way to look larger than life is to have a big pair of eyes. Some moths will spread their wings if disturbed. The underwings have two big eye-spots which look like part of a large face. The puss-moth caterpillar inflates its body until two large false eye-spots appear over its head, giving it a fierce face. One South American frog has large eye-spots on its backside. When threatened, it raises its rump to its attacker.

Did you know?

Ladybirds produce poisonous blood from their knee joints when threatened.

Some fish give a predator a short sharp shock – an electric shock.

Some plants can warn other plants of approaching predators by means of chemicals which they waft through the air.

More about animals in armour (pp.22, 23); warning colours (pp.56, 57); camouflage (pp.52, 53)

Mimicry

monarch

viceroy

Look-alikes

Some animals, called mimics, look so like other animals or plants, their models, that the two creatures are easily confused. These two butterflies are from different families. The one on the left is the monarch butterfly. Caterpillars of the monarch butterfly feed on poisonous milkweed plants, and, as butterflies, their flesh is poisonous to their predators. It makes the predators very ill, but does not kill them. Once a predator has tasted a monarch, it wants to avoid eating another one. It can easily recognize other monarchs by their bright colours. The butterfly on the right is the viceroy. It is harmless, but predators avoid it, mistaking it for the monarch.

Acting the part

An animal may mimic its model in behaviour to improve the deception. Perhaps the most surprising wasp mimic is the wasp beetle. It does not have transparent wings, but to look more convincing, it moves in short darting runs like a wasp.

Ant-mimic spiders have slender ant-like bodies. They hold their front legs up like feelers and dash to and fro like the ants they are hunting.

Stick caterpillars are coloured like twigs. To improve the deception they grip the branch and hold their stiff bodies away from the branch to look like twigs. They may not move all day.

Warning stripes

The bright black-and-yellow stripes of the wasp warn of its vicious sting. Lots of different insects have the wasp's colours — hoverflies, lacewings, beetles and even a moth which has a striped body and transparent wings.

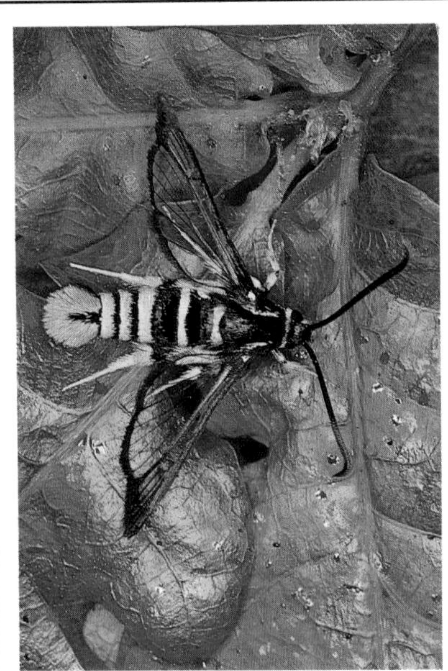
◀ Wasp-mimic moth.

▼ Wasp beetle.

▲ Red and yella', kill a fella'. ▼ Red and black, friend of Jack.

▲ Some plants look like animals. Bee orchids have furry bee-coloured petals, and give off a scent like that of a female bee. The orchid needs to receive pollen from another orchid flower in order to produce seeds. Male bees are attracted to the flower and try to mate with it. In the process, the orchid pollen sticks to their bodies. Pollen from other orchids the bees have visited rubs off on the orchid.

Red and black, friend of Jack

In North and South America there are many different species of coral snake. Many of them are very poisonous. Coral snakes have bright red, black and yellowish-white warning stripes. Harmless kingsnakes living in the same area also have red, black and whitish stripes. Local people distinguish between the harmful and harmless snakes by the order of colours of the stripes.

Dangerous deceits

Sometimes only one part of an animal mimics something else. The alligator-snapping turtle has a fleshy red flap of tissue on the floor of its mouth, which it wiggles so it looks like a worm. The turtle opens its mouth and wiggles its lure. Small fish, thinking they can catch the worm, swim right into the turtle's open jaws.

Anglerfish use the same deceit. Wiggly lures grow out from their chins or dangle above their mouths. Many have huge mouths. As soon as a small fish comes within reach, attracted by the lure, the mouth opens wide and the prey is sucked in.

Did you know?

The lantern bug of South America looks just like a miniature caiman (a South American alligator). Is it mimicking the caiman? Answer on page 152.

Some caterpillars coil round to look like snails when they are resting.

Tiny *Extatosoma* mantids look like ants when young. As they get too big for this disguise, their bodies change colour and shape and they mimic scorpions instead.

More about warning colours (pp.54, 55); anglerfish (p.119); look-alikes (p.25)

Tool users in the animal world

Do animals really use tools?

Many people have seen or heard a song thrush banging a snail shell against a large stone. Song thrushes often use the same stone over and over again. You can easily recognize the song thrush's 'anvil' by the many pieces of broken shell scattered around it. Song thrushes behave like this because they cannot get the snails out of their shells in any other way. Is the song thrush using the stone 'anvil' as a tool? Do animals, other than humans, really use tools? Some scientists think they do. A number of wild animals have been seen using simple objects to help them do certain jobs.

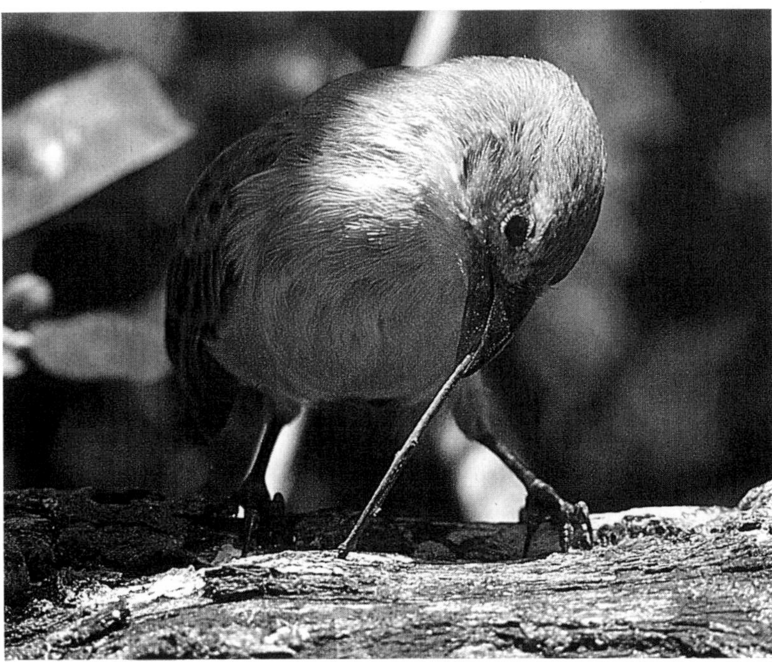

▲ Woodpecker finch using a twig to dig an insect out of the bark.

Making beaks and arms longer

The woodpecker finch lives on the Galapagos Islands in the Pacific Ocean. It feeds on small animals including insects and spiders. It looks for its prey on the bark of trees. However, insects and other small animals can easily hide in the cracks in the bark. When they do this they are difficult to reach. The woodpecker finch solves the problem by poking a twig into the crack to 'winkle' out its food. While it gobbles up its catch, it drops its twiggy tool. When it is ready to search for more food it holds the tool in its beak and starts poking between the cracks again.

Termite 'fishers'

Wild chimpanzees have been seen catching termites with tools they have made. They use a variety of objects including twigs and strong grass stems. The chimpanzees modify the tools by chewing the ends to make a kind of brush. They then push the tool into a termite mound in search of insects. Any termites disturbed by the chimpanzees bite the brush-like end of the tool and hold on. All the chimpanzee has to do is pull the tool out and eat the termites on the end. Using this tool, chimpanzees can catch food otherwise out of reach.

▲ The Egyptian vulture feeds on different kinds of food, including eggs. It can easily break open small eggs by picking them up in its beak and then dropping them on the ground. It deals with bigger eggs in a different way. It doesn't take the eggs to a stone. Instead, it drops a stone on the egg. It usually takes several attempts to break the shell, but the vulture nearly always succeeds. If a stone of the right size isn't available, birds may go some distance to find something they can use.

The bearded-vulture drops bones from a great height. The bones shatter on the rocks below. The vulture can then feed on the marrow inside the broken bones. Sometimes the vultures drop tortoises to break their hard shells.

Marine strongman

The sea otter lives in the Pacific, off the west coast of North America. When it gets hungry it dives to the sea bottom. It returns to the surface carrying a rock in one paw and a shellfish in the other. The otter then floats on its back and breaks the shellfish open by banging it against the rock held on its chest. Sometimes this hammering can be heard far away.

A sticky problem

A few animals are known to use sticky materials for gluing other things together. The satin bowerbird lives in north-eastern Australia. It squeezes bark from a particular tree to extract a sticky fluid. It mixes this with its own saliva. The mixture is then used to plaster the walls of its bower home. This bird also paints the inside of its bower with juice from wild berries. It uses a piece of bark as a paint brush.

Did you know?

Harvester ants, in south-east Asia, use bits of stick as plates to carry home food, or to soak up mud and sand. By doing this they can carry 10 times more food than if they swallowed it.

In south-east Asia some tailor ants squeeze their larvae and extract a glue. They use this to stick leaf edges together.

The dwarf mongoose, in Africa, holds an egg between its back legs, and breaks it by flicking it backwards against a rock.

More about animal skills (pp.60, 61); Galapagos finches (p.21)

Animal builders

Buildings large and small

Animals build for different reasons. They build homes in which to live and nests in which to rear their young. Some animals even build traps to catch other animals. The types of structures animals build vary in size and complexity, and they are made from many kinds of building material.

Some animals build tubes and tunnels where they can live. Certain marine molluscs can bore holes in hard rock. Worms living on the sea-bed often make complicated and delicate tubes which protect their soft bodies from predators. Other animals burrow in the soil. Moles, rabbits and badgers are good excavators. They are able to dig long, complicated underground passages. There are some birds which are also tunnel experts.

Insects are skilled architects and builders. Bees make intricate honeycombs based on sound mathematical principles. Weaver ants from tropical southern Asia glue leaves together by using their own larvae as a weaver uses a shuttle. Termites are even more skilled as planners and builders. They make huge mounds that have complicated air-conditioning systems.

Honey-bees: the mathematical builders

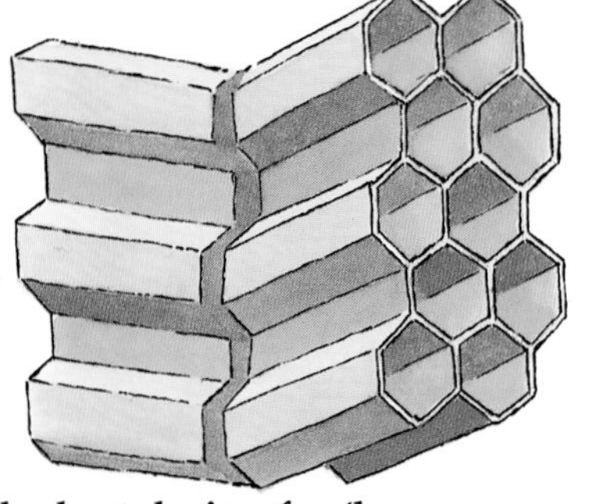

Honey-bees build the cells of their honeycomb very accurately. Each cell is hexagonal in cross-section. The hexagonal units fit together neatly, so that there are no spaces left between them. This means that the bees do not waste material in building the honeycomb. Hexagonal-shaped cells are the best design for 'honey warehouses'. A piece of honeycomb measuring 37 mm by 25 mm can hold 2.5 kg of honey. Yet it needs only 45 g of wax to build it.

Honey-bees are able to measure precisely. Each hexagonal cell in the honeycomb slopes downwards from the opening to the base. The slope is always 13°. Can you guess why? **Answer on page 152.** **The distance across a worker cell is 5.2 mm. It is 6.2 mm for a drone cell. Each cell wall is 0.073 mm thick.**

▲ Termite mounds are often very big structures made of sand or clay. The one in the picture is built by an African termite called Macrotermes. Inside there is a complicated system of ventilation shafts which help air circulate through the mound. This species of termite also grows fungus gardens. The humidity in the gardens must be carefully controlled. Some termites living in tropical rain forests put roofs with overhanging eaves on their buildings which make them look like pagodas. The roofs keep the heavy rain out. Other rain forest species build the whole mound in the shape of a mushroom.

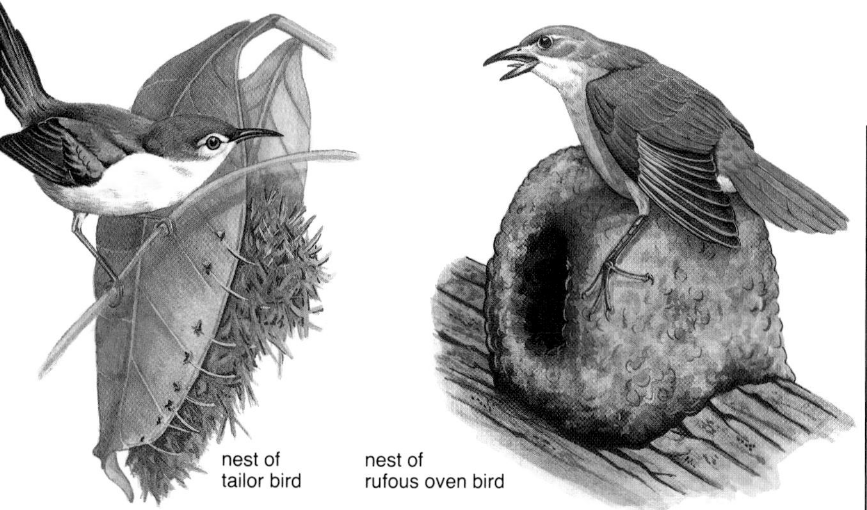

From potter to weaver

Birds are some of the most ingenious builders in the animal world. Some dig holes in the ground. Others bore holes in trees. They use all kinds of materials and building techniques. There are basket makers, weavers, carpenters and potters. The nests they build vary in size and complexity. The vervain hummingbird from the West Indies builds a nest no bigger than half a walnut shell. The brush turkey from Australia, on the other hand, makes a mound several metres in diameter in which the eggs are incubated. The social weaver-bird from Africa makes a communal nest in which fifty or more pairs of birds live together.

Male bowerbirds construct very elaborate structures with which to attract the females. Some bowers are built in the shape of a circle with a pole in the middle. Others are made to look like an avenue of small pillars. The orange-crested bowerbird from New Guinea makes a stage-shaped bower and decorates it with coloured berries and beetles.

Did you know?

There is enough limestone in the coral of the Great Barrier Reef to build 8 million of the biggest Egyptian pyramids.

Compass termites build mounds with two long and two short sides. The short sides always face exactly north and south so that the surface exposed to the hot midday Sun is small. The big surface of the long sides catches the cooler morning and evening Sun. This design keeps the mound cool.

The 'well-digger' jawfish digs a tube which it lines with pebbles and mollusc shells.

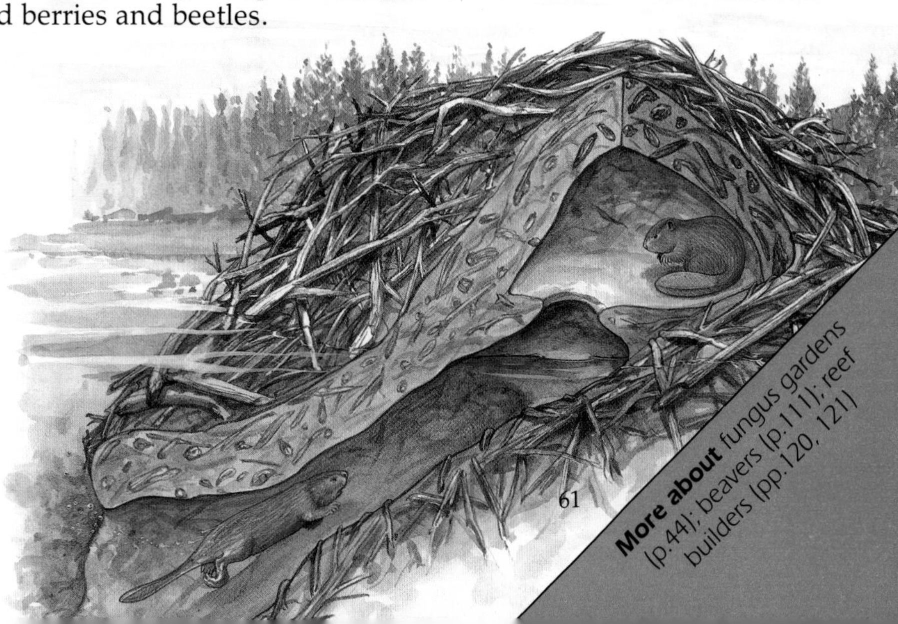

► Beavers are skilled engineers. They cut down trees and use the timber to build dams and lodges. They construct canals along which they float the trees to the building site. They build a dam across a stream which creates a pond. The beavers then build a lodge in the middle of the pond where they can live in safety.

More about fungus gardens (p.44); beavers (p.111); reef builders (pp.120, 121)

Territory

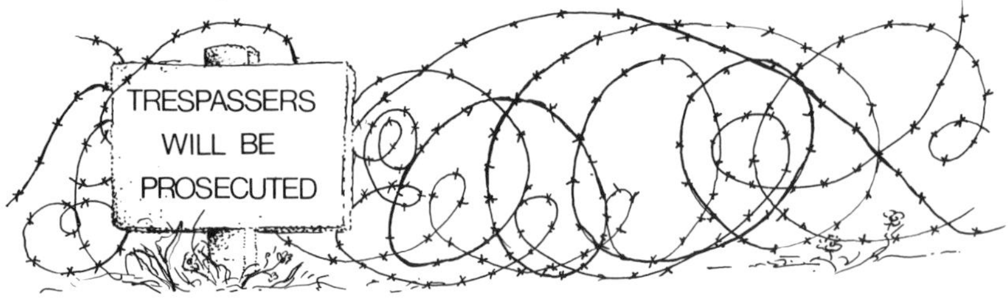

You have probably seen this sign before. We don't like other people walking on our property so we put up signs and build fences and walls to keep them out. Many animals also like their own property. They don't usually build walls around it, but they do mark its boundaries by using all kinds of signs. We can't easily see them but they are there for other animals to look out for, and they give the same message: 'Keep out'.

The home range

Many animals spend the whole of their lives in one particular area and they don't usually move away from it. They find their food there and they sleep there. They may even have 'lookout' posts in the area, and places where they can hide when danger threatens. An area like this is called the home range. The size of the home range varies from one species to another. For some species it is very big, and for others it may be quite small. Its boundaries are not usually defended, and other animals are allowed to enter.

Territory

Within the home range, animals may claim a special area which they defend against other animal trespassers, especially members of their own species. This area is called a territory. It can be defended by a single animal, by a pair or even by a group of animals. It may be defended all year round, or only during the breeding season.

◀ Territories are usually defended by males. A bull-elephant seal will attack any other male which enters his territory. He may even kill the trespasser to defend his harem of females.

Territory 'flags'

The African male agama lizard has a bright-red head and an orange tail which act as his advertising flags. The bright colours and his fierce behaviour tell other males to 'keep out'. Many male animals advertise themselves by their bright colours or by behaving in a certain way. This is how they keep their territory. Male robins claim their territory by singing loudly. This drives other males away. However, the male robin sings only on his own property.

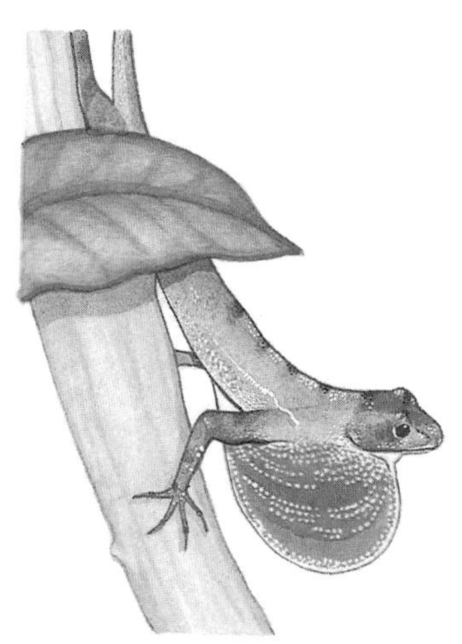

▲ Anolis lizard displaying throat pouch.

Mock fights

Quite often male animals claim and then defend their territory without hurting each other. They take part in 'mock fights' and the winner holds on to the territory. Antelopes and deer do this. At the beginning of the breeding season, the males fight amongst themselves. They fight in pairs by locking horns or antlers together. They push each other around until one gives up and is chased away. The strongest male wins and claims his territory. He also wins the collection of females that goes with it. Other males sometimes challenge him, and he may have to defend his territory and his harem of females.

Hear all about it

Animals living in thick forest find it difficult to advertise themselves and their territory. This is because they are not easily seen. They solve the problem by shouting. The sound of their screams can be heard several kilometres away and it warns other groups to keep their distance. Gibbons and howler monkeys do this. So do many birds including parrots and turacos.

War paint

A famous scientist called Konrad Lorenz was puzzled by the very bright colours of many coral reef fish. He decided to do some experiments to find out why they were so brightly coloured. He discovered that the special colours of each species act like a flag, telling other fish of the same species to keep away. The 'war paint' worn by each fish helps it to keep its territory and stops trespassers from entering.

Thinking through your nose

Although we can't see them, territories do have definite boundaries and animals mark these in different ways. Hippopotamuses spray their territory with a liquid diarrhoea. It works like an aerosol spray. By waving their tails in the spray they mark the surrounding vegetation. The message they leave behind warns other hippopotamuses to 'keep out'. Tigers urinate on trees and other plants. The marked trunks act like fence posts telling other tigers to stay away. Bush babies and tarsiers even urinate on their hands and then spread the 'message' by climbing through the branches.

More about communication (pp.72, 73); hearing, seeing, smelling (pp.50, 51); animal defences (pp.54, 55)

Display and courtship

Courtship

Most animals need to find a mate before they can reproduce. Courtship behaviour is used by male animals to attract a female and to get her into the mood to mate. Often several males compete for the attentions of a female. The male who puts on the most impressive display wins the lady.

Dressing up

Many animals use colour to attract a mate. Many male birds have a brighter plumage in the spring. The breast of the male stickleback turns red in the spring. The bright colour attracts females, and also serves as a warning to other males not to come too close. Many courtship displays have this double aim. Male sticklebacks will even attack red circles of cardboard in the mating season.

▲ Male birds of paradise grow special, long tail feathers which are used in a spectacular display which involves acrobatics, fluffing up of feathers, and strange calls.

Serenades

Many animals use sound to attract mates. Male frogs 'sing': many of them have large air sacs which make the sound louder. The females are attracted to the male frog with the loudest croak. A chorus of frogs can attract females from several kilometres away. Grasshoppers and crickets chirp a serenade. Mayflies and mosquitoes gather in huge clouds of dancing males. Their whirring wings attract the females, who are recognized by the different sounds of their wing beats.

Sight and sound

Often animals put on a special display to show off their bright colours. The peacock spreads its magnificent tail into a great fan. The frigate bird inflates its large, red throat sac. The throat sac also helps it to make a booming sound, which also helps to attract the attention of females flying overhead.

Dancing partners

Sometimes the courtship display is in the form of a dance. The male stickleback performs a zigzag dance in front of the female.

The scorpion grabs his female by the pincers and dances her across the ground. Before the dance, he wraps his sperms in a tiny packet which he leaves on the ground. During the dance, he guides the female over the packet so she can pick it up.

Waving the flag

Some male spiders wave their legs in a form of semaphore to signal to the female that they are mates and not meals. The male fiddler crab has one claw which is much larger than the others. He waves this claw like a big white flag to attract the females to his burrow.

Giving presents

Many animals give their intended mates presents of food. Terns offer fish, while the American road-runner gives his mate a lizard, which she continues to hold in her beak during mating. Road-runners are awkward birds, and some people think the female uses the big lizard to help her balance while mating!

Some spiders give their mates food, wrapped up in silk. The female spider is much bigger than the male, and would normally attack and eat him if he came too close. The food parcel acts as a distraction while he mates with her. Spiders who cheat by giving their mates an empty parcel often end up as dinner.

The lure of perfume

All animals give off special scented chemicals called pheromones. Many male moths have huge antennae loaded with smell sensors. They can detect the scent of a female from two or more kilometres away. Some animals can tell whether a female is ready to mate by her smell. You often see courting mammals sniffing near the tail of their partners.

▲ The male bighorn sheep sniffs near the tail of the female to discover whether she is ready to mate.

▲ Like these great crested grebes, many animals have courtship displays involving both partners.

Did you know?

During courtship, snakes tickle each other by rubbing their scales up the wrong way.

Mating snails inject chalky love darts into each other while courting.

The female baboon gets a very swollen bare pink bottom when she is ready to mate. She stands with her back to the male and her tail raised to show off her bottom.

More about how animals smell (p.51); how animals communicate (pp.72, 73); animal reproduction (pp.66, 67)

Reproduction

Why multiply?

No animal or plant lives for ever. Sooner or later it dies; it is eaten, has an accident or simply ages — its body wears out and becomes less efficient as it grows old. All plants and animals reproduce. They produce more plants or animals like themselves.

Simple multiplication

Very simple creatures reproduce by dividing in two. A few bigger, more complicated animals can also divide in two. Some sea anemones pinch in their bodies down the middle until they become two separate animals. The green hydras which live in ponds produce buds which grow rings of tentacles. The buds later drop off as baby hydras.

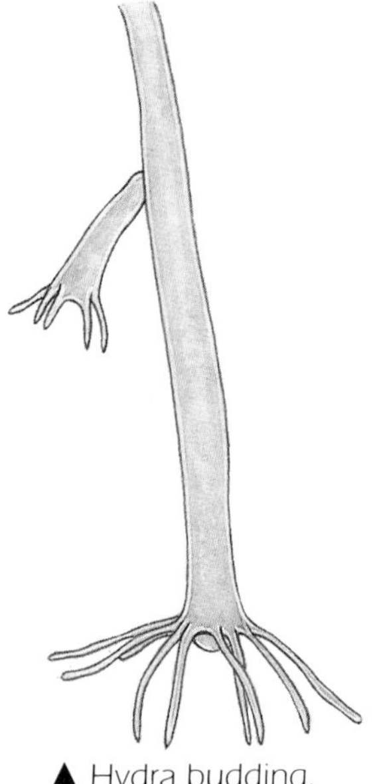

▲ Hydra budding.

Advanced multiplication

For bigger and more complicated animals or plants it is difficult just to divide in two. Imagine trying to divide a human being in two. How can a tree divide in two when the two halves cannot move apart?

Most animals and plants reproduce sexually. When they reproduce, they make special sex cells. In animals, the male sex cells are called sperms, and the female sex cells are called eggs. Each sex cell contains half the information needed to make a new animal. During 'fertilization' a sperm meets an egg and joins with it to form one new cell. This cell contains all the information for making a new animal. The cell then divides again and again until a new animal is formed.

Taking chances

Many animals mate in water. The sperms have tails and can swim to the eggs. The eggs attract the sperms by giving off special chemicals. Frogs and fish mate in water. This process is very wasteful: lots of eggs and sperms never meet each other, but drift away on water currents or get eaten by fish. Very large numbers of eggs and sperms have to be produced to make sure a new generation is made.

◀ In order to reproduce, sperms have to meet the eggs. This happens during mating, when a male animal and a female animal come together and shed their sex cells at the same time.

Playing safe

Sperms need water to swim in. Some animals which live on land, like frogs and toads, return to the water to breed. Other land animals use internal fertilization. The male has a special tube-like organ, called a penis, which he uses to inject sperms into a special opening in the female. The sperms fertilize the eggs inside her body. Mammals and reptiles have penes, and most male insects have some sort of organ for transferring sperms to the female. Birds do not. With internal fertilization there is a much better chance of a sperm meeting an egg, so far fewer sex cells are produced.

Eggs inside and outside

▲ Rattlesnake giving birth.

▲ Snakes hatching from eggs.

Some animals which reproduce by internal fertilization keep the eggs inside the mother's body in a special hollow, called a womb, until they have developed into baby animals. Then they are pushed out — they are 'born'. This happens in mammals, rattlesnakes and some lizards. In other animals, like birds, insects and most reptiles other than rattlesnakes, the eggs develop a tough waterproof shell. They are then released to the world outside. The baby animal goes on developing inside the egg until it is ready to hatch.

▼ Female trout laying eggs for male to fertilize.

Life before birth

While the baby animal is developing inside the egg or inside its mother's womb, it is called an embryo. Most eggs contain a bag of food called the yolk, which the embryo slowly absorbs. Baby mammals have an even better food supply. They are attached to their mother's womb by the umbilical cord. In this cord the embryo's blood vessels are very close to those of the mother, and they get food and oxygen from the mother's blood.

Did you know?

The ocean sunfish may produce 300 million eggs.

A newly hatched sunfish is 1575 times smaller than its mother.

An ostrich egg is so strong that a human adult can stand on it without breaking it. Why does it need to be so strong? Answer on page 152.

More about how animals find mates (pp.64, 65); how baby animals grow up (pp.68, 69); animal parents (pp.70, 71)

Metamorphosis

A human baby looks very much like a tiny adult, but many baby animals do not look anything like their parents. They undergo a dramatic change during the development from egg to adult. We call this change in form 'metamorphosis'. The young animals below are very different from their parents. Can you guess whose babies they are? You will find the answers on page 152.

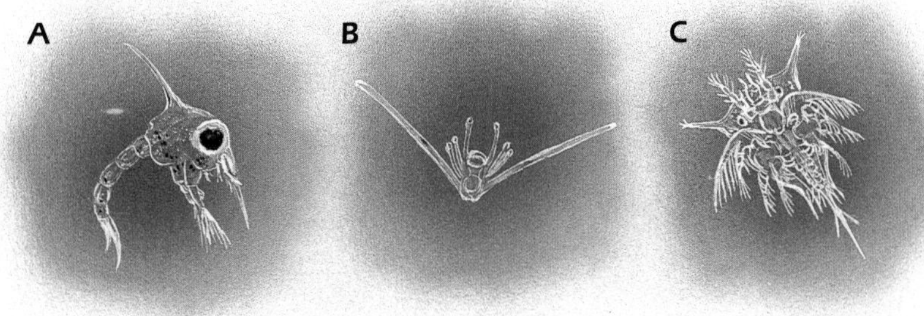

Larvae on the move

Many animals which live on the sea-bed cannot move around much. Mussels and barnacles are anchored to the rocks. Worms and starfish can only creep about very slowly, and even crabs cannot swim far. All these animals produce tiny larvae which drift in the plankton near the surface of the ocean. The larvae may be carried for hundreds of kilometres on the ocean currents. This helps to spread the species around the world.

A change of diet

The young of some animals are very different from their parents. They are called larvae. Butterflies and moths are elegant flying insects, but their larvae are slow, fat caterpillars. The adults and young feed on different things. Caterpillars feed on plants. They have hard, horny jaws for cutting up the leaves. The adults feed on nectar, which they sip through a long coiled tube called a proboscis.

The caterpillars are perfectly designed for growing fast. They have simple bodies, that are just fat food processors. As they grow, they moult often. They can move just enough to find another leaf to eat. The adults can fly far and wide in search of mates. They may lay their eggs some distance away. This helps the species spread to new places.

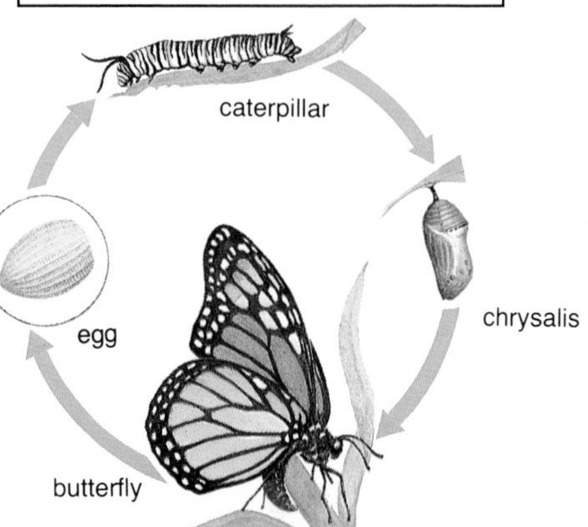

Reshuffling the building blocks

How does a caterpillar change into a butterfly? When it is fully grown, the caterpillar forms a hard case around itself. It is now called a pupa or chrysalis. Sometimes it spins a silken cocoon around the case. Inside the case, the caterpillar's tissues break down and the 'building blocks' of living material are rearranged to form the adult butterfly or moth. After a time, the pupal case cracks open, and the adult emerges. At first the wings are crumpled where they have been folded inside the pupa. Soon they stretch out as blood is pumped along their veins. Then they harden in the air.

Growing problems

Insects and crustaceans grow in a different way from other animals. They are covered in a hard shell or skin, called the cuticle, which limits how much they can grow underneath. Every so often, the shell splits open and comes off. Below is a new soft shell, which hardens quickly in air. Before it does so, the animal quickly puffs itself up with air, so the new shell sets as a bigger one. Then the insect or crustacean has room to grow under the shell.

Changing slowly

Not all insects go through dramatic changes like the butterflies and their caterpillars. Some newly-hatched insects, like grasshoppers and locusts, do not have proper wings. They are called nymphs. Every time they moult, the new cuticle forms around the growing wing buds. The tiny wings get bigger every time, until, at last, the insects are ready to fly.

Living like their ancestors

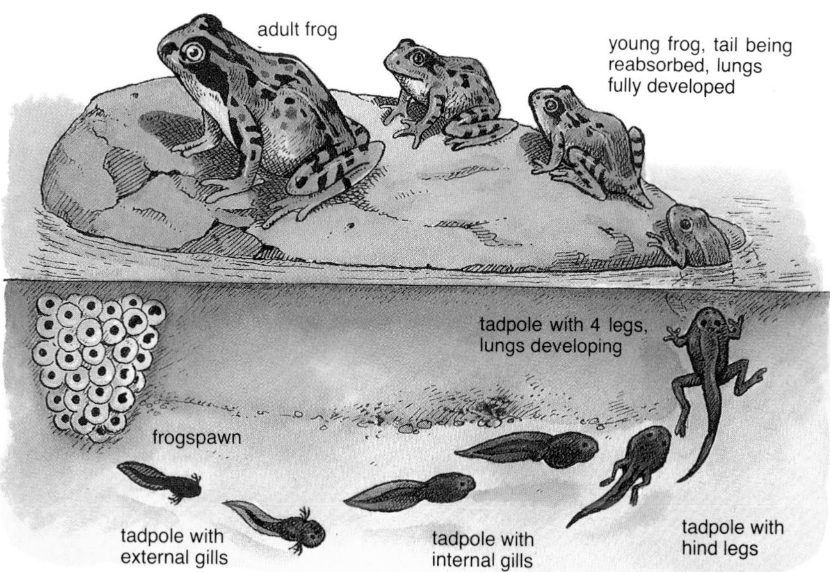

The vertebrates evolved in the sea. First came the fish. From them, the amphibians evolved. The amphibians have legs and can live on land. Frogs and toads are amphibians. They catch insects with their sticky tongues and have lungs for breathing air. But their larvae, or tadpoles, are still fish-like, as their ancestors were, with long, flat tails and no legs. They breathe with gills, like the fish.

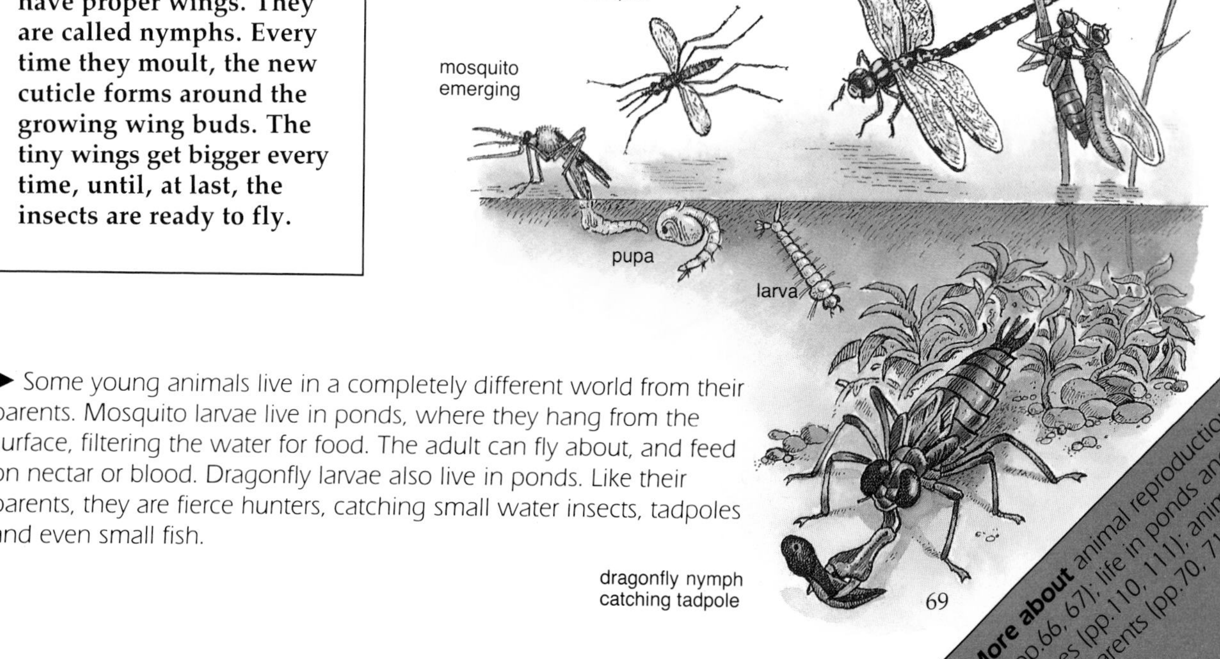

► Some young animals live in a completely different world from their parents. Mosquito larvae live in ponds, where they hang from the surface, filtering the water for food. The adult can fly about, and feed on nectar or blood. Dragonfly larvae also live in ponds. Like their parents, they are fierce hunters, catching small water insects, tadpoles and even small fish.

More about animal reproduction (pp.66, 67), life in ponds and lakes (pp.110, 111), animal parents (pp.70, 71)

Parental care

The numbers game

Have you ever wondered why some animals, like the cod, produce millions of young, while others, like the elephant, produce only one offspring at a time? Once the cod's eggs are fertilized, neither parent has anything more to do with them. The young cod are very small, and are eaten by many different predators. Because of this very few survive. However, the baby elephant stays with its mother for several years. A much higher proportion of baby elephants survive to become parents themselves compared with the cod, where perhaps only one young survives from several million eggs.

◀ New-born harvest mice in nest.

Helpless babies

Where vertebrates produce large numbers of offspring, their young are often small and helpless at birth. If they were to be born any bigger, the mother would not have enough room inside her to produce so many. Imagine an elephant trying to produce several baby elephants at once. Many baby birds and mammals are naked at birth — their feathers or fur grow later. Often their eyes and ears are still closed and they are quite helpless. They do not have warm coats, so they need to be close to their mother's warm body. Most mammals and birds make nursery nests, lined with soft grass or feathers.

Learning who's who

Many animals learn to recognize their own species from learning the characteristics of their parents. Goslings brought up in a swan's nest think that they are swans. When they find a mate they will court swans instead of geese.

Ready to run

The baby giraffe is born with a full coat of fur and is able to walk within a few hours of its birth. It has to be able to keep up with the herd right from the start. The young of ground-nesting birds like chickens and lapwings hatch fully-feathered. They can run around and find their own food within hours of hatching.

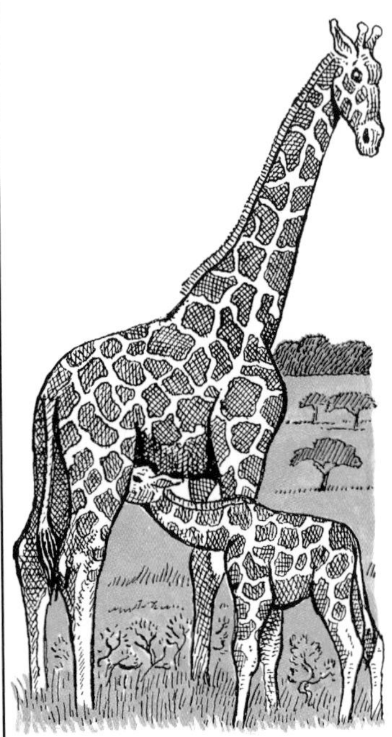

Food on tap

All baby mammals stay with their mother for a while after their birth because, at first, they feed on her milk. Once they can feed themselves, and no longer need the milk, they are said to be weaned.

Parents on the move

Not all animals stay in or near a nursery nest. Some spiders and scorpions carry their young on their backs, and so do some frogs. Crabs and lobsters carry their eggs and young in a fold of the abdomen, or among the bristly hairs on their back legs.

▲ Scorpion with babies.

Playing for the future

Even after they are weaned, some baby mammals stay with their mothers for a time. Carnivorous mammals like foxes and cats learn how to hunt. They do this by watching their parents. Lions and cheetahs bring back their prey alive so that the young can learn to kill. Foxes hold food just out of reach of their babies, then jerk it away as if it were still alive. Play is useful. It helps young animals become good at judging distance for pouncing. It also teaches them to react quickly. Baby animals at play seem to be rather rough.

▶ Baby bees and ants are cared for by the whole community. Bee larvae are kept in special cells in the comb, and are fed and cleaned by worker bees.

Colourful clues

Among birds, you can tell which parent cares for the young by the colour of its coat. If a bird has to spend a long time sitting on the nest, it must be well camouflaged. Compare the gaudy plumage of the male pheasant with that of his dull mate. Who incubates the eggs? In most thrushes both the male and the female are dull coloured. What does this tell you? Answer on page 152.

Caring creepy crawlies

Parental care is found in most animal groups almost all over the animal kingdom. Centipedes lick their eggs free of fungus spores and curl around the eggs to guard them. Parent bugs stand guard over their eggs and young. Spiders spin special webs, called cocoons, to protect their young.

Did you know?

A new-born kangaroo, or joey, is only 1/30 000th of its mother's weight.

A new-born panda grows so fast that its weight increases twenty-fold in the first 8 weeks of its life. If a human baby grew at the same rate, it would weigh 63 kg when it was just 8 weeks old.

More about why animals produce so many young (p.20); animal reproduction (pp.66, 67)

Communication

◀ This male moth has large, feathery antennae. They look a bit like tiny television aerials. They pick up chemical signals from a female moth. Often they can pick up the signals over very long distances. Chemical signals are called pheromones. Crabs, barnacles, spiders and insects all use them fo: communication. Mammals also use them for attracting a mate.

Animal communication

There are thousands of different human languages. They are all very complicated. We have to learn how to use a language correctly. This usually takes a long time. Animals do not have languages like ours, but they can communicate. For example, they use visual signals, sounds, smell, touch and even chemicals to tell each other what is going on. You might be surprised to learn that whales can sing and bees can dance.

Follow that tail

Animals which live together in groups or herds often flash signals to each other. White bottoms or tails with white underneath are good for giving a quick 'message'. A sudden white flash is a warning of danger. The signal is given when animals turn and start to run. Antelopes and rabbits signal like this. The African wart-hog runs away from danger with its tail held straight up. The tail acts like a flag pole and points the way for others to follow. The ring-tailed lemur from Madagascar uses its tail like a flag. The lemurs in a group feeding on the forest floor keep their tails upright so they can all see each other. This keeps the group close together.

A

B

C

▲ Chimpanzees make different faces to show their feelings. Here are three pictures showing a chimpanzee in three different moods. Can you match A, B and C against the feelings of excitement, fear and happiness. Answers on page 152.

Open wide!

Young birds communicate with their parents when they want food. They keep their mouths open wide so that their parents can pop the food inside. Often, the inside of the chick's mouth mouth is brightly coloured to make it easier for the parents to see.

Elephant 'talk'

Scientists have now discovered that elephants make low frequency sounds, too low for humans to hear. They may be used in communication.

Sea sounds

Whales and dolphins make all kinds of sounds. Some of these are used for navigation but others are for communication. Humpback whales sing long and complicated songs. Each whale has its own song which is different from those of other whales. They can be heard hundreds of kilometres away. Whales keep 'in touch' by singing to each other. It may be that one whale can talk to another whale on the other side of the world!

◀ Kiss me quick! Prairie dogs are small rodents from North America. They live in large groups in underground burrows. When two prairie dogs first meet, they kiss each other to find out if they are from the same group. If they recognize each other they start grooming each other's fur. If they are strangers they fight and the trespasser is sent away to find his own group.

Listen to me!

Shouting is a good way to communicate, especially if you live in thick vegetation. Groups of monkeys and flocks of birds shout to each other as they move amongst the branches. This keeps them together and stops anyone getting lost. Each species has its own 'voice' which members of its group can recognize. Insects use sound to communicate. So do frogs and toads.

Honeybees have a complicated dance language. They can tell each other where to find a new supply of food, how far away it is from the hive, and which direction to fly to find it. Bees have different languages. Russian bees cannot understand Italian bees and vice-versa.

Did you know?

Beavers slap the surface of the water with their tails as an alarm signal.

A rhinoceros has scent glands on its feet which it uses to pass on chemical messages to other rhinoceroses.

Humpback whale songs have made the record charts in the United States.

More about hearing, seeing and smelling (pp.50, 51); attracting a mate (pp.64, 65); whale songs (p.81)

Rhythms and 'clocks'

Various rhythms

Most animals and plants show some rhythmic behaviour. They do certain things at specific times and they repeat them regularly. Some rhythms follow a twenty-four hour pattern. Others occur once every month. Birds and other animals migrate from one place to another every year. Such journeys are examples of annual rhythms.

Day and night rhythms

Most animals become active at particular times every twenty-four hours. Some move about and feed during the daytime. These are called diurnal animals. Nocturnal animals are more active at night-time. Most moths, owls and bats are nocturnal. Within any twenty-four hour period there are often peaks of activity. For example, troops of gibbons in the rain forest canopy are very noisy at dawn. So are many birds. We even talk about the bird 'dawn chorus'. Gorillas and chimpanzees feed in the morning and rest in the heat of the afternoon. Howler monkeys shout at dawn and in the evening.

Many plants hold their flowers and leaves in one position during the day and in another position at night. The blooms of the moonflower plant open at night and close during the day. They are pollinated by moths and bats. The leaves of many plants change their position throughout the day as they follow the Sun's path across the sky.

South Pole roundabout

Karl Hamner wanted to learn more about daily animal rhythms so he went to the South Pole and did an interesting experiment. He put some small animals on a revolving turntable and watched their behaviour. The turntable went round at the same speed as the Earth, but in the opposite direction. The animals didn't experience night or day, or even time. They were 'standing still' in space. Even so, they still showed all their normal twenty-four hour rhythms. What do you think Karl Hamner concluded? Answer on page 152.

Regular deep sleep

South American humming-birds are very small and very active. They use up enormous amounts of energy. They also lose a lot of heat across their body surface. This creates many problems. They cannot supply their bodies with enough energy to keep active for more than twelve hours at a time. Because of this, they go into a deep sleep, rather like hibernation, for twelve hours every night. In this way they keep their energy demands under control.

▲ Green leaves have tiny pores on their surface called stomata. The stomata open and close following a daily rhythm.

► At the end of May every year, herds of wildebeeste begin their migration across the East African plains. They must start the journey on time to reach their feeding grounds. This yearly rhythm needs careful timing.

Moon rhythms and the tides

Other animals and plants show behaviour patterns which are related to the phases of the Moon and the rise and fall of the tides. Some fiddler crabs change colour between high and low tide. They also show different activity patterns. Crabs come out of their burrows to feed at low tide. When the tide returns they go back to their holes to hide. The palolo worm from the South Pacific is even more remarkable. Every year at dawn on one particular day in October the surface of the sea becomes frothy with writhing worms. The palolo worm is spawning and its cycle is linked to the Moon's phases. The day before there is no activity and the day after it is all over. Another year passes before the palolo worm spawns again. The life cycles of many seaweeds are also controlled by the rhythms of the Moon and tides.

Migratory and seasonal rhythms

Many animals and plants show behaviour rhythms which are linked to changes in length of daylight, temperature and even food supply. Butterflies, birds, mammals and even some reptiles make yearly journeys called migrations. These always take place at the same time each year. The animals which take part in these migrations seem to have a good sense of time. For example, between June and August every year, most of the world's female leatherback turtles gather at the Trengaunu Beaches in Malaysia to lay their eggs. How do they time this event? Answer on page 152.

Many trees lose their leaves in winter. This is a rhythmic activity related to the fall in temperature and light. In tropical countries other trees behave in a similar way, but this rhythm is linked to hotter temperatures and the dry season. Some animals start to hibernate as winter approaches. This shows another annual rhythm.

Time-keepers

Some mangrove swamp snails are remarkable time-keepers. At low tide they climb down from the trees to browse on the exposed mud. However, they need to return to the safety of the trees before the tide comes in. They are slow movers, so they have to start their journey back before the tide begins to turn. If they start back too late, they will be caught by the rising water. Their internal 'clock' allows the snails to forecast the tide's return. Why do they reset their 'clocks' every day? **Answer on page 152.**

Animal 'clocks'

Not all animal rhythms are controlled by changes in their surroundings, such as day or night, tidal movements or the seasons. Many rhythms still occur even when animals are put in surroundings which do not change. Karl Hamner discovered this at the South Pole. Animals which do this must have some way of telling the time. Scientists now think these animals have some kind of 'clock' inside their bodies. They are not sure how such 'clocks' work, but chemicals called hormones may be important.

More about migration (pp.78, 79); mangrove swamps (pp.114, 115); hibernation (pp.76, 77, 96)

The big sleep

▶ In winter, water freezes in the soil making it difficult for many plants to survive. The problem of survival is solved in different ways. Some trees and shrubs lose their leaves and grow new ones in the spring. Some plants 'die back' to the level of the soil. Their shoots grow again in warmer weather. Many plants pass the winter as seeds, bulbs or corms. These are all dormant stages which need no energy. They are the inactive part of the life cycle of plants.

Super seeds

Harold Schmidt found some Arctic lupin seeds in the frozen soil in the Yukon, Canada, in July 1954. The seeds were tested scientifically and found to be at least 10 000 years old. The seeds were germinated in 1966, 10 000 years after they fell off the plant. They had lain dormant all this time and had survived the coldest winters.

▲ Fish, amphibians and reptiles are cold-blooded. Their body temperature is always the same as their surroundings. As the outside temperature drops, they become sluggish and sleepy. The cold works like an anaesthetic which slowly puts them to sleep.

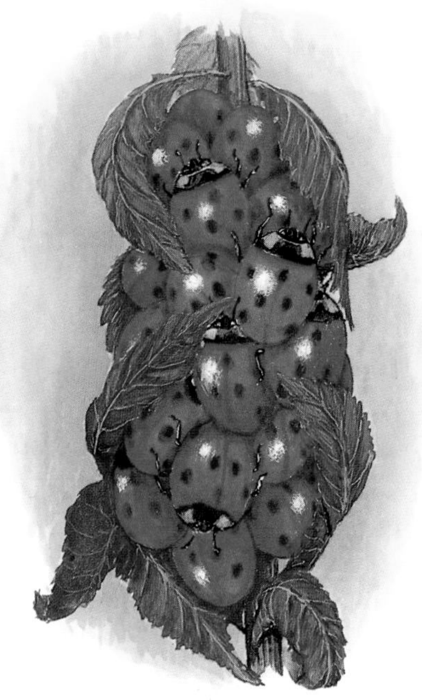

▲ All invertebrates are cold-blooded. They survive winter in different ways. Insects sometimes pass the winter in the pupal stage and emerge as adults in the spring. Some butterflies hide themselves away in a sheltered spot and slowly go to sleep as the temperature drops. This sleep-like state is called torpor. Flies, bees and ladybirds do the same thing, often huddling together in large numbers.

The problem of winter

Animals and plants which live in cold parts of the world face the problem of survival in winter. Food and water are scarce at this time of year, and keeping warm becomes difficult. Animals and plants solve the problem of winter in different ways. Many birds escape it altogether by migrating to warmer countries. They return in the spring. Some mammals, such as squirrels, store food in their larders during the summer and then visit these from time to time during the winter. Wolves grow a thicker coat to give them better protection against the cold winds. Shrews, voles and lemmings survive the Arctic winter by living and feeding beneath the snow. Some animals don't even try to find food in winter. Instead, they go to sleep. They hibernate.

Mammals

Mammals are warm-blooded. They have a high body temperature which is controlled by a kind of 'thermostat' in the brain. Keeping a high body temperature needs plenty of energy, especially for small mammals. This means they must eat a lot of food. Winter is a problem because food is scarce, and so some mammals hibernate. In order to survive winter, hibernating mammals must use less energy, so they must be less active. They limit their activity by turning down their 'thermostats', and lowering their heartbeats and breathing rates. Now the body 'ticks over' very slowly using very little energy. The fat stored up in the summer provides all the energy needed. Some mammals even have a kind of 'antifreeze' in the blood to stop it freezing up.

Some mammals go into a 'temporary' hibernation from which they wake up from time to time. Bats do this. Bears do something different again. The European brown bear and the American black bear simply go into a deep sleep. It isn't real hibernation because the body temperature never drops below 15°C. Female bears even give birth to their young during this time.

▲ The dormouse has a 'thermostat' in its brain which controls its body temperature, keeping it at just under 40°C. As winter approaches, the dormouse builds a nest, curls up in a ball, and goes to sleep. Can you think why it curls up? It turns its 'thermostat' down so its body temperature drops to about 4°C. Its heartbeat slows from 300 beats to about 10 beats per minute. Now it can survive the winter by using very little energy. It gets what energy it needs from its stored body fat. In spring it turns its 'thermostat' up again and starts to wake up. Perhaps the dormouse in Alice in Wonderland was hibernating!

The sleepy poorwill

Birds are warm-blooded. Not many birds hibernate, although some swifts and hummingbirds go into a deep sleep like hibernation to save energy. The poorwill, a type of nightjar from North America, does hibernate. As winter approaches it builds up fat reserves to help it survive. Then, when the weather gets colder, it crawls into a sheltered hole and goes to sleep. Its body temperature drops to below 15°C. It stays like this for several months, slowly using up its food reserves. It needs about 10 grams of fat for every 100 days of sleep.

The sleeping fish

The African lungfish survives drought in a remarkable way. If the lake in which it lives dries up, it burrows into the mud and surrounds itself with a waterproof cocoon. Breathing air through a ventilation shaft to the surface, it lives off its own muscle tissue. It soon revives when the rains come. Some tropical frogs and toads do the same thing. This kind of hibernation is called aestivation.

More about hibernation (p.96); life in cold climates (pp.100, 103); coping with dry weather (pp.96, 97)

Migration

On the move

Not all animals live in the same place all the time. Many animals live in one country in the summer and in another country, or even another continent, in the winter. Other animals spend the first part of their lives in one area, and their adult lives in another. These regular journeys are called migrations.

The Sun-seekers

The lands of the far north, especially the Arctic tundra, are favourite places for many animals to have their young. When the snow melts in the spring, there is plenty of new plant growth. In the melt-water pools, millions of insects thrive, providing food for many birds. The cold polar waters are also full of fish and small crustaceans, which are food for many seabirds. Because the winters are too cold for most animals to survive, there are no large resident populations of animals here to compete for the food.

Many geese, ducks, waders and terns breed in the tundra, but spend the winter in warmer climates, often south of the Equator. Swallows and warblers, which feed on insects, migrate every year from tropical regions to breeding grounds in northern Europe and America.

In mountainous regions of the world, wild goats and sheep move up to high alpine pastures in the summer. In the autumn, they move back to the shelter of the wooded valleys where they feed in the shelter of the trees.

◀ North American caribou spend the summer feeding on the tundra, but retreat hundreds of kilometres to the sheltered forests in the winter. Packs of wolves follow them.

From land to water . . .

Some animals need special conditions for mating or egg-laying. Frogs and toads are evolved from fish, and they still shed their eggs and sperms into water when mating. For most of the year they live on land, feeding on insects, but in the breeding season they gather together at favourite ponds to mate, often travelling several kilometres.

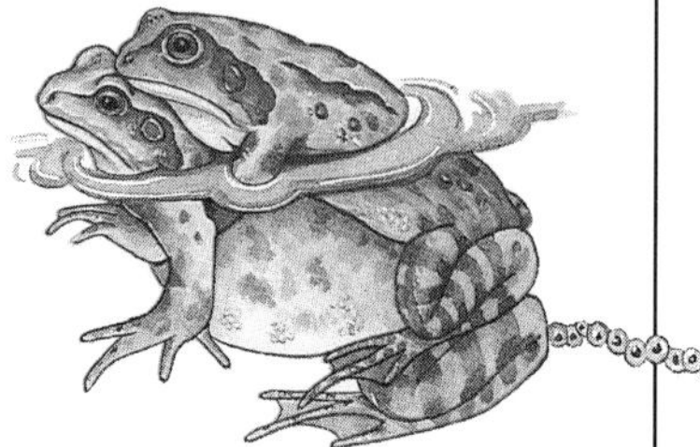

. . . and water to land

Other animals migrate from the sea to the land. The marine turtles evolved from land-dwelling ancestors. They return to sandy beaches to lay their eggs. Here the eggs incubate in the warm sand. When they hatch, the tiny turtles immediately make their way back to the sea.

Exploding populations

Sometimes animals multiply too fast, and run out of food in their home area. Vast numbers of animals then move out to find new feeding grounds. These one-way mass movements are called emigrations. They are common in lemmings, small vole-like animals that live in Scandinavia and Canada. In warmer climates, huge swarms of locusts also emigrate in search of food.

Following the rains

In the dry grasslands of Africa, and similar areas, large herds of grazing animals follow the rains, migrating in search of fresh, green vegetation. Elephants, antelopes and wildebeeste follow regular routes, hundreds of kilometres long, across the great plains.

Ocean wanderers

In the sea, whales migrate thousands of kilometres in search of food. Fish like herring and cod migrate to special shallow-water areas to breed. Salmon spend most of their adult lives at sea, but when the time comes for them to breed, they travel thousands of kilometres across the oceans to the rivers in which they were born, struggling upstream to lay their eggs. The young salmon return to the oceans to mature. Common eels make the opposite migration, spending their adult lives in fresh water, but returning to the ocean to breed.

▼ Insects also migrate. In Europe, large numbers of clouded yellows, red admirals and other butterflies frequently fly across the English Channel to the United Kingdom in the spring and summer. In the United States and Canada, monarch butterflies migrate some 2000 kilometres south to Mexico and the southern United States in the autumn. In the winter, monarch butterflies rest, crowded together in favourite roosting trees. In the spring, they migrate north to breed.

Did you know?

Most bird migration takes place out of sight of human eyes, 3000 m or more up in the atmosphere.

In Africa in the last century, a herd of migrating springbok may have contained one hundred million animals.

In the ocean, lanternfish migrate to the surface each night to feed, returning to depths of 1250 m at dawn.

More about migration (pp.75, 103, 104); how migrating animals find their way (pp. 80-83)

How animals find their way

Why do animals need to navigate?

Many animals are able to navigate accurately. They may have to find their way back home after hunting for food. They sometimes have to navigate to find a mate, or to escape from enemies. Some have to leave an area for a short time because the weather is very bad. For example, because the winter is too cold and harsh. Animals often navigate over long distances when they migrate. Migrations may involve journeys from one part of the world to another. Animals usually migrate when the seasons change.

The Sun is always up

It is important for an animal to know in which direction to travel. It is also important for the animal to know about the position of its body in space. Fish, insects and birds use the Sun to tell them about their own position. They also use gravity to tell them which way up they are. Other animals use chemicals to help them navigate. Salmon and eels migrate long distances. Chemicals in the Atlantic Ocean help them to find their way.

Local landmarks

During short journeys, animals often use local landmarks to help guide them. Insects, birds and mammals do this.

Electrical signals

Tropical lakes and rivers are often very muddy. Some species of fish which live in these conditions find their way about in a special way. The electric eel from South America sends out large numbers of electrical signals. It surrounds itself with these signals which make a special pattern. If the signals hit against something in its surroundings the pattern changes. This tells the eel that there is something close by. These signals can also be used to stun other fish on which the eel feeds.

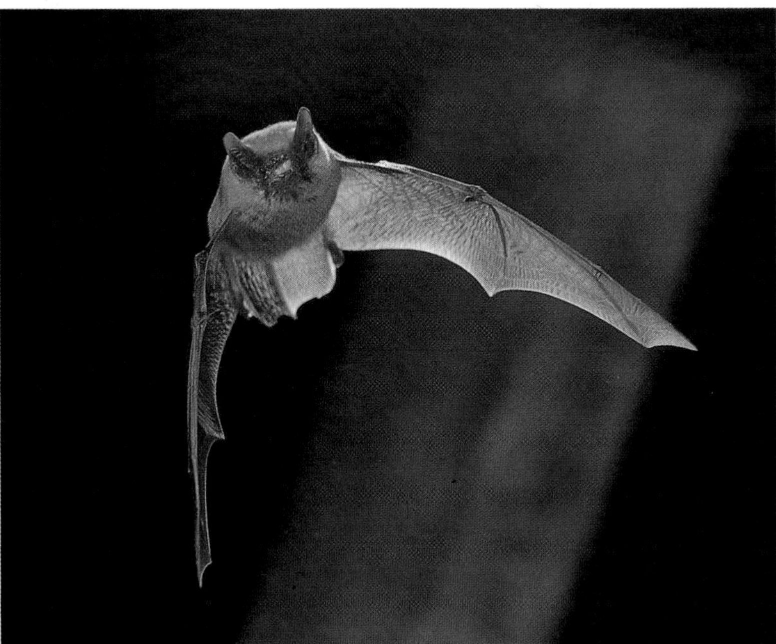

◀ Bats navigate by sonar. They produce high-pitched sounds which bounce back off objects in their flight path. They have very large ears to catch these echoes. This system of navigation is called echolocation. Bats use echolocation to find their way even in complete darkness. It works like radar and is very accurate. Bats also use sonar to catch insects. There are bats from Central America that use sonar to find the fish on which they feed.

Singing whales

Whales and dolphins make sounds to help them find their way and to keep in contact. The sounds are usually high-pitched like the sonar of bats, although lower sounds are also produced. Dolphins seem to 'talk' to each other by 'whistling'. Their high-pitched clicks help keep the group together. The humpback whale sings for long periods and it also sings different songs. A single song may last for thirty minutes. Whale songs can travel for hundreds of kilometres underwater. The songs may help in navigation during the whale's annual migration. They almost certainly help to keep the whales together. Only the male humpbacks sing, so their songs may help in finding a mate. Whales also follow the patterns of the Earth's magnetic field on the sea-bed. They follow these rather like cars on a motorway. Sometimes they come off the 'motorway', crash on a beach and become stranded.

Insect navigation

Butterflies navigate by sight and smell. Species which migrate also use the Sun's position to help them find their way. The monarch butterfly travels more than three thousand kilometres on its migration. It uses the Sun to help it. The Sun's position in the sky changes throughout the day. The monarch butterfly allows for this movement when it navigates. Not all migrating butterflies do this. The cabbage white and the red admiral butterflies also migrate over long distances. They do not seem able to compensate for the Sun's movement.

Dancing bees

Worker bees do a special dance on the face of the honeycomb when they want to tell each other about a group of flowers they have discovered. When it dances, the bee follows a path shaped like the figure 8. The line between the loops of the 8 acts as a pointer. It tells other bees how far to the left or right of the Sun they have to fly to find the flowers. The dancing bee also tells the others how far away the flowers are by wagging its abdomen. Quick wagging means the flowers are close to the hive. Slow wagging means they are a long way off.

Did you know?

The blue whale produces the loudest sound of any animal. It can be heard 850 km away.

The oil bird from Venezuela flies in complete darkness in the caves in which it lives. It echolocates like a bat.

Some moths 'jam' the sonar system of bats hunting them. This helps them escape capture.

Nose-leaf bats amplify the sound they produce, just like a megaphone.

More about bird navigation (pp.82, 83); animal senses (pp.50, 51); navigating in the dark (pp.126, 127)

Birds — master navigators

Long-distance travellers

Certain species of bird leave their winter feeding grounds and fly to summer breeding areas. This type of journey is called a migration. The birds may fly many thousands of kilometres during these journeys. After breeding they make the return trip back to the feeding grounds they came from.

Bird navigation

Arctic terns hold the record for the longest migration. The birds breed in the Arctic and the northern hemisphere. When breeding ends, they fly south to Antarctica where they spend the winter. Sometimes the birds fly for long distances over the open sea. They have no landmarks to guide them but they still manage to navigate accurately. After spending the winter near the South Pole, the birds fly north again to their breeding grounds. The round trip may be as much as 40 000 km. It requires accurate navigation to fly there and back safely.

▲ Arctic tern.

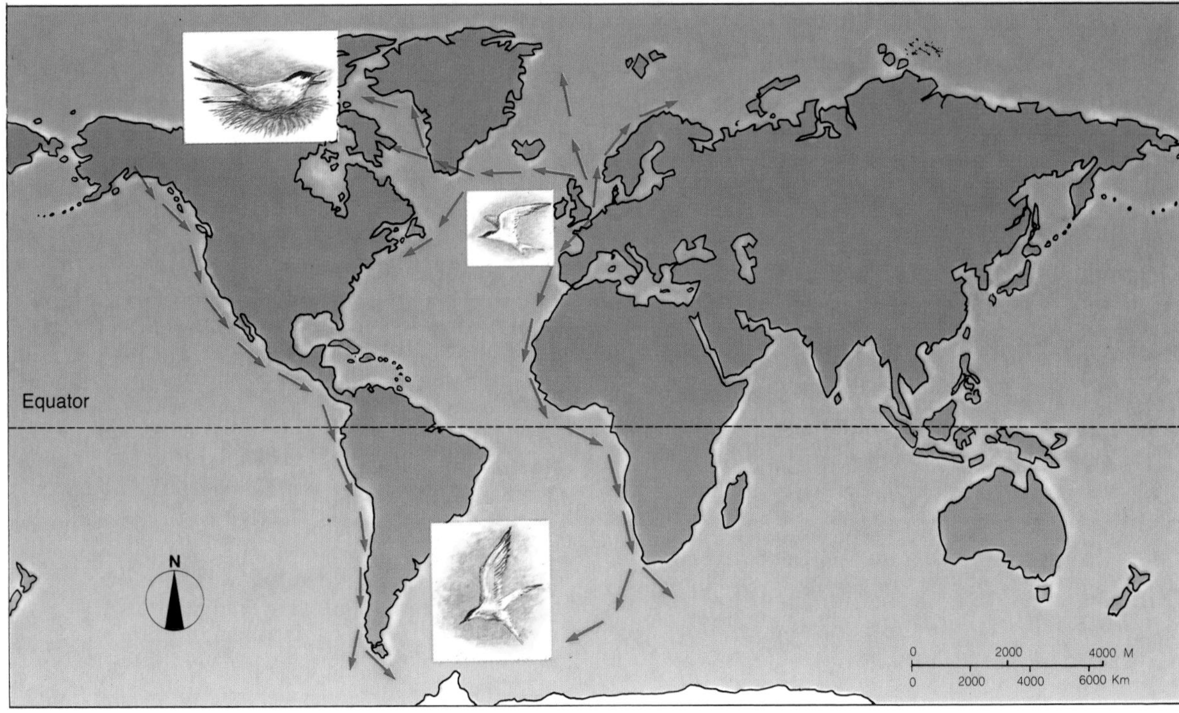

▼ Migration route of Arctic tern.

How do birds find their way about?

Scientists have puzzled for a long time about how birds navigate. Some species follow clear landmarks which they recognize using their keen eyesight. For example, they identify rivers, estuaries and coastlines. This is called visual navigation. Birds have much more sensitive eyes than we do. They can see very fine detail on the ground below them, which may help them to find their way.

Navigating over long distances

Birds flying over long distances probably navigate in a similar way to a trans-atlantic jumbo jet. In a jet, the captain uses a special kind of compass, a flight plan, and the computers on board to make sure the plan is followed accurately. The flight crew is able to tell exactly where the jumbo is at any time during the flight. The crew can tell the correct latitude and longitude. The captain also uses radio beams along the route.

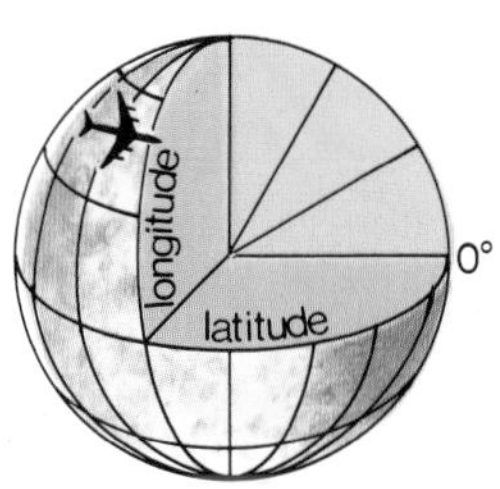

A bird probably carries a 'flight plan' in its brain. The brain also has a built-in clock, map and compass. All these things help birds to navigate very accurately. Birds use the position of the Sun and stars to help them find their way. The bird's brain allows for the Sun's movement when following its flight plan. This helps it work out its position of longitude. Some birds navigate during cloudy nights. It is likely that birds also use the Earth's magnetic field to help them navigate even when the Sun and stars are not visible.

The remarkable emperor penguin

During the breeding season, emperor penguins make several long journeys across the frozen Antarctic. The males and females separate at certain times, but they navigate so accurately that they are able to find one another at the end of each trip. There are few landmarks to help and the weather is poor. The birds may use the Earth's magnetic field to help them find their way.

Did you know?

Swallows, shearwaters and puffins return to the same nesting site every year.

Young wheatears make their first journey from Greenland to South Africa without the help of their parents.

Bar-headed geese fly over the Himalayas during their migration. They fly as high as 8000 m.

More about how animals navigate (pp.80, 81); migration (pp.78, 79)

Life in the water

The torpedo shape

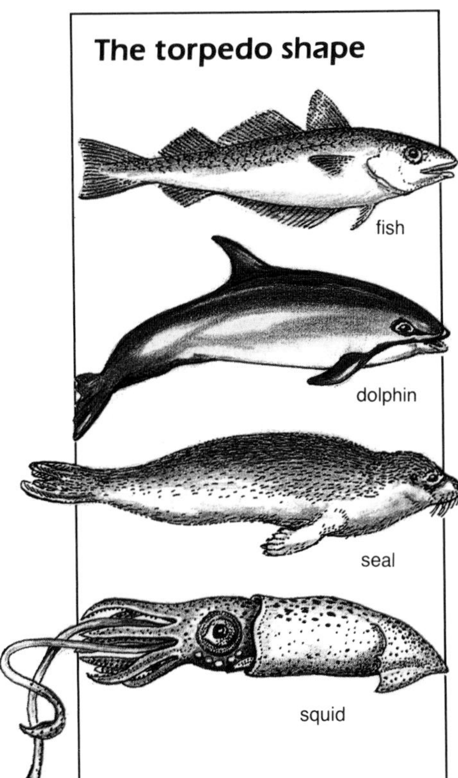

Many aquatic animals are torpedo-shaped. This makes them streamlined so they move easily through water. Whales and seals have extra layers of fat under their skin. The layers make their body outline smoother and more streamlined. Whales also have very short neck bones to make the front of the body more torpedo-shaped. Penguins become torpedo-shaped when chasing fish underwater. Octopuses and squids are not streamlined normally, but when swimming fast they change shape and become streamlined.

A watery world

Two-thirds of the Earth's surface is covered by water. There are many different kinds of animal and plant living in this aquatic habitat. Some animals and plants live on the surface of water. Others live below the surface at different depths. There are even animals in the deepest parts of the sea.

Floaters

Many animals and plants float on, or near, the surface of water. Plankton contains millions of tiny floating animals and plants. Animal plankton is called zooplankton. These animals often have unusual shapes which help them float. Some floating plants have air bladders which keep them afloat. Animals such as the Portuguese man-of-war have enlarged air bags which are used like sails. They are blown along by the wind.

Countershading

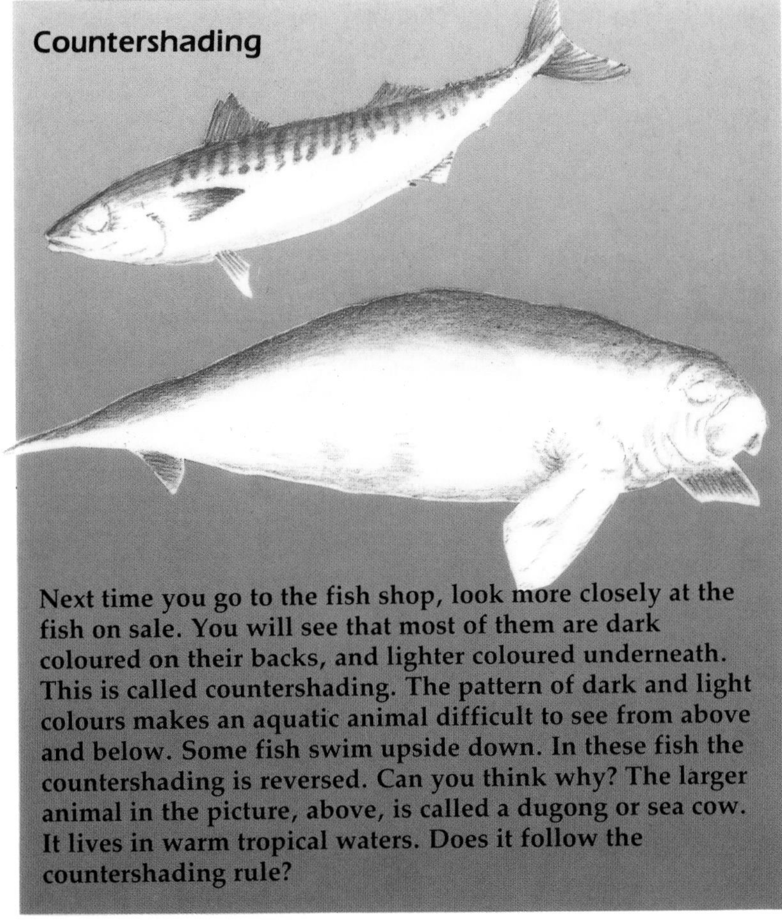

Next time you go to the fish shop, look more closely at the fish on sale. You will see that most of them are dark coloured on their backs, and lighter coloured underneath. This is called countershading. The pattern of dark and light colours makes an aquatic animal difficult to see from above and below. Some fish swim upside down. In these fish the countershading is reversed. Can you think why? The larger animal in the picture, above, is called a dugong or sea cow. It lives in warm tropical waters. Does it follow the countershading rule?

◀ A hippopotamus may weigh as much as 3 tonnes. Hippopotamuses live in tropical Africa. They are some of the biggest mammals. Even so, a fully-grown hippopotamus is able to lie submerged in water without being seen. Only its nose, eyes and ears are visible.

Many aquatic animals have their nose, eyes and ears sticking up on top of their head. They can remain under water and smell, hear and see without being seen. Frogs can do this, and so can crocodiles.

Staying afloat

Staying afloat is a problem which animals solve in different ways. Oil and fat are less dense than water. Animals make use of this fact to help solve their floating problems. Fish eggs contain oil droplets which keep them afloat. Sharks have oily livers to make them more buoyant. Other fish have small balloons, called swim bladders, inside them. The swim bladders work like tiny buoys. The amount of gas inside a swim bladder can be changed to make the fish float higher or sink lower in the water. The thick fat under the skin of seals and whales helps them float, and also keeps them warm.

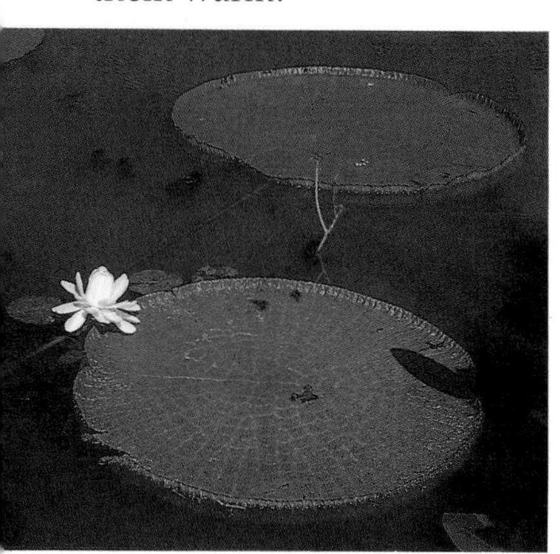

◀ Water plants float because they have large air spaces in their underwater stems and leaves. The trapped air makes them very buoyant. Some plants have leaves which float on the surface of water. Giant water lilies live in the River Amazon in South America. Their leaves may be two metres in diameter. Why do you think that the floating leaves have gaps in the rims? Answer on page 152.

Did you know?

A whale's nostrils open to a blow-hole on top of its head.

The sailfish is the fastest swimmer. It can swim more than 100 km/h.

Squids and octopuses swim by a kind of jet propulsion.

Sperm whales may dive to depths greater than 3000 m when hunting.

Fish called mudskippers are able to leave the water and come on to land. They carry their own water and air supply with them.

More about life in the water (pp.86, 87, 108-111); life in the oceans (pp.116-119); countershading (p.53)

Life in the water

Design for swimming

If you want to move you have to push or pull against something. When you walk, your feet push against the ground and drive your body forwards. The only thing animals living in water can push or pull against is the water. Aquatic animals have developed various structures for 'pushing' and 'pulling'.

Fish 'power'

A fish lashes its tail from side to side as it swims. Its tail pushes against the water and the fish moves forwards. The tail fin can also change shape and work like a propeller to push the fish even faster.

Fish watch

Look at a fish swimming in an aquarium. Watch how it uses its tail fin and then try to work out how it uses its other fins.

Here's a clue. The different fins have different jobs to do when a fish swims.

Super diver

The sperm whale dives deeper than any other animal. Its head is full of oil which the whale uses to help it sink and float. When the whale dives, the oil becomes solid, and is called wax. Wax is heavier than oil so a diving whale is 'heavy-headed'. This may help it dive quickly. When it starts to come up, the whale changes the wax back to oil. Now it is 'light-headed' and it comes to the surface quickly.

Turtles, seals and whales have flippers which they use like paddles to help pull themselves forward when they swim. They can even back-paddle. Penguins have small wings which are shaped like flippers. They are too small for flight in air but penguins use their flippers to 'fly' underwater.

▼ This water boatman has one pair of legs very much bigger than the others. It uses them like a pair of oars to 'row' through the water.

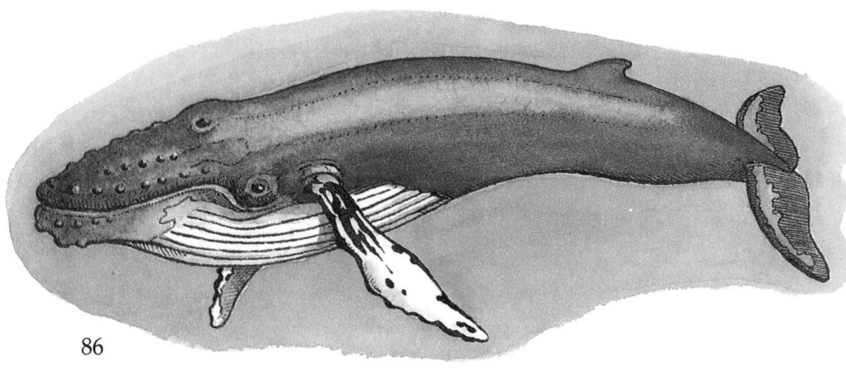

◀ Whales swim in a different way from fish. They have powerful muscles above and below the backbone. A whale's tail doesn't bend from side to side like the tail of a fish. Instead it moves up and down. Its flattened tail fin pushes against the water, and this pushes the whale forward.

Breathing in water

Animals living in water have two ways of getting oxygen. They can either gulp it from the air above the water, or they can get it from air dissolved in the water itself. Reptiles and mammals use their lungs to breathe atmospheric air, even when they live in water. They can swim underwater for long periods because they are good at holding their breath. However, they always return to the surface when they want more air. Crocodiles and turtles do this, so do seals and whales. Adult amphibians also use their lungs for breathing, but in the tadpole stage they use gills. These are special structures which many aquatic animals have for breathing air dissolved in the water. All fish and many invertebrates living in water breathe with gills.

Built-in snorkels

Mosquito larvae have tiny trumpet-shaped structures which they push above the surface of the water. The structures work like little breathing tubes or snorkels. Some tropical snails also get their air supply in this way.

On the surface

Some animals are able to live on the surface of ponds and lakes. Surface animals are very small and have a small mass. They are so light that their weight doesn't break the surface tension of the water. It is a bit like walking over the skin on a bowl of custard. Animals like pond skaters spread their weight by standing on legs spread wide apart.

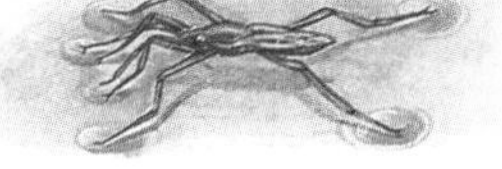

◀ A water spider's abdomen is covered with tiny hairs which trap air when it comes to the surface to breathe. When the spider has collected its new air supply it dives down to its little 'diving bell' anchored below the surface. Here it releases the air bubble into its underwater home. The water spider can even carry bubbles of air on its legs when it goes hunting under the water.

The monstrous coconut robber

The robber crab is a huge crab which lives on islands in the Indian and Pacific Oceans. Like all crabs it has gills. However, it is rather a special crab because it lives most of its life out of water. Coconuts are its favourite food. It even climbs coconut palms to get a tasty dinner. The robber crab can live out of water because it carries its own air supply. The crab keeps its gills soaked in sea water. This water contains the dissolved oxygen that the crab needs. It has to be renewed by washing the gills in sea water every day.

Did you know?

A 50 kg human would need feet with a total perimeter of 7 km in order not to break the surface tension when standing on the surface of a pond.

A bull sperm whale can hold its breath for nearly two hours in a deep dive.

The Indian climbing perch is a fish which can live for long periods out of water. It can even walk over land on its front fins.

More about life under water (pp.110, 111); life in the sea (pp.116, 117)

Life in the air

Floating in air

Many living things are able to float in air. Very small things can float because they have a small mass. They also have a large surface area compared to their volume. Air currents keep them airborne.

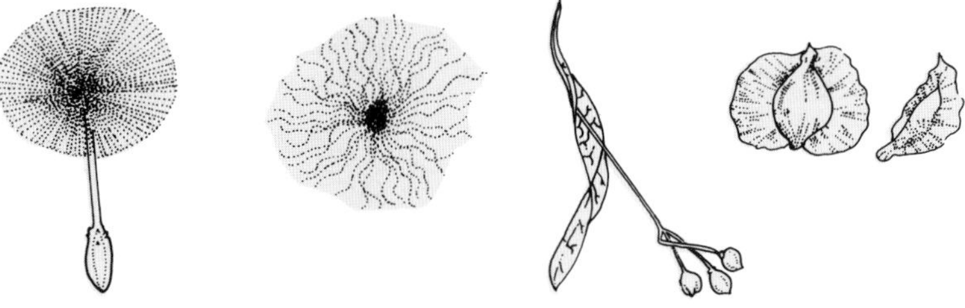

◀ These seeds have hairs and enlarged surfaces to help them float in air. These structures increase the seeds' surface area and this gives them greater resistance to falling in air.

Flying and gliding

As organisms increase in size they develop special structures to help them stay airborne. Many seeds have hairy parachutes and wings. Larger organisms face an even bigger problem of keeping airborne. Animals have developed ways of flying. There are two types of flight. These are powered flight and gliding flight.

Aerial plankton

Aerial plankton contains bacterial and fungal spores, pollen grains, small animals, such as tiny insects, and even minute spiders. It is found up to many thousands of metres above the Earth's surface.

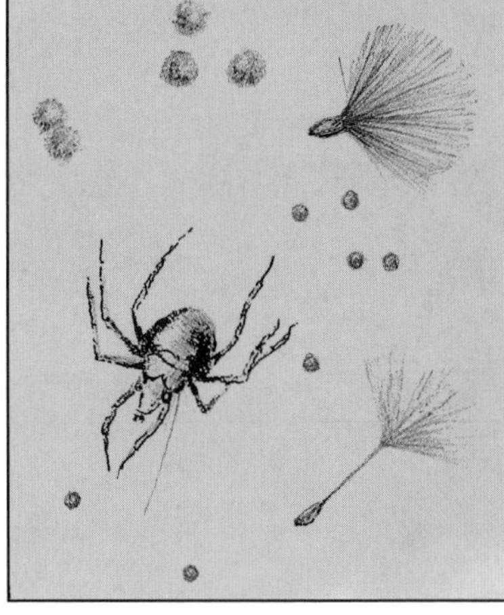

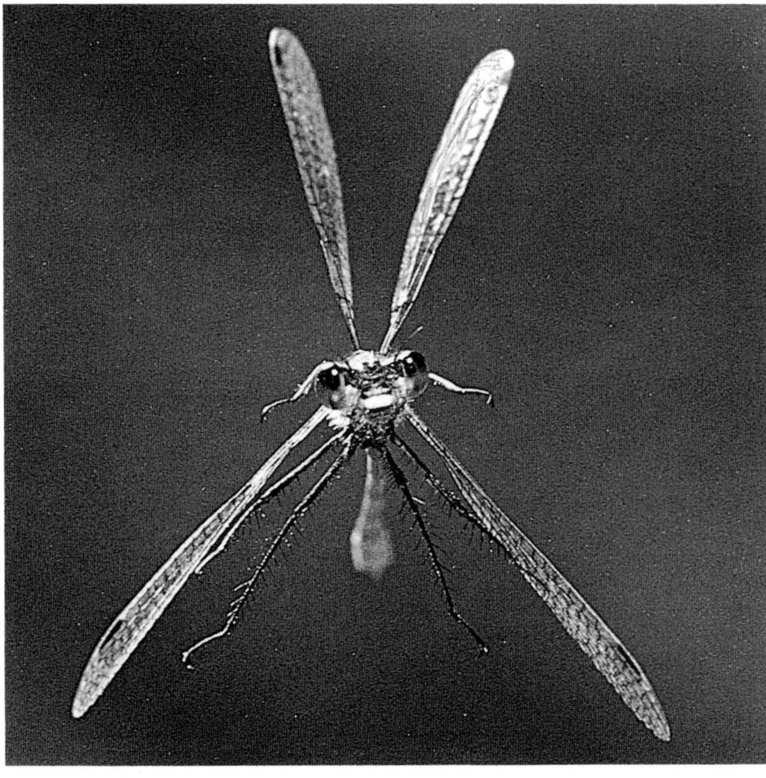

◀ Powered flight is found in insects, birds and one type of mammal, bats. The wings are formed in different ways, but they have the same function. They give the animals an increased surface area which helps them to resist falling through the air.

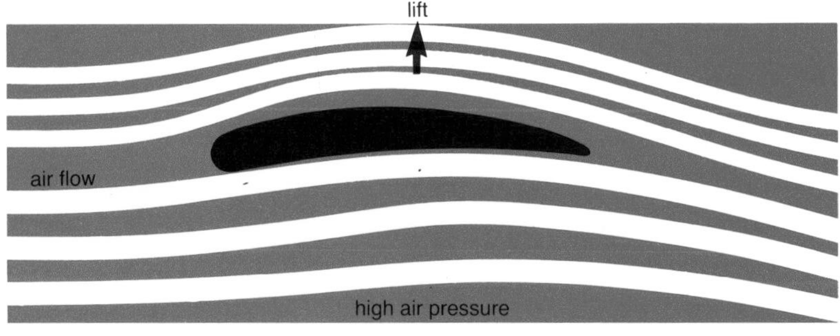

◀ A wing cut in section looks like this. Such a shape is called an aerofoil. The airflow above is different from the airflow underneath. The air pressure above the curved wing is lower than the pressure underneath, so air under the wing pushes upwards and gives lift. This keeps the bird airborne. The bird's muscles provide power for flight.

The aerofoil

Wings have a large surface. They are also moved by large flight muscles. They have a special shape and this is important in helping the wings gain lift. A bird's wing is curved on its upper surface, rather like in the diagram above. This curvature is important in controlling the movement of air as it passes over the wing. As air passes over the curved upper surface of a wing it has to move faster because it has further to go. This reduces the air pressure above the wing. The air pressure underneath the wing is higher than that above. This gives lift because the air pressing up under the wing pushes the wing upwards. A wing with a curved upper surface is called an *aerofoil*. A bird's wings are shaped like aerofoils. So are the wings of a jumbo jet. This aerofoil structure, together with the bird's muscles, keep a bird airborne. The muscles provide the power for flight.

▼ Gliding flight is found in a number of different types of animal. These are not true fliers but they can glide downwards from a higher place. All these animals have developed webs and flaps of skin to increase their body surfaces. This helps them resist falling through air, rather like a parachute.

A is a flying gecko. Its flattened tail helps it control its glide. **B** is a flying draco lizard. Its flaps of skin are supported by ribs and can be folded up when not in use. **C** is a flying squirrel. **D** is a flying frog. It has big membranes between its toes to increase its surface area. There is also a flying snake.

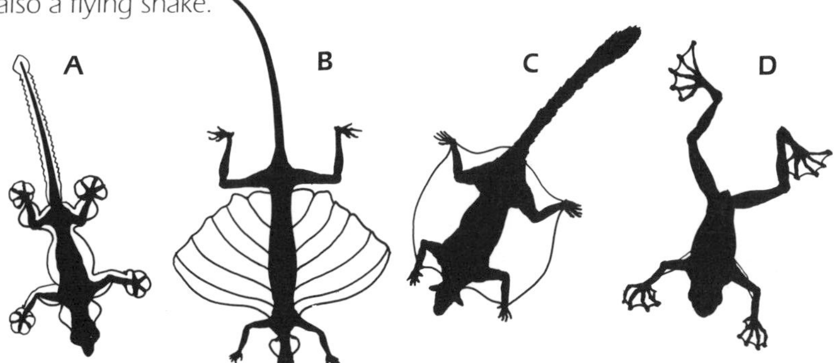

Did you know?

A dandelion seed may be carried 10 km or more by the wind before landing on the soil.

Small spiders are often carried thousands of kilometres by the wind on their silken parachutes.

A bumble bee's body is covered with a 'hair-like' material. This keeps the bee warm and helps its large flight muscles work more efficiently.

The paradise tree snake from south-east Asia turns its body into the shape of an aerofoil when it glides down from a high tree.

A flying fish can travel or glide more than 100 m across the surface of the sea.

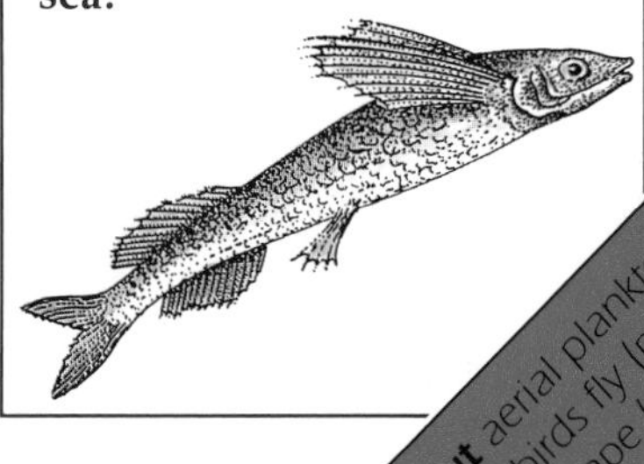

More about aerial plankton (p.117, 122); how birds fly (pp.90, 91); size and shape (pp.26, 27)

Masters of the air

Bird adaptation to flight

Birds are the most skilful fliers in the animal kingdom. They fly in different ways but they all have similar adaptations to help them. They have well developed wings providing a large surface area. The wings are shaped like aerofoils. The bird's body is covered with feathers. These help increase

The feathers keep the bird warm: They are also important for flight.

the surface area, and also keep the bird warm. It is important that the flight muscles are kept warm if they are to work efficiently. The bird's breast muscles are large and powerful to move the wings. Inside the body the bird's skeleton is specially modified for flight. The bones are hollow. This reduces weight. The lower part of the keel bone is large and flat. The powerful breast muscles are attached to it. A bird has air sacs inside its body. These help it to breathe more efficiently. They also reduce the bird's body weight. Birds have well developed senses, including good eyesight. This is very important for fast flight.

▲ The albatross is an expert glider. It has long, narrow wings to catch the wind above the surface of the sea.

Flapping flight

Although some birds are skilled gliders and soarers, most birds fly by flapping their wings up and down, using their powerful flight muscles. In fast flight the muscles pull the wings downwards and forwards. The movement of the wing downwards is called the downstroke. This movement pushes air backwards and the bird moves forwards. The movement of the wing upwards is called the recovery stroke. When the wings are pulled up the feathers at the tips of the wings become parted. This can be seen in the pictures below. The parted feathers allow air to pass easily between them and so there is less resistance to air as the wings move up to begin the downstroke again.

▲ The condor has very long, wide wings. It soars through the sky on currents of air.

Gliding and soaring

Some birds are experts at soaring and gliding. Vultures, buzzards and eagles have broad wings which help them to make use of warm air currents rising from the Earth's surface. These birds are soarers. Their wings spread out over a large surface. This allows them to sink slowly in air. If they find air rising faster than their sinking speed they will gain height. The slotted wings help the warm air to flow under the wings and out through the ends. They also help the bird to turn quickly.

Birds like albatrosses, fulmars and frigate birds have long, narrow wings which make them excellent gliders. These birds catch the high wind speeds above the surface of the sea. They make semicircular turns, climbing into the wind and then descending downwind. They don't have slotted feathers at the wing tips because there is no need to turn quickly like soarers.

Hovering flight

Some birds are able to hover in the air. This is achieved by very fast wing beats. Hummingbirds from South America and their African relatives, the sunbirds, are experts at this kind of flying. Hummingbirds are the smallest birds. They use their hovering flight to 'stand still' in the air while sipping nectar from tropical flowers. They can move up and down and even backwards in some cases. Because of their very small size and great use of energy, hummingbirds are not able to remain fully active for long periods. They go into a state which is rather like hibernation for about twelve hours every day.

Did you know?

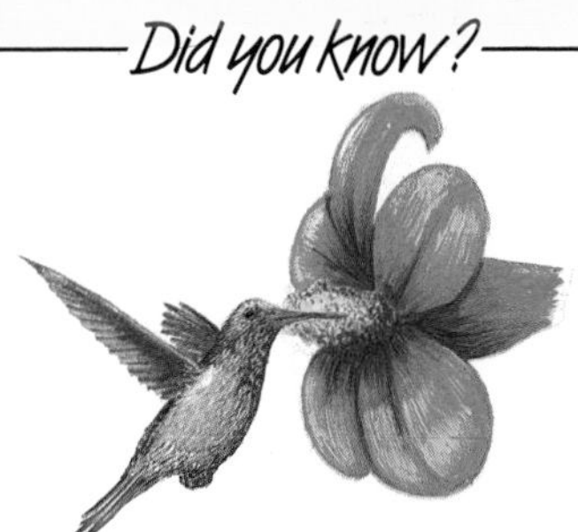

A hummingbird beats its wings as many as 50 times per second.

Albatrosses on remote islands need a clear runway which they use to take off into the wind.

The wandering albatross has a wingspan of more than 3 m.

The Andean condor weighs as much as 10 kg. It can travel more than 100 km without flapping its wings.

More about life in the air (pp.88, 89); long distance fliers (p.78); hibernation (pp.76, 77)

Life on land

Living on land

The first living creatures evolved in the sea. Then, about three hundred and fifty million years ago, some animals moved on to dry land. Water provides a good support for the bodies of plants and animals. Think how easy it is to float in a swimming-bath. But air does not provide such a good support. Terrestrial animals and plants (ones which live on land) need their own built-in supports.

▲ No legs, no speed!

Four legs and more

Worms and caterpillars move very slowly because they cannot lift their bodies off the ground. Most terrestrial animals have legs to lift them off the ground, and so increase their speed. Usually they have at least two pairs of legs, making it easy to balance. Frogs, salamanders, lizards and crocodiles have legs at the sides of their bodies. They cannot lift their bodies far off the ground, so they are not very efficient walkers. Mammals' legs are attached further underneath the body, giving better support. Insects and crustaceans have rather short legs, but they are not very heavy and can easily lift their bodies clear of the ground.

Bags of water

If you fill a large polythene bag with water and tie the top very tightly, you can sit on the bag. The water inside keeps it stiff. Plant cells are like lots of tiny bags of water. The water keeps the plant stiff. If a plant loses a lot of water, for example, on a hot day, it wilts. The leaves droop because they no longer have enough water to keep them stiff. Large plants need extra support. Trees have stiff wood to support them.

◀ Some monkeys use their tail like an extra limb. They curl it round branches for support, and even hang by it while they feed.

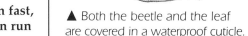

Waterproofing

Living on land with your body exposed to the air means that you may dry out. Land animals and plants usually have waterproof coats. Insects and crustaceans are covered in a hard, waxy layer, called the cuticle. The skin of mammals is also waterproof. Birds coat their feathers with waterproofing oil from special glands. Reptiles are covered in scales, and are so well waterproofed that many can live in hot, dry deserts and hunt in the heat of the day. Only frogs have a moist skin which easily dries out. Frogs are usually found only in damp places.

▲ Both the beetle and the leaf are covered in a waterproof cuticle.

How big are your feet?

Big feet make it easy to balance, but, if you want to run fast, they slow you down. Cheetahs and other cats which can run very fast walk only on the tips of their toes. Antelopes, horses and other grazing animals that travel large distances in search of food have feet reduced to hooves.

Did you know?

Millipedes don't have 1000 legs. The largest number of legs recorded is only 355 pairs (710 legs).

Four legs are better than two! The cheetah can reach speeds of 96 km/hour. The ostrich can run at almost 50 km/hour, and the kangaroo at 60 km/hour.

The heaviest land animal is the elephant, at 6 tonnes. But the heaviest plant, a giant sequoia or 'big tree', weighs 2179 tonnes, almost 360 times more.

More about life on land (pp.94, 95); moving through the treetops (p.131); waterproofing (p.22)

Life on land

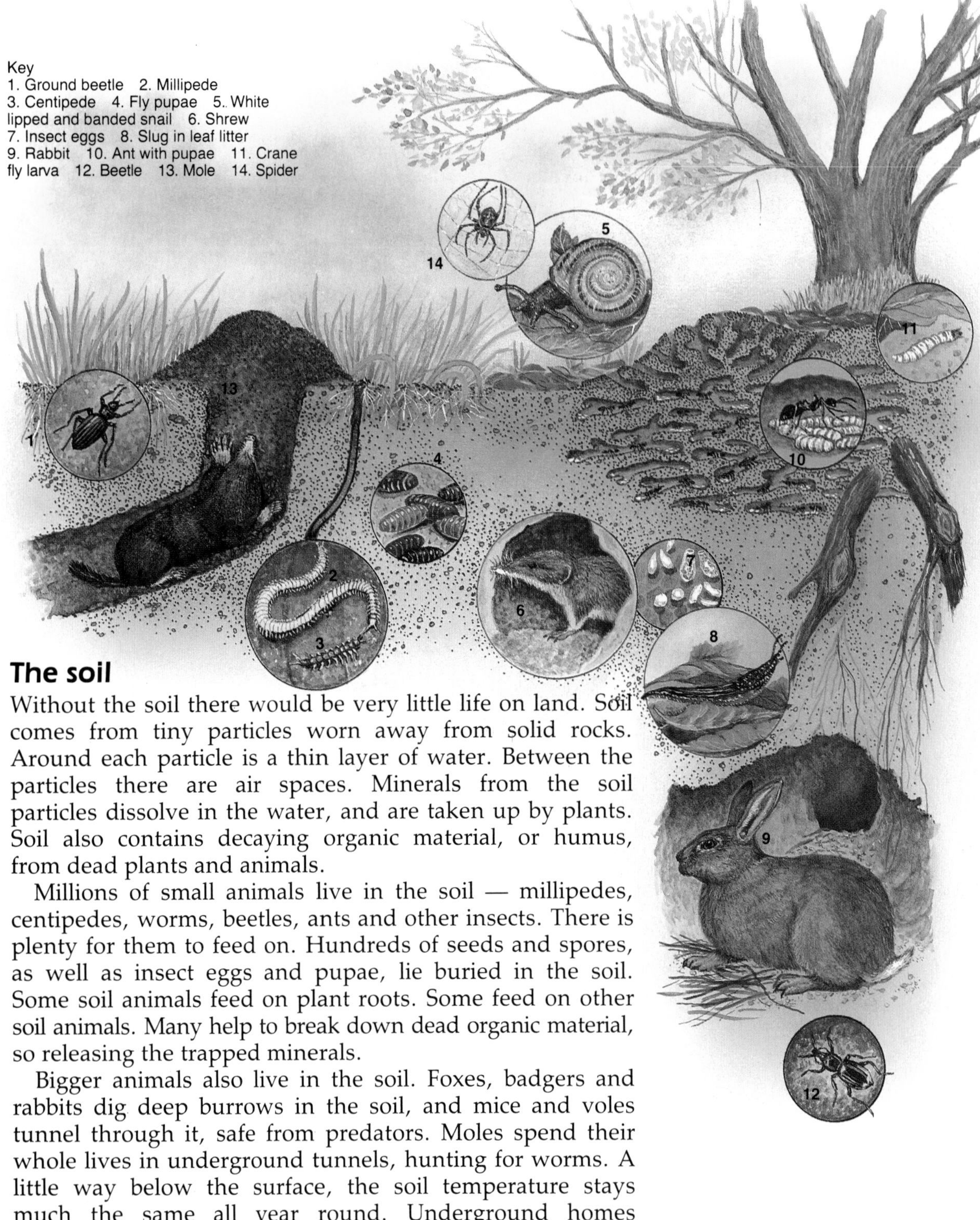

The soil

Without the soil there would be very little life on land. Soil comes from tiny particles worn away from solid rocks. Around each particle is a thin layer of water. Between the particles there are air spaces. Minerals from the soil particles dissolve in the water, and are taken up by plants. Soil also contains decaying organic material, or humus, from dead plants and animals.

Millions of small animals live in the soil — millipedes, centipedes, worms, beetles, ants and other insects. There is plenty for them to feed on. Hundreds of seeds and spores, as well as insect eggs and pupae, lie buried in the soil. Some soil animals feed on plant roots. Some feed on other soil animals. Many help to break down dead organic material, so releasing the trapped minerals.

Bigger animals also live in the soil. Foxes, badgers and rabbits dig deep burrows in the soil, and mice and voles tunnel through it, safe from predators. Moles spend their whole lives in underground tunnels, hunting for worms. A little way below the surface, the soil temperature stays much the same all year round. Underground homes provide warmth, shelter, and protection from bad weather.

The go-betweens

Flowering plants do not produce sperms. Instead, they produce pollen. In some plants, the pollen is carried from flower to flower by the wind. In other plants, it is carried by insects like honeybees. Many flowers contain a sugary liquid, called nectar, which insects like to drink. Colourful petals advertise the flower to passing insects. Sometimes there are patterns of lines and spots on the petals to lead the insects to the nectar. Each flower is designed so that insects searching for nectar will rub against the pollen-producing parts.

▲ When they reproduce, most animals living in water shed their sperms and eggs into the water. The sperms swim to the eggs. Except in damp places, there is not enough water for this to happen on land. Most land animals pass their sperms directly from the male into the female, who keeps the eggs inside her body until they have been fertilized and sometimes even longer.

► The honeybee acts as a go-between for the flowers.

▼ Pollen from hazel catkins blows away on the breeze.

Waterproof eggs

Most land animals lay eggs which have tough, waterproof coats. Only animals living in damp places have soft, moist eggs. Snails and slugs lay their eggs in the soil, which stops the eggs drying out. Some animals get round the problem by keeping the eggs inside them until they hatch. The young are born fully developed. Mammals do this, and so do some snakes and lizards.

Did you know?

One gram of soil may contain as many as 4000 million bacteria.

Termites use soil to build huge mounds up to 6m high. Some mounds have their own central heating system, using decaying vegetation to generate heat. Others have a complicated system of chambers and passages which form an air-conditioning system.

More about life on land (pp.92, 93); feeding on nectar (p.33); how animals reproduce (pp.66, 67)

Life without water

Deserts of the world

Deserts are usually found in areas which get very little rain, or where rain falls rarely, perhaps only once every seven years. In hot parts of the world, much of the rain falling on the scorching ground evaporates before it has time to sink into the soil.

Some deserts are sandy. They have rows of sand dunes that move with the wind. Others are bare and rocky, with high mountains and deep, dry canyons. Deserts are places of extremes, with blazing hot Sun by day, and very cold temperatures by night, and long periods of drought followed by sudden torrential rain.

The long sleep

Many plants and animals avoid drought altogether by sleeping for months at a time. This sleep is a kind of hibernation called aestivation. The dry season is also a time when food is scarce, so aestivation saves food as well as water. The African lungfish can survive for four years in the dried-up mud, breathing through a narrow tunnel from its burrow to the surface. The desert tortoise sleeps in a deep hole underground, storing water in its bladder.

Plants need water too. They rely on water in their tissues to keep them stiff. Without it they wilt. Many desert plants spend most of their lives as dormant seeds, or as underground bulbs and stems swollen with stored food. The soil protects them from the Sun's drying rays. When rain falls, their stored food is used to produce leaves, flowers and seeds quickly, while the water supply lasts.

◀ Even in rocky deserts some plants manage to survive.

◀ The spadefoot toad of North America uses a special horny pad on its hind feet for digging. It digs down as much as 3 metres below the desert surface to escape the heat of the dry season.

▼ The regal-horned lizard hunts in the early morning and later afternoon, when it is warm enough for a cold-blooded animal to be active, but not too hot for comfort.

Fish in the desert

After heavy rain, pools and lakes appear in the desert. Soon they are full of life — shrimps, water fleas, fish and even tadpoles. But where have all these creatures come from? Many of them have spent the dry period resting as eggs or pupae in the soil, protected by waterproof coats. Eggs and pupae do not move or grow, so they use very little stored food, and need very little water.

Like many desert plants, the animals of these temporary pools pass through all the stages of their life cycle in a surprisingly short time. The African bullfrog tadpole hatches from its egg less than a day after rain falls. In just four weeks it is an adult frog. After mating and laying eggs, it buries itself in the mud, protected from drying out by a cocoon of mucus and mud. Here it sleeps until the next rains.

Did you know?

Fairy shrimps survive the desert drought as tough-coated eggs. They can survive for 100 years without water, and still hatch successfully after rain.

The hottest land temperature ever recorded was 58°C in the Sahara Desert.

Desert frogs and toads can store up to 40 per cent of their body weight as water in their bladders.

A food store in the soil! The soil of the Californian desert receives about 1½ billion seeds a year, more than enough for all the animals that would like to eat them.

In the Arctic and Antarctic there is very little rain – only snow falls. These regions are cold deserts.

More about life without water (pp.98, 99); hibernation (pp.76, 77); eggs and pupae (pp.68, 69)

Life without water

Cacti, the desert specialists

The giant saguaro cactus lives for up to two hundred years. It grows to a height of seventeen metres, and weighs about ten tonnes. Four-fifths of this weight is water. Cacti like the saguaro are well adapted to the desert. They store vast amounts of water in their swollen stems. The stems are ribbed, like a concertina, so they can expand when full of water, and shrink as they dry out. Cactus roots are not very deep, but they spread sideways, for some distance, to trap rain-water. Their stems are green, and they make their own food by photosynthesis. They have thick, waxy, waterproof surfaces, and spines which keep off browsing animals.

Living through the drought

Some desert animals stay active throughout the year. Birds, and large mammals like the desert fox, the oryx and the kangaroo, can travel to find water. Many animals spend the hottest part of the day in burrows, only coming out to feed in the cool of the evening. The air inside the burrow becomes damp from the moist air that the animal breathes out. The kangaroo rat plugs the entrance to its burrow to keep in the moisture.

Weaver birds in the African deserts live in huge communal nests woven from dry grasses. A weaver bird colony looks rather like an untidy haystack. Inside the nest, the birds are protected from the Sun, and the air stays cool and moist.

Water-hoarding plants

Living in the desert is difficult for many plants. Some, like the tamarisk, have deep roots which reach permanent water supplies far below the ground. Others, like cacti, have shallow roots which are spread over a wide area to catch as much rain as possible before it evaporates. Many desert plants store water in their stems or leaves. Only a few plants, such as the strange resurrection plant, can survive being completely dried out. Some desert shrubs, like the ocotillo, even shed their leaves in dry weather so as not to lose water from them.

Plants are often the only source of moisture for desert animals. Many desert plants have spines to keep thirsty animals at bay. The stone plants, *Lithops*, rely on camouflage instead. They have only two leaves, which look like the pebbles which surround them.

▲ A kangaroo rat.

Lord of the desert

Everything about the camel is adapted to life in the desert. Its hump is full of fat, a store of food for the long dry season. The hump shields its back from the Sun. It acts like a large sun hat. When the camel is resting, the hump insulates it from the heat of the Sun, and keeps the body cool. The rest of the body has very little fat, and can easily lose heat from its surface. The camel can drink sixty-six litres of water at one time, one-third of its own body weight. It even swallows its own nose drippings to save water. The camel's faeces are so dry that they can be used to light fires. Its huge feet are wide and spreading to prevent the camel sinking into the sand.

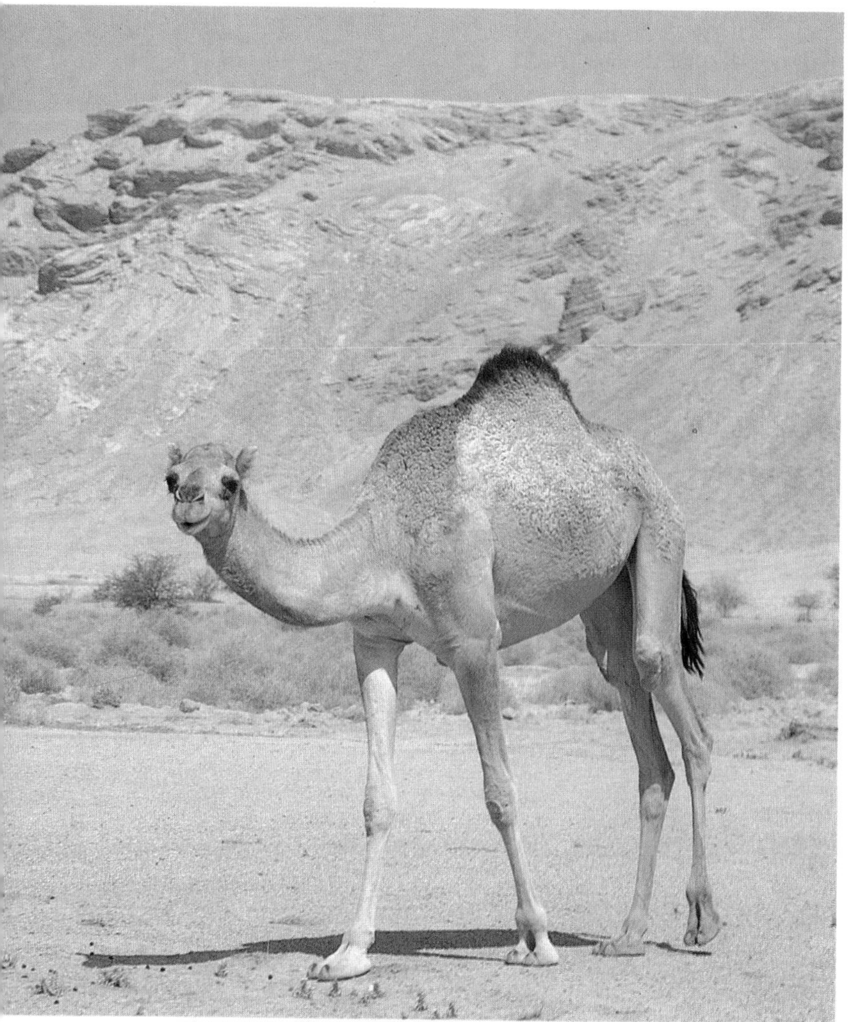

Cooling down

Some desert animals have large ears. As blood runs through the ears, it loses heat to the surrounding air, and cools down the animal.

Drinking the dew

There is another source of water in the deserts. As deserts get cold at night, moisture in the air condenses as dew. In the early morning, animals lick the droplets off the plants, or simply eat the wet leaves. In some deserts, such as the Namib Desert of South-west Africa, fog is common. Here, desert beetles stand on their heads, letting the fog condense on their bodies and trickle down into their mouths.

More about life without water (pp.96, 97); camouflage (pp. 52, 53); photosynthesis (pp.28, 29)

Life in cold climates

The long winter

In the Arctic and Antarctic it is cold throughout the year. There is seldom any rain — only snow falls. The winters are long. In midwinter the Sun never appears above the horizon. In summer the days are long, and the Sun does not set. The summer Sun is low in the sky, and does not give much warmth. Animals that live in these areas cope with these freezing conditions all year round.

Further away from the polar regions the weather is warmer, but the winters are still cold and snowy. There is a bigger difference between the seasons, and the summers are quite warm. Animals living here have a choice. Either they can hunt for food in the cold of winter, or they can avoid the worst of the weather by hibernating or migrating.

▲ Many animals put on extra fat during the late summer. This provides a food store for the winter. Fat is also a good insulator (it does not allow heat to escape). The extra fat helps to keep the animal warm. Mammals like seals and walruses, which live in the polar seas, have thick layers of fat rather than extra fur.

Growing your own blanket

Mammals that live in cold regions usually have thick fur. Often they grow extra-thick fur in the autumn, and moult to a thinner coat in the spring. The musk ox has some of the thickest fur. It grows an extra layer of soft, warm fur under the straggly, waterproof, outer layer. It looks as if it is draped in a shaggy old rug.

Snow can keep you warm

Small animals lose heat easily. Many birds and small mammals use the snow as an insulator. The ptarmigan scrapes a hollow in the snow to shelter from the icy winter wind. Lemmings tunnel under the snow, feeding on roots and seeds in the soil under the warm, white, snowy blanket.

Lying low

In the far north, the bitter, cold winds and lack of rain prevent trees growing. Only small, slow-growing plants survive. This treeless region is called the tundra. It is covered in lichens, mosses and cushion plants. These plants are low and rounded. Because they are so short, they can avoid the worst of the wind, and are protected under the snow in the winter.

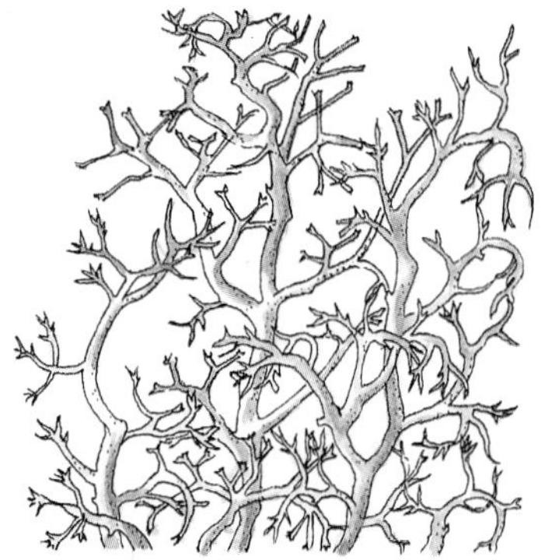

▲ There are lots of feathery lichens. These are called reindeer moss, because they are the favourite food of the reindeer.

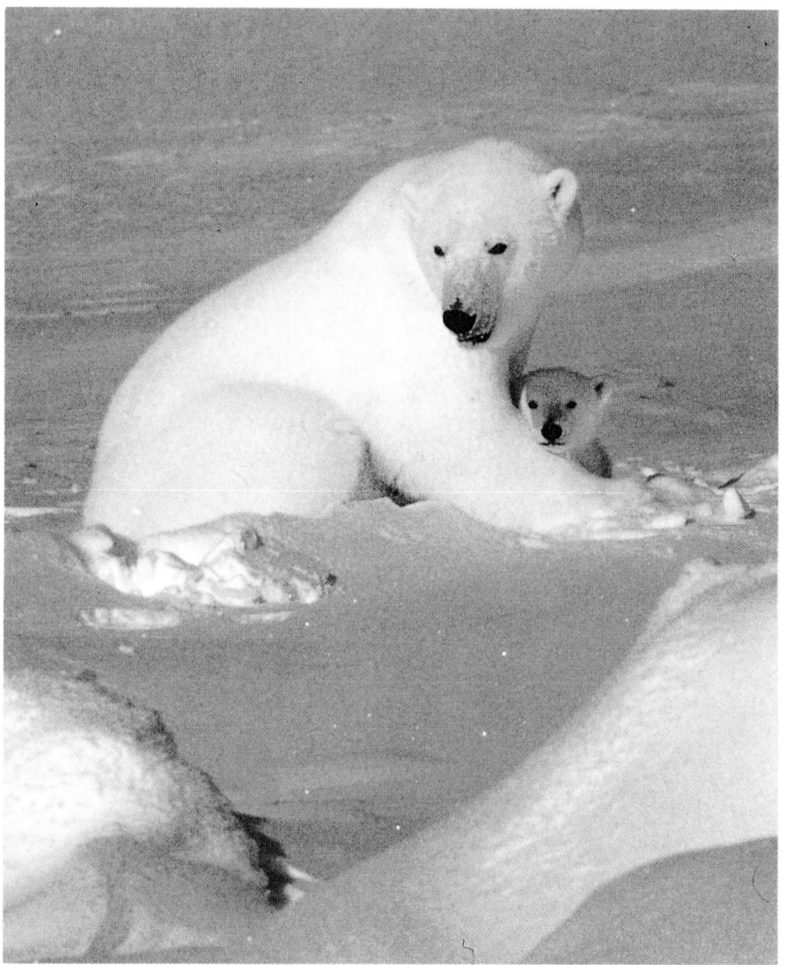

Born under the ice

The polar bear gives birth to her cubs in the middle of winter in a den inside the ice of the frozen polar sea. She remains with them, living on her store of fat, until they are big enough to explore the world outside. By this time spring has arrived, and there is plenty of food around.

Did you know?

In polar regions, insect eggs and pupae contain 'antifreeze' to help them survive the winter. So do plants.

Fish living in the polar seas have supercooled blood. Although the blood temperature can be below freezing point, 'antifreeze' in the blood prevents it freezing.

Many Arctic seabirds have very cold feet. This prevents them from losing heat from their feet, which are usually not protected with feathers.

Blood runs very near the body surface in ears. The Arctic fox has much smaller ears than any of its relatives. The tiny ears reduce heat loss.

More about life in cold climates (pp.102, 103); hibernation (pp. 76, 77); migration (pp.78, 79)

▲ In summer the ptarmigan has a dull, speckled coat that blends with the summer plants.

▼ By the winter the ptarmigan's coat is white to match the snowy landscape.

▲ Snowshoe hare.

The winter hunters

Animals that hunt in the snow all year round — the polar bear, Arctic fox and snowy owl — have permanent white camouflage. Many animals that feed on the tundra in summer change the colour of their coats with the spring and autumn moults. Ptarmigan blend perfectly with the summer tundra, but change to winter-white in the autumn. So do hares, foxes and stoats. The stoat's colour change is triggered by falling temperatures. Further south, in Britain, stoats turn white only in very severe winters.

Snowshoe feet

Winter hunters need to be able to walk on snow. The snowshoe hare has huge feet. They spread its weight over the snow, so it is less likely to sink down.

Reindeer and caribou also have large spreading feet. These help in spring, too, when the thawing snow makes the ground soft and boggy.

The ptarmigan grows its own snowshoes. In winter, it has extra feathers on its feet. These keep the feet warm as well as acting like snowshoes.

The snow leopard lives in Asia. It has thick hairs between its toes. These also act like snowshoes.

The polar spring

The insects of polar regions pass the winter protected in the soil as eggs or pupae. When spring comes, they emerge in their millions to feed on the new growth, and on the nectar in the tundra flowers. The melting snow produces a landscape full of pools, and mosquitoes thrive. They become such a nuisance that the caribou will sometimes go and stand in the sea to get away from them.

This wealth of food makes the tundra an attractive breeding ground for birds. Thousands of birds fly north, often travelling thousands of kilometres, to rear their young in the tundra. The long summer days allow plenty of time to find food to feed the growing families.

In early spring the weather is still very cold. But the birds must lay their eggs well before all the insects hatch, as the summer season is so short. Eider ducks line their nests with soft, downy feathers.

▲ Penguins incubate their single large egg on their feet. Their legs are very short, and they have a special hollow in their feathers which fits snugly over the egg.

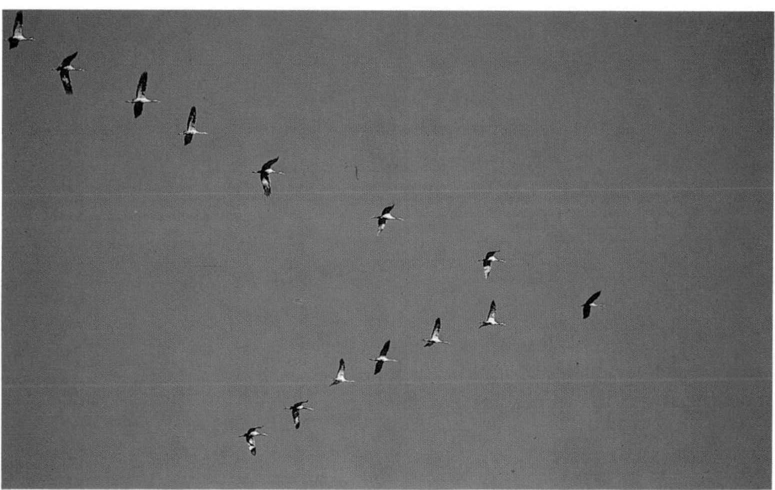

▲ Cranes fly south to avoid the winter.

Running away

Many animals avoid the polar winter by migrating to warmer areas. The North American caribou (reindeer) feed on the tundra in summer. In autumn they migrate 700 kilometres south to the forests. Here, the snow, although deep, is less frozen, and they scrape it away to reach the plants below. They are followed by packs of wolves and by scavengers.

Penguins in Antarctica spend the winter at sea. They may travel 100 kilometres back to their breeding sites in spring, partly swimming and partly walking across the pack-ice.

Did you know?

The polar bear is perfectly camouflaged except for the tip of its nose. When it is stalking prey, it will cover its black nose with a paw.

Arctic poppies can turn their heads to follow the Sun as it moves across the sky. This keeps the centres of the flowers warmer than the surrounding air, helping to attract insects.

Seals spend the winter hunting under the ice. They make their own breathing holes in the ice.

More about life in cold climates (pp.100, 101); camouflage (pp. 52, 53); migration (pp.78, 79)

Grasslands

▲ The pronghorn can run faster than any other American mammal.

The great plains

Stretching across the centres of most of the continents are vast areas of grassland, including the steppes of Europe and Central Asia, the savannas of Africa and Australia, the prairies of North America, and the pampas of South America. In some areas the grasses grow to over two metres tall; in others they are kept short by herds of grazing animals. Once there were millions of these grazing animals, but they have been hunted so much that their numbers are now a lot smaller. In Africa there are still large herds of antelopes and zebra, but the great herds of American bison have gone, the European bison are near-extinct (there are some in captivity), and the wild horses of Asia are rare.

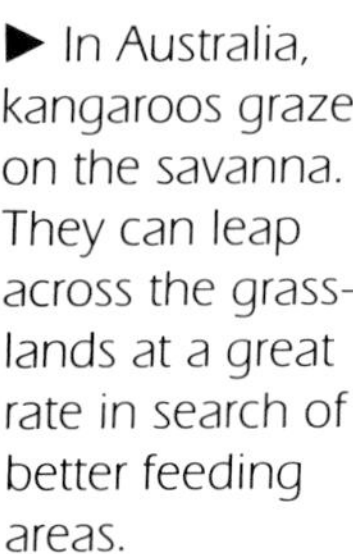

► In Australia, kangaroos graze on the savanna. They can leap across the grasslands at a great rate in search of better feeding areas.

Long distance travellers

The herds of animals on the grasslands roam far and wide in search of good grazing. Often they migrate with the seasons, following the rain. They are not the only long distance travellers. Ostriches (Africa), rheas (South America) and emus (Australia) also feed on grassland plants. They are large birds and cannot fly, but they have very long, powerful legs and can run very fast.

Life underground

The plains offer little shelter for small animals. Most live in underground burrows, which protect them from the heat of the day, and from the cold in winter. They also provide safe havens from predators and fire.

For many of these animals danger comes from both above and below. Snakes can slide into burrows unnoticed. Eagles and other birds of prey scan the plains from the air, alert to every small movement in the grass. Members of the dog family — foxes, coyotes, hunting dogs and dingoes — are common predators in grasslands. In Africa, big cats such as lions and cheetahs also prowl the plains, and in South America the puma stalks through the pampas. Vultures are a common sight, circling high above the grasslands in search of carcasses.

Builders of the plains

Large termite mounds are dotted across the grasslands. Ant- and termite-eating animals are common in the grasslands. For example, the giant anteater of the pampas, the aardvark and aardwolf of the African savanna, and the spiny anteater of Australia. They all use strong claws to tear into the ant or termite nest, and long sticky tongues to extract their prey.

Food for all

Grasslands are full of food for small mammals. Grasses and other flowering plants produce millions of seeds. The underground parts of plants provide more food, and the insects attracted to plants can be eaten, too. Grasslands are home to many different kinds of mice, rats and voles, and, in Europe and Asia, hamsters and gerbils. Many of them collect huge amounts of seeds and store them in their burrows for the winter or the dry season.

◀ In America, prairie dogs live in vast underground towns, building entrance mounds which serve as lookout posts.

Fire makes the grass grow

Many grassland plants flower only after a fire. Most of them rest underground while the grass is high, surviving as bulbs or underground roots and stems swollen with stored food. Fire is common on the plains. The thunderstorms that end the dry season produce lightning, which easily ignites the dry grasses. After the fire and rain, tender new shoots of grass appear, providing better fodder for the grazing animals. The plains are now full of colour from lilies, tulips, irises, anemones, gladioli and many other flowers. They have to produce their seeds before the grass grows tall and shades them again.

Did you know?

The mounds of some termites can be over 12 m high.

Although they have small brains, ostriches are quite intelligent, and can even be trained to herd sheep.

More about anteaters (p.39); migration (pp.78, 79); animals that eat plants (pp.32, 33)

Temperate forests

▲ Spotted deer in English forest.

Forests of the temperate regions

Temperate regions are parts of the world which have warm summers and cool or cold winters. At one time, large areas of the world's temperate regions were covered in forests of broad-leaved trees. These forests are mostly of deciduous trees, that is, trees which lose their leaves in winter. Many forests have been cleared for farming. The remaining forests are home to many different animals.

Vegetarians of the forest

In the summer there is plenty of food for plant-eaters. The caterpillars of many moths feed on the leaves. Mice and voles make their homes among the twisting roots, or burrow in the soft soil. They eat tender young buds and seeds. The American porcupine eats the bark as well. The sapsuckers of American forests are birds which look like woodpeckers. They drill holes in the bark of trees to get to the sap below. At dawn and dusk, deer browse on young shoots, and rabbits scamper across the forest clearings. In autumn, nuts and berries add to the feast, just as the leaves are beginning to fall.

► Once the leaves have come out in the spring, the forest floor does not get much light. Many forest herbs put out leaves and flowers before the trees come into leaf. They can do this because they have underground stores of food in swollen roots and stems, or in bulbs and corms. Snowdrops, anemones, daffodils, celandines, bluebells, and, in America, trilliums and hepaticas, form carpets of colour in the spring.

Hunters of the forest

Many predators hunt the plant-eaters. Shrews search for insects on the forest floor, and many small birds such as tits, warblers, wrens and thrushes feed on the caterpillars. There are not many wolves and mountain lions left, but there are plenty of foxes, weasels, wild cats and martens, as well as hawks and owls. After dark, badgers and hedgehogs hunt for small invertebrates, and bats chase night-flying insects through the trees.

Every forest has its all-rounder. In America it is the raccoon which feeds on almost anything — insects, mice, frogs, and even fruit and nuts. In Europe, wild boars root for nuts and fungi, and anything small enough to be caught without much effort.

◀ Young red fox.

► Woodpeckers use their strong beaks to break open bark and rotten wood. They use their long sticky tongues to extract the insects and spiders living there.

The winter woodland

In winter the leaves are gone, and it is not so easy to hide from predators. Animals which feed on leaves have very little food now, and soon even the nuts and berries will all have been eaten. Insect-eating woodland birds like the warblers migrate to warmer climates, where food is plentiful.

Some animals store food for the winter. Squirrels bury nuts in the woodland floor, and so do jays. Mice carry nuts and seeds off to their nests.

The insects spend the winter as eggs or pupae, buried in the soil or hidden in the crevices of the tree bark. Small animals like mice, voles and squirrels spend a lot of the winter sleeping in their warm nests. Some, like the dormouse and the chipmunk, actually hibernate during the coldest months. So do bats, which huddle together for warmth. Even the black bear of North America goes into a very deep sleep, waking up occasionally to search for food.

Did you know?

The acorn woodpecker of North America drills holes in old tree stumps and fills them with acorns, which it eats later when food is scarce.

More about forests (pp. 10, 11); animals that eat plants (pp. 32, 33); hibernation (pp. 76, 77)

Life in rivers and streams

Swimming against the current

Animals which live in rivers and streams are good swimmers. Most mammals push with their feet when they swim. Mammals like water voles and shrews, otters and mink, which regularly hunt in rivers and streams, have webbed hind feet to help them swim. Webbed feet also help them walk on the marshy ground beside the river.

Why is an otter like a crocodile?

The otter is especially well equipped for life in the water. Its fur is oily and waterproof. The otter's body is smooth and streamlined, and its ears are small. You might not think that an otter is like a crocodile, but they both have webbed feet, a flattened tail for pushing against the water when swimming, and ears and nostrils that can be closed when under the water.

Lazy grazers

In several parts of the tropics, the lush vegetation of large, slow-flowing rivers is grazed by manatees or dugongs, 'sea cows'. These large docile mammals swim slowly using flippers. They have smooth fat bodies rather like seals. They tear at the plants with their long muscular lips. Sadly, their numbers are low today because they are so easily caught for food.

Fishermen large and small

Many of the hunters in the world's rivers are very large indeed. Crocodiles and alligators are common in the tropics, where they bask in the Sun. They open their huge mouths to cool themselves – showing their long rows of teeth. River dolphins also have long rows of pointed teeth, over one hundred in all, for catching fish.

South American piranhas make up for their small size by their numbers. They hunt in groups of hundreds or even thousands. Mostly they catch other fish, and occasionally animals like capybaras (the biggest rodents in the world). They also clean up carcasses that fall into the water.

Danger on all sides

There are predators on the river banks, too. Kingfishers scan the water from overhanging branches, then dive directly on their prey. The heron stalks its prey through the shallower water. The purple gallinule, an American bird rather like a moorhen, lures prey into its mouth by wiggling its worm-like tongue.

Some river turtles eat crustaceans and even small fish. The matamata turtle can stay under water for long periods. It has a very long neck and its nose acts like a snorkel, taking in air from the surface. It catches the prey by waiting for it to come within reach. Then the turtle suddenly opens its huge mouth and sucks in the prey.

Holding on tight

In fast-flowing streams it is easy to be swept away. The eel-shaped river lamprey has a large, sucker-like mouth which helps it cling to rocks. The river lamprey can even hang on to rocks under waterfalls. The climbing catfish of South America also has a sucker-like mouth. Its belly fins have tiny tooth-like structures which stop the catfish slipping.

▲ A river lamprey clinging to a rock in a fast-flowing stream.

The world's biggest rodents

The plants of South American river banks are food for the capybara, the largest rodent in the world. An adult female may be up to 1.3 m long, and can weigh 55 kg. Capybaras have long legs with webbed hind feet, and are very good swimmers.

Did you know?

South American hatchet-fish leap out of the water to catch flying insects.

The largest freshwater fish in the world is the South American arapaima. It can grow to over 3 m long and can weigh 136 kg.

In the Amazon there is a fish with four eyes. It lives near the surface of the water, and has one pair of eyes for seeing under the water and one pair for seeing in the air above.

More about swimming (p.86); streamlining (p.84); life in the water (pp.110, 111)

Ponds, lakes and swamps

Life at the surface

Ponds, lakes and swamps have lots of places for animals to live. Some live right at the water's surface. Fishing spiders lie in wait on floating leaves, or on the surface of the water, trailing a foot on the surface film. They can sense the vibrations from small fish near the surface, and know just when to pounce.

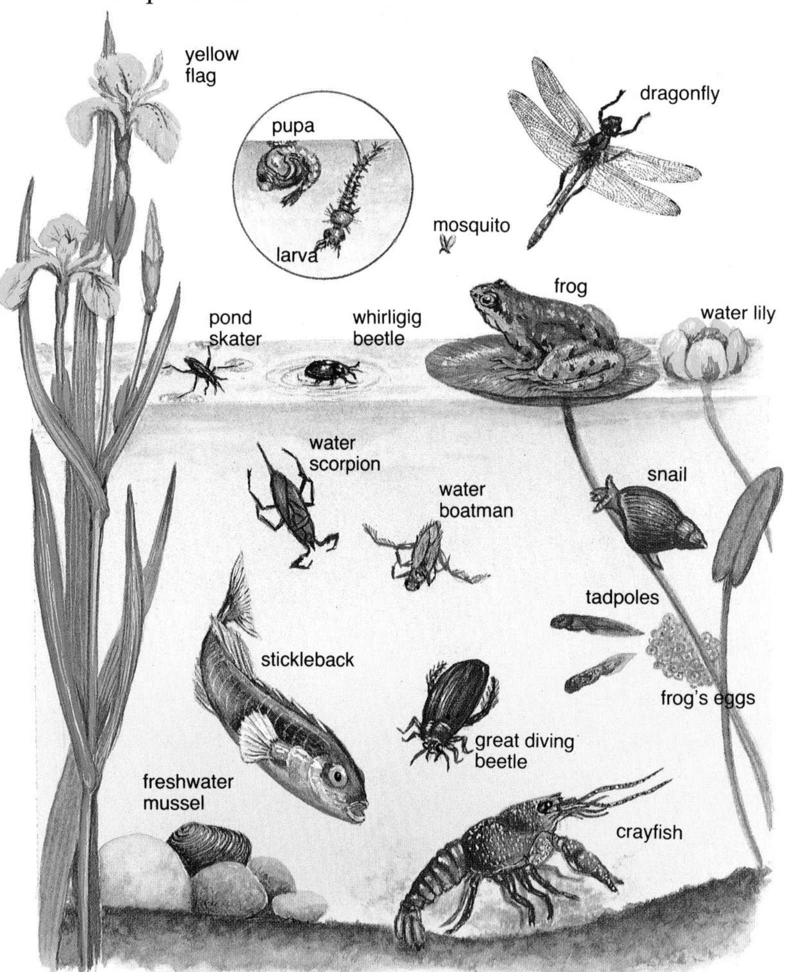

Life among the water weeds

The underwater plants are food for many small animals. Frog tadpoles graze on the algae coating the underwater leaves and stems. Pond snails glide over the leaves, depositing jelly-like masses of eggs behind them. Dragonfly nymphs and water beetle larvae lie in wait for other small water insects, tadpoles, and even tiny fish.

The big hunters

The edges of lakes attract many animals. While they are drinking they are easily caught by surprise. In tropical waters, crocodiles and alligators lie in wait just below the surface of the water, with only their eyes and nostrils showing. They will attack large mammals, like deer, when they come to drink. So will the anacondas, South American snakes up to 6m long. Even European grass snakes and American cottonmouths are good swimmers, and can catch frogs and toads.

The lakes themselves are full of fish, which are food for larger carnivores. In deep lakes some fish can grow very big. The European pike may weigh up to 23kg. It eats other fish, even smaller pike, as well as mammals like water rats.

Making their own lakes

Beavers make their own lakes by damming rivers with logs and branches, using their sharp teeth to fell trees. They build large lodges of branches and sticks, held together with mud. There are many entrances under the water. In these lodges the beavers bring up their young and store food for the winter. Beavers have changed the landscape of parts of North America, making large lakes and changing the flow of rivers and streams.

▲ For all their great size, hippopotamuses feed on grass. At night they leave the water and graze in the nearby water meadows, like giant lawnmowers. By day, they wallow in the water, stirring up the mud at the bottom. They pass huge amounts of dung into the water. The nutrients from the dung feed the algae which feed the fish, which feed the birds, and so on.

Danger from above

Around the edges of lakes there are often dense reed beds where birds can find safe nesting places out of sight of predators. Many birds hunt in lakes and ponds. Fish eagles swoop on their prey from above, seizing it in their talons. Fishing bats feed this way, too. Herons stalk their prey in the shallow water. Flamingoes and spoonbills sieve the water through special bills to filter out crustaceans. Pelicans scoop up fish in their huge throat pouches. Ducks paddle along the surface or dive and swim under the water, feeding on water weeds and small water creatures.

Did you know?

Giant otters weighing up to 35 kg live in South American lakes.

The deepest freshwater lake in the world is Lake Baikal, in the USSR. It is 1620 m deep, and contains one-fifth of the world's fresh water. Over 1200 different animals and about 600 different plants live in the lake.

More about life at the surface (p.87); pond animals (p.69); life in the water (pp.108, 109)

Life between the tides

The longest habitat in the world

The world has 312000 kilometres of coastline. Along these coasts the tide rises and falls every day. Between the high tide mark and the low tide mark lies the intertidal zone. Here live very special groups of plants and animals. In some places the intertidal zone is only a few metres wide, in others it may be up to three kilometres. Some shores are rocky, some have sandy beaches, and some are flat and muddy. They may look rather empty, with no life, but a square metre of rock in the intertidal zone may be home to a quarter of a million animals. You may not see many of them. Some will be too small to see, others come out only at night, or when the tide is covering them.

It's a hard life

Animals and plants which live in the intertidal zone have to cope with a lot of difficult conditions. When the tide comes in, the waves pound the shore, and the animals are at risk of being washed out to sea. At high tide they are under water, but at low tide they are exposed to the Sun and wind.

Life beneath the sand

On muddy and sandy shores, the animals can bury themselves in the sediments at low tide. Some make fairly permanent burrows. When the tide is in, they draw in water and extract food from it. Many worms and molluscs do this. Cockles and other molluscs with hinged shells send up tubes, called siphons, to the surface of the sediments to feed at high tide. When they die, their shells lie spread out on the sand and mud. Some marine worms make special protective tubes of sand and mud, and put out their feathery tentacles to feed at high tide. The ghost crab waits at the entrance to its burrow with only its stalked eyes showing. It will pounce on any small creature that comes within reach.

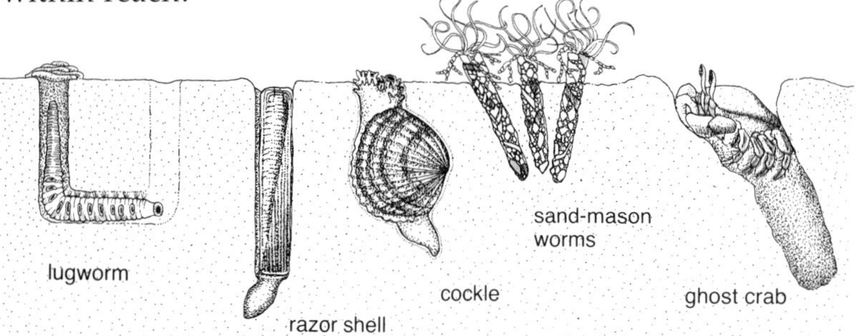

Tracking snails

Choose a piece of rock in the intertidal zone. Take some enamel paint, and paint some dots on the shells of a few limpets and winkles. Make a map to show their position. Wait until the tide has covered the rocks and gone out again, then look for your spotted shells. Compare them with your map, and see how far they have moved.

Exploring rock pools

Choose a rock pool and see how many different creatures you can find (don't forget the seaweeds). Try turning over the stones and lifting up the seaweed. If you want to fish, a small, strong net with a wooden edge is a good idea, as you can push this under weeds.

Dustmen of the seashore

The remains of many ocean-dwelling animals get washed up on the beach, especially after storms. They all collect along the drift line, together with the corpses of shore animals and broken-off seaweeds. Some animals, like the seagull, find them an easy source of food. Crabs are the 'dustmen' of the shore. They will eat almost anything. After sunset, the drift line is alive with sea slaters and sandhoppers, feeding among the decaying seaweeds.

The rock pool

1 **Lichens** Grow on bare rock. Different colours at different levels of the shore.

2 **Seaweeds** Cling to rocks with tough holdfasts. Flexible, so waves don't break them. Slimy mucus prevents them drying up. Different species occur at different levels on the shore.

3 **Sea slaters** Scavenge among rocks.

4 **Mussels** Have special threads to fix them to rocks. Close their shells to avoid drying out. Filter feeders.

5 **Barnacles** Permanent fixtures. Filter feeders.

6 **Limpets** Clamp on to rock so hard that they wear a groove in it. Graze on algae when tide in. Always return to same resting place.

7 **Periwinkles** Feed on seaweed. Shelter under weed, or in crevices at low tide.

8 **Whelks** Also shelter in crevices. Eat other animals.

9 **Crabs** Shelter under rocks or seaweed. Eat almost anything.

10 **Red coralline algae** Deposit skeletons of limestone.

11 **Anemones** Catch other animals with their stinging tentacles.

12 **Hydroids** Feed like anemones.

13 **Fan worms** Filter feeders.

14 **Sponges** Filter feeders.

15 **Sea squirts** Filter feeders.

16 **Starfish** Prey on other animals, including shellfish.

17 **Flatworms** Scavengers.

18 **Ribbon worms** Feed on other marine worms.

19 **Prawns** Filter feeders.

20 **Blennies** Eat other small animals. Camouflaged to escape attention of seagulls. Can change colour.

Forests on the march

▲ The tangled roots of the mangrove trees trap mud and pieces of vegetation carried to the swamps by rivers and the sea. As more and more mud collects, the mangrove forests gradually creep further into the sea, growing on top of the new layers of mud. In this way, the mangrove swamp slowly reclaims land from the sea.

The root of the trouble

Getting a hold in a layer of moving, sticky mud is not easy. It helps to have special roots for the job. Trees at the edge of the sea produce a platform of roots, rather like a raft, just below the surface of the mud which they sit on. These are the pioneers of the swamp. They colonize new ground. They also produce roots which grow upright above the surface of the mud. These are used for 'breathing'. Most of the food is found in the top few centimetres of the mud. A root raft just below the surface is just right for supporting the trees and for taking in food. Trees further from the sea grow special prop roots to hold them on the mud.

Life in a tangle

Mangrove swamps are found on sheltered tropical coastlines. They are a half-way house between the sea and the shore and are home for a fascinating group of animals and plants. They are muddy habitats which are covered twice every twenty-four hours by the tide. The main plants growing in these swamps are mangrove trees of various kinds. The trees are specially adapted for growing on mud, and they are also able to live in the very salty conditions.

One of the most common animals found in the swamps is a small fish called a mudskipper. At low tide the mudskippers flip across the mud using their fins like small crutches. One species even uses a modified fin to climb up the mangrove roots. Mudskippers can survive for long periods out of water. They carry their own oxygen supply trapped in water around their gills. This oxygen reservoir has to be renewed from time to time by dipping the gills in water. One species builds its own swimming pool on the mud and surrounds it with a wall. It defends its territory against all trespassers.

▼ Mudskippers live in mangrove swamps in coastal areas of many parts of the tropics.

The 'water-pistol' fish

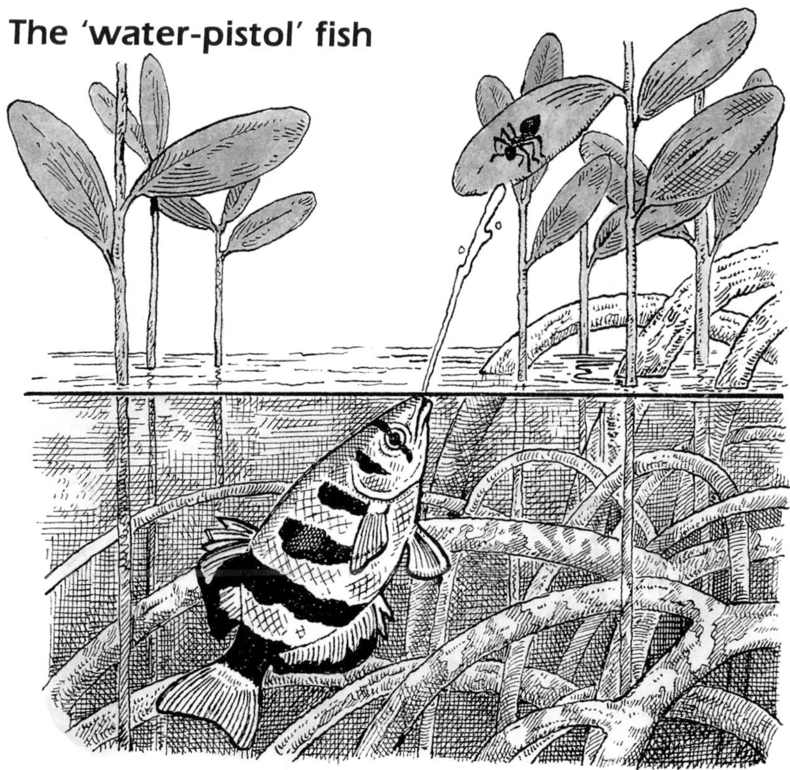

When the tide comes in, it brings with it an unusual fish with a remarkable way of catching food. It is called the archer fish, but a better name would be the 'water-pistol' fish. It swims round the underwater roots of the mangrove trees using its big eyes to focus on objects above the level of the water. If it spots an insect lurking on a leaf, it squirts out a jet of water and tries to knock the insect off its perch. It doesn't always succeed, but when it does it gobbles up the insect as soon as it falls into the water. The fish makes its aim more accurate by getting right underneath its prey before firing its water gun.

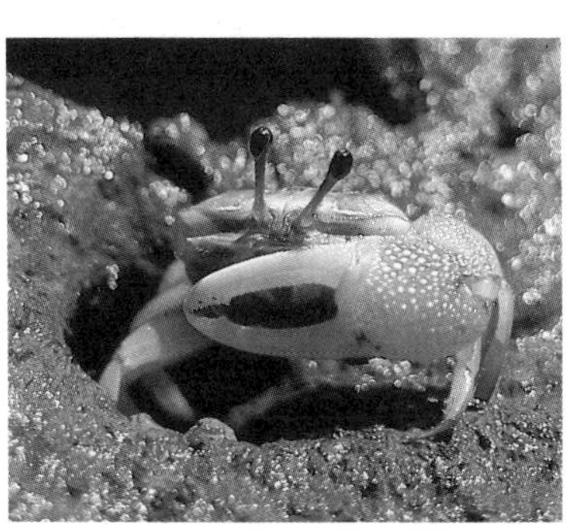

◀ At low tide the surface of the mud becomes alive with crabs of various kinds, including the fiddler crab. The male has one front claw which is very much bigger than the other. It is also much more brightly coloured. It is seldom used for fighting, but its bright colours are used for advertising, and attracting a mate and also for threatening a rival.

The mangroves of Borneo are home for the long-nosed or proboscis monkey. Only the male has a big nose. It probably works like an amplifier, increasing the sound of its honking among the forest trees. The monkey is an expert swimmer and often jumps into the water when crossing from one part of the forest to another.

Did you know?

The crab-eating frog is the only amphibian which can live in salty conditions. It lives in the mangroves of south-east Asia where it feeds on crabs, scorpions and insects.

More about breathing in water (p.87); advertising colours (p.64); life between the tides (pp.112, 113)

The open ocean

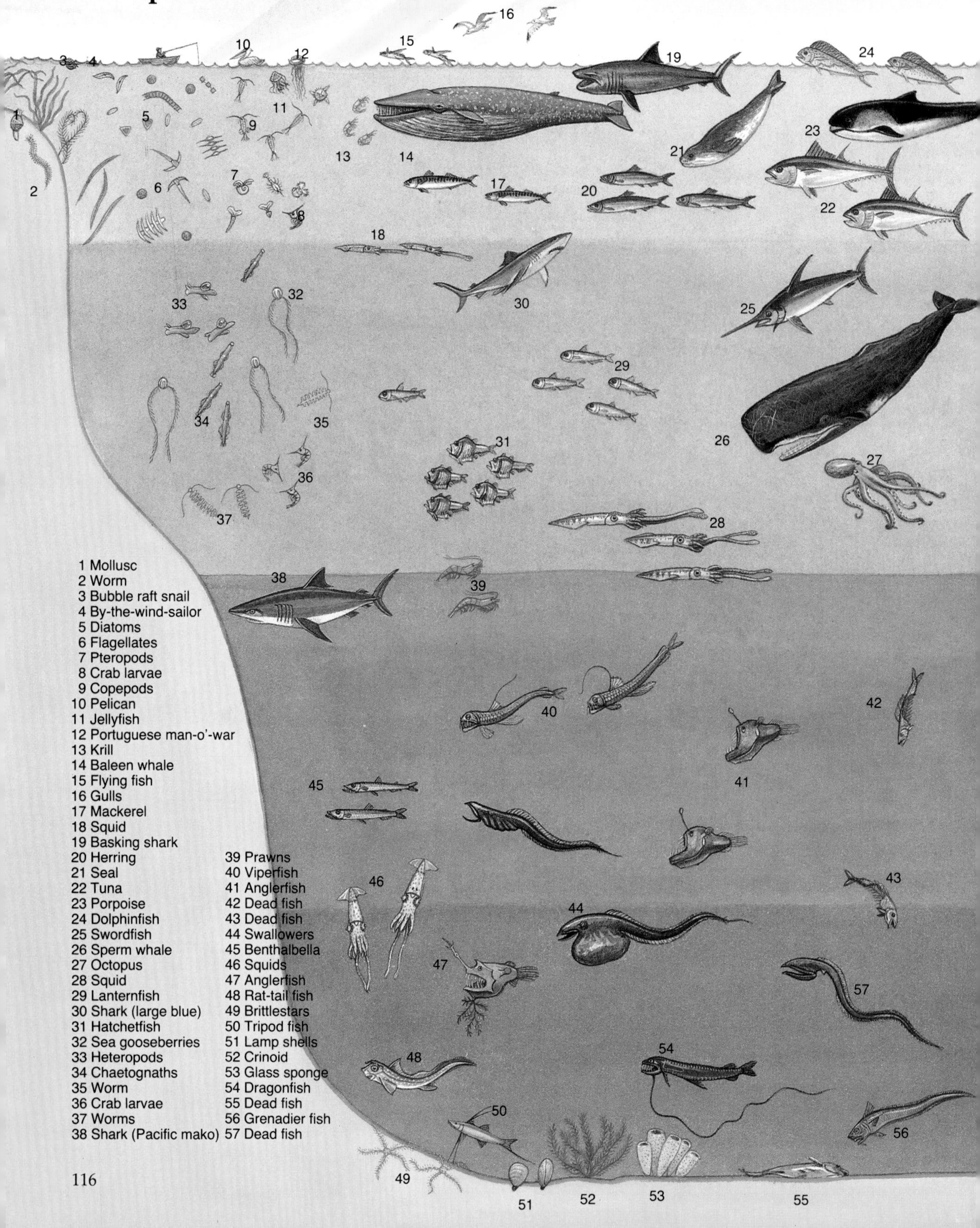

1 Mollusc
2 Worm
3 Bubble raft snail
4 By-the-wind-sailor
5 Diatoms
6 Flagellates
7 Pteropods
8 Crab larvae
9 Copepods
10 Pelican
11 Jellyfish
12 Portuguese man-o'-war
13 Krill
14 Baleen whale
15 Flying fish
16 Gulls
17 Mackerel
18 Squid
19 Basking shark
20 Herring
21 Seal
22 Tuna
23 Porpoise
24 Dolphinfish
25 Swordfish
26 Sperm whale
27 Octopus
28 Squid
29 Lanternfish
30 Shark (large blue)
31 Hatchetfish
32 Sea gooseberries
33 Heteropods
34 Chaetognaths
35 Worm
36 Crab larvae
37 Worms
38 Shark (Pacific mako)
39 Prawns
40 Viperfish
41 Anglerfish
42 Dead fish
43 Dead fish
44 Swallowers
45 Benthalbella
46 Squids
47 Anglerfish
48 Rat-tail fish
49 Brittlestars
50 Tripod fish
51 Lamp shells
52 Crinoid
53 Glass sponge
54 Dragonfish
55 Dead fish
56 Grenadier fish
57 Dead fish

The oldest environment on Earth

The open ocean is probably the oldest environment on Earth. The ocean has changed little over millions of years. Its surface area is twice the area of the land, and its average depth is four kilometres. This gives it a volume of 1370 million cubic kilometres, all of it occupied by living creatures.

The plankton

The surface waters of the ocean have the most animals. Here, billions of microscopic one-celled plants called diatoms, encased in glassy shells, are the main source of food and energy. In these sunlit waters lives a vast drifting community of tiny plants and animals called plankton. Most of the plankton animals are crustaceans, mainly tiny copepods, which swim using their two large antennae. There are also small shrimps and prawns, and the larvae of many other animals — starfish, sea urchins, sea snails, crabs, barnacles and a host of others. They include tiny herbivores, carnivores and filter feeders. There are so many of them that the great baleen whales eat nothing else.

Ocean surface drifters

Among the plankton are some larger animals, the ocean surface drifters. Many of them have gas-filled floats which act like sails, catching the wind and blowing the animals along. Jellyfish like the Portuguese man-o'-war and the by-the-wind-sailor drift across the sea, trailing their stinging tentacles behind them. Other drifters feed on them. The bubble raft snail has a float of bubbles, while the sea slug *Glaucus* gulps in air at the surface to help it float.

▼ Bubble raft snail eating by-the-wind-sailor.

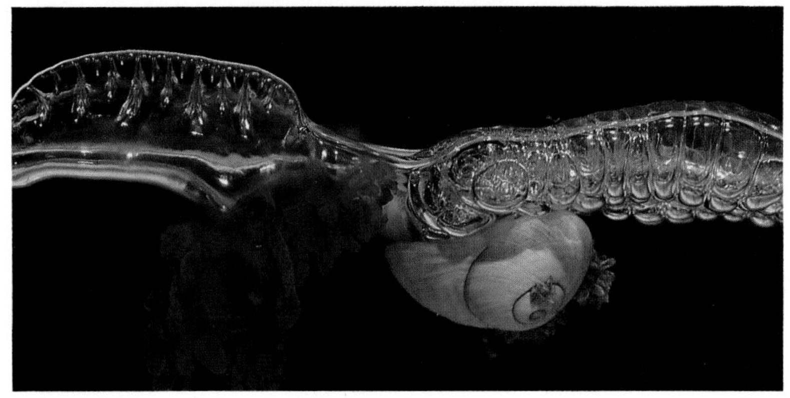

▲ Copepods are the most important animals in the plankton.

Surrounded by danger

The animals of the upper waters have enemies both from above and below. Seabirds like pelicans, boobies and gulls swoop on them from above, and seals and penguins chase them under water. Many of them are coloured deep-blue on their backs and white below. From above, their blue backs match the deep-blue of the ocean. From below, their white bellies blend with the light coming from above.

Fish great and small

In the deeper waters of the ocean are many fish. Some, like the herring, swim along with their mouths open, filtering the water to sieve out the plankton food. Other predators chase after their prey. The flying fish has wing-like fins and can glide through the air for several hundred metres to escape predators in the water below.

The ocean deeps

Life in the ocean deeps

The average depth of the ocean is four kilometres, and parts of it reach depths of eleven kilometres. The temperature falls as the ocean deepens, until, at very great depths, it may be below 0°C. At the same time, the pressure increases because of the great weight of the water above. This makes it difficult to move quickly.

The ocean twilight

The light is dimmer in the ocean depths. Blue light goes deeper than red light, so the scenery appears bluer as the ocean deepens. Animals adapt to the changes in light by using different camouflage. Deep-sea prawns are usually bright red. There is no red light at these depths, so they will normally appear black.

Many fish living at depths between one hundred and two thousand metres are dark on top, but have silvery mirror-like sides. By day, the sides match the light around them, and at night they appear dark. Some fish appear flat. They look very wide when seen from the side, but very thin when seen from other angles. They are not easily seen by predators above or below.

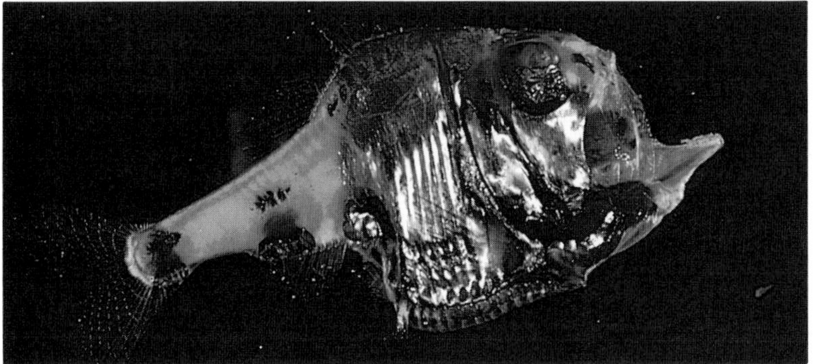

▲ The hatchetfish is well designed for hunting in the twilight. How many special features can you spot? Answers on page 152.

Finding food in the dark

Smell and taste are important senses at these depths. Deep-sea fish like the rat-tail fish often have long tails. These contain long lines of sensors, which detect vibrations in the water caused by the movement of other animals. The tripod fish (right) lives on the sea-bed. It has three extra-long fins which it uses as a tripod to prop itself up above the muddy waters so it can smell for prey in the clearer water above.

Food from above

All living creatures depend on plants for food. Either they eat plants, or they eat the animals that eat plants. The ocean is an unusual place because the plants can live only in a small part of it — near the surface, where there is enough light for photosynthesis. The animals in the rest of the ocean have to live either on other animals, or on the remains of dead organisms that sink down through the water.

Looking up

Predators try to see the silhouette (the dark outline) of their prey against the light coming from above. Many deep-sea fish have eyes that are directed upwards.

The prey need to camouflage their bellies. Often they use light-producing organs. Rows of tiny pockets of bacteria produce light by chemical reactions. This makes the fish invisible against the light from above.

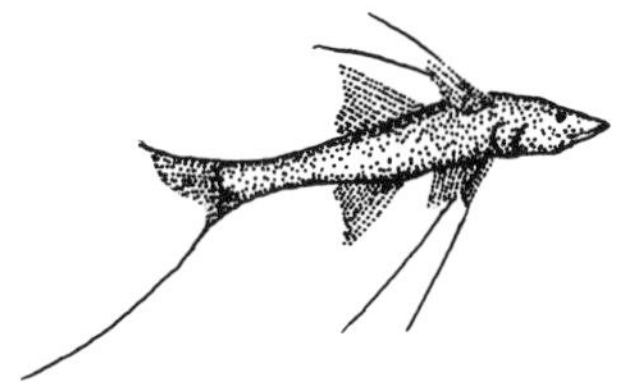

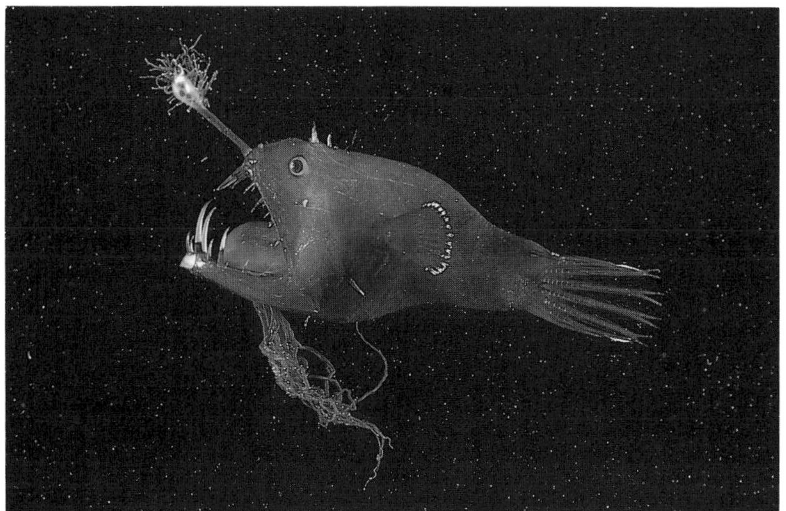

▲ Deep-sea anglerfish with luminous lure.

Animals that make light

In deeper water, where there is no light at all, many animals produce their own light. They do this to see their prey, or to deceive their predators. Anglerfish have luminous lures which they wiggle to attract other fish. When the fish comes within reach, the anglerfish opens its large mouth and sucks them in. Some tiny shrimps have spots of light on very long antennae, which make them seem much larger, so that predators will not attack them.

Some of the creatures in these dim waters move up to the surface to feed at night, when predators cannot see them. The lanternfish and the flashlight fish use light organs under their eyes like searchlights to find their prey.

◀ The deepest parts of the ocean have not been fully explored yet. Here, the environment has not changed for millions of years. Some of the animals found here cannot even be classified. They are not like any other living animals. This strange community of animals is found around hot springs, at great depths, near the Galapagos Islands.

Big mouths and stretchy stomachs

There is not so much food in the deep ocean, so the animals living there are few and far between. Many of the fish have very large mouths and elastic stomachs to take whatever prey they can catch. Some can even unhinge their jaws to catch prey larger than themselves. Their teeth curve backwards, making sure that once caught, the prey does not escape.

Did you know?

There are more than 10 000 different species of copepod.

The giant squid is the largest invertebrate in the world, up to 14.3 m long. It lives in the deepest parts of the ocean.

More about life in the oceans (pp.116, 117); camouflage (pp. 52, 53); animal senses (pp.50, 51)

Coral reefs

What are coral reefs?

Coral reefs are the most massive structures any living creatures have ever made. They are made up of the limestone skeletons of millions of reef animals, cemented together by sand. Living corals form only a thin layer on the surface of the reef. The dead coral rock underneath may be thousands of metres deep. Reef-building corals need light and warmth to grow, so living coral reefs are found only in shallow tropical seas.

Sand producers

Many fish, sea urchins, starfish and sea slugs feed on the corals. The parrotfish scrapes at the coral using its hard, beak-like teeth. As it feeds, bits of coral limestone fall off to form coral sand, which fills in cracks in the reef. Some sponges and clams bore into the rock for protection, producing more coral sand.

Corals are animals

Corals are animals. Each animal is cup-shaped and hollow and is called a polyp. It has a mouth at the top, surrounded by a ring of stinging tentacles which it uses to catch its prey. Many corals feed only at night. By day, the polyps shrink back into the cup for protection.

Corals are plants

The corals' tissues contain tiny plants called algae. For every square metre of coral surface there may be one and a half billion algae below. The algae produce food and oxygen by photosynthesis. Some of the food and oxygen is passed to the coral. In turn, the coral protects the algae, and provides them with carbon dioxide. This extra food makes it possible for the coral to grow fast enough to produce the massive coral reefs. The algae need light for photosynthesis. This is why corals grow only in shallow water where a lot of light reaches them.

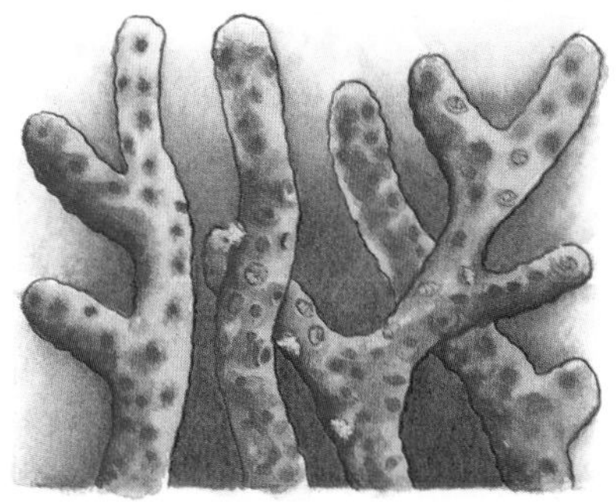

Hidden reef dwellers

Thousands of small animals live in the crevices in the reef. Crabs and shrimps scavenge for food among the corals. Butterflyfish use their long snouts to probe the crevices to get at them. Bristleworms and ribbon worms can wriggle into the thinnest cracks in the reef. Starfish are everywhere. They attack even the hard-shelled clams and scallops. Many reefs have large caves, and bigger predators lurk here — nurse sharks and octopuses, and the huge moray eel.

Some reef animals feed at night, and stay hidden during the day. Others have a wide range of camouflage. Some are coloured to match their background, or are shaped to look like fronds of seaweed. Many have stripes which break up their outlines, and some even have false eyespots to direct the predators to less vulnerable parts of their bodies.

Corals are minerals

Corals produce a limestone skeleton around their bodies. They form colonies by budding off new polyps, which do not completely separate from each other. There are many different shapes of colony. Some are large and branching, some are delicate and like large leaves, while others form massive boulders. The beautiful sea fans are also corals.

▲ These beautiful soft corals do not form hard skeletons. Instead, they have jelly-like coats with little spikes of limestone embedded in them for extra support.

A paradise for fish

All the thousands of small animals of the reef produce even smaller eggs and young. There is so much food on a reef that large fish shoals can be found everywhere, and bigger fish, such as reef sharks and barracuda, come to feed on them.

Filter feeders

Many of the reef creatures filter food from the water. Sponges and sea squirts form colourful crusts on the coral rock, fan worms and barnacles sweep their bristly combs through the water, and giant clams draw currents of water through their shells. At night, feather stars climb to the top of the sea fans and sweep their arms through the water to filter out food particles.

Corals are the oldest living animals on Earth. Some colonies may be several hundred years old, and contain over one million polyps.

Life on islands

▲ Insects, birds and bats are able to fly long distances. These animals can sometimes reach even the most distant islands. Many birds use islands as resting places on their long migration routes.

Islands: large and small

There are many different kinds of islands. There are large ones, and small ones. Some are covered with forests, and others are just bare rock.

Islands are formed in three main ways. Some islands appear when an underwater volcano erupts. The islands are formed from hot liquid rock, from the volcano, which solidifies in the sea. Many tropical islands are made of coral which builds up slowly in the sea. These islands take many thousands of years to form. An island is sometimes produced because the action of the sea begins to separate a small piece of land from the mainland.

Carried on the wind?

Many islands are a long way from land. Because of this, they are often difficult to reach. Even so, most islands have some plants and animals living on them. Scientists are interested in finding out how these plants and animals reached the islands.

Many microscopic plants and animals are carried by the wind. These tiny organisms are called aerial plankton. When these organisms are blown on to islands some of them survive and begin to live and grow there. We say that they colonize the island.

Seeds on the move

Birds and mammals often carry plant seeds, either clinging to their feathers or fur, or inside their digestive systems. In this way, many seeds reach islands. Later, they begin to grow into plants. The coconut is one of the best colonizers of islands. It floats inside its own husk which is resistant to sea water. Coconut palms are found on many tropical islands.

Adapting to needs

Many plants and animals become specially adapted to life on islands. A species of cormorant on the Galapagos Islands in the Pacific Ocean has very small wings. Over thousands of years its wings have gradually become smaller. Now they are too small for it to fly. Another bird, called a rail, lives on the island of Aldabra in the Indian Ocean. It, too, is flightless. Many islands have few large predators. Scientists think that some birds became flightless because there is no need to escape from predators.

Islands often have very large animals and plants living on them. The big island of Papua New Guinea is the home of giant birdwing butterflies. Giant tortoises and huge cacti are found on the Galapagos Islands, and on Aldabra Island. The world's biggest lizard lives on the island of Komodo in the East Indies.

Island stowaways

Large animals, such as reptiles and mammals, may float across the sea on rafts of vegetation. Sometimes these rafts reach islands by chance, and the stowaways come ashore, and survive. Large animals often carry smaller animals in their fur or feathers. In this way, many small animals, such as insects and spiders, are carried to islands hundreds of kilometres from land.

▲ Islands form safe places for arrivals to breed and bring up their young. Many islands have large colonies of birds, seals, and even walruses. Turtles come ashore on some islands to lay their eggs in the sand.

Too heavy to fly

Insects called lacewings live on some of the Hawaiian islands. Their huge wings are too big and too heavy for flight. This stops them being blown away by the wind.

Did you know?

The world's biggest butterfly, the Queen Alexandra birdwing, lives on Papua New Guinea. It has a wingspan of 30 cm.

The coco-de-mer is the biggest plant seed. It grows on only one island in the Seychelles. It hasn't reached other islands, unlike its relative the common coconut.

The world's most remote, inhabited, island is Tristan da Cunha. It is 2735 km from the coast of Africa.

More about aerial plankton (p.88); adapting to places (pp.20, 21); migration (pp.78, 79); size (p.27)

Life in caves

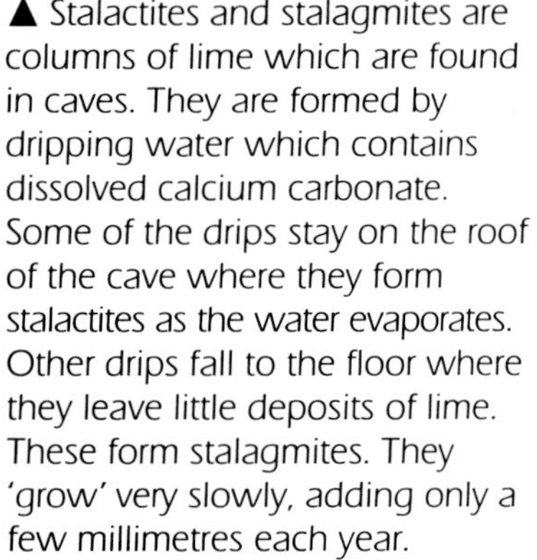

▲ Stalactites and stalagmites are columns of lime which are found in caves. They are formed by dripping water which contains dissolved calcium carbonate. Some of the drips stay on the roof of the cave where they form stalactites as the water evaporates. Other drips fall to the floor where they leave little deposits of lime. These form stalagmites. They 'grow' very slowly, adding only a few millimetres each year.

A cave usually has three zones or regions. The part nearest the outside is called the light zone. Further inside the cave it becomes dim. This is the twilight zone. The deepest part of the cave is called the dark zone. It is a very stable environment where temperature and humidity never change.

The world's biggest cave

Caves and underground tunnels are usually found in limestone rocks. Limestone is quite a soft rock, and it is easily eaten away by water containing dissolved carbon dioxide. As the water trickles through the limestone it begins to make small holes and tunnels. These slowly become deeper and bigger, and caves and caverns begin to form. This takes many thousands of years, and the caverns vary in size. The biggest 'cave room' so far discovered is in Sarawak, in south-east Asia. It was found by an expedition in 1980. It is 700 metres long, and its average width is 300 metres. Its roof is more than 70 metres high, and the whole cavern is big enough to park about 20 000 cars.

'Red-hot' tunnels

The lava tube (above) is in Hawaii. It was formed by volcanic action. When a volcano erupts it sends a stream of lava flowing down the side of the mountain. This is called the lava flow. The lava flow gradually cools down as it moves along. The outside cools first and soon becomes solid. The inside remains molten and carries on flowing like a red-hot river. The solid lava on the outside insulates the hot 'river' inside and stops it cooling. When the eruption stops, the flowing hot lava drains away leaving behind a long tunnel or lava tube. After the lava has cooled, some animals and plants are able to live there.

Light to twilight

Caves are home for a number of different animals and some plants. It is not easy living in a cave. One of the main problems is finding enough food. This becomes more difficult the deeper you go. There is plenty of food in the light zone. Plants can grow in this zone because there is enough light, and large numbers of insects are found here. Earthworms and snails live in this zone and so do frogs and toads. Other animals visit the light zone from time to time. There is less food in the twilight zone and fewer animals live here. Bits of dead animals and plants are brought in by the underground streams or are washed in by rain-water. This provides food for shrimps, and little animals called isopods, which are like woodlice. There are even small fish living in the underground streams.

Prisoners of the dark

Caves are very unusual habitats and only specially adapted animals can live in them. In fact, these animals cannot live anywhere else. They are 'prisoners' of the dark. The animals include certain spiders, crickets, centipedes and fish. Even a crayfish, a kind of freshwater lobster, lives here. Animal colours don't seem to form in the dark. Most of the dark zone species are colourless. They also have poorly developed eyes, or no eyes at all. Eyes are not much use in complete darkness. Instead, these animals have long antennae, and use their sense of touch to feel their way about. Some of the fish can detect tiny vibrations in the water.

The 'bat' bird

The oil bird lives in caves in parts of South America. Like bats, it uses the caves only for sleeping in during the day. Oil birds roost in large numbers. The oil bird has very good eyesight, but its eyes are not much use in complete darkness. Even so, it can fly around quite easily in the dark because it navigates in the same way as bats. This is why it is sometimes called the 'bat' bird. At night the birds leave their caves to feed on oil palm fruits.

▲ Bats are part-time lodgers in the dark zone. They use caves to sleep in during the day. The bats hang upside-down from the roof in large numbers. Their droppings collect on the cave floor and provide food for other animals.

Did you know?

The Proteus salamander lives in caves in Yugoslavia. At birth it has eyes and its body is coloured. However, it loses its eyes and its colour as it gets older. It never really becomes adult, and reproduces in the tadpole stage. It can go for several years without food.

More about how bats navigate (p.80); animal senses (pp.50, 51); hunting in the dark (pp.126, 127)

Night life

Life after dark

Many animals are active at night. We say they are nocturnal. Some plants even open their flowers at night and close them during the day. Animals are nocturnal for different reasons. Some only come out at night to avoid predators. Others hunt their prey at night because this is when it is moving about. Some animals are out at night because it is either safer or more comfortable. Spiders spin their webs at night, and many butterflies and moths emerge from their pupal cases under the safe cover of darkness. Earthworms come up to the surface of the soil at night to feed. At this time, the humidity is higher and there is less chance of the earthworm's skin drying out. Desert animals usually become active after dark when the air is cooler.

▲ One of the main problems facing nocturnal animals is finding their way. They solve this problem in different ways. Some, such as owls, bush babies and geckos, have large, sensitive eyes designed for seeing in dim light. Night eyes can open very wide to let in the maximum amount of light. They can also become very narrow in daylight.

▲ Nocturnal snakes such as pit vipers have pits on the head which sense the heat given off by the bodies of other animals. They use these organs to find their warm-blooded prey in the dark. Heat detectors only work because the prey's body is warmer than the snake's. Snakes can also detect vibrations on the ground through their chins.

Eye-spy

Most of the world's 130 species of owl are nocturnal. They have huge, forward-facing eyes used for hunting their prey in dim light. An owl's eyes are so big that they occupy most of the space in each eye socket in the skull. Because of this, there is no room for any eye muscles. An owl doesn't move its eyes. Instead it moves its head. The flexible neck allows the owl to turn its head either way to face backwards without moving its body. Other nocturnal animals such as tarsiers can also do this.

Big-ears

Nocturnal animals often have large, sensitive ears which they use for detecting prey and predators in the dark. Bats find their way and locate food by sonar. Their high-pitched cries bounce back off objects in their flight path. These echoes are picked up by their large, sensitive ears. The frog-eating bat from Central and South America finds its prey by picking up the frogs' night calls with its sensitive ears.

◀ This Australian frogmouth matches the bark on which it sleeps during the day. Many nocturnal animals are camouflaged to help avoid day predators. The South American potoo blends with the tree on which it roosts. It looks like a large, dead branch. Insects such as mantids and moths remain motionless during the day. Many tree frogs sleep with their legs drawn up and their eyes closed. This makes them more difficult to see.

Night 'talk'

Night life has developed various ways of communicating in the dark. Because vision is limited, many animals 'keep in touch' by sound, or by light signals. Insects such as crickets become very active at night. The males 'sing' for long periods by rubbing one wing over the other. Temperature affects the rate of chirruping. The speed of a cricket's song increases on warm evenings and decreases when it is cooler. Frogs also join in the night chorus, especially in the tropics. They often have large throat sacs which produce and amplify the noise they make.

South American tree frog

Many plants have flowers which open at night. These flowers are usually pale so they are easily seen in the dim light. This makes it easier for animals like the honey possum to find the plant and help pollinate the flowers. Night flowers also have a strong scent to help attract moths and bats. Flowers pollinated by bats usually hang free of the leaves so bats can easily find them by sonar.

Lighting-up time

Fireflies and glow-worms are light-producing beetles. In both cases the light is for sexual attraction. Only female glow-worms light up to attract the males. The male fireflies give off short bursts of light to attract females. Light-producing organs usually have a reflecting layer and a series of lenses to increase the strength of the signals.

Did you know?

The click beetle from the West Indies has an orange light that it turns on when taking off and landing.

The heat pits of a rattle-snake can detect a small mammal only 30 cm away.

In the Second World War, soldiers in the jungle of Malaysia carried branches with light-producing fungi on them. They acted like torches in the dark.

More about animal senses (pp.50, 51); communication (pp.72, 73); attracting a mate (pp.64, 65)

Wildlife goes to town

City dwellers

A large town, or city, with its many houses and factories does not seem a likely place to find wildlife. For years scientists paid little attention to the animals and plants living in our towns. Instead, they studied plants and animals in the countryside, and those in remote habitats. Recently, scientists have become more interested in town habitats, and in the plants and animals living in them.

▲ Some mammals have become very successful town invaders. Foxes are now quite common in many towns. They bring up their cubs in towns. Hedgehogs are also common town animals. They live in gardens where they are able to find plenty of food. In American cities, some raccoons raid dustbins at night. And some settlements in northern Canada are even visited by polar bears.

Where do the invaders come from?

All animals and plants living in towns have come from the surrounding countryside. Some animals enter the town and find a habitat like the one they left in the country. Many of our garden birds do this. Others find a very different habitat, and adapt to the new conditions.

The good life

Wildlife may find that living in a town has certain advantages over living in the country. People and buildings produce a lot of heat, which makes the town a warm place in which to live. The air temperature of a town in winter is higher than that of the surrounding countryside. Many animals are attracted by this warmth. The buildings of a town also give shelter from the wind. Some buildings serve as safe places where animals can breed. Food is in plentiful supply in the town's dustbins and rubbish tips. Many wild plants also find a home in the gardens of the town.

The artful alligator

In parts of Miami, in Florida, alligators have invaded private swimming pools, and lakes on golf-courses. They have started to do this because their natural habitats are being destroyed by human activity.

Water, water everywhere

Big towns and cities have plenty of watery habitats. There are lakes, rivers and reservoirs. In addition, many gardens have artificial ponds. All of these are places where aquatic plants and animals can live. The large lakes and reservoirs attract a lot of birds. The small garden ponds are good places for frogs, toads and newts to breed. Garden ponds are often stocked with fish of various kinds. Birds such as herons are attracted to the ponds to feed on the fish.

The big clean up

In recent years pollution of many town rivers has lessened or stopped altogether. Laws have been passed which prevent factories emptying poisonous chemicals into town waterways. The rivers are now much cleaner, and new species of fish are beginning to invade them. In recent years, more than one hundred species of fish have come back to the River Thames in London.

▲ Birds are well adapted to town life. Some birds are more common in towns and cities than in rural areas. Starlings and pigeons live in very large numbers in many cities. Sometimes their numbers become so great they begin to be a nuisance. They make a lot of noise, and they damage buildings with their droppings.

The rat invasion

Rats and mice are the most common town mammals. Some towns may have more rats than humans living in them. The rats cause damage, and may spread disease.

Mice in cold store

House mice have been reported living in cold meat stores, where the temperature never rises above freezing point. They have adapted to these cold conditions and even breed in them. These freezer-store mice have thicker fur, and are bigger than their relatives who live in ordinary conditions. Can you explain why? Answer on page 152.

Did you know?

In Venice, there are so many pigeons that they have been given birth control pills to keep their numbers down.

The chimney swiftlet once nested in hollow trees in North America. Now it prefers hollow ventilator shafts and disused chimneys in towns and cities.

Ospreys nest in sight and sound of the space shuttle launch pad at the Kennedy Space Centre in Florida in the United States.

More about adapting to places (pp.20, 21); pond life (pp.110, 111); size (p.27); life in cold places (p.100)

Tropical rain forests

Hot, wet and never changing

Tropical rain forests grow on lowlands and foothills in regions close to the Equator. They are found in equatorial Africa and South America, and there are smaller forests scattered throughout south-east Asia and Australasia. In these regions there are no seasons, and day and night are equal in length all year round. The air temperature remains between 20 and 30°C throughout the year, and the rainfall is always greater than 2032 millimetres per year. These hot, wet conditions are just right for rapid plant growth. Because there are no seasons, conditions in these regions never vary. This makes tropical rain forests very stable places for animals and plants to live in. The forests have been like they are today for millions of years. They are the richest habitat on Earth for wildlife and they contain an enormous variety of animals and plants. The picture shows the main layers which make up a tropical rain forest.

A few trees grow so tall that they stand well above the canopy layer. The atmosphere here is fresh and windy, and **emergent trees** use the wind to distribute their seeds.

The **canopy** is a dense and continuous layer of green leaves about 8 metres deep. Many animals live here, feeding on the rich supply of leaves and fruit.

The **understorey** receives very little light. It is the 'highway' along which many animals travel when moving through the forest from floor to canopy.

The **soil** in tropical rain forests is not very deep. The giant emergent trees put out shallow roots to catch the nutrients before the heavy rains wash them away. They also produce huge buttress roots which help to support their great height.

The **forest floor** is semi-dark and few plants grow here. It is covered with dead leaves. The humid conditions encourage decay. Fungi, ants and termites live here in large numbers.

▲ Each leaf in the canopy is positioned to catch the maximum amount of sunlight. Many leaves can even change their position during the day as they follow the Sun's path across the sky. The leaves have 'drip tips' which act like the spout of a jug and help the heavy rain-water to drain away quickly. They also have a waxy, protective covering which prevents the spores of small plants, such as moss and algae, from getting a hold and germinating on their surface.

Life in the forest canopy

Most of the animal life in a tropical rain forest lives in the canopy layer. It is only recently that scientists have been able to climb into this part of the forest habitat, 25 metres above the ground, and study the wildlife living there. The canopy forms the rain forest ceiling. The dense foliage encloses a warm, humid atmosphere which supports a variety of animals. There are browsers, such as sloths and monkeys, feeding on leaves and fruits. Hunters like the monkey-eating eagle feed on the browsers. There are also scavengers, and even some animals which steal food from others. When the animals of the 'day shift' have finished, nocturnal animals take over. Pottos, bush babies and lorises climb through the canopy. They have huge eyes to find fruits and insects in the dark. Large fruit-eating bats arrive and flap amongst the leaves, looking for ripe fruits on which to feed.

Climbing and hanging on

Life in the canopy requires special methods of locomotion. Birds can flap, jump or fly from one branch to another. Some clamber about the branches in search of food. Certain mammals have developed a tail for gripping, and extra large claws for hanging on to branches. It is also important to be able to judge distances very accurately. Because of this, many mammals have developed binocular vision for finding their way amongst the branches.

The living coat-hanger

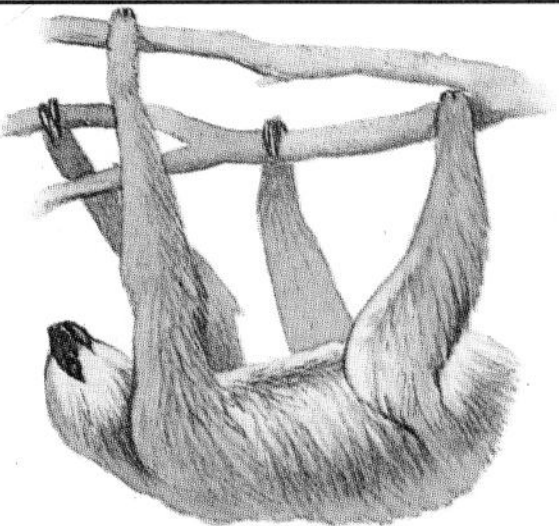

The two-toed sloth lives in the rain forests of South America. It is found in the canopy where it does everything upside-down. It feeds on fruit and leaves, and even sleeps, while hanging by its feet from the branches. The sloth is completely adapted to an upside-down life in the canopy. It hangs by stiff, rod-like legs and moves very slowly, gripping the branches with its hook-like claws. Even its fur grows in the opposite direction to that of other mammals so the rain can drip off easily. Green algae grow on its fur and these camouflage the sloth from its predators. It can move its head through nearly 360°, allowing it to see all round without moving its body.

Did you know?

The South American rain forest covers an area of 2.5 million km^2.

A dead leaf takes only 6 weeks to decay completely on the forest floor.

The world's tropical rain forests are being damaged or destroyed at the rate of 40 hectares per minute.

More about rain forest animals (pp.132, 133); forests (pp.10, 11, 106, 107); binocular vision (p.50)

FOREST RANGER'S NOTEBOOK

The tropical rain forest is one of the richest habitats in the world. It contains a wide variety of animals and plants. Although some large animals live on the forest floor, most animals live in the canopy, 25 metres above the ground.

1 **Toucan** Lives in rain forest of South America. Canopy dweller. Feeds on fruit, insects and even eggs.

2 **Howler monkey** Lives in groups in South American rain forest. Very noisy. Calls heard several kilometres away.

3 **Great blue turaco** Found in African rain forest. Noisy bird. Feeds on fruit and small grubs. Often travels in groups.

4 **African grey parrot** Lives in flocks in canopy of African rain forest. Feeds on fruit and seeds. Powerful beak for breaking seeds.

5 **Aye-aye** Lives in forests of eastern Madagascar. Nocturnal. Feeds on fruit and insect larvae.

6 **Malay fruit bat** From rain forest of south-east Asia. Largest of bats. Feeds mainly on bananas and figs.

7 **Slender loris** Lives in forests of southern India and Sri Lanka. Nocturnal. Feeds on insects and fruit.

8 **Lar gibbon** Found in canopy of rain forest of south-east Asia. Swings through canopy using its long arms. Feeds on fruit and some insects.

9 **Flying frog** Found in rain forest in Borneo. Has enlarged webs between toes. Can glide downwards using webs as parachutes.

10 **Orang-utan** Lives in Borneo and Sumatra. Feeds on fruit, leaves and insects. Lives alone or in family groups. Expert climber.

11 **Colugo** Found in forests of south-east Asia. Glides on large body membranes. Nocturnal. Lives on leaves, fruits and flowers.

12 **Great hornbill** Canopy dweller. Large beak, long eyelashes. Feeds in flocks on fruits and nuts. South-east Asia.

13 **Six-wired bird of paradise** Lives in rain forest of New Guinea. Male does special dance for female on forest floor.

14 **Okapi** Rare animal from African rain forest. Not discovered until 1900. Feeds mainly on leaves.

15 **Royal python** Lives in equatorial West Africa. Maximum length 1.5 metres. Curls up into a ball when attacked.

16 **Lowland gorilla** Lives in family groups in rain forest of West Africa. Adults too heavy to climb trees.

17 **Common iguana** Lives in forests of South America in trees along river banks. Feeds on fruits. Good swimmer.

18 **Tamandua** Found in rain forest of South America. Nocturnal. Uses tail to grip branches. Feeds on ants and termites.

19 **Spider monkey** Found in tropical American forests. Swings through canopy on long arms. Tail used to grip branches. Feeds on fruit.

20 **Kinkajou** Found in forests of Central and South America. Nocturnal. Mixed diet including plants, insects, mammals and birds.

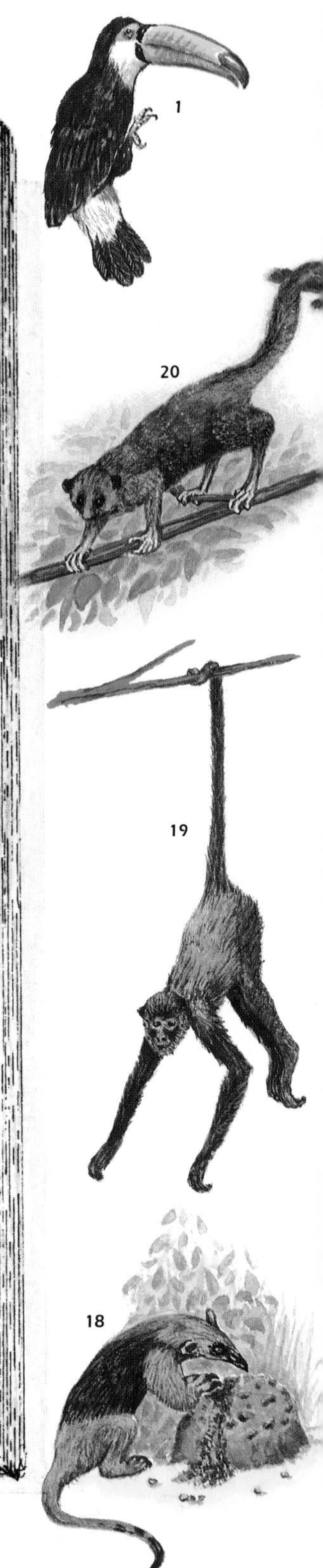

2
3
4
6
7
8
5
9
10
19
20
3
15
4
16
2
18
1
14
17
12
6
9
11
13
7
10
8
5
15
11
12
17
16
14
13

Endangered species

6

8

9

10

11

13

CONSERVATIONIST'S NOTEBOOK

Many animals are in danger of becoming extinct. This is because their habitats are gradually being destroyed by humans. The animals shown here are all endangered species.

1 **Californian condor** Found in mountains north-west of Los Angeles. Total population about 6.

2 **Polar bear** Found in Arctic regions around North Pole. Total population about 12000.

3 **Spanish lynx** Found in one small area of southern Spain. Population perhaps a few hundred.

4 **Walrus** Lives in Arctic region. Hunted by Eskimos. Atlantic race disappearing. Population 25000.

5 **Giant panda** Found in mountains and forests of Tibet and south-west China. Probably less than 1000.

6 **Caspian tiger** Found on border between Russia and Afghanistan. Farming has destroyed habitat.

7 **Monkey-eating eagle** Lives in Philippine Islands. Becoming very rare. Total population about 40.

8 **Orang-utan** Found only in parts of Borneo and Sumatra. Total population about 5000.

9 **Przewalski's horse** Found in south-west Mongolia. Very rare. Probably more in captivity than wild.

10 **Komodo dragon** World's largest lizard. Lives on 4 small islands near Indonesia. Only a few hundred exist.

11 **Tuatara** Rare burrowing lizard. Lives on islands near New Zealand. Perhaps 20000 survive.

12 **Kakapo** A large flightless parrot from New Zealand. Nocturnal. Less than 100 survive.

13 **Tasmanian 'wolf'** Thought still to exist in Tasmania. Tracks found and sightings made.

14 **Koala** Found in eastern Australia. Recently, population reduced because of virus disease.

15 **Indris** Largest of lemurs. Found in north-east Madagascar. Lives in forest habitat. Vegetarian.

16 **Cheetah** The African cheetah is becoming rarer. Total population probably less than 25000.

17 **Great Indian rhinoceros** Found in north-west India and Nepal. Population about 500.

18 **Mountain gorilla** Found near Virunga volcanoes in equatorial Africa. Population about 400.

19 **Leatherback turtle** Largest of turtles. Once common in tropical seas. Breeding sites threatened.

20 **Blue whale** Biggest animal that has ever lived. Suffered from over hunting. Population less than 2000.

21 **Green turtle** Used to be common in most tropical seas. Hunted for food. Eggs taken from breeding grounds.

22 **Giant armadillo** Biggest of the armadillos. Lives in South America. Threatened by increased farming activities.

23 **Flightless cormorant** Found on only one of the Galapagos Islands. Eggs collected. Also hunted for food.

24 **West Indian manatee** Found near coasts of Caribbean Sea and north-east South America.

25 **Southern sea otter** Thought to be extinct but rediscovered in 1938. Population now about 2000.

Conservation — saving wildlife

▲ Great areas of forest were cut down when the Trans-Amazon Highway was built. This also caused large numbers of animals to disappear.

As dead as a dodo

You have probably heard the phrase 'as dead as a dodo'. The dodo was a species of bird. The last dodo was killed on the island of Mauritius more than three hundred years ago. Since then, many other species of animals and plants have disappeared forever. When this happens, we say the species has become extinct. Animals and plants become extinct naturally. This is part of the process of evolution. However, in recent times, these disappearances have increased, and humans have been responsible for most of them.

Farms, industry, hunting and poaching

Many of the world's natural habitats are gradually being destroyed. More land is being claimed for farming. Areas of forest have been cleared and land drained to make room for factories. Land has even been flooded to make huge artificial lakes to provide hydroelectric power. Forests are cut down for timber and to make room for roads and highways. Drilling for oil has destroyed habitats on land and at sea. Other threats to wildlife are hunting and poaching. More than one million whales have been killed in the last eighty years by hunting. Poachers in Africa have reduced elephant and rhinoceros populations to near extinction.

Passenger pigeons

About one hundred years ago, the passenger pigeon was the most common bird in the world. One flock on migration was estimated to contain more than 2 billion birds. The pigeons were tasty, and were hunted for food. In 1869, 7½ million birds were caught at one spot. In 1879, 1 billion birds were captured in the state of Michigan in the United States. The last passenger pigeon died in Cincinnati Zoo in 1914, and so the passenger pigeon became extinct.

Every year, millions of animals and plants are shipped around the world. Many end up as pets and house plants. Other animals are killed and their skins used for furs and leather. Elephant tusks are made into trinkets and the wood of many rain forest trees is used for building.

► Operation Tiger started in 1972. Its main aim has been to find out how to protect the Indian tiger. Over the years, tigers have been moved from places where they are in danger to game reserves where they are protected. The project has been very successful and the Indian tiger has increased in numbers once again.

DON'T SQUASH ME!

Safe places to live

Many governments in different parts of the world have put aside areas of land for the preservation of wildlife. These areas vary in size. Some are quite small, but others cover many thousands of square kilometres. The Wood Buffalo National Park in Canada covers 45480 square kilometres. The Etosha Reserve in Namibia, in Africa, is the world's biggest reserve, covering 99525 square kilometres. North America and Canada have more than one hundred and sixty game parks and nature reserves. In these reserves wildlife can live without being disturbed, and hunting is banned. Park rangers and wardens stop poachers from killing the animals. Even so, many of the world's animals and plants are still in danger of dying out. Because of this, special projects have been set up by the World Wildlife Fund and other organizations to save those animals most in danger.

Panda problems

The giant panda is the symbol of the World Wildlife Fund. There are probably less than 1000 still alive in the mountains of central China. In 1975, many pandas starved because the bamboo plants on which they feed flowered and died. This put the giant panda in great danger. In 1980, the Chinese government began work with the World Wildlife Fund to study the giant panda in its natural habitat. Animals were fitted with radio transmitters so their movements could be followed. Scientists are finding out more about the pandas' way of life.

HELP SAVE US

WE ARE MOUNTAIN GORILLAS
THREATENED WITH EXTINCTION BY
POACHING AND FOREST DESTRUCTION
WE LIVE ONLY IN RWANDA, ZAIRE AND UGANDA
THERE ARE FEWER THAN 400 OF US LEFT
HELP
THE FAUNA AND FLORA PRESERVATION SOCIETY
RAISE FUNDS FOR THE
MOUNTAIN GORILLA PROJECT
Information/donations: Fauna and Flora Preservation Society, c/o ZSL, Regent's Park, London NW1 4RY

Only about 400 mountain gorillas survive in the rain forests of Central Africa. The Mountain Gorilla Project was set up in 1978 to protect these animals and help them survive. People living in the area have gradually cut down the gorillas' forest home to make more farming land. The Rwanda Government works closely with the Project to educate local people about conservation of the forests. A team with a special van goes to schools and villages to show films and give talks about the importance of the rain forest and its gorillas. School parties have been taken to see the gorillas in their natural habitat, and wildlife clubs have been set up in local schools.

Zoo news

Old and new

The first zoos were very different places from the zoos of today. In the beginning, people did not care about the animals, how they were kept or the cages they lived in. The animals' comfort was not very important to the zoo owners, or the visitors. If any of the animals died they could easily be replaced by catching more from the wild.

Today the situation is different. Many animals are rare in their natural habitats, and some have disappeared altogether. Several governments have banned the export of wild animals. For these reasons it is much more difficult for zoos to obtain new specimens. If a particular animal dies, the zoo cannot replace it easily unless it can breed its own specimens, or buy from another zoo.

◀ This is a picture of the Tower of London's menagerie in about 1820. The animals were kept in 'dens' under the arches. Compare this zoo with the modern one in the photograph below. If you were an animal, which zoo would you prefer to live in?

◀ In a modern zoo, animals are kept in well designed enclosures in surroundings similar to their natural habitats. Animals were often kept by themselves; but now many live in small groups. They are much happier like this. They are healthier and live longer. They also breed more easily.

Moonlight world

Until recently, nocturnal animals like this Australian spiny anteater were never seen in zoos. During the day, they slept in a corner of their cage and only became active after all the visitors had gone home. New ideas about keeping animals changed all this. 'Moonlight' houses are now found in most big zoos. Here day and night are reversed. The animals inside live in a moonlit world when there is daylight outside. This allows visitors to watch nocturnal animals moving about and feeding quite naturally. At night, the lights are turned on fully so the animals think it is daylight.

Breeding rare animals

As animals in the wild become rarer, zoos are becoming more important as places for breeding endangered species. For some very rare animals zoos may be their only hope of survival. There are probably more Przewalski's horses in captivity than in the wild. Capturing the few remaining Californian condors and keeping them in zoos may save them from extinction. Zoos set up breeding programmes for rare species. The ne-ne, or Hawaiian goose, has been successfully bred in captivity and even returned to the wild. In the future, zoos will probably become more involved in this kind of work. Perhaps history will be reversed. In the past zoos have taken animals from the wild. In future they may give some animals back.

▲ Like many zoos, Paignton Zoo in Devon has an educational centre where young people can learn more about the animals in the zoo. Programmes are organized for school parties, and there are young naturalist clubs for children to join. Workers at the centre give talks and show films. There are many other activities to help young visitors get more from a day at the zoo.

Zoo scientists

Zoos are not just places where animals are kept and bred. Many big zoos have large laboratories where scientists work to find out more about things like animal diseases and health. They also investigate animal diets in order to discover the best ways of feeding zoo animals. Much of what they find out helps other scientists working with animals in the wild.

Feeding time

Usually animals in zoos are not given the same food they would get in the wild. They are fed on carefully worked-out diets. Here are some daily menus.

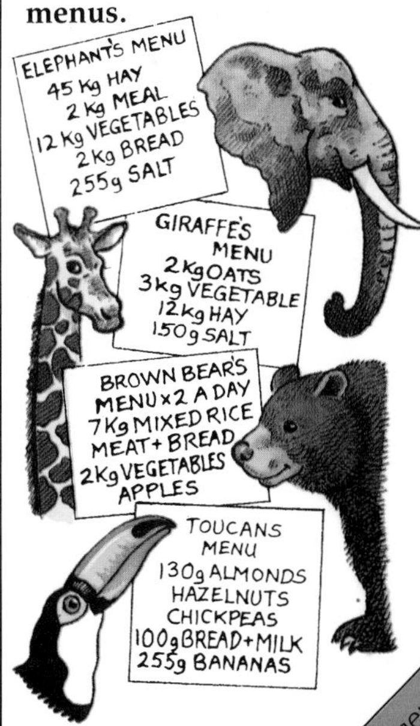

ELEPHANT'S MENU
45 Kg HAY
2 Kg MEAL
12 Kg VEGETABLES
2 Kg BREAD
255g SALT
GIRAFFE'S MENU
2 Kg OATS
3 Kg VEGETABLE
12 Kg HAY
150g SALT
BROWN BEAR'S MENU x 2 A DAY
7 Kg MIXED RICE
MEAT + BREAD
2 Kg VEGETABLES
APPLES
TOUCANS MENU
130g ALMONDS
HAZELNUTS
CHICKPEAS
100g BREAD + MILK
255g BANANAS

More about endangered species (pp.134, 135); nocturnal animals (pp.126, 127); mountain gorillas (p.19)

Looking for clues

Nature is all around you

Now you have read this book, you will probably want to go out and look at nature for yourself. But, at first, you may be disappointed because you may not see any animals. Yet the signs of animal activity are all around you, if you know how to look for them. You have to look for clues. Once you start following the signs, you will probably start to see the animals themselves.

Dropping clues

Animals have their own characteristic droppings. The droppings of a dog or fox are very different in size and shape from these gazelle droppings.

▲ Animal burrow in heather.

Be quiet

All animals have enemies. As humans are bigger than most animals, it is not surprising that animals hide away when they hear us coming. So try to be quiet. You will see more if you stop and wait than if you move about.

Listen!

Stop and listen. You can usually hear birds long before you see them. Every bird species has its own distinctive song. Birds sing most in the early morning, and in the late afternoon and evening. Listen for the alarm calls of birds that hear you coming.

Collectable clues

Thorny thickets and barbed-wire fences are good places to look for other clues – hairs of badgers, foxes, deer and other animals. Feathers are easy to find and collect. Do you often find the same hairs or feathers in the same place? There may be a nest nearby, or you may be standing on a path used regularly by animals.

Nests and holes

The burrows of mice and foxes are easy to see. The size of the burrow will give you a clue as to who made it. Look for signs that it is still occupied - remains of food nearby, droppings, hairs. Use your nose - many burrows have a very distinctive smell. You may find well-worn tracks leading away from the burrow. Badgers follow regular paths when they go out foraging, and so do mice and rats.

Bird nests are also quite easy to find. Note the size of the nest, and what it is made of - the outer structure, and the soft inner lining. Are there any features to give you clues?

Untidy eaters

Many animals leave the remains of their food on the ground. Different animals feed in different ways. Nutshells may be split in half by squirrels and hawfinches. Voles gnaw a round hole in nutshells. Dormice and voles leave a smooth edge to the hole, while wood mice leave tooth marks. Nuthatches and woodpeckers often wedge nuts in cracks in tree bark, either to hold them firm while they hammer them open, or to store them for later.

Look on the ground

Footprints are more easily found when the ground is soft, or if it is covered in snow. Good places to look are in the mud beside streams and ponds, in sandy areas, and areas where the soil is not covered by vegetation.

Note the size of the tracks, how many 'toeprints' they have, and how far apart the footprints are. Are the tracks fresh? Can you follow the trail and get close to the animal that made it? Look at the detail of the tracks. Has the animal got long claws? Are its feet webbed? See if you can work out which tracks belong to the fore feet and which belong to the hind feet. Are there any other clues - feathers, hairs, droppings? Have its wings or tail left their tracks too?

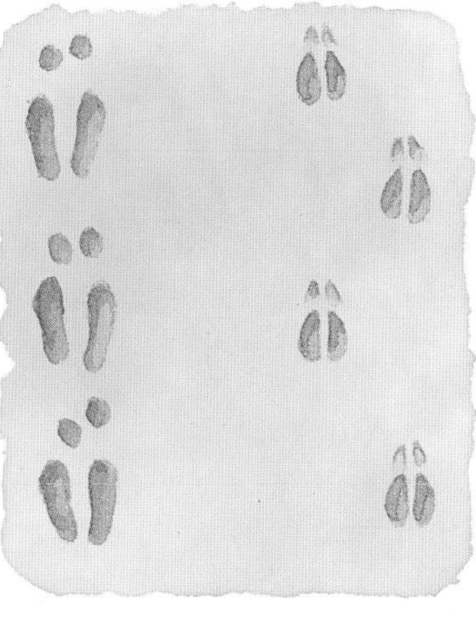

▲ Rabbits and hares put both their fore feet down at the same time. Deer put their feet down one after the other.

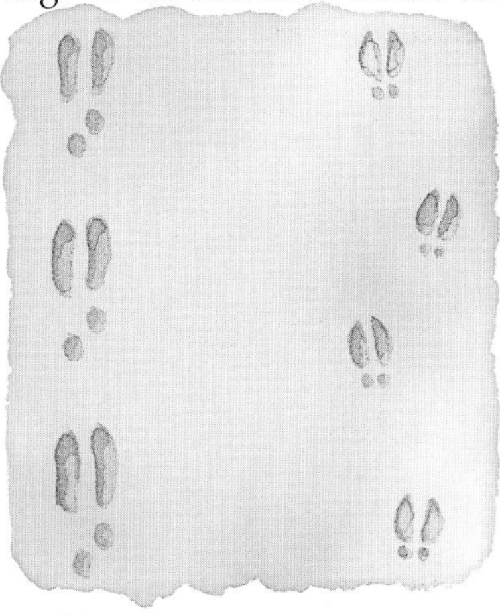

▲ Running and walking produce quite different patterns of tracks.

Beach combing

If you are at the seaside, the shore is a wonderful place for clues, not only to the life of the beach, but to life in the ocean beyond. Shells, eggs, skeletons, washed up jellyfish - all collect along the shore. The most exciting finds are often made after there has been a storm at sea.

◀ Looking at the ground can tell you what kind of plants there are above you. In tropical forests many plants grow on the branches of trees hundreds of metres up. Vines trail up other trees, but do not flower until they reach the top. But their flowers, fruits and leaves fall to the ground below, where you can see them.

More about animal homes (pp.60, 61); the beach (p.113)

Improving your nature photography

It's the ideas that count

There are so many different cameras that it is impossible in such a short space to tell you how to take good nature pictures with your particular camera. There are many good books on photography, including some which specialize in nature photography.

On this page, you will find ideas for making your pictures more interesting and fun. Even with a very basic camera, it is possible to take good nature photographs, good enough to publish. Your ideas can compensate for the limitations of your camera.

▲ Silhouettes can be impressive, and work well in black-and-white as well as in colour.

Lighting

You can get many interesting effects by varying the lighting. Instead of taking photographs with the Sun behind you, try lighting your subject from the side. Shadows can pick up the texture of skin or petals, and lots of small details which the rather flat lighting of bright sunlight does not show.

▲ Furry animals look quite dramatic when the light is coming from behind. The hairs show up as a bright line around the animal. Hairy plants produce the same effect.

If you have a single lens reflex camera, try under-exposing your picture. You can turn day into night by doing this. Sometimes it produces very dramatic effects. It can show up striking cloud groups, or turn the Sun into a starry form with shafts of light coming from it. Under-exposing is especially exciting in snowy conditions.

Coming in close

Even if you do not have the special equipment for taking really close-up pictures, you can get some interesting pictures by coming closer than usual to your subject. Think about photographing special features – feet, ears, eyes, noses, coats. A close-up of a zebra coat can be quite a puzzler for your friends!

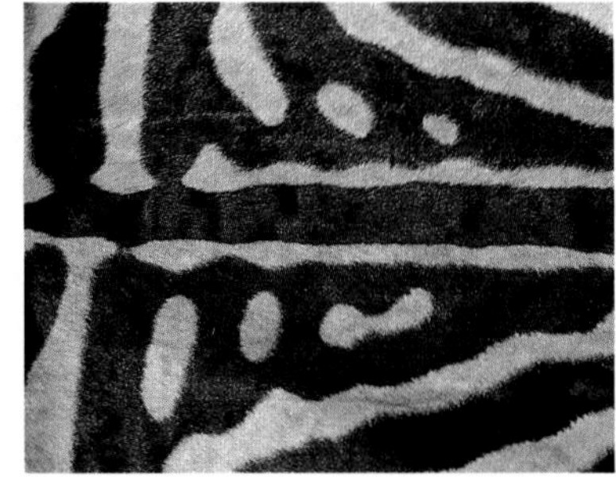

▲ Close-up of a zebra coat.

▼ Bold shapes and an unusual angle combine to make an interesting picture.

Shapes and patterns

Look for interesting patterns in nature, such as arrangements of leaves, patterns on tree bark, the shapes of trees and branches in winter. Try and find bold shapes to frame your pictures. Overhanging branches, twisting tree trunks, and grasses in the foreground will all help to add interest and a sense of depth.

Watch your background

Watch your background. Walk around your subject to find the best angle from which to photograph it. Brightly lit flowers or animals look even better photographed against a dark background. Dark subjects may look better against a light background. If the background is cluttered, it may take away interest from your main subject. On the other hand, if the background is important, use a wide-angle lens to give you greater depth of focus - this means that more of the background is in focus.

▲ A wide-angle lens can really show the subject in its natural habitat.

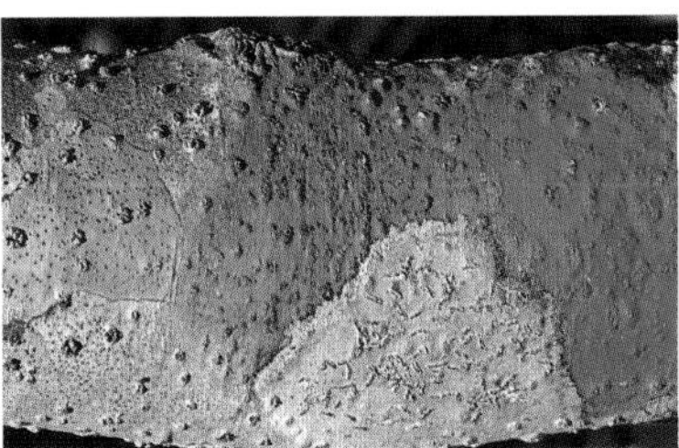

▲ Lichen patterns on tree bark.

Practice can be fun

You can get a lot of practice of photographing nature by visiting local parks, botanic gardens, zoos and wildlife parks. These are good places to try comparing long distance and close-up pictures, and to sort out any problems. Keep going back to photograph the same animals again and again until you get your picture just right. Butterfly houses are marvellous places to try out close-up photography.

Looking through the lens

A final word of warning. It is difficult to take good pictures if you are trying to do other things at the same time. It is no good going out and trying to look at birds as well as taking photographs. To get good pictures you need to be thinking photography. You have to be looking at the world around you as if you are seeing it through the lens of a camera.

Natural history art

Drawing animals and plants

You can learn a great deal about animals and plants by drawing them. To draw well, you must watch nature closely. It is this close study which leads to a greater understanding of the plants and animals that share the world with us. Here we show you how you can start drawing and painting living things.

Working against the clock

Time is very important. Animals move quickly. They seldom stand still, or 'pose' for you. So you must learn to put the maximum amount of information on paper in the shortest possible time. Drawing from life is the best way for you to become familiar with an animal because you can study its behaviour and movement. It is a good idea to draw a pet, or a farm animal, or even take a trip to the zoo to practice drawing quickly. When drawing a plant you will have more time to think about detail and use of colour.

Composing the drawing

Sketching your subject as a series of shapes in the form of circles, cylinders and eggs will help you to draw its outline. Compare the height with the width, and note the distances from head to tail and from head to feet. You can make your observations more accurate by using the pencil as a measuring device.

Materials

The most handy and useful piece of drawing equipment is the pencil. It is easy to handle, and can be used to work out the relative height and width of your subject. Charcoal is not so easy to use. It tends to smudge easily and, being brittle, is likely to snap.

Your basic equipment should include a wooden board or stiff pad to lean the paper on, a portable stool, a screw-top jar for water, and a choice of papers with rough and smooth surfaces. You should also have some graded pencils, a rubber and sharpener, some paint and water soluble crayons and pastels.

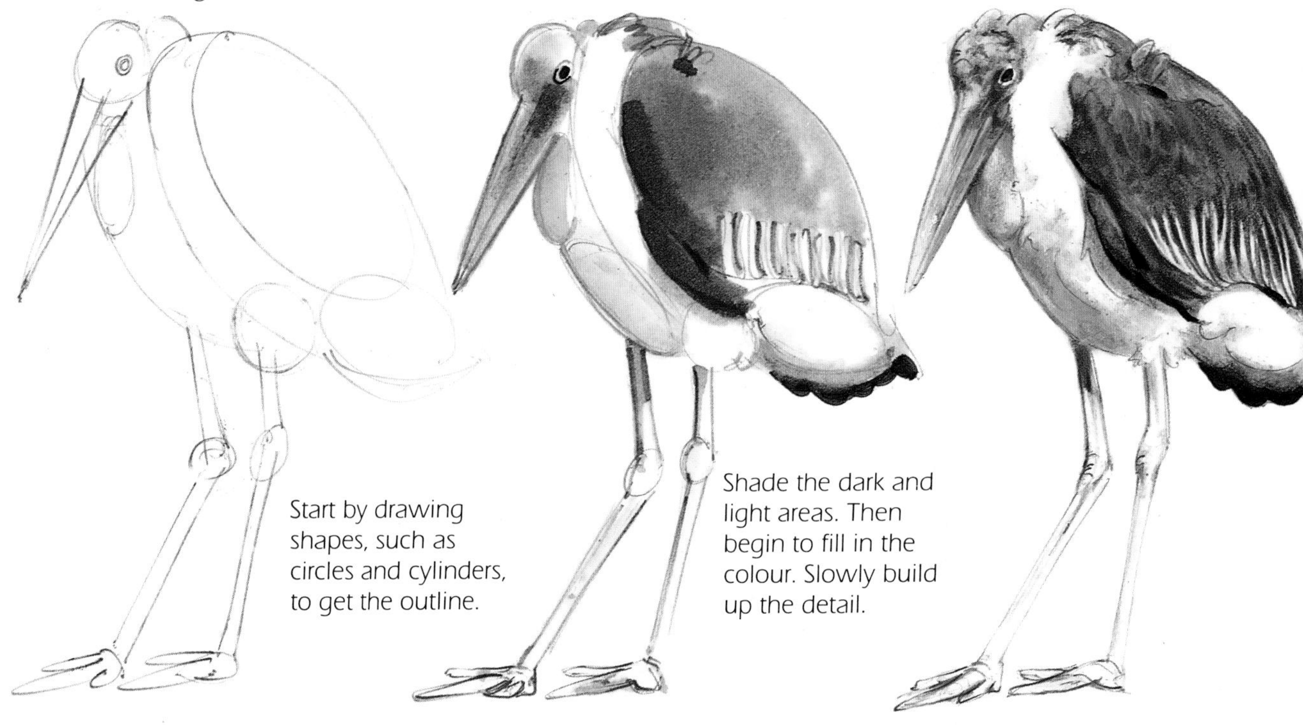

Start by drawing shapes, such as circles and cylinders, to get the outline.

Shade the dark and light areas. Then begin to fill in the colour. Slowly build up the detail.

Black and white

Half-closing your eyes can help you to pick out which areas are dark and which are light. You can draw different depths of light and shade by using different pencils. A very soft 4B used on its side gives the rough texture of the coat of a squirrel or fieldmouse. A harder 2H pencil will give the smoothness of a beak, hoof or horn.

Use the rubber as little as possible as it damages the surface of the paper. Mistakes can be covered by new lines or areas of tone.

Fur, hair or bushy tails are not easy to draw! This squirrel has been sketched using a very soft pencil to give the rough texture of its coat and tail.

Colour

Having drawn the outline and general shape, choose the basic overall colour. Cover the shape with a light coat of paint, except in the lightest parts. Using your crayons and pastels, build up the darker regions. Do not fill in the detail until the pattern of tones is completed. If a colour is too strong it can be diluted with a little water.

Colour can be used to fill in the details of your subject.

Attention to detail

Be aware of starting with distinctive markings and interesting patterns. Try to show exactly how the animal stands or moves and your picture will be much more life-like. The main advantage of drawing plants is that by touching them you can get a better feel for texture and form.

Practice makes perfect

Carry a sketch pad and pencil wherever you go so you can draw anything that catches your eye. As you get better you might like to try new materials and techniques and look at other pictures and books for new ideas.

Identikeys

Putting a name to it

When a scientist is talking about an animal or plant, scientists from other countries often like to know which particular species is being described. But scientists from different countries speak different languages. So how do they communicate? When they give a new animal or plant a name they use an international language. The name they give to each species is a special one. It is not an ordinary name like 'dog' or 'cat'. It is a special name, called the scientific name, and it is made up of two parts. The first is the genus part of the name. The second is the specific part of the name. The two parts together make up the species, or scientific, name. Let us look at a famous animal to see how this works.

New finds

New animals and plants are being discovered all the time. Each new species has to be classified and given a scientific name. Most of the world's biggest animals have probably been discovered, but there are still some surprises. In 1979 a new species of lizard was found on the Fiji Islands in the Pacific Ocean. Until 1979, nobody knew it existed.

A lion is a member of the cat family. It is one of the big cats, which include tigers, leopards and jaguars. The big cats belong to the genus *Panthera*. This word forms the first part of a big cat's scientific name. The second part is the specific word which separates one big cat from another. The lion's second name is *leo*. So its full scientific name is *Panthera leo*.

Here are three more big cats. Can you guess which scientific name belongs to which animal? You may have to use your imagination. Look for similar words.

A *Panthera pardus*
B *Panthera onca*
C *Panthera tigris*

Answers on page 152.

Imagine that you have just returned from an expedition to Africa. While you were there you discovered a new species of big cat. The cat is remarkable because it lives completely in water. Your expedition leader has asked you to give your new species a scientific name. Here's a clue. Think of another word which means something to do with water.

Answer on page 152.

How to identify animals and plants

When you want to identify an animal or plant you have to look for clues. There are lots of ways to begin. You can start by looking at pictures in a book. Sometimes a picture matches the plant or animal you are interested in and this helps you identify it. Sometimes you have to read a description, but you still have to look for clues. You may learn about the habitat in which a particular organism lives. Is it the same kind of habitat as the one where you found your animal or plant? You will probably collect a lot of evidence before you can be sure of your identification.

A
B
C
D
E
F
Remember
Look carefully at each penguin in turn. Start at the beginning. Think about each pair of clues. Then decide which step to go on to next. Good luck!

Using a key is like a treasure trail. An answer to one clue leads you to the next clue and soon.

Identification keys

You can identify an animal or plant even if you haven't seen it before. This is something scientists often have to do. To help them they use a 'key'. Just as a key opens a locked door, a scientist's key solves the mystery of an unidentified animal or plant.

Using a key

Jim is an Antarctic explorer. He is interested in penguins, but knows nothing about them. They all look the same to Jim. Maggie is an explorer friend who knows a lot about penguins. She decides to help Jim by making a key so he, too, can identify penguins. Here are 6 penguins and part of Maggie's key. Can you use the key to identify each penguin? **Answers on page 152.**

MAGGIE'S KEY

1	Penguin has long, thin beak	go to step **2**
	Penguin has short, thick beak	go to step **3**
2	Penguin has D-shaped patch on head	Emperor
	Penguin has comma-shaped patch on head	King
3	Penguin has completely black head	Adelie
	Penguin has light stripes or patches on head	go to step **4**
4	Penguin has tuft of feathers on head	Rockhopper
	Penguin has no tuft of feathers on head	go to step **5**
5	Penguin has thin line across face	Chinstrap
	Penguin has light patch above eye	Gentoo

Wildlife quiz

Try these knotty problems

Heads you win

Here are the heads of three different animals. Can you name them?

A

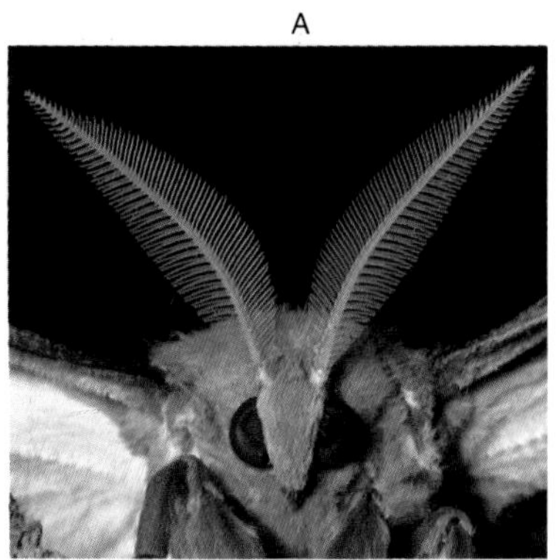

B

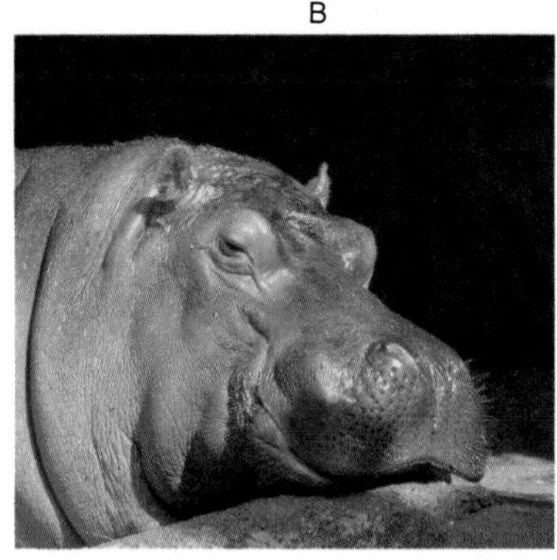

C

True or false

1 Birds have teeth.
2 Armadillos live in Africa.
3 Camels drink their own nose drippings.
4 Octopuses are molluscs.
5 Some insects can produce light.
6 Leopards live in South America.
7 There is a bat that can catch fish.
8 Sea-horses are mammals.
9 All birds can fly.
10 Corals are plants.
11 Some insects and spiders look like bird droppings.
12 Some coral fish can live among the tentacles of sea anemones.

Food

1 What does the blue whale feed on?
2 Name a group of birds which feeds on nectar.
3 Where do butterflies have their taste sensors?
4 How does a python kill its food?
5 What is an omnivore?
6 What does an aardvark feed on?
7 Name one animal which uses a tool when feeding.
8 How does an insect-eating bat find its food?
9 Which animal feeds mainly on bamboo?
10 What do leaf-cutter ants feed on?

What's this?

This is an unusual view of a well-known animal. Can you name it?

Close up

Can you name what each of these close-ups shows?

A

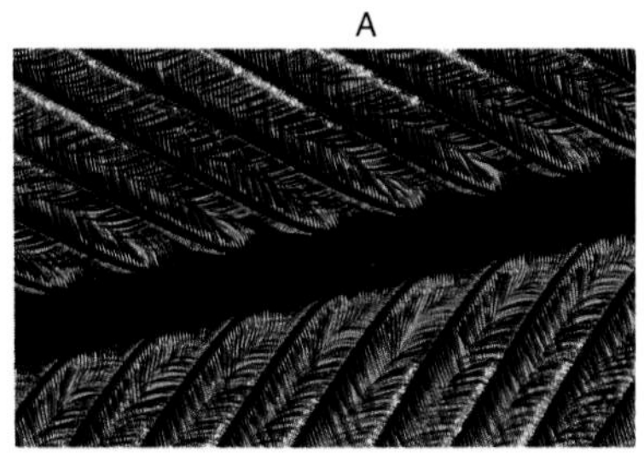

B

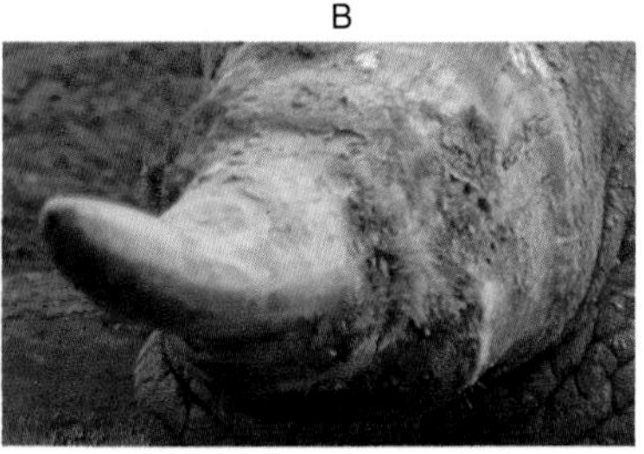

C

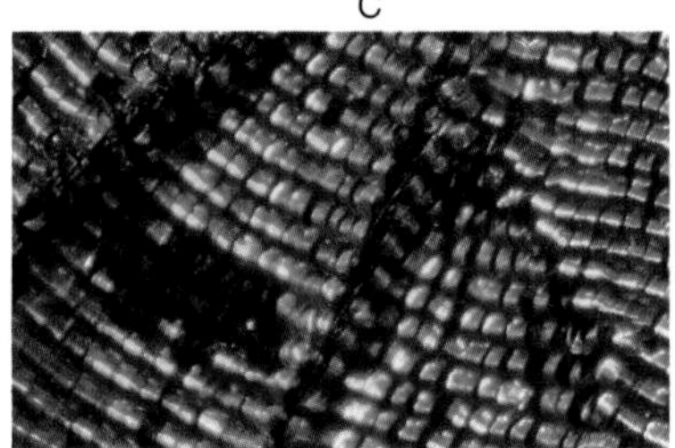

Eye spy

Which animal does each of these eyes belong to?

A

B

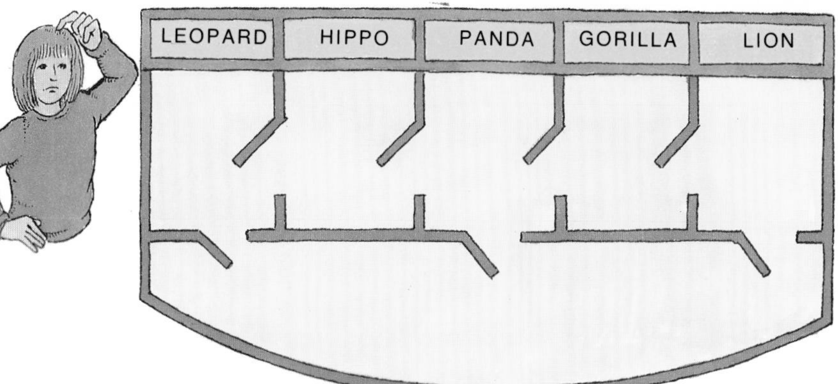

Zoo puzzle

Milly got the job of keeper at her local zoo. On her first day she inspected the animals. Each cage had the animal's name printed on it, but the animals were in the wrong cages. Here is what Milly found. The lion was in the leopard's cage. The gorilla was in the hippo's cage. The hippo was in the panda's cage. The leopard was in the gorilla's cage and the panda was in the lion's cage. When Milly told the zoo owner, he told her to put each animal back in its proper cage. But he warned her that all the animals were very fierce. Before she started to move them, she was told never to put two animals in the same cage at the same time. She was also told not to put two animals in the enclosure at the same time. How many moves will Milly have to make to put each animal in its proper cage?

Mixed bag

1 What is coral made of?
2 Where would you find an aye-aye?
3 What do vultures feed on?
4 What is symbiosis?
5 What is a sundew?
6 What is the symbol of the World Wildlife Fund?
7 What is countershading?
8 Name one animal which can change colour.
9 How does the African lungfish survive drought?
10 What does cold-blooded mean?
11 Where would you find a monkey-eating eagle?
12 How do flamingoes feed?
13 Which species of animal did Dian Fossey study?
14 Where do you find most marsupials?

Size

1 Name the world's largest mammal.
2 What is the world's biggest flower?
3 Name the world's smallest mammal.
4 Where does the world's biggest butterfly come from?
5 Name the world's biggest mollusc.
6 What is the world's biggest plant?
7 Name the world's biggest seed.
8 What is the world's biggest lizard?

Answers on page 152

Bookshelf

General natural history

Life on Earth: a Natural History DAVID ATTENBOROUGH, Collins/BBC, 1979. Enlarged edition Reader's Digest/Collins/BBC, 1980
The Natural History of the Garden MICHAEL CHINERY, Collins, 1977
The Young Naturalist NEIL ARNOLD, Ward Lock, 1983
Mysteries and Marvels of Nature series, Usborne:
Insect Life JENNIFER OWEN, 1984
Reptile World IAN SPELLERBERG and MARIT McKERCHAR, 1984
Bird Life IAN WALLACE, ROB HUME and RICK MORRIS, 1984
Ocean Life RICK MORRIS, 1983
Plant Life BARBARA CORK, 1983
Animal world KAREN GOAMAN and HEATHER AMERY, 1983
Science Around Us series, Usborne:
Living Things MARIT CLARIDGE, 1985
Hamlyn all-colour paperback series:
The Animal Kingdom. Bird Behaviour. Birds of Prey. Butterflies. Evolution of Life. Fishes of the World. A Guide to the Seashore. Life in the Sea. Mammals of the World. Monkeys and Apes. Natural History Collecting. The Plant Kingdom. Seabirds. Seashells. Snakes of the World. Trees of the World. Tropical Birds. Wild Cats

Things to do

The Amateur Naturalist GERALD DURRELL with LEE DURRELL, Hamish Hamilton, 1982
The Family Naturalist MICHAEL CHINERY, Macdonald & Janes, 1977
The Family Water Naturalist HEATHER ANGEL and PAT WOLSELEY, Joseph, 1982
Botanic Action with David Bellamy CLARE SMALLMAN and DAVID BELLAMY, Hutchinson, 1978

Field Guides

The Collins series of Field Guides and Pocket Guides

Animals around the world

The New Larousse Encyclopedia of Animal Life, Hamlyn, 1980
Let's Learn series, Mitchell Beazley:
Animals of our world
Watching Seashore Life ANDREW CLEAVE, Severn House, 1984
Discovering Nature series, Wayland:
Discovering Bees and Wasps. Discovering Birds of Prey. Discovering Hedgehogs. Discovering Snakes and Lizards. Discovering Spiders. Discovering Worms
The Birds R.T.PETERSON and THE EDITORS OF TIME-LIFE BOOKS, Time-Life Books, 1968
The Mammals R.CARRINGTON and THE EDITORS OF TIME-LIFE BOOKS, Time-Life Books, 1973

Reference 1968

Cambridge Illustrated Dictionary for Young Scientists JEANNE STONE, Cambridge University Press, 1985
The Guiness Book of Animal Facts and Feats

Energy and life

Nature at Work: an Introduction to Ecology, British Museum (Natural History)/Cambridge University Press, 1978

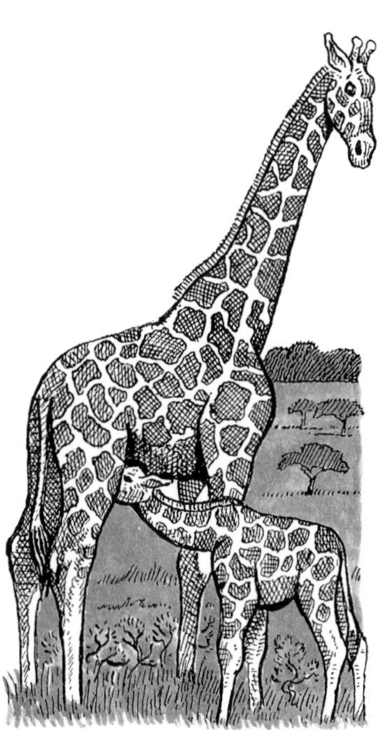

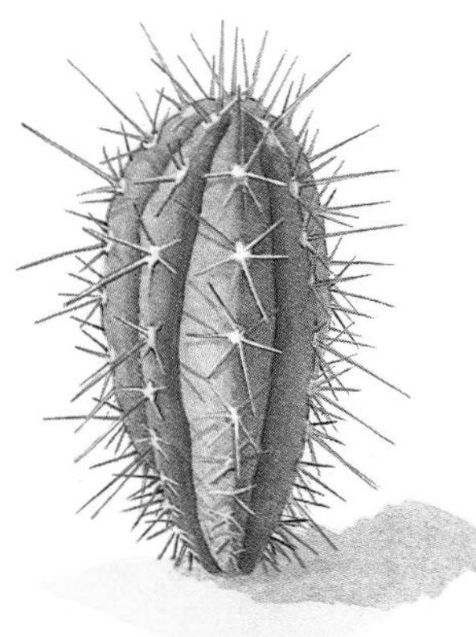

Evolution

Origin of Species, British Museum (Natural History)/Cambridge University Press, 1981

Reproduction

How Life Begins C.RANKIN and COLDREY, Collins, 1984

Life in cold climates

The Poles WILLY LEY and THE EDITORS OF TIME-LIFE BOOKS, Time-Life Books, 1976

Life without water

The Desert A.STARKER LEOPOLD and THE EDITORS OF TIME-LIFE BOOKS, Time-Life Books, 1976

Night life

Nature's Night Life ROBERT BURTON, Blandford Press, 1982

Wildlife goes to town

Animals in Towns series JOYCE POPE, Hamish Hamilton, 1984
Spotters Guide to Town and City Wildlife D.SHIP, Usborne, 1981
Town Birds ALAN RICHARDS, A. & C. Black, 1983

Rain forests

Jungles Edited by EDWARD S. AYENSU, Cape, 1980

Conservation

The Doomsday Book of Animals DAVID DAY, Ebury Press, 1981

Looking for clues

Nature Detective HUGH FALKUS, Gollancz, 1978
Mammals of Britain: their Tracks and Signs M.J.LAWRENCE and R.W.BROWN, Blandford Press, 1974
Collins Guide to Animal Tracks and Signs P.BANG and P.DAHLSTROM, Collins, 1974

A good read

My Family and Other Animals GERALD DURRELL, Penguin Books, 1959
The Bafut Beagles GERALD DURRELL, Penguin Books, 1958
The Drunken Forest GERALD DURRELL, Penguin Books, 1958
Encounters with Animals GERALD DURRELL, Penguin Books, 1963
The Whispering Land GERALD DURRELL, Penguin Books, 1964
Three Singles to Adventure GERALD DURRELL, Penguin Books, 1964
A Zoo in My Luggage GERALD DURRELL, Penguin Books, 1964
King Solomon's Ring KONRAD LORENZ, Methuen, 1964

Answers

page 12 The mammals.

page 18 The dachshund was bred for hunting badgers. Its name means badger-hound in German. The bull-dog is short and squat with very powerful jaws because it was bred for bull baiting. This was an old English sport in which a bull was matched against several bulldogs. The dogs had to be strong and fearless.

page 19 Picasso.

page 21 The spectacled bears have different face markings because they each received different information in the sperms and eggs from their parents.

page 21 The finches have different shaped beaks because they are adapted to eating different foods. The ground finch eats hard nuts and seeds. The warbler finch eats insects and grubs in crevices and under bark. The cactus finch probes in the flowers of cacti.

page 25 When an animal curls up into a ball it becomes a sphere. It now has a small surface compared to its volume. This means it loses less heat across its surface. This is important for hibernating mammals.

page 26 The mouse is affected more by the air than the human. It is affected less by gravity. Because of this, it is held up more by the air than the human as it falls. The mouse's relatively large surface helps it to float down more gently.

page 27 A small animal has a much bigger surface in relation to its volume than a big animal. This means it has relatively more surface to lose heat across. Small animals, therefore, lose heat more quickly.

page 30 *toucan* fruit, insects and even eggs – mainly a herbivore but really an *omnivore*.
orang-utan fruit, leaves and some insects – mainly a herbivore but really an *omnivore*.
python small animals such as birds and mammals – a *carnivore*.
aye-aye fruit and insect larvae – an *omnivore*
hummingbird nectar – a *herbivore*.
aardvark termites – a *carnivore*.
kinkajou plants, insects, small mammals and birds – an *omnivore*.
blue whale small shrimps called krill – a *carnivore*.

page 51 The tongue needs to be able to feel where food is, so that it can move the food around the mouth, and to detect hard objects like fish bones. The tongue is also used to clean bits of food out of gaps between the teeth. The fingertips are also very sensitive, but they are covered with tough, protective skin which makes them less sensitive than the tongue.

page 57 No. The lantern bug lives in the forest. The caiman is much bigger and lives in the river. Predators of the lantern bug are unlikely to mistake it for a caiman.

page 60 The slope stops the honey from flowing out of the cell.

page 67 The egg has to be strong to bear the weight of the adult ostrich when the egg is being incubated. An adult ostrich weighs about 125 kg, almost twice as much as a human adult.

page 68 **A** crab **B** sea urchin **C** barnacle.

page 71 Both parents take turr to incubate the eggs.

page 72 **A** happiness **B** fear **C** excitement.

page 74 Karl Hamner concluded that some animals have built-in rhythms which cannot be changed no matter what you do to the animals.

page 75 The female leatherback turtles time the return to their breeding grounds by means of their internal 'clocks', which tell them when to start making their journey.

page 75 The mangrove snails reset their 'clocks' every day because the times for high and low tide are different each day.

page 85 The margins of the giant water lily leaves have gaps in them to allow rain-water to drain off. Otherwise the leaf would sink under the weight of the water it collected.

page 118 Reflective mirror sides. Rest of body black. Body flattened from side to side. Upward-looking eyes. Large mouth.

page 129 Freezer store mice need thicker fur to give them better insulation. Because they are bigger than ordinary mice, they have a smaller surface area in relation to their volume compared to ordinary mice. This means they lose less heat across their surface, so they keep warmer.

page 146 *Panthera pardus* is the leopard. *Panthera onca* is the jaguar. *Panthera tigris* is the tiger.

page 146 *Panthera aquatica* or *Panthera waterus*.

page 147 **A** gentoo; **B** chinstrap; **C** rockhopper; **D** adelie; **E** king; **F** emperor.

WILDLIFE QUIZ

Heads you win: **A** moth **B** hippopotamus **C** giant tortoise.

True or false: **1** false; **2** false; **3** true; **4** true; **5** true; **6** false; **7** true; **8** false; **9** false; **10** false; **11** true; **12** true.

Food: **1** plankton (krill); **2** hummingbirds; **3** on their feet; **4** it constricts or strangles it; **5** an animal that eats plants and other animals; **6** termites; **7** song thrush or woodpecker finch or chimpanzee or Egyptian vulture or bearded-vulture or sea otter or satin bowerbird or harvester ant or tailor ant or dwarf mongoose; **8** by sonar or echolocation; **9** giant panda; **10** fungi which they grow in special underground gardens.

What's this?: the back view of a male ostrich.

Close up: **A** bird's feather; **B** the horn of a rhinoceros; **C** scales of a butterfly's wing.

Eye spy: **A** a chameleon's eye; **B** a frog's eye.

Mixed bag: **1** limestone; **2** in Madagascar; **3** carrion (dead animals); **4** two organisms living together; **5** an insect-eating (carnivorous) plant; **6** the giant panda; **7** when an animal's body is dark on top and light underneath. The shading is sometimes reversed; **8** chameleon or plaice or octopus; **9** it 'hibernates' or aestivates; **10** when an animal's body temperature is always the same as its surroundings; **11** in the Philippine islands; **12** they are filter feeders; **13** the mountain gorilla; **14** in Australia.

Zoo puzzle: Milly got all the animals into the right cages in twenty-five moves. Can you do it in fewer? Ask your mathematics teacher to help.

Size: **1** the blue whale; **2** Rafflesia; **3** Savi's white-toothed pigmy shrew; **4** Papua New Guinea; **5** giant squid; **6** giant sequoia or 'big tree'; **7** coco-de-mer; **8** komodo dragon.

Glossary

abdomen: the hollow part of an animal's body containing most of the gut and other internal organs.
adaptation: a characteristic which improves the chances of an animal or plant surviving and reproducing in its environment (its natural surroundings).
aerofoil: a surface which is specially shaped to help it stay in the air. The wings of birds and aeroplanes are aerofoils.
aestivation: a kind of hibernation or dormancy shown by some desert creatures during the dry season.
air sac: in birds, pouches formed from part of the lungs and filled with air. The air sacs make the bird very light for its size.
amphibian: an animal belonging to a group of vertebrates which live partly in water and partly on land. Frogs, toads, newts and salamanders are amphibians. Amphibians are cold-blooded. They live mainly on land, but return to the water to breed. When young they breathe with gills, but as adults they use their lungs. Adult amphibians usually have 4 legs and smooth, wet skins.
antennae: the pairs of feelers found on the heads of insects and other arthropods. Antennae are used for touch, taste, smell and for sensing changes in humidity and temperature.
aquatic: describes animals or plants that live in water.
binocular vision: the use of both eyes to look at the same object. Binocular vision is possible if the eyes are at the front of the head. Because each eye looks at the object from a different angle, two different pictures are seen. From this the brain can work out how far away the object is. Binocular vision is important for animals which need to judge distances for hunting or for movement.
bladder: a stretchy bag-like structure.
breeding ground: the place to which animals travel to breed and bring up their young.
breeding programme: the carefully-planned arrangements made to encourage animals in captivity to breed.
bulb: a short, underground stem surrounded by fleshy leaves swollen with stored food.
buoyancy: the way some objects tend to float in water or air.
camouflage: a form of disguise which helps an animal to blend with its background so that it is not noticed by other animals.
carbon dioxide: a gas made up of the elements carbon and oxygen. Carbon dioxide is present in the air, and is also dissolved in the water of rivers, lakes and oceans.
carcass: the dead body of an animal.
carnivore: a flesh-eating animal.
cell: the basic unit of living matter. It contains a jelly-like living material, called protoplasm, surrounded by a thin skin called the membrane. Plant cells also have a stiff cell wall around the outside of each cell.
cellulose: the material that forms the walls of plant cells.
characteristic: any shape, pattern, or way of behaving by which an organism can be recognized.
chitin: a hard, horny, waterproof substance found in the shells of crustaceans and the hard outer covering of insects and other arthropods.
chlorophyll: the green substance found in plants. It absorbs light, which the plant uses to make its own food by photosynthesis.
chrysalis: *see* **pupa.**
class: one of the groups used in the classification of plants and animals. Mammalia is the class to which the mammals belong.
classification: the arrangement of animals and plants in groups, chosen by looking at their characteristics.
cocoon: a fluffy ball of silk made by an animal. Some moth caterpillars spin cocoons around themselves when they are ready to turn into moths.
cold-blooded: describes an animal whose body temperature changes as the temperature of its surroundings changes. In cold weather, the animal's temperature falls, but in hot weather the body temperature rises, so its blood is not always cold.
colony: a group of organisms of the same species living together.
compound eye: an eye made up of many tiny units, each with its own lens.
conifers: trees and shrubs which produce cones.
copepod: microscopic crustaceans found in very large numbers in both fresh and salt water.
corm: a swollen underground stem which stores food and produces new plants from its bulbs.
countershading: a form of camouflage where the animal is coloured dark on top and lighter underneath.
courtship: a complex pattern of behaviour and signalling which takes place before mating.
crustacean: one of a group of hard-skinned animals with jointed legs and long antennae. The body is divided into three main parts, which may be further divided into segments. Crustaceans include crabs, shrimps, lobsters, barnacles, water fleas and copepods.
cuticle: a waterproof layer covering the outside of a living organism.
decomposer: a living organism which causes decay, breaking down the remains of dead plants or animals.
diurnal: describes an animal which is active only during the day.
dormant: describes an organism which is resting and not growing.
drag: the resistance an animal meets as it tries to move through the air or water.
drift line: the line marking the highest point the sea reaches on a beach at high tide. It is marked by an untidy line of drying seaweed, empty shells, drift wood and other objects washed up and left by the tide.

echolocation: a method of navigation using echoes. High-pitched sounds are sent out, and these sounds bounce back (echo) off solid objects in their path.
egg: a female sex cell both before and after it has been fertilized. Eggs are also the hard- or soft-shelled structures in which the embryos of some animals develop.
endangered species: species which have so few members that they are in danger of becoming extinct.
environment: the collection of physical, chemical and biological factors which affect an organism.
evolution: the way organisms change over many generations, giving rise to new species.
extinct: describes a species that has died out and no longer exists.
fertilization: the joining together of a male sex cell and a female sex cell (in animals, these are called sperm and egg) to produce a new living organism.
filter feeder: an animal which feeds by sieving out tiny particles of dead or living organic material from water as it flows through or past the animal.
fluke: the horizontal tail fin of a whale or dolphin.
food chain: a chain which shows the order in which food energy is passed from plants to animals. All food chains begin with a plant. This is eaten by an animal which is eaten by another animal and so on.
food web: a number of food chains linked together to form a web.
genus: one of the groups used in the classification of plants and animals. *Pinus* is the genus to which pine trees belong.
germination: the growth and development of a plant embryo, in a seed or spore, into an independent plant.
gestation time: the length of time that a female mammal carries her young inside her body. It starts when the egg is fertilized and ends when the young are born.
gills: structures used for breathing under water.
habitat: the place where a particular organism lives.
herb: a non-woody flowering plant.
herbivore: an animal that feeds mainly on plants.
hibernate: to go into a very deep sleep during cold weather.
hormones: chemicals produced by living organisms. They are used to coordinate body processes, such as growth and reproduction.
humidity: a measure of the amount of moisture in the atmosphere.
incubate: to keep eggs warm so that they will hatch.
insectivore: an animal that feeds mainly on insects.
insulate: to prevent heat from leaving or entering an object or animal.
internal 'clock': many living organisms have a built-in way of recognizing the time of day or the time of year. We say that they have an internal clock.
invertebrate: an animal without a backbone.
larva (pl. larvae): a young animal that looks quite different from its parents. Tadpoles are the larvae of frogs.
lichen: a small, plant-like growth found on trees and bare rocks. It is a mixture of an alga and a fungus.
lift: the lifting force which develops because of a difference in air pressure above and below the wings of a bird or aeroplane.
locomotion: movement from place to place. Walking, running, swimming and flying are types of locomotion.
magnetic field: the area around a magnet where its magnetic force acts. The Earth is rather like a giant magnet.
mammal: a backboned animal which is warm-blooded and whose body is usually covered with hair or fur. The female mammal gives birth to live young and feeds them on milk.
marsupial: a pouched mammal.
mass: the amount of material in a body or object.
metamorphosis: the change of shape in some animals during their life cycle.
microscopic: describes something so small that a microscope is needed to see it.
migration: the movement of animals from one place to another, often over long distances.
mimicry: copying the appearance, movement or sound of another species.
mollusc: a member of a large group of animals, without a backbone and with a soft body with a muscular foot. Many molluscs are protected by a hard shell.
mucus: a slimy fluid produced by animals. Mucus moistens and protects delicate surfaces and stops them drying out.
natural selection: in evolution, the gradual process during which some species survive and reproduce while others die out and become extinct.
navigation: the method used by an animal to find its way about.
nectar: a sweet liquid made by some flowers.
nocturnal: describes an animal or plant that is active at night.
nymph: one of the stages in the development of some insects before they become adults. Nymphs look similar to their parents but are smaller.
omnivore: an animal which eats plants and other animals.
order: one of the groups in the classification of animals and plants. It is a unit into which classes are divided. An order is divided up further into families.
organ: a distinct part of an animal or plant made of many specialized cells. Each organ has its own special job to do.
organic: describes any material which contains carbon. Carbon compounds are found in all living and dead cells.
oxygen: a gas that is found in air and water. It has no colour, taste or smell. It is necessary for plant and animal life.

parasite: an animal or plant which lives on, or inside, another organism (called the host). It gets food from its host, but the host suffers as a result.
pheromone: a chemical substance produced by animals which acts as a signal.
photosynthesis: a process by which green plants use energy from sunlight to make sugars from carbon dioxide and water.
plankton: microscopic animals and plants which float near the surface of the sea and freshwater lakes.
plumage: the feathers of a bird.
pollen: tiny yellow or orange grains produced by the male parts of flowering and cone-bearing plants. The pollen grains contain the male sex cells.
pollination: the transfer of pollen grains from the male parts to the female parts of a flowering plant.
population: the total number of organisms of a species living in a particular area at any one time.
polyp: a hollow, cup-shaped animal with a ring of tentacles round its mouth.
predator: an animal that hunts and eats other animals.
prey: an animal that is hunted and eaten as food by another animal.
primate: a group of mammals which includes monkeys, apes and humans.
prop root: a special type of root produced by some plants which helps support the main stem or trunk.
proteins: a group of complicated chemical compounds containing nitrogen. Proteins are important for plant and animal growth.
pupa: a stage in the life cycle of an insect during which the animal changes from a caterpillar to an adult insect. Usually the pupa is covered in a hard case. Inside, the body materials of the caterpillar are rearranged to form the adult butterfly or moth. The pupa of a moth or butterfly is sometimes called a chrysalis.
reproduction: the process by which living organisms produce offspring.
reptile: one of a large group of cold-blooded animals with backbones and a dry, scaly skin. Most reptiles live on land and lay eggs covered with a tough, leathery shell.
rhythm: an action which occurs at regular intervals.
scavenger: an animal which feeds on dead animal or plant material.
sensor: a group of cells which picks up signals from its surroundings.
sex cell: a special kind of cell produced when animals or plants reproduce. Sex cells are either male or female. In animals, male sex cells are called sperms. Female sex cells are called eggs. Male and female sex cells join together during fertilization.
single lens reflex camera: a type of camera which allows you to view the object you want to photograph through the camera's lens.
siphon: a tube-like structure that draws water into an animal.
sonar: a method of navigation using sound. High-pitched sounds are given out and these bounce back off any objects in their path.
species: a unit of classification of animals and plants. Members of one species can breed among themselves. They cannot usually breed with members of another species.
sperm: a male reproductive/sex cell.
spore: a special reproductive unit produced in large numbers by certain plants and other organisms. Spores are carried by wind and air currents.
stoma (pl. stomata): one of the many tiny pores or holes found in the outer layer of leaves and also on some plant stems.
streamlined: describes a shape that is pointed or rounded at the front end and tapers to a thinner shape at the back.
submerged: describes an object that is under the surface of a liquid such as water.
suckle: to feed a young mammal with milk from the special milk-producing glands. All female mammals suckle their young for the first part of their lives.
surface film *see* **surface tension.**
surface tension: the property of liquids that makes their surface appear to be covered by a thin, elastic film, called the surface film.
symbiosis: the living together of two different types of organism.
territory: an area of land or water in which an animal or a group of animals live, feed and breed.
thermostat: a device for controlling the temperature of an object.
torpor: the condition of being very sleepy and inactive.
tuber: an underground stem swollen with food.
ultraviolet light: invisible rays present in sunlight.
umbilical cord: a soft cord of living tissue that joins the developing baby mammal to its mother before birth.
under-exposing: in photography, not allowing enough light when taking a picture.
variation: differences between animals or plants of the same species.
vertebrate: any animal which has a skeleton of bone or cartilage. Fish, amphibians, reptiles, birds and mammals are all vertebrates.
warm-blooded: describes an animal which has a body temperature that stays the same whatever the temperature of the surroundings. Birds and mammals are warm-blooded.
weaned: describes a young mammal which has stopped feeding on its mother's milk and has started eating other food.
womb: the part of a female mammal's body where the baby develops before birth.
zooplankton: microscopic animals which float at the surface of the sea and freshwater lakes.

Index

INDEX

WILDLIFE RECORD BREAKERS

The biggest reptile is the estuarine or salt-water crocodile from South-east Asia and Australia. It grows to 4·5 m in length and weighs 500 kg.
The goliath frog is the world's biggest frog. It lives in West Africa. Fully stretched out it measures 80 cm and weighs 3 kg.
The heaviest brain belongs to the sperm whale. It weighs more than 9 kg.
The biggest marsupial is the red kangaroo from Australia. It stands over 2m tall and weighs 80kg.
In one day a new born blue whale drinks enough milk to fill over 2500 glasses.
The world's biggest fish is the whale shark. It lives in the warmer parts of the Atlantic, Indian and Pacific Oceans. It sometimes reaches a length of 18m and a weight of 40 tonnes.
The giraffe is the tallest animal. It lives in Africa and bulls often grow to a height of 5m - sometimes more.
The giant spider crab from Japan is the biggest crab in the world. It measures nearly 4m across its outstretched front legs.
The smallest flowering plant is a water plant called duckweed. It is 0·5mm in length and 0·2mm in width. It weighs 0·00015g.
TAPE MEASURE
The longest snake is the reticulated python from South east Asia. It often grows more than 6m in length.
IN METRES
The biggest leaves belong to the raffia palm tree from the Mascarene Islands in the Indian Ocean. A single leaf can measure more than 20m.
When climbing a 3-toed sloth moves at about 4m per minute. It is the slowest moving mammal.
The biggest bird's egg is laid by the ostrich. An average egg is 20cm in length and 12·5cm in diameter. It weighs nearly 1·8kg.

THE ENGLISH COMPANION'S MODERN GRAMMAR

von

BERNHARD BARTELS und HEINZ RÖHR

unter Mitarbeit von Eileen Rose Glynn, B.A.

bearbeitet von

BERNHARD BARTELS und KEITH MITCHELL

VERLAG MORITZ DIESTERWEG

Frankfurt am Main

Unter beratender Mitwirkung von

Helmuth Herfurth, Willy Rodermond, Rudolf Salewsky und Walter Scheffler

Illustrationen von Harald Bukor

Genehmigt für den Gebrauch an Schulen.
Genehmigungsdaten teilt der Verlag auf Anfrage mit.

ISBN 3-425-06648-X

16. Auflage

Beim Nachdruck wurden einige Verbesserungen vorgenommen.

Monophoto-Filmsatz: Oskar Brandstetter Druckerei KG, Wiesbaden
Druck und Bindung: Druckhaus Kaufmann, Lahr

CONTENTS

Lautschrift nach *Daniel Jones*, *English Pronouncing Dictionary*, *Thirteenth Edition*, *London 1967*

Das Zeichen △ hinter einem Wort oder einem Satz weist darauf hin, daß der Ausdruck oder die Satzkonstruktion im modernen Englisch nicht mehr gebräuchlich ist.
Das Zeichen ○ bedeutet, daß die so gekennzeichneten Wörter oder Satzkonstruktionen mehr der literarischen, poetischen Sprache zuzuordnen sind.
Die Abkürzungen *BE* und *AE* stehen für *British English* und *American English*.

PRONUNCIATION AND SPELLING

Aussprache und Schreibung

Sounds	Stress	Intonation
Laute	Druck	Intonation

The English Sounds — Die englischen Laute

The Basis of Articulation — Die Artikulationsbasis 1

Die englischen Laute erhalten die ihnen eigentümliche Klangfarbe durch die Lage, die die Sprechwerkzeuge in der Ruhe einnehmen und die die Grundlage für ihre Bewegungen beim Sprechen bildet. Diese Ruhelage nennt man Artikulationsbasis. Sie ist bei Völkern, die verschiedene Sprachen sprechen (oft sogar bei Gliedern desselben Volkes), verschieden. Wesentliche Eigentümlichkeiten der englischen Artikulationsbasis sind:

Der Unterkiefer ist etwas vorgeschoben.

Die Zunge ist von den Zähnen zurückgezogen; sie liegt flach und gesenkt mit nach oben gerichteter Zungenspitze im Munde.

Beim Sprechen werden die Lippen möglichst wenig bewegt, nicht vorgestülpt, nicht gespreizt und selten gerundet.

The Vowels — Die Vokale

List of English Vowels — Liste der englischen Vokale 2

Bei der Bildung der Vokale kann die Zunge hoch, mitten oder tief im Mund liegen. Sie kann sich nach dem Vorder-, Mittel- oder Hintergaumen bewegen.

Zunge	Vordergaumenlaute	Mittelgaumenlaute	Hintergaumenlaute
hoch	i: i		(u:) (u)
mitten	e ɛ	ə: ə	(o) ʌ
tief	æ a		(ɔ:) (ɔ)

( ) = mit Lippenrundung

3 Tongue-positions of Vowels — Lautbildungsstelle der Vokale

Das Diagramm zeigt die Stellen im Mund, an denen die einzelnen Vokale gebildet werden.

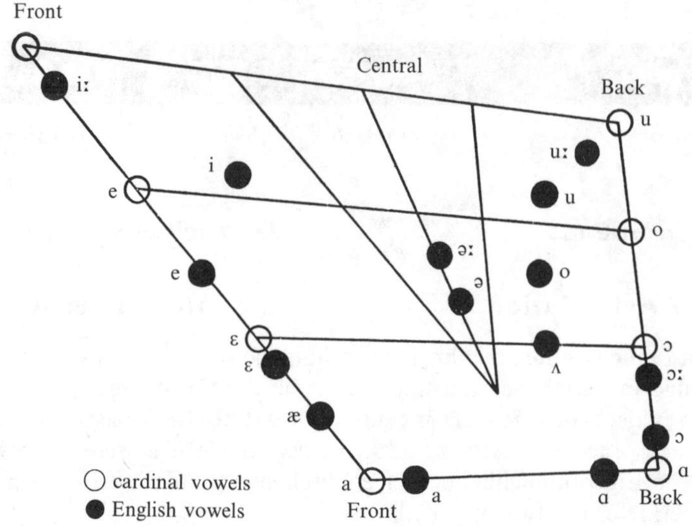

4 The Glottal Stop — Kehlkopfverschlußlaut

Im Deutschen geht den betonten Vokalen im Anlaut eines Wortes („der andere“) oder des zweiten Bestandteils eines Wortes („Ver/ein, Er/eignis, Vorder/achse“) ein Knackgeräusch, der sogenannte Kehlkopfverschlußlaut, voraus. Er entsteht durch das Schließen und plötzliche Wiederöffnen der Stimmritze im Kehlkopf. Die englischen Vokale werden (wie auch die französischen) stets ohne Knackgeräusch mit weichem Einsatz gesprochen.

The Consonants — Die Konsonanten

5 List of Consonants — Liste der englischen Konsonanten

Arten der Laute	Lippen-laute	Zahn-Lippen-laute	Zahn-laute	Zahn-fleisch-laute	Vorder-gaumen-laute	Hinter-gaumen-laute	Kehl-kopf-laute	Seiten-laut
Verschlußlaute	p b			t d			k g	
Reibelaute	w	f v	θ ð	s z ʃ ʒ r	j		h	l
Nasallaute	m			n		ŋ		

Stimmhafte Laute rot

Tongue-positions of Consonants — Lautbildungsstellen der Konsonanten 6

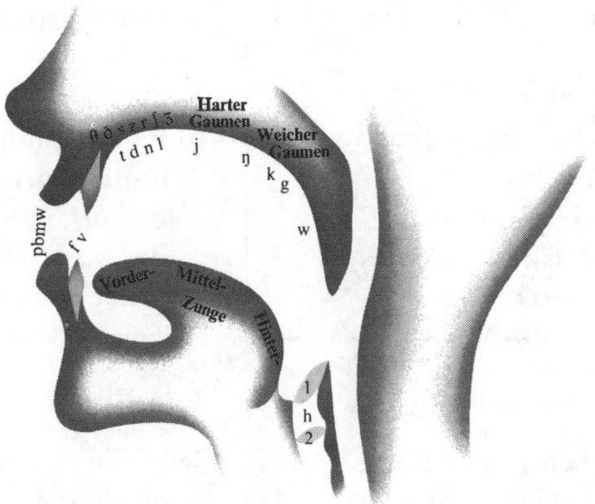

1 Kehldeckel
2 Stimmritze

Notes on Certain Consonants — Bemerkungen zu einigen Konsonanten 7

1. [l] ist das Zeichen für zwei verschiedene Laute:

a) lead [liːd]	let [let]	look [luk]
clear [kliə]	cling [kliŋ]	fill in [fil′in]
illume [i′ljuːm]	allure [ə′ljuə]	
b) old [əuld]	help [help]	
people [piːpl]	all [ɔːl]	
fill [fil]	wool [wul]	

a) *clear* [l]; ein helleres l, dem deutschen Laut l gleich. Es wird nur vor Vokalen und vor [j] gesprochen.

b) *dark* [l]; ein l mit dunklem Klang (Heben der Hinterzunge, Senken der Mittelzunge!). Es wird vor Konsonanten und im Wortauslaut gesprochen.

2. [r] ist Reibelaut, wird aber nicht gerollt wie das deutsche r. (Die Zungenspitze ist beim englischen [r] nach oben zurückgebogen.)

a) read [riːd]	rose [rəuz]	narrow [′nærəu]
for ever and ever [fər‿′evər‿ən‿′evə]		
b) farm [fɑːm]	bird [bəːd]	born [bɔːn]
far [fɑː]	fir [fəː]	nor [nɔː]
c) share [ʃɛə]	pure [pjuə]	fire [′faiə]
power [′pauə]	here [hiə]	there [ðɛə]

a) Das [r] ist nur vor Vokal erhalten (vgl. 8, b).

b) Vor Konsonanten und im Wortauslaut ist es geschwunden (dabei ist Längung des vorausgehenden Vokals eingetreten).

c) Nach Vokal und Diphthong und vor stummem Auslauts-e ist es zu [ə] geworden.

3.

a) heir [ɛə]	honest [ˈɔnist]	hour [ˈauə]
heiress	honesty	hourly
heirless	honour	
heirloom	honourable	

b) If he [ˈifi] keeps his [ˈkiːpsiz] ideas to himself [tuimˈself], it won't do him [ˈduim] much good. Mary has [ˈmɛəriəz] asked me to give her [ˈgivə] the book.

a) Das h in den nebenstehenden Wörtern ist stumm.

b) Es verstummt oft als Anlaut unbetonter Vortonsilben, z.B. bei *he, him, her, his, himself, herself* und bei *have, has, had*, wenn sie als Hilfsverb gebraucht werden (vgl. auch *Weak Forms*, 17,1 u. 3).

8 The Linking in the Sense-group — Die Bindung in der Sinngruppe

Die einzelnen Laute stehen in der Sprache nicht allein. Sie erscheinen in einer durch den Sinn zusammengeschlossenen Wortgruppe, der Sinngruppe. Innerhalb der Sinngruppen ist die Verbindung der einzelnen Laute sehr eng.

a) He asked if we had only old iron.
[hi‿ˈɑːskt‿if wi hæd‿ˈəunli‿ˈəuld‿ˈaiən]
Most Americans take an interest in their ancestry. [ˈməust‿əˈmerikənz ˈteik‿ən‿ˈintrist‿in ðər‿ˈænsistri]

b) here is [ˈhiər‿ˈiz] where is [ˈhwɛər‿ˈiz]
far away [ˈfɑːr‿əˈwei]
our own [auər‿ˈəun]
more agreeable [ˈmɔːr‿əˈgriəbl]
a pair of boots [əˈpɛər‿əvˈbuːts]

c) to prefer [priˈfəː] preferring [priˈfəːriŋ]
to enter [ˈentə] entering [ˈentəriŋ]

a) Die mit einem Vokal anlautenden Wörter werden eng mit dem Auslaut des vorangehenden Wortes (Vokal oder Konsonant) verbunden.

b) In der Bindung vor einem Vokal wird ein r am Wortende, das sonst in der Aussprache geschwunden ist, häufig wieder hörbar.

c) Ebenso erklärt sich das Wiederlautwerden eines (sonst stummen) r am Wortende eines Verbs vor vokalisch anlautenden Endungen.

9 Influence of a Sound on Its Neighbour — Beeinflussung eines Lautes durch den Nachbarlaut

1. Vowels — Vokale

back [bæk]	bag [bæ·g]
cap [kæp]	cab [kæ·b]
mat [mæt]	mad [mæ·d]

Vor stimmhaften Konsonanten wird ein kurzer Vokal etwas gedehnt (halblang).

Umgekehrt sind lange Vokale vor stimmlosen Konsonanten etwas kürzer als vor den entsprechenden stimmhaften Konsonanten: in *the use* [juːs] und *he used to* [ˈjuːstə] ist der Vokal etwas kürzer als in *to use* [juːz], in *heart* [hɑːt] etwas kürzer als in *hard* [hɑːd].

2. Consonants — Konsonanten

Ein Konsonant beeinflußt oft den Lautwert des benachbarten Konsonanten

a) five [faiv] fifth [fifθ] twelve [twelv] twelfth [twelfθ]	a) im Innern eines Einzelwortes;
b) news [nju:z] newspaper [ˈnju:speipə] cup [kʌp] cupboard [ˈkʌbəd]	b) in einer Wortzusammensetzung;
c) He's old [hi:zˈəuld]. It's time [itsˈtaim]. He used [ˈju:zd] a knife. He used to [ˈju:stə] get up late.	c) in einer Sinngruppe.

Stress — Druck (Betonung) 10

Im Wort ist gewöhnlich nur eine Silbe druckstark (*single stress*); die übrigen sind druckschwach.

inconvenience [ˌinkənˈvi:njəns] inability [ˌinəˈbiliti] administration [ədˌminisˈtreiʃən]	In drei- und mehrsilbigen Wörtern ruht jedoch auf einer weiteren Silbe ein Nebenton. Diese Nebentonsilbe ist von der Haupttonsilbe gewöhnlich durch eine unbetonte Silbe (oder mehrere) getrennt.

Der Gegensatz zwischen druckstarken und druckschwachen Silben ist im Wort und in der Sinngruppe sehr groß. Die druckschwachen Silben werden vernachlässigt. Dies hat im Laufe der Sprachentwicklung dazu geführt, daß die Vokale der druckschwachen Silben ihre Klangfarbe verloren haben und zum *neutral vowel* [ə] oder [i] geworden oder ganz verstummt sind.

a) doom [du:m]	kingdom [ˈkiŋdəm]	a) Nachtonsilben
less [les]	hopeless [ˈhəuplis]	
some [sʌm]	troublesome [ˈtrʌblsəm]	
able [eibl]	enjoyable [inˈdʒɔiəbl]	
b) today [təˈdei]	observe [əbˈzə:v]	b) Vortonsilben
accord [əˈkɔ:d]	forget [fəˈget]	
believe [biˈli:v]	expect [iksˈpekt]	
accept [əkˈsept]	unless [ənˈles]	

In dieser sprachlichen Erscheinung wirkt sich das Streben des Engländers aus, mit möglichst wenig Kraftaufwand auszukommen und ruhig und beherrscht zu sprechen. Sie erklärt auch den Reichtum des Englischen an einsilbigen Wörtern.

11 Stress in the Single Word

Der Druck im Einzelwort

1\. 'worker 'postman 'greatness

a'shore be'fall for'get

In Wörtern germanischer Herkunft ist in der Regel die erste Silbe druckstark.
Nur die Wörter mit den Vorsilben *a-*, *be-*, *for-* bilden hier eine Ausnahme.

2\. Für die Wörter lateinisch-französischen Ursprungs lassen sich keine festen Betonungsgesetze geben. Als Anhaltspunkte seien genannt:

a) creature ['kri:tʃə] empire ['empaiə]
figure ['figə] history ['histəri]
honourable ['ɔnərəbl] nature ['neitʃə]

a) Die aus dem romanischen Wortschatz entlehnten Wörter, die im 13. bis 15. Jahrhundert aufgenommen und im Englischen heimisch geworden sind, haben nach germanischer Betonungsweise den Ton auf der ersten Silbe.

b) august [ɔ:'gʌst] (= *erhaben*)
machine [mə'ʃi:n] police [pə'li:s]
saloon [sə'lu:n] moustache [məs'tɑ:ʃ]

b) Dagegen behalten die Wörter, die erst später (nach 1500) aufgenommen worden sind, die fremde Betonung.

Notice:
Häufig gebrauchte und dadurch eingebürgerte Wörter werden dagegen, selbst wenn sie erst in neuester Zeit übernommen worden sind, auf der ersten Silbe betont, z. B. garage ['gærɑ:dʒ, 'gæridʒ], massage ['mæsɑ:ʒ, 'mæsɑ:dʒ]; solche Wörter sind ein Beweis für die Leichtigkeit und Unbekümmertheit, mit der der Engländer Wörter aus fremden Sprachen in seinen eigenen Wortschatz übernimmt.

c) a'bolish di'minish scien'tific
re'public in'sipid 'valid
ex'plicit de'posit

c) Verben auf *-ish*, Adjektive u. Substantive auf *-ic*, *-id*, *-it* betonen die zweitletzte Silbe.

d) po'litical his'torian par'ticular
'demonstrate 'institute ex'perience
'circumstance 'permanent sig'nificant
fa'cility di'minutive ri'diculous
ack'nowledg(e)ment

'memory speci'ality phot'ography

d) Bei Substantiven, Adjektiven und Verben auf
-al, -an, -ar, -ate, -ute,
-ence, -ance, -ent, -ant,
-ty, -ive, -ment, -ous
ist meist die drittletzte Silbe betont, ebenso bei Substantiven auf *-y*.

e) 'adversary 'commentary 'admiralty
'casualty 'matrimony 'testimony

e) Substantive und Adjektive auf *-ary* und Substantive auf *-alty* und *-ony* betonen die viertletzte Silbe.

at'tentive dis'tribute ele'mentary

Ausnahmen zu d) und e) sind selten.

Change of Stress in the Same Word — Verschiedene Betonung desselben Wortes (Druckwechsel)

Oft haben Substantiv oder Adjektiv und Verb die gleiche Form. (Grund: Schwinden der alten Endungen in frühengl. Zeit). Ein wichtiges Unterscheidungsmerkmal ist der Druck (die Betonung). Substantive und Adjektive haben meistens den Ton auf der ersten Silbe, Verben auf der Stammsilbe (vgl. deutsch: 'Übertrag – über'tragen u. a.).

Substantiv (oder Adjektiv)		Verb	
'absent (adj.)	abwesend	to ab'sent o.s.	sich entfernen
'abstract (adj.)	abstrakt	to abs'tract	abstrahieren
'attribute	Beifügung	to at'tribute	beifügen
'compound	zusammenges. Wort	to com'pound	zusammensetzen
'conduct	Führung	to con'duct	führen
'contact	Berührung, Fühlung	to con'tact	Verbindung herstellen
'desert	Wüste	to de'sert	im Stich lassen
'desert (adj.)	wüst, öde, verlassen		
'exploit	Heldentat	to exp'loit	ausbeuten
'export	Ausfuhr	to ex'port	ausführen (Waren)
'frequent (adj.)	häufig	to fre'quent	häufig besuchen
'insult	Beleidigung	to in'sult	beleidigen
'object	Gegenstand, Objekt	to ob'ject	einwenden, etwas dagegen haben
'permit	Erlaubnis	to per'mit	etwas erlauben
'present	Geschenk	to pre'sent	(be)schenken
'present (adj.)	anwesend; jetzig		
'produce	Erzeugnis	to pro'duce	erzeugen
'rebel	Rebell	to re'bel	rebellieren
'record	Bericht	to re'cord	berichten
'retail	Kleinhandel	to re'tail	im kleinen verkaufen
'subject	Gegenstand, Untertan	to sub'ject	unterwerfen
'survey	Überblick	to sur'vey	überblicken
'transport	Transport	to trans'port	transportieren

Notice:

the envy ['envi] – to envy ['envi]
the reply [ri'plai] – to reply [ri'plai]

In vielen Fällen lauten aber Substantiv (bzw. Adjektiv) und Verb gleich.

13 The Stress in a Sense-Group

Der Druck (die Betonung) in der Sinngruppe

> The stresses of the words in a group depend on their importance.
> [ðə ˈstresiz əv ðə ˈwəːdz in əˈgruːp diˈpend ən ðɛər imˈpɔːtəns]

In der Sinngruppe sind, wenn keine besonderen Verhältnisse vorliegen, folgende Wortarten druckstark: Substantive, Zahlwörter, Adjektive, Demonstrativ- und Interrogativpronomen, Verben und verneinte Hilfsverben, die Ortsadverbien und die bestimmten Zeitadverbien, ferner *Mr.*, *Mrs.*, *Miss.*

I	never	gave	you	that	book.
[ˈai	nevə	geiv	juː	ˈðæt	ˈbuk]
[ai	ˈnevə	geiv	ˈjuː	ðət	buk]
[ai	ˈnevə	ˈgeiv	ju	ˈðæt	buk]

Es kann aber jedes Wort einer Sinngruppe betont (druckstark) werden, wenn es hervorgehoben werden soll.

14 The Level Stress

Der „ebene“ Druck (Die schwebende Betonung)

Im Englischen stehen sehr häufig zwei druckstarke Silben oder Wörter nebeneinander. Man nennt diese Erscheinung *level stress.*

Level Stress haben im Englischen:

1.

a) ˈcold ˈwater	ˈred ˈink	a) adjective + noun
b) ˈFred ˈMiller	ˈLondon ˈBridge	b) name + name
c) ˈMother's ˈbirthday	ˈPat's ˈfriend	c) possessive case + noun
d) the ˈtime of ˈday	the ˈCity of ˈLondon	d) noun + of + noun (name)
e) she ˈworks ˈhard	we ˈgo ˈout	e) verb + adverb
f) ˈall ˈright	ˈpretty ˈgood	f) adverb + adjective
g) ˈvery ˈearly	ˈquite ˈwell	g) adverb + adverb

Zu diesen Beispielen kommen Wortzusammensetzungen und Wortableitungen mit *level stress.*

2.

'four'teen	'seven'teen
'twenty-'three	'forty-'four

Die Zahlwörter von *thirteen* bis *nineteen* und *twenty-one*, *twenty-two*, etc. haben *level stress*, wenn sie allein stehen (vgl. aber 15 und 118, 2).

3.

'arch'bishop	'ex-'president	'half-'time
'mis'place	'non-'payment	'over-'anxious
'over'do	'pre'pay	'pre'fabricate
're'fill	're'write	'under'feed
'under'sell	'under'pay	
'under'statement		
But:		
ex'haust	ex'hort	under'stand
over'cloud	re'mind	

Ebenso haben viele Wörter *level stress*, die eine betonte Vorsilbe haben, jedoch nicht zu einer festen Verbindung geworden sind. Vorsilben dieser Art sind:

arch-, ex-, half, mis-, non-, over-, pre- [priː], re- [riː], under-.

'un'able	'un'asked	'un'button
'un'aided	'unbe'lief	'uncon'cealed

He was un'able to write his name.
He was 'unable to write his name.

Wortableitungen, die mit der Vorsilbe *un-* gebildet werden, haben meist *level stress.*
In gewissen Zusammenhängen können diese Wörter aber auch *single stress* haben.

4.

'down'stairs	'in'side	'mean'while
'up'stairs	'out'side	'first-'class
'red-'hot	'second-'hand	'old-'fashioned

Viele Wortzusammensetzungen haben *level stress.*

The Stress in Connected Words

Das Drei-Silben/Wörter-Gesetz 15

Hyde Park	Hyde Park Corner
'fif'teen	'fifteen 'days
'ups'tairs	the 'upstairs 'rooms
'red-'hot	a 'red-hot 'iron
'second-'hand	a 'second-hand 'car

Wenn zwei Silben, die *level stress* haben, mit einer dritten betonten Silbe verbunden werden, so verliert die zweite Silbe den Druck.
Das gleiche gilt für zwei Wörter, denen ein drittes betontes Wort folgt.

16 The Influence of the Stress on the Quality of Vowels

Einfluß des Druckes (der Betonung) auf die Qualität der Vokale

1.

courage ['kʌridʒ]	courageous [kə'reidʒəs]	
family ['fæmili]	familiar [fə'miljə]	familiarity [fəˌmili'æriti]
famous ['feiməs]	infamous ['infəməs]	
photograph ['fəutəgrɑːf]	photography [fət'ɔgrəfi]	photographic [ˌfəutə'græfik]

Bei stammverwandten Wörtern wird der Stammvokal häufig sehr verschieden ausgesprochen. Der Grund für diese sprachliche Erscheinung liegt in den Druck-(Betonungs-)Verhältnissen.

2.

land [lænd]	England ['iŋglənd]
shire ['ʃaiə]	Yorkshire ['jɔːkʃiə]
day [dei]	Monday ['mʌndi]
head [hed]	forehead ['fɔrid]
less [les]	merciless ['məːsilis]

In den unbetonten (druckschwachen) Silben werden die Vokale stark abgeschwächt. Sie sind dann meist zu dem *neutral vowel* [ə] oder [i] geworden (vgl. 10).

3.

able [eibl]	agreeable [ə'griəbl]
payable ['peiəbl]	recommendable [ˌrekə'mendəbl]
populace ['pɔpjuləs]	parentage ['pɛərəntidʒ]

Die Vokale in den Nachsilben *-able*, *-ace*, *-age* werden zum *neutral vowel* abgeschwächt.

4.

to deliberate [di'libəreit]	deliberate [di'libərit]
to desolate ['desəleit]	desolate ['desəlit]
to elaborate [i'læbəreit]	elaborate [i'læbərit]
to separate ['sepəreit]	separate ['seprit]

Die Nachsilbe *-ate* behält ihren Lautwert [eit] beim Verb; sie wird abgeschwächt beim Adjektiv und Substantiv zu [it].

5.

to recollect [ˌrekəˈlekt]	**to remember** [riˈmembə]
preparation [ˌprepəˈreiʃən]	**to prepare** [priˈpɛə]
exploit [ˈeksplɔit]	**to exploit** [iksˈplɔit]
prominent [ˈprɔminənt]	**to promote** [prəˈməut]
compliment [ˈkɔmplimənt]	**compatriot** [kəmˈpætriət]

Bei den Vorsilben *re-*, *pre-*, *ex-*, *pro-*, *com-* werden, wenn sie druckstark sind oder einen Nebenton haben, die vollen Vokale [e] und [ɔ] gesprochen.
In druckschwacher (unbetonter) Silbe haben sie dagegen den *neutral vowel* [ə] oder [i].

6.

to rebuild [ˈriːˈbild]	**to reconquer** [ˈriːˈkɔŋkə]
to reconstruct [ˈriːkənsˈtrʌkt]	**to re-address** [ˈriːəˈdres]
to re-elect [ˈriːiˈlekt]	**to preconceive** [ˈpriːkənˈsiːv]
to prepay [ˈpriːˈpei]	

Die druckstarken (betonten) Vorsilben *re-* und *pre-* werden [riː] bzw. [priː] gesprochen, wenn dem Sprechenden ihre Grundbedeutung „wieder" bzw. „vor" voll bewußt ist. Die mit diesen druckstarken Vorsilben gebildeten Verben haben ebenen Druck.

Notice:

to recover	[riˈkʌvə]	sich erholen
	[ˈriːˈkʌvə]	wieder bedecken
to reform	[riˈfɔːm]	reformieren
	[ˈriːˈfɔːm]	sich wieder formieren

Beachten muß man bei nebenstehenden Wörtern das Nebeneinander der Aussprache [ri] und [riː] bei Verben mit gleicher Schreibung, aber verschiedener Bedeutung!

7.

a) **to excavate** [ˈekskəveit]	**exercise** [ˈeksəsaiz]
exit [ˈeksit]	**excitation** [ˌeksiˈteiʃən]
b) **exact** [igˈzækt]	**exaggerate** [igˈzædʒəreit]
exalt [igˈzɔːlt]	**examination** [igˌzæmiˈneiʃən]
example [igˈzɑːmpl]	**exhibit** [igˈzibit]
c) **to exploit** [iksˈplɔit]	**to exceed** [ikˈsiːd]
exchange [iksˈtʃeindʒ]	**excite** [ikˈsait]
excuse [iksˈkjuːz]	**expand** [iksˈpænd]

Die Vorsilbe *ex-* wird gesprochen
a) [eks], wenn sie druckstark ist oder einen Nebenton trägt;

b) [igz], wenn sie (in der Aussprache!) vor einem betonten Vokal steht;

c) [iks], wenn sie druckschwach (unbetont) ist und ein Konsonant folgt.

17 Strong Forms and Weak Forms — Druckstarke und druckschwache Wörter

"Are you ready?" – "Yes, I am."	[ˈɑːju ˈredi – ˈjes aiˈæm]
"I am not ready, but you are."	[ˈaim ˈnɔtˌredi bət ˈjuː ɑː]
They played hide-and-seek.	[ðei pleid ˈhaidnˈsiːk]
He is a friend of mine.	[hiːzə ˈfrend əv main]
My father is taller than I.	[mai ˈfɑːðəriz ˈtɔːlə ðn ˈai]
I have seen them.	[aiv ˈsiːn ðm]

Viele englische Wörter verändern sich in der Aussprache, wenn sie unbetont, druckschwach gebraucht werden. Dies ist vor allem der Fall bei einsilbigen Wörtern, z. B. bei:

1. Auxiliary Verbs — Hilfsverben

	Strong Form	Weak Forms		Strong Form	Weak Forms
am	æm	əm, m	do	duː	du, də, d
are	ɑː	ə	does	dʌz	dəz, dz
is	iz	z, s	shall	ʃæl	ʃəl, ʃl
was	wɔz	wəz, wz	should	ʃud	ʃəd, ʃd, ʃt
were	wəː	wə	will	wil	əl, l
been	biːn	bin	would	wud	wəd, əd, d
has	hæz	həz, əz, z, s	can	kæn	kən, kn
have	hæv	həv, əv, v	could	kud	kəd, kd, kt
had	hæd	həd, əd, d	must	mʌst	məst, məs, ms

Die druckstarken Formen der Hilfsverben werden nicht nur gebraucht, wenn diese wirklich betont sind, sondern erscheinen auch stets am Ende, oft auch am Anfang der Sinngruppe (vgl. das erste Satzbeispiel oben).

2. Article — Artikel

	Strong Form	Weak Forms
the	ðiː	ði, ðə
a, an	ei, æn	ə, ən

Der bestimmte Artikel lautet [ði] vor Vokalen, [ðə] vor Konsonanten: *the* [ði] *apple*, *the* [ðə] *pear*. Der unbestimmte Artikel lautet [ən] vor Vokalen, [ə] vor Konsonanten: *an* [ən] *apple*, *a* [ə] *pear*.

3. Pronouns — Pronomen

	Strong Form	Weak Forms		Strong Form	Weak Forms
he	hiː	hi, i	them	ðem	ðəm, ðm, m
she	ʃiː	ʃi	my	mai	mi
we	wiː	wi	his	hiz	iz
you	juː	ju	your	jɔː (juə)	jo, jə
me	miː	mi	their	ðɛə	ðə
him	him	im	some	sʌm	səm, sm
her	həː	hə, ə	one	wʌn	wən
us	ʌs	əs, s	that	ðæt	ðət

4. Prepositions — Präpositionen

at	æt	ət	of	ɔv	əv, v
for	fɔː	fə	to	tuː, tu	tu, tə, t
from	frɔm	frəm			

Das Wort *to* lautet [tu] vor Vokalen, [tə] vor Konsonanten: *to open* [tu'oupən], *to shut* [tə'ʃʌt];

5. Conjunctions and other Words — Konjunktionen und andere Wörter

not	nɔt	nt	whereas	wɛər'æz	wərəz
and	ænd	ənd, ən, n	just	dʒʌst	dʒəst
but	bʌt	bət	that (*Konj.*)	ðæt	ðət
as	æz	əz	there	ðɛə	ðə
than	ðæn	ðən, ðn	saint	seint	snt, sn
because	bi'kɔːz	bi'kɔz, bikəz	sir	səː	sə

Intonation — Intonation 18

Die Tonführung ist in der englischen Sprache viel ruhiger, gleichmäßiger, sogar eintöniger als im Deutschen. Das starke Auf und Ab in der Stimmführung und in der Tonstärke, das der deutschen Sprache eigen ist, kennt das Englische nicht.

Die englische Intonation ist in abgeschlossenen Aussagen, in Ausrufen und in Fragen, die mit einem Fragewort beginnen, in der Regel fallend; sie sinkt allmählich von der ersten, mit hoher Tonlage gesprochenen druckstarken Silbe bis zur letzten, mit tiefer Tonlage gesprochenen druckstarken Silbe. Der ersten druckstarken Silbe etwa vorausgehende Silben werden in der Regel entweder tief oder mit allmählich zur Tonhöhe der druckstarken Silbe ansteigender Melodie gesprochen.

Die Wendung der Satzmelodie am Schluß der Sinngruppe ist entscheidend für deren Wesen und deren Bedeutung. Es ergeben sich zwei Grundmelodien: eine fallende und eine steigende.

19 Falling Intonation — Fallende Intonation

In der letzten druckstarken Silbe fällt die Melodie; etwa noch folgende druckschwache Silben werden tief gesprochen. Diese Melodie findet sich

1. in abgeschlossenen Aussagen;

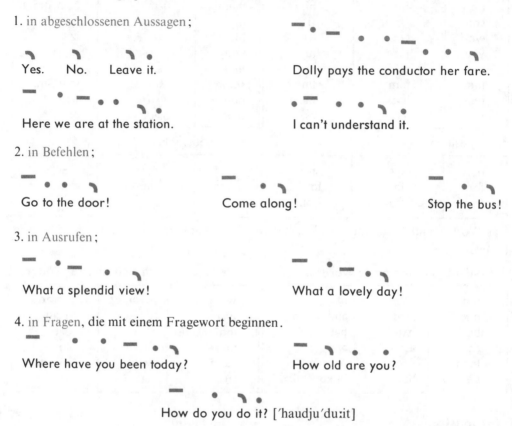

Yes. No. Leave it.

Dolly pays the conductor her fare.

Here we are at the station.

I can't understand it.

2. in Befehlen;

Go to the door!

Come along!

Stop the bus!

3. in Ausrufen;

What a splendid view!

What a lovely day!

4. in Fragen, die mit einem Fragewort beginnen.

Where have you been today?

How old are you?

How do you do it? ['haudju'du:it]

20 Rising Intonation — Steigende Intonation

Wenn die Satzmelodie in der letzten betonten Silbe ihren Tiefpunkt erreicht hat, bewegt sie sich aufwärts. Folgen keine weiteren unbetonten Silben, so geschieht das Steigen in der letzten betonten Silbe selbst. Diese Melodie findet sich

1. in Entscheidungsfragen, also in Fragen, die die Antwort „ja“ oder „nein“ erfordern;

Will you go to town today?

Is this your parcel?

2. in Bitten;

Excuse me. 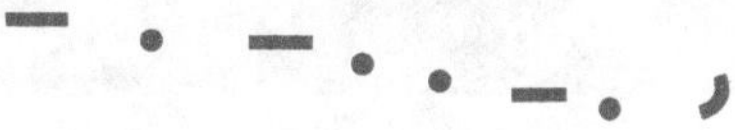 Will you pass me the butter, please.

3. in Sinngruppen, die nicht abschließend wirken sollen, sondern so, daß etwas unausgesprochen zu bleiben scheint;

It won't take long.  I hope I'm not disturbing you.

4. in Sinngruppen, die nicht abgeschlossen sind, sondern Fortführung durch die nächste Sinngruppe erfordern.

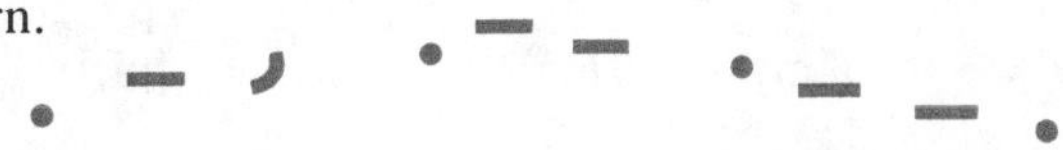

The door opens, and in come the two children.

Emphatic Intonation — Der Druck in emphatischer Rede 21

Wenn in emphatischer Rede ein besonders wichtiges Wort hervorgehoben werden soll, wird im Englischen (wie im Deutschen) das betreffende Wort stärker betont. Wesentlicher als die Betonung selbst ist aber der Umstand, daß die Melodie innerhalb der betonten Silbe stark abfällt. Damit wird von der gewöhnlichen Intonation abgewichen (emphatische Intonation). Die starke Betonung eines Wortes im Satz hat zur Folge, daß andere Wörter, die normalerweise auch betont wären, nun unbetont sind. Infolgedessen wird bei der ersten Grundmelodie alles, was auf die betonte Silbe folgt, in tiefer Tonlage gesprochen.

I don't touch such things.

Besonders häufig sind in der Umgangssprache emphatische Abwandlungen der zweiten Grundmelodie. Dabei setzt das Steigen der Melodie entweder unmittelbar nach dem Abfallen der Stimme in der betonten Silbe des hervorgehobenen Wortes ein oder erst mit der letzten, verhältnismäßig stark betonten Silbe.

Work? There isn't any work.  That's why we won the match today.

I'm sorry to have kept you waiting.

(In den Beispielen bezeichnen Striche druckstarke Silben, Punkte druckschwache Silben, ↘ Silben mit fallendem, ↗ Silben mit steigendem Ton.)

Spelling — Syllabication — Punctuation

Schreibung — Silbentrennung — Zeichensetzung

Spelling — Schreibung

22 The English Alphabet — Das englische Alphabet

a	b	c	d	e	f	g	h	i
[ei]	[biː]	[siː]	[diː]	[iː]	[ef]	[dʒiː]	[eitʃ]	[ai]
j	k	l	m	n	o	p	q	r
[dʒei]	[kei]	[el]	[em]	[en]	[əu]	[piː]	[kjuː]	[ɑː]
s	t	u	v	w		x	y	z
[es]	[tiː]	[juː]	[viː]	[ˈdʌbljuː]		[eks]	[wai]	[zed]

23 Capital Letters — Großschreibung

Mit großen Anfangsbuchstaben werden geschrieben:

a) Look! There is a jet in the sky.	a) der Satzanfang;
b) I am sorry I cannot read the letter.	b) das Personalpronomen *I;*
c) George, England, London	c) alle Eigennamen, z. B. Personen, Länder, Städte;
Christmas, Easter, Whitsuntide	Feste;
January, March, December Wednesday, Thursday, Saturday	Monate und Wochentage;
a Christian, a Protestant, a Catholic, a Puritan, a Quaker	Namen, die das religiöse Bekenntnis angeben;
the Liberals, the Conservatives, the Republicans	Namen der Parteien;
Father, Mother, Uncle, Aunt, Cook, Nurse, etc.	Namen von Familienmitgliedern (falls sie als Eigennamen betrachtet werden);
d) English, French, Roman, German	d) die von Eigennamen abgeleiteten Adjektive (*vgl. lingua Latina, populus Romanus*)*;*
e) Elizabeth the Second The Queen (Elizabeth the Second) went to Ghana. Lord Salisbury [ˈsɔːlzbəri], Professor Jones	e) Titel, mit und ohne Namen; und Ordnungszahlen zur Unterscheidung gleichnamiger Fürsten;

f) God, He (God), Our Lord, the Almighty
Heaven, Hell, the Holy Bible

f) religiöse Bezeichnungen;

g) The English Companion
The First Postage-stamp
The President and His Family

g) Substantive, Adjektive, Zahlwörter und alle Wörter, die ganz besonders hervorgehoben werden sollen, in Büchertiteln und Überschriften;

h) Sing one, two, three
Come follow me.

h) die Zeilenanfänge von Gedichten und Liedern.

Rules for Joining Endings

Regeln für das Anfügen von Endungen 24

a) to love – loved loving – lovable
noble – nobler – noblest
blue – bluish ice – icy

a) Stummes *e* am Wortende fällt weg vor Endungen, die mit einem Vokal beginnen.

b) care – careful nice – nicely
to excite – excitement

b) Stummes *e* am Wortende bleibt jedoch erhalten vor Endungen, die mit einem Konsonanten beginnen.

c) to argue – argument due – duly
awe – awful true – truly
nine – ninth whole – wholly

c) Eine Ausnahme von dieser Regel bilden die nebenstehenden Wörter.

2. a) to agree – agreeing – agreeable
to see – seeing

to see – seer
free – freer – freest

a) Alle Wörter, die auf *-ee* enden, behalten *-ee* vor den Endungen *-ing* und *-able.*
Vor den Endungen, die mit *e-* beginnen, verlieren diese Wörter ein *e.*

b) to shoe – shoeing
to canoe – canoeing
to hoe – hoeing

b) Bei Wörtern, die auf *-oe* enden, bleibt das stumme *e* am Wortende erhalten (Vermeidung von *-oi-* und damit von falscher Lautung).

c) to die – dying to tie – tying
to lie – lying (= *„liegend“ und „lügend“*)

c) Auf *-ie* endigende Verben verwandeln vor der Endung *-ing* das *-ie-* in *-y-.*

Notice:

to dye (= *färben*) – dyeing

Bei *to dye* bleibt vor *-ing* das *-e* erhalten.

	d) to change – changeable service – serviceable courage – courageous notice – noticeable	d) Stummes *e* am Ende eines Wortes bleibt auch nach *g* und *c* erhalten vor *-ous, -able*.
3.	to envy – envied – envious – enviable to cry – cried – crier (*But*: crying) merry – merrier – merriest twenty – twentieth victory – victorious happy – happily beauty – beautiful mercy – merciless holy – holiness	*y* am Wortende, dem ein Konsonant vorausgeht, wird vor Endungen (mit Ausnahme von *-ing*) in *i* verwandelt.
	a) lady – ladies body – bodies duty – duties reality – realities *But:* the Barrys the Kennedys	a) Substantive auf *-y* mit vorangehendem Konsonanten verwandeln im Plural *y* zu *i* und fügen die Endung *-es* an. (Ausnahme: Eigennamen).
	b) to try – he tries to fly – he flies to carry – he carries	b) Verben auf *-y* mit vorangehendem Konsonanten verwandeln in der 3. Pers. Singular Präsens *y* zu *i* und fügen die Endung *-es* an.
	c) dry – dryness – dryly shy – shyness – shyly sly – slyness – slyly	c) Als Auslaut einsilbiger Adjektive bleibt *y* vor den Endungen *-ness* und *-ly* erhalten.
4.	to begin – beginning – beginner to run – running – runner to stop – stopped – stopping to stir – stirred – stirring to occur – occurred – occurring to prefer – preferred – preferring	Werden *-ed, -er* oder *-ing* an ein Wort angehängt, das auf einen Konsonanten endet, so wird dieser verdoppelt, wenn ihm ein einfacher und betonter Vokal vorausgeht.

Notice:

to look – looked – looking to book – booked – booking to conquer – conquered to answer – answered	Keine Verdoppelung nach Doppelvokal! Keine Verdopplung nach unbetontem Vokal!
bus – buses (*Am.* busses) gas – gases	Ausnahmen!

to travel – travelled – traveller to equal – equalled – equalling to quarrel – quarrelled – quarrelling to patrol – patrolled – patrolling	Der Endkonsonant *l* wird nach einfachem Vokal bei Anhängen von *-ed*, *-er* oder *-ing* etc. immer verdoppelt, und zwar auch wenn der Vokal unbetont ist (vgl. aber 30, 5).

full – beautiful, careful, wonderful to fill – to fulfil till – until all – almost, alone, already, also, although, always, altogether	Einsilbige Wörter auf *-ll* verlieren in Wortzusammensetzungen eins der beiden *l* (vgl. 30, 6).

The Division of Syllables — Die Silbentrennung 25

Die Regeln für die Silbentrennung sind im Englischen recht kompliziert. Während im Deutschen die Silbentrennung im wesentlichen nach Sprechsilben erfolgt, wird im Englischen teils nach Wortbestandteilen, teils nach Sprechsilben getrennt. Die Schwierigkeiten bei der Trennung englischer Wörter sind sicherlich der Grund dafür, daß die Engländer die Silbentrennung weitgehend vermeiden.

Für die Fälle, in denen die Silbentrennung unvermeidlich erscheint, kann man sich folgende Richtlinien zu eigen machen:

1.

came wife	knives [naivz]	Einsilbig gesprochene Wörter können nicht getrennt werden.
moved [mu:vd]	cleaned [kli:nd]	

2.

Eng-land	Ox-ford	Lincoln-shire	Zusammengesetzte Wörter werden nach ihren Bestandteilen getrennt.
land-lord	with-out	power-ful	
to-wards	an-other	no-body	

3. Zwei- und mehrsilbige Wörter werden nach Sprechsilben getrennt.

a) po-em	li-on	cru-el	a) Zwei Vokale werden getrennt, wenn jeder einer eigenen Sprechsilbe zugehört.
re-al	Febru-ary	cre-ate	
b) at-tack	bril-liant	sug-gest	b) Von zwei oder mehr Konsonanten gehört der erste zur ersten Trennungssilbe.
cor-rect	sis-ter	sol-dier	
mon-ster			

c) emp-ty sculp-tor	part-ner punc-ture	punc-tual	c) Von drei Konsonanten wird nur der letzte zur zweiten Trennungssilbe gezogen, wenn der zweite und dritte Konsonant zusammen nicht am Anfang eines Wortes stehen könnten.
d) na-tive fa-ther	he-ro hy-phen	wa-ter tro-phy	d) Ein einfacher Konsonant (dazu werden auch *th*, *ph*, *ch*, *sh*, *ng*, *dg*, gezählt) tritt nach langem Vokal oder Diphthong zur zweiten Trennungssilbe.
e) pleas-ure rich-es	col-our moth-er	bach-elor noth-ing	e) Nach einem kurzen betonten oder auch einen Nebenton tragenden Vokal tritt aber der Konsonant zur ersten Trennungssilbe.
f) ta-ble ha-tred conse-quence anti-quity	cy-clist cathe-dral re-quire re-quest	mea-sles pro-gress li-queur li-quid	f) Zur zweiten Trennungssilbe treten Konsonant + *l*, Konsonant + *r*, und *-qu-*.
But:			
prob-lem sec-retary	pub-lic theat-rical	pub-lish	Konsonant + *l*, Konsonant + *r* werden aber getrennt, wenn ihnen ein kurzer betonter Vokal vorausgeht.
g) wick-et ex-ample lux-ury	rock-et ex-ist anx-ious	tick-et Sax-on	g) *ck* und *x* treten stets zur ersten Trennungssilbe.

4. Der Stamm eines Wortes muß bei der Abtrennung von Vorsilben oder Endungen erhalten bleiben

a) re-member	intro-duce	ex-treme	a) Vorsilben (*re-*, *intro-*, *ex-*, *etc*);
b) wish-es	greet-ed	work-ing	b) Flexionsendungen (*-es*, *-ed*, *-ing*);
c) high-er	high-est		c) Steigerungsendungen (*-er*, *-est*);
d) farm-er profit-able diction-ary serv-ice	west-ern read-able short-age journal-ist	child-ish assist-ant special-ize mechan-ism	d) Viele Ableitungssilben, wie -er, -ern, -ish, -able, -ant, -ary, -age, -ize, -ice, -ist, -ism können im allgemeinen vom Stamm des Wortes getrennt werden.

Einsilbig gesprochene Endungen können nicht getrennt werden, z. B.

5.

ex-plo-sion	ex-po-si-tion	ex-plo-sive
ex-po-sure	sen-si-tive	ad-ven-ture

-sion, -tion, -sive, -sure, -tive, -ture.

Punctuation — Zeichensetzung 26

The Punctuation Marks — Die Interpunktionszeichen

. full stop, period
: colon [ˈkəulən]
; semicolon [ˈsemiˈkəulən]
' apostrophe [əˈpɔstrəfi]
? question mark, note (mark) of interrogation
! exclamation mark, note of exclamation
, comma

— dash
– hyphen [ˈhaifən]
" " quotation marks
' ' inverted commas
( ) parenthesis [pəˈrenθisis], *plur.* parentheses [iːz]; round brackets
[ ] square brackets

The Use of Commas — Der Gebrauch der Kommata 27

Die englische Zeichensetzung ist von der deutschen sehr verschieden. Im Englischen werden durchweg viel weniger Kommata gesetzt als im Deutschen. Während das Komma im Deutschen grammatisches Zeichen zur Trennung von Satzteilen und Sätzen ist, zeigt es in der englischen Sprache die Sprechpause an und teilt den Satz in Sinngruppen ein.

I. When to use a Comma — Wann setzt der Engländer ein Komma?

1.

a) We had tea, eggs, buttered toast, and bread for breakfast.
Father, Mother, and the children went for a walk.
The United Kingdom consists of England, Scotland, Wales, and Northern Ireland.

b) Our first lesson begins at eight o'clock, and is over at 8.45.

a) Bei Aufzählungen von mehr als zwei Gliedern trennt der Engländer diese durch Kommata, selbst wenn eins dieser Glieder durch *and* angeschlossen ist.

b) Vor *and* steht auch ein Komma, wenn es ein zweites Prädikat an dasselbe Subjekt anknüpft.

2.

He is not rich, but happy.
He is happy, though not rich.

Zwischen Satzteilen, die durch Konjunktionen wie *but*, *though*, etc. verbunden sind, steht ein Komma.

3.

a) Off Cape Trafalgar, Nelson met the French and Spanish fleets. On a fine summer's night in August, the underground had taken us . . .	a) Stehen adverbiale Bestimmungen am Anfang des Satzes, setzt der Engländer gern ein Komma.
b) My dear boy, you ought to work more carefully. Sir, Can any of your readers explain . . .	b) Das gleiche gilt für Anreden am Anfang des Satzes.
c) Oh, splendid! Ah, how nice! Oh, I am so happy. Oh! how nice!	c) Hinter Ausrufen (*Interjections*) setzt man gern ein Komma. Es kann natürlich auch ein Ausrufezeichen stehen.
d) While in the country, we went for nice walks every day. Where bees are, there is honey.	d) Nebensätze, die einem Hauptsatz vorausgehen, trennt man durch ein Komma vom Hauptsatz ab. Das gilt auch für verkürzte Nebensätze.
e) His friend, after many efforts, succeeded in getting the job. When, at last, we arrived at home, we were dead tired. It was raining; Father, therefore, proposed to go to the cinema. The children, of course, wanted to go to the zoo.	e) Adverbiale Bestimmungen in der Satzmitte, besonders aber die Adverbien however too indeed therefore in fact of course werden durch Kommata abgetrennt.

4.

He said, "I'm glad to see you."	Vor der kurzen wörtlichen Rede (*Direct Speech*) setzt man statt des Doppelpunktes gern ein Komma.

5.

July 16, 1962 *or* 16 July (,) 1962	Vor Jahreszahlen nach den Monatszahlen steht ein Komma.

6.

My dear Parents, As I have been staying here in London for a fortnight, and . . .	Nach der Anrede in Briefen setzt der Engländer ein Komma, kein Ausrufezeichen.

II. When not to use a Comma

Wann setzt der Engländer kein Komma?

Im Englischen wird kein Komma gesetzt, wenn die Satzteile oder die Haupt- und Nebensätze dem Sinne nach eng zusammengehören und folglich nicht durch eine Pause getrennt werden.

1. Everyone who attended the concert enjoyed it.
All I need is a cup of tea.
Where is the book that you were reading?
The people who bought the pictures he painted made a fortune.

Abweichend vom Deutschen fehlt das Komma im Englischen vor notwendigen Relativsätzen (vgl. 91). (Ausmalende Relativsätze dagegen werden durch ein Komma vom Hauptsatz getrennt, vgl. 90, 2).

Notice:

I am sure that he will arrive soon.

Auch vor *that* (= daß) steht kein Komma.

2. Das Komma wird im Englischen nicht gesetzt

a) It is a pity that you weren't at home.
Where he is now living is a mystery.
What surprises me is that no one protested.
b) He did not know what to do.
Can you tell me where your friend went?

a) vor und nach Subjektsätzen (vgl. 236, 1);

b) vor Objektsätzen (vgl. 236, 3).

3. Kein Komma steht im Englischen

a) They rang me to come.
I asked him to do it for me.
He wanted to know if we had got his letter.
b) He left the room without saying a word.
You must finish this job before leaving for Scotland.

a) vor dem Infinitiv und dem erweiterten Infinitiv;

b) vor der Gerundialkonstruktion.

4. Wait until I am ready.
He was older than I had expected.

Vor kurzen Adverbialsätzen, die sich eng an den regierenden Hauptsatz anschließen, steht im Englischen oft kein Komma.

29 The Pronunciation of American English

Die Aussprache des amerikanischen Englisch

In der folgenden Übersicht werden phonetische Haupteigentümlichkeiten des *American English* (AE), die den verschiedenen amerikanischen Aussprachegruppen (vgl. 264) mehr oder weniger gemeinsam sind, mit dem *British English* (BE) verglichen.

		British English		American English		Explanation
a) task	ask	tɑːsk	ɑːsk	tæ(ː)sk	æ(ː)sk	a) BE [ɑː] AE [æ(ː)]
can't	class	kɑːnt	klɑːs	kæ(ː)nt	klæ(ː)s	
dance	half	dɑːns	hɑːf	dæ(ː)ns	hæ(ː)f	
laugh	past	lɑːf	pɑːst	læ(ː)f	pæ(ː)st	
castle	fasten	ˈkɑːsl	ˈfɑːsn	ˈkæ(ː)sl	ˈfæ(ː)sn	
b) hot	box	hɔt	bɔks	hɑt	bɑks	b) BE [ɔ] AE [ɑ][1])
shop	sock	ʃɔp	sɔk	ʃɑp	sɑk	
job	dog	dʒɔb	dɔg	dʒɑb	dɑg	
coffee	often	ˈkɔfi	ˈɔːf(t)n	ˈkɑ(ː)fi	ˈɑftn	
probable	novel	ˈprɔbəbl	ˈnɔvəl	ˈprɑbəbl	ˈnɑvəl	
conference		ˈkɔnfərəns		ˈkɑnfərəns		
c) hurry	worry	ˈhʌri	ˈwʌri	ˈhəːri	ˈwəːri	c) BE [ʌr] AE [əːr]
courage		ˈkʌridʒ		ˈkəːridʒ		
d) due	suit	djuː	sjuːt	duː	suːt	d) BE [juː] AE [uː] Der j-Vorschlag bei [uː], der heute auch in England vor gewissen Konsonanten vernachlässigt wird, fehlt im AE fast ganz, besonders nach Dentalen.
knew	news	njuː	njuːz	nuː	nuːz	
student	duty	ˈstjuːdənt	ˈdjuːti	ˈstuːdənt	ˈduːti	
presume	tube	priˈzjuːm	tjuːb	priˈzuːm	tuːb	
enthusiasm		inˈθjuːziæzm		enˈθuːziæzm		
e) boat	rope	bəut	rəup	boːt	roːp	e) BE [əu] AE [o(ː)] Auffällig ist im AE auch eine verhältnismäßig geringe Diphthongierung der Vokale (besonders nach stimmlosen Konsonanten und in unbetonter, auslautender Silbe).
nose	o no!	nəuz	ˈəuˈnəu	noːz	ˈoːˈnoː	
break	late	breik	leit	breːk	leːt	Ähnliches gilt für BE [ei].
fade	sail	feid	seil	feːd	seːl	BE [ei] AE [eː]

[1]) Der AE-Laut [ɑ] ist ein kurzes, „dunkles“, ein wenig nach [ɔ] klingendes a, deutlich vom „hellen“ deutschen a unterschieden; Hinterzungenvokal. Die Zunge liegt tief; Mund ziemlich weit geöffnet; keine Lippenrundung. (Entsprechender langer Vokal ist [ɑː], wie in BE *father*.)

			British English		American English		Explanation
f)	bird	first	bəːd	fəːst	bəːrd	fəːrst	f) Besonders charakteristisch ist die Aussprache des postvokalischen r vor Konsonant (im Inlaut und im Auslaut, [r][1]). Er wird im AE auch dort gesprochen, wo im BE das r vokalisiert ist.
	part	more	pɑːt	mɔː	pɑːrt	mɔːr	
	finger	arm	ˈfiŋgə	ɑːm	ˈfiŋg(ə)r	ɑːrm	
	sort	form	sɔːt	fɔːm	sɔːrt	fɔːrm	
	sir	Mr.	səː	ˈmistə	səːr	ˈmist(ə)r	
g)	red	break	red	breik	red	breːk	g) Das AE [r] im Anlaut und vor Vokalen wird ebenfalls weiter hinten im Mund gebildet.
	very		ˈveri		ˈveri		
h)	stand	time	stænd	taim	stæ̃nd	tãim	h) Vor einem Nasallaut werden Vokale und Diphthonge im allgemeinen nasaliert (sog. „*Nasal Twang*").
i)	leave	like	liːv	laik	liːv	laik	i) Das AE l ist immer ein „dunkles" l (*dark* l, vgl. 7).
	float	plan	fləut	plæn	floːt	plæn	
	silly	believe	ˈsili	biˈliːv	sili	biliːv	
j)	library		ˈlaibrəri		ˈlaiˌbreri		j) Im AE erscheint bei drei- oder mehrsilbigen Wörtern eine Nebentonsilbe. Der stärkere Druck auf dieser Nebentonsilbe bewirkt eine andere Qualität des Vokals der Nebentonsilbe (*Strong Form*).
	dictionary		ˈdikʃənəri		ˈdikʃəˌneri		
	territory		ˈteritəri		ˈtərəˌtɔːri		
	nominative		ˈnɔminətiv		ˈnɑməˌneːtiv		
	ceremony		ˈseriməni		ˈserəˌmoːni		
	secretary		ˈsekrətəri		ˈsekrəˌteri		
	extraordinary		iksˈtrɔːdnri		iksˈtrɔːdiˌneri		
k)	advertisement		ədˈvəːtismənt		ˌædvərˈtaizmənt		k) Bei einigen Wörtern liegt im AE der Druck auf einer anderen Silbe als im BE.
	laboratory		ləˈbɔrətəri		ˈlæbrəˌtɔːri		
	frontier		ˈfrʌntiə		frʌnˈtiər		
	address		əˈdres		ˈædres		
l)	actual		ˈæktjuəl, ˈæktʃuəl		ˈæktʃuəl		l) Verschiedene Aussprache von Einzelwörtern.
	either	neither	ˈaiðə	ˈnaiðə	ˈiːðər	ˈniːðər	
	government		ˈgʌvənmənt		ˈgʌvərmənt		
	lieutenant		lefˈtenənt		luːˈtenənt		
	literature		ˈlitəritʃə		ˈlitərəˌtʃur		
	schedule		ˈʃedjuːl		ˈskedjuːl		

[1]) [*r*] ist ein vokalischer r-Laut (Reibelaut). Die Zungenspitze wird dabei stark gegen den harten Gaumen zurückgebogen. Die Artikulationsstelle dieses AE [*r*] liegt also weiter hinten als die des BE [r]. (Nach *Jones*, "*An Outline of English Phonetics*").

Notice:

BE

Did it all happen yesterday?

AE

Die amerikanische Intonation ist viel gleichförmiger als die englische. Der Amerikaner vermeidet die (oberen und unteren) Tonhöhenextreme und wählt in normalen Sprechsituationen eine Mittellage.

30 American Spelling of English Words

Zur Schreibung des amerikanischen Englisch

Einige der wichtigsten Abweichungen in der Schreibung des amerikanischen Englisch vom britischen Englisch sind in der folgenden Tabelle zusammengefaßt.

	British English	American English	Explanations British	Explanations American
1.	a) armour humour favour favourite honour honourable parlour colour	armor humor favor favorite honor honorable parlor color	-our	-or
	b) mould (= *Gußform*) to smoulder (= *schwelen*) moustache	mold to smolder mustache	-ou-	-o-
	c) gauntlet (= *Stulphandschuh*) to staunch (stanch)	gantlet to stanch (= *hemmen*)	-au-	-a-
2.	medieval (mediaeval) manœuvre	medieval (= *mittelalterlich*) maneuver	æ (ae), œ (oe) (in griech. Lehnwörtern)	-e-
3.	theatre centre fibre litre meagre sombre spectre	theater center fiber (= *Faser, Faden*) liter meager (= *mager, dürftig*) somber (= *düster, finster*) specter (= *Gespenst*)	-re	-er

	British English	American English	Explanations British American
4.	defence licence (= *Lizenz, Erlaubnis*) offence pretence (= *Vorwand*)	defense license offense pretense	-ce -se (nur in den nebenstehenden 4 Wörtern)
5.	travelled-travelling traveller modelled marvellous woollen	traveled-traveling traveler modeled marvelous woolen	-ll- -l- Im amerikanischen Englisch tritt nach unbetontem Vokal keine Verdopplung ein(vgl. 24, 5).
6.	to fulfil fulfilment wilful wilfulness to enrol	to fulfill fulfillment willful willfulness to enroll (= *Namen eintragen; registrieren*)	Im amerikan. Englisch wird bei Wortzusammensetzungen *-ll* oft nicht vereinfacht (vgl. 24, 6).
7.	gramme programme (program) axe plough	gram program ax plow	In manchen Substantiven ist im amerikanischen Englisch Verkürzung des Wortendes eingetreten.
8.	cheque (check) abridgement (abridgment) acknowledgement (acknowledgment) judgement (judgment)	check abridgment (= *Ab-, Verkürzung*) acknowledgment judgment	Die kürzere amerikan. Schreibweise wird hier auch im brit. Englisch geduldet.

THE PARTS OF SPEECH AND THEIR USE IN THE SENTENCE

Die Wortarten und ihr Gebrauch im Satz

The Noun

Das Substantiv

31 The Gender of Nouns

Das Geschlecht der Substantive

1. "What is Bob doing?" – "He is playing with his ball."
"Where is Pat?" – "She is on her way to school."
"Where is your book?" – "It is in its place."

Im Englischen wird das grammatische Geschlecht durch das natürliche Geschlecht bestimmt. Männliche Wesen werden als männlich, weibliche Wesen als weiblich, Sachen und Begriffe als sächlich behandelt.

2. The baby was lying in his (her, its) little bed.
The child is eating her (his, its) porridge.

baby und *child* werden nach dem natürlichen Geschlecht männlich oder weiblich gebraucht. Ist das Geschlecht unbekannt oder ist die Angabe des Geschlechts für die Aussage unwichtig, so werden *baby* und *child* sächlich gebraucht.

32 The Gender of Persons

Bezeichnung des Geschlechts von Personen

1. Both husband and wife are very fond of music.

Das natürliche Geschlecht von Personen wird gekennzeichnet durch verschiedene Wörter, z. B.

boy	– girl	man	– woman	nephew	– niece
son	– daughter	father	– mother	uncle	– aunt
brother	– sister	husband	– wife	king	– queen

2.	Both our host and hostess were very kind people.	Es kann ferner gekennzeichnet sein durch besondere Endungen, z. B. *-ess* und *-ine*

master – mistress
host – hostess
heir[ɛə] – heiress ['ɛəris]

emperor – empress
duke – duchess ['dʌtʃis]
prince – princess [prin'ses]

actor – actress
steward – stewardess
hero['hiərəu] – heroine ['herəuin]

3.	Pat went to the Tower with her cousin Jill. The captain of the visiting team was a very nice girl. I should like to have Betty as (for) a friend.	Im Englischen gelten einige Personenbezeichnungen für beide Geschlechter Eine besondere Kennzeichnung des Geschlechts ist nicht notwendig, wenn sich die Geschlechtszugehörigkeit aus dem Zusammenhang ergibt.
4.	John has a charming girl-friend. Nowadays cotton mills employ many female workers. A lady-clerk gave me the tickets. He has a male and a female assistant in his shop.	Erscheint aber bei diesen Wörtern eine Kennzeichnung des natürlichen Geschlechts notwendig, so kann das durch Zusatzwörter geschehen, z. B. durch: man – gentleman – boy – male woman – lady – girl – female
	Bob has a lady-teacher for French. In the House of Commons there are several women-politicians. The first to congratulate the winner was the lady-captain of the golf-club.	Diese Zusätze werden vor allem bei den Personenbezeichnungen auf *-er* und *-ian* benutzt. Sie werden ferner verwendet bei den folgenden Wörtern:

assistant	Verkäufer(in)	customer	Kunde, Kundin
captain	(Mannschafts-)Kapitän(in)	doctor	Arzt, Ärztin
companion	Begleiter(in), Gefährte, Gefährtin	friend	Freund, Freundin
cook	Koch, Köchin	officer	Offizier, Beamte(r)
clerk	(Büro-)Angestellte(r)	pupil	Schüler, Schülerin
cousin	Vetter, Kusine	servant	Diener, Dienerin

33 The Gender of Animals

Bezeichnung des Geschlechts bei Tieren

1. At the race, a horse fell and broke its neck.

Die Namen der Tiere werden gewöhnlich sächlich behandelt.

a) Don't go near the big bear; he is dangerous.
We have a lazy cat; she likes to lie by the fire.

a) Ist das natürliche Geschlecht eines Tieres bekannt, so kann die männliche oder weibliche Bezeichnung gebraucht werden. (Große Tiere, z. B. *bear*, *lion*, *elephant*, *etc.*) meist männlich; kleine Tiere, z. B. *cat*, *mouse*, *etc.* meist weiblich).

b) Once upon a time there was an old donkey who was too old to work, so he ran away from home.

b) In Tiergeschichten, Fabeln und Märchen werden die Tiere wie Personen behandelt.

2. Das natürliche Geschlecht von Tieren kann bezeichnet werden

a) Farmer Jones has a bull and sixteen cows.
The lion was coming towards us while the lioness remained with her cubs (= the young lions).

a) durch verschiedene Wörter oder Zusatzendungen. Verschiedene Bezeichnungen gibt es u. a. für:

bull, ox	– cow	dog	– bitch
cock	– hen	drake	– duck
gander	– goose	lion	– lioness
horse	– mare	tiger	– tigress

b) In the clearing we saw a number of female elephants with their young.
A she-wolf is more dangerous than a he-wolf when defending her cubs.
Have you a he-cat (tom-cat, male cat) or a she-cat (female cat)?

The empress sent the little prince a cock-robin.

b) Bei Tiernamen, die für beide Geschlechter nur eine Bezeichnung haben, fügt man
male oder *female*,
he oder *she*,

bei Vögeln *cock* oder *hen* hinzu.

The Personal Gender of Things

Das persönliche Geschlecht bei Sachen

34

1. England can be rightly proud of her great sailors.
Oxford taught him as much as she could.

Länder und Städte werden oft wie Personen gesehen und dann weiblich gebraucht. (Vgl. die Darstellung von Ländern und Städten als weibliche Personen, z. B. *Britannia*, *Hibernia*, *Germania*, *Berolina*.)

2. The ship met with a terrible storm and lost both her masts.
"That must be her (= the plane)!" shouted Bob. "She is losing height very rapidly."
I am very pleased with my old car; she still does thirty miles to the gallon.

Die Bezeichnung für Schiffe, Flugzeuge, Maschinen, Lokomotiven, Motore, Autos usw. werden meist weiblich gebraucht. (Grund: Enges persönliches Verhältnis des Menschen zur Maschine.)

3. There was plenty of sun yesterday, and it (= the sun) was very hot too.
The sun has set in all his glory.○
The moon has hidden her face behind the clouds.○

sun wird auch männlich gebraucht (lat. *sol* = der Sonnengott, frz. *le soleil*); *moon* wird auch weiblich gebraucht (lat. *luna*, die Mondgöttin, frz. *la lune*); so vor allem in der Dichtung.

The Plural of Nouns

Der Plural der Substantive

The Formation of Plurals

Die Bildung des Plurals

35

Der Plural der Substantive wird im allgemeinen durch Anfügung eines *-s* an den Singular gekennzeichnet. Das Endungs-s wird gesprochen:

a) dogs [dɔgz] zebras ['ziːbrəz]

b) cats [kæts] books [buks]

c) faces ['feisiz] hedges ['hedʒiz] noses ['nəuziz]

a) stimmhaft [z] nach stimmhaften Konsonanten und nach Vokalen;
b) stimmlos [s] nach stimmlosen Konsonanten;
c) silbisch [iz] nach Zischlauten.

Notice:

house [haus] houses ['hauziz]

Die Aussprache des Wortes ['hauziz] ist besonders zu merken.

1.

a box – boxes	a class – classes	
a bush – bushes ['buʃiz]		
a match – matches ['mætʃiz]		

Wenn im Singular dem Zischlaut nicht schon ein stummes *-e* folgt, wird die Endung *-es* angefügt. Diese Endung wird silbisch [iz] gesprochen.

2.

family – families	ally – allies
pony – ponies	lady – ladies
But:	
day – days	journey – journeys

Substantive auf *-y* mit vorausgehendem Konsonanten verwandeln *y* in *i* und hängen die Endung *-es* an (vgl. 24, 3a).

3.

potato – potatoes [pə'teitəuz]
tomato – tomatoes [tə'mɑːtəuz]
hero – heroes ['hiərəuz]

Viele Substantive auf *-o* mit vorausgehendem Konsonanten fügen im Plural die Endung *-es* an.

Notice:

canto – cantos	dynamo – dynamos
photo – photos	solo – solos
studio – studios	radio – radios

Substantive auf *-o*, die noch als Fremdwörter empfunden werden, bilden den Plural nur mit *s*

4.

calf – calves	sheaf – sheaves
half – halves	shelf – shelves
knife – knives	thief – thieves
leaf – leaves	wife – wives
life – lives	wolf – wolves
loaf – loaves	-self – -selves

Substantive, die mit *-f* oder *-fe* enden, bilden den Plural mit *-ves* [vz]-. Diese Wörter sind alle germanischer Herkunft. – Auf *-ves* endet auch der Plural von *-self*.

5.

chief – chiefs	safe – safes
proof – proofs	roof – roofs

Alle Wörter romanischer Herkunft auf *-f* und *-fe*, ebenso die auf *-oof* bilden den Plural mit *-s* und behalten den stimmlosen Auslaut [fs].

Peculiarities of Pronunciation — Besonderheiten der Aussprache **37**

a) bath [bɑ:θ] – baths [bɑ:ðz]
path [pɑ:θ] – paths [pɑ:ðz]
mouth [mauθ] – mouths [mauðz]
oath [əuθ] – oaths [əuðz]

b) cloth [klɔθ] – cloths [klɔθs]
moth [mɔθ] – moths [mɔθs]
myth [miθ] – myths [miθs]

a) Der stimmlose Konsonant [θ] am Wortende wird im Plural stimmhaft [ð] nach vorausgehendem langen Vokal oder Diphthong.

b) Er bleibt stimmlos [θ] nach vorausgehendem kurzen Vokal.

Notice:

truth [tru:θ], *pl.* truths [tru:ðz], [tru:θs]

Für *truths* gibt es zwei Möglichkeiten der Aussprache.

Special Plural Forms — Besondere Pluralformen **38**

1.

man	[mæn]	– men	[men]
woman	['wumən]	– women	['wimin]
foot	[fut]	– feet	[fi:t]
tooth	[tu:θ]	– teeth	[ti:θ]
goose	[gu:s]	– geese	[gi:s]
mouse	[maus]	– mice	[mais]
louse	[laus]	– lice	[lais]

Notice the pronunciation:

postman ['pəustmən] – postmen ['pəustmən]
Englishwoman ['iŋgliʃwumən] – Englishwomen ['iŋgliʃwimin]

Einige Substantive (alte germanische Wörter) bilden den Plural wie die entsprechenden deutschen Wörter durch Umlaut.

2. ox – oxen   child – children
[tʃaild] – [tʃildrən]

Die Substantive *ox* und *child* bilden den Plural durch Anhängen von *-en* bzw. *-ren*.

3. Einige Substantive haben zwei Pluralformen mit verschiedener Bedeutung:

He put several pennies into the slot-machine.

You can get an ice-cream for four pence.
Anne has one sister and two brothers.
The parson began to address the congregation: "Dear brethren . . ."
These cloths are good for cleaning the car.
She always wears beautiful clothes.
The children had lost their dice and so they could not play Ludo.
Making dies for coins is very skilled work.

penny	pennies	=	einzelne Pennymünzen (-stücke)
	pence	=	Wertangabe
brother	brothers	=	leibliche Brüder
	brethren	=	Mitbrüder
cloth	cloths	=	Tücher
	clothes	=	Kleider, Kleidung
die	dice [dais]	=	Würfel
	dies [daiz]	=	Münzstempel

4. Since the end of World War II statesmen have had to deal with many crises.
He found it difficult to memorize the chemical formulae.

Fremdwörter haben oft besondere Pluralformen, d. h. sie behalten oft die Pluralform der Herkunftssprache, z. B.

crisis [ˈkraisis]	– crises [ˈkraisiːz]	Krise
thesis [ˈθiːsis]	– theses [ˈθiːsiːz]	These, wiss. Arbeit
synthesis [ˈsinθisis]	– syntheses [ˈsinθisiːz]	Synthese
parenthesis [pəˈrenθisis]	– parentheses [pəˈrenθisiːz]	runde Klammer, Parenthese
analysis [əˈnæləsis]	– analyses [əˈnæləsiːz]	Analyse
terminus [ˈtəːminəs]	– termini [ˈtəːminai]	Fachwort; Endstation
phenomenon [fiˈnɔminən]	– phenomena [fiˈnɔminə]	Phänomen
datum [ˈdeitəm]	– data [ˈdeitə]	*sg.* gegebene Tatsache, Voraussetzung; *pl.* (techn.) Daten, Angaben, Unterlagen
erratum [iˈreitəm]	– errata [iˈreitə]	Druckfehler, -verzeichnis
medium [ˈmiːdiəm]	– media [ˈmiːdiə]	Medium
formula [ˈfɔːmjulə]	– formulae [ˈfɔːmjuliː]	Formel (math., chem., phys.)
index [ˈindeks]	– indices [ˈindisiːz], indexes	Index, Register, Inhalts-, Stichwortverzeichnis

39 The Plural of Compound Nouns

Der Plural zusammengesetzter Substantive

1. His uncle in the USA has two motor-cars.
Her brothers-in-law live in Australia.
He lost some dollar bills.

Bei zusammengesetzten Substantiven erhält das Grundwort das Pluralzeichen, z. B.

fellow-travellers	Reisegefährten	lookers-on, onlookers	Zuschauer
apple-trees	Apfelbäume	standers-by, bystanders	Umstehende
boy scouts	Pfadfinder	passers-by	Vorübergehende
tooth-brushes	Zahnbürsten	sons-in-law	Schwiegersöhne
reading-rooms	Leseräume	fathers-in-law	Schwiegerväter

2. You are a pair of good-for-nothings.
She is very fond of forget-me-nots.

Ist in einem *Compound Noun* kein Grundwort vorhanden, so wird das Pluralzeichen dem letzten Bestandteil der Zusammensetzung angefügt. Weitere Beispiele dieser Art sind:

grown-ups	Erwachsene	merry-go-rounds	Karussels
pull-overs	Pullover	six-year-olds	Sechsjährige

3. He quickly drank three mouthfuls of tea and rushed out.
Take: three table-spoonfuls of milk . . .

Das Pluralzeichen tritt ans Ende des *Compound Noun* bei den Mengenbezeichnungen:
cupful handful mouthful plateful spoonful

4. They prefer to go to women-doctors.
In former times there were more men-servants than nowadays.

Bei Zusammensetzungen mit *man* und *woman* zur Bezeichnung des Geschlechts werden beide Bestandteile des *Compound Noun* in den Plural gesetzt.

Peculiarities of Singular and Plural

Besonderheiten im Gebrauch von Singular und Plural 40

Die meisten Substantive können im Singular und im Plural gebraucht werden, und die meisten von diesen haben verschiedene Singular- und Pluralformen (vgl. 35, 1; 36; 38). Oft aber können wir an der Form des Substantivs nicht erkennen, ob es im Singular oder Plural gebraucht wird. Das ist dann nur aus dem Zusammenhang (bzw. aus anderen Wörtern des Satzes, z.B. Verben, Pronomen, Artikeln, Zahlwörtern usw.) zu erschließen.

He is going to sell that sheep to a Chinese. *(Singular)*
The Chinese are going to import ten thousand English sheep. *(Plural)*

40 Nouns with One Form for Singular and Plural

Substantive mit gleicher Form für Singular und Plural

1\. They killed a sheep for the feast.
I could see ten sheep in the meadow.
A few deer were grazing in the clearing.
130 craft made up the Invincible Armada.
Four aircraft took off in five minutes.
The company now owns two hovercraft.
The Apollo spacecraft was the first to land men on the moon.

Die Substantive *sheep, deer, craft* (und die damit zusammengesetzten Wörter, wie z.B. *hovercraft*) haben die gleiche Form im Singular und Plural.

2\. How many fish did you catch?
Trout are delicious fried in butter.
The trawlers returned with their catch of cod.
They proudly displayed the four salmon they had caught.
He spends his weekends shooting pheasant and duck.

The ducks in the park are quite tame.
There are usually six sardines in a tin.

Das Substantiv *fish,* die Namen fast aller Fischarten sowie die Namen vieler Vögel und Tiere werden im Plural meist in der Singularform (ohne -s-Endung) gebraucht, besonders wenn die Aussage im Zusammenhang mit der Tätigkeit des Fischens oder Jagens steht.

Notice:

How many different fishes are there in this river?

Der Plural *fishes* (= Fischarten) wird immer seltener gebraucht.

3\. a) three dozen eggs
five thousand miles
two hundred sheep
six hundred thousand inhabitants
ten million pounds
a few hundred people
several thousand refugees

b) dozens of fish
thousands of people
many hundreds of pounds

a) *dozen, hundred, thousand, million* etc. erhalten kein Plural-s, wenn sie mit einem Zahlwort oder mit *a few, several* verbunden sind.

b) Ohne Verbindung mit einem Zahlwort und nach *many* steht aber die Pluralform. (Hier sind sie Substantive!)

4. a) I weigh twelve stone, but John weighs only ten stone six.

b) I am six foot (feet) tall and John five foot (feet) ten.

a) Von den Maßangaben hat im modernen Englisch nur *stone* (= 14 lbs. = 6,35 kg) eine unveränderliche Form.

b) *foot* und *feet* werden gleich häufig als Plural gebraucht.

5. I'm trying to find a means of persuading him to help us.
There are several means of transport to choose from.
I watched a series of television programmes about Scotland.
They discovered a rare species of monkey.
The ironworks is just outside the town.

Die Substantive *means, series, species, gallows, headquarters, barracks, works* (= *factory*) enden immer auf -s, sowohl im Singular als auch im Plural.

Nouns used only in the Plural

Substantive, nur im Plural gebraucht

41

1. These stairs are very steep.
The surroundings of Edinburgh are very picturesque.
In the Middle Ages innumerable people died of the Black Death.
The average man's earnings have risen by six per cent.

Einige Substantive, die Einzeldinge zu einem Ganzen zusammenfassen, stehen nur in Pluralform (vgl. aber 42). Vor diesen Substantiven können keine Zahlwörter stehen. Substantive dieser Art sind:

arms	Waffen, Bewaffnung
clothes	Kleidung
stairs	Treppe
goods	Ware(n)
ashes	Asche
contents	Inhalt (auch Sg.: content)
oats	Hafer
premises	Grundstück
thanks	Dank
straits	Meerenge
victuals ['vitlz]△	Lebensmittel
doings	Tun
earnings	Verdienst
riches	Reichtum
lodgings	Wohnung
wages	Lohn
surroundings	Umgebung
the Middle Ages	das Mittelalter

Notice:

Wages in Australia are high, the minimum wage is now about £ 100 a week.	*wages* (Lohn) wird mit Adjektiven auch ohne das Endungs-s gebraucht.
She removed the ashes from the fireplace.	*ashes* (= Asche, die sich im Kamin oder im Ofen befindet; menschliche Überreste nach Verbrennung)
There was cigarette-ash all over the carpet.	*ash* (= wenn es sich um Zigaretten- oder Tabakasche handelt)

2. Bob's trousers are very dirty.
Bobs Hose ist sehr schmutzig.
These scales are accurate.
Diese Waage ist in Ordnung.
I must buy some sun-glasses.
Ich muß eine Sonnenbrille kaufen.

Namen von gewissen Werkzeugen und Kleidungsstücken, die aus zwei gleichen Teilen bestehen, werden auch nur im Plural gebraucht. Hierzu gehören:

pliers	Flachzange	spectacles, glasses	Brille	breeches△	enge Kniehose
pincers	Kneifzange	goggles	Schutzbrille	knickerbockers△	weite Kniehose
tongs	Feuerzange	binoculars	Fernglas	jeans	Niethose, Jeans
scissors	(kleine) Schere	trousers	lange Hose	pyjamas	Schlafanzug
shears	(kräftige) Schere (Blech-, Hecken-)	shorts	kurze Hose	tights	Strumpfhose
scales	Waage	pants	Unterhose *(BE)*, Hose *(AE)*	braces *(BE)*, suspenders *(AE)*	Hosenträger

Notice:

I need a pair of pliers for this job.
I bought a pair of scissors yesterday.
She has three pairs of scissors.
He has several pairs of trousers.

Wenn man von einer Schere (Hose, usw.) sprechen will, steht bei diesen Substantiven *a pair of*. Im Plural (nach Zahlwörtern usw.) steht oft *pairs of*.

3. a) He owns five hundred (head of) cattle.
Those cattle don't look healthy.

b) There are two people waiting to see you.
People say he is very mean.
Have you met the people next door?
She enjoys helping people.

a) *cattle* (= Vieh) steht immer im Plural, obgleich das Wort keine Pluralform auf -s hat.

b) *people* (= Leute, Personen, Menschen) steht ebenfalls immer im Plural.

Notice:

Churchill wrote a 'History of the English-speaking Peoples'. The pygmies were a very friendly people.	*people* (= Volk) wird gewöhnlich im Singular und Plural mit verschiedenen Formen gebraucht: *a people – peoples*

Nouns used only in the Singular (Uncountable Nouns)

Substantive, nur im Singular gebraucht

42

1\. Horses eat hay.
Bring me some water.
Smoke rose from the chimneys.
The Indians eat a lot of rice.

Stoffnamen werden im Englischen wie im Deutschen nur im Singular gebraucht. (Sie stehen nie mit unbestimmtem Artikel.)

2\. For further information apply to the manager.
Her knowledge of English and German is very good.
He gave me plenty of advice.
He is making good progress with his Latin.
All this furniture was my grandmother's.
The news is very bad, isn't it?
I've got good news for you.
This news is not going to please you.

Einige Substantive, deren deutsche Entsprechungen entweder im Singular oder im Plural gebraucht werden können, erscheinen im Englischen nur im Singular und ohne unbestimmten Artikel.

Zu diesen Substantiven gehören:

advice	Rat, Ratschläge	merchandise	Ware(n)
business	Geschäft(e)	equipment	Ausrüstung(sgegenstände)
expenditure	Ausgabe(n)	produce	Erzeugnis(se)
furniture	Möbel(stücke)	progress	Fortschritt(e)
homework	Hausaufgabe(n)	remorse	Reue, Gewissensbisse
information	Auskunft, Auskünfte	strength	Kraft, Kräfte
knowledge	Kenntnis(se)	news	Nachricht(en)

Notice:

I have a piece of advice for you.
I'd like just one simple piece of information.
Here is an interesting piece of news.
I have three pieces of homework to do.
This old cupboard is a beautiful piece of furniture.

Einzelbegriffe wie „ein Ratschlag", „eine Auskunft", „eine Nachricht", „ein schönes Möbelstück" usw. werden im Englischen mit Hilfe von *a piece of* oder *(Zahlwort) + pieces of* ausgedrückt.

3\. a) Mathematics is an exact science.
Phonetics was taught by a London professor.
Athletics provides plenty of variety.
b) Measles is not a serious illness, nor is mumps.
c) Draughts is one of my favourite games, and so is dominoes

Drei kleine Gruppen von Substantiven, die im Englischen zwar immer auf -s enden, werden niemals im Plural gebraucht. Hierzu gehören:

a) Namen von Wissenschaften mit der Endung *-ics*
b) Namen von Krankheiten
c) Namen von Spielen

4\. There is a hair in my soup.
He has no hairs on his chest.
She has fair hair and blue eyes.

He never eats fruit.
Pineapple is a delicious fruit.
He never saw the fruits of his work.

a hair = ein (einzelnes) Haar
hairs = die (einzelnen) Haare
hair = das Kopfhaar, die (Kopf)haare

fruit = Obst, Früchte
a fruit = Obstsorte
fruits = Ergebnis, Erfolg (= Früchte), Resultat

43

Collective Nouns

Sammelnamen

The family have left the house.
The army are putting on a gymnastics display this afternoon.
The police are busy making inquiries.
The team are all under 25.

Substantive in Singularform, die eine Gruppe von Personen bezeichnen, können mit einem Verb im Singular oder im Plural gebraucht werden.

Das Verb steht im Plural, wenn an die einzelnen Glieder der Gruppe gedacht wird.

The family goes back to the fifteenth century.
Napoleon's army was obliged to retreat.
The police is not a very old institution.
The team consists of eleven men.

Das Verb steht im Singular, wenn man an die Gruppe als eine Einheit denkt.

Hierzu gehören:

army	crowd	team
police	class	group
party	parliament	company
crew	government	majority
family		

Das *AE* bevorzugt bei Sammelnamen die Singularform des Verbs.

Names of Countries and Nationalities

Ländernamen und Nationalitätsbezeichnungen

44

1. The United States is a powerful country. The Netherlands exports mainly agricultural produce.

The United States und *The Netherlands* haben gewöhnlich das Verb im Singular.

2. The passengers included two Portuguese, three Dutchmen, two Swiss, four Czechs, five Greeks, three Danes and five Italians.

Völkernamen auf *-se* und *-ss* haben im Singular und Plural die gleiche Form.

Notice:

Adjective	Noun
English	an Englishman
French	a Frenchman
Spanish	a Spaniard
Swedish	a Swede
Polish	a Pole
Turkish	a Turk
Dutch	a Dutchman

Adjektive (Nationalitätsbezeichnungen), die auf [ʃ] oder [tʃ] enden, können nicht als Substantive im Singular gebraucht werden. Sie haben ein besonderes Wort für den Singular.

Partitive Phrases with of

Mengenbezeichnungen mit 'of'

45

1. A number of the children have fallen ill. A few of the books are missing. A good many of the audience fell asleep.

Die Ausdrücke
a number of, a few (of), a good many (of)
können nur mit Substantiven und Verben im Plural gebraucht werden.

2. A good deal of time was wasted. A certain amount of patience is necessary. A bit of help is always welcome.

a good deal of　a great deal of
a certain amount of　a bit of
können nur mit Substantiven und Verben im Singular gebraucht werden.

3. Plenty of information is available.
Plenty of letters remain unanswered.
A lot of / Lots of } progress was made.
A lot of / Lots of } children like mathematics.
Part of the library was destroyed by fire.
Part of the class were late for the train.

plenty of, a lot of, lots of, part of können mit einem Substantiv im Singular oder Plural gebraucht werden. Die Form des Verbs richtet sich dann nach dem Substantiv.

46 Plurals with More than One Meaning

Plural mit doppelter Bedeutung

Christmas customs in America do not differ much from those in Britain.
At Dover, they had to pass through the customs.
The colours in her frock are very pretty.
When he was eighteen he was called to the colours.△

Bei manchen Substantiven hat der Plural neben der ursprünglichen noch eine zweite, erweiterte Bedeutung, z. B.

Singular		Plural	1. Bedeutung	2. Bedeutung
colour	Farbe	colours	Farben	Fahne
force	Kraft	forces	Kräfte	Streitkräfte
manner	Art	manners	Arten	Sitten, Benehmen
scale	Schale; Schuppe (von Fischen)	scales	Schalen; (Fisch-)Schuppen	Waage
spectacle	Schauspiel	spectacles	Schauspiele	Brille
step	Schritt, Stufe	steps	Schritte, Stufen	(Steh-)Leiter
spirit	Geist, Spiritus	spirits	Geister; Spirituosen	Laune, Stimmung
wit	Witz, witziger Mensch	wits	Witze△; geistreiche Menschen	Verstand
custom	Sitte, Brauch	customs	Sitten, Bräuche	Zoll
trouble	Mühe	troubles	Mühen	Sorgen
work	Arbeit	works	(Kunst-)Werke	Werke (Fabriken), das Werk (Fabrik)
mountain	Berg	mountains	Berge	Gebirge

Plural in English – Singular in German

Plural im Englischen – Singular im Deutschen 47

The boys stood there with their hands in their pockets. (*mit der Hand in der Tasche*)
Englishmen do not take off their hats in a shop. (*nehmen nicht den Hut ab*)

Bezeichnungen für Körperteile, Kleidungsstücke stehen im Plural, wenn sie sich auf mehrere Personen beziehen. Im Deutschen steht hier meist Singular. (Über den Gebrauch des Possessivadjektivs vgl. 74, 1).

Millions of soldiers lost their lives in the Second World War.
After the deaths of the founders, the work was carried on by their nephew.
The minds of children are easily set at ease.

Dasselbe gilt für Substantive wie

life, death, mind, etc.

The English and French languages have many words in common.
You have only read us the first and third stories in the book.
The thirteenth, fourteenth, and fifteenth centuries are called the late Middle Ages.

Stehen vor einem Substantiv mehrere durch *and* verbundene Adjektive, die verschiedene Dinge bezeichnen, so steht das Substantiv im Plural.

The Noun in the Sentence

Das Substantiv im Satz 48

Da im Englischen die Deklinationsendungen der Substantive seit der altenglischen Zeit allmählich verschwunden sind, kennt das heutige Englisch nur noch zwei Kasusformen, einen *Common Case* und den *Possessive Case*.

Als Subjekt, als direktes Objekt und auch als indirektes Objekt erscheint das Substantiv im Englischen in der gleichen Form (*Common Case*). Die Beziehungen eines Substantivs zu den anderen Satzteilen werden entweder durch die Wortstellung (S-P-O, vgl. auch *Indirect Object*, 213) gekennzeichnet oder durch Präpositionen (*of* und *to*, vgl. 51 und 213) hergestellt.

The boy calls the dog.	*Subject* (*Common Case*)
Pat gets her mother's shopping-bag. Mr. Black opens the door of the cupboard.	*Possessive Case* *of* + *Common Case*
Mrs. Black gives her daughter some money.	*Indirect Object* (*Common Case*). Meist steht das *Indirect Object* ohne *to* vor dem direkten Objekt.
She gives some money to her daughter, not to her son.	*to* + *Common Case* Bei Hervorhebung kann das *Indirect Object* mit *to* hinter das *Direct Object* treten (vgl. 213).
Mrs. Black leaves the shop.	*Direct Object* (*Common Case*)

49 The Possessive Case — Der Besitz-Fall

1\.

The shopping-bag belongs to Pat's mother.
It is her mother's shopping-bag.
The book is not quite free from printer's errors.

Der *Possessive Case* bezeichnet den Besitzer einer Sache oder auch den Urheber einer Handlung.

2\.

a) Pat gets her mother's shopping-bag.
At the beginning of this century the suffragettes fought for women's rights.
Nowadays there are children's playgrounds in many parts of our city.

a) Der *Possessive Case* wird gebildet durch Anfügung von Apostroph + s (*'s*).

b) my sisters' handbags
his brothers' friends

b) Nach Plural-s wird nur der Apostroph angefügt.

c) St. James's ['dʒeimziz] Park
Ross's ['rɔsiz] Hotel
Dickens's ['dikinziz] novels
Keats's ['kiːtsiz] poems

c) Auf -s endigenden Eigennamen wird entweder *'s* oder nur ein Apostroph angefügt, jedoch ist *'s* gebräuchlicher.

d) my fellow-traveller's rucksack
his father-in-law's farm
the Queen of England's castles
Charles I's reign

d) Bei zusammengesetzten Substantiven und Substantiven mit einer Apposition tritt der Apostroph an den letzten Bestandteil.

The Use of the Possessive Case

Der Gebrauch des Besitz-Falles

50

Der *Possessive Case* wird vor allem gebraucht

1. a) Bob's bicycle is in the garage.
Everybody's friend is nobody's friend.
b) a bird's song, the lion's roaring
c) Britain's glory, London's history, theatres
a ship's captain, crew, doctor, etc.

a) bei Personenbezeichnungen;

b) bei Tiernamen;

c) bei Personifizierungen.

2. A friend of Bob's came to see me.

Three friends of my sister's came to see her.

I like this poem of Stevenson's very much.

Some nephews of Mr. Brown's called.

Der *Possessive Case* steht gewöhnlich vor dem Substantiv, das er bestimmt. Ist dieses Substantiv jedoch mit dem unbestimmten Artikel, einem Zahlwort, einem hinweisenden oder unbestimmten Pronomen verbunden, so tritt der *Possessive Case* hinter das zu bestimmende Substantiv und wird mit *of* verbunden. (In Gedanken ist hier hinter dem *Possessive Case* immer das Wort zu ergänzen, das näher bestimmt wird, z. B. *A friend of Bob's* [*friends*] *came to see me.*)

3. Whose is this coat? – I think it is father's.
Whose fault was it? – It was the carpenter's.

Nach *to be* wird der *Possessive Case* prädikativ gebraucht. Er weist dann auf vorher erwähnte „Besitztümer" hin. (Zu ergänzen sind hier *coat, fault.*)

4. Der *Possessive Case* steht ferner bei Angaben

a) We went for a three hours' walk.
He did a good day's work.
b) He followed them at ten yards' distance.
c) She bought a pound's worth of books.

a) der Zeit;

b) des Maßes;

c) des Wertes.

5. Der *Possessive Case* steht bei Ortsbezeichnungen. Es sind gemeint

a) The two friends visited St. Paul's.	a) ein öffentliches Gebäude (es wäre *cathedral* zu ergänzen);
b) You can buy pencils at the stationer's.	b) ein Geschäft oder Laden (man könnte *shop* hinzufügen);
c) We shall go to my aunt's tomorrow.	c) ein Haus oder eine Wohnung (es handelt sich um *my aunt's house or home*).

Keep in Mind:

the sun's rays	for God's sake	um Gottes willen
the earth's surface	for goodness' sake	
the needle's eye△	for Heaven's sake	um Himmels willen
his life's work	for pity's sake	
a hair's breadth escape	to one's heart's content	nach Herzenslust
at death's door	in my mind's eye	nach meiner Ansicht
the journey's end	to be at one's wits' ends	weder aus noch ein wissen

51 The of-Attribute — Die Beifügung mit of

1.

The pilot of the aeroplane flew northwards.
We went to see the sights of the city.
James Watt was the inventor of the steam-engine.

Zur Bezeichnung des Besitzers oder Urhebers einer Handlung bei Substantiven, die keine lebenden Wesen bezeichnen, steht die Beifügung mit *of*. (*Possessive Case* bei lebenden Wesen, vgl. 50).

2. Die Beifügung mit *of* steht an Stelle des *Possessive Case*

a) The voice of Parliament is the voice of the people.	a) bei Sammelnamen,
b) He spent all his fortune for the good of the poor.	b) bei substantivierten Adjektiven,
c) In the days of Queen Elizabeth I the English theatre flourished. This is the pencil of my friend Arthur, who forgot it last night.	c) bei Bezeichnungen für Einzelwesen, wenn sie durch Zusätze erweitert sind oder wenn es die Klarheit oder der Satzrhythmus notwendig macht.

3. The fear of the Lord (*die Furcht des Herrn = die Furcht vor dem Herrn*) is the beginning of wisdom.
The love of God (= *die Liebe zu Gott*).
(*But*: God's love = *die Liebe Gottes, die von Gott ausgehende Liebe*).

Die Beifügung mit *of* steht zur Bezeichnungen einer Person, die Gegenstand einer Handlung ist.

(Vgl. lat. *metus mortis*
frz. *la peur des revenants*)

Keep in Mind:

His mistrust of doctors cost him his life.	Mißtrauen gegen
She would not fly for fear of an accident.	Furcht vor
I have a real horror of heights.	Abscheu vor
His loss of blood was so great that he almost died.	Verlust an, von
Her love of money makes her save every penny.	Liebe zu
The thought of the coming school-reports spoilt my fun.	Gedanke an
The plants died from lack of water.	Mangel an

4. a) the Duke of Edinburgh
the Prince of Wales
the Archbishop of Canterbury

b) the Battle of Waterloo
the Treaty of Paris
the Congress of Vienna

c) the town of Stratford (frz. *la ville de Paris*)
the Isle of Wight
the month of June (frz. *le mois de juillet*)
the title of duke
the dignity of a peerage

Eine Beifügung mit *of* steht ferner:

a) nach Titeln;

b) nach Bezeichnungen für geschichtliche Ereignisse zur Angabe des Ortes, wo diese geschehen sind.

c) Eine Beifügung mit *of* steht ferner zum Anschluß eines Eigennamens an den zugehörigen Gattungsnamen,

z. B. city, town, country, kingdom, dignity, title, month, hour, name

Notice:

Mount Everest, the river Thames
in the year 1962 the number 14
The word 'exaggerate' is not easy to pronounce.

of steht nie nach
mount, river, year, number, word.

5.

a cup of tea	a glass of water
a slice of bread	a number of passengers
all of you	a large part of Scotland
each of us	some of my friends
most of the accidents	

Die Ergänzung mit *of* steht nach Substantiven und Pronomen, die eine Menge bezeichnen.
(Vgl. frz. *une tasse de café*;
un grand nombre de personnes)

Notice:

dozens of eggs	two dozen eggs
thousands of people	ten thousand people
millions of insects	five million insects

Die Zahlwörter *hundred*, *thousand*, *million* und der Mengenbegriff *dozen* stehen ohne *of*, wenn ihnen eine Grundzahl vorausgeht.

The Article

Der Artikel

The Definite Article — Der bestimmte Artikel

Form and Pronunciation — Form und Aussprache 52

Der bestimmte Artikel hat für alle drei Geschlechter (*genders*), für Singular und Plural und für alle Fälle (*cases*) nur eine Form: *the.*

Der bestimmte Artikel wird gesprochen:

a) the book [ðə buk] the university [ðə juːniˈvəːsiti]
the Europeans [ðə juərəˈpiənz]

b) the arm [ði ɑːm] the eye [ði ai] the hour [ði auə]
the honest man [ði ˈɔnist ˈmæn]

c) This is the [ðiː] haircut for a hot day.
Das ist der richtige Haarschnitt für einen heißen Tag.
He was the [ðiː] footballer of the year.
Er war der Fußballer des Jahres.

a) [ðə] vor Wörtern mit konsonantischem Anlaut (es kommt auf den Laut an, nicht auf die Schreibung!);

b) [ði] vor Wörtern mit vokalischem Anlaut (wobei zu beachten ist, daß in vielen Fällen *h* am Anfang stumm ist und damit das Wort vokalisch anlautet);

c) [ðiː] wenn der bestimmte Artikel besonders betont ist, d. h. wenn er einen besonders starken hinweisenden Charakter hat.

The Use of the Definite Article — Der Gebrauch des bestimmten Artikels 53

Der bestimmte Artikel ist im Englischen aus dem Demonstrativpronomen (*this*, *that*, *etc.*) entstanden und hat stark hinweisenden Charakter.

The boys and the girls of the fifth form are to be at school not later than 8.30 a.m.
The history of languages is the history of mankind.
Children love cats.
Iron is not a particularly precious metal.

Der bestimmte Artikel hebt Einzelvorstellungen aus einer Menge gleichartiger heraus.

Er steht also nicht, wenn die Heraushebung überflüssig ist oder eine Heraushebung nicht beabsichtigt ist.

The Noun without the Definite Article — Das Substantiv ohne den bestimmten Artikel

54 I. Ohne den bestimmten Artikel stehen Eigennamen jeder Art.

1.

Bob and Hans met at the airport. Father and Mother are already having their breakfast.	Bei Personennamen und bei Bezeichnungen für Mitglieder der Familie steht kein bestimmter Artikel.

2. Geographische Eigennamen stehen ohne den bestimmten Artikel:

a) The Puritans left Europe and found a new home in America.	a) Erdteile
b) He spent his holidays in Sicily.	b) Inseln
c) The Normans came over from France.	c) Länder
d) London is one of the biggest cities in the world.	d) Städte
e) Snowdon is in Wales. Ben Nevis is the highest mountain in Scotland.	e) Namen der englischen Berge

3. Zeitbestimmungen stehen ohne den bestimmten Artikel:

a) Which season do you like better, spring or autumn? (The winter of 1941 was extremely cold.) We shall be back in January. My friend has invited me for Wednesday.	a) Namen der Jahreszeiten, Monate und Wochentage (außer wenn sie näher bestimmt sind, z. B. durch einen Zusatz mit *of*)
b) He arrived at midnight. At dawn the birds began to sing. We shall travel at night. *But*: She fell ill in the night.	b) Namen der Tageszeiten in Verbindung mit *at* (*at night*, *midnight*, *midday*, *noon*, *dawn;* vgl. aber 56, 3d)
c) Christmas comes but once a year. Easter is in spring. Thanksgiving Day is on the fourth Thursday in November.	c) Namen der Fest- und Feiertage
d) Dinner is ready. We had lunch at one o'clock.	d) Namen der Mahlzeiten

4. Ohne den bestimmten Artikel stehen ferner Eigennamen in Verbindung mit einem Attribut.

a) Uncle Tom, Aunt Mary, Cousin Jill

a) Verwandtschaftsname + Eigenname

b) Queen Elizabeth, Lord Nelson, Sir Francis (Drake)

b) englischer Titel + Eigenname

c)

Oxford Street	Fleet Street
Broadway	Riverside Drive
5th Avenue	Mount Crescent
Times Square	Piccadilly Circus
Central Park	St. James's Park
Westminster Abbey	Marble Arch
Oakland Bay Bridge	Tower Bridge

c) Bezeichnungen für Straßen, Plätze, Parks, Gebäude, Brücken usw.

d)

Mount Everest	Cape Horn
Lake Michigan	Lake Windermere

But: the Cape of Good Hope
the Lake of Geneva

d) Namen der Berge, Vorgebirge, Seen, wenn *Mount*, *Cape*, *Lake* unmittelbar vorangehen.

Aber: Mit bestimmtem Artikel, wenn der Eigenname mit *of* angefügt ist.

e)

dear old Bill	Young Percy
Little Jim	St. Paul's
Poor Richard	St. George
Tiny Tim	Good Queen Bess

e) Ohne den bestimmten Artikel stehen Personennamen in Verbindung mit den folgenden Adjektiven:

young	old	dear	little
tiny	poor	good	saint (St.)

f)

Continental Europe	Central Africa
East Anglia	Ancient Greece
Medieval London	Christian England
Merry Old England	Pagan Rome
Southern England	Pre-historic Britain
modern Europe	

f) Ohne den bestimmten Artikel stehen Länder- und Städtenamen in Verbindung mit Adjektiven wie

continental	east	west
southern	northern	central
ancient	modern	medieval
Christian	pagan	pre-historic etc.

g)

English literature	modern art
natural history	private property
brown bread	public welfare
French wine	foreign policy
domestic affairs	human nature
African industry	American ingenuity

g) Ohne den bestimmten Artikel stehen Abstrakta und Stoffnamen in Verbindung mit Adjektiven wie

English	foreign	domestic
human	natural	private
public	African	American
brown	modern	etc.

h) Most houses in this village are thatched.
Most people think that English is easy.

h) *most* in der Bedeutung „die meisten, fast alle" steht in Verbindung mit einem Substantiv ohne den Artikel.

55 II. Der bestimmte Artikel wird ferner nicht gebraucht bei Allgemeinbegriffen

1.

Beispiele	Erläuterung
Time is money. Hunger is the best cook. It was a matter of life and death. Nature is at its best in spring. One of the worst evils is poverty.	bei Abstrakten: time, hatred, life, virtue, nature, art, history, love, fortune, poverty, avarice, hunger, simplicity, fate, Congress, Parliament etc.
School will be over at four o'clock. Her parents wanted her to go to university. On Sundays, I go to church at nine o'clock. He was in prison for many years. Bob was very tired and went to bed.	ferner bei: school, university, church, prison, bed, wenn sie im Sinne von Unterricht, Studium, Gottesdienst, Gefangenschaft, Nacht-, Bettruhe gebraucht werden.

2.

Beispiele	Erläuterung
Iron and coal have made England great. Blood is thicker than water. Gold is a precious metal.	bei Stoffnamen: blood, coal, cotton, gold, iron, stone, wool, water etc.

3.

Beispiele	Erläuterung
Man proposes, but God disposes. Woman is the helpmate of man. By her acts of humanity Florence Nightingale proved herself a true friend of mankind; her name will go down to posterity.	*man* und *woman* im allgemeinen Sinne werden ohne Artikel gebraucht; ebenso mankind, humanity, posterity.

4.

Beispiele	Erläuterung
Horses are bigger than oxen. Children and fools speak the truth. Boys will be boys. They fight like cats and dogs.	Ohne Artikel stehen auch Gattungsnamen im Plural, (vgl. 56, 1), z. B. dogs eggs horses oxen children

5.

Beispiele	Erläuterung
Help yourself, and Heaven will help you. He fought against Satan and Hell. With the help of Providence, he was saved.	Religiöse Begriffe, z. B. Paradise, Heaven, Hell, Providence, etc. stehen ebenfalls ohne Artikel.

Keep in Mind:			
to be at hand	bei der Hand sein	to shake hands	sich die Hand geben
to be of the opinion	der Meinung sein	to set sail	die Segel setzen
to turn tail at	davonlaufen vor	on account of	wegen
on condition (that)	unter der Bedingung	in case	falls
to pronounce judgment	das Urteil sprechen	in fact	in der Tat
to set to work	sich an die Arbeit begeben	in memory of	zur Erinnerung an
to be at work	an der Arbeit sein	by way of	vermittels, zwecks
to give up business	das Geschäft aufgeben	at first sight	auf den ersten Blick
to give permission to	die Erlaubnis geben	within reach of	im Bereich von

The Noun with the Definite Article — Das Substantiv mit dem bestimmten Artikel 56

1. a) The boys are playing in the field.
When the cat is away, the mice will play.

b) Many great poets lived at the time of Queen Elizabeth I.
When the courageous Edmund Hillary returned from the ascent of Mount Everest he was knighted by the Queen.
The coal that is found in the Midlands is very good.

Der bestimmte Artikel wird gebraucht
a) bei Gattungsnamen, wenn nur ein oder mehrere Vertreter (Einzelwesen) aus einer Gattung bezeichnet werden sollen (vgl. dazu 55, 4);
b) bei Eigennamen, Stoffnamen und Abstrakten, wenn der Begriff durch ein Substantiv mit *of*, durch ein Adjektiv oder durch einen notwendigen Relativsatz näher bestimmt ist (vgl. 55, 1; 54, 4g).

2. a) The Blacks spent the week-end at the seaside.
The Tudors governed England well; they were succeeded by the Stuarts.
b) The Bermudas are not very far from the American mainland.
The West Indies are sometimes called Antilles.
Which do you like better, the Highlands or the Lowlands?
c) London is on the Thames.
The Americans fought the Japanese in the Pacific.

Ferner steht der bestimmte Artikel
a) bei Familiennamen im Plural;

b) bei geographischen Namen im Plural, z. B. bei Inselgruppen und Bergketten (vgl. aber 54, 4d und f);

c) bei den Namen von Flüssen und Meeren.

3. a) The Alps are the highest mountains in Europe. The ascent of the Matterhorn in winter is highly dangerous.	Der bestimmte Artikel steht ferner: a) bei den Namen der nichtenglischen Berge (vgl. 54, 2e);
b) Russia lies in the east. The Armada turned to the north.	b) bei den Himmelsrichtungen.
But: We travelled through Great Britain from north to south. They crossed the USA from east to west.	Der bestimmte Artikel steht aber nicht bei: from north to south — from east to west
c) The Tower (of London) The (English) Channel The City (of London) The Atlantic (Ocean)	c) Der bestimmte Artikel steht ferner bei Gattungsnamen, mit oder ohne Attribut, die als Eigennamen gebraucht werden.
d) He works in the morning and in the afternoon. On the morning of May 7th, 1985, he got up early. In the evening he comes home at seven o'clock. During the afternoon she went shopping.	d) Bei Tageszeiten in Verbindung mit *in*, *on* und *during* steht der bestimmte Artikel (vgl. 54, 3b).

Notice:

I was at home last night. Next time you will come earlier.	Zeitbestimmungen mit *last* und *next* stehen ohne Artikel, wenn der Sprechende von der Gegenwart aus rechnet.
But: One evening my friend got wet through, and the next day he was ill. I shall fly to Stockholm next Monday and journey to Upsala the next day.	Aber: Der Artikel steht manchmal, wenn von einem Zeitpunkt der Vergangenheit oder der Zukunft aus gerechnet wird.

Keep in Mind:

it is the custom	es ist Sitte	at the expense of	auf Kosten von
it is the fashion	es ist Mode	with the help of	mit Hilfe von
with the exception of	mit Ausnahme von	in (the) presence of	in Gegenwart von

Special Position of the Definite Article

Besondere Stellung des bestimmten Artikels 57

All the boys ran on to the playing field. In half the time you can earn double the money. Both (the) children were extremely tired.

Der bestimmte Artikel steht hinter

all (= alle) (both) half
double twice treble.

Bei *both* kann der bestimmte Artikel auch wegfallen.

Notice:

All the girls of the fifth form assembled in the School Hall. All boys are fond of playing cricket.

all mit Artikel = „alle aus einer bestimmten Zahl"
all ohne Artikel = „überhaupt alle"

The Repetition of the Article

Die Wiederholung des Artikels 58

1. The brother and sister (= *die Geschwister*) went shopping together.
The pepper and salt are on the table.

Der Artikel wird nicht wiederholt, wenn zusammengehörende Dinge oder Personen aufgezählt werden.

2. The parents and the children were glad at their visitor's arrival.
Not only the men, but also the women and the children had to work hard.

Der Artikel wird wiederholt, wenn die einzelnen Personen oder Dinge besonders hervorgehoben und gegenübergestellt werden.

3. The Old and the New World have much in common.
The North and the South Pole are the ends of the Earth's axis.

Der Artikel wird wiederholt, wenn mehrere Adjektive unterschiedlicher (gegensätzlicher) Bedeutung vor einem Substantiv im Singular stehen.

4. In the 11th, 12th, and 13th centuries, the French and English languages were spoken side by side in England.

Im gleichen Falle wird der Artikel nicht wiederholt, wenn das Substantiv im Plural steht (vgl. 46, 3).

The Indefinite Article — Der unbestimmte Artikel

59 Form and Pronunciation — Form und Aussprache

Der unbestimmte Artikel heißt im Englischen für alle drei Geschlechter (*genders*) und für alle Kasus (*cases*) *a* oder *an*.

a) a boy, a man, a girl, a woman a car, a hero, a university [ə ˌjuːniˈvəːsiti]	a) Der unbestimmte Artikel lautet *a* [ə] vor Wörtern mit konsonantischem Anlaut;
b) an uncle, an aunt, an hour [ənˈauə], an honest [ˈɔnist] man	b) er lautet *an* [ən] vor Wörtern mit vokalischem Anlaut.
c) Did you say 'the ship' or 'a [ei] ship'? Should I write 'the animal' or 'an [æn] animal'?	c) Wenn er besonders betont ist, wird der unbestimmte Artikel [ei] oder [æn] ausgesprochen.

60 The Use of the Indefinite Article — Der Gebrauch des unbestimmten Artikels

1. Der unbestimmte Artikel bezeichnet Einzelwesen und Einzeldinge. Er ist aus dem Zahlwort *one* entstanden. In einigen Ausdrücken ist noch der Charakter eines Zahlwortes erhalten:

Father killed three flies at a blow.	mit einem Schlage, auf einen Schlag
She took in the situation at a glance.	mit einem Blick
In a word, I missed the bus.	mit einem Wort
Not a hair of the child's head was hurt.	nicht ein Haar
They came forward one at a time to cast their votes.	einer nach dem anderen
Rome was not built in a day.	in einem Tag
He drank the glass of beer at a (one) draught [draːft].	mit einem Zuge

Im Gegensatz zu dem bestimmten Artikel, der ein Einzelwesen aus einer Gesamtheit heraushebt (vgl. 53), ordnet der unbestimmte Artikel das Einzelne in eine Gesamtheit ein.

2. Der unbestimmte Artikel bezeichnet die Zugehörigkeit eines einzelnen zu einer größeren Gruppe. Er steht besonders nach den Verben des Seins und Werdens zur Angabe

a) My brother is a doctor, but I should like to become a teacher.	a) des Berufes oder Standes;
b) David is an Englishman, and Alice is a Red Indian.	b) der Nationalität oder Rasse;
c) William Bradford was a Puritan. My friend is a Protestant, I am a Catholic.	c) der Religion.
d) I will give it to him as a birthday present.	d) Der unbestimmte Artikel steht außerdem nach *as*.

Notice:

a) F. D. Roosevelt was elected President of the United States three times. Dr. Arnold was headmaster of Rugby. The pupils made my cousin captain of the football team.	a) Der unbestimmte Artikel steht nicht, wenn eine Stellung oder Würde nur einmal vorhanden ist.
b) He turned Protestant. The famous general turned politician.	b) Der unbestimmte Artikel steht ferner nicht nach *to turn* (= werden) und
c) He got the title of doctor. He rose to the rank of colonel.	c) nach Bezeichnungen für Titel, Beruf und Rang, wenn eine Beifügung mit *of* angeschlossen wird.

3. Der unbestimmte Artikel steht ferner zur Bezeichnung

a) I shall travel only 300 miles a day, though my car does a hundred miles an hour.	a) der Zeiteinheit;
b) The price of salt is only 10 ¢ a pound. This material sells at 82p a yard (metre).	b) der Gewichts- und Maßeinheit;
c) The wine at 90p a bottle is quite good. This farmer sells his apples at 80p a box.	c) der Mengeneinheit.

Notice:

Pat got plenty of chocolates. John and Bob had plenty of time. He spent (a) part of the year in the country.	Der unbestimmte Artikel steht nicht vor plenty of (= eine Menge) und meistens nicht vor part of (= ein Teil).

Keep in Mind:

to be in a hurry	Eile haben	to take a seat	Platz nehmen
to be in a rage	in Wut sein	to bring to an end	zu Ende bringen
to be at a loss	in Verlegenheit sein	to come to an end	zu Ende kommen
to have a cough	Husten haben	to draw to an end	zu Ende gehen
to have a headache	Kopfschmerzen haben	it is a pity	es ist schade
to have an earache	Ohrenschmerzen haben	what a pity!	wie schade!
to have a stomachache	Bauchschmerzen haben	in a loud voice	mit lauter Stimme
to have a sore throat	Halsschmerzen haben	on (an) average	im Durchschnitt
to have (a) toothache	Zahnschmerzen haben	a merry Christmas	fröhl. Weihnacht
to have an appetite	Appetit, Hunger haben	as a rule	in der Regel
to have a fancy for	Gefallen haben an, mögen	in a high degree	in hohem Maße

61 The Position of the Indefinite Article

Die Stellung des unbestimmten Artikels

1.

I cannot work on such a hot day (on so hot a day). They walked for many a mile.△ What a lovely coat she has got! Can you lend me half a dollar? Last night we had quite a nice party. My friend had rather a bad cold. *Also*: a half-dollar, a half-year, a rather bad cold	Der unbestimmte Artikel wird nachgestellt bei such, many (= manch, manche) what (= Was für ein . . . !); oft steht er hinter half, quite, rather.

2.

This was as good a match as I have ever seen. We do not like so difficult a Maths problem (such a difficult Maths problem). No doubt it was too heavy a blow for her.	Der unbestimmte Artikel steht ferner immer hinter einem Adjektiv, das mit as, so, too, how, however eng verbunden ist.

Pronouns and Pronominal Adjectives

Pronomen und Pronominaladjektive

Pronomen vertreten im Satz Substantive und Adjektive. Sie können alleinstehend (substantivisch, pronominal) oder als Beifügung (adjektivisch) gebraucht werden. Die Pronomen ermöglichen es, die ständige Wiederholung derselben Substantive und Adjektive zu vermeiden. Sie sind damit ein wesentliches Mittel der Satzverkürzung und der Abwechslung.

The Personal Pronouns — Die Personalpronomen 62

	1st Person		2nd Person	3rd Person	
	Sing.	Plur.	Sing. Plur.	Singular	Plural
Subject Case	I	we	you	he, she, it	they
Object Case	me	us	you	him, her, it	them
			General Pronoun: one		

If I were her, I should not go to see him.
'It was me!' Kathy shouted.
'That's him!' Bob exclaimed.
'It's them!'

In der Umgangssprache (vgl. Fußn. S. 76) steht häufig die Objektsform des Personalpronomens an Stelle der Subjektsform, besonders nach *it is* (*was*) oder *that is* (*was*).

Dear me!

Die Objektsform *me* steht auch in Ausrufen

Turn again, Whittington, thou worthy citizen, Lord Mayor of London.△
Be near me, Lord Jesus, I ask Thee to stay . . .△
O blow, ye winds, over the ocean . . .△
Good-bye (= God be with you(ye)).

Früher hatte das Englische für die Subjekts- und Objektsformen im Singular die Formen *thou* und *thee*, im Plural *ye* und *you*. *Thou*, *thee* und *ye* leben nur noch in der Sprache der Bibel, in Sprichwörtern, in der Poesie und in Dialekten weiter.

63 The General Pronoun one — Das allgemeine Pronomen one

1.

One cannot be in two places at once.

One never knows oneself sufficiently.

One should always do one's duty.

Das allgemeine Personalpronomen *one* bezeichnet (wie deutsch "man") keine bestimmte, sondern eine allgemeine Person.
Es bildet mit *-self* das Pronomen *oneself* (vgl. 71).
Es kann den *Possessive Case* bilden (vgl. 49).

2.

One should love one's neighbour as oneself.
One can't have one's cake and eat it.

Das allgemeine Pronomen *one* steht besonders in allgemeingültigen Sätzen und Sprichwörtern

3.

a) In America people celebrate Thanksgiving Day in every state.
Men are blind in their own cause.

a) Für *one* können eintreten:
people
man (vgl. 63,2)
men (vgl. 63,2)

b) We often do what we repent the next day.
You may take a horse to water, but you cannot make it drink.
He did not mind what they said about him.

b) *One* kann ferner ersetzt werden durch *we*, *you*, *they*, je nachdem der Sprechende sich in die Aussage einschließt oder nicht.

c) Tea-shops are found everywhere.
(One finds tea-shops everywhere).
The doctor was sent for.
They were sent away.

c) Statt des *one* gebraucht der Engländer gern das persönliche Passiv (im Deutschen meist „man").

d) There was dancing and singing.
Man tanzte und sang.
There is no trusting the weather in April.

d) Ferner steht an Stelle von *one* öfter *there is* (*was*) + Gerundium.

The Use of the Personal Pronouns, 3rd Person

Der Gebrauch der Personalpronomen der 3. Person

64

Please, go and help Father; he is working in the garden.

he bezieht sich auf eine vorher genannte männliche Person;

"Where is Mother?" – "There she comes."

she auf eine weibliche Person;

I can't find my knife; I must have lost it.
My brother has a dog; he is very fond of it.

it auf ein Ding oder Tier;

"Can you see the smugglers?" – "Yes, I can. They are climbing up the rocks."
"Look at these beautiful summer frocks. – Aren't they nice?"

they auf Personen, Tiere und Dinge.

The German 'es' and Its English Equivalents

Deutsches „es" und seine englischen Entsprechungen

65

Besonders zu beachten ist die Wiedergabe des deutschen Personalpronomens „es".
„es" kann im Englischen wiedergegeben werden
a) durch *he*, *she* oder *they;* b) durch *it;* c) durch *there;* d) durch *so*.

he, she, they
Equivalent to German "es"

he, she, they
für das deutsche „es"

"Who is that boy?" – "He is a friend of mine." *Es (Das) ist einer meiner Freunde.*
"Who is this lady?" – "She is my cousin." *Es (Das) ist meine Kusine.*
"Who are these gentlemen?" – "They are friends of my father's."
Es (Das) sind Freunde meines Vaters.

Wird eine Aussage über eine vorher schon genannte Person gemacht, so stehen im Englischen die Personalpronomen *he* oder *she* oder *they*.

Notice:

"Who is knocking at the door?" – "It is the postman."
"Who brought these flowers?" – "It was the gardener's boy."

Wenn die Frage das Geschlecht der Person, nach der gefragt wird, nicht erkennen läßt, steht das unpersönliche *it*.

Keep in Mind:

Go to it!	Feste! (Gib ihm!)
Hang it all!	Hol's der Henker!
Hop it!	Verdufte!
Run for it, Jack!	Lauf, was du kannst, Hans!
He will have it that he spoke the truth.	Er behauptet, daß er die Wahrheit gesagt habe.
The first colonists in Australia had to rough it.	Die ersten Kolonisten in Australien mußten sich mühsam durchschlagen.
You will catch it.	Du wirst deine Strafe (Prügel, Schelte) schon bekommen.
The ayes [aiz] have it.	Die Mehrzahl ist dafür.
She was queening it over the younger girls.	Sie spielte die große Dame gegenüber den jüngeren Mädchen.
The butler lorded it over the other servants.	Der erste Diener spielte den Herren gegenüber den anderen Dienern.
I take it that you know when to stop.	Ich nehme an, du weißt, wann du aufhören solltest.

66 It Equivalent to German "es"

it für deutsch „es"

1. In winter it freezes and it snows.
It is eight o'clock and school is beginning.
It appears that we can't go.

Witterungs- und Zeitangaben sowie einige unpersönliche Verben haben das Neutrum *it* als Subjekt (wie im Deutschen).

Notice:

a) He succeeded in scoring a goal.
Es gelang ihm, ein Tor zu erzielen.
I am sorry that I couldn't come yesterday.
Es tut mir leid, daß ich gestern nicht kommen konnte.

a) Oft steht im Englischen die persönliche Ausdrucksweise, wenn im Deutschen ein unpersönliches Verb gebraucht wird, z. B.

I am glad	es freut mich
I am warm, cold	es ist mir warm, kalt
I am well	es geht mir gut (gesundheitlich)
I am unwell	es geht mir nicht gut
I am sorry	es tut mir leid
I succeed in	es gelingt mir
I fail	es gelingt mir nicht
I like	es gefällt mir
I want	es fehlt mir an
I am fine	es geht mir gut, großartig

Vgl. lat. pluit, frz. il pleut; lat. ningit, frz. il neige.
frz. j'ai froid, j'ai chaud; je m'étonne: je réussis à; je suis fâché, je me réjouis, etc.

b) He seems to be tired.
Er ist anscheinend müde.

We happened to meet him.
Wir trafen ihn zufällig.

b) Die Vorliebe des Englischen für die persönliche Ausdrucksweise zeigt sich auch bei nebenstehenden Beispielen. Im Englischen stehen verbale Ausdrücke, im Deutschen Adverbien (vgl. 132).

it bezieht sich (rückweisend) auf einen Gedanken, der ausgedrückt ist

a) We are trying to get tickets for tonight's show, though it might be difficult.
Fred was forced to give up smoking. I expected it, for smoking never agreed with him.

a) in einer vorausgehenden Wortgruppe, die meist einen Infinitiv mit *to* enthält;

b) My mother is quite well again, and I am very glad of it (= *darüber*).
"I hope you realise that there is a difficult task ahead of you." – "Yes, you have made it quite clear."

b) in einem vorausgehenden Satz

"There is a knock at the door. What (who) is it?" – "It is the postman."
"I heard a ring. Is it the children already?" – "No, it is Father."

Auf die Frage *what (who) is it?* antwortet immer *it is (was)* und zwar auch dann, wenn das folgende Substantiv oder Personalpronomen im Plural steht.

It is she who wanted to buy a new car.
It is they who won the match.
It is we who are making that noise.
It was his cousins whom we met at the races.

She is the one who wanted to buy a new car.

it is (was) . . . who (whom, that) . . . wird zur Hervorhebung von Satzgliedern gebraucht (vgl. 232). Nach unpersönlichem *it* als Subjekt steht immer nur *is* bzw. *was*, auch wenn das Bezugswort im Plural erscheint. Diese Form der Hervorhebung ist im modernen Englisch kaum noch gebräuchlich. Man sagt: *She is the one who...*

At first Robert found it difficult to speak English.
She thought it her duty to support her mother.
I consider it a shame that he should have escaped.

it weist bei den Verben des Dafürhaltens
to consider, to find, to think, to believe
(= halten für)
als vorläufiges Objekt auf das eigentliche Objekt hin, das in der Form eines Infinitivs oder eines Nebensatzes folgt.

67 it as a Preparatory Subject — it als Vorsubjekt

it weist in unpersönlichen Ausdrücken als grammatisches Subjekt (Vorsubjekt) auf das folgende logische (Sinn-)Subjekt hin,

a) It is difficult to learn German. It is easier to pull down than to build up.	a) wenn dieses ein Infinitiv mit *to* ist;
b) It is no good fishing in troubled waters. It is worth listening to him as he is always interesting.	b) wenn es ein Gerundium ist;
c) It is obvious that something must be done. It was a pity that he had to leave so early.	c) wenn es ein Nebensatz ist (vgl. *there*, 68).

68 there Equivalent to German "es" — there für deutsch „es"

1.	There was a knock at the door. There has been much talk about Germany lately. There is a mouse in our house. There are a hundred pence in a pound.	*there* steht als grammatisches Subjekt (Vorsubjekt = *Preparatory Subject*), wenn das Verb des Satzes *to be* und das nachfolgende Subjekt ein Substantiv ist (vgl. *it*, 67). *there is – there are* werden im Sinne des deutschen „es gibt, es ist", gebraucht; sie werden aber häufig im Deutschen gar nicht übersetzt.
2.	Luckily there were no people in the house when the fire broke out. Unfortunately there was no sunshine when we went for our picnic. At six o'clock there was a loud ringing of bells. At Easter there were many daffodils in our garden.	*there is* (*are*, *was*, *were*, *etc.*) muß auch dann stehen, wenn der Satz durch ein Adverb oder durch eine adverbiale Bestimmung der Zeit eingeleitet wird.
3.	In Westminster (there) are the Houses of Parliament and Westminster Abbey.	Nach Ortsbestimmungen kann *there* fehlen.

4. There came no sound from the studio. There arrived thousands of people after the match had started. There seemed to be plenty of food left after the party.	*there* als *Preparatory Subject* ist auch bei anderen (intransitiven) Verben möglich; es dient dann zur Hervorhebung des Subjekts (vgl. Inversion, 228 f).

5. There were more difficulties than we had expected. On the shelf there is a good book for you.	Nach *there* als *Preparatory Subject* richtet sich das Prädikat nach dem folgenden Sinnsubjekt.

so Equivalent to German "es" — so für deutsch „es“

69

1. Die Beziehung auf den Gedankeninhalt eines vorausgehenden Satzes wird durch *so* ausgedrückt. Im Deutschen steht oft „es“ (oder „auch“). *so* ersetzt einen längeren Nebensatz, der den vorausgehenden Gedanken bestätigt.

a) "Will it be fine tomorrow?" – "I hope so." (*Ich hoffe es*). "Shall we get tickets for the next performance?" – "I think so."	a) *so* steht oft nach den Verben des Sagens und Denkens, wie to believe to hope to say to suppose to think to be afraid to expect
b) "Open the gate, please." – "I'll try to do so." In England you take off your hat to a lady, but it is not customary to do so to a gentleman.	b) *so* steht ferner nach druckstarkem *to do*.

Notice:

I am asking you to send him an invitation and want you to do it at once. "I am going to break the door open." – "Don't do that."	Nach druckstarkem *to do* werden an Stelle von *so* auch das bestimmtere *it* und das nachdrücklichere *that* gebraucht.

2\. a) "Can you ride a bicycle?" – "Yes, I can."
"May Jack come in?" – "Yes, he may."
b) "Did you give him the letter?" – "No, I forgot."
"His uncle has returned from London." – "Yes, I know."
c) "Are you tired?" – "Yes, I am."
"Did he come in time?" – "Yes, he did."

so steht nicht
a) nach unvollständigen Hilfsverben;
b) nach Verben des Sagens und Denkens, wenn sie druckstark gebraucht werden, z. B. nach to forget, to know, to tell, to try;
c) ferner nicht in kurzen Antworten nach to be, to have, to do.
(Auch im Deutschen steht hier meist kein „es").

70 so, nor Equivalent to German „auch (so)", „auch nicht"

so, nor für deutsch „auch (so)", „auch nicht"

1\. Old men are wise, young men may become so.
He is wrong, and he thinks me to be so.
"He seems to be a happy boy." – "Yes, he looks so."
His wages are low, but they might not remain so.

so weist zurück auf ein vorausgegangenes Prädikatsnomen nach den Verben

to be,	to become,	to grow,
to look,	to remain,	to seem.

2\. a) "You should have warned him in time." – "So I did."
I told her to go by train, and so she did.

so tritt oft an die Spitze eines Satzes, der eine vorausgehende Aussage nachdrücklich bestätigt. Das Prädikat der vorausgehenden Aussage wird in dem mit *so* eingeleiteten Satz durch *to do* ersetzt.

b) His brother wrote a letter last week, and so did he.
They prefer the mountains, and so do we.
You are tired, and so am I.
He came back from the station, and so did I.
"I like the seaside." – "So do I."
We have a good television set, and so have they.
I must change from train to bus, and so must John.

so tritt ferner oft an die Spitze eines Satzes, der einen Vergleich zu vorher genannten Personen oder Dingen zieht. Das Prädikat des voraufgehenden Satzes wird durch *to be*, *to do*, *to have* oder durch *Defective Auxiliary Verbs* ersetzt.
Nach *so* tritt in diesen Fällen Inversion ein (vgl. 228), so daß die verglichenen Dinge am Anfang und am Ende, also an den stark betonten Stellen des Satzes stehen.

John does not like to play baseball, nor do I. They never wanted to go there, nor did we.

In negativen Sätzen steht für die unter 2b) genannten Fälle *nor* am Anfang des vergleichenden Satzes.

Notice:

Tuesday was a miserable day, and Wednesday wasn't very nice either. You could not tell him what it was? I am afraid I could not have told him either.

not – either heißt ebenfalls „auch nicht". Es tritt hier keine Inversion ein! *either* tritt ans Ende des Satzes.

The Reflexive Pronouns — Die Reflexivpronomen 71

The Forms — Die Formen

Person	Singular	Plural
1st	myself	ourselves
2nd	yourself	yourselves
3rd	himself, herself, itself	themselves
	General Pronoun: oneself	

The Use of the Reflexive Pronouns — Der Gebrauch der Reflexivpronomen 72

Die mit *-self* zusammengesetzten Pronomen werden druckstark und druckschwach gebraucht. Der Akzent (die Betonung) liegt immer auf dem *-self* ([mai'self], [auə'selvz]).

a) My father himself answered the phone.
I want to read the book itself.
We ourselves could not have done better.

a) Das druckstarke Reflexivpronomen dient zur Hervorhebung von Personen und Dingen. Es steht gewöhnlich unmittelbar hinter dem Wort, das es hervorheben soll.

b) My brother has made the model yacht himself.
My sister has seen it herself.

b) Wird das Subjekt hervorgehoben, so wird das Pronomen oft auch durch die Verbgruppe von dem Subjekt getrennt.

c) My friend and (I) myself saw him off.
I spoke to himself, not to his wife.

c) Wird die hervorzuhebende Person durch ein Personalpronomen bezeichnet, so fällt dieses meist weg.

2. The children enjoyed themselves.
The boy made himself useful on the farm.

Druckschwach wird das Reflexivpronomen bei den reflexiven Verben gebraucht (vgl. 215).

3. a) He has a lot of money with him.
She shut the door behind her with a bang.
We saw nothing but the sky above us and the sands around us.

b) I don't want to be left up here all by myself.
The children were beside themselves with joy when their parents returned.

a) Nach Präpositionen steht rückweisend das Personalpronomen (nicht das Reflexivpronomen).

b) Wenn aber das Pronomen druckstark ist, so steht auch hier das Reflexivpronomen.

73 The Possessive Adjectives and the Possessive Pronouns

Die Possessivadjektive und die Possessivpronomen

The Forms

Die Formen

	Possessive Adjectives		Possessive Pronouns	
Person	*Singular*	*Plural*	*Singular*	*Plural*
1st	my	our	mine	ours
2nd	your		yours	
3rd	his, her, its	their	his, hers (its own)	theirs
General Pronoun:	one's		one's own	

Bill's friend is also my friend.
We visited his (your friend's) garden.
This bicycle belongs to a friend of mine.
I met a friend of hers (one of her friends).

Die Possessivadjektive und die Possessivpronomen bezeichnen den Besitzer (vgl. *Possessive Case*, 49, 50).

The Use of the Possessive Adjective

Der Gebrauch des Possessivadjektivs

1. You should not put your hands in your pockets.
Du solltest die Hände nicht in die Taschen stecken.
He fell off his bicycle and broke his arm.
Er fiel vom Fahrrad und brach sich den Arm.

Das Possessivadjektiv steht im Englischen zur Bezeichnung von Körperteilen und von Kleidungsstücken, die dem Subjekt eigen sind; ebenso ist es bei *house*, *bicycle*, *car*, *work*, etc. (Im Deutschen steht hier meist der bestimmte Artikel).

Notice:

Im Englischen steht aber nicht das Possessivadjektiv, sondern der bestimmte Artikel,

a) The policeman took the child by the hand.
The villain gave me an awful crack on the head.
b) King Harold was shot through the eye.
Suddenly I was hit in the face by a snowball.
c) He had a cold in the head.
She went red in the face.

a) wenn der bezeichnete Körperteil dem Objekt eigen ist;

b) wenn die Person, deren Körperteil genannt wird, Subjekt eines passivischen Satzes ist;

c) in einigen Redewendungen.

2. That would be the death of her.
She hates the very look of him.
I couldn't for the life of me remember his phone number.

Statt des Possessivadjektivs steht in Redewendungen die Beifügung von *of* + der Objektsform des Personalpronomens.

3. All his friends have left for the holidays.
With all my heart. (*Von ganzem Herzen*)
He lost both his sons in the war.
She has eaten only half her porridge.
He will get double his present salary in his new job.

Das Possessivadjektiv wird wie der bestimmte Artikel (vgl. 57) nachgestellt bei

all both half double

(vgl. frz. Il consacrait toute sa fortune aux pauvres. – De tout mon cœur).

4. He drives his own car.
Why don't you use your own fountain-pen instead of always writing with mine?

Zur Verstärkung des Possessivadjektivs dient das Wort *own*.

5. *own* tritt mit *of* angeschlossen hinter das Substantiv, wenn vor diesem steht:

a) Jack has a room of his own.	a) der unbestimmte Artikel;
b) They have no house of their own. I have not many books of my own.	b) ein unbestimmtes Pronominaladjektiv (z. B. *no*, *much*, *many*, *any*, *some*, *etc.*);
c) Father's friend has two motor-cars of his own.	c) ein Zahlwort.

75 The Use of the Possessive Pronoun — Der Gebrauch des Possessivpronomens

1. "This is not my spoon, is it yours?" – "Yes, thank you, it is mine."
Your house is bigger than theirs.

Das Possessivpronomen steht immer ohne Artikel.

2. The cuckoo lays its eggs in other birds' nests, not in its own.

Das Possessivpronomen *its* erscheint immer zusammen mit *own*.

3. Das *Possessive Pronoun* wird dem Substantiv mit *of* angeschlossen, wenn vor diesem stehen:

a) I can lend you a coat of mine. He is a school-fellow of ours.	a) der unbestimmte Artikel;
b) Bob visited London with some friends of his.	b) ein unbestimmtes Pronominaladjektiv (*some*, *any*, *both*, *every*, *etc.*);
c) This school of ours is very old.	c) ein Demonstrativadjektiv (*this*, *that*, *these*, *those*).

4. Your father and my father went to town together.
Your father and mine went to town together.

Wenn man vermeiden will, daß sich zwei Possessivadjektive (mit *and* verbunden) vor demselben Substantiv befinden, so hängt man ein Possessivpronomen mit *and* an. Das Beispiel macht das deutlich; die zweite Art ist viel gebräuchlicher als die erste.

5. Yours truly (Truly yours) *Hochachtungsvoll*
Yours faithfully *Hochachtungsvoll*
Yours sincerely *Ihr (Mit freundl. Grüßen)*
Yours *Ihr (Dein)*
Yours very sincerely *(Herzlich) Ihr (Dein)*

Das Possessivpronomen *yours* steht in Höflichkeitsformeln am Ende von Briefen.

The Reciprocal Pronouns

Die Pronomen der Gegenseitigkeit 76

We have not seen each other for ten years.
You must help one another.

The teams played each other for the first time.

Wenn man ausdrücken will, daß etwas wechselseitig geschieht (deutsch: sich, einander), so setzt man *one another* oder *each other* hinter das Verb.
Bei zwei Personen bzw. Gruppen wird *each other* bevorzugt.

Notice:

We do not work for one another.
The two friends shook hands with each other.

Präpositionen stehen vor, nicht zwischen *one another* und *each other*.

The Demonstrative Adjectives and Demonstrative Pronouns

Das Demonstrativadjektiv und Demonstrativpronomen 77

The Forms

Singular	*Plural*
this that	these those

Die Formen

Die Formen der Demonstrativadjektive und der -pronomen sind gleich. *this* und *these* weisen auf das räumlich und zeitlich Nähere hin, *that* und *those* auf das Entferntere.

The Use of the Demonstrative Adjective

Der Gebrauch des Demonstrativadjektivs 78

This boy (here) is Jack's cousin, and that boy (over there) is his younger brother.
I like these tulips (here) better than those lilies (there).

Die Demonstrativadjektive *this, these* und *that, those* stehen in Verbindung mit Bezeichnungen für Personen und Sachen.

The Use of the Demonstrative Pronoun

Der Gebrauch des Demonstrativpronomens 79

1. I want to tell you this.
"What do you think of that?"

In der Bedeutung „dies" und „das" können *this* und *that* substantivisch gebraucht werden.

2.	a) This is Mr. Wilkins, Robert's uncle. That is Westminster Hall. b) These are my friends Bill and Jim. Those over there are Pat's friends.	a) *this* und *that* weisen hin auf ein prädikativ gebrauchtes Substantiv im Singular b) *these* und *those* weisen hin auf ein prädikativ gebrauchtes Substantiv im Plural. (Beachte den Plural im Englischen! Im Deutschen heißt es „Dies sind . . .“ und „Das da sind . . .“)
3.	"Which of the boys got the prize?" – "This one." This girl is more intelligent than that one. This room is longer than that (one). This story is more thrilling than that (one).	Wenn ein vorher genanntes Substantiv im Singular aus dem Zusammenhang zu ergänzen ist, so steht mit Bezug auf die Person immer, mit Bezug auf eine Sache in der Regel *this one, that one* (vgl. 117).
4.	These businessmen have been more successful than those. Are those your friends? Which flowers do you like better, these here or those over there?	*these* und *those* werden dagegen alleinstehend (d. h. ohne *one*) auf Personen und Sachen im Plural bezogen.

Keep in Mind:

this morning	heute morgen	that's it	richtig
this evening	heute abend	that'll do	das genügt
this week	in dieser Woche	that won't do	so geht's nicht
this month	in diesem Monat	that's all right	schon recht
this year	in diesem Jahr, heuer	that's why	deshalb
That's how he did it.	So hat er es gemacht.		
Those were happy times.	Das war eine glückliche Zeit.		

80 The Use of such — Der Gebrauch von such

1.	Such is life. Such is my reward. Such kindness is not often met with.	*such* hat demonstrative Bedeutung: „von dieser Art“, „solcher“. Es wird substantivisch und adjektivisch gebraucht.

2. We had such (= much) fun.
They take such pleasure in watching television.

such kann auch im Sinne von *much* gebraucht werden.

3. Mother bought all sorts of food, such as bread, butter, meat, milk, sugar, etc.

such as steht vor Aufzählungen und heißt „wie zum Beispiel".

4. He is such a nice fellow (= a very nice fellow).
It was such a difficult problem that I could not solve it myself.
They had such a pleasant time.

such a (= ein solcher, solch ein, so ein) bezeichnet einen hohen Grad; es hebt hervor und unterstreicht.

The Determinative Adjectives and Determinative Pronouns

Das Determinativadjektiv und Determinativpronomen

81

The Use of the Determinative Adjective

Der Gebrauch des Determinativadjektivs

1. That boy who broke the window will have to pay for it.
Do not trust those men who have never proved true.
The boy who broke the window ...
Do not trust the men who have never ...

Mit Bezug auf Personen lautet das Determinativadjektiv (*determinative* = näher bestimmend)
that ... who im Singular,
those ... who im Plural.
Statt *that, those* wird in der Umgangssprache *the* gebraucht.

2. That (the) part of London which is called the City is full of banks and offices.
Those (the) books which you lent me were very interesting.

Mit Bezug auf Sachen lautet das Determinativadjektiv
that ... which im Singular,
those ... which im Plural.
Statt *that, those* wird in der Umgangssprache *the* gebraucht.

82 The Use of the Determinative Pronoun

Der Gebrauch des Determinativpronomens

	a) *with an Attribute following*	b) *with a Relative Clause following*
Persons	that of those of	he who they who she who those who
Things	that of those of	that which those which what

1. a) Your rooms are larger than those of his house.
I like this book better than that of my cousin Robert.
I like this book better than my cousin Robert's.
John's bicycle is older than that of his brother.
John's bicycle is older than his brother's.

a) Dem Determinativpronomen *that*, *those* folgt eine Beifügung mit *of*. Bei Personen kann statt der präpositionalen Ergänzung mit *of* auch der *Possessive Case* stehen.

b) He who laughs last laughs loudest.△
Heaven helps those who help themselves.△
They who talk least do most.△

b) Dem Determinativpronomen folgt ein Relativsatz.

c) Who lies in the mud will rise dirty.△
Who keeps company with the wolf will learn to howl.△
Who is born to be hanged cannot be drowned.△

c) Statt *he who* steht manchmal, besonders in älteren Sprichwörtern, nur *who*.

(Vgl. frz. Qui se lève tard, dîne tard.)

d) Jack was the one whom I wanted to see.
He placed his chair near the one on which I was sitting.
I have read many Red Indian stories, and these are the ones (which) I like best.

d) Für *he who*, *they* (*those*) *who* kann eintreten *the one who*; für *that which*, *those which* können *the one which*, *the ones which* eintreten.

2. Never trust to another what you can do yourself.
What soberness conceals, drunkenness reveals.

Für *that which* tritt in der literarischen Sprache oft, in der Umgangssprache (vgl. Fußn. S. 76) stets *what* ein.

The Interrogative Adjectives and Interrogative Pronouns

Die Interrogativadjektive und Interrogativpronomen

83

The Use of the Interrogative Adjective

Der Gebrauch des Interrogativadjektivs

what boy? what book?	which boy (of this group)? which book (of those on the table)?

1. What man could be so cruel?
What subject do you like best?
In what year were you born?
At what time did your friend leave?

what fragt ganz allgemein nach Personen und Sachen.

2. Which school (of those in your town) does your friend attend?
Which poem (of those in your English reader) have you learnt by heart?
Which Mr. Walter do you want to see, the elder or the younger?

which fragt nach einer Person oder Sache aus einer bestimmten Anzahl.

3. What fun we had! What nonsense!
What lovely flowers!
What valuable presents you have got!

Im Ausruf steht *what* (deutsch: was für).

Notice:

What a rage he is in! (He is in a rage.)
What a beautiful view! (It is a beautiful view.)
What a pity! (It is a pity.)
What a fool you are! (You are a fool.)

Das auf *what* folgende Substantiv hat den unbestimmten Artikel, wenn es diesen auch als Prädikatsnomen hätte (deutsch: was für ein).

84 The Use of the Interrogative Pronoun

Der Gebrauch des Interrogativpronomens

	Relating to		
	Persons	*Things*	*Persons and Things*
Subject Case	who?	what?	which?
Possessive Case	whose?	—	—
Object Case	whom (who)?	what?	which?
with Prepositions	of whom?	of what?	of which?
	to whom?	to what?	to which?
	with whom?	with what?	with which?

1. Who brought this letter?
Who is now the Leader of the Opposition, and who are the ministers in his Shadow Cabinet?
Whom did they meet in the town?
To whom did you deliver the message?
Who did you deliver the message to?
Who did you visit yesterday afternoon?
Who did you ask for the key?
Who did you meet at the races?

who, whose, whom fragen nach Personen.

An Stelle der Objektform *whom*, vor der auch Präpositionen stehen können, gebraucht die heutige Umgangssprache* meist *who;* dieses darf jedoch keine Präposition vor sich haben (vgl. 85).

2. Whose books are those lying on the table?
On whose farm did the family spend their holiday?

Whose is this coat?
Whose are those books?

whose ist *Possessive Case* und fragt nach dem Besitzer.

whose kann auch prädikativ verwandt werden.

* Unter Umgangssprache ist hier und auch sonst in dieser Grammatik das gemeint, was *H. E. Palmer* als *Spoken English* bezeichnet:

The terms "spoken" and "written" are open to more than one interpretation. The term Spoken English should be taken to mean "that variety of English which is generally used by educated people (more especially in the South of England) in the course of ordinary conversation or when writing letters to intimate friends." The term Written English may be taken to cover those varieties of English that we generally find in printed books, reviews, newspapers, formal correspondence, and that we expect to hear in the language of public speakers and orators, or possibly in formal conversation (more especially between strangers).
The terms "spoken" and "colloquial" are frequently used synonymously; when this is the case, the term "colloquial" is assumed to have the connotation used above, and not that connotation which would make it synonymous with "vulgar" or "slangy". Similarly the term "written" is frequently used as a synonym of "classical" or "literary". (Harold E. Palmer: A Grammar of Spoken English, p. XXXIII)

3. What is in this parcel?
What did you say?
What are you talking about?

what fragt nach Sachen.

4. Which do you prefer, tea or coffee?
Which of these books do you want to read?
Which of the London cathedrals are the best known?

which fragt nach Personen und Sachen aus einer bestimmten Anzahl; es trifft eine Auswahl.

Compare:

"Who was here?" – "A boy." – *lat. Quis erat hic? Puer.*
frz. Qui était là? Un garçon.
"What boy?" – "A son of my uncle's." – *lat. Qui puer? Filius avunculi.*
frz. Quel garçon? Un fils de mon oncle.
"Which boy?" – "The youngest." – *lat. Quis puerorum? Minimus natu.*
frz. Lequel? Le cadet.

85

The Position of the Preposition in an Interrogative Sentence

Die Stellung der Präposition im Fragesatz

Who(m) are you speaking of?
(Of whom are you speaking?)
Who(m) are you working for?
What school do you go to?
Which girl did you give the letter to?
Who is your father playing golf with?
Who are you laughing at?

Die mit einem Interrogativadjektiv oder -pronomen verbundenen Präpositionen treten in der Umgangssprache fast immer hinter die Verbgruppe.

In diesem Falle tritt im Umgangsenglisch für *whom* meist *who* ein.

Keep in Mind:

What do you call this?	Wie nennt man das?
What is "Wasserhahn" in English?	Was heißt „Wasserhahn" auf Englisch?
What is the English word for"Wasserhahn"?	(water-tap)
What is his name?	Wie heißt er?
What is the time?	Wieviel Uhr ist es?
What age is he?	Wie alt ist er?
What kind (sort) of fellow is he?	Was ist es eigentlich für ein Mensch?
What colour is it?	Welche Farbe hat es?

86 The Relative Pronouns — Die Relativpronomen

The Forms — Die Formen

	Persons	Relating to: Things	Persons or Things
Subject Case	who	which	that
Possessive Case	whose	—	—
Object Case	whom, (who)	which	that
with Prepositions	of whom to whom	of which to which	(that . . . of) (that . . . to)

87 The Use of the Relative Pronouns — Der Gebrauch der Relativpronomen

who

1. The children, who were eager to see everything on the farm, did not want to rest after lunch.
He was on his way to his uncle, whose home in Wisconsin is about 700 miles from New York.
The man whom we saw was about forty years of age.
She did not know who she was speaking to.
She did not know to whom she was speaking.

who und seine Ableitungen *whom, whose, to whom, of whom* beziehen sich auf Personen. (Vgl. *who* an Stelle von *whom*, 84, 1).

= Umgangssprache
= Schriftsprache

Notice:

a) We have a cat who likes to sit by the fire.
England, for whom they died, has not forgotten her brave sons.
Oxford, to whom he owed so much, honoured him for his learning.

a) Gelegentlich wird *who* auf Tiere und auf personifizierte Länder- und Städtenamen bezogen (vgl. 33 bzw. 34, 1).

b) He joined the party which was in power.
They cheered the team which had won the match.
The team who played this afternoon were all very tired after the match.
He joined the group of tourists who were sitting in the garden.

b) Mit Bezug auf Substantive in Singularform, die eine Anzahl von Personen bezeichnen, steht *which*, wenn die Gruppe als solche gemeint ist;
es steht aber *who*, wenn an die Einzelwesen gedacht wird (vgl. 43).

which

2. a) Give me the letter which arrived yesterday.
He looks like a doctor, which he is.
When I met her first, I thought she was French, which in fact she is.

b) We asked her who she was, to which she answered that she was a foreigner spending her holidays in England.

a) *which* bezieht sich auf Sachen oder Begriffe
which bezieht sich als Prädikatsnomen auch auf Personen, wenn eine Klassifizierung vorgenommen wird.

b) *which* bezieht sich auf den Inhalt eines vorausgehenden Satzes oder Satzteiles (vgl. *what*, 89).

that

3. This is the girl that (who) is good at reading.
Tell us the story that you told us yesterday.
The pony that was grazing in the meadow came when the farmer whistled.

that bezieht sich auf Personen, Sachen und Tiere (vgl. 91).
(*that* bei Personen wird im modernen Englisch immer seltener gebraucht; man bevorzugt *who.)*

Notice:

Here is the letter (that) I have been waiting for.

Vor dem Relativpronomen *that* darf nie eine Präposition stehen!

whose – of which

4. a) Is there anybody whose name has not been called?
Bob, whose eleventh birthday it is today, is having a party.
b) The church, the steeple of which you can see from here, stands in the middle of the village.

a) *whose* bezeichnet den Besitzer oder Urheber einer Handlung bei Personen. Es steht immer vor dem regierenden Wort.
b) *of which* bezeichnet den Besitzer bei Sachen oder Tieren.

Notice:

We saw the tree whose leaves were already yellow.
The church whose steeple you can see . . .

Um das schwerfällige nachgestellte *of which* zu vermeiden, gebrauchen die Engländer heute auch in den unter 4b) genannten Fällen *whose*.

of whom – of which

5. a) The boy, for the love of whom his parents had worked hard, has become a great painter.
The girl looked at her plant, the blossoms of which were so delicate and pretty.
b) His grandfather, of whom he was so fond, died unexpectedly.
The picture of which we are speaking hangs in the Tate Gallery.
c) The boys, most of whom are fond of skating, went to the pond.
The boats, many of which were decorated, came back from the regatta.

of whom und *of which* stehen
a) als präpositionale Beifügung zu Substantiven;
b) als präpositionale Ergänzung zu Verben;
c) zur Bezeichnung eines Teilverhältnisses nach Ausdrücken der Menge.

88 Generalizing Relative Pronouns

Verallgemeinernde Relativpronomen

Whoever told you that did not know anything about British history.
Take whichever of these books you like.
Whatever you do, think of the consequence.

Die verallgemeinernden Relativpronomen sind:
whoever „wer auch immer"
whichever „welche(r) auch immer"
whatever „was auch immer"
(Letzteres neben einfachem *what* = „alles was").

89 what instead of a Relative Pronoun

what an Stelle eines Relativpronomens

a) She supports her parents, and, what is more, (she) looks after them very well.
The 'Tin Lizzy' made Henry Ford famous and wealthy and, what was more important, it put America on wheels.

what kann als Relativpronomen stehen
a) mit Bezug auf einen folgenden Satz (deutsch: was);

b) What Florence Nightingale did, she did whole-heartedly.
What annoyed him very much was that he could not get the car to start.

c) You will get what you need in good time.
With this money you can buy what you want.

b) im Sinne von *that which*, *all that* (deutsch: das, was);

c) im Sinne von (*all*) *the* . . . (*that*).

Relative Pronouns in Clauses

Relativpronomen im Satz

Non-defining Relative Clauses

Ausmalende (nicht notwendige) Relativsätze 90

1. He met his friend, who had been ill.
Mr. Adam's guests, who were eager to see everything on the farm, did not want to rest after lunch.
My old car, which I sold last week, did 70 m.p.h.
(My old car did 70 m.p.h. – I sold it last week.)

Einen Relativsatz, den man auslassen könnte, ohne den Sinn des Hauptsatzes zu entstellen, nennt man ausmalenden (erweiternden) Relativsatz; er wird mit *who* oder *which* eingeleitet. (Ausmalende Relativsätze könnten auch in der Form eines Hauptsatzes folgen.)

2. Sir Walter Raleigh, who was standing nearby, quickly took off his costly cloak.
A big crane swung its arm over the hold of the vessel, which had already been opened, and lifted the luggage on to the quay.

Vor ausmalenden Relativsätzen tritt in der Sprache eine deutliche Pause ein. Sie werden deshalb durch ein Komma vom Hauptsatz getrennt (vgl. 28).

Defining Relative Clauses

Notwendige Relativsätze 91

1. I'll buy a car. – Any car?
I'll buy a car that does 100 m.p.h.
Boys like books. – What books? –
Boys like books that were written by Cooper.
In the self-service restaurant the boys picked out some sandwiches from the various kinds of food that were laid out on long counters.

Einen Relativsatz, der dem Begriff des Beziehungswortes im Hauptsatz ein wesentliches Merkmal hinzufügt, (den man also nicht weglassen kann, ohne den Sinn des Hauptsatzes zu verfälschen), nennt man einen notwendigen Relativsatz.
Notwendige Relativsätze schließen sich in der Sprache eng und ohne Pause an ihr Beziehungswort an; sie werden deshalb nicht durch ein Komma abgetrennt (vgl. 28).

2. I have found the pocket-knife I had lost.
This is the man I gave the letter to.
There is the hand-bag that (which) was stolen yesterday.
Is that the letter which has just arrived?
That's the beggar who came to your house yesterday.

Ein notwendiger Relativsatz wird meist unmittelbar, d. h. ohne Relativpronomen, an sein Beziehungswort angefügt, wenn das Relativpronomen als Objekt hinzuzudenken wäre.
Ist *that* Subjekt des Relativsatzes, so kann es nicht weggelassen werden, weil die Klarheit ein Subjekt im Relativsatz erfordert; vgl. Bsp. unter 91, 1).

Notwendige Relativsätze können aber mit einem Relativpronomen (meist *that*, aber auch *which* und *who*) angeschlossen werden. *who* wird besonders dann gebraucht, wenn das zu bestimmende Wort im Relativsatz die Rolle des Subjekts spielt.

3. All that glitters is not gold..
Everything that I did was wrong.
Is there anything that I can do for you?
In the little village shop they found nothing that pleased them.
Edward I was one of the best kings that ever ruled England.
She was the first girl that jumped into the water.
He was the only boy that could do it.
He stammered something that (which) I did not understand.

Notwendige Relativsätze werden immer mit *that* angeschlossen nach

all („alles"), everything, anything, nothing, much, little, few;

sie werden vorzugsweise mit *that* angeschlossen nach Superlativen und ähnlichen Ausdrücken wie z. B.
the first, the last, the only.

Nach *something* kann auch *which* stehen.

92 The Position of Prepositions in Relative Clauses

Die Stellung der Präpositionen in Relativsätzen

1. Do you know the man (whom) I sold the dictionary to?
This is the book (that) you were asking for.
This is the car (that) I heard of.

Ist das Relativpronomen von einer Präposition abhängig, so tritt diese gewöhnlich hinter die Verbgruppe. Dies muß geschehen, wenn der Relativsatz mit *that* oder ohne Relativpronomen angeschlossen ist.

2. I'd like to know what you are waiting for.
He failed in more enterprises than he succeeded in.
He got more money than he had hoped for.

Die Präposition muß auch am Ende von Nebensätzen stehen, die mit *what* angefügt sind; das gleiche gilt für Komparativsätze, die mit *as* oder *than* angeschlossen sind.

Relative Conjunctions — Relativkonjunktionen 93

Neben den Relativpronomen gibt es relative Anknüpfungen anderer Art.

1. We had such peaches as you never saw before.
Give me the same chocolate as (that) I had yesterday.

as dient zur Anknüpfung von Relativsätzen nach *such* und *the same*.
Nach *the same* kann auch *that* stehen.

2. The village reminds me of the time when I was a boy.
Do you remember the place where you were born?

when und *where* dienen zur Anknüpfung von Relativsätzen nach Zeit- und Ortsangaben

3. Can you really understand the reason why he never comes to see us?
There is no reason why you shouldn't come with us.

why dient zur Anknüpfung von Relativsätzen an *reason*

The Indefinite Pronominal Adjectives and Pronouns — Die indefiniten Pronominaladjektive und Pronomen 94

1. You can see British ships in every part of the world.
Many a brave sailor lost his life.
There is no rose without a thorn.

Nur als Pronominaladjektive werden gebraucht:

every	jeder (allgemein)
many a	mancher
no	kein

2. There are ships of the Royal Navy and of the Merchant Navy; each navy has a tradition of its own.
Each of them came at a different time.

Als Pronominaladjektive und als Pronomen werden die folgenden Wörter gebraucht:

all	all, ganz, alle, alles
some	etwas, irgendein, einige
any	etwas, irgendein, irgendwelche
both	beide
each	jeder (einzelne aus einer bestimmten Anzahl)
little	wenig
a little	ein wenig
few	wenige
a few	ein paar

much	viel
many	viele
most	die meisten
several	mehrere, verschiedene
either	einer von beiden, jeder von beiden, beide
neither	keiner von beiden
other	ander, -e
another	ein anderer, noch einer

3. a) Here are two bats; this one is mine, the other (one) is yours.
They have shown you one; now we shall show you another.
I went to the playground; the others went to see the new film.
He must have taken my gloves, for I cannot find the ones I wore last night.

a) Als reine Substantive werden nur die indefiniten Pronomen *one*, *other*, *another* behandelt. Sie können den *Possessive Case* bilden.
one und *other* erhalten in der Mehrzahl ein Plural-s.

b) All I know is that he was never heard of again.
He that knows little soon repeats it.○
Don't ask much to have little.○

b) *all* (= alles), *little* (= weniges), *much* (= vieles) können nur als neutrale Substantive gebraucht werden.

c) All the inhabitants went to the village green; all danced round the maypole.

A little girl asks: "May I have some sweets, please?" Her mother replies: "Sorry, dear, I have not got any. If I had any, I should give you some."

c) *all* zur Bezeichnung der Mehrzahl „alle" und die übrigen unter 2. genannten Pronominaladjektive können nur dann pronominal gebraucht werden, wenn sie sich an ein vorhergehendes oder folgendes Substantiv anlehnen können oder dieses leicht aus dem Zusammenhang zu ergänzen ist.

4. In allen übrigen Fällen treten für die indefiniten Pronomen Zusammensetzungen ein:

a) no one (none△)	keiner	a) Zusammensetzungen mit *one*;
everyone	jedermann	
each one	jeder	
someone	jemand	
anyone	irgendeiner	
b) everybody	jedermann	b) Zusammensetzungen mit *body*;
nobody	niemand	
somebody	jemand	
anybody	irgend jemand	
c) everything	alles	c) Zusammensetzungen mit *thing*.
something	etwas	
anything	irgend etwas	
nothing	nichts	

some – any

"I want some note-paper, can you give me any?"
"Sorry, I have not got any."

"I should like some sweets." – "Have you got any?"

some weist auf eine tatsächlich vorhandene oder als vorhanden gedachte Person, Sache oder Menge hin (= *a particular one, particular ones*).
any ist unbestimmt (= *it does not matter which one*) und besagt, daß das Vorhandensein bezweifelt oder verneint wird.

some and any as Pronominal Adjectives 95

some und any als Pronominaladjektive

Die indefiniten Pronominaladjektive *some* und *any* werden im Singular und im Plural gebraucht.

some steht meist in bejahenden Sätzen.

1. a) I'd like some [səm] tea, please.
I need some [səm] money to pay for the tickets.
b) Some [sʌm] boy rang up while you were out.
I had to wait for some [sʌm] time before I got served.

a) Im Singular bezeichnet *some* eine unbestimmte Menge von etwas oder
b) eine besondere, aber nicht im einzelnen bestimmte Person oder Sache.

c) Some people were swimming in the water.
I had bought some fine books as birthday presents.

c) Im Plural bezeichnet *some* eine unbestimmte Anzahl.

2\. a) He has not got any money.
We have not any time to lose.

b) Is there any cake left?
"Have you got any ink in your bottle, Tom?" – "No, I haven't got any."

c) If I had any money with me, I would lend you some.
If you have any milk, give me some, please.

any steht überwiegend

a) in verneinten Sätzen;

b) in fragenden Sätzen;

c) in Bedingungssätzen.

3\. Any work is better than none at all.
You may come at any time.
Any doctor will tell you that you are ill.

In bejahenden Sätzen hat druckstarkes *any* die Bedeutung von „jeder beliebige" (= *it does not matter which one*).

4\. a) "May I have some more meat?" – "Yes, of course."
"May I help you to some more soup?" – "Yes, thank you, that would be nice."
"Have you got some money for me?" – "I think I have, yes."

b) He never comes home without bringing some presents for us.
They rarely go to the woods without shooting some game.

a) In Fragesätzen und bei höflichen Aufforderungen steht *some* (statt *any*), wenn eine bejahende Antwort erwartet wird.

b) In verneinten Sätzen steht *some* (statt *any*), wenn der Sprechende auf etwas wirklich Vorhandenes oder Geschehenes hinweist.

96 some and any as Pronouns

some und any als Pronomen

1. Werden *some* und *any* wie ein Substantiv gebraucht, so bezeichnet

a) Some approve of the decision, some disapprove of it.

a) *some* [sʌm] eine unbestimmte Anzahl;

b) Some of the water had turned smelly.
Some of my friends helped me to pitch the tent. The others just watched.
Any of the needles will do.
You may use any of the towels lying around.

b) *some* [sʌm] und *any* mit einer präpositionalen Beifügung mit *of* vor einem Stoffnamen oder Gattungsnamen im Plural bezeichnen eine unbestimmte Menge oder Anzahl.
some = a particular one, particular ones
any = it does not matter which one(s)

"Somebody came to see you." – "Was anybody here?"
"Is there anything else, Miss Black?" – "There was something else."
"Someone must do the job." – "Do you think anyone would do it voluntarily?"

Wie *some* und *any* werden gebraucht:

somebody – anybody

something – anything

someone – anyone

Summary*

Übersicht

97

	some	any
Affirmative	If you want pears, pick some from the tree. Pick some pears from the tree.	Did you say you have too many lamps? I'm ready to buy any you don't want. I'm ready to buy any lamps you don't want.
Negative	I don't need some of these stamps: (I've already got ones like them in my collection, so could I just take those I want and leave the rest?) (Why are you so angry!) Because the store hasn't delivered some biscuits that I asked them to send for this afternoon's tea-party.	Here's one newspaper, but I'm afraid I don't have any more. I'm afraid I don't have any more newspapers.
Interrogative	(Here's a flower-seller.) Would you like some? Would you like some flowers?	I've forgotten to bring my money. Do you have any? Do you have any money?

* Beispiele aus ELT, Vol. XVI, 2, von L. A. Hill.

98 every – each

1. *every*, vor Substantiven im Singular, ist nur indefinites Pronominaladjektiv.

Every child is fond of playing. Every man has his faults. Everybody's business is nobody's business. Everyone in the town was busy. Everything must have a beginning. The sailors were saved, every one of them.	Es bedeutet „jeder ganz allgemein", „jeder ohne Ausnahme". Wie *every* werden auch die Zusammensetzungen behandelt. everybody everyone everything every one = zwei Wörter, wenn zur Hervorhebung verwendet.

2.

There are twenty-eight girls in our class; each of them is fond of sweets. Tom and David went to a self-service restaurant; each boy took a tray, and each picked out some sandwiches. Mother bought us some apples; she gave us two each. He spoke to each of us.	*each*, Pronominaladjektiv und Pronomen, bezeichnet „jeden aus einer bestimmten Anzahl"; jeder einzelne wird für sich betrachtet. (Es ähnelt somit dem Interrogativpronomen *which*.) Als Pronomen wird *each* alleinstehend und mit einer präpositionalen Beifügung mit *of* gebraucht.

3.

I spoke to each one of the girls separately.	*each one* betont die Vereinzelung besonders stark.

Keep in Mind:

every other day	jeden zweiten Tag
every four days (fourth day)	jeden vierten Tag
every now and then every now and again	dann und wann, von Zeit zu Zeit
every five miles	alle fünf Meilen

all; whole

99

a) We stayed in the museum all day long.
He has spent all his money.
All men must die.

b) All I know is that he was never heard of again.
All agree that he is an excellent pupil.
All of us know him.

a) *all*, adjektivisch gebraucht, steht sowohl im Singular (= ganz, all) als auch im Plural (= alle). *all* bezeichnet ein ungeteiltes Ganzes.

b) Substantivisch gebraucht, bezeichnet *all* im Singular „alles", im Plural „alle" (vgl. 94, 2).

We stayed in the museum the whole day.
He travelled round the whole country, round the whole of Great Britain.

Das Adjektiv *whole*, substantivisch *the whole of*, bezeichnet ein unteilbares Ganzes und betont die Ganzheit stärker als *all*.

Keep in Mind:

all day (long)	den ganzen Tag (hindurch)	all of a sudden	ganz plötzlich
all night (long)	die ganze Nacht (hindurch)	nothing at all	überhaupt nichts
all the better	um so besser	if at all	wenn überhaupt
all over	ganz durch; überall	all but (one)	alle außer (einem)
all right	ganz richtig, in Ordnung	first of all	zu allererst
all round	ringsumher, überall	last of all	zu allerletzt
all along	die ganze Zeit, schon immer	at all events	auf alle Fälle
all in all	im ganzen gesehen	all at once	auf einmal
after all	schließlich, trotz allem	all the same	gleichviel, trotzdem
not at all	durchaus nicht, keineswegs	all the world	die ganze Welt
once and for all	ein für allemal		

beyond all question	ganz außer Frage
with all my heart	von ganzem Herzen
from all over Germany	aus allen Teilen Deutschlands
news from all over	Nachrichten von überall her
That's Bob all over.	Das ist typisch Bob.
He is not all there.	Er ist nicht ganz gescheit.
It's all the same to me.	Es (Das) ist mir ganz gleich.
All's well that ends well.	Ende gut, alles gut.

100 both – two either – neither

1\. Both men were captured.
Both these fountain-pens are mine.
They both refused to come.

both (deutsch: alle beide), adjektivisch und substantivisch gebraucht, betont die Zusammengehörigkeit zweier Personen oder Dinge.

2\. The two friends went for a walk.
The two companies were great rivals.

Wird auf die Betonung der Zusammengehörigkeit kein Wert gelegt oder sogar die Gegensätzlichkeit betont, so steht *the two + noun*.

3\. London is situated on either bank of the Thames (on both banks).
"Which of the two teams will win?" – "That is difficult to say, either may win."
The passengers may leave the boat on either side of the river.

either, adjektivisch und substantivisch gebraucht, bedeutet:
der eine (oder der andere) von zweien, jeder von zweien (= beide)
(vgl. *either . . . or*, 222).

4\. I could use neither of my hands.
"Which of us is right, Bill or me?"– "Neither of you is right."

neither (deutsch: keiner von beiden, weder der eine noch der andere) ist die Verneinung von *either* (vgl. *neither . . . nor*, 222).

101 one; other, another

1\. This is the one way to do it.
The two towns are really one.

a) There are two hats; this one is mine, the other (one) is yours.
. . . , the second (one) is yours.
b) One captain Smith has disappeared.△
At one time I felt rather sick.

one, substantivisch und adjektivisch gebraucht, bezeichnet und betont die Einheit oder Einzelheit.

a) Unter zweien wird der erste mit *one*, der zweite mit *the other* oder *the second* bezeichnet.

b) *one* hat manchmal die Bedeutung von *a certain* „ein gewisser". (vgl. *one* als Personalpronomen, 63; *one* als Stützwort, 116).

2. a) Many Puritans sought a home on the other side of the Ocean.

b) I do not want this book; please, give me the other (one).

I enjoyed that piece of cake; may I have another (one)?

I went to the playground, the others went to see the new film.

other wird
a) adjektivisch und

b) substantivisch gebraucht.

In Vertretung eines vorhergegangenen Substantivs steht meist *the other one, another one* für den Singular,
the others, the other ones für den Plural.

3. a) This pen is bad, give me another, please.
If this hat does not suit you, try another.

b) Give me another glass of beer, please.
Robert will stay another three weeks in London.

a) *another*, ohne ein Substantiv gebraucht, bedeutet „ein anderer, ein neuer".
b) *another*, mit einem Substantiv verbunden, bedeutet „noch ein, ein zweites, ein weiteres, weitere". (vgl. *each other, one another*, 76).

Keep in Mind:

The other day we had special coaching by our sports master.	neulich
The other night I was woken up by a thunderstorm.	neulich nacht
We used to have a game of tennis every other day.	ein über den anderen Tag
Though he does not like shaving, he will have to do it some time or other.	doch einmal, dereinst
Geese like to walk one after the other.	einer hinter dem anderen
Somehow or other she managed to persuade her mother to let her go to the dance.	irgendwie

no; none; no one; nobody; nothing 102

1. No work is too difficult for him.
No intelligent person would believe that.
No books are to be removed.
No smoking (is) allowed.

no (deutsch: kein) wird nur adjektivisch gebraucht.

2. None of the work was very difficult.
None of the people believed me.
None of these books is interesting.

none of muß an Stelle von *no* gebraucht werden, wenn es heißt „keine (-r, -s) von“ (aus einer bestimmten Anzahl).

3. No one can deny his courage.
Nobody came to meet me at the station.
Nothing had been touched by the intruders.

no one, nobody = keiner, niemand
nothing = nichts

Notice:

Man beachte, daß in den Beispielen, die in 102, 1, 2 u. 3 angeführt worden sind, die negativen Formen *no*, *none of*, *no one*, *nobody*, *nothing* immer in Subjektstellung erscheinen.

He gave me no advice.°
You shall speak to no one.°
He ate nothing for a week.°
He opened none of her letters.°

He didn't give me any advice.
You are not to speak to anyone.
He didn't eat anything for a week.
He didn't open any of her letters.

Stehen diese Formen in Objektstellung (was selten vorkommt), so sind sie stark betont, und die Aussage wirkt sehr formell.

Im modernen Englisch gebraucht man in diesen Fällen meist die Konstruktion:
(negative verb) + any, anyone, anybody, anything.

103 little, few; much, many

little, *few* und *much*, *many* werden substantivisch und adjektivisch gebraucht. Sie können gesteigert werden.

1. a) She has very little knowledge of the Russian language.
She is content with the little she has.
He that knows little soon repeats it.
Shakespeare learned a little Latin and less Greek.
May I have a little water, please?

b) Little money, few friends; less money, fewer friends.
Only a few people were very loud.
The less trouble there is, the fewer worries you have.

a) *little* (= wenig) ist Singular und bezeichnet eine geringe Menge,
a little (= ein wenig, etwas),
a little water = *some water* (= etwas Wasser);

b) *few* (= wenige) ist Plural und bezeichnet eine geringe Anzahl.
a few (= einige, ein paar),
a few minutes = *some minutes*,
the less . . . the fewer

2\.

a) There is not much time left. Don't ask much to have little.	a) *much* (= viel) bedeutet eine große Menge (nicht zählbar; Singular).
b) He has neither much money nor many friends.	b) *many* (= viele) bezeichnet eine große Anzahl (zählbar; Plural!).

3\. In der heutigen Umgangssprache werden *much* und *many* nur in verneinenden Sätzen und in Fragesätzen gebraucht. In bejahenden Sätzen treten dafür andere Ausdrücke ein:

a) You get a lot of information about the weather by watching animals. I like to have lots of spare time. He's got plenty of money. I've seen a lot of interesting places. There were lots of children playing in the playground. Give me plenty of potatoes.	a) für *much* oder *many*: a lot of lots of plenty of
b) He has a great deal of patience. We have a good deal of time left. They spend a considerable amount (of money) on clothes. He drinks enormous quantities of beer.	b) für *much* (nur mit Substantiven im Singular): a good deal of a great deal of a + *(Adj.)* + amount of *(Adj.)* + quantities of
c) A large number of people came to the meeting. He speaks several languages.	c) für *many* (nur mit Substantiven im Plural): a + *(Adj.)* + number of several

Summary **Übersicht**

	much	many
Negative	He doesn't eat much (cabbage).	She doesn't have many friends.
Interrogative	Does he eat much (cabbage)?	Does she have many friends?
Affirmative	He eats { a lot / lots / a great deal / a huge amount / incredible quantities } (of cabbage).	She has { a lot of / lots of / plenty of / several / a good number of } friends.

The Adjective

Das Adjektiv

104 The Function of the Adjective — Die Funktion des Adjektivs

Das Adjektiv hat die Aufgabe, die Eigenschaft einer mit einem Substantiv bezeichneten Person oder Sache anzugeben, d. h. diese zu kennzeichnen. Im Englischen sind die Adjektive unveränderlich, sie werden nicht flektiert.

a) John is a clever boy.
London is a large town.

b) Lake Windermere is beautiful.
Richard is very small.

Das Adjektiv kann
a) als Attribut zu einem Substantiv treten (vgl. 112) oder

b) als Teil der Satzaussage, als Prädikatsnomen, stehen (vgl. 114).

105 The Comparison of Adjectives — Die Steigerung der Adjektive

Positive	Comparative	Superlative
a) Anne is tall.	Pat is taller.	Jill is the tallest (. . . tallest).
b) This rose is beautiful.	That one is more beautiful.	Those ones are the most beautiful.

Im Englischen gibt es zwei Arten der Steigerung:

a) Komparative und Superlative werden durch Anfügung von *-er* und *-est* gebildet. Diese Art der Steigerung nennt man Germanische Steigerung.
b) Komparative und Superlative werden durch Vorsetzen von *more* und *most* gebildet. Diese Art der Steigerung nennt man Romanische Steigerung.

Vgl. deutsch	reich	reicher	der reichste
frz.	riche	plus riche	le plus riche
lat.	pius	magis pius	maxime pius

deep	deeper	deepest
long [lɔŋ]	longer [ˈlɔŋgə]	longest [ˈlɔŋgist]
brave	braver	bravest

Alle einsilbig gesprochenen Adjektive werden auf germanische Art gesteigert. Die meisten dieser Adjektive sind germanischen Ursprungs.

beautiful	more beautiful	most beautiful
difficult	more difficult	most difficult

precarious	impressionable
more precarious	more impressionable
most precarious	most impressionable

Alle drei- und mehrsilbigen Adjektive werden auf romanische Art gesteigert. – Die meisten dieser Adjektive sind romanischen (frz. od. lat.) Ursprungs.

Notice:

My uncle grows the most beautiful flowers imaginable.
He is very good at mathematics, and solves the most difficult problems.

most steht mit dem bestimmten Artikel, wenn etwas oder jemand aus einer größeren Gruppe herausgehoben wird, d. h. besonders, wenn ein Vergleich vorliegt (*most* = mehr als alle andern).

Für die zweisilbigen Adjektive gelten folgende Richtlinien (vgl. dazu aber *Notice*, S. 96):

a) happy	happier	happiest
noble	nobler	noblest
clever	cleverer	cleverest
narrow	narrower	narrowest

a) Germanisch gesteigert werden gewöhnlich die zweisilbigen Adjektive mit den Endungen *-y*, *-le*, *-er*, *-ow*.

b) polite	politer	politest
remote	remoter	remotest
sincere	sincerer	sincerest

b) Germanisch gesteigert werden gewöhnlich auch die zweisilbigen Adjektive mit dem Ton auf der zweiten Silbe.

c) pleasant	pleasanter	pleasantest
stupid	stupider	stupidest
quiet	quieter	quietest

c) Auf germanische Art werden ferner die folgenden Adjektive gesteigert, wenn sie vor Substantiven stehen: *pleasant*, *solid*, *stupid*, *civil*, *common*, *cruel*, *quiet*.

d) terrible	more terrible	most terrible
splendid	more splendid	most splendid
decent	more decent	most decent

d) Die meisten zweisilbigen Adjektive mit dem Ton auf der ersten Silbe werden auf romanische Art gesteigert.

Notice:

Das Wörtchen „gewöhnlich“ in den unter 105, 3 gegebenen Richtlinien weist schon darauf hin, daß in bezug auf die Steigerung vieler zweisilbiger Adjektive im Englischen keine bindende Regel gegeben werden kann. Absicht des Sprechenden (Hervorhebung), Wohlklang, Rhythmus und Geschmack sind dem Engländer für den Gebrauch der einen oder anderen Art der Steigerung ausschlaggebend. Einige Beispiele mögen dies deutlich machen.

bitter	That was the bitterest medicine I ever tasted. From being friends, they have become the most bitter enemies.
clever	Rusty was the cleverest little dog you could imagine. She is more clever than her brother at inventing excuses.
shallow	The Thames at Windsor is shallower than at Greenwich. Is this side of the swimming-pool more shallow than that?
intense	The cold became intenser. The excitement grew more and more intense.
severe	The team took the severest beating they had ever had at home. This winter the frost was more severe than last year.
sincere	"With sincerest greetings from your old friend Joe." I think Peter is more sincere than his brother Paul.
civil	Even the civilest policeman will take your number if you park your car here. A stranger is more civil and polite to me than you are.
common	The daisy is one of the commonest flowers. It is more common to say: "Sorry!" than "I beg your pardon!"
cruel	King John was the cruellest king that ever sat on the English throne. A lion is more cruel than an elephant.
pleasant	The pleasantest days last August were those I spent in Scotland. Her voice is more pleasant than her sister's.
solid	It was the solidest cake imaginable; it was even more solid than concrete.
stupid	Even the stupidest boy must be able to understand the instructions. That was one of the most stupid mistakes I ever made.
handsome	It was the handsomest reward he could have hoped for. His father was more handsome than either of his sons.

4. Zu beachten ist die Rechtschreibung bei den Steigerungsformen.

a) pretty	prettier	prettiest
happy	happier	happiest
b) big	bigger	biggest
fat	fatter	fattest
hot	hotter	hottest

a) *y* wird zu *i*.

b) Der Endkonsonant wird verdoppelt, wenn diesem ein einfacher, betonter Vokal vorausgeht (vgl. 24).

5. The path became steeper and steeper and more and more slippery.

The time appeared longer and longer, and he grew more and more impatient.

Die allmählich zunehmende Steigerung (deutsch: immer) wird bei den nach germanischer Art gesteigerten Adjektiven durch Wiederholung des Komparativs; bei den nach romanischer Art gesteigerten Adjektiven durch *more and more* ausgedrückt (vgl. 133).

Comparison with Exceptional Forms — Steigerung mit besonderen Formen 106

good	gut	better	best
well	wohl, gesund		
bad	schlecht	worse	worst
ill	krank		
evil	böse		
little	gering, wenig,	less	least
	klein	smaller	smallest
much	viel	more	most
many	viele		

Double Comparatives and Superlatives — Doppelform im Komparativ und Superlativ 107

Einige Adjektive haben im Komparativ und Superlativ Doppelformen mit verschiedener Bedeutung. (Vergleiche die folgende zusammenfassende Aufzählung dieser Doppelformen und die entsprechenden Erläuterungen.)

a) Jill is older than her brothers Peter and Philip; she is the eldest child of Mr. and Mrs. Slack.
The Norwoods have two boys, Roy and David; Roy is the elder (one).

b) His fame spread to the farthest end of Britain.
She said no further words.

c) The next turning to the right is not the nearest way to the station.

d) We arrived later than usual.
His latest book will not be his last.
"Which books do you like better, amusing or instructive ones?" – "I prefer the former to the latter."

a) old	older	oldest	(bezeichnet das wirkliche Alter; frz. *âgé*)
	elder	eldest	(steht gewöhnlich nur im Vergleich von Familienmitgliedern und attributiv; frz. *aîné*)
b) far	farther	farthest	(von der Entfernung)
	further	furthest	(bildlich; oft auch von der Entfernung) [*further* ist heute gebräuchlicher als *farther*.]
c) near	nearer	nearest	(von der Entfernung: näher-, nächstliegend, -stehend)
		next	(von der Reihenfolge: nächstfolgend)
d) late	later	latest	(von der Zeit: später, spätest, neueste)
	the latter	last	(von der Reihenfolge: der letztere, letzt)

108 Comparisons without Positives

Steigerungsformen ohne Positiv

The quality of this cloth is superior to that.
This man is superior to flattery.
He hit the ball to the extreme edge of the cricket field.
The highest court in the USA is the Supreme Court.

Im Englischen gibt es einige Adjektive, die keinen Positiv haben und nur als Komparative und Superlative vorkommen. Diese wurden aus dem Lateinischen übernommen; schon dort fehlten zum Teil die Positive.

inferior to	niedriger, tiefer, geringer als
superior to	höher als, überlegen; erhaben über
interior	inner; binnenländisch
exterior	außenliegend; äußerlich
major	größer, wichtiger
(major =	*of age* „volljährig")
minor	kleiner, geringer; minderjährig
(Asia Minor	„Kleinasien")
(minor point	„Nebensache")
extreme	äußerst, fernst
supreme	höchst, oberst
senior to	älter als; ranghöher
junior to	jünger als; untergeordnet

Vgl. frz. inférieur, supérieur, intérieur, extérieur, majeur, mineur – extrême, suprême.

Comparison in the Sentence — Der Vergleich im Satz — 109

Will man mit Hilfe von Adjektiven Vergleiche anstellen, so kann man benutzen:

That blue shirt is nicer than this one. Better late than never.	than (= als) nach einem Komparativ;
He is as old as my friend. We have nothing as nice as that.	as . . . as (= ebenso . . . wie);
Your friend is not as old as his cousin. Our town is not so small as your town.	not as . . . as not so . . . as } (= nicht so . . . wie); (Beide Ausdrucksweisen stehen heute gleichberechtigt nebeneinander.)
All the better. – All the worse. The more danger, the more honour. The more I see her, the better I like her.	all the + *Comparative* (= umso); the + *Comparative* . . . the + *Comparative* (= je . . . desto).

Emphatic Comparison — Verstärkung der Steigerungsformen — 110

1. He is very clever and a most learned ['lə:nid] man.

Um ein Adjektiv im Positiv zu verstärken, gebraucht man im Englischen *very* (= sehr) und *most* (= überaus).

2. He is much more intelligent than his brother.
Today he looks even better than last week.
John is tall, but Peter is still taller.
He is far weaker at maths than at French.

Zur Verstärkung des Komparativs dienen:
much (= viel)

even (= sogar noch)
still (= noch)
far (= weit)

Notice:

Your exercise is better by far.

by far (= bei weitem) steht immer hinter dem Komparativ.

3. Alfred was by far the greatest of the Anglo-Saxon kings.
Alfred was the greatest of all (the) Anglo-Saxon kings.

Zur Verstärkung des Superlativs dient *by far* („bei weitem").
(*the greatest of all* „der allergrößte").

Notice:

Piccadilly Circus is in the very heart of London. (= *mitten im Herzen von London*)
The tree stands on the very edge of the river. (= *genau am Rand des Flusses*)
There was a knock at the door, and at that very moment the telephone rang. (= *gerade in diesem Augenblick*)

very kann auch vor Substantiven stehen. Es bedeutet Hervorhebung bzw. genauere Bestimmung des Begriffes (deutsch: genau, gerade; vgl. frz. *vrai*).

111 Negation of the Comparative

Verneinung des Komparativs

He is tired, and I am no less so.
They are no more prosperous than their neighbours.
The Tower is no longer a prison.

Zur Verneinung des Komparativs dient in der Regel *no*, besonders in *no less, no more, no longer*.

Notice:

There cannot have been more than fifty people at the concert.
They will offer him not less than £10,000.

not more (= höchstens)
not less (= mindestens, nicht weniger als)

112 The Adjective as an Attribute

Das Adjektiv als Attribut

1. Our little son has broken his arm.
But: Our son is very small for his age.
Cats are his favourite animals.
But: He likes cats best of all animals.

Einige Adjektive werden nur attributiv gebraucht. In prädikativer Verwendung stehen dafür sinnverwandte Adjektive.

Adjektive, die nur attributiv gebraucht werden, sind z. B.

a little child	an average wage	ein Durchschnittslohn
his favourite animals	spare parts	Ersatzteile
the left wing of the party	a spare tyre	ein Reserverad
the right side of the wood	a spare room	ein Gast-, Fremdenzimmer
the outer wall of the house	the late president	der verstorbene Präsident
the upper floor	the inner side of the story	der verborgene Gehalt der Erzählung
the former Prime Minister	in utter despair	in äußerster Verzweiflung
his elder brother	an oak chair	ein Stuhl aus Eichenholz
a wooden toy	the latter statement	die letztere Feststellung
a woollen stocking	an earthen pot	ein irdener Topf
	a drunken person	eine betrunkene Person

Notice:

silken hair	Seidenhaar
a silk dress	ein Seidenkleid
a golden age	eine goldene Zeit
a gold watch	eine goldene Uhr
a leaden sleep	ein bleierner (tiefer) Schlaf
a lead pencil	ein Bleistift

Die abgeleiteten Adjektive *golden silken, leaden* werden fast nur in übertragener Bedeutung gebraucht.

2. The driver of the up train (= *des nach London fahrenden Zuges*) saw the obstacle on the line and stopped; the driver of the down train, however, could not see the obstacle as there was a curve in the down line, and the train crashed.

Auch einige Adverbien werden als attributive Adjektive verwendet.

Weitere Beispiele dieser Art sind:

the then minister – der damalige Minister
the above remark – die obige Bemerkung

in after years△ – in späteren Jahren
in an off street – in einer Seitenstraße

3. Auch andere Wortarten können wie attributive Adjektive verwendet werden, z. B.

London Bridge	a steel pen	Windsor Castle	a ballpoint pen
a March wind	a leather coat	afternoon tea	a fountain pen
evening dress	paper money	April showers	the top shelf
the Berlin question	a Southampton merchant		

113 Position of the Adjective used as an Attribute

Stellung des attributiv gebrauchten Adjektivs

1. It was an unusually cold day, and there was a strong cutting east wind.

Das attributiv gebrauchte Adjektiv steht gewöhnlich vor dem zugehörigen Substantiv, auch wenn es durch ein Adverb näher bestimmt ist.

2. a) The girls took their seats at a table laden with wonderful things.
A wall ten feet high surrounded the prison.
b) They used every means possible to get there in time.
Most of the books available are here.
c) Things seen are mightier than things heard.
Money lent is money spent.
d) They worked all day long.
"Mother dear, may I have some money?"
The best way imaginable is this.
(Der best vorstellbare Weg . . .)
The Pyramids have looked down on us from time immemorial.
(. . . seit undenklichen (uralten) Zeiten)

a) Wenn das attributiv gebrauchte Adjektiv eine andere Bestimmung als ein Adverb bei sich hat, tritt es hinter das Substantiv.
b) Auch wenn das Adjektiv stark betont ist, kann es hinter das Substantiv treten.
c) Adjektive, die noch ihre verbale Kraft besitzen, treten ebenfalls hinter das Substantiv.
d) Hinter dem Substantiv stehen die Adjektive in einigen Redewendungen.

e) Merken muß man sich vor allem einige Wendungen, die dem Französischen oder Lateinischen nachgebildet sind. Hier stehen die Adjektive immer hinter den zugehörigen Substantiven:

Princess Royal	die älteste Tochter des Königs
the Lords Spiritual and Temporal	die geistlichen und weltlichen Lords des Oberhauses
Prince Consort	Prinzgemahl
court martial	Kriegsgericht
Solicitor General (*BE*)	Oberstaatsanwalt (*AE:* Attorney General)
Poet Laureate	(lorbeerbekränzter) Hofdichter

Notice:

The members present passed the motion.	die anwesenden Mitglieder
The British have kept their love of tradition up to the present day.	bis zum heutigen Tag

The Adjective as a Predicative Complement

Das prädikativ gebrauchte Adjektiv

114

a) His uncle was sad and lonely; he had grown old.
It is getting dark.
She looks pale.
What seems easy to you seems difficult to me.

b) The child stood white with terror.
His father returned happy.
They arrived home safe and sound.
The train left London empty.
He remained calm in spite of the danger.

a) Nach den Verben, die ein Sein, Werden oder Scheinen bezeichnen:

to be — to become — to get
to seem — to grow — to look

steht das Adjektiv als prädikative Ergänzung zum Subjekt.

b) Ebenso steht das Adjektiv als prädikative Ergänzung zum Subjekt nach den Verben der Ruhe und der Bewegung, z. B.

to remain — to stand — to lie — to sit
to leave — to arrive — to return

Notice:

to go wrong	schief gehen	to come true	sich bewahrheiten
to go mad	verrückt werden	to run short (of)	knapp werden (an)
to fall ill	krank werden	to turn Catholic	katholisch werden
to fall asleep	einschlafen	to keep quiet	sich ruhig verhalten

a) He made his point clear.
We consider his decision wrong.
Mary Stuart was found guilty.
I call his behaviour foolish.

b) Did he pronounce the vowel long or short?
Open the door wide.
Sweep the floor clean.
Cut the bread thin.
Shut your eyes tight.

a) Nach den Verben des Machens, Dafürhaltens und Erklärens (vgl. 209) steht das Adjektiv (nicht etwa das Adverb!) als prädikative Ergänzung zum Objekt.

b) Als prädikative Ergänzung zum Objekt kann das Adjektiv auch nach anderen Verben stehen, wenn es mehr über das bezügliche Substantiv oder Pronomen aussagt, als es die Tätigkeit näher kennzeichnet.

He was very ill.
But: He was a sick man.

The boy is well again.
But: He is a healthy boy.

Einige Adjektive können in bestimmter Bedeutung nur prädikativ gebraucht werden. – In attributiver Verwendung stehen dafür sinnverwandte Adjektive. Weitere Adjektive dieser Art sind auf Seite 104 aufgeführt.

Predicative Use Only	Substitutes
Stand (keep) still while I take your photograph.	As the wind was still, the sailing-ship hardly moved through the calm sea.
This stamp is worth a lot.	Whittington, thou worthy citizen!
The snake he caught is still alive.	He brought home a living snake. He brought home a live snake.
When I looked at her, she was fast asleep.	I found a sleeping squirrel.
Is he awake or asleep?	She has a very alert (wide-awake) mind.
Scott was aware of the dangers when he set out for the Antarctic.	He kept a watchful eye on the enemy's movements.
When his parents left him, he was alone in the house.	In some parts of Nevada you only meet a lonely traveller now and then.
The sailor was drunk.	What shall we do with the drunken sailor?

115 The Adjective as Noun — Das Adjektiv als Substantiv

Das Adjektiv kann durch Vorsetzen des bestimmten Artikels substantiviert werden. Es bezeichnet dann

1. a) We must help the poor (= *den Armen*). Florence Nightingale nursed the sick and the wounded. Helen Keller worked to help the blind.

a) die Gesamtheit der durch das Adjektiv charakterisierten Personen (keine Pluralform möglich);

b) Hope for the best (= *das Beste*) and expect the worst (= *das Schlimmste*).

b) ein Abstraktum;

c) The English, the Scottish, the Welsh, and some of the Irish form one nation. The French settled in a large part of North America.

c) das ganze Volk bei den folgenden Adjektiven:

British English Scottish Dutch
Welsh Irish French

a) Many English people find German very hard to learn.
He translated many books from Latin into French.
b) His father is American, his mother is Irish.
His cousin is English.

a) Zur Bezeichnung der Sprache eines Volkes verwendet das Englische das Adjektiv ohne Artikel.

b) Zur Bezeichnung der Zugehörigkeit zu einem Volk steht oft *to be* + entsprechendes Adjektiv (dtsch. meist Substantiv, z. B. „Er ist Engländer.“)

a Japanese	ein Japaner
the Japanese	die Japaner
a Swiss	ein Schweizer
the Swiss	die Schweizer

Die Völkernamen auf *-se* und *-ss* haben im Singular und Plural die gleiche Form. (vgl. 44, 2 Not.)

a German	the Germans
a Roman	the Romans
a Saxon	the Saxons
a Briton	the Britons
an Italian	the Italians
a Greek	the Greeks

Eine große Anzahl von Adjektiven ist zu wirklichen Substantiven geworden. Diese Adjektive können wie Substantive die Pluralform bilden. Es sind dies die Völkernamen auf *-an* und *-on*; ferner *Greek*.
Außerdem sind die folgenden Adjektive echte Substantive geworden:

a black	ein Schwarzer	a patient	ein Patient	a Catholic	ein Katholik
a white	ein Weißer	a savage	ein Wilder	a Protestant	ein Protestant
a noble	ein Adliger	a daily	eine Tageszeitung	a Conservative	ein Konservativer
a saint	ein Heiliger	my equal	meinesgleichen	a Liberal	ein Liberaler
a mortal	ein Sterblicher	(my) inferior	(mein) Untergebener	a Republican	ein Republikaner
a native	ein Eingeborener	(my) superior	(mein) Vorgesetzter	a Democrat	ein Demokrat

There is no customs charge on goods in transit.
The Commons meet regularly at certain intervals.

Manche Adjektive können nur als Substantive im Plural gebraucht werden, z. B.

drinkables	Getränke	goods	Güter, Waren
eatables	Eßwaren	sweets	Süßigkeiten
empties	Leergut	the Commons	die Mitglieder des Unterhauses, das Unterhaus

116 The Adjective with a Prop-word — Das Adjektiv mit einem Stützwort

1. Sollen ein oder mehrere Einzelwesen aus der durch das Adjektiv charakterisierten Gruppe herausgehoben werden, so muß dem Adjektiv ein Stützwort beigegeben werden, weil sonst Sinnverschiebungen eintreten.

> You can help the poor fellow (= *dem Armen*).
> *But*: A rich man always ought to help the poor (= *den Armen*).
> It was the first thing (= *das erste*) he said.
> Wise men (= *Weise*) will change their minds, fools never.

Als Stützwörter dienen z. B. Substantive wie:

man	gentleman	woman	lady
fellow	person	people	thing

117 The Prop-word one — Das Stützwort one

1.

> His aunt has two cats, a brown one and a black one.
> At the corner I saw a blind man and a lame one.
> These oranges look nice, please give me two big ones.

Als Stützwort dient besonders das unbestimmte Pronomen *one*, Plural *ones*. Es wird verwendet, um die Wiederholung desselben Substantivs zu vermeiden (vgl. 79, 3 u. 4).

2.

> a) Is this book your own?
> I don't want your pen; I shall use my own.
>
> b) He had three cups of coffee, I only two.
> She was given twenty stamps, he only nineteen.
>
> c) He had a lot of apples, but he gave me only a few, whereas my friends got many.
>
> d) Is there a difference between English steel and Swedish?
> Many people prefer brown bread to white.

Das Stützwort steht nicht

a) nach Possessivpronomen + *own*;

b) nach attributiv gebrauchten Grundzahlen.

c) Ferner steht das Stützwort nicht nach *few* und *many*.

d) Das Stützwort entfällt ebenfalls, wenn ein Stoffname zu ergänzen ist.

3. Meist ohne Stützwort steht das Adjektiv

a) Of all nations the United States is the richest. Which of the two brothers is your friend, the elder or the younger?	a) nach Superlativen und Komparativen in Verbindung mit dem bestimmten Artikel;
b) The second volume is more interesting than the first.	b) nach Ordnungszahlen, besonders nach the first, the second, the third;
c) Most Christians know the New Testament better than the Old. Is the Palace of Westminster on the right bank of the Thames or on the left?	c) bei zweigliedrigen Gegensätzen.

The Numerals

Die Zahlwörter

Numbers and Fractions — Zahlen und Brüche

118 The Cardinal Numbers — Die Grundzahlen

0	nought	21	twenty-one
1	one	22	twenty-two
2	two	30	thirty
3	three	31	thirty-one
4	four	40	forty
5	five	50	fifty
6	six	60	sixty
7	seven	70	seventy
8	eight	80	eighty
9	nine	90	ninety
10	ten	100	a (one) hundred
11	eleven	101	a (one) hundred and one
12	twelve	180	a (one) hundred and eighty
13	thirteen	183	a (one) hundred and eighty-three
14	fourteen	200	two hundred
15	fifteen	600	six hundred
16	sixteen	1 000	a (one) thousand
17	seventeen	1 007	a (one) thousand and seven
18	eighteen	2 000	two thousand
19	nineteen	100 000	a (one) hundred thousand
20	twenty	1 000 000	a (one) million
		1 000 000 000	a thousand millions (*Brit.*), a billion (*Am.*)

1.

a) Eight minus eight leaves nought.

b) The temperature has fallen below zero.

c) They beat them 2–0 (two nil).
The team won (by) 3–0 (three nothing).

d) He won the first set (by) 6–0 (six love).

e) 66503 = double six-five-o[əu]-three

a) *nought* [nɔːt] bezeichnet den Zahlenwert Null.

b) *zero* ['ziərəu] bezeichnet den Nullpunkt einer Skala.

c) *nil* [nil] steht im *BE* zur Angabe der Punktzahl bei Sportereignissen. Im *AE* heißt es *nothing*.

d) *love* [lʌv] ist die Bezeichnung für Null beim Tennis.

e) *o* [əu] sagt man für Null bei Fernsprechnummern.

2\. a) thirteen [ˈθəːˈtiːn] nineteen [ˈnainˈtiːn]
fourteen [ˈfɔːˈtiːn]

b) fourteen boys [ˈfɔːtin ˈbɔiz]
sixteen girls [ˈsikstin ˈgəːlz]

a) Bei den Zahlen *thirteen* bis *nineteen* werden beide Silben gleichmäßig stark betont (*level stress*), wenn sie allein stehen (vgl. 14).

b) In Verbindung mit einem Substantiv haben sie den Ton auf der ersten Silbe.

3\. twenty-two [ˈtwenti ˈtuː]
forty-eight [ˈfɔːtiˈeit]

Zwischen Zehnern und Einern steht ein Bindestrich (*hyphen* [ˈhaifən]).

4\. a (one) hundred and one,
one (a) thousand and ten,
one (a) million two thousand one (a) hundred and seventy-one

Bei Zahlen über 100 steht vor Zehnern und Einern *and*.

5\. a (one) hundred pupils,
a (one) thousand miles
Two hundred are twice (as many as) one hundred.
In (the year) one hundred and twenty-two Emperor Hadrian decided to build a stone-wall across Northern Britain.

hundred, thousand, million werden stets mit dem unbestimmten Artikel (oder einer Zahl) gebraucht. Bei Hervorhebung des „ein" kann *one* (statt *a*) stehen, bei Jahreszahlen steht *one* immer.

6\. London has eight million inhabitants.
The new canal cost three million pounds.

million wird als unveränderliches Zahlwort (Adjektiv) gebraucht.

Notice:

a) There were hundreds of people at church.
In Birmingham (there) live hundreds of thousands of people.
The new motor-works will cost 14 millions to build (*or*: 14 million pounds).
London has millions of inhabitants (*but*: eight million inhabitants).

a) *hundred, thousand, million* können auch als Substantiv gebraucht werden. Im Plural erhalten sie das Plural-s. Eine Ergänzung wird mit *of* angeschlossen.

b) She is a girl in her teens. In the thirties of the last century British industry expanded rapidly. They walked in threes and fours (= *zu dreien und zu vieren*).	b) Auch Einer- und Zehnerzahlen können als Substantive gebraucht werden.

Keep in Mind:

We were two.△ There were two of us.	Wir waren zu zweit.	two pound three△ two and three△	2 Pfund 3 Schilling 2 Schilling 3 Pence	(bis 15. 2. 1971)
to walk on all fours	auf allen vieren gehen	five foot seven	5 Fuß 7 Zoll	

119 The Ordinal Numbers

Die Ordnungszahlen

1st	the first	21st	the twenty-first
2nd	the second	22nd	the twenty-second
3rd	the third	23rd	the twenty-third
4th	the fourth	24th	the twenty-fourth
5th	the fifth	25th	the twenty-fifth
6th	the sixth	30th	the thirtieth
7th	the seventh	40th	the fortieth
8th	the eighth	50th	the fiftieth
9th	the ninth	60th	the sixtieth
10th	the tenth	70th	the seventieth
11th	the eleventh	80th	the eightieth
12th	the twelfth	90th	the ninetieth
13th	the thirteenth	100th	the hundredth
14th	the fourteenth	101st	the hundred and first
15th	the fifteenth	105th	the hundred and fifth
16th	the sixteenth	129th	the hundred and twenty-ninth
17th	the seventeenth	212th	the two hundred and twelfth
18th	the eighteenth	1 000th	the thousandth
19th	the nineteenth	2 003rd	the two thousand and third
20th	the twentieth ['twentiiθ]	1 000 000th	the millionth

a) Elizabeth II Richard III (*read*: Elizabeth the Second, Richard the Third)	a) Die Ordnungszahlen werden gebraucht zur Unterscheidung von Herrschern gleichen Namens. (Hinter der Ordnungszahl steht hier kein Punkt!);

b) Chapter III (*read*: [the] third Chapter, *or*: Chapter three)

c) September 30th, 1973;
or: 30th September 1973
(*read*: the thirtieth of September)
May 13th, 1973 *or*: 13th May, 1973
June 29, 1974 *or*: 29 June 1974

d) *Brit.*: 30. 9. 73 13/5/75 *Am.*: 9/30/73 5/13/75

b) zur Bezeichnung der Kapitel eines Buches u. ä.;

c) zur Angabe des Datums.
Vor der Jahreszahl muß ein Komma stehen, wenn eine Zahl unmittelbar vorausgeht. – Das *th* wird heute, besonders in Zeitungen, oft weggelassen.

d) In Geschäftsbriefen oder auf Rechnungen findet man auch die nebenstehenden Kurzformen. Die Amerikaner halten eine andere Reihenfolge ein.

The Multiplying Numbers

Die Wiederholungs- und Vervielfältigungszahlen 120

a) I see my uncle once a year.
Their house is twice as big as ours.
We met them three times last month.

b) Use double, not single, thread when sewing on a button.
He put in quite a lot of money; however, he got it back fivefold.△

Zu diesen Zahlen gehören:

a)	once	einmal
	twice	zweimal
	three times	dreimal
	four times	viermal etc.
b)	single	einfach
	double	doppelt
	triple (treble), threefold△	dreifach
	fourfold△	vierfach
	fivefold△	fünffach, etc.

Keep in Mind:

He has played for England more than a hundred times.	hundertmal
Last June it rained five times as much as in the same month last year.	fünfmal so viel
Please, read the sentence once more.	noch einmal
Once upon a time there was . . .	Es war einmal . . .
When her mother called her, she got up at once.	sofort
Don't speak all at once!	auf einmal
All at once I caught sight of him.	plötzlich
I have told you once and for all.	ein für allemal
He got back half as much again.	anderthalbmal soviel

121 The Adverbial Numbers

Die Zahladverbien

1. First she lived in New York, then in Boston. Last, but not least I welcomed my friend.

Die Reihenfolge wird bezeichnet durch *first* („zuerst", als erstes"), *then, last.*

2. At first I thought she was very good. At last he reached his aim.

Der Gegensatz wird ausgedrückt durch *at first* („anfangs"), *at last* („schließlich").

3. Firstly (in the first place) we were tired, and secondly (in the second place) we were hungry.

Bei Aufzählungen steht
firstly (or: *in the first place*);
secondly (or: *in the second place*);
thirdly, fourthly
und dann gewöhnlich
in the fifth place, etc.

122 The Vulgar Fractions

Die gemeinen Brüche

a) $^1/_2$ a (one) half $^1/_3$ a third
$^1/_4$ a fourth, a quarter $^1/_5$ a fifth
$^2/_5$ two fifths
$3^5/_6$ three and five sixths ['faiv'siksθs]

b) A fourth and one eighth are three eighths.
a quarter of an hour
three and a quarter miles of good road . .
(or: three miles and a quarter)

a) Im Plural erhält der Nenner der Bruchzahl ein s.

b) Ein Viertel heißt *a fourth*, wenn kein Substantiv darauf folgt; andernfalls muß es *a quarter* heißen. Die Benennung (hier *an hour* bzw. *good road*) wird mit *of* angeschlossen.

123 The Decimal Fractions

Die Dezimalbrüche

An inch is 2.54 cm (*read*: two point five four centimetres).
A foot is 30.48 cm (*read*: thirty point four eight centimetres).
A yard is 91.44 cm (*read*: ninety-one point four four centimetres).
0.349 (*read*: point three four nine, *or*: nought point three four nine).

Measures and Weights — Maße und Gewichte 124

Measures of Length — Längenmaße

1 yd. (yard) = 3 ft. (feet) = 36 in. (inches) = 91.44 cm. (centimetres)
1 mile = 1760 yds. = 1609.34 m. (metres)

Weights — Gewichte

1 ton = 20 cwts. (hundredweights) = 1016 kg.	(kilogram[me])
1 cwt. = 8 stone = 112 lbs. (pounds)	c = lat. *centum*
1 lb. (pound) = 16 oz. (ounces) = 0.453 kg	lb. = lat. *libra*
1 oz. (ounce) = 28.35 g.	lbs. = lat. *libras* (= pounds)

Measures of Capacity — Hohlmaße

1 gal. (gallon) = 4 qt. (quarts) = 8 pints [paints] = 4.54 l.
1 bush. (bushel [buʃl]) = 8 gal.

Temperatures — Wärmegrade

0° C. (Celsius) = 32° F. (Fahrenheit) : freezing-point
100° C. = 212° F. : boiling-point
1° C. (Celsius, one centigrade) = 1,8 + 32° F.

British and American Money — Britisches und amerikanisches Geld 125

£1 (one pound) = 100 pence
coins: 50p (50 pence), 10p (10 pence), 5p (5 pence), 1 p (1 penny), ½p (½ penny)

$1 (one dollar) = 100 ¢ (cent)
coins: 50¢ (a half dollar), 25¢ (a quarter), 10¢ (a dime), 5¢ (a nickel), 1¢ (a penny)

Bis zum 15. Februar 1971 galt in Großbritannien folgendes Währungssystem:

£1 (pound) = 20s. (shillings); 1s. = 12d. (= pence; lat. *denarius*);
£2/5/6 = two pound five (shillings) and six (pence).

126 Time by the Clock

Uhrzeit

1.

a) 12.30 = half past twelve
2.24 = twenty-four minutes past two
5.04 = four minutes past five
7.33 = twenty-seven minutes to eight
8.45 = a quarter to nine

10.52 = eight (minutes) to eleven
3.56 = four minutes to four
9.02 = two minutes past nine

a) Bei Angaben der Uhrzeit bezieht man die 1. bis 30. Minute mit *past* auf die vorhergehende Stunde, die 31. bis 59. Minute mit *to* auf die folgende volle Stunde.

Das Wort *minutes* kann wegbleiben, wenn es sich um mehr als 4 Minuten handelt (bei einer bis 4 Minuten muß es jedoch stehen).

b) 5.31 = five thirty-one
12.56 = twelve fifty-six
12.03 = ['twelv əu 'θriː]
9.11 = nine eleven
11.06 = eleven six
13.00 = thirteen hundred (hours)
20.10 = twenty ten
23.05 = ['twenti θriː əu 'faiv]

b) Bei der Angabe der Abfahrts- und Ankunftszeit von Zügen (der Abflugs- und Ankunftszeit von Flugzeugen o. ä.) werden die Grundzahlen genannt. Das ist so wie im Deutschen; nur verzichtet der Engländer auf die Benennung *o'clock* (deutsch: Uhr).

c) The train leaves at 7.06 a.m. (seven six a.m.)
The plane arrived at London Airport at 12.15 p.m. (twelve fifteen p.m.).

c) Die Engländer kennzeichnen die Zeit von
12 Uhr nachts bis 12 Uhr mittags durch *a.m.* (= *ante meridiem*), von 12 Uhr mittags bis 12 Uhr nachts durch *p.m.* (= *post meridiem*).

2.

a quarter of an hour	¼ Stunde
half an hour	½ Stunde
three quarters of an hour	¾ Stunde
an (one) hour and a half	1½ Stunde

Die nebenstehenden Ausdrücke bezeichnen einen Zeitraum.

. Englische Zeitangaben über mehr als einen Tag unterscheiden sich oft von ihren deutschen Entsprechungen.

Twice a week he used to go to the theatre.	zweimal die Woche
A week today our holidays will begin.	heute in 8 Tagen
The accident happened a week ago today.	heute vor 8 Tagen
They stayed with their uncle for a fortnight.	14 Tage (lang)
A fortnight today our holidays will be over.	heute in 14 Tagen
My birthday was a fortnight ago yesterday.	gestern vor 14 Tagen
The day before yesterday my father got a new car.	vorgestern
He is going to take us to London the day after tomorrow.	übermorgen
three months (a quarter of a year)	ein Vierteljahr
six months (half a year)	ein halbes Jahr
eighteen months (a year and a half)	anderthalb Jahre

The Adverb

Das Adverb

127 The Function of the Adverb — Die Funktion des Adverbs

Adverbien übernehmen im Satz die Aufgabe, den Begriffsinhalt eines Wortes oder auch eines ganzen Satzes näher zu bestimmen.

1. Durch Adverbien können näher bestimmt werden:

a) Jack usually drives very fast. He is a man who always says what he really thinks.	a) ein Verb;
b) Our dog has a beautifully shiny coat. She is seriously ill.	b) ein Adjektiv;
c) Pat can play the piano very well. He has done his task surprisingly well.	c) ein Adverb;
d) She is only a beginner. His father is quite an expert in repairing cars.	d) ein Substantiv.

Notice:

I am (very) much obliged to you. I am very surprised.	Vor einem *Past Participle* steht im allgemeinen *much* oder *very much*. In der modernen Sprache steht *very*, wenn die verbale Verwendung des *Past Participle* nicht klar ist.

2. Perhaps we shall be late for the train. That is very strange news, indeed. This is not altogether true.	Durch Adverbien kann auch ein ganzer Satzinhalt näher bestimmt werden. Adverbien dieser Art sind z. B. perhaps still altogether indeed surely possibly

Form and Formation of Adverbs — Form und Bildung der Adverbien

Classification of Adverbs — Einteilung der Adverbien 128

Nach ihrer Form unterscheidet man drei Arten von Adverbien:

a) here, not, just, quite, often, etc.	a) ursprüngliche Adverbien;
b) always, already, today, tomorrow, etc.	b) durch Zusammensetzung gebildete Adverbien;
c) happily, usually, wonderfully, etc.	c) abgeleitete Adverbien.

Man kann die Adverbien auch nach ihrer Bedeutung einteilen. Besonders wichtig sind die folgenden vier Arten:

a) yesterday	today	tomorrow	etc.	a) die Adverbien der bestimmten Zeit (*Adverbs of Definite Time*);
b) afterwards	ever	now		b) die Adverbien der unbestimmten Zeit (*Adverbs of Indefinite Time*);
already	immediately	seldom		
before	late	since		
early	never	soon	etc.	
c) above	here	near		c) die Adverbien des Ortes (*Adverbs of Place*);
below	there	far		
in	everywhere			
out	nowhere		etc.	
d) well	badly	easily		d) die Adverbien der Art und Weise (*Adverbs of Manner*).
quickly	quietly	slowly	etc.	

Formation of Derived Adverbs — Bildung der abgeleiteten Adverbien 129

Adverbien kann man aus Adjektiven und aus Partizipien durch Anfügung der Endung *-ly* bilden.

a) quick	– quickly	a) Adverb aus Adjektiv gebildet;
beautiful	– beautifully	
b) surprising	– surprisingly	b) Adverb aus Partizip Präsens gebildet;
moving	– movingly	
c) hurried	– hurriedly	c) Adverb aus Partizip Perfekt gebildet.
excited	– excitedly	

2.	a) due – duly; true – truly b) idle – idly; simple – simply; possible – possibly; terrible – terribly c) pale – palely; sole – solely *But:* whole – wholly	Vor der Endung *-ly* verlieren a) die Adjektive *due* und *true* das *-e*; b) die Adjektive auf *-le* mit vorausgehendem Konsonanten das *-le*. c) Geht dem *-le* ein Vokal voraus, so bleibt *-le* erhalten. Aber: Ausnahme!

3. Adjektive auf *-ly* bilden das Adverb durch Umschreibung, z. B. die Adjektive

They treated me in a friendly way. He acted like a coward. She came in time.	friendly freundlich cowardly feige timely rechtzeitig

4. *difficult* bildet das Adverb ebenfalls durch Umschreibung:

It is difficult for us to believe what he tells us. She could only make herself understood with difficulty.	it is difficult } with difficulty } schwerlich, kaum

130 Adverbs in the Form of Adjectives — Adverbien in der Form eines Adjektivs

1. Einige Adjektive und Adverbien haben gleiche Form und gleiche Bedeutung:

a) He returned from his daily walk. Many accidents happen daily in the streets of London. b) He has not enough money, for he does not work hard enough. c) "Which of these three books is the best one?" – "I like this one best."	a) daily early hourly weekly monthly quarterly yearly nightly fortnightly b) enough far fast hard little long much c) better best last less least worse worst

2. Einige Adjektive und Adverbien haben gleiche Form, aber verschiedene Bedeutung:

His only son died last night.
He was only twenty years old.
It was a pretty picture.
We are pretty tired.
He is well again after his illness.
She gets on well at school.
"Give me a clean shirt," he said.
I am clean out of bread, I must go to the baker's.

	adj.	*adv.*
only	einzig	nur
pretty	hübsch	ziemlich
still	still	noch
well	wohl	gut
ill	krank	schlecht
	böse	böse
clean	rein	gänzlich

Adverbs with Two Forms and Different Meanings

Adverbien mit zwei Formen und verschiedener Bedeutung

131

Einige Adverbien haben eine endungslose Form und eine mit *-ly* gebildete Form; die letztere wird meist in übertragener Bedeutung gebraucht.

I bought this pair of shoes cheap (or: cheaply)	billig
He won the prize in the competition cheaply.	leicht
He stood close beside him.	dicht
He was closely watched.	genau, scharf
Buy cheap, sell dear, and you will be a rich man.	teuer
They love each other dearly.	zärtlich
The sailor sold his life dearly.	teuer
He went on working deep into the night.	tief
He is deeply interested in mathematics.	sehr
The team played fair.	fair (ehrlich, offen)
They are fairly well.	recht, ziemlich
The boy climbed high up the mountains.	hoch
She is highly interested in history.	sehr, höchst
We had to work hard.	hart, schwer, angestrengt
They could hardly find their way.	kaum
It was just half past seven when he heard the ring.	gerade
Our teachers have always treated us justly.	gerecht
She got up very late this morning.	spät
Have you been to the concert lately?	kürzlich, vor kurzem
Sometimes he laughs too loud (or: loudly).	laut
A gentleman does not dress loudly.	auffallend, prahlerisch
The pupil bent low over the book.	niedrig, tief
Some of them are lowly paid workers.	gering, niedrig
My grandparents live quite near.	nahe
I nearly made a mistake.	beinahe, fast
He often runs short of pocket money.	kurz, knapp
The chairman cut him short in the middle of his argument.	unterbrechen
The runaway horse stopped short at the gate.	stehenbleiben; steckenbleiben
To cut a long story short, I missed the train.	kurz gesagt; um es kurz zu machen
Shortly after the lunch he came home.	kurz (da)nach
I shall be seeing him shortly.	in kurzem, bald

vgl. frz. parler haut – parler hautement; parler bas, acheter cher, vendre cher, chanter juste, etc.

132 Verbs instead of Adverbs — Verben an Stelle von Adverbien

Im Englischen stehen häufig verbale Ausdrücke dort, wo wir von der deutschen Sprache her Adverbien gewohnt sind.

I happened to meet him in London. He chanced to be at home when I called. It so happened that I saw him last week. As it happens, I have enough money with me.	zufällig
I hope he will return soon.	hoffentlich
I am sure to meet him in the library.	sicherlich, bestimmt
He is likely to be at home. I expect that she will come.	wahrscheinlich, voraussichtlich
He is said to be a good driver. People say that she is a good housewife. It is said that there has been a big earthquake in Italy.	angeblich
He finished by saying that he wished us all the best for the future.	zuletzt, schließlich
I don't suppose to be back until 10 o'clock. It is to be supposed that he will finish his new book at the end of this year.	vermutlich
On February 28th, that is to say a fortnight next Wednesday, we'll meet again.	nämlich
It is true (I admit) that we left the party early, but we did not find it uninteresting, we were just tired.	zwar
Children prefer playing to working.	lieber
It seemed that nobody knew anything about the matter.	anscheinend
The plane was about to land. The train was on the point of leaving.	gerade
After the fire the workers continued (went on, kept on) working as if nothing had happened.	weiter
He is fond of pop music. He likes to listen to classical music.	gern

Vgl. frz. venir à faire qch., finir par faire qch., aimer (à) faire qch., continuer à faire qch., espérer que, on dit que, il est vrai.

133 The Comparison of Adverbs — Die Steigerung der Adverbien

1. Nach germanischer Art werden gesteigert

a) The sooner you do it, the better you will help him.

b) The earlier you begin, the sooner you will finish.

a) die ursprünglichen Adverbien wie *soon*, *fast*, *hard* (vgl. 128, 1);

b) viele Adverbien, die gleiche Formen wie die entsprechenden Adjektive haben (vgl. 130);

c) He laughs best, who laughs last.
She walked farther than she had intended to.

c) die Adverbien mit besonderen Steigerungsformen; ihre Komparative und Superlative gleichen denen der entsprechenden Adjektive (vgl. 106).

Positive		*Comparative*	*Superlative*
well	gut, wohl	better	best
badly, ill	schlimm	worse	worst
little	wenig, gering	less	least
much	viel	more	most
far	weit	farther further	farthest furthest

2. You must work more carefully.
English is the most widely spoken of all languages.

Auf romanische Art werden die abgeleiteten Adverbien mit Endung *-ly* gesteigert.

3. Die allmähliche Zunahme und Steigerung (deutsch: immer, vgl. 105) wird

a) He ran faster and faster.
Your composition gets worse and worse towards the end.

b) We had to work more and more quickly.
She writes more and more carelessly when she gets tired.

a) bei den nach germanischer Art gesteigerten Adverbien durch Wiederholung des Komparativs ausgedrückt;
b) bei den nach romanischer Art gesteigerten Adverbien geschieht das durch *more and more*.

4. He tried again and again to climb the mountain.

„immer wieder" heißt *again and again*.

5. a) All the better if you get there early.

b) The more you practise, the better you will become.

a) *all the* vor einem Komparativ bedeutet „um so".
b) *the . . . the* vor Komparativen heißt „je . . . desto".

6. He very seldom plays the piano nowadays.
She goes to the theatre very regularly.

Manche ursprünglichen Adverbien, z. B. *often*, *seldom*, werden durch *very* gesteigert, wenn es sich nicht um einen Vergleich handelt.

134 The Position of Adverbs and Adverbial Phrases

Stellung der Adverbien und der adverbialen Bestimmungen

Die Stellung der Adverbien und der adverbialen Bestimmungen wird bedingt durch die Bedeutung, die sie für den Satzinhalt haben:

druckstarke Adverbien treten also an das Ende oder auch an den Anfang des Satzes, druckschwache Adverbien stehen an den druckschwachen Stellen, d. h. vor dem Hauptverb, in zusammengesetzten Zeiten nach dem ersten Hilfsverb.

Aber auch der Wohlklang des Satzganzen und das Streben, den Zusammenhang von Sinngruppen nicht durch die Einfügung von Adverbien zu stören, sind für die Stellung der Adverbien bedeutsam.

Im allgemeinen lassen sich für die Stellung der Adverbien folgende Richtlinien geben:

1. It was extremely interesting.
The team defended themselves very bravely.
This is a very pretty frock; of course it was quite expensive.

Bestimmt das Adverb ein Adjektiv oder auch ein anderes Adverb, so steht es unmittelbar vor diesem.

Notice:

a) Are you warm enough?
He sings well enough.

a) *enough* steht stets hinter einem Adverb oder einem prädikativ gebrauchten Adjektiv;

b) This tie is very smart and cheap, too (. . . *und auch billig*).

b) *too* („auch") steht hinter dem Wort, zu dem es gehört. Das *too* wird meist durch Komma abgetrennt.

c) Did you meet anybody else?
Where else did you go on Sunday?

c) *else* („sonst") wird grundsätzlich nachgestellt.

d) Only you can know it.
You only can know it.

d) *only* kann als nähere Bestimmung zu dem einzelnen Wort vor oder hinter diesem stehen, je nach der Satzmelodie.

I can tell you only what he said.
I can only tell you what he said.
I can tell you what he said only.

Wird durch *only* ein ganzer Satz näher bestimmt, kann es, je nach dem Sinn, am Ende oder in der Mitte stehen.

2. Für Adverbien, die den Satzinhalt näher bestimmen, gilt:

a) I met him yesterday.
Tomorrow we will go to London; we will see St. Paul's there.

b) He seldom works after supper.
Mother quickly laid the table.
I had never seen him before.
She has quietly gone to bed.

c) Suddenly he felt a hand on his shoulder.
Fortunately she returned just in time.
The bells were ringing merrily

a) Adverbien des Ortes und der bestimmten Zeit stehen meist am Anfang oder am Ende des Satzes.

b) Adverbien der unbestimmten Zeit und Adverbien der Art und Weise stehen in einfachen Zeiten vor dem Verb, in zusammengesetzten Zeiten nach dem ersten Hilfsverb.

c) Bei Hervorhebung stehen jedoch auch die Adverbien der Art und Weise und die der unbestimmten Zeit am Anfang oder am Ende des Satzes.

Vgl. frz. On nous a cherchés ici. – Je l'ai vu hier. – Je fus agréablement surpris. – Tu t'es souvent trompé. – Déjà la nuit tombait.

3. She worked very hard at school last week.
He spoke well at the debate this morning.
She played the piano well at the competition last night.

Treffen am Satzende Adverbien verschiedener Art zusammen, so ist die Reihenfolge gewöhnlich:
Art und Weise – Ort – Zeit

4. He left his home never to return there again.
My parents asked me not to forget my promise.

Als Bestimmung zu einem Infinitiv stehen die Adverbien meist vor dem Infinitiv; *not* steht immer vor dem Infinitiv.

Notice:

Ein Adverb zwischen *to* und den Infinitiv zu setzen (*Split Infinitive*), sollte man vermeiden.

5. I shall give her the letter immediately.
They often took a walk together.

Prädikat und direktes Objekt werden im allgemeinen nicht durch ein Adverb getrennt. (Auch keine Sprechpause!)

(Adverb) – **Subject** – (Adverb) – **Predicate** – **Object** – (Adverb)

The Verb

Das Verb

135 The Function of Verbs — Die Funktion der Verben

Das Verb hat die Aufgabe, Vorgänge zu bezeichnen, d. h. das auszudrücken, was im Leben des Menschen und der Natur geschieht. Außerdem beschreibt es Zustände.
Das Englische hat, wie das Deutsche, eine schwache und eine starke Konjugation; sie unterscheiden sich in der Bildung des *Past Tense* und des *Past Participle*.

136 The Weak Verbs — Die schwachen Verben

	Infinitive Present	*Past*	*Past Participle*
1.	(to) ask (to) call (to) wait	asked called waited	asked [ɑːskt] called [kɔːld] waited [ˈweitid]

Die schwachen Verben bilden das *Past Tense* und das *Past Participle* durch Anfügung der Endung *-ed* an die Stammform (= Infinitiv). Nach dieser Konjugation gehen mit wenigen Ausnahmen die Verben romanischen Ursprungs und alle neu entstehenden Verben.

Notice:

Aussprache des *-s* in der *3. Pers. Sg. Present Tense*		
he calls [kɔːlz] he waits [weits] he washes [ˈwɔʃiz] he boxes [ˈbɔksiz]	he opens [ˈəupənz] he stops [stɔps] he dresses [ˈdresiz] he watches [ˈwɔtʃiz]	stimmhaft [z] nach stimmhaften Lauten; stimmlos [s] nach stimmlosen Lauten; silbisch [iz] nach Zischlauten.

Aussprache der Endung *-ed*		
he called [kɔːld] he stopped [stɔpt] he waited [ˈweitid]	he opened [ˈəupənd] he wished [wiʃt] he ended [ˈendid]	stimmhaft [d] nach stimmhaften Lauten; stimmlos [t] nach stimmlosen Lauten; silbisch [id] nach *d* und *t*.

2. Viele Verben der schwachen Konjugation bilden das *Past Tense* und das *Past Participle* nicht regelmäßig oder haben neben der regelmäßigen Form noch eine besondere. Sie sind in der Tabelle der „Verben mit besonderen Formen" (vgl. S. 285 ff.) aufgeführt und durch* gekennzeichnet.

The Strong Verbs — Die starken Verben 137

Infinitive Present	*Past*	*Past Participle*
(to) sing (he sings)	sang	sung
(to) begin	began	begun
(to) find	found	found

Die starken Verben bilden das *Present Tense* und das *Present Participle* wie die schwachen Verben, das *Past Tense* und das *Past Participle* jedoch durch Wechsel des Stammvokals (Ablaut).

Notice:

Eine Liste aller *Strong Verbs* und aller *Weak Verbs* mit unregelmäßigen Formen findet sich auf den Seiten 285 ff. Mit Hilfe der dort aufgeführten Stammformen *(principal forms)* lassen sich alle Zeitformen *(Tenses)* der Verben (vgl. S. 126 ff. und S. 149 ff.) bilden.

The Conjugation — Die Konjugation 138

Im Englischen hat das Verb (bis auf die 3. Person Sg. Präsens) alle Personalendungen verloren.

Das Englische hat nur zwei einfache, durch Person und Zahl bestimmte Zeiten: *Present Tense* und *Past Tense*. Man nennt diese auch „finite Zeiten" (*finite* [ˈfainait] *tenses*).

Ferner hat das Verb drei nicht durch Person und Zahl bestimmte Formen: *Infinitive*, *Past Participle* und die aus der Stammform mit der Endung *-ing* gebildete Form (vgl. 176, f). Man nennt diese „infinite" Verbformen (*non-finite forms*).

Alle Zeiten außer dem *Present Tense* und dem *Past Tense* werden durch Zusammensetzung der drei infiniten Formen mit Hilfsverben gebildet. Wie das im einzelnen geschieht, geht aus der folgenden Übersicht hervor.

1. The Active Voice — Das Aktiv

Tenses	Auxiliary Verbs		Ordinary Verbs: Weak Verbs	Ordinary Verbs: Strong Verbs
	to have	**to be**	**to call**	**to write**
Present Tense	I have you have he, she, it } has we have you have they have	I am you are he, she, it } is we are you are they are	I call you call he, she, it } calls we call you call they call	I write you write he, she, it } writes we write you write they write
Past Tense	I had you had he, she, it } had we had you had they had	I was you were he, she, it } was we were you were they were	I called you called he, she, it } called we called you called they called	I wrote you wrote he, she, it } wrote we wrote you wrote they wrote
Future Tense	I shall (will) have you will have he, she, it } will have we shall (will) have you will have they will have	I shall (will) be you will be he, she, it } will be we shall (will) be you will be they will be	I shall (will) call you will call he, she, it } will call we shall (will) call you will call they will call	I shall (will) write you will write he, she, it } will write we shall (will) write you will write they will write

Future in the Past and Conditional	I would (should) have you would have he / she / it } would have we would (should) have you would have they would have	I would (should) be you would be he / she / it } would be we would (should) be you would be they would be	I would (should) call you would call he / she / it } would call we would (should) call you would call they would call	I would (should) write you would write he / she / it } would write we would (should) write you would write they would write
Present Perfect	I have had	I have been	I have called	I have written
Past Perfect	I had had	I had been	I had called	I had written
Future Perfect	I shall (will) have had	I shall (will) have been	I shall (will) have called	I shall (will) have written
Future Perfect in the Past and Conditional Perfect	I would (should) have had	I would (should) have been	I would (should) have called	I would (should) have written

2. The Progressive Form — Die Verlaufsform

Present Tense:	I am calling you are calling he, she, it is calling we are calling you are calling they are calling	Past Tense:	I was calling you were calling he, she, it was calling we were calling you were calling they were calling
Future Tense:	I shall (will) be calling	Past Perfect:	I had been calling
Future in the Past:	I would (should) be calling	Future Perfect:	I shall (will) have been calling
Present Perfect:	I have been calling	Future Perfect in the Past:	I would (should) have been calling

3. The Non-finite Forms (Active) — Die infinitiven Verbformen

Infinitives		Participles	
Present:	to call	Present:	calling
Present Progressive:	to be calling	Past:	called
Perfect:	to have called	Perfect:	having called
Perfect Progressive:	to have been calling		

4. The Passive Voice — Das Passiv

Simple Present:	I am called	Simple Past:	I was called
Present Progressive:	I am being called	Past Progressive:	I was being called
Present Perfect:	I have been called	Past Perfect:	I had been called
Future:	I shall (will) be called	Future in the Past:	I would (should) be called
Future Perfect:	I shall (will) have been called	Future Perfect in the Past:	I would (should) have been called

Notice: Andere Kombinationen im Passiv sind theoretisch möglich, z. B. *Future Progressive (I will be being called)* und *Future Perfect Progressive (I will have been being called)*, aber derartige Formen sind außerordentlich selten.

5. The Non-finite Forms (Passive) — Die infinitiven Formen

Present Infinitive:	to be called	Present Participle:	being called
Perfect Infinitive:	to have been called	Perfect Participle:	having been called

Contractions — Kurzformen

a) Zusammenziehungen, auch Kurzformen genannt, sind bei Hilfsverben in der Umgangssprache sehr gebräuchlich.

to be	to have	shall/will	should/would
I'm (calling)	I've (called)	I'll (call)	I'd (call)
you're	you've	you'll	you'd
he's	he's	he'll	he'd
she's	she's	she'll	she'd
it's	it's	it'll	it'd
we're	we've	we'll	we'd
you're	you've	you'll	you'd
they're	they've	they'll	they'd

b) Zusammenziehungen bei der Verneinung mit 'not'

to be		to have		to do	
I'm not	I wasn't	I haven't	I hadn't	I don't	I didn't
you aren't	you weren't	you haven't	you hadn't	you don't	you didn't
he / she / it isn't	he / she / it wasn't	he / she / it hasn't	he / she / it hadn't	he / she / it doesn't	he / she / it didn't
we / you / they aren't	we / you / they weren't	we / you / they haven't	we / you / they hadn't	we / you / they don't	we / you / they didn't

can	could	must
cannot = can't [kaːnt]	could not = couldn't	must not = mustn't [mʌsnt]

shall	should	will
shall not = shan't [ʃaːnt]	should not = shouldn't	will not = won't [wəunt]

would	dare	need
would not = wouldn't	dare not = daren't	need not = needn't

to have

139

to have as an Ordinary Verb — to have als selbständiges Verb

1. *to have* wird als selbständiges Verb gebraucht in der Bedeutung

He has a lot of money. I have a nice book on the USA. He had a big car 10 years ago. Now he has (got) a small one.	besitzen;
They often have guests in their country home. Can you have us next week-end?	empfangen, aufnehmen;
I had lunch in a tea-shop. We were having tea when your telegram arrived.	(ein)nehmen, essen, trinken usw.

2.

I hope you are having a good time. My cousin was having his dinner when I came to see him. While Frank was in the bathroom the family were already having their breakfast.	Während das Vollverb *to have* in der Bedeutung „besitzen, haben" keine *Progressive Form* zuläßt, kann es in Verbindung mit bestimmten Substantiven in der *Progressive Form* gebraucht werden. Solche Verbindungen sind z. B.

to have a good time	es schön haben
to have dinner, breakfast	essen, frühstücken
to have fun	sich amüsieren
to have a rest, break	eine (Ruhe-)Pause einlegen
to have a bath	baden

3. Das selbständige Verb *to have* wird in Fragesätzen und in verneinten Sätzen mit *to do* umschrieben,

a) We don't have fish for breakfast. What do you usually have? Where do you usually have lunch?	a) wenn *to have* die Bedeutung (ein)-nehmen, essen, trinken usw. hat.
b) Did you have a bath this morning? Did they have a rest before leaving? Did they have a go at cricket?	b) In der Verbindung *to have + noun* muß ebenfalls die Umschreibung mit *to do* stehen.

The Mellors have got a house in the country. Have you got a house in the country, too? – Yes, we have. Or: Do you have a house in the country? – No, we don't. Many people have got a dish-washer. Has your mother got a dish-washer? – Yes, she has. Or: Does your mother have a dish-washer? – Yes, she does.	In der Umgangssprache gebraucht das *BE* im *Present Tense* immer häufiger neben *have* in der Bedeutung „besitzen, haben" die Form *have got.* In Fragen und verneinten Sätzen erfolgt in diesem Falle keine Umschreibung mit *to do*. Das *AE* zieht im allgemeinen *have* vor. Hier wird dann in Fragen und verneinten Sätzen mit *do* umschrieben.

to have as an Auxiliary Verb — to have als Hilfsverb 140

. Als Hilfsverb dient *to have* mit dem *Past Participle* zur Bildung des *Present Perfect*, *Future Perfect* und *Future Perfect in the Past* (vgl. 138).

a) I have to write my letters. We had to wait for a long time. They had to get up very early.	a) In Verbindung mit einem Infinitiv mit *to* bezeichnet *to have* eine Notwendigkeit (deutsch: müssen, zu tun haben; vgl. 158).
b) I had my hair cut the other day. Have your coat mended!	b) Mit einem direkten Objekt und *Past Participle* hat *to have* die Bedeutung „lassen", „veranlassen" (vgl. 200, 2b).

The Strong and Weak Forms of to have — Die druckstarken und druckschwachen Formen von *to have* 141

I have [aiv] given him the letter. He has [hi:z] made many mistakes. She had [ʃi:d] forgotten your phone number. I've given . . . he's made . . . She'd forgotten . . .	Die druckschwachen Formen [əv, v], [əz, z, s], [d] werden hauptsächlich gebraucht, wenn *to have* Hilfsverb in zusammengesetzten Zeiten ist. In der direkten Rede werden sie oft *'ve, 's, 'd* geschrieben.

2. Dagegen stehen die druckstarken Formen von *to have*

a) I have not [hævnt] met him. Hasn't [hæznt] she answered your letter?	a) wenn unbetontes *not* [nt] folgt;
b) He has [hæz] a lot of books.	b) wenn *to have* selbständiges Verb ist;
c) Had [hæd] he got the tickets?	c) in einer Frage, die mit einer Form von *to have* beginnt.

Notice:
Geschrieben und gedruckt werden die druckschwachen Formen heute nur, wenn eine direkte Rede wiedergegeben wird. (Als direkte Rede gilt auch der Brief; doch gebraucht man die „Kurzformen" nur in Briefen an gut bekannte Personen.)

to be

142 to be as an Ordinary Verb — to be als selbständiges Verb

1. He was in the garden.
Are there no taxis here?

to be wird in der Bedeutung „sich befinden, vorhanden sein" als selbständiges Verb gebraucht.

2. He is a clever boy.
They were very brilliant.
The Tower was a fortress in former times, but now it is a peaceful armoury.

Auch zur Verbindung von Subjekt und Prädikatsnomen wird es als selbständiges Verb gebraucht.

Notice:

Don't be silly.
Don't be angry with me.

Der verneinte Imperativ von *to be* wird stets mit *to do* umschrieben.

143 to be as an Auxiliary Verb — to be als Hilfsverb

1. They are playing in the garden.
Father is reading the newspaper.

to be + Present Participle
= Progressive Form (vgl. 138, 2; 171).

2. A loud noise was heard outside.
All the sweets had been eaten by the children.

to be + Past Participle
= Passive Voice (vgl. 138, 4; 168).

3. Mit folgendem Infinitiv mit *to* werden das *Present Tense* und das *Past Tense* von *to be* gebraucht

a) We were to meet at Euston Station. (*sollten*)
Father says you are to come at once. (*sollst*)

b) How is he to know what she will do?
How am I to do all this work today?

a) zum Ausdruck einer bestehenden Verabredung oder des Willens eines Dritten;

b) zum Ausdruck einer Frage, die einen Zweifel enthält.

I hoped to spend my holidays at the seaside, but it was not to be.○
He went to India and was to die there.○
With the Norman conquest a new period in English history was to begin.○

Das *Past Tense* von *to be* mit einem folgenden Infinitiv mit *to* bezeichnet eine Fügung, das Walten des Schicksals.

The Strong and Weak Forms of to be

Die druckstarken und druckschwachen Formen von *to be* 144

You are [juə] to go at once.
It is [its] easy.

You're to go at once.
It's easy.

Die Formen des *Present Tense* werden druckschwach gesprochen [m], [z, s], [ə], wenn der Sinngehalt des Satzes von anderen Wörtern getragen wird. In der direkten Rede werden sie oft *'m* *'re* und *'s* geschrieben.

Die druckstarken Formen von *to be* werden benutzt

a) you aren't [ɑːnt]
it isn't [iznt]
b) Are [ɑː] you happy now?

c) What is it? [wɔt'izit]
But:
What's [wɔts] that?

a) vor folgendem druckschwachen *not*;

b) in einer Frage, die mit einer Form von *to be* beginnt;

c) wenn die Form von *to be* den Druck im Satz trägt.

Notice:

Dieselben Grundsätze gelten für die druckstarken und druckschwachen Formen von *was* [wəz, wz] und *were* [wəː, wə].

Keep in Mind:	
How are you?	Wie geht es Dir?
What are you up to?	Was machen Sie denn da?
What is that to you?	Was kümmert Sie das?
Be off!	Mach', daß du fortkommst!
As it were (= so to speak), they were glad to get the money.	sozusagen
You are right (wrong).	Du hast recht (unrecht).
You are mistaken.	Du irrst dich.

My watch is fast (slow).	Meine Uhr geht vor (nach).
This book is my own.	Dies Buch gehört mir.
Here you are.	Hier! (Hier haben Sie das Gewünschte.)
There you are.	Da hast du's. (Da haben Sie das Gewünschte.)

to do

145 to do as an Ordinary Verb

to do als selbständiges Verb

Whatever you do, do it with your might.
After dinner I shall do my homework.
She does her hair with a brush every evening.

to do mit eigener Bedeutung („tun", „machen") wird als selbständiges Verb gebraucht.

He doesn't do his hair with a brush.
Did she do her homework carefully?

Das selbständige Verb *to do* wird in fragenden und verneinten Sätzen mit den Formen des Hilfsverbs *to do* verbunden.

146 to do as an Auxiliary Verb

to do als Hilfsverb

'to do' in Interrogative Sentences

to do in Fragesätzen

1. Do you know him?
Did they not go to Westminster?
Does he drive a car?
Do they do their homework carefully?

What did the man shout?
Whom did David thank for the gift?
Where does Pat live?

With whom do you go to school in the morning?
Which of the songs in your reader do you like best?
On whose farm did the family spend their holiday?

Eine Frage wird mit Hilfe von *to do* gebildet, wenn das Prädikat ein Vollverb in einer einfachen Zeit ist (*Present Tense*, *Past Tense*; Grund: Erhaltung der Wortstellung S-P-O).

. Was she reading when you entered the room?
Will he be coming home for lunch?
Can you see the plane?
What are you looking for?

Das Hilfsverb *to do* wird im Fragesatz nicht gebraucht, wenn im Prädikat des Fragesatzes ein Hilfsverb steht.

. Who came to see you?
What makes you say so?
Whose friend arrived in London?
Which boy goes to school by car?

Who did not want to go for a swim?
Whose father does not drive a car?

Ferner wird das Hilfsverb *to do* in Fragesätzen nicht gebraucht, wenn das Fragefürwort Subjekt oder mit dem Subjekt verbunden ist.

In der verneinten Frage steht natürlich auch hier *to do*.

to do in Negative Sentences — *to do* in verneinten Sätzen 147

. He does not know what to do.
Many people do not like to get up early.
There are not many boys who do not like swimming.
The water is dangerous; don't go in too far!
Please, do not cry.
Don't be so noisy, boys.

Das Hilfsverb *to do* wird in allen verneinten Sätzen gebraucht, wenn das Prädikat ein Vollverb in einer einfachen Zeit (*Present Tense*, *Past Tense*) oder ein Imperativ ist.

2. You must not cry.
The little boy could not write the word 'teeth'.
He has not come home yet.
She will not be at home in time.

Das Hilfsverb *to do* wird nicht gebraucht, wenn im Prädikat des verneinten Satzes ein Hilfsverb steht.

3. John never answers my letters.
Never mind!

Ferner steht *to do* in verneinten Sätzen nicht, wenn die Verneinung durch *never* ausgedrückt wird.
(Vgl. aber 228, 2).

4. "Is Charlie ill?" – "I hope not." "Have they come back yet?" – "I imagine not".	*to do* steht ebenfalls nicht, wenn *not* nicht den Begriff des Verbs, sondern den im vorausgehenden Satz ausgedrückten Gedanken verneint.

148 Emphatic to do — *to do* zur Hervorhebung

Durch *to do* wird der im Verb ausgedrückte Vorgang nachdrücklich hervorgehoben, und zwar

a) Bob, do get up now! Oh, do come, we'll have great fun. Children, do be quiet!	a) beim *Imperative*;
b) She does talk a lot. You do look pale. "Why didn't you call your sister?" – "I did call her, Mummy."	b) beim *Present Tense* und beim *Past Tense*.

149 to do as Substitute — *to do* als Ersatz

to do tritt als Ersatz für ein vorausgehendes selbständiges Verb ein

1. a) He does not run as fast as I do. You knew him better than I did.	a) in Vergleichssätzen;
b) "Do you understand this?" – "Yes, I do." – "No, I don't." "I like Shrewsbury." – "So do I." "I don't like working after supper." – "Nor do I."	b) in kurzen Antworten, besonders nach *yes* und *no* (vgl. *so* und *nor*, 70).

2. Erwartet der Sprechende von jemandem, den er anredet, eine Bestätigung seiner Aussage (deutsch: nicht wahr?), so wiederholt er im Englischen diese Aussage in kurzer Frageform.

My fountain-pen writes well, doesn't it?
They like swimming, don't they?
You did not go to town, did you?
He scarcely walks at all, does he?
She did not take the early train, did she?

Das Subjekt wird durch das entsprechende Personalpronomen, das Verb durch ein Hilfsverb ersetzt. – Das Hilfsverb (hier: *to do*) wird nach einer bejahenden Behauptung mit *not* verneint, nach einer verneinten Behauptung ohne *not* gebraucht.

Notice:

a) These are beautiful flowers, aren't they?
Her frock is very pretty, isn't it?
This story is not very exciting, is it?
The boys' bicycles are not particularly clean, are they?
Mrs. Rogers has got a new handbag, hasn't she?
Mr. Brown had not got a new car, had he?
You can't come today, can you?
That will do, won't it?

a) Wie *to do* im Sinne des deutschen „nicht wahr?" können auch andere Hilfsverben gebraucht werden, z. B. *to be*, *to have*, *can*, *will*, *etc.*

b) She can scarcely write her own name, can she?
Hardly anybody believes that, does he?

b) *scarcely* und *hardly* („kaum") geben dem Satz einen negativen Sinn, deshalb wirken sie wie eine Verneinung.

. Die bejahende Aussage wird nicht verneint wiederholt

a) Stop shouting, will you!
Pass the butter, will you?
Let's go home now, shall we?

a) wenn der Satz einen Imperativ enthält (Die Wiederholungsformen sind in diesem Falle immer *will you* oder *shall we*.);

b) You found this money in the street, did you?
She's thinking of marrying him, is she?
'The doctor told me to stay in bed.' – 'Did he?'
'You can leave early today.' – 'Can I really? Thank you.'

b) wenn in der Wiederholungsfrage Erstaunen, Zweifel, Freude, Erregung oder Überraschung ausgedrückt werden soll. (Die Wiederholungsfrage kann vom Sprecher selbst oder von seinem Gesprächspartner ausgesprochen werden.)

Keep in Mind:	
How do you do?	Wie geht es Ihnen? (Grußformel)
That will do.	Das genügt.
That won't do.	Das genügt nicht.
I can do without it.	Ich kann ohne es auskommen.
I cannot do without my cup of tea.	Ich kann nicht ohne meinen Tee auskommen.
It will do you good.	Es wird Ihnen gut tun.
It will do no good.	Es wird nichts helfen.
This act does him little credit.	Diese Handlung macht ihm wenig Ehre.
Have done!△	Hör' auf!
Have you done?△	Sind Sie fertig?
I have done eating.△	Ich bin fertig mit Essen.
Well done!	Bravo!
I am done.	Ich bin erschöpft.
I am done for.	Es ist um mich geschehen.
I have done with him.	Zwischen ihm und mir ist es aus.

150 Special Use of to do

Besonderheiten im Gebrauch von *to do*

1. They did not have a nice summer holiday.
Did you have a nice time?
Did you have a good concert?
We did not have much rain this summer.

Sehr häufig findet sich die Umschreibung mit *to do* neben vereinzelten nicht umschriebenen Formen bei *to have* in der Bedeutung: „erleben, geistig genießen, verbringen".

2. Ein Vordringen der Umschreibung mit *to do* ist zu beobachten in Fällen, in denen *to have* folgende Bedeutungen hat:

a) Do English boys all have pocket-money?
They did not have walking-sticks, because they did not want them.
Why do you all have red and yellow shirts?

a) „zur Verfügung haben (halten), zur Hand haben"
„bei sich führen"
„an sich tragen"

b) Do they have many visitors in winter?
We don't have children here.

b) „Verwandte, Freunde, Gäste usw. haben"

c) They did not have the ability to carry on the argument.

c) „als geistiges Eigentum besitzen",

d) Do you have much time for your garden?
I don't have colds as a general rule.
Do you often have headaches?

d) „Zeit haben"
„Krankheiten haben"
„Schmerzen haben"

Ein Vordringen der Umschreibung mit *to do* ist ferner zu beobachten

a) Do you have much work to do? Most popular histories do not have much to say about that event.	a) in der verneinten oder fragenden Verbindung *to have* + Objekt + Infinitiv;
b) I don't often have my window open now. Does she have your dinner ready? Didn't you have your names or numbers pinned on you? Why do you have that workman here?	b) in der Verbindung *to have* + Objekt + prädikatives Adjektiv, Partizip oder Adverb

Die Umschreibung mit *to do* erfolgt meistens in Allgemeinfällen oder in der Emphase. Daneben spielt auch der Satzrhythmus eine Rolle.

The Defective Auxiliary Verbs — Die unvollständigen Hilfsverben 151

Die unvollständigen Hilfsverben (Man nennt sie auch modale Hilfsverben, *modal auxiliaries,* von Lat. modus = Art und Weise.) bringen zum Ausdruck, wie der Sprechende sich innerlich zu dem im Verb angegebenen Vorgang verhält oder welche Stellung er dazu einnimmt. Sie drücken aus, daß eine Tätigkeit ausgeführt werden

kann	darf	soll	muß
konnte	durfte	sollte	mußte
(könnte)	(dürfte)	(sollte)	(müßte).

Simple Present	*Simple Past*	*Substitutes*
I can	I could	to be able to
I may	I might	to be allowed to, to be permitted to
I shall	I should	to be to, to be supposed to
I will	I would	to want, to wish, to desire, to mean, to intend to
I must	—	to have to, to be obliged to, to be forced to, to be compelled to
—	I ought to	—
—	I used to	I was in the habit of; I would
dare	dared	to dare
need	—	to need

Wie der Name schon andeutet (*defective* = unvollständig), kann man von den *Defective Auxiliaries* nicht alle Zeiten bilden; sie haben keinen Infinitiv und keine Partizipien. Sie kommen nur im *Present Tense* und *Past Tense* vor. Infinitive, Partizipien und die zusammengesetzten Zeiten müssen durch Umschreibung oder durch sinnverwandte Verben (*Substitutes*) ersetzt werden. Beim Gebrauch der *Defective Auxiliaries* ist zu beachten:

a) He must go to school. She can sing well.	a) Die 3. Person des Präsens Singular hat kein *s*.
b) Can you lend me fifty pence? "May I come in?" – "No, you may not (come in)."	b) Die fragenden und verneinenden Formen werden nicht mit *to do* umschrieben.
c) I can do it (= *Ich kann* es). I can speak English (= *Ich kann Englisch*). I must go home (= *Ich muß nach Hause*).	c) Die Defective Auxiliaries können kein direktes Objekt bei sich haben; ihnen folgt stets ein Infinitiv ohne *to*.
d) "Can you speak English?" – "Yes, I can." He will do what he can.	d) Der Infinitiv wird ausgelassen, wenn er unmittelbar vorher gebraucht wurde.

The Defective Auxiliaries in Particular

Die unvollständigen Hilfsverben im einzelnen

152

can – could

1. He can see better with his glasses on.
They cannot speak Russian.
I could not see his point.

can, could bezeichnen die körperliche und geistige Fähigkeit (deutsch: kann, können; konnte, konnten);

2. That seat is empty. You can sit down.
You can't go in there. It's private.
I couldn't leave, because there was a rail strike.

But:
There was an empty seat behind her, so she was able to sit down.
As we had a day off yesterday, we were able to spend the afternoon at the beach.

can, could bezeichnen ferner die durch äußere Umstände gegebene Möglichkeit (deutsch: kann, können; konnte, konnten).

Aber:
In bejahenden Sätzen, in denen eine in der Vergangenheit erfüllte Möglichkeit ausgedrückt wird, muß *was able, were able* an Stelle von *could* gebraucht werden.

3. You can go for a swim after lunch.
She can have this book when I have read it.

can bezeichnet oft die Erlaubnis (deutsch: kann, darf).

Can I go to the cinema tonight? Can we go for a swim in the afternoon? Can we go to the art exhibition in the museum?	Eine Bitte um Erlaubnis wird im Umgangsenglisch oft mit *can* ausgedrückt.
What can he mean? What can they want?	Druckstarkes *can* drückt in Fragen Erstaunen oder Ungeduld aus (deutsch: „Was kann er nur meinen?").
We could tour Europe in a fortnight if we had got a car. I could come earlier if necessary.	*could* bezeichnet auch Handlungen, die nur unter gewissen Voraussetzungen möglich sind (deutsch: könnte). Vgl. 238 f.

Notice:

He knows English (= He can speak English). She knew how to make her own dresses (= She could make her own dresses).	*can* + Vollverb im Sinne von „wissen, verstehen", kann auch durch *to know* wiedergegeben werden.

Substitute Form for can, could	
We have been able to buy the tickets. Florence Nightingale was convinced that she would be able to help the wounded. As soon as the strike ended, I was able to leave the town.	to be able to

may – might 153

May I take my tennis racket with me? They asked their parents if they might go to play in the field.	*may, might* bezeichnen die Erlaubnis (deutsch: darf, durfte, dürfte). Vgl. 152.4.

Notice:

"May I go out now?" – "No, you may not, Father does not want you to go."	*may not* (= darf nicht) ist nur in der Antwort auf eine Frage mit *may* möglich; sonst aber heißt es *must not* (vgl. 158, 2).

2. It may rain today. His story may not be true. She has not come yet; she might have missed the bus.	*may, might* bezeichnen die denkbare Möglichkeit (deutsch: kann, könnte möglicherweise).

Notice:

He might have read the book. *Er hätte das Buch eigentlich lesen können.*	Aus dem Zusammenhang und der Intonation geht hervor, wie das *might* zu verstehen ist. Hier ist das *read* [red] betont, und der ganze Satz enthält einen Vorwurf.

Substitute Forms for may, might	
If they had asked their father, they would have been allowed to go to London („ . . . *hätten fahren dürfen.*“).	to be allowed to
Stanley said to Livingstone: “I thank God, Doctor, I have been permitted to see you.”	to be permitted to

154 shall – should

1. *shall* dient neben *will* zur Bildung der 1. Pers. Sg. und Pl. *Future Tense* (164) und mit *have* zur Bildung der 1. Pers. Sg. und Pl. *Future Perfect* (165). *should* kann neben dem heute gebräuchlicheren *would* zur Bildung der 1. Pers. Sg. und Pl. *Future in the Past* (166) und *Condiional,* mit *have* zur Bildung der 1. Pers. Sg. und Pl. *Future Perfect in the Past* (167) und *Conditional Perfect* gebraucht werden.
In der Umgangssprache wird für *shall* mehr und mehr *will* (gesprochen [l] und oft geschrieben *'ll*), für *should* in dieser Bedeutung heute fast ausschließlich *would* gebraucht.

2. Shall I open the window? Shall I tell him our secret? Shall we meet at your house next time? Shall we lay the table?	*shall* wird im heutigen Englisch in Fragen nur in der 1. Person Sg. (*shall I?* = soll ich? = Angebot) und in der 1. Person Pl. (*shall we?* = sollen wir? = Vorschlag) gebraucht. Der Sprecher fragt nach dem Willen des Angeredeten.

3. You should not speak to him like that.
He should be more careful.
I should really visit my grandmother more often.
Should teachers be better paid? What do you think?
You should have helped that poor man.
(„Du hättest . . . helfen sollen.")

should drückt eine sittliche Verpflichtung aus (deutsch: ich sollte eigentlich; vgl. *ought to*, 155).

4. *shall* wird heute nur noch selten gebraucht, um Befehle, Versprechen und Drohungen auszudrücken. In den folgenden Beispielen wird gezeigt, welche Wendungen im modernen Umgangsenglisch an die Stelle von *shall* in dieser Bedeutung treten.

a) (You shall not smoke.△)
(They shall start work immediately.△)
You are not to smoke.
You mustn't smoke.
I don't want you to smoke.
They are to start work immediately.
They must start work immediately.
I want them to start work immediately.

a) Befehl des Sprechenden

b) (You shall go to the cinema if you are good.△)
You can go to the cinema if . . .
You'll be allowed to go to the cinema if . . .
I'll let you go to the cinema if . . .

b) Versprechen des Sprechenden

c) (He shan't have any ice-cream unless he behaves himself.△)
He won't have any ice-cream unless . . .
He's not going to have any ice-cream unless . . .
He won't be allowed to have any ice-cream unless . . .
I won't let him have any ice-cream unless . . .

c) Drohung des Sprechenden

Substitute Forms for shall, should

5\. a) I am to be at the station at six o'clock, so I am told.
Apparently Mr. Smith is not to be disturbed: he has an important visitor in his office.
Father says you are not to use his typewriter.
The exhibition is to be opened by the Queen.

a) to be to
wird gebraucht, wenn der Sprecher Anweisungen, die von anderen gegeben werden, oder Vereinbarungen, die von anderen getroffen werden, wiedergibt.

b) The hockey match was to have taken place yesterday.
I was to have met her at the station but I completely forgot.

b) *Past Tense of* 'to be' + *Perfect Infinitive*
wird gebraucht um auszudrücken, daß Vereinbarungen oder Verabredungen (in der Vergangenheit) nicht erfüllt bzw. eingehalten worden sind.

c) The hockey match was supposed to take place yesterday.
I was supposed to meet her at the station, but I completely forgot.
You were supposed to be here at nine o'clock. Why are you late?

c) Im gesprochenen Englisch wird sehr häufig der Ausdruck
was (were) supposed to
gebraucht, um auszudrücken, daß eine Vereinbarung oder Verabredung nicht eingehalten, eine Anweisung nicht befolgt worden ist.

d) Don't tell anyone you've seen me: I'm not supposed to be here.
Don't open the window like that. This is how you're supposed to open it.

d) to be supposed to
wird im Present Tense an Stelle von *should* gebraucht, um einen ähnlichen Sachverhalt wie in c) auszudrücken.

e) His father is said (supposed) to be very rich.
The west coast of Ireland is said (supposed) to be very beautiful.

e) Deutsch „sollen" heißt im Englischen to be said to oder
to be supposed to
wenn von Gerüchten oder vom Hörensagen die Rede ist.

ought to 155

1. | Never put off till tomorrow what you ought to do today.
I ought to have done it at once. | *ought to* bezeichnet noch stärker als *should* (vgl. 154, 3) eine sittliche Verpflichtung (deutsch: ich sollte eigentlich). |
|---|---|

2. | As the bicycle was so expensive, it ought to be good.
If it is a travel film, it ought to be interesting. | *ought to* drückt ferner eine große Wahrscheinlichkeit aus. |
|---|---|

will – would 156

1. I most certainly will tell him what I think of him.
He really will help you, I assure you.
This time we will win the tournament.
I really will not tolerate this nonsense.
Of course people laughed at him; he would ask such silly questions.
He was tired, but he simply wouldn't go home.

will, would drücken, wenn sie stark betont werden, den Willen, die Entschlossenheit aus. Die starke Betonung wird häufig durch vorangestellte Adverbien erzielt.

Notice:

I would it were true. △
I wish it were true.

An Stelle von *would* („wollte, wünschte") in Verbindung mit der Konjunktivform *were* wird heute *wish* gebraucht.

2. In the morning he will go for a walk.
He would sit up late in the night working.

will und *would* bezeichnen Handlungen, die gewohnheitsmäßig (vgl. 157) geschehen (deutsch: „pflegen" oder ein Adverb wie „oft", „immer").

3.	Boys will be boys. Accidents will happen.	*will* drückt allgemeingültige Erfahrungstatsachen aus (deutsch: „eben“, „halt“, „nun einmal“).

Substitute Forms **for will, would**	
Peter Minuit said that he wanted to buy the Island which the Indians called Manhattan. Henry Hudson had wished to find a passage to China. I had intended to go to town now. He meant to do it immediately. What are you going to do now? *Was willst du jetzt tun?* At first Dick Whittington was not willing to part with his cat.	to want to wish to intend to to mean to to be going to to be willing to

157 used to

She used to live in the country. He used to be a keen footballer. We used to have a game every other day.	*used to* in Verbindung mit dem Infinitiv drückt aus, was früher dauernd oder gewohnheitsmäßig geschah (deutsch: pflegte [zu tun]).

Notice:

My father is in the habit of smoking his pipe when reading the newspaper. My mother had the habit of lying down for an hour after lunch. He was used to getting up early and working till late in the night.	Neben *used to* und *will, would* für deutsch „zu tun pflegen“ kann auch stehen: *to be in the habit of + Gerund; to have the habit of + Gerund; to be used to + Gerund.*

158 must

1. *must* steht in Hauptsätzen nur im *Present Tense*. Für die anderen Zeiten treten Ersatzformen ein.

a) All men must die. We must leave earlier tomorrow. He told us: “You must all be at the station at six o'clock.”	a) *must* bezeichnet eine Notwendigkeit oder einen Zwang, oft auch einen Befehl (deutsch: muß, müssen).

b) They must be at home now.
He must be successful, for he has studied hard.
"Why isn't she here?" – "She must have missed the bus."
You must have known (you surely knew) what I meant.

b) *must* bezeichnet ferner eine Wahrscheinlichkeit, die Vermutung, daß etwas fast sicher ist (deutsch: muß, müssen, „es ist kaum anders denkbar", „es ist sicher").

You must not touch the ball with your hands.
Children must not play here.

must not drückt ein Verbot aus (deutsch: darf nicht, dürfen nicht). (Vgl. *may not*, 153, 1; Notice.)

He said that he must leave in a minute.
She said they must do as they were told.

In Nebensätzen kann *must* auch das *Past Tense* bezeichnen. Das ist der Fall, wenn der Sinnzusammenhang eindeutig auf die Vergangenheit hinweist.

Substitute Forms for must	
The Celts had to build roads for the Romans.	to have to
I have (got) to write a letter to my uncle. You have (got) to do this, haven't you?	to have (got) to
In most countries children are obliged to go to school.	to be obliged to
He was forced to work hard.	to be forced to
They were compelled to stop playing as it began to rain (began raining).	to be compelled to

(to) dare; (to) need 159

(*to*) *dare* und (*to*) *need* werden sowohl als selbständige Verben wie als Hilfsverben gebraucht. Den Hilfsverben *need* und *dare* folgt ein Infinitiv ohne *to*; die 3. Person Präsens erhält kein Endungs-s; in den fragenden und verneinten Formen werden *dare* und *need* nicht mit *to do* umschrieben.

1. How dare you speak to your mother like that?
She dared not return home.
He dare not come.
Dare he go alone?
He hardly dared speak to her.

Das Hilfsverb *dare* (deutsch: wagen, sich getrauen) wird im *Present Tense* und im *Past Tense* fragender und verneinter Sätze gebraucht.
Adverbien wie *hardly, never* wirken wie eine Verneinung.

2. He does not dare (to) ask.
Don't dare (to) touch me.
I would never dare (to) disturb him when he sleeps.
She would never dare (to) interrupt his speech.

dare kann in verneinenden und fragenden Sätzen auch mit *do* umschrieben werden. Dem *dare* kann dann entweder ein Infinitiv mit oder ohne *to* folgen.

3. He dares to criticize her.
We dared to call him a fool.

In bejahenden Sätzen folgt dem *dare* ein Infinitiv mit *to* und die 3. Pers. Sg. Präs. enthält ein Endungs-s.

4. American engineers dared new ways to keep the expanding piles of waste down to a manageable size.

Folgt ein direktes Objekt, so steht das Vollverb *to dare.*

Notice:

I dare say she will come soon.

„ich kann wohl sagen; ich glaube wohl; vermutlich"

5. I need not tell you that I was highly delighted.
You need not mention that you expect me to work.
He need not write the letter immediately.

Das Hilfsverb *need* steht nur im *Simple Present* und nur in Sätzen mit negativem Sinn; zu *need not, needn't* gehört immer ein Infinitiv ohne *to* (deutsch: ich brauche nicht zu ...).

6. He did not need any help.
They do not need any more money.
Does he really need to go?
He does not need a dictionary to translate this newspaper article.
His hair needs cutting badly.

need (deutsch: notwendig sein, nötig haben, müssen) wird wie ein selbständiges Verb gebraucht, in bejahenden, verneinenden und fragenden Sätzen. Das Vollverb *need* bildet also die verneinte und die fragende Form mit *do* und schließt einen nachfolgenden Infinitiv mit *to* an.

Notice:

There was no need to run.
There was no need for him to complain.

„Ich brauche (brauchte) nicht zu ..." wird oft durch *there is (was) no need (for s.b.) to* ausgedrückt.

The Tenses

Die Zeiten

The Present Tense

Das Präsens

160

1. It is 8 o'clock in the morning;
Bob leaves the house for school.
He goes to the garage and gets his bicycle.

Das *Present Tense* wird gebraucht, um Tatsachen und Vorgänge der Gegenwart darzustellen.

2. Tigers live in India.
Postmen deliver mail.
It's the early bird that catches the worm.
Christmas comes but once a year.

Das *Present Tense* drückt ferner aus, daß etwas immer so ist oder immer wieder geschieht.

3. I write my letters with a fountain-pen.
After supper, he works a little in the garden, and then he goes to bed early.

After dinner we go for a walk.
Many people go to the seaside in summer.
John often arrives at school late.
Most people wear woollen clothes in winter.

Das *Present Tense* bezeichnet immer wiederkehrende, gewohnheitsmäßige Handlungen.

Das *Present Tense* steht in diesen Fällen oft in Verbindung mit einem Adverb oder mit einer adverbialen Bestimmung der Zeit.

4. Bob is riding his bicycle.
His sister is writing a letter.

Gegenwärtige Vorgänge von vorübergehender Dauer werden durch die *Progressive Form Present Tense* dargestellt (vgl. *Progr. Form*, 171).

5. She loves her mother dearly.
I like my English lessons very much.
We often remember the pleasant holiday we had with you.

Bei den Verben, die Handlungen oder Vorgänge von Dauer ausdrücken, steht das *Simple Present Tense*, nicht die *Progressive Form* (vgl. 171,5).

Notice:

I saw him once, but I forget where it was.

Man beachte den Gebrauch des *Present Tense* von *to forget* im Sinne von „ich kann mich jetzt nicht mehr erinnern".

6. In der Umgangssprache können für die Zukunft geplante Handlungen oder Vorgänge durch das *Present Tense* ausgedrückt werden, und zwar

a) We leave for Edinburgh tomorrow and then we go to the Highlands. I come to see you next Sunday.	a) in Hauptsätzen, wenn Zeitbestimmungen auf die Zukunft hinweisen (vgl. aber 164);
b) I'll come to see you before you leave. I can't wait till he comes.	b) in Nebensätzen mit einer in die Zukunft weisenden Konjunktion wie: before till until

161 The Present Perfect — Das Perfekt

Das *Present Perfect* stellt eine Beziehung zwischen der Vergangenheit und der Gegenwart her.

1.

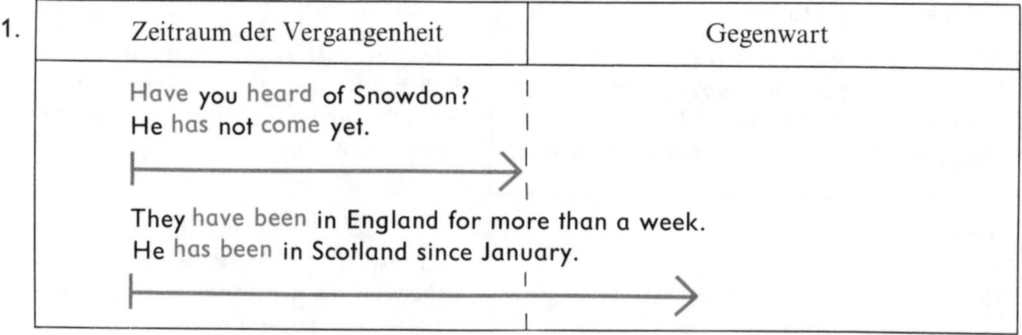

Zeitraum der Vergangenheit
Gegenwart
Have you heard of Snowdon?
He has not come yet.
They have been in England for more than a week.
He has been in Scotland since January.

Das *Present Perfect* wird gebraucht, wenn ein Vorgang oder ein Zustand, der in der Vergangenheit begonnen hat, bis an die Gegenwart heranreicht oder in der Gegenwart noch andauert. (Das Deutsche gebraucht in diesen Fällen oft das Präsens mit „schon"; vgl. obiges Bsp.: „Sie sind schon länger als eine Woche in England.")

2.

I met him two years ago and he has been a good friend of mine ever since. Our cat has been losing a lot of hair lately. Several space-ships have been launched recently. The plane has just passed a big ocean liner.	Wenn Zeitbestimmungen auf einen bis zur Gegenwart reichenden Zeitraum hinweisen, steht das *Present Perfect*. (Bei den in der folgenden Liste rot gedruckten Zeitbestimmungen kann auch das *Past Tense* stehen; vgl. 162, 4.)

up to the present up till now up to now so far as yet	bis jetzt
not yet	bis jetzt noch nicht
since then	seit damals bis heute
ever since	seitdem
for two years	während der jetzt vergangenen zwei Jahre, zwei Jahre lang
these last five years	während der jetzt vergangenen fünf Jahre

in my life	in meinem Leben, während meines Lebens
this year	in diesem Jahr (schon)
this week	in dieser Woche
this morning	heute morgen
lately	kürzlich, vor kurzem
recently	unlängst, vor kurzem
already	schon
just	gerade

Notice:

Bei *since* und *for* steht das *Present Perfect*, wenn der Zeitraum bis an die Gegenwart heranreicht (vgl. *Past Tense*, 162).

a) He has lived in New York since Easter 1961. I have known Uncle Eric since his first visit to England.	a) *since* bezeichnet den Zeitpunkt, seit wann eine Handlung oder ein Zustand andauert.
b) "How long has he been here?" – "He has been here for three months." (= *drei Monate lang; seit drei Monaten*) She has not slept for two nights.	b) *for* bezeichnet einen Zeitraum.

3.

Zeitraum der Vergangenheit	Gegenwart
have opened	(and it is still open).
has lost	(and he has not found it yet).
have had	(and here it is).

Das *Present Perfect* bezeichnet ferner einen Vorgang, der zwar in der Vergangenheit abgeschlossen ist, dessen Ergebnis oder Folge aber für die Gegenwart noch gilt. Das in der Gegenwart liegende Ergebnis soll hier noch mitberücksichtigt werden. (Enthält ein Satz aber eine Zeitbestimmung wie *ago*, *last night*, *yesterday*, *last week* etc., so muß natürlich *Past Tense* gebraucht werden.)

4.	
He has been writing letters for three hours. *Er schreibt schon seit drei Stunden (drei Stunden lang) Briefe.* How long have you been learning English? *Wie lange hast du schon Englisch?*	Zur Bezeichnung eines Geschehens, das in der Vergangenheit begonnen hat und in der Gegenwart noch andauert, steht meist die *Progressive Form* des *Present Perfect* (vgl. 171).
I have always disliked washing-up. The house has belonged to my grandfather since 1952.	Die *Ordinary Form* des *Present Perfect* steht nur bei den Verben, die keine *Progressive Form* bilden können (vgl. 171).

162 The Past Tense — Die Vergangenheit

1.

Zeitraum der Vergangenheit	Gegenwart
Last year my father flew to New York.	

Das *Past Tense* bezeichnet Vorgänge oder Handlungen, die der Vergangenheit angehören und in ihr völlig abgeschlossen wurden.

The Normans conquered England. In 1588, Sir Francis Drake defeated the Armada. I saw him yesterday. Last week we visited the zoo. He met her the other day. When was your friend born? Six weeks ago, he returned from the States. He did it many years ago. Formerly I used to go for a walk every evening.	Das *Past Tense* steht dabei vor allem bei geschichtlichen Tatsachen (Frage: *when?*) und bei Zeitangaben, die auf die Vergangenheit hinweisen, wie yesterday — last night — last week last year — once — the other day when? ago (= heute vor) (long) ago, long since△ (= vor langer Zeit) formerly (= früher) not long ago (= vor kurzem)

2. “Once upon a time, there was a donkey who was too old to work, so he ran away from home. He wanted to go to Bremen to make music there . . .”

Das *Past Tense* ist die Zeitform des Erzählers. Im *Past Tense* werden aufeinanderfolgende Vorgänge der Vergangenheit wiedergegeben.

3. When I was cycling home from school yesterday, I met Uncle Jim.
They were having supper when the lights went out suddenly.

Vorgänge von vorübergehender Dauer, die sich im Zeitraum der Vergangenheit abspielen, werden durch die *Progressive Form, Past Tense* dargestellt (vgl. 171).

4.

Past Tense	*Present Perfect*
I saw him this morning on my way to school.	I have not seen him this morning, but I hope to see him before I go to bed.
She did not sleep for two nights; last night, however, she slept soundly.	She has not slept for two nights; before going to bed tonight she must take some sleeping-pills.
He lived in London for two years; that was between 1970 and 1972.	He has lived in London for two years and is getting on very well there.

Bei einer Reihe von Zeitbestimmungen kann das *Past Tense* oder das *Present Perfect* stehen, je nachdem, ob der Sprechende den Zeitraum als in der Vergangenheit abgeschlossen oder ihn als bis zur Gegenwart reichend ansieht. Solche Zeitbestimmungen sind z. B.

today	this morning	always	never	for (some time)
recently	a short time ago	ever	since	

(Vgl. 161, 2)

The Past Perfect — Das Plusquamperfekt 163

1.

The train had already arrived	when I got to the station.
Bob had finished his homework	before his father came home.
Past Perfect	Past

Das *Past Perfect* bezeichnet (wie das Plusquamperfekt im Deutschen) Vorgänge oder Zustände, die vor einem in der Vergangenheit liegenden Zeitpunkt abgeschlossen waren. Ein Satz im *Past Perfect* steht immer im Sinnzusammenhang mit einem Satz im *Past Tense*.

2. How long *had* you *known* him before he moved to the country?
We had *been wandering* for hours when we arrived at a small village.

Past Perfect — Past

Das *Past Perfect* bezeichnet ferner Handlungen oder Zustände, die vor einem Zeitpunkt der Vergangenheit begannen und zu diesem Zeitpunkt noch andauerten. (Im Deutschen steht in diesen Fällen oft die Vergangenheit mit „schon".)

164 The Future — Das Futur

1.

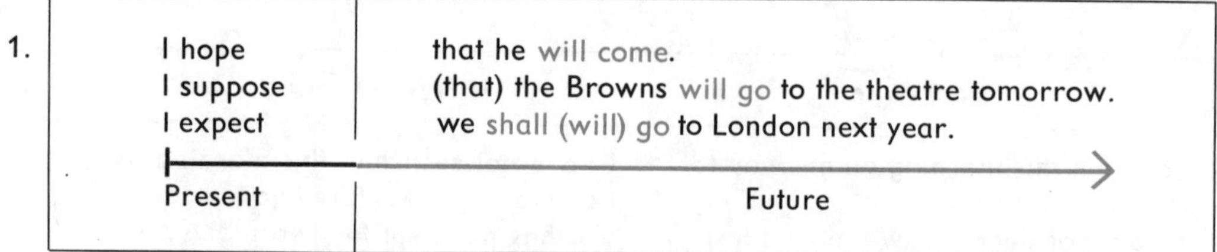

I hope
I suppose
I expect
that he will come.
(that) the Browns will go to the theatre tomorrow.
we shall (will) go to London next year.
Present
Future

Das Futur bezeichnet einen Vorgang, der, von der Gegenwart aus gesehen, in der Zukunft liegt. Das Englische hat mehrere Möglichkeiten, zukünftige Geschehnisse auszudrücken.

2. Eine dieser Möglichkeiten ist das *Future Tense*. Die 2. und 3. Pers. Sg. und Pl. des *Future Tense* wird gebildet durch *will* + Infinitivform.
Das Hilfsverb für die erste Pers. Sg. und Pl. ist zwar immer noch *shall*, aber in der Umgangssprache wird dafür mehr und mehr *will* (gesprochen [l] und oft *'ll* geschrieben) gebraucht.

Das Englische ist in der Kennzeichnung zukünftiger Ereignisse genauer als das Deutsche.

a) Tomorrow they will drive to the sea.
Morgen fahren sie an die See.
I shall (will) leave for the USA next week.
In der nächsten Woche fahre ich ab nach den USA.
When shall (will) we see you again?
Wann sehen wir dich wieder?

b) I hope she will soon be well again.
Do you think that he will leave tomorrow?
I expect they will be back soon.
I suppose (that) you will get a prize.
You must promise that you will visit us.
(You must promise to visit us.)

a) Im Englischen steht in der literarischen Sprache meist auch dann noch das Futur, wenn schon durch eine Zeitbestimmung deutlich gemacht wird, daß die Handlung oder der Vorgang sich in der Zukunft abspielt (vgl. aber 160, 6). Im Deutschen steht hier meist das Präsens.

b) Das *Future Tense* muß stets gebraucht werden bei Verben, die in die Zukunft weisen, z. B.
to hope — to expect — to suppose
to promise — to think
(Auch Infinitivkonstruktion bei einigen dieser Verben möglich!)

Englische Aussprache, Schreibung, Wortwahl und Grammatik müssen auch in der Oberstufe noch gefestigt werden.
Diese Aufgabe erleichtert:

How to Avoid Mistakes

Ein Lernbuch + 3 Übungsbücher + Compact-Cassette
von Hans Brinkmann.

»How to Avoid Mistakes« bietet: eine Zusammenstellung wichtiger Wörter, die häufig falsch ausgesprochen oder falsch geschrieben werden / eine übersichtliche Darstellung der Veränderungen in Wortbildung und Flexion / Besonderheiten der englischen Rechtschreibung / ausgewählte Synonyme / Behandlung der wichtigsten Präpositionen / kurze Darstellung typischer Schwierigkeiten bei den übrigen Wortarten in einfachen Mustersätzen / stammverwandte, leicht verwechselbare Wörter in Beispielsätzen / trügerische Wörter, die oft zu falschen Deutungen führen, einschließlich der richtigen Übersetzung.

Die Übungsbücher befassen sich mit: »Pronunciation and Spelling« (+ Compact-Cassette), »Choice of Words« und »Forms and Structures«.

Alles in allem:
Ein ideales Lern- und Trainings-Paket für die Sekundarstufe II

Hiermit bestelle ich:

.... **How to Avoid Mistakes**
VIII + 148 Seiten — Linson DM 24,80 (MD-Nr. 4101)

Dazu die Übungsbücher:

Practise Avoiding Mistakes

.... **Part I: Pronunciation and Spelling** — 57 Seiten, DM 10,80 (MD-Nr. 4121)

.... **Tonmaterialien zu Part I** (Compact-Cassette)
Laufzeit ca. 74 Min. — unverbindlich empf. Preis DM 30,— (MD-Nr. 8621)

.... **Part II: Choice of Words** — 68 Seiten, DM 12,80 (MD-Nr. 4122)

.... **Part III: Forms and Structures** — 132 Seiten, DM 18,80 (MD-Nr. 4123)

Außerdem benötige ich:

.... **Grammar in Review**
Grammatischer Intensivkurs Englisch Sekundarstufe II
VIII + 155 Seiten — DM 23,80 (MD-Nr. 4124)

....

Datum — Unterschrift (ggf. des Erziehungsberechtigten)

Die angegebenen Preise verstehen sich ggf. zuzüglich Versandkosten und Nachnahmegebühren.

Preise gültig für 1993 · Änderungen vorbehalten · Bitte Absenderangaben auf der Rückseite nicht vergessen!

Zukünftige Geschehnisse werden sehr häufig durch *to be going to* ausgedrückt.

a) Jack said that he was going to write the letter tomorrow.
I am certainly not going to put up with this noise any longer.
I am going to visit my aunt on Sunday. (I intend to visit her ...)
My brother is going to start learning Russian soon. (He intends to start ...)

a) *to be going to* wird besonders dann gebraucht, wenn eine Absicht des Sprechenden ausgedrückt werden soll.

b) The weather forecast says that it is not going to rain this weekend.
People say we are going to have a cold winter this year.
If he goes on driving as recklessly as that he is going to kill himself some day.

b) *to be going to* drückt (außer einer Absicht) auch eine Wahrscheinlichkeit oder eine Zuversicht aus.

They are about to leave the house.
I was on the point of doing my maths when the telephone rang.

Wenn eine Handlung unmittelbar bevorsteht, drückt man das gern durch *to be about to* oder *to be on the point of* aus.

They are going to Brighton for the weekend.
Is Bill coming tonight?
Are you leaving with your friend?
I am writing to him tomorrow.
He is arriving in town tomorrow.

Eine meist für die nahe Zukunft geplante oder beabsichtigte Handlung wird bei Verben der Bewegung wie *to go*, *to come*, *to arrive*, *to leave* und bei einigen anderen Verben auch durch die Form von *to be* + *Present Participle* ausgedrückt (vgl. 172,2).

In der Umgangssprache können für die Zukunft geplante Handlungen durch das *Simple Present Tense* ausgedrückt werden. Vgl. dazu 160,6.

The Future Perfect — Das zweite Futur 165

I shall (will) have finished my letter by midnight.
Next May, they will have lived in this town for ten years.

Das *Future Perfect* bezeichnet wie im Deutschen einen Vorgang, der an einem Zeitpunkt der Zukunft abgeschlossen sein wird.

166 The Future in the Past and the Conditional

Das Futur der Vergangenheit und das Konditional

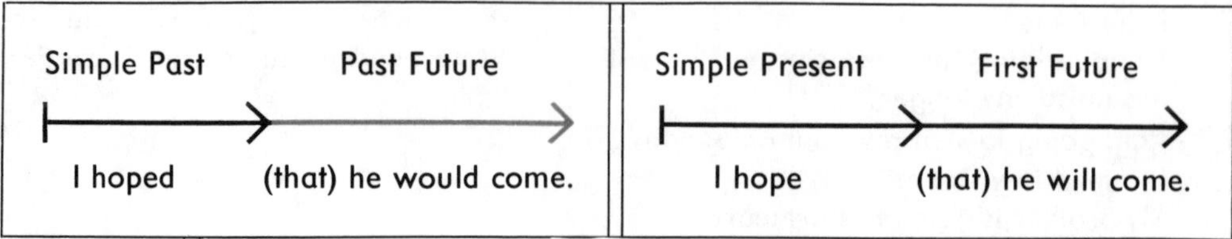

1. She sent us a letter to tell us that she would be back on Sunday.

   He came to see me in the hope that I would (should) help him.

   The manager informed his secretary that he would not be in the office on Monday.

Das *Future in the Past* bezeichnet, von einem Zeitpunkt der Vergangenheit aus gesehen, einen Vorgang, der noch nicht geschehen war, also (von diesem Zeitpunkt aus gesehen) noch in der Zukunft lag.

2. If wishes were horses, beggars would ride.
   If he had any money at all, he would give me some.
   If Father had a holiday, we would (should) go to the seaside.

Formgleich mit dem *Future in the Past* ist das *Conditional*. Das *Conditional* drückt aus, was geschehen würde, wenn eine Bedingung oder Voraussetzung erfüllt wäre (vgl. *Conditional Clauses*, 238, 239).

167 The Future Perfect in the Past and the Conditional Perfect

Das zweite Futur der Vergangenheit und das zweite Konditional

1. He thought that he would have finished his work on Monday.
   She believed that she would have got her examination result by 1st October.

Das *Future Perfect in the Past* bezeichnet Handlungen oder Vorgänge, die, von einem Zeitpunkt der Vergangenheit aus gesehen, an einem Zeitpunkt in der Zukunft abgeschlossen sein werden.

It would have been better you had stayed at home.
If Edward's brave wife had not immediately sucked the poison from the wound, her husband would probably have died.

Formgleich mit dem *Future Perfect in the Past* ist das *Conditional Perfect*. Das *Conditional Perfect* drückt aus, was geschehen wäre, wenn eine Bedingung oder Voraussetzung erfüllt gewesen wäre (vgl. 238, 239).

Active and Passive (Voices)

Aktiv und Passiv 168

a) The manservant opened the door.
Heat affects musical instruments.
Mother cooked this meal.

b) The door was opened by the manservant.
Musical instruments are affected by heat.
This meal was cooked by Mother.

a) Das Aktiv drückt eine Tätigkeit aus, die das Subjekt ausführt.

b) Das Passiv bezeichnet dagegen eine Tätigkeit, die am Subjekt vollzogen wird.

The Passive (Voice)

Das Passiv 169

Criminals are punished.
The enemy was defeated.
The table has been moved.
An inquiry will be held.

Das Passiv wird gebildet aus einer Form von *to be + Past Participle.*

Das Passiv kann von allen Zeiten gebildet werden:

a) She ordered the tea to be brought.
The traffic had to be stopped.

b) The traffic is stopped.
The traffic has been stopped.

c) Many problems were discussed by them.
Many problems had been discussed by them.

a) *Infinitive*

b) *Present Tense*
Present Perfect

c) *Past Tense*
Past Perfect

d) The sound of the bells will be heard. The sound of the bells would be heard. The work would be finished in time if we were not interrupted so often.	d) *Future* *Future in the Past* *Conditional*
e) I shall (will) have been told about the exam by next week. They would have been told about their exams yesterday. I would have been eaten alive if you had not shot the lion.	e) *Future Perfect* *Future Perfect in the Past* *Conditional Perfect*
f) Don't be deceived by him. May he be remembered for ever!△	f) *Imperative*
g) The house is being built. The meeting was being held.	g) Die *Progressive Form* wird im Passiv nur im *Present Tense* und *Past Tense* gebraucht.

170 The Use of the Passive (Voice)

Der Gebrauch des Passivs

1.

Subject	Predicate	Object
Pat	wrote	the letter.
The letter	was written	by Pat.

Bei der Umwandlung eines Aktivsatzes ins Passiv wird das direkte Objekt des Aktivsatzes zum Subjekt des Passivsatzes.

2. A tent was pitched by the boys.
The first real steam-engine was invented by James Watt.

Soll bei der Umwandlung eines Aktivsatzes ins Passiv das Subjekt des Aktivsatzes genannt werden, so wird es mit der Präposition *by* angefügt.

A new railway-line was built.
A prize of £500 was offered for the fastest steam-engine.

Bisweilen bleiben allerdings *by* und das Objekt des Passivsatzes ganz weg. Man läßt beide fort, wenn es nicht recht interessiert, durch wen etwas getan wird bzw. wurde etc.

3. | The typewriter is repaired. You can use it. *Die Schreibmaschine ist repariert ...* The typewriter is repaired once a year. *Die Schreibmaschine wird ... repariert.* The window was shut when I arrived. *Das Fenster war geschlossen ...* The window was shut by the maid. *Das Fenster wurde ... geschlossen.*

a) The road is being built.
The typewriter is being repaired.

b) Three glasses got broken last night.
The details of the theft became known.

Das Passiv kann doppeldeutig sein bei Sätzen, deren Verb einen Zustand („ist", „war") und eine Zustandsänderung („wird", „wurde") zugleich ausdrücken kann. Welche Bedeutung gemeint ist, ergibt sich meist aus dem Zusammenhang.

Wenn die einfachen Zeiten keine volle Klarheit geben, verwendet die Sprache

a) die *Progressive Form* des Passivs zur Bezeichnung des Vorgangs (deutsch: werden);

b) *to get* und *to become* zur Bezeichnung des Zustands.

4. Das Passiv wird im Englischen viel häufiger gebraucht als im Deutschen. Seine sachliche (objektive) Aussageform entspricht einem wesentlichen Zug der englischen Sprache (vgl. 263).

a) My brother was called by me.
The farmer's wife had been helped by some girls.
The animals are allowed to run free in the field.
He was advised by the teacher.
The factory is run by the owner's nephew.

a) Alle Verben, die ein direktes Objekt bei sich haben (= transitive Verben, vgl. 210), können das Passiv bilden. Es kann also auch in den Fällen gebildet werden, wo im Deutschen unpersönliche Ausdrücke stehen.

b) The blackboard has been written on.
(Someone has written on the blackboard.)
The doctor was sent for.
(Mother sent for the doctor.)
The singer was listened to with pleasure.
(They listened to the singer with pleasure.)

b) Auch von Verben mit einem präpositionalen Objekt (vgl. 212) wird das Passiv gebildet. Verb und Präposition sind hier so eng verbunden, daß sie als eine Einheit empfunden werden und einem transitiven Verb entsprechen.

c) The thief was laid hold of.
(They laid hold of the thief.)
The old man was taken good care of.
(They took good care of the old man.)
The invention was made use of by few people.
(Few people made use of the invention.)

c) Auch Verben mit einem direkten (sachlichen) Objekt (ohne Artikel) und (persönlicher) präpositionaler Ergänzung (vgl. 214) lassen diese unter b) angeführte Konstruktion zu.
Solche Verben sind z. B.

to find fault with	tadeln	to pay attention to	beachten
to lay hold of / to take hold of	ergreifen	to take account of	berücksichtigen
to keep hold of	festhalten	to take advantage of	ausnutzen
to lose sight of	aus den Augen verlieren	to take care of	sorgen für
to make fun of	Spaß treiben mit	to take notice of	beachten, Kenntnis nehmen von
to make use of	gebrauchen	to take possession of	in Besitz nehmen

5. Bei Verben, die zwei Objekte bei sich haben (vgl. 213), kann sowohl das *Direct Object* als auch das *Indirect Object* zum Subjekt des Passivsatzes werden.

The inhabitants were told wonderful stories.

The sailors told the inhabitants wonderful stories.

Wonderful stories were told (to) the inhabitants.

Notice:

He announced his arrival to his friend.
His arrival was announced to his friend.

Bei den Verben mit einem direkten Objekt und einer persönlichen Ergänzung mit *to* (vgl. 214) kann nur das direkte (sachliche) Objekt zum Subjekt des Passivsatzes werden.

6. **It is to be hoped that she will pass the exam.**
It cannot be denied that he is clever.

Das unpersönliche Passiv ist im Englischen selten. Es findet sich nur, wenn das *it* auf einen folgenden Subjektsatz hinweist.

7. **This poor boy is to be pitied.**
A copy of Magna Carta is to be seen in the British Museum.

Der Infinitiv des Passivs wird gebraucht nach den Formen von *to be.*

8. **There was no time to lose (to be lost).**
There was a lot of work to do (to be done).

Als Beifügung zu einem Substantiv, Adjektiv oder Pronomen steht, besonders nach *there is, there was*, der Infinitiv des Aktivs oder der Infinitiv des Passivs.

That is easy to do.
There was nothing to see.
Rooms to let (*Zimmer zu vermieten*).
Who is to blame?

Im allgemeinen bevorzugt der Engländer den kürzeren Infinitiv des Aktivs.

The Progressive Form — Die Verlaufsform — 171

1. Die *Progressive Form* dient dem Engländer dazu, den Verlauf eines Geschehens anschaulich darzustellen. Sie drückt aus, daß zu einer bestimmten Zeit „gerade“ etwas geschieht bzw. geschah.
Die *Progressive Form* kann in allen Zeiten des Aktivs und im *Present* und *Past Tense* des Passivs gebildet werden.

Active

Present Tense	"What is the weather like?" – "The sun is shining."	Die Sonne scheint (gerade).
Past Tense	When I entered the room, he was writing a letter.	Als ich ins Zimmer trat, schrieb er gerade einen Brief.
Present Perfect	They have been waiting there for more than an hour.	Sie warten dort schon länger als eine Stunde.
Past Perfect	Before the bus started, we had been walking up and down the street.	Bevor der Bus abfuhr, waren wir die Straße auf und ab gegangen.
Future	In August we will be walking along Miami Beach.	Im August werden wir am Strande von Miami spazierengehen.
Past Future	My friend told me that his father would be returning from America tomorrow.	Mein Freund erzählte mir, daß sein Vater morgen von Amerika zurückkehren werde.

Passive

Present Tense	The road is being built.	Die Straße ist (gerade) im Bau.
Past Tense	When I crossed the bridge yesterday, it was being repaired.	Als ich gestern über die Brücke fuhr, wurde sie gerade ausgebessert.

2.

	Die *Progressive Form* steht ferner
a) While we were rowing up the river, many small motor-boats were darting past us. While I was playing the piano, my sister was doing her homework.	a) wenn zwei Vorgänge von vorübergehender Dauer sich zum gleichen Zeitpunkt abspielen;
b) We were sitting in the garden, when my mother called us. John's father was cleaning the new car, when Bob came along.	b) wenn eine Handlung noch andauert, während eine andere eintritt.

3. Eine Reihe von Verben können nur dann in der *Progressive Form* verwendet werden, wenn sie in veränderter, übertragener oder erweiterter Bedeutung gebraucht werden, z. B.

Do you see that small house over there? He is seeing his friend off. George is seeing her home.	to see	sehen begleiten, fortbringen nach Hause bringen
I hear you have got a prize. I am hearing lectures at the university.	to hear	hören, erfahren Vorlesungen hören
It smells nice. She is smelling the flower.	to smell	duften, riechen riechen an
It tastes good. Cook is tasting the soup.	to taste	(gut, schlecht) schmecken kosten, probieren, ab- schmecken

4. Auch Verben der Bewegung, deren Begriff eine Augenblickshandlung ausdrückt, bilden die *Progressive Form* nur dann, wenn sie in einer erweiterten Bedeutung gebraucht sind.

When did he arrive?	to arrive	ankommen
The houses became more and more numerous, the plane flew over the Thames, we were arriving at London Airport.		gelangen
What did he see when he entered?	to enter	eintreten
When we came on deck, our ship was entering the Channel.		gerade hineinfahren in, einlaufen

5. This box contains the new books.
They love each other dearly.
The sun fades the carpet.
I don't know to whom these things belong.

Die *Progressive Form* kann nicht gebraucht werden bei Verben, deren Bedeutung schon eine Dauer in sich schließt (vgl. aber 172).
Solche Verben sind z. B.

to agree to	übereinstimmen mit / zustimmen	to own / to possess / to have	besitzen
to believe in	glauben an	to prefer	vorziehen
to belong to	gehören zu	to remember	sich erinnern
to contain	enthalten	to resemble	sich ähneln / gleichen
to deserve	(Belohnung) verdienen	to seem	scheinen
to doubt	zweifeln	to suffice	genügen, ausreichen
to exist	sein, existieren	to suppose	vermuten
to hate	hassen	to want / to wish / to desire	wünschen
to know	wissen		
to like	gern haben		
to dislike	nicht mögen, mißbilligen		
to love	lieben		
to mind (don't mind)	etwas dagegen haben		

. Die *Progressive Form* kann ferner nicht gebraucht werden, wenn ausgedrückt wird,

a) London lies on the Thames.
His friend lives in Manchester.
John's house stands in Church Road.
In America boys and girls go to school together.

a) daß etwas immer so ist oder das Ende des Vorgangs nicht abzusehen ist (vgl. 160,5);

b) Every week-day Bob goes to school along Church Road.
Every Saturday John's father cleans his car.

b) daß etwas immer wieder geschieht (vgl. 160, 2).

. Die *Progressive Form* wird ferner nicht gebraucht

a) William and his army defeated the English. He conquered Kent and marched to London. He brought the country under his control and built up a kingdom under Norman rule.

a) bei der Darstellung von aufeinanderfolgenden Vorgängen (vgl. 162);

b) Bob turned on the television set.
Pat switched off the light.

b) bei Vorgängen, die nur einen Augenblick dauern, z. B.

to turn on   to switch off   to notice
to recognize   to understand

172 Durch eine Form von *to be + Present Participle* kann einem Geschehen besonderer Nachdruck verliehen werden, und zwar

1. a) I'm loving every minute of my holidays.
Ich genieße jede Minute meiner Ferien.
I've been wanting to speak to this actor.
Ich habe mir schon immer sehr gewünscht . . .

a) bei Verben, die im allgemeinen nicht in der *Progressive Form* gebraucht werden;

b) "Have you ever heard a nightingale in this valley?" – "Now you are hearing one." – "I hear it clearly now."

b) bei einigen Verben der sinnlichen Wahrnehmung, die sonst ebenfalls nicht die *Progressive Form* bilden (vgl. 171, 3);

c) He is forgetting everything today.
Er vergißt aber auch alles heute.
I am hoping to see him.
Ich hoffe doch, daß ich ihn sehe.
How are you liking this novel?
Wie gefällt Ihnen denn dieser neue Roman (bis jetzt)?
I have been wanting to go home for months.

c) bei Verben, die geistige Fähigkeiten, Tätigkeiten und Neigungen ausdrücken;

d) The child is always crying.
Das Kind schreit (aber auch) immer!
He is continually contradicting me.
Er widerspricht mir aber auch dauernd.
He is always telling me of his good qualities.
Er erzählt mir (aber auch) immer (wieder) von seinem Können.

d) bei wiederholten Handlungen; wobei die umschreibende Form (oft in Verbindung mit *always*, *constantly*, *continually*) einen besonderen Gefühlswert (Vorwurf, Tadel, Unwillen) enthält.

2. Eine Form des Präsens von *to be + Present Participle* (statt des einfachen Futurs) steht oft zur Bezeichnung eines zukünftigen Geschehens, z. B.

a) I am leaving for London tomorrow.
Where are you going next Sunday?

b) What are you wearing for the party?
The Dolmen Press is publishing Jack's latest book next week.

a) bei Verben der Bewegung (vgl. *Future Tense*, 164, 5)

b) bei to do, to dine, to lunch, to play, to publish, to sleep, to stay, to wear

The Moods — Die Modi (Aussageweisen)

The Indicative — Der Indikativ 173

1. Der Indikativ stellt eine Aussage als Tatsache, als Wirklichkeit dar.

> What cannot be cured must be endured.
> Dogs that bark at a distance never bite.

2. Abweichend vom Deutschen steht im Englischen (wie im Französischen) der Indikativ auch

a) in der indirekten Rede (vgl. *Reported Speech*, 240);

> a) He says that he is ill.
> *Er sagt, daß er krank sei (er sei krank).*
> She said that her mother was not at home.
> *Sie sagte, daß ihre Mutter nicht zu Hause sei (. . . ihre Mutter sei nicht zu Hause).*

b) in indirekten Fragesätzen (vgl. 243).

> b) Robin wanted to know how much the butcher had hoped to get for his meat (. . . *gehofft habe*).
> Fred asked if they had heard the cry (. . . *gehört hätten*).

The Imperative — Der Imperativ 174

1. Der Imperativ drückt einen Befehl oder eine Aufforderung aus.

> Go to the door, please.
> Stop talking!

2. Der verneinte Imperativ drückt ein Verbot aus. Er wird stets mit *to do* gebildet (vgl. 146).

> Don't enter the room.
> Don't be so noisy.

3. Als Ersatz für die 1. Person des Plurals, die 3. Person des Singulars und die 3. Person des Plurals steht die Umschreibung mit *let*.

> Let's go now.
> Let him try to do it.
> Let them stay here.

4. Do be quiet, children!
Pat, do be careful on the road.

Dem Imperativ kann durch Hinzutreten von *do* mehr Nachdruck verliehen werden (vgl. 148).

5. Bob, you go to bed now.
Don't you forget what I said.

Durch Hinzusetzen des Subjekts wird ein Befehl sehr bestimmt.

6. Try and come early.
Versuche, früh zu kommen!
Mind and bring your ball with you.
Denke daran, deinen Ball mitzubringen!

Im Englischen stehen oft zwei Imperative mit *and* verbunden nebeneinander; im Deutschen entspricht dem zweiten Imperativ meist ein Infinitiv mit „zu".

Notice:

Be quiet !– Mind the step !
Don't be so noisy !
Come here.

Nach einem Imperativ(-satz) steht nur dann ein Ausrufezeichen, wenn es sich wirklich um einen Ausruf handelt.

7. Häufig wird der Sprechende seine Willensäußerung in die Form einer höflichen Bitte kleiden wollen; dafür gibt es eine ganze Reihe von Ausdrucksmöglichkeiten:

Please mend my coat.
Please could you tell me the way to the station?
Will you please mend my coat.
Come here, will you?
Come here, won't you?
Would you mind repeating that name?

Would you mend this coat for me?
Would you kindly . . .
Would you be so good as to . . .
Could you possibly . . . ?
You might as well do this. (= eine sehr bestimmte Aufforderung)

Der Konjunktiv drückt eine Nichtwirklichkeit aus. Die Aussage wird als nur gedacht oder gewünscht dargestellt.

Es gibt nur noch wenige Konjunktivformen im Englischen:

Be that as it may, he nevertheless was a great help to me.

I wish it were over.
If I were you, I would go.

Heaven help him. – God bless you.
Long live the Queen. – God save the Queen.

be für alle Personen (sg. u. pl.) des *Present Tense*;

were für die 1. und 3. Person des *Past Tense* (vgl. 239, 2 Notice);

eine endungslose Form für die 3. Person (sg.) Präsens der Vollverben.

2\. Though a lie be clever, the truth will come out.△

Die Konjunktivformen *be* und *were* werden meist nur im geschriebenen English gebraucht, und zwar
be in Einräumungssätzen;

Even if it were true, it would not make any difference.
I wish it were over.
I wish I were a bird and could fly where I wanted to.

were in Bedingungssätzen und in Nebensätzen, die von einem Hauptsatz abhängen, der einen Wunsch oder eine Willensäußerung ausdrückt (vgl. 245 ff.).

3\. May you be happy in the life you have chosen.△
May I ask you for the salt, please?
We might take a boat up the river.

In der Umgangssprache ist der Konjunktiv recht selten geworden. Wenn ein Wunsch, eine höfliche Bitte oder eine Möglichkeit ausgesprochen werden sollen, so gebraucht man die Formen der unvollständigen Hilfsverben (vgl. 174, 7; 245 ff.).

Infinitive — Gerund — Participle

Infinitiv — Gerundium — Partizip

176 Der Infinitiv, das Gerundium und die Partizipien werden nominale Verbformen genannt, weil sie als Satzteile an die Stelle eines Nomens (Substantivs oder Adjektivs) treten können. Infinitiv und Gerundium haben substantivischen, die Partizipien adjektivischen Charakter.

Infinitiv, Gerundium und Partizipien sind die wichtigsten Mittel des Englischen für die Satzverkürzung, da sie oft längere Nebensätze entbehrlich machen. Sie ermöglichen jene Kürze und Straffung des Satzbaus, die wesentliche Merkmale der englischen Sprache sind.

The Infinitive — Der Infinitiv

177 The Forms — Die Formen

a) **Active Voice**	
Present Infinitive: to call *Perfect Infinitive:* to have called	rufen gerufen haben
b) **Passive Voice**	
Present Infinitive: to be called *Perfect Infinitive:* to have been called	gerufen werden gerufen worden sein

1. a) Do you intend to come with me?
   They hoped to visit the Empire State Building.
   b) Pat should help you with your homework.
   He must go to bed now.

Der Infinitiv wird gebraucht
a) mit *to*;
b) ohne *to*.

2. You could do it if you had to.
   He may go with you if he wants to.
   I cannot come with you though I should love to.

Ein vorher erwähnter Infinitiv braucht nicht wiederholt zu werden; er wird dann durch *to* ersetzt.

178

a) To swim is healthy.△
She promised to come.
His sister seems to be ill.
We eat to live, but we do not live to eat.

b) I am delighted to see you.
Eric decided to stay at home.

a) Wie ein Substantiv kann der Infinitiv stehen
als Subjekt;
als Objekt;
als prädikative Ergänzung;
als adverbiale Bestimmung.

b) Wie ein Verb kann der Infinitiv ein Objekt nach sich haben und durch Adverbien näher bestimmt sein.

The Infinitive with to

The Infinitive with to as a Subject

Der Infinitiv mit 'to' als Subjekt

179

1. To err is human, to forgive divine.
To know him is to like him.△
To go by car is comfortable, to walk is healthier.△

Der Infinitiv mit *to* steht als grammatisches Subjekt.

2. It is a pleasure to listen to her songs.
It is advisable to leave early.

Der Infinitiv mit *to* steht nach unpersönlichen Ausdrücken als logisches (Sinn-)Subjekt.
Das grammatische Subjekt ist hier das *it*.

Notice:

It is time for me to go.
It was kind of her to lend me an umbrella.

Nach unpersönlichen Ausdrücken wie *it is time*, *it is kind*, etc. kann das Sinnsubjekt des Infinitivs mit *for* oder *of* dem Infinitiv vorangehen.

Vgl. lat. Mentiri turpe est. – Adulescentis est maiores natu vereri. –
frz. Mentir est une action honteuse. – Promettre et tenir sont deux. Il faut servir ses parents et ses amis.

180 The Infinitive with to as an Attribute

Der Infinitiv mit 'to' als Beifügung

Der Infinitiv mit *to* tritt als Beifügung

1. a) Everybody hoped for better days to come.
   We have plenty of time to get there.
   Here is a pen to write with.

a) zu Substantiven;

   b) She was delighted to see me.
   That is hard to believe.
   He was unable to do it.

b) zu Adjektiven.

Der Infinitiv mit *to* steht ferner

2. a) He was the fastest runner to compete for our school.
   It was the funniest play ever to be staged by the local theatre club.
   The next speaker to come forward was a delegate from Sheffield.

a) nach Superlativen;

   b) He was the last to go to bed.
   Drake was the first Englishman to sail round the world.
   Work is the best thing to make us love life.
   That is the very thing to upset her.

b) nach Zahlwörtern, wie
the first, the last,
the only (best) thing,
the very thing, etc.

Im Deutschen stehen in diesen Fällen Relativsätze.

Vgl. frz. un homme facile à tromper. – l'espoir de vaincre. – prêt à quitter – Il sera le premier à faire cela.

181 The Infinitive with to as an Object

Der Infinitiv mit 'to' als Objekt

Der Infinitiv mit *to* steht als Objekt nach vielen transitiven Verben.

1. She promised to come early.
   We decided to go for a walk.
   She hopes to become a veterinarian.
   Our father refused to sign the contract because he did not agree with its contents.
   Mr. Smith wanted to buy a house.
   Anne offered to help her mother.
   Bob pretended to work, but actually he was listening to jazz music.
   We managed to get to the concert-hall in time.

(. . . weigerte sich zu unterzeichnen . . .)

(. . . tat so, als ob . . .; . . . gab vor zu arbeiten . . .)
(Es gelang uns . . .; Wir schafften es . . .)

Notice:

Nach einigen transitiven Verben kann als direktes Objekt der Infinitiv oder das Gerundium stehen (vgl. 192,2). Bei anderen transitiven Verben hängt es von der Bedeutung ab, ob ihnen ein Infinitiv oder ein Gerundium folgt (vgl. 192,3 bis 5).

We do not know what to do, or where to stay. He told me when to come. She showed us how to open the window. She did not tell me why to do it. We wondered whether to repeat the performance. Do you understand how to work the pump? Have you learnt yet how to mend a puncture? He did not know how to start the car.	Der Infinitiv mit *to* steht als Objekt an Stelle von indirekten Fragesätzen, die mit what where when whether why how beginnen. Dies ist oft der Fall nach Verben wie to know to show to tell to understand to learn to teach Das Fragewort bleibt vor dem Infinitiv erhalten.

The Infinitive as a Predicative Complement to the Direct Object (Direct Object + Infinitive)

Der Infinitiv als prädikative Ergänzung zum direkten Objekt (Direktes Objekt + Infinitiv) 182

David wanted to visit his relations. I should like to learn English. David wanted Tom (him) to go with him. I should like you to learn English too.	In den nebenstehenden Sätzen drückt der Infinitiv aus, was das Subjekt selbst zu tun wünscht. Was es (das Subjekt) aber eine andere Person tun lassen möchte, drückt der Engländer mit dem *Direct Object + Infinitive* aus. Diese Satzform wird im

Englischen sehr häufig verwandt, da sie es dem Engländer gestattet, sich kurz auszudrücken (vgl. 183; 188).

Direct Object + Infinitive with to

Direktes Objekt + Infinitiv mit to 183

Subject + Verb	Direct Object	Infinitive with to
I asked	him	to show me the town.
She expected	me	to do her homework for her.
Mother told	Anne	to clean the house.
He likes	his sister	to dress well.
We should prefer	our uncle	to come next week.
Our headmaster warned	us	not to be late.
The teacher could not get	the boy	to do his homework carefully.
I hate	you	to speak to your sister like that.

Direct Object + Infinitive with to steht nach Verben des Veranlassens (Befehlens, Bittens), nach Verben des Zulassens (Erlaubens) und nach Verben des Wünschens und Nichtwünschens, z. B.

to advise	raten	(I should like	ich möchte gern, daß)
to allow	erlauben, lassen	to love	lieben
to ask	bitten	to order	befehlen
to beg	(dringend) bitten	to permit	erlauben
to cause	(veran-)lassen; der Grund sein, daß	to prefer	vorziehen, etw. lieber haben, (lieber sehen)
to command	befehlen	I should prefer	es wäre mir lieber, wenn
to desire	wünschen	to teach	lehren
to expect	erwarten; verlangen von jem., daß	to tell s.o. to do s.th.	befehlen, jem. sagen, er solle etw. tun
to forbid	verbieten	to warn s.b. to do s.th.	jem. mahnen, etw. zu tun
to force	zwingen	to warn s.b. not to do s.th.	warnen, dringend raten, etw. nicht zu tun
to get	jem. dazu bringen, veranlassen	to want	wünschen
to hate	hassen, etwas nicht leiden können	to wish	wünschen
to invite	einladen		
to like	lieben, gern haben		

2. The mother told the boys to cut the lawn.

Im nebenstehenden Beispiel wird die Person, welche die Handlung ausführen soll, genannt.

She ordered the meal to be served in her room.
I expect the letter to be written soon.

Wenn die Person, welche die im Infinitiv ausgedrückte Handlung ausführen soll, nicht genannt wird, gebraucht man den *Infinitive Passive* (*Voice*).

3. a) We believe him to know a lot of English.
I know him to be an honest man.
They suppose this news to be true.
They proved him to have done it.
I recommended him to take a short cut.
We imagined him to be a fool.
I considered him to be very clever.
They declared him (to be) guilty.
He denied it to be a fact.

a) *Direct Object + Infinitive with to* steht in der literarischen Sprache nach den Verben des Sagens und Denkens, z. B.

to believe	to guess	to suppose
to consider	to imagine	to think
to declare	to prove	to understand
to deny	to recommend	

b) We believe that he knows a lot of English.
I know (that) he is an honest man.
They suppose that this news was true.
They proved that he had done it.

b) Im Umgangsenglisch würde man dasselbe durch einen Nebensatz mit *that* ausdrücken. Im Deutschen steht meist ein Nebensatz mit „daß“.

c) He told me (that) he would be back at six o'clock.

I hope (that) my friend will come to see me soon.

c) Nach *to say, to tell,* (= sagen), *to answer, to hope, to reply* ist *Direct Object + Infinitive with to* nicht möglich, es muß ein Nebensatz (mit oder ohne *that*) folgen.

4. They knew themselves to be wrong.
He imagines himself to be a great poet.

Wenn das Objekt ein Personalpronomen ist und sich auf das Subjekt zurückbezieht, so steht das mit *-self* gebildete Pronomen.

The Infinitive with to as a Predicative Complement to the Subject

Der Infinitiv mit to als prädikative Ergänzung zum Subjekt 184

1. The best attitude is to do what has to be done and say nothing.
Your father seems to work very hard; he appears to feel very well, though.

Nobody was to be heard.
That remains to be seen.
Many letters are still to be written.

Der Infinitiv mit *to* steht als prädikative Ergänzung zum Subjekt nach den Verben

to be   to seem
to appear   to remain

(vgl. 114, 1).

Hat der Infinitiv passive Bedeutung, so muß im Englischen auch die passive Form stehen (vgl. 170, 6, 7 u. 8).

2. The boy was told to do his work more carefully.

The children were not allowed to leave the garden.

He is supposed to come back today.
Do not believe him; he is known to be a liar.

Der Infinitiv mit *to* steht als prädikative Ergänzung zum Subjekt nach dem Passiv vieler Verben, die im Aktiv ein *Direct Object + Infinitive with or without to* nach sich haben.

3. The old man was seen to come up the street.
But:
They saw the old man come up the street.

The ship was seen to disappear in the mist.
But:
David saw the ship disappear in the mist.

The monks were made to copy Latin books by hand.
But:
Alfred the Great made the monks copy Latin books by hand.

Man beachte besonders, daß nach dem Passiv der Verben

to see to hear to feel
to make

der Infinitiv mit *to* steht. (Im Aktivsatz steht nach diesen Verben der *Infinitive without to*. Vgl. 188).

185 for, with, on, without + Noun or Pronoun + Infinitive with to

Die hier aufgeführten Satzkonstruktionen haben im modernen Englisch weite Verbreitung gefunden:

a) I waited for the rain to stop.
The house is too small for us to live in.
The parcel was too heavy for him to carry.
Have you got some paper for me to write on?

a) for + (Pro) Noun + Infinitive with to

b) It rests with you to decide what to do.

b) with + (Pro) Noun + Infinitive with to

c) When you engaged him, you asked me if you could rely on him to be honest.
Ireland very much depends on her tourist traffic to balance her budget.

c) on + (Pro) Noun + Infinitive with to

d) They would fall apart without God to hold them together (May Sinclair).
(*Also possible*: . . . without God holding them).
For eighteen years I was not allowed to go downstairs without somebody to hold my hand (Laurence Housman).
(*Also possible*: . . . without somebody holding my hand).

d) without + (Pro) Noun + Infinitive with to

The Infinitive with to as an Adverbial Phrase

Der Infinitiv mit to als adverbiale Bestimmung

1. At first, the Danes came to plunder, not to settle in Britain.
The boy hurried off to fetch the doctor.
She went to the grocer to buy some eggs.
Stephenson took part in the race in order to prove that his locomotive was the fastest.
In order to punish the boy, he forbade him to go to the cinema.

Als adverbiale Bestimmung zu Verben steht der Infinitiv mit *to* zur Bezeichnung der Absicht.

Zur Verstärkung der Absicht kann *in order to* vor dem Infinitiv stehen.

2. Zur Bezeichnung einer Folge oder eines Ergebnisses steht der Infinitiv mit *to* nach

a) They were too tired to walk back.
He spoke too softly to be understood.
She was kind enough to lend me the book.
They were lucky enough to get seats at all.

a) *too + adjective (adverb)*;

adjective (adverb) + enough.

b) Will you be so good as to fetch me the newspaper?
His cruelty is such as to frighten even the strongest.○

b) Nach *so* und nach *such* steht der Infinitiv als adverbiale Bestimmung der Folge mit *as to.*

3. To be brief, I cannot pay the rent any longer.
To be sure, he is rather old for such an important position.

Als Satzbestimmung steht der Infinitiv mit *to* ohne eigenes Subjekt in einer Reihe von Redewendungen:

to be quite frank (plain) to tell the truth	ich will ganz ehrlich sein; rundheraus
to be brief to cut the matter short	um mich kurz zu fassen; kurz
to be sure	sicherlich; wahrhaftig
to begin with	um es gleich zu sagen; zunächst einmal
to hear him talk	wenn man ihn reden hört
to judge from his looks	seinem Aussehen nach
to cut a long story short	kurz und gut
to speak frankly	um offen zu reden; rundheraus
so to speak so to say△	sozusagen
to sum up	ich fasse zusammen
to take an example	um ein Beispiel herauszugreifen

The Infinitive without to

187 The Infinitive without to as an Object — Der Infinitiv ohne 'to' als Objekt

1.

He can play football very well.
You may stay if you wish.
Do tell me what has happened.
She does come regularly.

Der Infinitiv ohne *to* steht als Objekt nach *Defective Auxiliaries* und nach dem Hilfsverb *to do*.

2. Der Infinitiv ohne *to* steht ferner nach den Ausdrücken:

You had better go now as I have not done my maths yet.
They would (had) rather walk than work.
They would (had) sooner read than write.
I could not but laugh at his jokes.△

I had better	= ich täte gut daran
I would (had△) rather I would (had△) sooner	= ich möchte lieber
I cannot but△ I could not but△	= ich kann (konnte) nicht umhin

188 Direct Object + Infinitive without to — Direktes Objekt + Infinitiv ohne to

Der Infinitiv steht als prädikative Ergänzung zum direkten Objekt auch ohne *to*, und zwar

a) Mother made me water the flowers.
Our teacher did not let us swim in the river.

b) David watched the policeman control the traffic and heard him blow his whistle.
Later he watched a ship disappear in the mist.
I saw the man enter the building.

a) nach den Verben
to make – veranlassen
to let – zulassen (vgl. 183);

b) nach dem Aktiv der Verben der sinnlichen Wahrnehmung (*Verbs of Perception*) (vgl. 184).
Hierzu gehören:

to see	to hear	to feel
to watch	to observe	to notice

The Gerund — Das Gerundium

Character and Function — Charakter und Funktion 189

Das Gerundium ist eine substantivische Verbform, die durch Anfügen der Endung *-ing* an das Verb gebildet wird. Wie der Infinitiv (vgl. 177 ff.) hat das Gerundium teils substantivische, teils verbale Eigenschaften. Auf Grund dieser Mittelstellung kann es vielseitig verwendet werden. Es gestattet dem Engländer, sich kurz, klar und anschaulich auszudrücken. Das Gerundium wird daher sowohl in der Umgangssprache als auch in der Schriftsprache sehr häufig verwendet.

Die Doppelnatur des Gerundiums wird aus den folgenden Beispielen besonders deutlich.

. Wie ein Substantiv kann das Gerundium sein

a) Walking is a healthy exercise for all car-drivers.	a) Subjekt;
b) Do stop talking.	b) Objekt;
c) Seeing is believing it.	c) prädikative Ergänzung.
d) We thank you for helping us.	d) Wie ein Substantiv kann das Gerundium nach Präpositionen stehen.
e) Would you mind my opening the window? Mother did not object to my brother's smoking.	e) Es kann wie ein Substantiv ein Possessivadjektiv oder einen *Possessive Case* bei sich haben.

. Wie ein Verb kann das Gerundium

a) The boys began playing games.	a) ein direktes Objekt anschließen;
b) She spoke of having been ill last year.	b) in verschiedenen Zeiten erscheinen;
c) He objected to being called greedy.	c) Aktiv und Passiv bilden;
d) It is worth while working hard.	d) durch ein Adverb näher bestimmt werden.

Notice:

a) The singing of the birds announces the coming of spring. A good beginning makes a good ending. b) There was a continuous humming of voices. He was disturbed by a loud knocking at the door. c) The writing of novels	Wie andere Substantive kann das Gerundium a) mit dem (bestimmten oder unbestimmten) Artikel verbunden werden; b) es kann ferner durch Adjektive näher bestimmt werden und c) eine Beifügung mit *of* bei sich haben.

In dieser Verwendung wird das Gerundium oft „Verbalsubstantiv" genannt, weil hier die Vorstellung des Vorgangs (die verbale Eigenschaft) so sehr in den Hintergrund tritt, daß man die *-ing*-Form fast wie ein echtes Substantiv empfindet. Da eine Unterscheidung von sogenanntem Verbalsubstantiv und Gerundium für den Sprachgebrauch letztlich nicht wesentlich ist, wird im folgenden nur vom Gerundium gesprochen.

3.	Some English words have the same form, but different meanings. Busy crossings are usually controlled by traffic-lights. Misunderstandings may lead to war.	Viele Gerundien sind längst echte Substantive geworden und können auch den Plural bilden, z. B.

being(s)	Wesen	meaning(s)	Bedeutung
beginning(s)	Anfang	meeting(s)	Versammlung
blessing(s)	Segen	misunderstanding(s)	Mißverständnis
building(s)	Gebäude	painting(s)	Gemälde
crossing(s)	(Straßen-)Übergang	reading(s)	Lesung
ending(s)	Endung	saving(s)	Ersparnisse
feeling(s)	Gefühl	saying(s)	Sprichwort
gathering(s)	Versammlung	suffering(s)	Leiden

4.	For a walking-tour you need strong walking-shoes; also a walking-stick may be useful. The captain told the passengers that there was no more drinking-water on board.	Das Gerundium wird häufig zur Bildung von zusammengesetzten Substantiven verwendet. In solchen Zusammensetzungen liegt der Ton auf dem ersten Bestandteil, z. B.

'booking-office	'housing-office	'sailing-boat	'waiting-room
'dining-room	'living-room	'sewing-machine	'walking-stick
'driving-licence	'drinking-water	'sitting-room	'walking-tour

The Gerund as a Subject

Das Gerundium als Subjekt

190

> Swimming is healthy.
> Travelling is most interesting.

Das Gerundium kann (wie der Infinitiv) grammatisches Subjekt eines Satzes sein.

> There is no denying the fact that the Romans built excellent roads in Britain.
> It is no good talking to her as she never listens.
> It is worth while watching birds.
>
> It is no use crying over spilt milk.
> It is no use to cry over spilt milk.
> It is useless trying to talk sense to him.
> It is useless to try and talk sense to him.

Als logisches (Sinn-)Subjekt muß das Gerundium stehen nach:

there is no ...	man kann nicht
it is no (not much) good	es hat keinen (nicht viel) Zweck
it is (not) worth while	es lohnt sich (nicht)

Nach *it is no use, it is useless* (= es nützt nichts) läßt der heutige Sprachgebrauch neben dem Gerundium auch den Infinitiv zu.

The Gerund as a Predicative Complement

Das Gerundium als prädikative Ergänzung

191

> My hobby is playing football.
> Seeing is believing.
> She was busy writing letters.
> London is well worth seeing.

Das Gerundium steht als prädikative Ergänzung nach *to be*, besonders nach:

to be busy	(= beschäftigt sein mit)
to be worth	(= wert sein)

The Gerund as a Direct Object

Das Gerundium als direktes Objekt

192

> Would you mind opening the window?
> (= May I ask you to open the window?)
> I could not help smiling.
> Boys enjoy playing cricket.

Bei einigen Verben muß als direktes verbales (!) Objekt das Gerundium stehen. Zu diesen Verben gehören:

to admit	zugeben	to escape	entkommen
to avoid	vermeiden	to excuse	entschuldigen
to delay	verzögern	to fancy	sich etwas vorstellen (in Ausrufen)
to dislike	nicht gern tun, nicht mögen	to finish	etwas beendigen, fertig werden mit
to enjoy	Freude haben an	to mind	etwas dagegen haben (verneint od. frag.)

to miss	vermeiden; verpassen	to burst out	herausplatzen
to practise	üben	to go on to keep on	fortfahren mit
to risk	wagen	to put off	aufschieben
to stop	aufhören mit	to give up	aufgeben, aufhören (mit)
to suggest	vorschlagen		
I cannot avoid I cannot help	ich kann nicht umhin, vermeiden		

2. Lincoln began studying (to study) law.
He intends going (to go) to Edinburgh tomorrow.
He has never ceased loving (to love) the theatre.

Nach einigen Verben kann als direktes Objekt das Gerundium oder der Infinitiv stehen. Zu diesen Verben gehören:

a) to begin to start	anfangen mit	b) to dread to fear	fürchten
to cease	aufhören mit	to hate	nicht mögen, hassen
to continue	fortfahren mit	to like	mögen, gern haben
to intend	beabsichtigen, vorhaben	to love	sehr gern mögen, lieben
		to prefer	lieber tun, vorziehen

Notice:

I like reading (to read) books (= *immer, überhaupt).*
I liked to read this interesting book.
I hate getting (to get) up early in the morning.
I hated to get up early this morning.

Bei Verben der Gemütsbewegung (siehe 2b) drückt das Gerundium oft etwas Allgemeines, Gewohnheitsmäßiges aus, während der Infinitiv einen besonderen Einzelfall kennzeichnet.

3. Nach den Verben *to remember, to stop, to try, to propose* steht je nach der Bedeutung Gerundium oder Infinitiv

Do you remember seeing her in the park?	sich erinnern an
You must remember to post my letter.	daran denken, nicht vergessen
We stopped working late in the night.	aufhören mit, beendigen
He stopped to buy some flowers.	innehalten, eine Pause machen, anhalten (um etw. zu tun)
Try cleaning it with this stain remover.	ausprobieren, testen
He tried to open the door, but couldn't.	versuchen, einen Versuch *(attempt)* machen
He proposed resting for an hour or two.	vorschlagen *(to suggest)*
She proposed to fly to Paris on Saturday.	beabsichtigen, vorhaben *(to intend)*

4. Nach den Verben *to regret* und *to forget* weist das Gerundium auf die Vergangenheit, der Infinitiv auf die Zukunft hin.

I regret following (having followed) his advice.	Ich bereue, daß ich ... befolgt habe.
I regret to say that you are wrong.	Ich bedaure, sagen zu müssen ...
I shall never forget hearing her recite Wordsworth.	... vergessen, daß ich gehört habe ...
I must not forget to buy the tickets for tonight's concert.	... vergessen, daß ich ... kaufen muß.

He frankly admitted that he had been wrong.
She remembered that she had promised to be there early.
They regretted that they had not come earlier.
We feared that she might have hurt herself.

Einige der Verben, die in diesem Paragraphen (192) aufgeführt sind, können neben Gerundium (bzw. Infinitiv) auch einen Nebensatz als Objekt haben. Das ist in der Umgangssprache oft der Fall.

The Gerund after Prepositions — Das Gerundium nach Präpositionen 193

He must apologize for	having been impolite.
He excused his friend for	being late.
She insisted on	being taken to the seaside.
They are looking forward to	visiting New York.
She does not object to	going to the seaside.
They prevented the Indians from	attacking the settlers.
The pupil prides himself on	having got the prize.
Did they succeed in	winning the match?
Father thanked the boys for	having helped him.

Das Gerundium steht immer nach Verben, die eng mit einer Präposition verbunden sind. Hierzu gehören die obigen Verben und die folgenden:

to accuse of	anklagen wegen	to keep from	hindern an
to believe in	glauben an	to quarrel about	streiten über
to delight in	Vergnügen finden an	to think of	denken an
to depend on	sich verlassen auf, abhängen von	to worry about	sich beunruhigen wegen
to despair of	verzweifeln an	to rely on	sich verlassen auf

I am tired of saying it again and again.
I am interested in meeting him.

Das Gerundium steht immer nach Adjektiven, die fest mit einer Präposition verbunden sind, z. B.

absorbed in	vertieft in	capable of	fähig zu
engaged in	beschäftigt mit	incapable of	unfähig zu
fond of (doing)	gern (tun)	interested in	interessiert an
far from	weit entfernt von	responsible for	verantwortlich für
		tired of	müde

Notice:

a) He was proud of having attained his aims.
He was proud to have attained his aims.
They were accustomed to using a dictionary. (...to use...)
He was angry at finding the gate locked. (...to find...)

b) The rain looks like lasting.
I do not feel like working today.
The train is near starting.
The pain was almost past bearing.
I am far from blaming her.

a) Bei den Ausdrücken

to be proud (of)	stolz sein auf
to be accustomed to	gewöhnt sein an
to be angry (at)	ärgerlich sein über

kann sowohl das Gerundium als auch der Infinitiv stehen.

b) Wie Präpositionen werden verwandt: like, near, past, far from.

3. Have I the pleasure of speaking to (with) Mr. Black?
He takes a great interest in studying languages.
That is the reason for my leaving England.

Das Gerundium steht ferner immer nach Substantiven, die eng verbunden sind, z. B.

to be in danger of	to have a reason for	to have some experience in
to be in the habit of	to have no objection to	to take an interest in
to be on the point of	to have the pleasure of	to take pleasure in

4. How about going to bed now?
What about making an early start?

Das Gerundium steht nach *what about* und *how about* („wie steht's mit . . . ?", „wie wäre es, wenn wir . . . ?").

194 The Gerund Equivalent to an Adverbial Clause — Das Gerundium als adverbiale Bestimmung

Mit Präpositionen verbunden wird das Gerundium als adverbiale Bestimmung gebraucht. Im Deutschen entspricht der Konstruktion *Preposition + Gerund* in der Regel ein Nebensatz mit einer entsprechenden Konjunktion.

Das Gerundium steht als adverbiale Bestimmung

a) After spending a fortnight on the south coast, we went to the Isle of Wight. You must finish this job before leaving for Scotland. On hearing the news of the Armada sailing up the Channel, the Plymouth townfolk got excited. Since coming to Brighton I have had a swim every day.	a) der Zeit nach *after*, *before*, *on*, *since*;
b) The pupil was punished for having been late three times. He got sunstroke from lying too long in the sun. He was annoyed at being kept waiting so long.	b) des Grundes nach *for*, *from*, *at*;
c) Livingstone educated himself by reading books. In doing so he proved to be a master-mind.	c) des Mittels nach *by*, *in*; (*in doing so* = dadurch, daß)
d) He left the house without saying good-bye. Instead of helping his father the boy ran away.	d) der Art und Weise nach *without*, *with*, *in*, *instead of*.
e) In spite of (its) hitting the chimney, the plane did not crash.	e) der Einräumung nach *in spite of*;
f) In the event of his not being there, ask his wife to give you the money.	f) der Bedingung

Notice:

Zu a): Da *after* und *before* auch als Konjunktionen gebraucht werden (vgl. 224 a), wäre es möglich, die *ing*-Form hier auch als Partizip anzusehen. Der Einfachheit halber wird diese sprachliche Erscheinung hier nur unter Gerundium behandelt.

After reading the book . . . *or:* Having read the book . . . *Possible, but clumsy*: After having read the book . . .	Nach *after* gebraucht man meist die einfache Form; die Perfektform nach *after* wird im modernen Englisch als umständlich empfunden.

195 The Subject of the Gerund — Das Subjekt des Gerundiums

1. He insisted on doing it himself.
I am looking forward to visiting my aunt.

Ist der Träger der Gerundalhandlung dieselbe Person wie das Subjekt des Hauptsatzes, so wird er nicht besonders genannt.

2. Ist der Träger der Gerundalhandlung eine andere Person als das Subjekt des Hauptsatzes, so muß er besonders bezeichnet werden. Das kann geschehen

a) He insisted on your doing it yourself.
Do you object to our smoking?
I am looking forward to your visiting my aunt.

a) durch das *Possessive Adjective*;

b) I insist on his brother's paying the bill.
She objected to her husband's smoking.
We are looking forward to our uncle's visiting us.

b) durch den *Possessive Case* (= formelles Englisch).

3. I insist on you doing it yourself.
They are looking forward to him visiting them.
Does she object to her husband smoking?
I am looking forward to my uncle visiting me.

In der Umgangssprache findet man für das *Possessive Adjective* und den *Possessive Case* sehr häufig den *Object Case* des Personalpronomens oder die endungslose Form des Substantivs.

The Participle — Das Partizip

196 The Forms — Die Formen

a)	**Active Voice**				
	Present Participle:	having	being	calling	writing
	Past Participle:	had	been	called	written
	Perfect Participle:	having had	having been	having called	having written
b)	**Passive Voice**				
	Present Participle:	being called		being written	
	Perfect Participle:	having been called		having been written	

Character and Function — Charakter und Funktion 197

Das Partizip nimmt eine Mittelstellung zwischen Adjektiv und Verb ein. Wie die beiden substantivischen Verbformen Infinitiv und Gerundium ist das Partizip ein oft gebrauchtes Mittel, sich knapp und klar auszudrücken. Viele englische Partizipialkonstruktionen lassen sich im Deutschen nur durch einen längeren Nebensatz ausdrücken.
Die Doppelnatur des Partizips wird aus den folgenden Beispielen deutlich.

Wie ein Adjektiv können die Partizipien

a) The lot of the unemployed is very hard.
b) The match was more exciting than we had expected.
c) His father returned unexpectedly.
She looked strikingly healthy.

a) substantiviert werden;
b) gesteigert werden;
c) Adverbien bilden.

Wie ein Verb können die Partizipien

a) He saw the boy crossing the road.
b) Though speaking in a low voice, he was well understood by everybody.
c) Having arranged everything, he left for New York.
Having been welcomed by the chairman, the speaker began his lecture.

a) ein Objekt regieren;
b) durch Konjunktionen näher bestimmt werden;
c) zusammengesetzte Zeitformen der Vergangenheit und des Passivs bilden.

The Use of the Participle — Der Gebrauch des Partizips

Das Partizip wird im englischen Satz gebraucht
a) attributiv, b) prädikativ, c) an Stelle von Nebensätzen.

The Participle as an Attribute — Das Partizip als Attribut 198

the surrounding country
a terrifying sight
a well-known sportsman
a well-aimed blow
a grown-up person

Das Partizip steht attributiv zur näheren Bestimmung des Substantivs. Es steht vor dem Substantiv, auch wenn es durch ein Adverb erweitert oder mit anderen Wörtern zusammengesetzt ist.

199 The Participle as a Predicative Complement to the Subject

Das Partizip als prädikative Ergänzung zum Subjekt

1. He was standing at the window and he looked depressed.
The bell was rung.
The weather looks threatening.
He seems disappointed.
She felt tired.
I felt daring and courageous.
Your words do not sound encouraging.
He sounded annoyed on the phone.
He appeared worn out after the journey.
She appears (seems) demanding and selfish and to care only for herself.

Als prädikative Ergänzung zum Subjekt stehen beide Partizipien *(Present Participle* und *Past Participle)* nach den Verben:

to be (*Progr. Form, Passive Voice*)
to look (= aussehen)
to appear (= seem)
to seem
to feel
to sound

2. Als prädikative Ergänzung zum Subjekt stehen ferner

a) She stood listening to the music.
Remain sitting.
He lay injured at our feet.
There lies still unexplored a great white continent of ice and snow.

b) He came running into the room.
They went along singing and whistling.
He that goes borrowing goes sorrowing. △

a) beide Partizipien nach den Verben der Ruhe
to sit to remain
to lie to stand etc.

b) das *Present Participle* nach den Verben der Bewegung
to go, to walk, to run, to come etc.

200 The Participle as a Predicative Complement to the Object (Direct Object + Participle)

Das Partizip als prädikative Ergänzung zum Objekt (Direktes Objekt + Partizip)

1. I heard her singing a nice song.
David heard the band playing a gay tune.
He saw some women talking to each other.
He never heard an unkind word spoken at home.
He heard a hymn played by the band.

Als prädikative Erganzung zum Objekt stehen beide Partizipien nach den Verben der sinnlichen Wahrnehmung (vgl. *Direct Object + Infinitive without to*, 188).

Notice:

They watched the thief running away. She noticed a cat walking on the roof.	Das *Present Participle* (*Direct Object + Participle*) wird gebraucht, wenn man den Ablauf eines Vorgangs anschaulich darstellen will; darin ähnelt das Partizip der *Progressive Form*.
David saw a ship disappear in the mist. They watched me dive into the pool.	Der Infinitiv (*Direct Object + Infinitive without to*) wird verwendet, wenn man nur das Ergebnis, das Geschehene feststellen will.

Als prädikative Ergänzung zum Objekt stehen ferner

a) Leave the children undisturbed; let them play. Mother sent her shopping. I am sorry to have kept you waiting.	a) beide Partizipien nach den Verben des Lassens, wie *to keep, to leave, to send*;
b) We shall have the house painted. I have my hair cut every month. She must get her coat mended. Please get your shoes cleaned.	b) das *Past Participle* besonders nach *to have* und *to get* (deutsch: lassen).

Compare:	
I have bound my book.	Ich habe mein Buch (selbst) gebunden.
I am going to have my book bound.	Ich lasse mir mein Buch binden.
He has labelled his luggage.	Er hat sein Gepäck mit Zetteln versehen.
He has his luggage labelled.	Er läßt sein Gepäck mit Zetteln versehen.

The Participle instead of a Subordinate Clause — Das Partizip an Stelle eines Nebensatzes 201

Die Partizipien können – wie Infinitiv und Gerundium – an Stelle von Nebensätzen stehen; sie schließen sich entweder an ein Satzglied des Hauptsatzes an (= verbundenes Partizip), oder sie haben ein eigenes Subjekt (= unverbundenes Partizip).

202 The Participle instead of a Relative Clause

Das Partizip an Stelle eines Relativsatzes

The man speaking on the radio was telling a story.
(The man who spoke on the radio was telling a story.)

'Steel City' was the name given to Pittsburgh.
('Steel City' is the name that was given to Pittsburgh.)

Das „verbundene" Partizip steht oft an Stelle eines Relativsatzes.

The Participle instead of an Adverbial Clause

Das Partizip an Stelle eines Adverbialsatzes

203 In der Schriftsprache steht das „verbundene" Partizip oft an Stelle von Adverbialsätzen. Die Umgangssprache bevorzugt den Adverbialsatz (vgl. die Beispiele in den Klammern).

Das „verbundene" Partizip steht an Stelle eines Adverbialsatzes•

1.
a) Going to school, he met his friend.
(When he went to school, he met his friend.)
b) Having no money, she could not buy any sweets.
(As she had no money, she could not buy any sweets.)
c) They entered the classroom, laughing heartily.
He sat there crying.
d) If posted at once, the letter will arrive in time.
(If the letter is posted at once, it will arrive in time.)

a) der Zeit (*time*);

b) des Grundes (*cause*);

c) der Art und Weise (*manner*)
(deutsch: . . . und lachten herzlich.)
. . . und weinte.)

d) der Bedingung (*condition*);

Vgl. lat. Alexander moriens anulum suum dederat Perdiccae. –
frz. La ville refusant de capituler fut bombardée.

Notice:

Though seated near the window, he could not see the road. Unless forced by bad weather to turn back, we should reach the summit before noon. He stood there as if rooted to the ground. The crowd waited patiently near the palace gates until ordered away by the police. If properly trained, Rex should become an excellent police-dog.	Der Sinn eines Partizips, das an Stelle eines Adverbialsatzes gebraucht wird, ist nicht immer eindeutig. Um Unklarheiten zu vermeiden, müssen deshalb oft entsprechende Konjunktionen vor das Partizip treten, z. B. if though unless as if until while

In der Schriftsprache steht manchmal das „unverbundene" Partizip an Stelle eines **204**
Adverbialsatzes. Das Umgangsenglisch gebraucht hier fast ausschließlich Adverbialsätze (vgl. Bsp. in Klammern).

Das „unverbundene" Partizip steht an Stelle eines Adverbialsatzes

a) The battle finished, William the Conqueror marched to London. (When the battle was finished, William . . .)	a) der Zeit (*time*);
b) The weather being too bad, we could not go for a walk. (As the weather was too bad, we . . .)	b) des Grundes (*cause*);
c) Time permitting, I shall come to see you. (If time permits, I shall come . . .)	c) der Bedingung (*condition*);
d) A month passed, each day making life more and more unbearable. (. . . and each day made life . . .)	d) an Stelle eines mit „und" anschließenden Hauptsatzes (. . . und jeder Tag machte . . .).

Vgl. lat. Regibus expulsis, consules rei publicae praeerant. –
frz. La ville refusant de capituler, le bombardement fut résolu.

205 with + Noun + Participle — with + Substantiv + Partizip

With their hands clasping the raft, the ship-wrecked sailors tried to keep themselves above the water. We sat together at the fireplace, with the door of the living-room shut. Next to the railway was a field, with men and youths playing football for their lives (D. H. Lawrence).	Die Partizipien mit eigenem Subjekt werden oft mit *with* eng an den Hauptsatz angeschlossen. Diese Partizipialkonstruktion verleiht der Aussage des Satzes besondere Anschaulichkeit und Ausdruckskraft.

206 Peculiar Participles — Besondere Partizipien

1. Eine Reihe von Partizipien wird „unverbunden" ohne eigenes Subjekt gebraucht, da ein unbestimmtes Subjekt „man" vorschwebt, das unausgesprochen bleibt. Dies ist der Fall in einer Anzahl von oft gebrauchten Redewendungen, die man sich merken sollte.

Allowing for the fact that he was tired, he did not do too badly.	wenn man berücksichtigt
He is still a very good cricketer, considering his age.	wenn man bedenkt
Generally speaking, the British are a very tolerant people.	allgemein gesagt, gesprochen
Roughly speaking, there are 200 million inhabitants in the USA.	allgemein gesagt
Judging from what you told me, the play must have been very exciting.	zu urteilen nach
Properly speaking, what he said is not quite true.	genau genommen
What they did was, strictly speaking, against the law.	streng genommen
Supposing you had fallen ill, you could not have travelled either.	angenommen

2. Die folgenden Partizipien sind zu Präpositionen geworden:

Your friend called during your absence.	während
We have no doubt concerning the best policy to be pursued.	was anbetrifft
There were about three hundred people present, including children.	einschließlich
Notwithstanding her laziness she managed to make the next grade.	ungeachtet, trotz
Words are put into classes according to the work they do in sentences.	gemäß

Verbs and Their Complements — Das Verb und seine Ergänzungen

Predicative Nouns and Adjectives — Das Prädikatsnomen 207

Das Prädikatsnomen kann ein Substantiv oder ein Adjektiv sein. Es bezeichnet eine Eigenschaft oder einen Zustand

a) Her father is a doctor. He had become rich. It is getting dark.	a) des Subjekts;
b) Keep the children quiet. The Queen made him a peer. The President appointed him Secretary of State.	b) des Objekts.

The Predicative Complement to the Subject — Die prädikative Ergänzung zum Subjekt 208

Ein Prädikatsnomen steht mit Bezug auf das Subjekt bei Verben, die einen Zustand ausdrücken, wie bei

a) He was clever and brave. They seemed quite proud of his success. She looks very young. He appeared quite well.	a) den Verben des Seins, Scheinens, Aussehens to be to seem to appear (= seem) to look to prove to show
b) After the football match, we lay quiet for an hour. He stood silent at the door. The weather will continue fine. The patient must keep very quiet.	b) Verben der Ruhe to lie to sit to stand to keep to remain to continue (bleiben)

2. Ferner steht ein Prädikatsnomen mit Bezug auf das Subjekt nach den Verben des Werdens:

a) It is getting misty. I am getting excited.	a) to get + adjective
b) David soon became acquainted with American life. The novel is becoming more and more thrilling.	b) to become + adjective
On leaving school she became a student of philosophy. Rockefeller became one of the richest men in the world.	to become + noun
c) Time is growing short. The farmer grew furious.	c) to grow + adjective
d) My left shoe-string has come loose. Everything will come all right in the end.	d) to come + adjective
e) He went red with anger. Poor man! He's gone blind.	e) to go + adjective
f) The weather is turning much warmer. The leaves are beginning to turn red.	f) to turn + adjective
He turned Protestant. Some people do not think it wise for a great general to turn politician.	to turn + noun
g) The well was beginning to run dry. Supplies were running short.	g) to run + adjective
h) Soon after his return he fell ill. After the long cricket match the boys soon fell asleep.	h) to fall + adjective
The girl fell in love.	to fall in love
My bicycle is so old that it might fall to pieces any time.	to fall to pieces
The chancellor fell out of favour with the King and had to resign.	to fall out of favour
As he has never modernized his production methods, his business has fallen behind the times.	to fall behind the times

3. Do you feel tired?
These flowers smell sweet.
These apples taste nice.
His proposals sound all right.
The tide rose high.
They arrived safe in the harbour.

Das Prädikatsnomen mit Bezug auf das Subjekt steht auch bei anderen intransitiven Verben, wenn eine Eigenschaft des Subjekts angegeben werden soll, und nach Verben der Bewegung, so z. B. nach Verben wie

to feel	to taste	to rise
to smell	to sound	to arrive

4. Drake was made a knight.
He is considered thorough and careful.
Queen Elizabeth II was crowned Queen of England on June 2nd, 1953.

In passivischen Sätzen steht ein Prädikatsnomen als Ergänzung zum Subjekt bei den Verben des Ernennens, Erwählens und Dafürhaltens (vgl. 209, 3).

Vgl. lat. Socrates oraculo Delphico sapientissimus iudicatus est. – Nemo ante mortem beatus habendus est. –
frz. Victor Hugo fut élu président. – Le fils du roi d'Angleterre fut proclamé roi de France.

The Predicative Complement to the Direct Object — Die prädikative Ergänzung zum Objekt 209

Das Prädikatsnomen mit Bezug auf das Objekt steht

1. New York's police keep their eyes open day and night.
They made me responsible for everything.
Try to hold the camera still.

nach Verben, die ein Verharren oder Versetzen in einen Zustand ausdrücken, wie
to keep, to hold, to leave, to make, (to render△);

2. Everybody thinks him guilty.
We consider him a reliable friend.
Have I made this clear?
I think it my duty to tell my friends the truth.

nach Verben des Denkens, Dafürhaltens, der sinnlichen Wahrnehmung, wenn dem Objekt eine Eigenschaft zugeschrieben werden soll;

3. Elizabeth made Drake a knight.
Robin Hood appointed Little John the second in command.
The boys elected my cousin captain of the cricket team.

nach den Verben des Ernennens und Erwählens:

to appoint	to create	to call
to declare	to elect	to crown
to name	to proclaim	to make

Vgl. lat. Post Romulum populus Numam regem creavit. – Senatus Antonium hostem patriae declaravit. –
frz. Les Français nommèrent Napoléon général après la prise de Toulon; en 1799 ils l'élurent premier consul.

4.	Guy Fawkes is regarded as a traitor. Florence Nightingale is recognized as the founder of modern nursing. I think of him as a great man.	Mit *as* muß das Prädikatsnomen angeschlossen werden bei: to regard as — betrachten als to look upon as — ansehen als to recognize as, to acknowledge as — anerkennen als to think of as — halten für

Notice:

5.	She chose him as (for) her partner in the mixed doubles.	Das Prädikatsnomen kann nach *to choose* mit *as* oder *for* angeschlossen werden.

Vgl. frz. choisir pour, considérer comme, prendre pour, reconnaître pour, regarder comme.

210 Verbs with a Direct Object — Verben mit direktem Objekt

1.	We saw a ship. He welcomed his visitors.	Viele englische Verben haben ein direktes Objekt.

Diese Verben nennt man transitive Verben (*Transitive Verbs*), weil die im Verb ausgedrückte Handlung unmittelbar (direkt) auf das Objekt „übergeht" (lat. *transire*), also zielgerichtet ist. Alle anderen Verben, d. h. alle Verben ohne *Direct Object*, werden im Englischen als intransitive Verben (*Intransitive Verbs*) bezeichnet.

2.	Do not believe him. The Puritans followed Mr. Brewster's advice. He had advised them to go to New England. Robin escaped his enemies.	Im Englischen gibt es keine dem deutschen Dativ und Akkusativ entsprechenden besonderen Deklinationsformen mehr (vgl. 48). Aus diesem Grunde werden viele englische Verben, denen im Deutschen intransitive Verben entsprechen, transitiv gebraucht, d.h. sie haben ein direktes Objekt bei sich. Solche Verben sind z.B.

to advise	jem. raten	to allow, to permit	erlauben
to aid, to help, to assist	helfen	to answer	antworten
		to approach	sich nähern

to believe	glauben	to oppose	sich widersetzen
to command / to order	befehlen	to pardon	verzeihen
to congratulate	Glück wünschen	to please	gefallen
to contradict	widersprechen	to remember / to recollect	sich erinnern
to enter	eintreten in	to renounce	entsagen
to flatter	schmeicheln	to resemble	gleichen, ähneln
to follow	folgen	to resist	sich widersetzen
to imitate	nachahmen	to serve	dienen
to invade	eindringen in	to succeed	folgen
to join	sich anschließen	to thank	danken
to meet	jem. begegnen	to threaten	drohen
to obey	gehorchen	to trust	vertrauen

Vgl. lat. iuvare, adiuvare, frz. aider, secourir, seconder;
lat. sequor, frz. suivre; lat. imitari, frz. imiter;
lat. adulari, frz. flatter, etc.

211 Verbs used with and without a Direct Object

Verben, sowohl mit als auch ohne direktes Objekt gebraucht

1. He plays football. – He plays well.
She opened the door. – The door opened.
We are leaving London. – We shall leave tomorrow.
Cook tasted the soup. – The soup tasted good.
He began his lecture. – When does the lecture begin?
Do you smell the sea? – The wine smells sour.
The doctor felt the boy's arm to see whether it was broken. – The boy felt comfortable.

Einige Verben können sowohl mit direktem Objekt (transitiv) als auch ohne direktes Objekt (intransitiv) gebraucht werden, z. B.

to play, to feel, to open, to smell, to leave, to taste, to begin

2. They flew to London by British Airways.
Bobby flew his kite.

The boys worked very hard.
The sports master worked the boys very hard.

Many Spanish ships sank in the Channel.
The English sank many Spanish ships.

Manche Verben, die häufig ohne Objekt (intransitiv) gebraucht werden, können in bestimmter Bedeutung auch mit einem direkten Objekt stehen. Man nennt diese Verben auch faktitive (bewirkende) Verben (*Causative Verbs*). Im Deutschen müssen diese Verben oft mit „lassen" wiedergegeben werden. Hierzu gehören:

to dance	tanzen	tanzen lassen
to descend	herabsteigen	durch Erbschaft zufallen
to drop	fallen	fallen lassen
to enter	eintreten	eintragen
to fly	fliegen	fliegen lassen
to grow	wachsen	anbauen
to jump	springen	zum Springen bringen *(a horse)*
to leap	springen	springen lassen
to march	marschieren	marschieren lassen
to mount	besteigen, reiten	beritten machen
to pass	vorübergehen	reichen
to race	rennen	rennen lassen
to rėturn	zurückkehren	zurückgeben
to run	laufen	laufen lassen, leiten, betreiben
to sink	sinken	versenken
to stand	stehen	stellen, aushalten
to work	arbeiten	arbeiten lassen

212 Verbs with Prepositional Objects

Verben mit Präpositionalen Ergänzungen

a) This book belongs to Jack.
He turned to his boys and told them to listen to his words.
Nobody knows what has happened to him.

a) Eine Reihe von Verben verlangt stets eine (persönliche oder sachliche) Ergänzung mit *to*. Zu diesen Verben gehören:

to agree to / to consent to	zustimmen
to allude to	anspielen auf
to amount to	sich belaufen auf
to appear to / to seem to	scheinen
to apply to	sich wenden an, gelten für
to attend to	bedienen
to belong to	gehören
to bow to [bau]	sich verneigen vor
to happen to / to occur to	zustoßen
to introduce to	vorstellen
to listen to	zuhören
to object to	Einspruch erheben gegen
to propose to	vorschlagen
to refer to	sich beziehen auf
to speak to (with) / to talk to	sprechen mit
to turn to	sich wenden an
to set fire to	anzünden, in Brand stecken

b) What has become of him?
You must not laugh at the poor.
My father immediately sent for the doctor.
What are you talking about?

b) Andere Verben schließen die Ergänzung mit anderen Präpositionen an, z. B.

Verbs + about:

to hear about	hören von (= über)
to quarrel about	streiten über
to speak about	sprechen über
to talk about	reden über
to think about	nachdenken über
to worry about	sich beunruhigen über, sich Sorgen machen um

Verbs + at:

to aim at	zielen nach, auf	to point at	zeigen auf
to fire at	feuern auf	to shoot at	schießen auf
to gaze at	blicken nach, auf	to smile at	lächeln über
to glance at	blicken nach, auf	to sneer at	spötteln, höhnisch grinsen über
to look at	blicken nach, auf	to stare at	starren auf, anstarren
to grumble at	murren über	to throw at	werfen nach
to laugh at	lachen über	to weep at	weinen über
to mock at	spotten über	to wonder at	sich wundern über

Verbs + for:

to advertise for	annoncieren	to long for	sich sehnen nach
to apply for	sich bewerben um	to look for	suchen nach
to ask for	fragen nach, bitten um	to pay for	bezahlen für
to beg for	bitten um	to praise for	loben wegen
to call for	rufen nach	to send for	schicken nach jem. oder etwas
to care for	sorgen für	to struggle for	kämpfen um
to exchange for	eintauschen gegen	to wait for	warten auf
to change for (dinner)	sich umkleiden		
to hope for	hoffen auf		

Verbs + from:

to arise from	ausgehen von	to part from	sich trennen von
to conceal from	verbergen vor	to prevent from	hindern an
to conclude from	schließen aus	to protect from	schützen vor
to defend from	verteidigen gegen	to recover from	sich erholen von
to differ from	sich unterscheiden von	to separate from	trennen von
to distinguish from	unterscheiden von	to shelter from	schützen vor
to escape from	entkommen	to shrink from	zurückschrecken vor
to flee from	fliehen vor	to steal from	stehlen
to hide from	(sich) verbergen vor	to suffer from	leiden unter, an
to hinder from	hindern an	to take from	nehmen

Verbs + in:

to abound in	Überfluß haben an	to fail in	mißlingen, nicht schaffen
to believe in	glauben an	to join in	sich beteiligen an
to deal in	handeln mit	to persist in	beharren auf
to delight in	sich erfreuen an	to take part in	teilnehmen an
to succeed in	Erfolg haben mit(gelingen)	to trust in	vertrauen auf

Verbs + of:

to become of	werden aus	to dream of	träumen von
to boast of	sich rühmen	to hear of	hören von (= über)
to complain of	sich beklagen über	to judge of	urteilen über
to consist of	bestehen aus	to know of	wissen von
to despair of	verzweifeln an	to smell of	riechen nach

to die of	sterben an	to speak of	sprechen von
to dispose of	verfügen über	to think of	denken an

Verbs + on :

to agree on	übereinstimmen in	to live on	leben von
to call on	vorsprechen bei, jem. besuchen	to make war on	Krieg führen gegen
to congratulate on	Glück wünschen zu	to rely on	sich verlassen auf
to depend on	sich verlassen auf	to set on fire	anzünden
to feed on	sich nähren von	to wait on sb.	jemandem dienen, aufwarten
to insist on	bestehen auf		

Verbs + with :

to agree with	einverstanden sein mit	to meddle with	sich einmischen in
to be (make) friends with	befreundet sein, (Freundschaft schließen) mit	to part with	sich trennen von
to faint with	schwach werden vor	to tremble with	zittern vor

213 Verbs with Two Objects — Verben mit zwei Objekten

1.

Verb	Indirect Object	Direct Object
He offered	his friend	some sweets.
She gave	the grocer	fifty pence.

Zahlreiche Verben haben zwei Objekte bei sich, ein direktes (meist sachliches) und ein indirektes (meist persönliches) Objekt. Das indirekte Objekt steht im allgemeinen vor dem direkten Objekt.

Verb	Direct Object	Indirect Object	
He offered	the sweets	to Bob,	not to Pat.
She gave	the money	to the grocer,	not to the shop-assistant.

Nur wenn das indirekte (persönliche) Objekt besonders betont ist, tritt es mit *to* hinter das direkte Objekt.

Die wichtigsten Verben mit zwei Objekten, die diese beiden Ausdrucksweisen gestatten, sind:

to allow	bewilligen, gewähren	to get	besorgen, verschaffen
to award	anerkennen, verleihen	to give	geben, schenken
to bring	bringen	to grant	gewähren
to cost	kosten	to hand	überreichen, geben
to deny	jem. etw. versagen	to leave	überlassen
to forgive	jem. etwas erlassen	to lend	jem. etw. (aus)leihen

to offer	(an)bieten	to sell	verkaufen
to owe	schulden, verdanken	to send	schicken
to pass	reichen	to show	zeigen
to pay	bezahlen	to teach	lehren
to promise	versprechen	to tell	erzählen
to refuse	verweigern, versagen	to wish	wünschen
to return	zurückbringen, -senden	to write	schreiben

2. He gave the book to the boy.
He gave it to the boy.
He gave the boy the book.
He gave him the book.
Offer her a sweet.
Offer one to your sister.

Ist eines der beiden Objekte ein Pronomen, so steht dieses gewöhnlich an erster Stelle, gleich ob es direktes oder indirektes Objekt ist.

3. a) He gave it to him.
Offer one to her.
I'll send them to you.
Bring them to us.

b) Will you show me one?
I'll buy you some.
Did he leave us any?

a) Sind beide Objekte Pronomen, so ist die übliche Wortstellung:
Direct Object + to + Indirect Object

b) Ist (bei zwei Pronomen als Obj.) das direkte Objekt ein unbestimmtes Pronomen (z. B. *one*, *some*, *any*), so ist die Wortstellung *Indirect Object – Direct Object* gebräuchlicher.

4. John gave Mary that book.
Mary was given that book by John.
John gave that book to Mary.
That book was given to Mary by John.

Jede der in 213, 1 angeführten Satzstrukturen im Aktiv hat ihre Entsprechung im Passiv. Das Passiv wird gebildet, indem das erste Objekt zum Subjekt gemacht wird. Die Form des zweiten Objekts ändert sich nicht.

Verbs + Direct Object + Prepositional Object

Verben + Direktes Objekt + Präpositionales Objekt 214

1. He explained the plan to his friends.
The teacher dictated the words to the boys.
She mentioned the problem to her mother.
They concealed the facts from the public.

Bei einer Reihe von Verben, die zwei Objekte haben können, muß das *Indirect Object* immer mit einer Präposition (z. B. *to* oder *from*) angeschlossen werden. Es steht gewöhnlich hinter dem *Direct Object*.

Notice:

> He explained to his friends the plan for the trip.
> She related to her father what she had seen in town.
> His friends suggested to him that he should consult a doctor.

Das *Direct Object* kann jedoch auch bei diesen Verben nachgestellt werden, wenn es mehr Nachdruck erhalten soll oder viel länger ist als das indirekte Objekt.

Zu den Verben mit zwei Objekten, die das indirekte Objekt mit einer Präposition anschließen müssen, gehören:

Verbs + to

to announce	s.th. to s.o.	ankündigen
to add	s.th. to s.th	zufügen
to address	s.th. to s.o.	richten an
to admit	s.th. to s.o.	zugeben
to ascribe	s.th. to s.o.	zuschreiben
to confide	s.th. to s.o.	anvertrauen
to declare	s.th. to s.o.	erklären
to deliver	s.th. to s.o.	zustellen, liefern
to demonstrate	s.th. to s.o.	am Beispiel zeigen
to describe	s.th. to s.o.	beschreiben
to dictate	s.th. to s.o.	diktieren
to distribute	s.th. to s.o.	verteilen
to explain	s.th. to s.o.	erklären
to introduce	s.o. to s.o.	vorstellen
to mention	s.th. to s.o.	erwähnen
to prefer	s.th. to s.th. / s.o. to s.o.	vorziehen
to propose	s.th. to s.o.	vorschlagen
to prove	s.th. to s.o.	beweisen
to read	s.th. to s.o.	lesen
to relate	s.th. to s.o.	erzählen
to repeat	s.th. to s.o.	wiederholen
to reply	s.th. to s.o.	erwidern
to say	s.th. to s.o.	sagen
to seem	s.th. to s.o.	scheinen
to suggest	s.th. to s.o.	vorschlagen

Verbs + from

to hide	s.th. from s.o.	verbergen
to conceal	s.th. from s.o.	verbergen
to take	s.th. from s.o.	nehmen
to steal	s.th. from s.o.	stehlen
to snatch	s.th. from s.o.	entreißen
to buy	s.th. from s.o.	kaufen
to borrow	s.th. from s.o	borgen
to hire	s.th. from s.o	mieten
to inherit	s.th. from s.o.	erben
to order	s.th. from s.o.	bestellen

2.
> The teacher explained the problem to us.
> The problem was explained to us by the teacher.

Da diese Verben nur eine Aktivstruktur haben (214, 1) gibt es auch nur eine Passivstruktur (vgl. 213,4).

3.
> We had the problem explained to us by the teacher.
> I had the accident described to me by an eye-witness.
> I like having stories read to me.
> She had £ 10 stolen from her.

Die „fehlende" zweite Passivform können wir bilden mit Hilfe der Konstruktion
have + Dir. Obj. + Past Participle + to/from + Pronoun

"To pride oneself on" is a reflexive verb. How did you enjoy yourself at the party?

Reflexive Verben sind im Englischen viel seltener als im Deutschen. Hier folgt eine Aufstellung der Verben, die

a) stets mit Reflexivpronomen
b) nur in der hier angegebenen Bedeutung mit Reflexivpronomen gebraucht werden.

a)	to absent	o.s. from	fernbleiben
	to apply	o.s. to	sich widmen
	to avail	o.s. of	(Gelegenheit) benutzen
	to exert	o.s. to	sich bemühen
	to plume	o.s. on	sich brüsten
	to pride	o.s. on	sich brüsten mit, stolz sein auf
	to confine	o.s. to	sich beschränken auf

b)	to enjoy	o.s.	sich gut unterhalten
	to amuse	o.s.	sich gut unterhalten
	to accustom	o.s. to	sich gewöhnen an
	to distinguish	o.s.	sich auszeichnen
	to hurt	o.s.	sich verletzen
	to defend	o.s.	sich verteidigen
	to help	o.s.	sich bedienen
	to introduce	o.s.	sich vorstellen

Eine Reihe von Verben kann im Englischen sowohl mit als auch ohne Reflexivpronomen gebraucht werden.

a) Bob washed and dressed quickly. The squirrel hid behind the tree. He doesn't like shaving.
b) Pat dressed herself carefully for the party. Bob prepared himself very carefully for the interview.

a) Das Verb steht ohne Reflexivpronomen, wenn ausgedrückt werden soll, daß die Handlung gewohnheitsmäßig geschieht bzw. wenn nicht besonders betont werden soll (oder muß), daß der Handelnde selbst etwas tut.

b) Das Verb wird dagegen mit dem Reflexivpronomen gebraucht, wenn man ausdrücken will, daß die Handlung bewußt vonstatten geht.

Zu den Verben, die mit oder ohne Reflexivpronomen gebraucht werden können, gehören:

to behave	(o.s.)	sich betragen
to dress	(o.s.)	sich ankleiden
to hide	(o.s.)	sich verbergen
to offer	(o.s.)	sich erbieten
to prepare	(o.s.)	sich vorbereiten
to prove	(o.s.)	sich erweisen
to shave	(o.s.)	sich rasieren
to spread	(o.s.)	sich ausbreiten
to submit	(o.s.)	sich unterwerfen
to surrender	(o.s.)	sich ergeben
to wash	(o.s.)	sich waschen

The cloth feels soft. This book sells well. The gate opened and closed again.

Bei Sachsubjekten wird das Verb in der Regel nicht reflexiv gebraucht.

4. The accident happened at ten o'clock.
The weather often changes very quickly in England.
He turned to his friend for help.
She does not remember his name.

Viele englische Verben sind im Gegensatz zum Deutschen nicht reflexiv.

Zu diesen Verben gehören:

to amount to	sich belaufen auf
to approach	sich nähern
to boast of	sich rühmen
to bow to [bau]	sich verbeugen vor
to care about	sich kümmern um
to care for	sich etwas machen aus
to change	sich ändern
to complain of	sich beklagen über
to depend on	sich verlassen auf
to differ from	sich unterscheiden von
to endeavour	sich bemühen
to fancy	sich vorstellen (in Ausrufen)
to happen	sich ereignen
to imagine	sich einbilden, sich vorstellen
to increase	sich vermehren
to join	sich anschließen, Mitglied werden
to lie down	sich hinlegen
to meet	sich treffen
to move	sich bewegen
to realize	sich klarmachen, begreifen
to remember, to recollect	sich erinnern
to recover	sich erholen
to refuse	sich weigern
to rejoice△	sich freuen
to rely on	sich verlassen auf
to retire	sich zurückziehen, in Pension gehen
to rise	sich erheben
to sit down	sich setzen
to turn to	sich wenden an
to withdraw	sich zurückziehen
to wonder at	sich wundern über

5. Bob was interested in the book on birds.
He got accustomed to life in America.
It became cloudy again.
The weather grew worse

In gewissen Fällen vermeidet die englische Sprache das Reflexivpronomen und gebraucht Konstruktionen wie to be / to get / to become / to grow + *Past Participle* / *Adjective* / *Adverb*

Konstruktionen dieser Art sind z. B.

to be interested in	sich interessieren für
to be mistaken	sich irren
to be glad of	sich freuen (über)
to be satisfied with, to be contented with	sich begnügen (mit)
to get accustomed to	sich gewöhnen an
to get excited over	sich ereifern, aufregen über
to get engaged to	sich verloben (mit)
to get married to	sich verheiraten (mit)
to get rid of	sich entledigen
to get shaved (get a shave)	sich rasieren lassen
to become acquainted with	sich kennenlernen
to become cloudy	sich bewölken
to grow better	sich (ver)bessern
to grow stiff	sich versteifen
to grow worse	sich verschlechtern

The Prepositions

Die Präpositionen

The Function and Classification of Prepositions

Die Funktion und Einteilung der Präpositionen 216

Die Präpositionen hatten ursprünglich vorwiegend die Funktion, das örtliche oder zeitliche Verhältnis von Personen oder Dingen zueinander zu bezeichnen. Später wurden sie dann auch in übertragener, bildlicher Bedeutung gebraucht.

Nach dem Verfall der Deklinationsendungen haben die Präpositionen (neben der Wortstellung) auch die Funktionen der alten Endungen übernommen und dadurch eine entscheidende Bedeutung gewonnen. Die Präpositionen drücken die Beziehungen der Wörter im Satz zueinander deutlicher und klarer aus, als die alten Kasusendungen es tun konnten, und tragen dazu bei, der englischen Sprache ihre große Anschaulichkeit zu verleihen. – Die wichtigsten Präpositionen, die syntaktische Aufgaben übernommen haben, sind *of* und *to*.

1.

a) after, at, by, down, for, from, in, of, off, on, over, since, through, till, under, up, with, out, to

b) about, above, across, against, along, amid(st), among(st), around, before, behind, below, beneath, beside(s), between, beyond, despite, inside, into, onto, out of, outside, throughout, towards, until, upon, within, without

c) concerning, considering, during, except, past

d) around, near, opposite, close to

Nach ihrer Form unterscheidet man

a) ursprüngliche Präpositionen;

b) zusammengesetzte Präpositionen;

c) Präpositionen, die aus Verbalformen (Partizipien) entstanden sind;

d) Präpositionen, die aus Adjektiven entstanden sind.

2.

according to, by means of, owing to, in front of, in consequence of, because of, instead of, for the sake of, with regard (respect) to, in spite of, as far as, thanks to, with the exception of

Zu den Präpositionen kann man auch die präpositionalen Ausdrücke zählen.

217 The Use of the Prepositions — Der Gebrauch der Präpositionen

1\. He came running into the room.
A big crane swung its arm over the hold of the vessel.

Die Präpositionen sind unveränderlich und stehen im allgemeinen vor Substantiven (prae-position = Vor-Stellung).

2\. Die Präpositionen können nachgestellt werden in

a) What are you looking for?
Where do you come from?

a) Fragesätzen (vgl. 85);

b) The gentleman we are speaking about is a friend of my father's.
The film we went to was very exciting.

b) Relativsätzen (vgl. 92);

c) He was never heard of again.
The animals in the zoo are well cared for.

c) im passivischen Satz (vgl. 170);

d) It was an answer to smile at.
The lecturer gave them a good deal to think about.

d) beim Infinitiv als attributive Bestimmung (vgl. 180).

3\. The children came from behind the door.
I bought the dictionary for about three pounds.
The dog crawled out from under the table.
He shot the arrow to within an inch of the bull's eye.

Im Englischen treten häufiger als im Deutschen zwei Präpositionen zusammen, wenn ein bestimmtes Verhältnis genauer gekennzeichnet werden soll.

4\. They talked about, and laughed at, his strange manners.
Some people are interested in, others obsessed with, photography.

Verben mit verschiedenen Präpositionen können eine gemeinsame Ergänzung haben. (Die Konjunktion und das zweite Verb werden in Kommata eingeschlossen.)

The Most Important Prepositions of Place

Die wichtigsten Präpositionen des Ortes

218

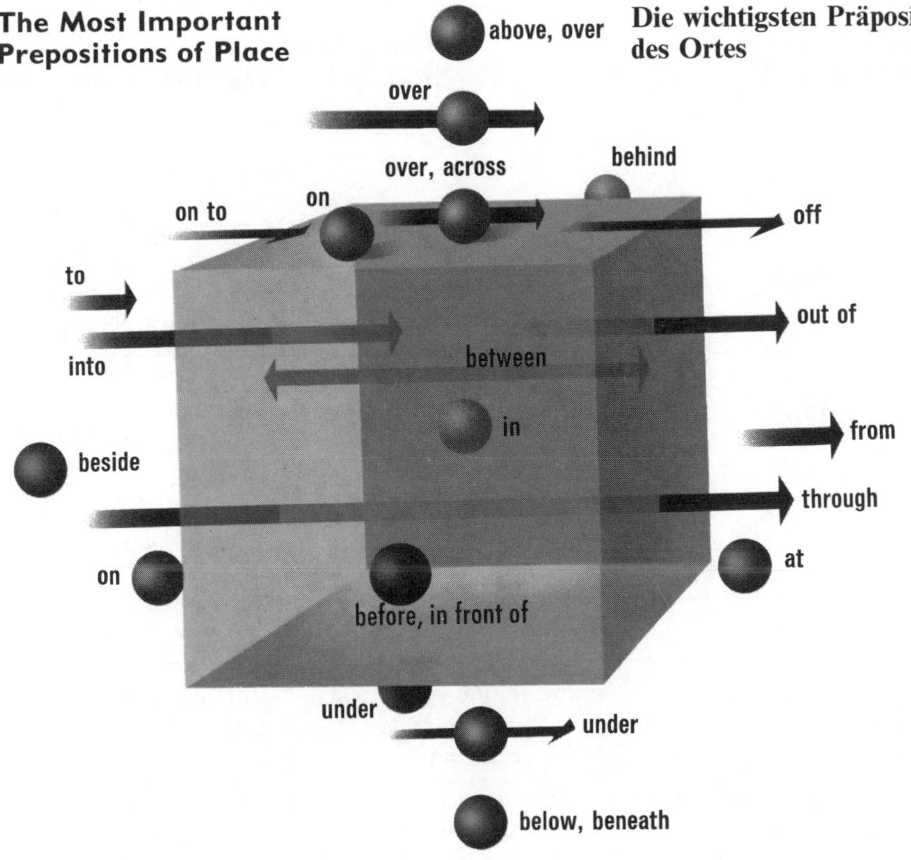

	Prepositions Indicating	
Rest	**Motion**	
Question: where?	*Question: where to?*	*Question: where from?*
He stood at the corner. He is sitting in his room. The book is on the table. The picture is on the wall. The dog is lying under the table. The lamp is over (above) the table. The bus stopped in front of the theatre.	He went to the river. He jumped into the water. Put the book on (to) the table. The dog crept under the table. The plane is flying over the river. He swam across the river.	He came from the river. He came out of the water. Take the book off the table.

219 The Most Important Prepositions of Time

Übersicht über die wichtigsten Präpositionen der Zeit

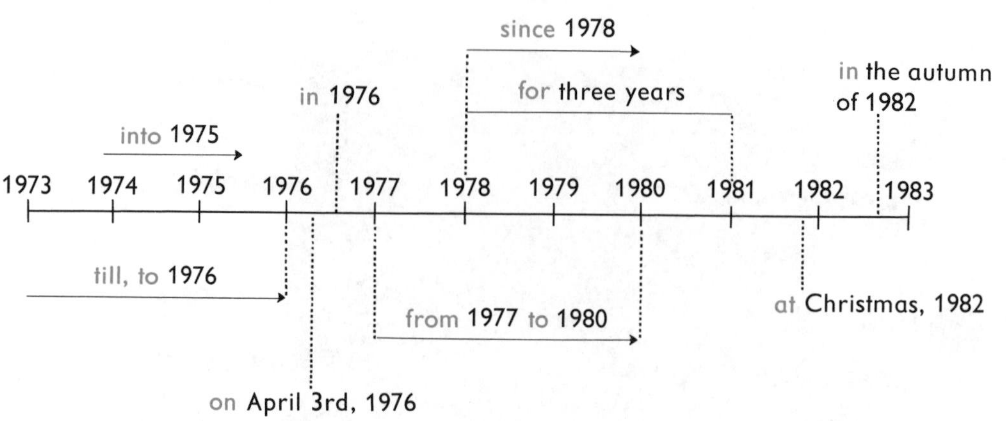

Zeitpunkt	Zeitraum	Zeitdauer
at: at Christmas, at midnight at dawn on: *an einem bestimmten Tag*: on April 3rd, 1984 on Monday since: *von einem Zeitpunkt ab*: since 1970 to, till: *bis zu einem Zeitpunkt*: to, till 1990	in: in (the year) 1603 in January 1983 in spring into: *in einen Zeitraum hinein* We drove on into the night.	for: for three years from . . . to: *von . . . bis* from 1966 to 1976

220 The Prepositions in Particular

Die Präpositionen im einzelnen

In der folgenden Liste der Präpositionen, die natürlich nicht vollständig sein kann, bedeuten die Abkürzungen

(r) = räumliche; (z) = zeitliche; (ü) = übertragene Bedeutung.

Da einige Präpositionen in derselben Form auch als Adverbien und als Konjunktionen erscheinen können, wird an den entsprechenden Stellen auf den Gebrauch in diesen Funktionen hingewiesen (*adv.*, *conj.*).

about

He must be somewhere about the house. They walked about the market place.	(r) in . . . umher, herum, irgendwo
I looked about me. I lost it somewhere about here.	um . . . herum
The boys talked about cars. Tell us about it. What about you?	(ü) über, darüber
There was a lot of excitement about his visit. He has gone to see his uncle about the money.	wegen
My friend comes about three o'clock every day. She is about seventeen.	*adv.* ungefähr, etwa
The policemen were running about looking for the thief.	herum

above

Antonym: below, beneath
Compare: over

Do you see the dome of St. Paul's above the surrounding houses? The seagulls flew above the masts of the ship.	(r) über (einem Gegenstand, ohne Berührung) oberhalb von, höher als
A captain is above a lieutenant. I should have liked an MG above all.	(ü) über, höher als
This is above me (= too difficult for me). She is above criticism (= too great to be criticized). They are above suspicion (= too honest to be suspected).	erhaben über

according to

According to Magna Carta no man was to be put into prison before having been properly tried. You will be paid according to your efforts.	gemäß, nach

4. **across**

Draw a line across the sheet. The plane flew straight across London. There is a tea-shop just across the road. They built a bridge across the Thames.	(r) quer über . . . hin, quer durch jenseits, über (eine Fläche)
I came across him yesterday.	*to come across* = jem. (zufällig) begegnen

5. **after** *Antonym:* before
Compare: behind

He ran after his dog. The police have been after this thief ever since. After supper we usually go for a walk. After ten minutes he left the house. He is a man after my own heart. She dresses after the fashion of the twenties.	(r) hinter . . . her, nach (z) nach (ü) nach
He drove into a tree and died the day after. Bob went ahead, and the others came after.	*adv.* da(r)nach hinterher
He died a few days after he had crashed into the tree.	*conj.* nachdem

6. **against**

I fell against him. Two tug-boats were pushing the ship against the quay. The cupboard stands against the wall. The boy was leaning against the door. The Britons fought against the Romans. This is against the rule.	(r) gegen, wider; an, gegen (mit Berührung eines Gegenstandes). (ü) gegen, wider

. along

A police-car comes along the street. Drake sailed along the western coast of America.	(r) entlang, längs
Please work along these lines.	(ü) nach, gemäß
Come along!	*adv.* *(to come along)* Komm mit! Mach schnell!

. amid(st)

I found him amidst his friends. The miners had their meal amid the coal-dust and dirt.	(r) mitten in, mitten unter, inmitten
Amidst the cheers of the girls, the head-mistress announced that they were to have the day off.	(ü) unter

. among(st) *Compare*: between

There was a foreign lady among the passengers. The boys hid among the trees.	(r) zwischen (mehreren), unter (einer Menge)
I feel much honoured to be numbered among his friends.	(ü) *to number among* = zählen zu
We divided the apples among the children.	*to divide among* = teilen unter, zwischen

. around (round)

There were several children around (round) the ice-cream stand.	(r) um . . . herum
We went on a motor-trip around the island.	ringsherum

. at *Compare*: in

	Bezeichnung eines Punktes im Raum:
Pat is standing at the door (at the corner).	(r) an
My mother is at the grocer's.	bei
He is at the zoo (at school, at the store).	in
My father is not at home.	zu
Have a look at the title at the top of page 253.	oben (*at the top*)
The pages are numbered at the bottom.	unten *(at the bottom)*
She prefers to sit at the front of the car.	vorne *(at the front)*
Will you sit at the back?	hinten *(at the back)*

We sleep at night. At the moment he is feeling quite well. They go to school at eight o'clock. I hope we shall have snow at Christmas. At the beginning of the meeting there were only very few people present. He arrived at a gallop. I risk it at my own cost. She bought it at half the price. The bank lent me the money at 8% interest. He is very good at his studies. In 1941 Germany was at war with Great Britain.	Bezeichnung eines Zeitpunktes: (z) zu, an im (Augenblick) um zu bei (ü) in (Bezeichnung der Art u. Weise) auf (bei Bezeichnung des Preises) für gegen Zinsen in, bei in

a) Phrases with at:

at table	bei Tisch	at length	ausführlich; schließlich
at a distance	in einiger Entfernung	at full speed	eiligst
at work	bei der Arbeit	at a high price	um einen hohen Preis
at once	sofort	at any price	um jeden Preis
at first	zuerst, anfangs	at the age of	im Alter von
at last	zuletzt, schließlich, endlich	at your risk	auf deine Verantwortung
at present	jetzt, zur Zeit	at a loss	in Verlegenheit
at sunrise	bei Sonnenaufgang	at a reduced price	billiger
at dawn	im Morgengrauen	not at all	keineswegs
at noon	zu Mittag	at any rate	auf jeden Fall
at sunset	bei Sonnenuntergang	at least	mindestens, wenigstens

b) Adjectives + at

alarmed at	beunruhigt über	furious at	wütend über
astonished at surprised at	erstaunt über	frightened at	erschrocken über
		happy at	glücklich über
delighted at	entzückt über	shocked at	entsetzt über

c) Verbs + at (see 212)

12. **because of** (= on account of, owing to)

She could not run as fast as the other girls because of her swollen leg. (We were late, owing to the icy roads.)	(ü) wegen

13. **before** *Antonyms:* behind, after

They walked before us in the park. The police-car stopped in front of the town hall.	(r) vor (einer Person oder Sache) Häufiger als *before* (im räumlichen Sinne) steht *in front of*.

My sister came before eleven o'clock. My aunt arrived the day before yesterday. Patricia is excellent at school; she is before the other girls in her class.△	(z) vor (einem Zeitpunkt der Vergangenheit oder Zukunft) (ü) vor (Rangordnung; Häufiger ist in diesem Sinne *ahead of*.)
She met her yesterday, but she had never seen her before. "Have you ever been to Chester before?" – "I have never been here before."	*adv.* zuvor (vgl. *ago*, 220, 13 Not.) schon einmal noch nie
It was not long before I got to know him well. Think before you speak.	*conj.* Es dauerte nicht lange, bis . . . ehe, bevor

Notice:

I went to see him a week ago. Six months ago, he returned from York.	*ago* (= vor, heute vor) rechnet von der Gegenwart zurück. Es steht hinter der Zeitangabe.
John left Paris on 2nd April. He had arrived there from Rome two days before. She thought he looked much more relaxed than he had been a couple of hours before.	Wenn aber die Zeitdauer von der Vergangenheit zurückgerechnet wird, gebraucht man *before*. Es steht ebenfalls hinter der Zeitangabe.

behind *Antonym:* in front of

The assistant is standing behind the counter. She came behind me.	(r) hinter, nach
He was ten minutes behind the winner of the cross-country race.	(z) hinter
When she died she left nothing but debts behind her.	(ü) hinter
You are behind the times (= old fashioned). The train arrived twenty minutes behind time (= 20 minutes late).	*behind the times* = rückständig *behind time* = verspätet
Everything had been arranged behind the scenes (in secret) beforehand.	hinter (im Hintergrund)
Bob must stay (remain) behind after school. Have you left anything behind? They are three months behind with the rent.	*adv.* zurück im Rückstand

15. **below** *Antonym:* above, over
Compare: under, beneath

Looking out of the plane he saw London lying below him. Below us was a very rapid river. It is very cold today; it must be a few degrees below zero.	(r) unter, unterhalb (ohne gegenseitige Berührung)
A lieutenant is below a captain in rank. Why do you think it is below your dignity to sweep the footpath?	(ü) unter (im Rang, einer Würde)
Looking out of the plane he saw London lying below.	*adv.* unten
Let's go below (= below the deck on a ship).	nach unten

16. **beneath** *Antonym:* above, over
Compare: under, below

The submarine remained beneath the surface of the water for 38 days.	(r) unter, unterhalb (ohne gegenseitige Berührung)
That's beneath my dignity.	(ü) unter (einem Rang, einer Würde usw.)
They are beneath contempt.	*beneath contempt* = verachtenswert, unter aller Kritik.

17. **beside** *Compare:* besides

Let me sit beside you. Our school is beside the church.	(r) neben, an der Seite von
Tom's drawing is poor beside David's.	neben, im Vergleich zu
The boy was beside himself with joy.	(ü) außer
That's beside the question. Her argument was beside the point.	außerhalb (nicht zur Sache gehörend)

18. **besides** *Compare:* except, but, beside

Besides me five boys were invited. Besides coal, iron-ore is found in the Midlands.	(ü) außer, neben (zusätzlich)

Unfortunately we did not have time to visit the Roman Gardens when we were in York. Besides they were closed that day.	*adv.* außerdem

9. between *Compare:* among

There is a meadow between our house and the river.	(r) zwischen (zweien bzw. zwei Gruppen u. a.)
How many stops are there between Marble Arch and St. Paul's, please?	
All the work was done between ten and four p.m.	(z) zwischen
Between Christmas and New Year's Day there was no work done.	
There was a quarrel between the parents and their children.	(ü) zwischen
Between ourselves (= between you and me) I do not trust him.	unter (uns gesagt)
There was another meeting between the unions and the employers.	
In the eighteenth century there was much rivalry between the English and the French in North America.	
From London to Stratford is somewhere between 30 and 40 miles.	etwa (zwischen)
A portable typewriter weighs between 10 and 15 pounds.	
A mule is a cross between a horse and a donkey.	zwischen

10. beyond

Are you travelling beyond Manchester?	(r) über . . . hinaus
My relatives live beyond the frontier.	jenseits
He worked beyond his usual eight hours.	(z) über . . . hinaus
He likes the mountains beyond everything	(ü) „. . . über alles."
His behaviour was beyond all blame.	„. . . über jeden Tadel erhaben."
That's beyond me.	„Das geht über meine Begriffe."

21. **but** *Compare:* besides, except

All but one were saved. She eats hardly anything but fruit. He talked nothing but nonsense. Have a look at the last line but one.	(ü) außer, ausgenommen (nach *all*, *any*, *every*) als (*the last but one* =) vorletzte
They have but few friends.△ Mary, Queen of Scots, became queen when but five days old.△	*adv.* nur erst
He is good at mathematics but bad at sports. They do not begin school at five but at six.	*conj.* aber sondern

22. **by**

The policeman catches the thief by the arm. I like to sit by the open fire. He went to England by the Hook of Holland. They came by the lane, not by the main road. He must be back by six o'clock. I hope to have finished my work by Easter. My mother does not like travelling by night; she always travels by day. When we stayed in Florida last year we swam by moonlight. The carpenter will have repaired the roof by tomorrow. Britain was conquered by the Romans. Please let me know by telegram (letter) when you come. They won by force of arms. Formerly most locomotives and ships were driven by steam. They preferred travelling by rail, by train, by boat, by steamer, by plane; by land, by sea, by air. They went to see the headmaster one by one. This poem is by Robert Frost. They beat their opponents by two goals.	(r) an über durch (z) gegen, um (ungefähre Zeit) bis spätestens in, an bei bis (ü) von (beim Passiv!) durch, mittels mittels, mit über; durch nach (Aufeinanderfolge) von um
We watched the ship pass by. The troops were standing by. He will become more sensible by and by.△	*adv.* vorbei in Bereitschaft halten allmählich

Keep in Mind:

Manual workers are often paid by the day, by the week, by the month.	täglich, wöchentlich, monatlich
My American uncle will come back to see us in three years' time; I shall be fourteen by then.	dann
When she is by herself she likes to read.	allein
Joseph Conrad was a Pole by birth.	von Geburt
Little Frank is timid by nature.	von Natur aus
I find it difficult to learn anything by heart.	auswendig
She knows him only by name.	dem Namen nach
We know him by sight.	vom Sehen her
We met Aunt Alice by chance.	durch Zufall
The criminal was taken to prison by force.	mit Gewalt
You must not do it all at once, you must do it by degrees.	allmählich
You can lift heavy loads by means of big cranes.	mit Hilfe von
Don't hesitate, do it by all means.	auf jeden Fall
By no means must you forget to keep left.	keineswegs
He went to the wrong house by mistake.	aus Versehen
What do you mean by that?	damit
One should not only judge people by their clothes.	nach ihrer Kleidung
You must learn a language step by step.	Schritt für Schritt

. **despite**

Despite their bravery the Britons could not defeat the Romans. Despite all her efforts she failed the exam.	(ü) trotz

. **down** *Antonym:* up

The boat glided down the Mississippi. He is coming down the hill. The two boys were pushed down the gangway by the crowd of passengers.	(r) herunter, hinunter
Down the ages, York has kept traces of its Roman origin.	(z) durch (die Jahrhunderte bis heute)
At the outing they all enjoyed themselves, from the managing director down to the youngest lift-boy.	(ü) *from . . . down* = von . . . herunter bis

The sun goes down in the west. The farmhouse burnt down in half an hour. My grandfather was knocked down by a motor-car.	*adv*. nieder, herunter

25. **during**

During the last century, industry became highly developed. During my stay in London I went to all the museums.	(z) während

Notice:

While driving along the A I we saw several accidents. She has remained poor, while her brother became a millionaire.	Der deutschen Konjunktion „während" entspricht im Englischen *while* (vgl. 224).

26. **except** *Compare:* but, beside

I've spent all my money, except for two pounds. No one was present except myself. Except for a few slips of the tongue his reading was good.	(ü) außer, ausgenommen

27. **for**

The boys started for school. We took the train for Windsor.	(r) zu(r) (Bezeichnung des Zieles), nach
He has been working for two hours. We have not seen each other for years. The thrush has been looking for worms for a good while (for some time). He was so badly hurt that he will be a cripple for life.	(z) . . . lang, seit (vgl. since)
Here is a letter for you. For his age he is rather clever.	(ü) für
Are you working for money? He was blamed for his laziness.	wegen, (für)
They were struggling for a prize.	um
The little girl wept for joy.	vor, aus
The bears are looking for food.	nach

Bob called a policeman, for a thief had stolen his bicycle. He is always surrounded by children, for he is very good-natured.	*conj.* denn

Keep in Mind:

There are many wild cats, for example (for instance) lions and tigers.	zum Beispiel (Abkürzung im Englischen e. g. = lat. exempli gratia)
On Sunday afternoons our family usually goes for a walk.	spazieren gehen
He did not do it for money, he did it for fun, as he is not greedy for money.	des Geldes, des Spaßes wegen, aus Freude, geldgierig
Through the woods the children walked very fast for fear of robbers.△	aus Furcht vor
He felt very weak for want of food.△	aus Mangel an
In the suburbs we saw a few houses for sale.	zum Verkauf
For goodness sake, drink milk!	um Himmels willen
We live far from the city; for this reason we bought a car recently.	aus diesem Grunde
Once and for all I forbid you to enter my house.	ein für allemal
As for me I love pancakes.	was . . . anbetrifft
For all I know he is a bachelor.	soviel ich weiß
Find out the meaning of the word for yourself.	selbst
Oh, for a long holiday!	Oh, hätte ich . . .
For my part I wouldn't hesitate to go to Australia.	was mich betrifft
He won't eat beef – or any other meat for that matter.	übrigens, was das (an)betrifft
He could not say for certain when the doctor would come.	sicher

Verbs + for (see 212)

to depart for to leave for	abreisen nach	to sail for	segeln nach
to embark for	sich einschiffen nach	to set sail for	aufbrechen (mit einem Schiff) nach
to make for	sich begeben nach	to start for	aufbrechen nach

Nouns + for

desire for	Verlangen nach	preference for	Vorliebe für
love for	Liebe zu	taste for	Geschmack an

Adjectives + for

anxious for	begierig auf	known for	bekannt wegen
celebrated for famous for	berühmt wegen	remarkable for	bemerkenswert wegen
		responsible for	verantwortlich für

28. from *Antonym:* to
Compare: of

He is coming from school. The boy nearly fell from the tree. From the top of the hill we had a fine view of the country.	(r) von (weg) (Bewegung von einem Ort weg)
He worked from morning to night. Queen Elizabeth I reigned from 1558 to (till) 1603. From the end of December, the days grow longer.	(z) von . . . an (Anfangspunkt einer Zeitspanne)
The nobleman hid from his enemies. Protect us from harm and protect us from our enemies.	(ü) vor
I know him from my own experience.	aus (Erfahrung)
Steel is made from iron. Chocolate is made from cocoa and milk and sugar.	aus (Das Material [hier: *iron*] wird in einen anderen Stoff verwandelt; vgl. dagegen *of*).

Verbs + from (see 212)

Nouns + from

difference from	Unterschied zu	protection from	Schutz vor
escape from	Flucht von (aus)	shelter from	

Adjectives + from

different from	verschieden von	safe from	sicher vor
far from	fern von, weit von	secure from	
free from	frei von		

29. in *Compare:* into, at, on

The children were sitting in a plane. He lives in London.	(r) in (Frage: Wo?) bezeichnet einen Aufenthalt in einem Raum, Land, auf einer Insel, auf einem Platz etc.
I prefer living in the country to living in town. The boys play in the street, in the field, in the playground.	in, auf

It was cold in the morning, in the afternoon, in the evening.	(z) am
He was born in 1949.	im (Jahre)
He will be back in five minutes, in a month.	in
He was in great danger.	(ü) in
They were in a hurry.	
She asked in a low voice, in a whisper.	mit
What is that in English?	auf (English)
Are you in earnest? (=Are you serious?)	Ist das dein Ernst?
Don't put your hands in your pockets.	Nach *to put* steht heute vorwiegend *in*.
Is anybody in? Come in!	*adv*. drinnen; herein
When does the next train get in?	ein(laufen)

Keep in Mind:

In my opinion she is a very lucky girl.	nach meiner Meinung
The monument was erected in memory of the airmen who died in the war.	zum Gedächtnis von, im Andenken an
A dinner was given in honour of the famous visitor.	zur Ehre von
Three Conservatives and one Liberal M.P. spoke in favour of the Government motion.	zum Besten, zu Gunsten von
I personally am in favour of going to the races and not to the football match.	dafür (sein)
She was in good health when I visited her last summer.	bei bester Gesundheit
As far as things in general are concerned I have little to complain about.	im allgemeinen
What struck me in particular about the play was the excellent acting by the leading lady.	besonders, insbesondere
He tried in vain to reach the drowning man.	vergeblich
In vain did he shout for help; no one heard him.△	
He is always in a (great) hurry in the morning as he never gets up in time.	in Eile (recht)zeitig
He spoke in a loud voice so that everyone in the room would hear him.	mit lauter Stimme
In a word, I consider him a liar.	kurz (gesagt), mit einem Wort
If you go on in this way you will soon have no money left at all.	auf diese Weise
In this manner, by being very willing and helpful, he soon succeeded in making himself well liked.	auf diese Weise
Although he is still young in years he is a world-famous politician.	jung an Jahren

Verbs + in (see 212)

Nouns + in

confidence in	Vertrauen auf	interest in	Anteilnahme an
delight in	Vergnügen an	pleasure in	Vergnügen an

Adjectives + in

abundant in	überreich an	interested in	beteiligt bei; interessiert an
concerned in	beteiligt an	poor in	arm an
employed in	beschäftigt mit	rich in	reich an

30. **inside** *Antonym*: outside

Outside it is raining; inside it is warm and dry.	(r) innerhalb
The cups are in the cupboard; she put them inside the cupboard.	in . . . hinein
Inside a week he recovered.	(z) in weniger als

31. **into** *Compare*: in
Antonym: out of

He jumps into the car. The plane rose into the air. David stood on deck and peered into the fog.	(r) in . . . hinein (Frage: Wohin? Bewegung in den Raum hinein)
Our visitor stayed on well into the summer (into the night).	(z) bis in
He flew into a passion, into a terrible rage. He got into difficulties.	(ü) in . . . hinein
They divided the apples into quarters. Translate that sentence into English.	in
Take it into consideration.	in Betracht ziehen
She burst into tears.	in Tränen ausbrechen

. of *Compare:* from

Die Präposition *of* bezeichnete ursprünglich den räumlichen und zeitlichen Abstand und in übertragener Bedeutung die Herkunft. In diesen Bedeutungen ist *of* aber durch andere Präpositionen (*from, off*) bis auf einige Redensarten verdrängt worden. (Über *of* als Satzbeziehungsmittel vgl. 48; 51).

This ship is made of good wood. This chain is made of steel. The house is built of brick.

Heute dient *of* noch zur Angabe des Stoffes, aus dem etwas hergestellt wird. Das Material (hier: *steel, wood* etc.) bleibt unverändert. (vgl. *from,* Bsp. S. 218)

Keep in Mind:

Cambridge is (to the) north of London.	nördlich von London
Mr. Jones, of London, will advise our clients tomorrow.	aus London
In days of old people's lives were often endangered by plagues.△	früher, ehemals
"Do you like swimming?" – "Of course, I do."	natürlich
All of a sudden the train stopped.	plötzlich
At twenty-one young people come of age.	mündig werden
He comes of a very respectable family.△ (*now usually:* come from)	herkommen, abstammen
Let go of me!	Laß mich los!

Verbs + of (see 212)

Nouns + of (see 51, 3 K. i. M.)

Adjectives + of

characteristic of	bezeichnend für	typical of	bezeichnend für
conscious of	bewußt	vain of	eingebildet auf
desirous of	begierig auf	weary of	müde, überdrüssig
envious of	neidisch auf	(un)worthy of	(un)würdig
glad of	froh über	to be ashamed of	sich schämen
innocent of	unschuldig an	to be aware of	sich bewußt sein
jealous of	eifersüchtig auf	to be afraid of	sich fürchten vor
proud of	stolz auf	to be fond of	etwas gern haben
sure of	sicher	to be ignorant of	etwas nicht verstehen, etwas nicht wissen
tired of	müde, überdrüssig		

33. off *Antonym*: on
Compare: from

The child fell off the chair.	(r) von . . . herunter
Take the book off the table.	von . . . weg
Keep off the grass, please.	
Get off that bicycle.	von . . . herunter
The ship sailed off Cape Horn.	auf der Höhe von (geographisch)
Supper was not ready in time because the gas was off.	*adv.* weg

Keep in Mind:	
The men now on strike laid off work at 6 p.m.	die Arbeit niederlegen
She is looking somewhat off colour, I hope she is not going to get (be) ill.	blaß, ungesund
The policeman was not wearing his uniform as he was off duty.	dienstfrei
She has been off her food for several days.	ohne Appetit
A weight fell off my mind.	„vom Herzen“

34. on, upon *Antonym*: off

Der Unterschied zwischen *on* und *upon* ist sehr gering; *upon* wird viel seltener und nur in der Schriftsprache gebraucht. In zeitlicher Bedeutung ist *upon* nur in der Verbindung *once upon a time* zu verwenden (Anfang eines Märchens).

He is sitting on a chair.	(r) auf (oben auf)
The picture is hanging on the wall.	an
to go on board, on horseback	an Bord, zu Pferde
On Sunday the children go to the zoo.	(z) am (Sonntag)
On wet days they play in the house.	an
On 5th September . . .	
In the famine years, the Irish lived chiefly on potatoes.	(ü) von
The wealth of Great Britain depends on her trade and industry.	
Put your cap on.	*adv.* auf

Verbs + on (see 212)

Keep in Mind:

On an average it takes me an hour and a half to do my homework.	im Durchschnitt
They are on no account to leave the house after dark.	unter keinen Umständen
My father has gone to London on business.	geschäftlich, in Geschäften
The train was on time.	pünktlich
I shall only go with you on condition that you pay all my travelling expenses.	unter der Bedingung
When I was in hospital the nurse on duty used to take my temperature twice a day.	im Dienst
When his car broke down he had to continue his journey on foot.	zu Fuß
While on leave from the army my brother spent three days in London.	auf Urlaub
She told the lie on purpose so that she would not be punished.	absichtlich
He is not an honest man; on the contrary I consider him a thief.	im Gegenteil
On the whole I prefer the mountains to the seaside.	im ganzen
On this occasion he was very friendly, although he is usually not so.	bei dieser Gelegenheit
While on a visit to my grandmother, I fell and broke my arm.	zu Besuch
While on his travels through France and Switzerland he saw many interesting things.	auf Reisen
He was ordered to recapture the escaped prisoner on pain of death if he failed.	bei Todesstrafe
In war time a soldier always has to be on his guard against the enemy.	auf der Hut sein
The apples on sale at the greengrocer's this morning were very dear.	zum Verkauf
She showed her dependence on her mother by asking her permission before doing anything.	Abhängigkeit von
My first view of the Niagara Falls made a great impression on me.	Eindruck auf
David Livingstone took pity on the unfortunate slaves and did all he could to help them.	Mitleid haben mit
The revenge they took on their enemy was complete and horrible.	Rache nehmen an
She is very keen on swimming and rarely misses a chance to bathe.	erpicht auf, begierig auf
He was so intent on his work that he did not hear me enter the room.	begierig auf, vertieft in

35. **out, out of** *Antonym*: in, into

David dressed in a hurry and dashed out of his cabin.	(r)	aus, heraus
Bob came out of his house.		
They prefer living out of town.		außerhalb
He did it out of anger, out of jealousy.	(ü)	aus (Beweggrund)
To walk was out of the question.		außer Frage
Bob's and Pat's parents are out tonight.	*adv.*	aus(gegangen)

36. **outside** *Antonym*: inside

Let's meet outside the theatre.	(r)	außerhalb
The park is outside the town.		
We went outside the house to talk.		
Is there anybody outside?	*adv.*	draußen
She is outside; shall I call her in?		

37. **over** *Antonym*: under, below, beneath
Compare: above, across

There is a bridge over the river.	(r)	über
The lamp hangs over the table.		
The dog jumped over the wall.		über . . . hin (mit und ohne Berührung)
We wandered over melting snow.		
Did he stay over night?	(z)	über (einen Termin hinaus)
Will he stay over Sunday?		
It is no use crying over spilt milk.	(ü)	über
He must be over ninety years old.		mehr als
The boys were dirty all over.	*adv.*	über und über, ganz
The storm is not over yet.		vorbei
He keeps telling the same stories over and over again.		immer wieder

Keep in Mind:	
Queen Elizabeth II has reigned over the United Kingdom since 1952.	regieren über
He ruled over his family like a tyrant.	herrschen über
He must learn to keep control over his temper and not get angry so easily.	im Zaum halten
By putting on her most charming smile she tried to win him over.	jemanden für sich gewinnen
She has fallen head over heels in love with him.	Hals über Kopf
After the race the jockeys were splashed all over with mud.	völlig
Many Americans travel all over the Continent when they 'do Europe'.	durch ganz Europa
You will see the German VW all over the world.	überall in der Welt

past

Motor-boats were darting past us. Crowds of people were running past our house.	(r) an . . . vorbei
It is half past ten.	(z) nach (Uhrzeit)
This news is past belief. (*now usually:* beyond belief) His strength was past its peak.	(ü) über . . . hinaus (vgl. *beyond*)

Keep in Mind:	
The noise in the classroom is past endurance and must stop at once. (*now usually:* beyond endurance)	unerträglich
His honesty and integrity is past doubt, and I have the very highest opinion of him. (*now usually:* beyond doubt)	außer Zweifel
The old man is now past work and lives on his pension.	zu alt zur Arbeit
Although she is well past seventy she still does all her own housework.	über siebzig

39. **round** *Compare:* around

If I ever won in the football pools I should travel round the world. York is one of the few old English cities with a wall round the town. At the cricket match there were enthusiastic people all round us.	(r)	um . . . herum
When I called after her she turned round. Nowadays you can get ice-cream all the year round. He was so tired that he slept round the clock.	*adv.*	sich umdrehen durch . . . hindurch „einmal um die Uhr“

40. **since**

I have been ill since last Friday. He has been in London since May 1st.	(z)	seit (einem Zeitpunkt)
He left for the USA in 1949, and I have never seen him since.	*adv.*	seitdem
What have you been doing since I last saw you? Since we have no money we can't buy the television set.	*conj.*	seit da

41. **through**

David agreed to walk with Tom through Central Park. Suddenly the sun broke through the fog. Queen Victoria reigned through the latter half of the nineteenth century. I found a job through my friend. He caught a cold through walking in the rain.	(r) (z) (ü)	durch durch (über einen Zeitraum) durch, mit Hilfe von durch (Ursache, Grund)
They danced the whole night through. The train runs through to Manchester.	*adv.*	hindurch

. throughout

That day was celebrated throughout the Commonwealth of Nations.	(r) durch . . . hindurch
The inhabitants suffered terribly throughout the winter.	(z) hindurch

. till, until

We must wait till after lunch.	(z) bis
I shall not be back until Sunday.	erst

. to *Antonym*: from

Come back to me.	(r) zu (Richtung auf, ein Ziel)
Will you fly to America?	nach
Take the next turning to the left.	
He goes to the wrong side.	
He works from morning to night.	(z) bis (zu einem Zeitpunkt)
It is a quarter to ten.	
She is married to an American.	(ü) mit
The long quarrel came to an end.	zu
He thought to himself that she was behaving very stupidly.	bei (sich)
The old vase fell down and broke to pieces.	in (Stücke)
She spoke to her teacher about her homework.	zu, mit

Neben dieser Eigenbedeutung als Präposition hat *to*, ähnlich wie die Präposition *of*, syntaktische Aufgaben übernommen.

Über *to* als Satzbeziehungsmittel vgl. *Indirect Object,* 213. Über *to* als Ersatz für einen Infinitiv vgl. 177. Über *to* vor dem Infinitiv vgl. 179.

Verbs + to **(see 212, 1)**

Nouns + to

to put in a (to lay) claim to s. th.	Anspruch erheben auf etwas
to have a claim to s. th.	Anspruch haben auf etwas
to be the heir to s. th.	etwas erben
to be of some (no, much) help to s. b.	jem. eine (keine, große) Hilfe sein
to have no objection to s. b.	nichts gegen jem. haben
to make an objection to s. th.	gegen etwas einen Einwand erheben
to have a right to s. th.	Anrecht haben auf etwas
to call attention to s. th.	die Aufmerksamkeit auf etwas lenken
to pay attention to s. th. or s. o.	etwas oder jem. Beachtung schenken
cruelty to	Grausamkeit gegenüber
faithfulness to	Aufrichtigkeit gegenüber
indifference to	Gleichgültigkeit gegenüber

Adjectives + to

accustomed to / used to	gewöhnt an
attentive to	aufmerksam auf
blind to	blind für
cruel to	grausam gegen
deaf to	taub gegen
due to s.th.	zuzuschreiben, zurückzuführen auf
equal to	gleich
inferior to	untergeordnet
faithful to	treu
favourable to	günstig für
grateful to	dankbar
helpful to	hilfreich
hostile to	feindlich
indifferent to	gleichgültig gegen
just to	gerecht gegen
kind to	freundlich gegen
obedient to	gehorsam gegen
polite to / civil to	höflich gegen
responsible to	verantwortlich (jem.)
severe to	streng gegen
similar to	ähnlich
superior to	überlegen, stärker als
thankful to	dankbar
true to	ehrlich gegen
unjust to	ungerecht gegen
welcome to	willkommen

45. **towards** *Antonym*: away, from

[tə'wɔːdz, tɔːdz]

They marched towards the coast. The aeroplane flew towards the north of London.	(r) auf . . . zu (Richtung)
We arrived towards evening.	(z) gegen (ungefähre Zeit)
He doesn't feel very kindly towards me.	(ü) zu (Verhältnis zu einer Person)
Don't forget the duties you have towards your parents.	Pflicht gegenüber einer Person oder einer Sache
His attitude towards modern music is well known. What is your attitude towards jazz?	Haltung zu jemandem oder etwas
His behaviour towards his parents was disgraceful.	Betragen einer Person gegenüber

46. **under** *Antonym*: over
Compare: below, beneath

The dog is asleep under the table.	(r) unter
Little boats can pass under the bridge.	unter . . . her (mit oder ohne Berührung)
She is a girl under twenty.	(ü) unter

Keep in Mind:	
Under such circumstances his behaviour is quite understandable.	unter diesen Umständen
Under Queen Elizabeth I the English became a great seafaring nation.	unter der Regierung von
He became ill on Saturday and is now in hospital under medical treatment.	in ärztlicher Behandlung
While my car was under repair I travelled to the office by bus.	in Reparatur sein
Under these conditions I am not willing to do work for you.	unter diesen Bedingungen

. **up** *Antonym*: down

We went up the hill. The boat goes up the river.	(r) hinauf
We need rain and sunshine to make the seeds come up.	*adv.* heraus
Please, speak up!	lauter
He lived in Edinburgh up to 1955.	bis
Eat up your porridge.	auf
Drink up your juice.	aus

Keep in Mind:	
If you don't know the word, look it up in the dictionary.	im Wörterbuch nachsehen
After all we had heard about him beforehand, the soloist did not come up to my expectations.	meinen Erwartungen entsprechend
He is an honest and upright man and always lives up to his principles.	nach seinen Grundsätzen
I am very tired and do not feel up to a long walk today.	nicht in der Lage zu etwas sein
He had to give up driving his car in town as his nerves were not up to the traffic.	aufgeben gewachsen sein
It is no use letting her go in for the exam as she is not up to it yet.	

3. **via** *Compare*: by

We went to London via Ostend.	(r) über

49. with

A woman is coming along with her daughter.	mit
He spends his holidays with his uncle.	bei (bei Personen!)
She lives with her grandmother.	
I am stiff with cold.	vor
He kissed his mother with joy.	aus
"Will you join us for lunch?" – "Thank you, with pleasure."	mit

with bezeichnet die Gemeinschaft, das Zusammensein oder die Zusammengehörigkeit, ferner kann es eine Einschränkung ausdrücken und außerdem das Mittel, das Werkzeug, die Art und Weise, den Grund oder die Ursache angeben.

Keep in Mind:

These glasses are very fragile and must be handled with care.	vorsichtig
It was only with great difficulty that they managed to rescue the trapped miners.	unter schwierigen Umständen
She was beside herself with fear and pain.	vor Furcht
The boy was trembling with rage and disappointment.	vor Wut
He was white with rage and in a furious temper.	
As I had no money with me I could not buy the book.	bei (mit) mir
I'm sorry I have not got my book with me.	
With regard to your last question I can only repeat what I have already said.	hinsichtlich
I was very sorry to have to part with my camera.	sich trennen von
I really cannot put up with the noise any longer.	ertragen
John was very angry with his sister when she broke his new fountain pen.	ärgerlich über
They went mad with joy when their team won the match.	außer sich geraten vor
The poor woman went almost out of her mind with grief when her child died.	
One gets so bored with having to answer the same questions all the time.	einer Sache müde werden
My father was not a bit satisfied with my last school report.	zufrieden mit (über)
Before the examination she was pale with excitement and tension.	blaß vor (Erregung)
On hearing this, he went pale with anger.	

Adjectives + with

charmed with	entzückt über	pleased with	erfreut über
delighted with	entzückt von	displeased with	nicht erfreut über
ill, sick with	krank an	struck with	betroffen von

Verbs + with (see 212)

within

They are looking for a house within the city boundary.	(r) innerhalb
We must finish this piece of work within a week.	(z) innerhalb

Keep in Mind:

I shall help you if it is within my power.	in meiner Macht
She is very careful to live within her income as she does not want to run into debt.	ihrem Einkommen gemäß
Although he was very much annoyed, he kept his anger within bounds.	in Grenzen halten
The children must keep within bounds and are not to leave the school-yard without permission.	innerhalb der Grenzen bleiben
Please keep your demands within the bounds of reason!	in vernünftigen Grenzen
That's true within limits, but you have not told me the whole story.	begrenzt wahr sein

without

There is no rose without thorns.	ohne
He does his work without my help.	
Without further delay he took his hat and left.	
Without difficulty we found the house in the dark.	
He is without doubt the best actor we have.	
It goes without saying that we should be delighted to see you any time you come to London.	„Es ist selbstverständlich . . .“

The Conjunctions

Die Konjunktionen

221 Function — Funktion

Die Konjunktionen (Bindewörter) sind eine unveränderliche Wortart. Sie dienen dazu, Teile eines Satzes oder ganze Sätze miteinander zu verbinden.

I said nothing, but John said a great deal.
This is either my pencil or yours.
Thick fog surrounded the ship, and David could see neither the coast nor the ships.

Die Konjunktionen, die gleichartige Satzteile oder Sätze miteinander verbinden, nennt man beiordnende Konjunktionen (*Coordinating Conjunctions* [kəu'ɔːdineitiŋ kən'dʒʌŋkʃənz]).

You may stay in my room, as long as you are quiet.
Though he was very tired, he went on working.
The Romans built a wall so that the tribes of the north should not invade England.

Verbinden die Konjunktionen einen Hauptsatz und einen Nebensatz miteinander, so spricht man von unterordnenden Konjunktionen (*Subordinating Conjunctions* [sə'bɔːdineitiŋ kən'dʒʌŋkʃənz]). Vgl. Adverbialsätze.

222 The Co-ordinating Conjunctions — Die beiordnenden Konjunktionen

a) and, also, too, besides, further, likewise, moreover, as well as, both . . . and, not only . . . but (also) — a) anreihende (*copulative*)

b) or, nor
either . . . or, neither . . . nor. — b) trennende (*disjunctive*)

c) but, however, yet, nevertheless, notwithstanding, still (= *doch*, *jedoch*) all the same, it is true . . . but (yet); (= *trotzdem*), (= *zwar . . . aber* [*und doch*]) — c) entgegenstellende (*adversative*)

d) for — d) begründende (*causative*)

e) so, thus, therefore, consequently, hence (= *daher*), then (= *also*). — e) folgernde (*consecutive* [kən'sekjutiv])

Particular Use of Co-ordinating Conjunctions 223

Besonderheiten im Gebrauch beiordnender Konjunktionen

a) "You have seen him today?" – "I also (*Auch ich*) met him this morning."

a) *also* steht in der Regel nicht am Anfang des Satzes.

b) I think he is dishonest; I may, however, be mistaken.
The murder was committed by a woman. Mrs. Smith was the only woman present; therefore she is the murderer.
The ship was three days overdue; the company, nevertheless, did not give up hope.

b) *however, therefore, then* („also"), *nevertheless*, stehen gewöhnlich nicht an der Spitze des Satzes. Sie können, durch Komma abgetrennt, hinter das Subjekt treten.

c) His friends, too, are working in a factory.
The peaches were excellent, and cheap, too.

c) *too* tritt, meist durch Komma abgetrennt, hinter das hervorzuhebende Wort oder an das Ende des Satzes.

d) Both my father and my mother have returned.

d) *both . . . and* werden stets getrennt. *both* tritt vor das Vergleichspaar und bleibt im Deutschen unübersetzt.

e) My father as well as my mother have returned.

e) *as well as* steht ungetrennt hinter dem ersten Glied.

The Subordinating Conjunctions 224

Die unterordnenden Konjunktionen

Zur Bezeichnung

a) when, whenever, as, while, before, after, until, till, since, now (that),
as long as, as soon as, as often as,
scarcely (hardly) . . . when,
no sooner . . . than (*kaum . . . als*)

a) der Zeit (*time*);

b) where, wherever, whence (= from where), whither (= where, to what place)

b) des Ortes (*place*);
(*whither* = alte, heute selten gebrauchte Form)

c) as, because, since
seeing (that), in that

c) der Ursache (*reason*);
(*as* = im vorgestelltem und im nachgestellten Nebensatz; *because* = nur im nachgestellten Nebensatz)

d) that, so that, in order that, lest△ (= *damit nicht*), in case	d) des Zweckes (*purpose*);
e) that (*nach vorhergehendem so oder such*), so that, to such an extent that	e) der Folge (*result*);
f) if, supposing (that), so long as, provided that, on condition (that), unless (= *wenn nicht*)	f) der Bedingung (*condition*);
g) though, although, however (*mit folgendem Adjektiv oder Adverb*) as (*nach vorhergehendem Substantiv oder Adjektiv*)	g) der Einräumung (*concession*);
h) whereas, while, whilst	h) des Gegensatzes (*contrast*);
i) as . . . as, not so . . . as, than, the . . . the, as if, as though	i) des Vergleichs (*comparison*).

Notice:

after, *before*, *but* und *since* erscheinen auch als Präpositionen (vgl. 220).

The Interjections

Die Interjektionen

Character and Function — Charakter und Funktion 225

Interjektionen sind, wie die deutsche Bezeichnung „Gefühlswort“ schon verrät, Wörter, die einem Gefühl aus unmittelbarer Reaktion auf ein Geschehnis Ausdruck verleihen. In den meisten Fällen sagt eine Interjektion ebensoviel aus wie ein ganzer Satz: ein “Ah!“ als Ausdruck der Überraschung oder des Staunens entspricht etwa einem Satz wie „Der Anblick ist wundervoll, ist herrlich.“

Die Interjektionen sind Einzelsilben, die ganz verschiedene Gefühle bezeichnen können. Das hängt von dem Ereignis ab, durch das die Interjektion ausgelöst wird. Intonation, Tonhöhe und begleitende Mienen oder Gesten ermöglichen vielfältige Abstufung im Bedeutungsgehalt der Interjektionen.

Da der typische Engländer sich scheut, seine Gefühle zu zeigen, bedient er sich gern der Interjektion. Sie gestatten es ihm, seine Empfindungen in knapper Form zum Ausdruck zu bringen.

Die gebräuchlichsten Interjektionen und ihre Bedeutungen sind:

ah!	[ɑː]	Freude, Überraschung, Befriedigung, Verachtung, Mitleid, Klage
aha!	[ɑːˈhɑ]	Überraschung, Freude, Hohn
alas!	[əˈlɑːs]	Enttäuschung, Bedauern, Kummer
boo!	[buː]	Verachtung; Ausruf, um jemanden zu erschrecken
eh!	[ei]	„was!“ (Bedeutungen wie *oh*!), manchmal fragend
ha!	[hɑː]	Überraschung, Freude, Kummer
hey!	[hei]	Überraschung, Vergnügen, Anfeuerung
hm!	[hm]	zögernde Zustimmung
oh!	[əu]	Ach! Wehe mir!
oh! o dear!		plötzliche Erregung, Rührung; Neckerei
oho!	[ə(u)ˈhəu]	Erstaunen; Neckerei
wo(e)!	[wəu]	große Sorge, Kummer
whew!	[huː]	„huh!“ Erstaunen, Verblüffung, Bestürzung, Schrecken
hush!	[hʌʃ]	still, pst!
pooh!	[puː]	pah! dummes Zeug!
gosh!	[gɔʃ]	herrjeh!
gee!	[dʒiː]	ei!

Notice:

O for the wings of a dove!△ O worship the King!△ Oh! What a lie! Oh, how do you know that?

Es ist heute üblich, *O* (*o*) zu schreiben, wenn kein Komma, Ausrufezeichen oder Punkt folgt; aber vor irgendeinem dieser drei Zeichen schreibt man am besten *Oh!* (*oh!*).

Die folgenden Wörter können wie Interjektionen gebraucht werden; sie nehmen dann eine andere Bedeutung an.

well!	nun, na!, wohlan!	indeed!	in der Tat!
what!	was! wie!	really!	wirklich! in der Tat!
why!	ei!, ja!, nun!	I say!	höre(n Sie) mal!
Dear me!	o du meine Güte!	There, there!	na, na! nun! (Besänftigung oder Beruhigung)
Oh, dear! O dear!	verwünscht!		
Dear, dear!	ach herrjeh!	attaboy!	bravo!, so ist's richtig!
for shame!	pfui! (schäme dich!)	By jove!	bei Gott!
		right! (= right so!)	richtig!

The Sentence

Der Satz

Word Order

Wortstellung

The Normal Word Order

Die normale Wortstellung 226

Subject	*Predicate*	*Object*
He	saw	his father.
Pat	is writing	a letter.
Father	drives	a car.

Durch das Schwinden der alten Deklinationsendungen sind die Subjekts- und die Objektsform heute gleich. Das einzige Mittel für ihre Kennzeichnung im Satz ist die feste Wortstellung: Subject – Predicate – Object

Diese Wortstellung wird (im Gegensatz zum Deutschen) auch beibehalten

a) At eight o'clock Frank left the house.
Suddenly he saw a thief.
b) When I entered the room, my friend was reading a newspaper.
c) He had received the letter before he left for London.
He has broken his leg.

a) wenn eine adverbiale Bestimmung an der Spitze des Satzes steht;
b) wenn ein Nebensatz dem Hauptsatz vorausgeht;
c) bei zusammengesetzten Zeiten.

Special Word Order

Besonderheiten der Wortstellung 227

Die Grundform der Satzstellung erfährt unter dem Einfluß der Betonungsverhältnisse (Druckverhältnisse) im englischen Satz und unter dem Einfluß der Sprechweise des Sprechenden Abwandlungen.
Die Druckstelle im englischen Satz liegt am Ende des Satzes bzw. der Sinngruppe. Es ergibt sich also manchmal die Notwendigkeit, Wörter, die einen starken Druck tragen, an die Druckstelle, d. h. an das Ende des Satzes bzw. der Sinngruppe zu stellen (= *Final Placing*).
Auch der Satzanfang ist eine Stelle stärkeren Druckes, so daß ein druckstarkes Wort unter einer gewissen Druckgebung auch an den Anfang des Satzes treten kann (= *Initial Placing*), wobei es meist an das Vorangehende anknüpft.
Die Stelle zwischen Subjekt und Verb ist druckschwächer als die vor dem Subjekt oder die nach dem Verb (vgl. 134).

Initial Placing with Inversion for Emphasis

Spitzenstellung mit Inversion als Mittel zur Hervorhebung

228 Inversion Necessary

Inversion muß eintreten

1. Such is life.
Great was the joy of the children when their parents returned.△
Terrible were the battles which followed, and long was the quarrel.△
Content will he never be.△

In gefühlsbetonter Rede kann das prädikativ gebrauchte Adjektiv (Prädikatsnomen) an die Spitze des Satzes treten. In diesen Fällen muß auch das Prädikat bzw. der erste Teil des Prädikates) vor das Subjekt treten (Umstellung des Subjektes = *Inversion*).

2. Seldom does it happen that misfortunes come singly.
Never did he cross a street without looking right and left.
He does not like working after supper. Nor do I.
No sooner did the band begin to play than everybody was silent.

Stehen am Satzanfang Adverbien oder Konjunktionen mit verneinendem oder einschränkendem Sinn, so muß das Prädikat vor dem Subjekt stehen (= *Inversion*).
Die einfachen Zeiten der Vollverben werden in diesen Fällen mit *to do* umschrieben. Ausdrücke mit verneinendem oder einschränkendem Sinn sind z. B.

little	wenig	in vain	vergeblich
seldom, rarely	selten	nor	und auch nicht
never	nie(mals)	neither . . . nor	weder . . . noch
scarcely . . . when, hardly . . . when, no sooner . . . than	kaum . . . als	not only . . . but	nicht nur . . . sondern

Vgl. frz. En vain le pauvre voyageur se défendit-il le plus vaillamment. – A peine le chevalier se fut-il couché dans l'herbe qu'il vit venir à lui deux vierges.

3. May he rest in peace.△
May God forgive you.△
Be it so.△

In Wunschsätzen tritt das Hilfsverb an die Spitze des Satzes (also vor das Subjekt).

4. Had I met him sooner, all would have been well.
Should it be wet tomorrow, I shall stay at home.
Were my daughter here, she would help me.

Die Umstellung des Subjekts (*Inversion*) tritt auch ein in Bedingungssätzen ohne Konjunktion

Inversion Possible — Inversion kann eintreten 229

Inversion kann erfolgen in Sätzen, deren Subjekt ein Substantiv ist und die kein Objekt enthalten, wenn

a) After rain comes sunshine.△
In the year 1776 began the American War of Independence.△
Merrily rang the bells.△
Then arose a quarrel.△
There comes Robert at last.

b) Off went the train.
The door opened, and in came Father.

a) eine adverbiale Bestimmung oder ein betontes Adverb wie

here so thus then there

an der Spitze des Satzes steht;

b) das mit einem Verb eng verbundene Adverb am Satzanfang steht.

"Come quickly here, Roy," said David, "I see something not far from the shore."
"That must be a fishing-boat," said Roy.

"If I lose my way," he said, "I can always ask a policeman."

Inversion kann auch stehen im Zwischen- oder Nachsatz bei direkter Rede, wenn das Subjekt ein Substantiv ist.
Ist das Subjekt des Zwischen- oder Nachsatzes ein Personalpronomen, so steht das Pronomen vor dem Verb

Vgl. "Faites comme vous voulez," repartit mon frère (repartit-il), "je m'en lave les mains."

Initial Placing without Inversion — Spitzenstellung ohne Inversion 230

His daughter he did not meet alive, and his wife he found badly wounded.
About Shakespeare's life we know very little.
To every Englishman England is the dearest country.
That offer I declined.
This job he did when he returned home.

In Spitzenstellung ohne Inversion stehen betonte direkte Objekte und präpositionale Ergänzungen. Sie werden dadurch mehr hervorgehoben. – Zum Anschluß an das Vorhergehende stehen in diesen Fällen die direkten Objekte oft in Verbindung mit *this*, *that*, *such a* u. ä.

Vgl. frz. Ce nom modeste, il ne l'eût échangé contre un autre. – Les cris de joie, on pouvait les entendre.

2. In Scotland they drink their whisky neat. Yesterday they went to Manchester.	In Spitzenstellung ohne Inversion stehen auch die Adverbien und adverbialen Bestimmungen des Ortes und der bestimmten Zeit (vgl. 134).

231 Final Placing

Endstellung

Please take your coat off.	Ist das mit dem Verb eng verbundene Adverb betont, so steht es am Ende des Satzes.
He took off his clothes and went to bed.	Ist das mit dem Verb eng verbundene Adverb nicht besonders betont, so tritt es unmittelbar hinter das Verb.

	In Endstellung stehen
a) The pupils asked some questions.	a) die Objekte;
b) He was dreaming of a lion.	b) die präpositionalen Ergänzungen (vgl. 212);
c) I met him yesterday.	c) Adverbien und adverbiale Bestimmungen (vgl. 134).

232 Other Ways of Emphasizing

Andere Mittel der Hervorhebung

	Andere Mittel zur Hervorhebung sind
a) It's Mary who is wrong. It's I (me) who (that) should apologize. It's you who are wrong.	a) die Umschreibung des Subjekts durch *it is* (*was*) . . . *who* (*which*, *that*);
b) It is your father that I want to see. It was John whom the postman gave the letter to.	b) die Umschreibung des direkten Objekts durch *it is* (*was*) . . . *whom* (*which*, *that*);
c) It is to your brother that I wanted to speak. It was then that we saw the danger.	c) die Umschreibung der präpositionalen Ergänzung mit *to* und jedes anderen Satzteiles durch *it is* (*was*) . . . *that* (deutsch: daß).

The Word Order in Interrogative Sentences

Die Wortstellung in Fragesätzen

Questions without Inversion

Fragesätze ohne Inversion 233

Fragesätze verlangen gewöhnlich Inversion. Es gibt nur zwei Ausnahmen:

You live here?
She said that?
You went to London?

In der Umgangssprache kann die Frage allein durch die Satzmelodie zum Ausdruck kommen. Die Satzmelodie steigt zum Ende des Satzes hin an (vgl. 20).

Who told you that news?
What boy brought this letter?
How many boys are on this farm?
Whose uncle left last night?
Which of these boys go to your school?

Der Fragesatz wird ohne Inversion gebildet, wenn das Fragewort Subjekt des Satzes ist oder wenn es mit dem Subjekt verbunden ist (vgl. *to do*, 145–148).

Inversion in Interrogative Sentences

Inversion in Fragesätzen 234

Has he made a mistake?
Is your sister ill?
Are those books on the shelf yours?

Does your friend know English?
Did he like porridge in the morning?

In Fragen ohne Fragewort tritt das Subjekt hinter die erste Verbform; diese muß die Form eines Hilfsverbs sein.
Ist kein Hilfsverb vorhanden, so tritt eine Form des Hilfsverbs *to do* ein (vgl. 146).

What is Father doing?
Why don't you take the bus?
Where will he spend his holidays?
Whom did you meet in the street?
Which tie do you prefer?
Whose book did you find in the cupboard?
Where will they spend their holidays?

Die Inversion des Subjekts tritt ein in Fragesätzen mit Fragewort, wenn dieses nicht Subjekt des Satzes ist (vgl. 147, 2).

The Compound Sentence — Der zusammengesetzte Satz

235 Coordinated Sentences — Die Satzreihe

After dinner sit a while, after supper walk a while. He saw his father and he asked him for money. The Indians pointed to the south-west, for they wanted to indicate the time.

In der Satzreihe stehen zwei oder mehrere Sätze entweder unverbunden nebeneinander oder sie werden verbunden durch nebenordnende Konjunktionen wie *and, but, for, or* etc. (vgl. 222).

236 Complex Sentences — Das Satzgefüge

Ein Satzgefüge besteht aus einem oder mehreren Hauptsätzen *(Principal Clauses)* und einem oder mehreren Nebensätzen *(Subordinate Clauses)*. Ein Nebensatz kann für jeden Satzteil außer dem finiten Verb eintreten. Je nach dem Satzteil, den sie ersetzen, unterscheidet man

1. That he should now have run away from home is hardly surprising.
Whoever told you that was a fool.
What people don't realise is that she is very shy.

   Subjektsätze;

2. You may be sure he is not what he seems to be.
The worst thing is that he never knows when to speak and when to be silent.

   Prädikatsätze;

3. He told me that his brother would go to America.
Can you tell me where your friend went?
What soberness conceals, drunkenness reveals.△

   Objektsätze;

4. The man who lives next door is ill.
I remember the place where I was born, and the time when I was a boy.

   Attributsätze (vgl. Relativsätze, 90, 91);

5. We ran as fast as our legs could carry us. When we got there, it was already dark.

Adverbialsätze.

Adverbial Clauses in Particular

Adverbialsätze im besonderen

237

1. Where there are bees, there is honey. Wherever I put the scissors, they disappear. As far as I could see the countryside was flooded.

Adverbialsätze des Ortes (*place*) werden eingeleitet durch:

where	= wo, wohin
wherever	= wo, wohin (auch immer)
as far as	= soweit

2. When the cat is away, the mice will play. As long as you are quiet, you may stay in the room.

Adverbialsätze der Zeit (*time*) werden eingeleitet durch:

when	als
whenever	wenn (auch) immer
once	wenn einmal
as soon as	sobald als
no sooner .... than	kaum ... als
hardly ... when	kaum ... als
scarcely .... when	kaum ... als
after	nachdem
since	seit

before	bevor
until	bis
till	bis
now (that)	nun da
the moment	sobald als
as	als, während
as long as	so lange als
while, (whilst)	während (whilst = veraltete Form)
as often as	so oft als

Notice:

As soon as I get the necessary money I shall emigrate to Australia.
We shall go on protesting till we achieve our aim.
I'll see you when you return.
He will leave the moment he is ready.

In Adverbialsätzen der Zeit steht kein Futur.

3. As it is raining hard, we have to stay at home.
Since you raise so many objections, we will drop our plan.

Our master punished him, because he was often late.

Adverbialsätze des Grundes (*cause*) werden eingeleitet durch as (= da), since (= da), seeing (= da ja), wenn sie am Anfang des Satzgefüges stehen; sie werden eingeleitet durch because (= da, weil), wenn sie am Ende des Satzgefüges stehen.

4. I shall speak more distinctly so that everybody can understand me.
(We eat that we may live, we do not live that we may eat.△)

Adverbialsätze des Zweckes, der Absicht (*purpose*) werden eingeleitet durch

so that, in order that, (that△).

5. I shall not leave you, unless I am told to.
What would you do if you were in England?
If it should rain tomorrow, we shall stay at home.
Provided that he passes his exam, he can go to university.

Adverbialsätze der Bedingung (*condition*) (vgl. 238). beginnen mit

if	(= wenn; falls),
unless	(= es sei denn; wenn nicht),
provided that	(= vorausgesetzt daß; unter der Bedingung, daß).

6. He spoke very softly, so that nobody could hear him.
I was so tired (that) I could hardly walk on.
He did such excellent work that he was made an engine-man.

Adverbialsätze der Folge werden angeschlossen durch

so that, so . . . that, such . . . that.

7. He did not get the prize although he had worked hard.
Even if it were true, it would not make any difference.
However rich he may be, he is not happy.

Adverbialsätze der Einräumung (*concession*) werden eingeleitet durch:

though, although	(= obgleich, obwohl),
even if even though	(= selbst wenn),
as, though	(= wenn auch, obwohl),
however	(= wie auch immer)

8. He works very hard whereas (while) his brother is lazy.
Uncle Eric took a cup of coffee whereas the boys had a glass of milk each.

Adverbialsätze des Gegensatzes werden angeschlossen durch *whereas, while, whilst* (= während).

9. We speak as we think.
He is as wise as you are foolish.
Take as much as you like.
The more one has, the more one wants.
They look as if they had not slept for days.
It isn't as if you were poor.

Adverbialsätze des Vergleichs (Komparativsätze) werden eingeleitet durch as, as if, as though, as . . . as, not so . . . as, not as . . . as, than (nach einem Komparativ), the + Kompar. . . . the + Kompar. (Nach as if steht immer eine Zeit der Vergangenheit.)

10. I always carry an umbrella in case it rains. (= because it might rain)
It's wise to have a medical insurance in case you have a skiing accident.

Keep quiet lest you wake the baby.△
They remained silent for fear that they might be heard.△

Adverbialsätze, die den Grund einer Vorsichtsmaßnahme ausdrücken, werden eingeleitet durch in case (= im Falle, daß);
sie enthalten nie ein Verb im Futur.
lest und *for fear that* werden in dieser Bedeutung heute nicht mehr gebraucht.

Conditional Clauses — Bedingungssätze 238

Die *Conditional Clauses* sind eine besonders wichtige Form von Adverbialsätzen. Sie können eingeleitet werden durch die Konjunktionen:

if	wenn, falls	supposing (that)	angenommen (daß)
if not / unless	wenn nicht, falls nicht	provided (that)	vorausgesetzt, daß
		on condition (that)	unter der Bedingung, daß

Ein Bedingungssatz kann dem Hauptsatz vorangehen oder ihm folgen. – Die Voraussetzungen, die durch den Bedingungssatz ausgedrückt werden, haben einen verschiedenen Grad der Gewißheit oder Wahrscheinlichkeit. Der Unterschied kommt im Englischen durch den Gebrauch der Zeiten oder die Aussageform (*Mood*) des Verbs zum Ausdruck.

The Sequence of Tenses in Conditional Clauses — Die Zeitenfolge in Bedingungssätzen 239

1.

Conditional Clause	*Principal Clause*
Present, Pres. Perfect, Past, Past Perfect	Future, Present, Imperative and Auxiliaries
If you give us a ring	we shall come to your house.
Unless it rains	they will go for a picnic on Sunday.
If you want a thing done well	do it yourself.
If you are in a hurry	take your bicycle.
If it is too cold	we cannot play tennis.
If one knows a little Latin	the meaning of the word becomes clear.
If you have read my letter carefully	you will understand what I meant.
If he slept until nine o'clock	he must be pretty well rested.

Wenn der Sprechende die Verwirklichung oder die Erfüllung der Bedingung für durchaus möglich hält, steht im Bedingungssatz und im Hauptsatz der Indikativ. Das ist so wie im Deutschen. – In den meisten dieser Fälle steht der Bedingungssatz im *Present Tense*, der Hauptsatz im *Future Tense*. – Wie die Beispiele aber zeigen, können sinngemäß auch andere Zeiten stehen.

2.

Conditional Clause	Principal Clause
a) Past Tense	a) Conditional
If Father had a holiday	we would (should) go to the seaside.
If it stopped raining	they would start the match.
If he had any money	he would give me some.
If I were rich	I would (should) buy a sports car.
If you gave them a ring	they would come to your house.
If my friend came to see me	I would (should) be delighted.
If I were you	I would (should) go to the doctor.
If they had time	they would go for a walk.
If it rained tomorrow	the reservoir would fill up quickly.
b) Past Perfect	b) Conditional Perfect
If he had died	he would have left his family in great distress.
If I had left you earlier	I would (should) not have missed the last train.
If you had worked harder	you would not have failed the exam.
If Bob had eaten all those chocolates	he would have been sick.
If I had not fallen ill	I would have taken part in the meeting.
If she had done as I told her	she would have succeeded.
If my watch hadn't been slow	I wouldn't have been late.
If you had invited him	he would have come

a) Hält der Sprechende die Verwirklichung der Bedingung für unwahrscheinlich oder für unmöglich, so steht in Bezug auf die Gegenwart und Zukunft im Bedingungssatz *Past Tense,* im Hauptsatz *Conditional.*

b) Wenn ausgedrückt werden soll, was in der Vergangenheit geschehen wäre, wenn eine Bedingung oder Voraussetzung erfüllt gewesen wäre, so steht im Bedingungssatz *Past Perfect,* im Hauptsatz *Conditional Perfect.*

Notice:

If I were given permission	I would (should) travel to Russia.
If he were healthy	he would be a good rugby player.
If it were true	it would be sensational news.
If he were a sportsman	he would play fairly.

Für die 1. und 3. Person Sg. von *to be* wird hier (239, 2a) die alte Konjunktivform *were* gebraucht. Immer häufiger aber gebraucht die Umgangssprache *was*

Conditional Clause	Principal Clause
Past Tense, Past Perfect	could **(have)**, might **(have)**
If we had a plane	we could fly to America.
If I had a yacht	I could sail round Britain.
If Father drove us to Buckingham Palace	we might see the Queen leave for the opening of Parliament.
If he drove us to the airport	we might still see the Queen arrive.
If the Titanic had had more life-boats	many more passengers could have been saved.
If the performance had lasted longer	I could not have stayed to see the end.
If the brakes had worked properly	the racing-driver might have avoided the collision.
If the time had not been so very short,	we might not only have seen the National Gallery, but also the Tate.

Für das *Conditional* bzw. *Conditional Perfect* im Hauptsatz (vgl. 239, 2) können auch *could* und *might* gebraucht werden.

Conditional Clause	Principal Clause
should	Present, Future, Imperative, Conditional, Auxiliaries
If Helen should call	please tell her to ring.
If you should happen to need a pronouncing-dictionary	I can lend you one.
If you should lose your way in London	you might ask a policeman to direct you.
If the train should be late tonight	you could (might) take a taxi home.

Drückt der Bedingungssatz aus, daß etwas zufällig eintreten könnte (bloße Möglichkeit oder Annahme), und enthält der Hauptsatz eine sich darauf beziehende Bitte oder einen Vorschlag, so steht im Bedingungssatz ebenfalls *should*. Im Hauptsatz können sinngemäß folgende Zeiten stehen: *Present, Future, Imperative, Conditional* oder entsprechende Hilfsverben.

5.

Conditional Clause	Principal Clause
Should the atomic fall-out increase,	drastic measures will have to be taken by all governments.
Should more and more people be killed on the roads,	driving-tests will have to be more strictly enforced.
Should it be wet tomorrow,	I shall (will) stay at home.
Had I met him sooner,	all would have been well.

Der Bedingungssatz ohne Konjunktion ist eine besondere Form des Bedingungssatzes in der Gestalt eines Fragesatzes mit vorangestelltem *should, had* oder einem anderen Hilfsverb, dem dann das Subjekt folgt (vgl. 228).

240 Reported Speech — Die indirekte Rede

Jack says: "My brother is in America."
Jack says (that) his brother is in America.

Im Englischen steht auch in der indirekten Rede der Indikativ. Die indirekte Rede kann mit *that* eingeleitet werden.

The Sequence of Tenses in Reported Speech — Die Zeitenfolge in der indirekten Rede

241 I. Wichtig ist die Zeitenfolge in der indirekten Rede; sie ist anders als im Deutschen. Im Englischen hängt die Zeit des Nebensatzes von der des einführenden Hauptsatzes ab.

1. a) Pat replies: "I see the plane."
Pat replies (that) she sees the plane.
Pat replies: "I shall (will) go to the seaside."
Pat replies (that) she will go to the seaside.
Pat will reply: "I like swimming."
Pat will reply that she likes swimming.

a) Steht der Hauptsatz in einer Zeit der Gegenwart, *Present Tense, Present Perfect* oder *Future Tense*, so ändert sich die Zeit der direkten Rede bei der Umwandlung in die indirekte Rede nicht.

b) Pat replied: "I see the plane."
Pat replied (that) she saw the plane.
. . . , *sie sehe das Flugzeug.*
My friend said: "My brother is in America."
My friend said that his brother was in America.
. . . sagte, daß sein Bruder in Amerika sei.
. . . sagte, sein Bruder sei in Amerika.

b) Steht der Hauptsatz aber in einer Zeit der Vergangenheit (*Past Tense, Past Perfect*, etc.), so muß auch im Nebensatz der indirekten Rede eine Zeit der Vergangenheit stehen.

Summary

Übersicht

Past Tense in the Principal Clause	*Direct Speech*	*Reported Speech*
Pat replied(:) Pat had replied(:) Pat would have replied(:)	Simple Present "I see the plane."	Simple Past (that) she saw the plane. *. . . sie sehe das Flugzeug.* *(Konjunktiv!)*
Pat replied(:) etc.	Present Perfect "I have seen the plane."	Past Perfect (that) she had seen the plane. *. . . sie habe schon gesehen.*
Pat replied(:) etc.	Simple Past "I saw the plane."	Past Perfect (that) she had seen the plane. *. . . sie habe. . . gesehen.*
Pat replied(:) etc.	Past Perfect "I had seen the plane."	Past Perfect (that) she had seen the plane. *. . . sie habe . . . gesehen.*
Pat replied(:) etc.	Simple Future "I shall (will) see the plane."	Future in the Past (that) she would see the plane. *. . . sie werde . . . sehen.*
Pat replied(:) etc.	Future Perfect "I shall (will) have seen the plane."	Future Perfect in the Past (that) she would have seen the plane. *. . . sie werde (würde) . . . gesehen haben.*

Notice:

Pat replied: "London lies on the Thames." Pat replied (that) London lies on the Thames. „The tide is caused by the attraction of the moon." I was taught that the tide is caused by the attraction of the moon.	Wird im Nebensatz der indirekten Rede eine an sich bestehende Tatsache ausgedrückt (d. h. ein objektiver Tatbestand gekennzeichnet), so gebraucht man (trotz einer Zeit der Vergangenheit im Hauptsatz) in der indirekten Rede das Präsens.

242 II. Bei der Verwandlung der direkten Rede in die indirekte Rede gehen folgende Veränderungen vor:

1.

a) I said: "I must leave in a minute." I said I had to leave in a minute.	a) *must* wird zu *had to* (*must* drückt hier aus die Notwendigkeit im Augenblick des Sprechens);
b) We said: "We must go to London next month." We said we should (would) have to go to London the following month.	b) *must* wird zu *should* (*would*) *have to* (*must* drückt hier aus die Notwendigkeit für die Zukunft, steht also im Sinne von *shall have to*);
c) My mother said: "You must not read in bed." My mother said that I was not to read in bed.	c) *I* (*you*, etc.) *must not* wird ersetzt durch *I* (*you*, etc.) *was not to*.
d) Father said: "You mustn't cross the road against the red light." He told us we must not cross the road against the red light.	d) *must* (*not*) wird auch in der indirekten Rede in unveränderter Form gebraucht, wenn dadurch eine ständig gültige Regel oder ein ständiges Verbot ausgedrücktwird (vgl.158, 2).

2.

Bob shouted: "They will be here soon."
Bob shouted that they would be there soon.
Robin said: "I must be off now."
Robin said he had to be off at once.
Pat told her friend: "I went shopping yesterday."
Pat told her friend that she had gone shopping the day before.
"What about tomòrrow morning?" asked the Sheriff.
The Sheriff asked if the next morning would suit Robin.
He said: "I think I know this place."
He said he thought he knew that place.

Es werden ferner bei der Umwandlung der direkten in die indirekte Rede

here	zu	there
now	zu	then, at once
yesterday	zu	the day before
tomorrow	zu	the next day
next week (month)	zu	the following week (month)
last week (month)	zu	the week before (month)
ago	zu	before
this, these	zu	that, those
	etc.	

Reported Questions — Indirekte Fragesätze 243

1\.

Mr. Green asked: "What is your name?" Mr. Green asked him what his name was. They were asked: "Do you like these cakes?" They were asked if (whether) they liked those cakes. He asked me: "Have you seen him anywhere?" He asked me if (whether) I had seen him anywhere.	Die Wortstellung im indirekten Fragesatz ist die gleiche wie im einfachen Aussagesatz. Entscheidungsfragen (Antwort: ja oder nein) werden mit *whether* oder *if* eingeleitet; *whether* ist das zutreffendere Wort, weil es die Bedeutung von *if* oder *if not* einschließt; aber *if* wird viel öfter gebraucht, einfach weil es kürzer ist.

2\. Fragesätze, die in direkter Rede mit *shall* eingeleitet werden, sind bei der indirekten Rede besonders zu behandeln. Man unterscheidet hier zwei Arten:

a) Shall I ever meet her again? Shall we have time to finish our meal? b) Shall I turn on the light? Shall the children go ahead and buy the tickets?	a) solche, die nach der Zukunft fragen, („Werde ich . . . ?"); b) solche, die erkunden, ob der Fragende etwas tun soll (einen Befehl oder eine Anweisung erwartend; „Soll ich . . . ?").

In der indirekten Rede erscheinen diese Fragen in folgender Form:

a) He wondered: "Shall I ever meet her again?" He wondered if he would ever meet her again.	a) *shall* wird zu *would* (*Conditional*) (= werde, würde);
b) He asked: "Shall I turn on the light?" He asked if he should turn on the light.	b) *shall* wird zu *should* (= solle, sollte).

Reported Imperative — Der Imperativ in der indirekten Rede 244

Der Imperativ der direkten Rede wird in der indirekten Rede wiedergegeben

a) The teacher said: "Interrupt me, children, if anything is not clear." The teacher said to the children (that) they should interrupt him if anything was not clear.	a) durch *should* nach *to say*;

b) The teacher {ordered / told} them: "Interrupt me . . ."
The teacher {ordered / told} them to interrupt him if anything was not clear.

b) durch *Direct Object + Infinitive with to* nach den Verben des Veranlassens und des Zulassens (vgl. 183, 1).

The Defective Auxiliaries in Subordinate Clauses

Die unvollständigen Hilfsverben in Nebensätzen

Da das Englische nur noch wenige Formen des Konjunktivs kennt, reichen diese oft nicht aus, um die verschiedenen Willensäußerungen und gefühlsmäßigen Stellungnahmen auszudrücken. Deshalb bedient sich das Englische in diesen Fällen der Defective Auxiliaries, in erster Linie *might*, *should*.

245 Subordinate Clauses expressing a Wish or Will

Nebensätze der Willensäußerung

should – might – would

1. Eine Willensäußerung kann ausgedrückt werden durch *should* oder (seltener) *might*

The judge ordered that the prisoner should be pardoned.
I am determined that nobody should enter this area.
He demanded that the money should be paid at once.
After much talk it was decided that they should fight the matter out.
The officer commanded that nobody should move.
He suggested that we might (should) go out for a meal.

nach den Verben des Befehlens, Anordnens und Beschließens, z. B. nach:

to order	to decide
to command	to resolve
to expect	to determine
to agree	to arrange
to settle	to make up one's mind
to demand	to suggest
to desire	to recommend
to ask	etc.
to request	
to insist	

2. Eine Willensäußerung kann ferner ausgedrückt werden durch *should*

a) It is desirable that he should help his friend.
It is natural that he should be angry with you.
It is important that you should be present.
It is better that you should apologise.

b) We burnt the letter lest he should find it.△
He told me to leave lest I should miss the train.△

a) nach unpersönlichen Ausdrücken, deren Bedeutung einen Wunsch oder ein Verlangen einschließt, z. B. nach:

it is desirable	it is natural
it is better	it is right
it is important	it is essential

b) in verneinten Finalsätzen (vgl. 237, 4), deren Verb im *Past Tense* steht, nach *lest* = damit nicht.
(Nur literar. Gebrauch).

3. Eine Willensäußerung kann auch ausgedrückt werden durch *would*

I wish (that) they would come back.
He wishes (that) he would pass the examination.
I wish I were a bird.
I wish I had never met him.

nach *I wish* .

Bei *to be* steht im *Past Tense were*! Zusammengesetzte Zeiten stehen im *Past Perfect*.

Subordinate Clauses expressing Personal Feelings

Nebensätze der gefühlsmäßigen Stellungsnahme 246

may – might – should

1. Die gefühlsmäßige Stellungnahme kann ausgedrückt werden durch *may, might* (neben *should*)

I am afraid that I may be late for school.
I am afraid he might not understand me.
He was afraid that he might never see his home again.
It was feared that the prisoners might escape.
He is working hard for fear that he might fail the examination.△ (= in case he fails)

nach den Verben des Fürchtens:

to be afraid, to fear	fürchten
for fear	aus Furcht

Notice:

I am afraid lest you should have done a foolish thing.△	*lest* (△) nach Verben des Fürchtens heißt „daß". Nach *lest* steht immer *should* (vgl. 237, 10; 246, 2).

2. Die gefühlsmäßige Stellungnahme kann ferner ausgedrückt werden durch *should*

a) I am pleased that you should have remembered my birthday.
I am sorry that you should have lost so much time.
I am astonished that he should act like this.
I regret very much that I should be the last to know this news.

b) It is strange that they should refuse to visit her.
It is funny that you should say that.
It is disgraceful that the refugees should be neglected.
It is a pity that we should not have met earlier.

a) nach den Verben und Ausdrücken der Gemütsbewegung (Freude, Trauer, Ärger usw.) z. B.

to wonder	to be angry
to regret	to be surprised
to be pleased	to be astonished
to be sorry	

b) nach unpersönlichen Ausdrücken, z. B.

it is strange	it is disgraceful
it is odd	it is a shame
it is a pity	it is regrettable
it is funny	it is surprising
it is curious	it is incredible

247 Subordinate Clauses expressing Uncertainty — Nebensätze der Unsicherheit

may – might – should

1. Zum Ausdruck der Unsicherheit stehen *may, might*

a) His family thought that he might still succeed.
I supposed that he might not be at home.
It is probable that you may meet him at the theatre.
It seemed at last that he might overcome the difficulties.

b) I shall (will) not do it, whatever he may say.
I cannot believe the news although it may be true.

a) nach Verben oder Ausdrücken, die ein Zweifeln oder eine Annahme bezeichnen, z. B.

to think	it is probable
to suppose	it is likely
it is doubtful	it seems;
it is possible	

b) in Einräumungssätzen (vgl. 237, 7) zur Bezeichnung einer Einräumung oder eines Zugeständnisses.

Zum Ausdruck der Unsicherheit steht ferner *should*

a) It is impossible that he should avoid this.
It is unlikely that he should have seen us.
It is improbable that she should catch the train.
It is inexplicable that he should not have heard me.
It is inconceivable that he should have been killed.

a) nach unpersönlichen Ausdrücken, die eine Unwahrscheinlichkeit oder eine Unmöglichkeit bezeichnen, z. B.
it is impossible
it is unlikely
it is improbable
it is inexplicable („unerklärlich")
it is inconceivable („unbegreiflich");

b) If he should call while I am out, ask him to wait.
If you should meet him, give him my best regards.
If it should rain tomorrow, we must make our trip another day.

b) in Bedingungssätzen der bloßen Möglichkeit oder Annahme (deutsch: sollte; vgl. *Conditional Clauses*, 239, 4).

WERDEN UND WESEN DER ENGLISCHEN SPRACHE

(Development and Character of the English Language)

Übersicht über die Geschichte der englischen Sprache (History of the English Language) 248

Die englische Sprache ist in einem höheren Maße als irgendeine andere eine Mischsprache. Im Laufe der Geschichte fielen in England sehr verschiedene Völker und Volksstämme ein, und jeder dieser Invasoren hat größere oder kleinere Teile seiner Sprache im Englischen zurückgelassen und mehr oder weniger Einfluß auf dessen Gestaltung gehabt.

Die altenglische Zeit (bis 1066) (The Old English Period)

Die ältesten Einwohner der britischen Inseln, von denen wir sichere Kunde haben, waren die den Kelten zugehörigen Briten. Sie fand Julius Caesar vor, als er in den Jahren 55 und 54 v. Chr. mit einem römischen Heer an der Küste der Insel landete (vgl. 249).

Die planmäßige Unterwerfung Britanniens durch die Römer setzte unter Kaiser Claudius (41 bis 54 n. Chr.) ein, dessen Feldherr Plautius Südbritannien 43 n. Chr. zur römischen Provinz machte. Unter Domitian (81–96 n. Chr.) wurde der römische Machtbereich bis Schottland ausgedehnt. Da Rom außerstande war, die langen Küsten Englands auf die Dauer zu verteidigen, gab es 410 n. Chr. freiwillig die Provinz Britannien auf. Obwohl die Römer über 350 Jahre die Insel beherrschten, hat die lateinische Sprache aus jener Zeit nur geringe Spuren in der Sprache Englands hinterlassen (vgl. 250).

Schon zur Römerzeit hatte es Angriffe germanischer Stämme auf die Insel gegeben. Vom 5. Jahrhundert an begann nun eine stärkere Einwanderung germanischer Stämme aus den nordwestlichen Küstengebieten Deutschlands, aus dem Land zwischen Elbe und Ems, aus Schweswig, Holstein und Jütland.

Angeln, Sachsen, Jüten, und wahrscheinlich auch Teile anderer germanischer Stämme, gründeten in Britannien mehrere rein germanische Reiche. In ihnen wurden, der Herkunft der Stämme entsprechend, verschiedene germanische Dialekte gesprochen: das Jütische im Südosten, das Sächsische südlich und das Anglische nördlich der Themse. Das Sächsische wurde allmählich der vorherrschende Dialekt und die Grundlage für die Entwicklung der englischen Sprache.

Die Dialekte der germanischen Stämme hatten auf niederdeutschem Gebiet die erste Lautverschiebung mitgemacht, dagegen, wie auch das Niederdeutsche, nicht die zweite, die Hochdeutsche Lautverschiebung. Hieraus erklärt es sich, daß das Englische dem Niederdeutschen viel näher steht als dem Hochdeutschen. Über den Stand der Konsonanten im Englischen im Vergleich mit dem Niederdeutschen und Hochdeutschen gibt die folgende Zusammenstellung einen Überblick:

	Englisch	Nieder-deutsch	Hochdeutsch		Englisch	Nieder-deutsch	Hochdeutsch
b	rib	Ribbe	Rippe	k	to make	maken	machen
d	day	Dag	Tag		book	Bauk, Bok	Buch
	door	Dor	Tor		to speak	spreken	sprechen
	garden	Gaden	Garten	v	seven	säven	sieben
g	bridge	Brügg	Brücke	f	wife	Wif	Weib
p	pipe	Piepe	Pfeife		half	half	halb
	apple	Appel	Apfel		deaf	dof	taub
	to sleep	slapen	schlafen	th	that	dat, dit	das
	deep	deip	tief		brother	broder	Bruder
t	ten	tain	zehn		father	Vadder	Vater
	to tell	vertellen	erzählen		mother	Modder	Mutter
	water	Water	Wasser	gh	night	Nacht	Nacht
	heart	Hat	Herz		daughter	Dochter	Tochter

Von 787 an begann eine neue Einwanderung germanischer Stämme aus Skandinavien: Norweger und Dänen strömten in das fruchtbare England. Von 1016 bis 1042 beherrschten die von den Angelsachsen als „Dänen“ bezeichneten Skandinavier das Land (vgl. 251).

Die mittelenglische Zeit (1066–1500) (The Middle-English Period)

Das folgenschwerste Ereignis für die Sprachgeschichte Englands war die normannische Eroberung (1066). Die Normannen, ein nordgermanischer Volksstamm, hatten im Anfang des 10. Jahrhunderts Nordwestfrankreich erobert und dort sehr bald ihre Muttersprache aufgegeben. Als sie 1066 unter Wilhelm dem Eroberer England in Besitz nahmen, sprachen sie Französisch und waren Träger der französischen Kultur.

Nach der Thronbesteigung Wilhelms wurde Französisch die Sprache des Hofes, der Gerichte, der Kirche und der Schulen. Das angelsächsische Volk hielt aber zäh an der Sprache seiner Väter fest. So wurden fast 300 Jahre lang Englisch und Französisch nebeneinander gesprochen. Während dieser Zeit fand aber eine gegenseitige Durchdringung der beiden Sprachen statt. Viele französische Wörter, besonders Bezeichnungen für Dinge und Begriffe, die den Angelsachsen fremd waren, drangen in das Englische ein (vgl. 252 und 255).

Aus dem Ringen der beiden Sprachen miteinander ging das Englische als Sieger hervor: Das Englische ist bis auf den heutigen Tag seinem Wesen, seinem inneren Aufbau und dem Wortschatz des täglichen Lebens nach eine germanische Sprache geblieben. 1362 wurde durch einen Erlaß Eduards III. Englisch neben Französisch als Sprache der Gerichte zugelassen. 1363 wurde das Parlament mit einer königlichen Botschaft in englischer Sprache eröffnet, und 1483 wurden schließlich auch die Gesetze in englischer Sprache veröffentlicht.

Das Englische hatte aber während dieser 300 Jahre starke Veränderungen erfahren: zahlreiche französische Wörter waren eingedrungen, die alten, klangvollen germanischen Endungen waren zu e abgeschwächt worden, und die Funktionen der alten bedeutungsvollen Flexionsendungen hatten Hilfsmittel (Präpositionen usw.) übernommen.

Die neuenglische Zeit (seit 1500) (The Modern English Period, since 1500)

Gegen Ende des Mittelalters gewinnt der Dialekt des Ostmittellandes, in dem die Hauptstadt London liegt, immer mehr an Bedeutung. In dem ostmittelländischen Dialekt dichtet Chaucer (etwa 1340–1400) seine Werke und veröffentlicht Caxton die in der ersten englischen Druckerei (1476 in Westminster eröffnet) hergestellten Bücher. Schon zur Zeit der Königin Elisabeth I. (1558–1603) ist der ostmittelländische Dialekt allgemein als Schriftsprache anerkannt.

Während der neuenglischen Zeit ist eine weitere Bereicherung des Wortschatzes der englischen Sprache eingetreten durch die Übernahme zahlreicher Wörter aus den klassischen Sprachen und dem Französischen zur Zeit der Klassik und der Pseudoklassik (17. und 18. Jahrhundert).

In diesem Zeitraum hat das Englische auf dem Gebiet der Flexion keine weiteren umgestaltenden Entwicklungen durchgemacht, wohl auf dem Gebiet der Syntax und vor allem der Aussprache. Die Schreibung der Wörter ist aber im wesentlichen auf dem Stand der frühneuenglischen Zeit stehengeblieben; zwischen der Schreibung und der Aussprache hat sich dadurch eine so tiefe Kluft aufgetan, daß die Schreibung oft keinen Anhalt für die Aussprache eines Wortes bietet. Bestrebungen, die englische Rechtschreibung zu reformieren, haben bisher – wohl infolge der stark konservativen Einstellung der Engländer – noch zu keinem nennenswerten Erfolg geführt.

The English Vocabulary

Der Wortschatz des Englischen

Celtic Words

Keltische Bestandteile 249

Snowdon	(*don* = Hügel)
Ben Nevis	(*ben* = Berg)
Avon, Ouse [u:z]	= (Wasser)
Aberdeen	(*aber* = Flußmündung)
Kent, Thames	

Nur geringe Reste des Keltischen sind in das Altenglische (bis 1066) eingedrungen. Die meisten dieser Wörter sind Eigennamen.

bard	(= Barde)
cradle [kreidl]	(= Wiege)
crag	(= Klippe, Felsspitze)
glen	(= Schlucht)

Eine Reihe von Wörtern haben erst in neuerer Zeit Eingang ins Englische gefunden.

plaid [plæd]	= Reisedecke, Überwurf
whisky, whiskey	= Branntwein, Whisky

Heute wird noch Keltisch gesprochen in Wales, im schottischen Hochland, auf der Insel Man und in Irland.

250 Latin Words

Lateinische Bestandteile

a) cheese	*lat. caseus*	street	*lat. via strata*
mile	*lat. milia*	pound	*lat. pondus*
mint	*lat. mentha*	wall	*lat. vallum*
plum	*lat. prunum*	wine	*lat. vinum*

a) Schon in Germanien war durch die Berührung mit römischen Kaufleuten eine Reihe von lateinischen Lehnwörtern in die Sprache der Angeln, Sachsen und Jüten eingedrungen.

b) bishop	*lat. episcopus*	pope	*lat. papa*
clerk	*lat. clericus*	to preach	*lat. praedicare*
creed	*lat. credo*	priest	*lat. presbyter*

b) Mit der Christianisierung des Landes (um 600) wurden viele religiöse Bezeichnungen aus dem Lateinischen übernommen.

c) to describe	extravagant	picture
ingenious	obscure	regal

c) Zur Zeit der Klassik und Pseudoklassik (17. und 18. Jahrh.) sind wieder viele lateinische Wörter ins Englische aufgenommen worden.

d) emphasis = Betonung	aeroplane
recipe = Rezept	propeller
tonic = Stärkungsmittel	telegraph
aerial = Antenne	telephone
locomotive	television etc.

d) Durch Wissenschaft und Technik dringen fortgesetzt neue Wörter lateinischen und griechischen Ursprungs ins Englische ein.

251 Scandinavian Words

Altnordische Bestandteile

anger	fellow	harbour	knife
law	skin	sky	tree
to call	to cast	to die	to take
to get	to hit	to scream	

Der Einfluß des Altnordischen (Skandinavischen) auf die englische Sprache war sehr stark. Dies zeigt sich schon darin, daß dieser Sprache ganz alltägliche Wörter entlehnt worden sind, wie z. B. auch die Pronomina *they*, *their*, *them*, *both*, *some* und die Verbform *are*.

252 French Words

Französische Bestandteile

1. In mittelenglischer Zeit (1066–1500) wurden übernommen:

a) government	reign	sovereign	parliament
fief (= Lehen)	feudal	state	nation
session	party	commons	vassal

a) Bezeichnungen für Regierung, Verwaltung und staatliche Einrichtungen;

b) duke	duchess	marquis	peer	b) Titel, Würden und Ämter;
prince	princess	count	baron	
chancellor	treasurer	minister	secretary	
c) chivalry	armour	harness	lance	c) Rittertum und Kriegführung;
battle	victory	dart (= Wurfspeer)		
standard	banner	mail (= Kettenpanzer)		
officer	soldier	enemy	ransom	
d) art	science	astronomy		d) Künste und Wissenschaften;
mathematics	arithmetic	architecture		
e) religion	service	cloister	Trinity	e) Kirche, Gottesdienst, Schule;
to baptize	lesson	rule	friar	
clergy	school	pupil	master	
f) justice	judge	court	jury	f) Rechtswesen und Rechtsprechung;
cause	prison	to plead	crime	
to accuse	trial	to try	to defend	
g) commerce	merchant	banker	apprentice	g) Handel und Gewerbe.
tailor	barber	printer	mason	
joiner	carpenter	actor	butcher	

attack	garage	massage	palace	In der Neuzeit wurden u. a. die nebenstehenden Wörter übernommen.
hotel	group			

Loan-Words from Other Languages — Entlehnungen aus anderen Sprachen 253

a) balcony	folio	piano	opera	a) aus dem Italienischen
b) armada	cigar	potato	tobacco	b) aus dem Spanischen
c) skipper	yacht [jɔt]	wagon		c) aus dem Holländischen
d) iceberg	hinterland	quartz	blitz	d) aus dem Deutschen
kindergarten	meerschaum	rucksack		
frankfurter	wanderlust	[ˈruksæk]		
e) admiral	alcohol	sofa		e) aus dem Arabischen
f) bey	bosh	horde		f) aus dem Türkischen
g) chess	lilac	shawl		g) aus dem Persischen
h) tea	kowtow [ˈkauˈtau]	(= Berühren des Bodens mit der Stirn als Gruß)		h) aus dem Chinesischen
i) jungle	bungalow	dinghy		i) aus dem Indischen
k) canoe	tomahawk	wigwam		k) aus der Indianersprache

254 American Words — Amerikanische Wörter

Aus dem Amerikanischen Englisch sind u. a. die folgenden Wörter in den englischen Wortschatz übernommen worden:

ballyhoo [bæli'hu]	= Reklamegeschrei; übertriebene Anpreisung oder Propaganda; Reklamerummel
to ballyhoo	= übertrieben anpreisen
blurb [bləːb]	= Reklame, „Waschzettel" (auf Bücherumschlägen)
boost [buːst]	= Propaganda, Reklame; Preistreiberei; Aufschwung
to boost	= lebhafte Reklame für etwas machen; Preise in die Höhe treiben
boom [buːm]	= Hochkunjunktur, Hausse, geschäftlicher Aufschwung
to boom	= für eine Sache geräuschvolle Reklame machen; in die Höhe treiben
chore [tʃɔː]	= leichte (Haus-, Gelegenheits-) Arbeit
doodle ['duːdl]	= kritzeln, Männchen malen
quiz [kwiz]	= Fragespiel, Aus-, Befragung
to quiz	= prüfen, befragen, ausfragen
set-up ['setʌp]	= arrangierter Kampf, Spiel; Plan, Entwurf; Zusatz (zu alkoholischen Getränken)

255 The Vocabulary as a Reflection of Civilization — Der Wortschatz als Spiegelbild der Kultur

Englische Ortsnamen geben ein Bild von der Besiedlung des Landes durch die verschiedenen Stämme und Völkerschaften.

1. a) Aberdeen, Carnarvon, London, Dunbar, Carlisle, Cardigan, Dundee, Strathmore

   a) Ortsnamen, die mit *aber* („Mündung"), *carr* („Burg", „Festung"), *dun* („Hügelfeste"), *strath* („Tal") gebildet sind, bezeichnen keltische Siedlungen.

   b) Lancaster, Winchester, Lincoln, Leicester, Chester

   b) Ortsnamen auf *-caster, -cester, -chester* (lat. *castra*); *-coln* (lat. *colonia*) bezeichnen Orte, an denen sich römische Lager befanden.

c) Birmingham	Northampton	
Hampstead	Bradford	
d) Warwick	Berwick	Hardwick
Ipswich	Harwich	
Mablethorpe	Whitby	
e) Ashby-de-la-Zouch [ˈæʃbidəlɑːˈzuːʃ]		

c) Ortsnamen auf *-ham*, *-ton*, *-stead*, *-ford* sind Namen angelsächsischer Siedlungen.

d) Siedlungsnamen auf *-wick* (*vik* = Bucht), *-thorpe* (= Dorf), *-by* (= Stadt), gehen auf Gründungen der Nordländer zurück.

e) Auch der Umstand, daß Ortsnamen französischer Herkunft sehr selten sind, ist sehr aufschlußreich. Die Normannen saßen auf ihren Burgen und Schlössern, gründeten aber keine Städte und Dörfer.

2.

Wessex	Essex	Sussex
Middlesex	East Anglia	

Die Landschaftsnamen auf *-sex* erinnern an die altgermanischen Reiche (Sachsen); an das Siedlungsgebiet der Angeln erinnert *East Anglia*.

3. In den Namen englischer Wochentage und Feste leben die Namen germanischer Gottheiten weiter.

Tuesday	mhd. ziestac	= der Tag des Ziu
Wednesday		= der Tag des Wotan
Friday		= der Tag der Frigg, Freia
Easter		= Fest der *ags.* Göttin *ēastre*

4. Weitere Beispiele, aus denen kulturgeschichtliche Erkenntnisse gewonnen werden können, sind:

town	(Zaun, Stadt) läßt erkennen, daß die altgermanischen Siedlungen mit einem Zaun umgeben waren.
spoon	(Span, Löffel) weist darauf hin, daß ursprünglich die Löffel aus Holz geschnitzt wurden.
cattle fee	*cattle*, aus lat. *capitalis* (= Eigentum), auf das auch das deutsche Wort „Kapital" zurückgeht, und *fee* (= Vieh; Lohn, Bezahlung, Gebühr) erinnern an die Zeit, in der das Vieh der Hauptbesitz war und als Zahlungsmittel diente.
window	= niederdeutsch *windoge*, berichtet uns von den kleinen glaslosen, augenförmigen Öffnungen in den Wänden der Häuser für den Abzug des Rauches.

lord lady	*lord,* altengl. *hlaford* (= Brotgeber) und *lady* altengl. *hlafdige* (= Brotkneterin) lassen erkennen, daß ursprünglich die Dienerschaft und Gefolgschaft im Hause des Herrn wohnte und von ihm unterhalten wurde.
book to write to read	Diese Wörter erinnern an die Sitte, aus in „Buchenholz" (*book*) „geritzten" (*to write;* vgl. Reißbrett) Runenzeichen die Zukunft zu deuten oder zu „raten" (*to read*). Als die Kunst des Schreibens die Runenschrift verdrängte, erhielt *book* die Bedeutung „Buch", *to write* die Bedeutung „schreiben".
to spell	Das Verb *to spell* bedeutete früher „bezaubern". Im heutigen Englisch hat sich die ursprüngliche Bedeutung noch in *to spell away* („wegzaubern") erhalten.
a fortnight the Twelfth-night	*a fortnight* (= vierzehn Tage, mhd. vierzehn nahte) und *the Twelfth-night.* (= Dreikönigstag) sind Reste der altgermanischen Zeitrechnung nach Nächten.

5. Die nach der normannischen Eroberung ins Englische übernommenen Wörter lassen Schlüsse zu auf die Lebensweise und Lebensart der Angelsachsen.

stool = Schemel, Stuhl ohne Lehne
chair = Stuhl mit Lehne, Sessel; frz. *la chaire*
board = Tischplatte auf zwei Stützen (vgl. „die Tafel aufheben")
table = Tisch mit fester Platte auf vier Beinen; frz. *la table*

Diese Wörter zeigen, daß die Angelsachsen mit den französischen Wörtern auch die bequemeren Möbel übernommen haben. *Stool* bezeichnet heute noch „Schemel" (*footstool, office-stool*); *board* hat sich erhalten in der Bedeutung „Aufsichtsrat" und in der Verbindung *board and lodging* (*residence*) „Kost und Logis".

6.

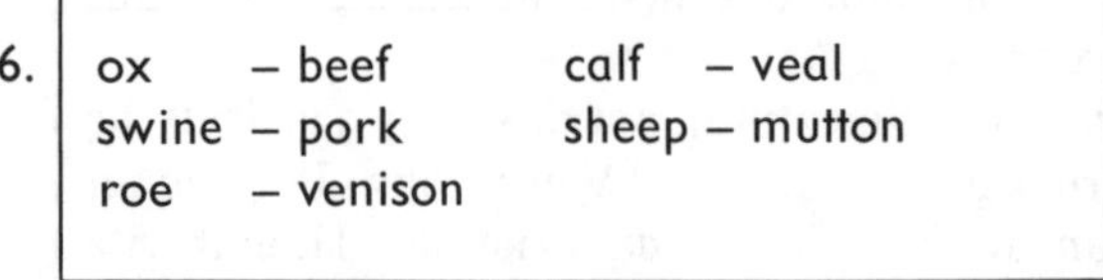

ox	– beef	calf	– veal
swine	– pork	sheep	– mutton
roe	– venison		

Die Namen der Tiere sind im allgemeinen germanischen Ursprungs, die Namen der aus ihrem Fleisch bereiteten Speisen jedoch romanischer Herkunft. – Die Normannen waren den Angelsachsen in der Kochkunst überlegen; mit der von den Normannen erlernten verfeinerten Zubereitung wurden auch die Namen für das nach der neuen Art bereitete Fleisch übernommen.

to boil	to fry	to roast
sauce	pie	paste
toast	dinner	supper

So sind auch die Bezeichnungen für die verschiedenen Arten der Fleischzubereitung romanischen Ursprungs, ebenso die Namen der Mahlzeiten *dinner* und *supper*.

breakfast	bread	loaf
honey	milk	to bake

Die Namen der einfachen Speisen und Mahlzeiten sind germanisch.

weapon	sword	spear
arrow	bow	shield

Die Namen der einfachen Waffen, deren sich der alte Germane auf der Jagd und im Kampfe bediente, sind germanischen Ursprungs.

harness	mail	banner
dart	lance	armour

Die Namen für die vornehme Ausrüstung des Ritters sind romanischer Herkunft.

father	mother	brother
sister	son	daughter
child		

Die Bezeichnungen für die nahe Verwandtschaft sind germanisch.

uncle	aunt	nephew
niece	cousin	family

Die Bezeichnungen für die entferntere Verwandtschaft sind romanisch. (*grandfather*, *grandmother* u. ä. bestehen aus romanischen und germanischen Wörtern.)

smith	baker	miller
weaver	shoemaker	shepherd

Die Namen für die verschiedenen Gewerbe, soweit es sich nicht um kunstvolle Arbeiten handelt, sind germanischer Herkunft.

tailor	barber	printer
mason	joiner	carpenter
actor	butcher	merchant

Dagegen sind die Gewerbe, die Kunstfertigkeit verlangten und die Angelsachsen mit den Normannen, für die sie arbeiteten, in Berührung brachten, romanischen Ursprungs.

nail	hammer	ax(e)
saw	spade	tongs

Die Namen der einfachen Werkzeuge sind germanisch

10.				
germ.	red	blue	black	white
rom.	violet	crimson	scarlet	
germ.	father	mother	brother	
rom.	family	relatives		
germ.	nose	mouth	eye	chin
	forehead			
rom.	face			

Die Bezeichnungen für das Einfache sind meist germanischer Herkunft, dagegen die Bezeichnungen für das Zusammenfassende oder Zusammengesetzte meist romanischen Ursprungs.

11.		
sun	moon	weather
rain	hail	thunderstorm
sea	storm	wind
house	hut	window
door	yard	field
plant	corn	
ship	boat	board
keel	sail	etc.

Germanischer Herkunft sind auch die Namen für Erscheinungen in der Natur, mit der die alten Germanen aufs engste verbunden waren.
Germanischer Herkunft sind außerdem die Bezeichnungen für Haus, Hof und Feld
und die Namen für Schiffe und Schiffsteile.

256 Change in the Meaning of Words — Wandel in der Wortbedeutung

Jedes Wort hat ursprünglich eine bestimmt umgrenzte Bedeutung; es ist die Bezeichnung einer bestimmten Vorstellung. Häufig aber hat sich ein Wandel in der Bedeutung des Wortes vollzogen.

1. Begriffsverengung

Das Wort:	bedeutete ursprünglich:	es bedeutet heute:
maw [mɔː]	Magen (ganz allgemein)	Magen der Tiere
wife	Weib, jede Frau überhaupt	Ehefrau
to starve	sterben	verhungern, Hungers sterben
stove [stəuv]	Stube	Ofen; heizbare Stube
harbour	Unterkunftsort (im Althochdeutschen hieß das Wort: heriberga)	Hafen
deer	Tiere	Rotwild
fiend [fiːnd]	Feind	Teufel, Satan

queen (altengl. cwēn)	Frau	Königin	Hier spricht man von einer Bedeutungsverbesserung.
knight	Knecht	(Ritter) Adelsrang	
churl knave villain	Kerl (im guten Sinne) Knabe Dorfbewohner, Bauer	Rüpel Schelm, Schurke Schurke, Tölpel	Hier spricht man von einer Bedeutungsverschlechterung.

. Begriffserweiterung

Das Wort:	bedeutete ursprünglich:	bedeutet heute aber:
town	Zaun (später: umzäunter Hof, umzäunter Bezirk eines Dorfes)	Stadt
glee	Unterhaltung, Spiel, Sport, später: musikalische Unterhaltung, Musik	Freude

. Begriffsänderung durch Übertragung der Bedeutung. Sie kann dadurch veranlaßt werden:

a) cock	Hahn	Hahn (allgemein); Hahn am Faß und am Gewehr	a) daß zwischen 2 Dingen eine Ähnlichkeit der Form besteht;
eye	Auge	Auge; Öhr der Nadel, Stielloch d. Hammers, Öse	
b) hand	Hand	Hand; Arbeiter; Zeiger (der Uhr);	b) daß zwei Dinge denselben Zweck oder dieselbe Eigenschaft haben;
head	Kopf	Kopf; Spitze eines Berges; Vorsteher (einer Schule); Führer (einer Gruppe); Überschrift	
c) spoon	Holzspan später: der aus Holz geschnitzte Löffel	Löffel (aus jedem Material)	c) daß zwei Gegenstände aus demselben Stoff verfertigt sind.
copper	Kupfer	Kupfermünzen, -kessel	

Word-building — Wortbildung

Neue Wörter entstehen (im Englischen wie in anderen Sprachen) durch Neuschöpfung, durch Übergang von einer Wortart in eine andere, durch Zusammensetzung und Zusammenrückung, durch Ableitung von einem vorhandenen Wortstamm.

257 The Building of New Words — Neuschöpfung von Wörtern

1. Imitation of Sounds — Lautnachahmung

cuckoo	Kuckuck	peewit	Kiebitz
bow-wow	Hund (in der Kindersprache)	to mew	miauen
to cackle	gackern	to moo	wie eine Kuh brüllen
to caw	wie ein Rabe krähen	to bang	(die Tür) zuschlagen
to buzz	summen; sausen		

2. Abbreviated Words — Abkürzungen

cab	(cabriolet)	'varsity	(University)
exam	(examination)	bike	(bicycle)
zoo	(Zoological Gardens)	pram	(perambulator)
lab	(laboratory)	Bakerloo Line	(Baker Street + Waterloo)
prep	(preparation)	fancy	(fantasy)
pub	(public house)	movie	(moving pictures)
bus	(omnibus)	cablegram	(cable-telegram)
phone	(telephone)	fridge	(refrigerator)
plane	(aeroplane)	flu	(influenza)
plot	(complot)	prefab	(pre-fabricated)
cycle	(bicycle)	soccer	(Association Football)
van	(caravan)	gipsy, gypsy	(Egyptian)

3. Initial Words — Wörter aus Anfangsbuchstaben

B. A.	Bachelor of Arts	UNESCO	United Nations Educational, Scientific, and Cultural Organization
M. A.	Master of Arts	UN(O)	United Nations (Organization)
M. D.	Doctor of Medicine	U. S. A.	United States of America
B. B. C.	British Broadcasting Corporation	Y. M. C. A.	Young Men's Christian Association
		R. S. P. C. C.	Royal Society for the Prevention of Cruelty to Children

Change from One Part of Speech to the Other

Übergang von einer Wortart in die andere 258

a) post	die Post	to post	auf die Post geben
shop	der Laden	to shop	einkaufen gehen Einkäufe machen
b) to hope	hoffen	hope	Hoffnung
to dress	sich ankleiden	dress	Anzug, Kleid
c) calm	ruhig	to calm	beruhigen
dry	trocken	to dry	trocknen
d) up oben	to up hochheben	the ups and downs of life das Auf und Ab des Lebens	
down nieder	to down tools die Arbeit niederlegen, streiken		
d) light	hell	the light	das Licht
half	halb	the half	die Hälfte
f) London		a London merchant ein Londoner Kaufmann	
average		the average wage	

a) Substantive werden zu Verben;

b) Verben werden zu Substantiven;

c) Adjektive werden zu Verben;

d) Adverbien werden zu Verben und Substantiven;

e) Adjektive werden zu Substantiven;

f) Substantive werden zu Adjektiven.

Notice:

Auch aus Eigennamen sind einige neue Wörter entstanden, z. B.

boycott, to boycott	nach dem irischen Grundbesitzer Captain Boycott, der 1880 von seinen Nachbarn geächtet wurde;
to lynch	nach dem virginischen Farmer Lynch (1736 bis 1796);
mackintosh	Name des Erfinders des „Regenmantels", des Schotten Mackintosh
sandwich	nach dem Earl of Sandwich

Word-building through a Change of the Stem Vowel

Wortbildung durch Veränderung des Stammvokals 259

a) a sale – to sell; a tale – to tell
a fall – to fell (= *Bäume fällen*)
b) to abide – an abode to bite – a bit
to shoot – a shot to sing – a song
to bind – a band, bond, bundle

Neue Wörter haben sich gebildet
a) durch Umlaut;

b) durch Ablaut.

260 Word-building through Composition and Moving together — Wortbildung durch Zusammensetzung und Zusammenrückung

1. Im Englischen lassen sich wie im Deutschen (vgl. Hoftor, Fensterflügel, graubraun usw.) zwei Wörter zu einem neuen Wort verbinden, und zwar ohne ihre Form zu verändern. – In der Regel hat das erste Wort den Ton, jedoch ist *level* (*double*) *stress* häufig.

Zusammensetzungen dieser Art sind:

a)	'arm'chair 'fireworks 'playfellow	'business-man 'goldsmith 'playboy	'farm'yard 'pea-'soup 'suit-case	a) Noun + Noun
b)	'seasick 'snow-'blind	'sky-'blue	'snow-'white	b) Noun + Adjective
c)	'handwriting 'writing-table	'yacht-'racing	'sitting-room	c) Noun + Gerund
d)	'commonwealth 'pennyworth	'free-'trade 'redbreast	'highway	d) Adjective + Noun
e)	'dark-'brown 'good-'looking	'dead-'tired 'red-'hot		e) Adjective + Adjective (or: Participle)
f)	'bystander	'looker-'on	'passer-'by	f) Adverb + Noun
g)	'evergreen	'everlasting		g) Adverb + Adjective
h)	'ever'more	'never'more	'roundabout (= *Karussell*)	h) Adverb + Adverb
i)	'breakfast	'drawbridge	to 'typewrite	i) Verb + Noun
k)	to 'blindfold to 'whitewash	to 'safeguard		k) Adjective + Verb

Notice the Difference:

a 'blackbird	die Amsel
a 'black 'bird	ein schwarzer Vogel
a 'French-master	ein Lehrer des Französischen
a 'French 'master	ein französischer Lehrer

2.

doll's house	Puppenhaus	stay-at-home	Stubenhocker
ship's captain	Schiffskapitän	son-in-law	Schwiegersohn
man-of-war	Kriegsschiff	good-for-nothing	Taugenichts
matter-of-fact	sachlich, nüchtern	will-to-peace	Friedenswille
man-at-arms	Gewappneter		

In Zusammenrückungen werden Wörter miteinander verbunden, die in einer syntaktischen Beziehung zueinander stehen.

Word-building with Extra Syllables — Wortbildung mit Ableitungssilben

Germanische Ableitungssilben werden mit Wörtern germanischer und romanischer Herkunft, romanische Ableitungssilben mit Wörtern romanischer und germanischer Herkunft verbunden.

Word-building with Prefixes — Wortbildung mit Vorsilben 261

Vorsilbe	Herkunft und Bedeutung	Silbe dient zur Bildung von	
be-	dtsch. be-	Subst., Adj. u. trans. Verben	behest bespectacled to becloud to bedew to befriend to belittle to bemoan to besiege to behold
for-	dtsch. ver-	transitiven Verben	to forbear to forbid to forget to forgive to forsake
fore-	dtsch. Vorder-, vorher-	Subst., Verb	′forecast ′foreground ′foretaste to ′forecast to fore′see to fore′taste
mis-	dtsch. miß-, schlecht, falsch (tun)	Subst., Verb	′mis′deed mis′fortune ′mis′trust to ′mis′manage to ′mis′read to mis′take to ′misunderstand
out-	dtsch. aus-, mehr oder länger als	Subst., Verb	′outbreak ′outcry ′out′sider to out′cry to out′do to out′live to out′number
over-	dtsch. über; zuviel, zu lang	Subst., Verb	′overcoat ′overflow to ′over′do to ′over′eat to ′over′sleep to ′over′work
un-	dtsch. un-, kehrt den Begriff des Grundworts um	Subst., Adj., Verb	′unbe′lief ′unem′ployment ′un′rest ′un′truth ′un′able un′happy un′kind ′unim′portant to ′un′button to ′un′do to ′un′dress to ′un′tie
with-	dtsch. wider-, ab-, ent-, zurück-	Verb	to with′draw to with′hold to with′stand
ante	lat. ante, frz. ante-, „vor-“	Subst., Adj. (Verb)	′anteroom ′ante-refor′mations (time) ′anteme′ridian to ′ante′date (vgl. pre-)
anti-	griech., gegen	Subst., Adj.	′antichrist ′anti′militarist ′antipope ′anti-′aircraft ′anti-′German

Vorsilbe	Herkunft und Bedeutung	Silbe dient zur Bildung von:	
arch-	griech., „Erz-"	Subst.	′archangel ′arch′bishop ′arch-′enemy ′arch-′liar
co-	frz. con-, lat. cum „zusammen"	Subst., Adj., Verb	co′adjutor ′coedu′cation ′coope′ration co′equal co-′ordinate to ′co-exist to co-′operate to co-′ordinate
counter-	frz. contre-, lat. contra- „gegen"	Subst., Verb	′counter-attack ′counterclaim to counter′act to counter′balance
dis-	frz. dis-, lat. dis-; hebt den Begriff des Grundworts auf, „ent-, ver-, zer-"	Subst., Adj., Verb	dis′honour dis′order dis′trust dis′honest ′disin′clined diso′bedient to disap′pear to dis′arm to dis′close to ′disem′bark to dis′miss
en-; em-	frz. en-, dtsch. ein-	kausative Verben von Subst., Adj., Verb	to en′danger to en′large to en′rage to en′rich to en′slave to em′bark to em′bed to em′bitter
ex-	lat. ex- „aus, früher"	Subst.	ex-′chancellor ′ex-′emperor ′ex-′prime minister
in-	frz. in-; Gegensatz; dtsch. un- (Assimilation)	Subst., Adj.	inaction inattention inconvenience; inapt inaudible incomplete (*vor Labial:*) impossible improper (*vor* l:) illiberal illegible (*vor* r:) irresistible irresolute
post-	lat. post	Adj. (Verb)	′post-′war(time) to ′post′date
pre-	frz. pré-, lat. prae-	Adj., Verb	′pre-ar′rangement preface [′prefis] ′pre-′Roman ′pre-′war (times) to ′pre-ar′range to pre′cede to pre′dict (vgl. 16,4)
pro-	lat. pro-, „für"	Adj.	′pro-′Boer ′pro-′German
re-	frz. ré-, re-, lat. re-, „wieder zurück, noch einmal"	Subst., Adj., Verb	′recons′truction ′re-′eligible to re′claim to re′fresh to re′fuse to re′move to re′turn (vgl. 16, 6)

Word-building with Suffixes

Wortbildung mit Nachsilben

. Suffixes for the Formation of Personal Nouns

Nachsilben zur Bildung von Personenbezeichnungen

Nachsilbe	Herkunft und Bedeutung	Funktion: dient zur Ableitung von			
a) für die handelnden Personen					
-er	dtsch. -er	Verben	baker hunter teacher	employer painter writer	glover speaker
		Subst., Adj.	Londoner cottager	Dubliner villager	Britisher
-or, -ar	lat. -or	Verben	actor visitor	possessor beggar	sailor liar
-ess	frz. -eresse, bezeichnet weibl. Personen	Subst.	actress hostess	authoress stewardess	empress waitress
-eer	frz. -ier	Subst.	engi'neer volun'teer	mountai'neer	profi'teer
b) für die von der Handlung betroffene Person					
-ee	frz. -é	Verb.	address'ee pay'ee	employ'ee train'ee	evacu'ee refug'ee
c) Zugehörigkeit zu einem Beruf, Staat, Ort					
-ian	frz. -ien	Subst.	historian Italian Christian	librarian Austrian Presbyterian	mathematician Prussian
-ist	griech.	Subst., Adj., Verb	archaeologist novelist dramatist pacifist	linguist philologist colonist socialist	Latinist dentist loyalist copyist
-ite	urspr. hebr.	Personen- u. Ortsname	Durhamite („Einwohner von Durham") Ibsenite Wagnerite (= *Verehrer von Ibsen, Wagner*) Jacobite (= *Anhänger der Stewarts*) Pre-Raphaelite ['priː'ræfəlait] (= *Anhänger einer Kunstrichtung*)		

d) für die Bezeichnungen des Ortes einer Handlung, einer Geschäfts- oder Berufs tätigkeit

-age	frz. -age	Subst.	garage ['gærɑːdʒ, 'gæridʒ]	pasturage ['pɑːstjuridʒ]	vicarage ['vikəridʒ]
-ery	frz. -erie	Subst.	bakery	brewery	fishery

2. Suffixes for the Formation of Collective and Abstract Nouns

Nachsilben zur Bildung von Sammelbegriffen und Abstrakten

Nach-silbe	Herkunft und Bedeutung				
-d	dtsch. -t	blood	deed	flood	seed
-dom	dtsch. -tum	boredom	freedom	martyrdom	officialdom
-hood	dtsch. -heit	boyhood falsehood	brotherhood likelihood	childhood neighbourhood	manhood
-ness	dtsch. -nis	blindness happiness	darkness kindness	fearfulness sweetness	goodness wickedness
-t	vgl. dtsch. „Gewicht“	draught height	drift weight	gift	flight
-th	dtsch. -t	birth length	death strength	growth truth	health youth
-age	frz. -age	bondage	courage	shortage	peerage
-al	frz. -aille	approval revival	arrival refusal	denial trial	proposal
-ance, -ence	frz. -ance, -ence	distance difference	resistance vehemence	hindrance	forbearance
-ation	frz. -ation	foundation representation	operation starvation	reformation	

-cy	frz. -ce	accuracy elegancy secrecy	constancy legacy	currency privacy	decency supremacy
-ion	frz. -ion	agitation passion	creation rebellion	conversion solution	motion
-ism	lat.; frz. -isme	baptism egoism Puritanism	Bolshevism egotism	Christianism militarism	communism patriotism
-ment	frz. -ment	acknowledgement engagement punishment	amazement fulfilment treatment	argument judgment	astonishment merriment
-ry	frz. -erie	gentry rivalry	peasantry drudgery	poultry	yeomanry
-ty	frz. -té	cruelty piety	dignity society	gaiety	honesty
-y	frz. -ie, -é, e	army remedy	family study	misery	philosophy

. Diminutive Endings — Verkleinerungssilben

Nachsilbe	Herkunft				
-ette	frz. -ette	kitchenette	sermonette	maisonette	novelette
-ie, -y	Koseform von Eigennamen	Annie Daddy Tommy	auntie darky Peggy	doggie Johnny Bobby	lassie pussy Granny
-kin	deutsch: -chen	lambkin	napkin	Peterkin	
-let	deutsch: -lein	booklet ringlet	brooklet riverlet	hamlet streamlet	leaflet
-ling		seedling nestling	darling sapling (= *junger Baum*)	duckling	gosling
-ock	ags.	bullock	hillock	paddock (= *Pferdekoppel, Sattelplatz; Kröte*△, *Frosch*)	

4. Suffixes for the Formation of Adjectives — Nachsilben zur Bildung von Adjektiven

Nachsilbe	Herkunft u. Bedeutung	Funktion: leitet ab von	
-ed	dtsch. -et, -t	Subst., Verb.	blessed crooked gifted learned wooded wretched 'blue-'eyed 'fair-'haired Die Endung -ed wird [id] gesprochen in: crooked [id] dogged [id] learned [id] naked [id] rugged [id] wretched [id] etc.; ebenso stets in -edly: assured [ə'ʃuəd] assuredly [ə'ʃuəridli]
-en	dtsch. -en, -ern	Stoffnamen	earthen flaxen golden leaden silken wooden woollen
-ful	dtsch. -voll	Subst.	awful careful fearful hopeful joyful painful pitiful powerful sinful
-ish	dtsch. -isch	Subst.	Bezeichnung der Zugehörigkeit: English Irish heathenish outlandish Vergleich, „wie ein . . .", oft mit verächtlichem oder verkleinerndem Sinn: boyish clownish foolish girlish Schwache Farbe: blackish greenish reddish yellowish
-less	dtsch. -los	Subst.	bootless careless endless fearless hopeless joyless penniless restless sinless wireless
-like	dtsch. -gleich	Subst.	boylike childlike gentlemanlike godlike ladylike lifelike warlike
-ly	dtsch. -lich	Subst.	cowardly earthly godly lively lovely manly soldierly hourly yearly
-some	dtsch. -sam	Subst., Adj.	burdensome irksome quarrelsome tiresome troublesome wearisome
-ward	dtsch. -wärts	Ortsadv., Subst.	backward downward forward inward onward outward upward eastward landward seaward
-y	dtsch. -ig	Subst.	bony earthy hungry mighty shady smoky stormy wealthy

-able, -ible	frz. -al, -ial	trans. Verben	agreeable favourable responsible	drinkable unbearable flexible	eatable audible visible
-al, -ial	frz. -able, -ible	Subst.	annual national papal	educational natural essential	coastal occasional imperial
-an	frz. -ain	von geographischen Namen auf -a und Personennamen	African Mohammedan Lutheran Elizabethan	American [məu'hæmidən] ['lu:ðrən] Gregorian	Australian Victorian
-ic(al)	(Die Ableitungen auf *-ic* gehören meist der gelehrten, die auf *-ical* der Alltagssprache an.)		classic(al) historic(al) energetic critical	comic(al) politic(al) phonetic logical	domestic(al) systematic(al) emphatic musical
-ous	frz. -eux, -euse	Subst.	conscious glorious	dangerous mountainous	fabulous furious

The Formation of Verbs with Suffixes

Die Bildung von Verben mit Nachsilben

Nachsilbe	Herkunft	Funktion		
-en	dtsch. -en	bildet Verben von Substantiven und Adjektiven germanischer Herkunft, die die Überleitung oder den Übergang in den im Grundwort bezeichneten Zustand ausdrücken;	to blacken (= *schwarz machen und schwarz werden*) to darken to fasten to sharpen to shorten to widen to whiten	 to deepen to harden to strengthen to sweeten to weaken to heighten
-fy	frz. -fier	bildet solche Verben von Stammwörtern romanischer Herkunft;	to certify to glorify to purify	to fortify to justify to satisfy
-ize, -ise (vgl. S. 272)	frz. -iser	bildet Verben, die eine Überführung, seltener einen Übergang, von einem Zustand in einen anderen bezeichnen.	to civilize to fertilize to realize	to colonize to organize to tyrannize

Zur Schreibung *-ise* oder *-ize*:
-ise wird geschrieben, wenn *-ise* ein Teil eines in das Englische eingegangenen, aber nicht mehr lebendigen Stammwortes ist (man kann dies daran erkennen, daß nach Abstreichen von *-ise* weder ein englisches Wort noch ein erkennbarer Teil eines solchen bleibt: *to advertise, to advise, to chastise* („züchtigen"), *to comprise, compromise* (S. u. V.), *to despise, exercise* (S. u. V.), *to paralyse, merchandise, to supervise, surprise* (S.u.V.), Ausnahmen: *to baptize* („taufen"), *to capsize* („kentern").
Die Verben auf *-ize* sind von Wörtern der heutigen Sprache gebildet: *-ize* wird entweder an das unveränderte Grundwort angefügt: *to authorize, to centralize, to characterize, to civilize, to realize, to terrorize, to vulcanize*, oder die Endung des Grundwortes (z. B. *-al, -e, -ie, -y*) wird vor der Endung *-ize* abgeworfen: to *fraternize* (*fraternal*), *to temporize* („Zeit zu gewinnen suchen"); *to sterilize* (*sterile*), *fertilize* (*fertile*), *to dramatize* (*dramatic*), *to magnetize* (*magnetic*); *colonize* (*colony*), *to tyrannize* (*tyranny*).
Endung der Substantivbildung: *-ization: colonization, realization.*
In AE stehen oft die Schreibungen *-ise* und *-ize* nebeneinander, doch wird *-ize* allgemein bevorzugt.

6. The Formation of Adverbs — Die Bildung von Adverbien

Ableit.-silbe	Herkunft						
Vorsilben							
a-	*on* + Subst. oder Adj.	abroad aside	adrift asleep	afoot away	alive	along	apart
be-	*by* + Subst. oder Adverb	before	behind	below	beneath	besides	betimes
Nachsilben							
-ly	dtsch. -lich	badly	contentedly	quickly	richly	sweetly	
-ways	vgl. allerwege	lengthways	sideways				
-wise	vgl. pfennigweise	lengthwise	nowise	likewise	otherwise		
-ward(s)	dtsch. -wärts	backward(s)	forward(s)	homeward(s)	upward(s)		

263 Characteristic Features of the English Language — Wesenszüge der englischen Sprache

1. Wealth of Vocabulary

Germanic:	Romanic:
wife	spouse
welcome	reception
hearty	cordial
lucky	fortunate
tale	story, history
house, building	mansion, edifice
kingly	royal, regal

Das Englische hat nicht nur zu allen Zeiten neue Wörter für neue Begriffe und Gegenstände übernommen, sondern hat oft neben ein schon vorhandenes Wort ein fremdes Wort gleicher Bedeutung gestellt. Häufig stehen Wörter germanischer Herkunft neben Wörtern romanischen Ursprungs.

Wenn für denselben Begriff Wörter germanischer und romanischer Herkunft vorhanden sind, so läßt sich allgemein sagen, daß die Umgangssprache die Wörter germanischer Herkunft bevorzugt, während die literarische, gewähltere Sprache (bes. das Amts-, Kaufmanns- und Zeitungsenglisch) diejenigen französischer Herkunft wählt.

a lucky fellow	a fortunate individual
a nice house	a desirable mansion
a loving wife	an amiable spouse
a hearty welcome	a cordial reception

Manchmal wird in der literarischen und in der Amtssprache die Verwendung von Wörtern französischen Ursprungs so weit getrieben, daß die Ausdrucksweise sogar für einen weniger gebildeten Engländer schwer verständlich werden kann. In Carrol's "*Alice in Wonderland*" sagt *Dodo:* '*In that case I move* („vorschlagen") *that the meeting adjourn* („sich vertagen") *for the adoption of more energetic remedies . . .*' („um sofort energischere Maßnahmen zu ergreifen"), worauf *Eaglet* sie unterbricht: '*Speak English! I don't know the meaning of half those long words, and what's more, I don't believe you do either!*' Heute wird von namhaften englischen Philologen entschieden für den Gebrauch der Wörter germanischer Herkunft und gegen den Mißbrauch romanischer Wörter Stellung genommen.

Der Wortreichtum des Englischen wird noch dadurch vermehrt, daß es nach dem Verfall der Flexion dasselbe Wort in verschiedenen Funktionen verwenden kann.

dog,	to dog	dogged ['dɔgid]
paper	to paper	a paper-weight
in after years		
the then prime-minister (vgl. 258)		

. Shortness and Conciseness — Kürze und Gedrängtheit

Die große Zahl der einsilbigen germanischen Wörter, die durch den Verfall der Flexion entstanden sind, kommt dem Streben des Englischen nach Kürze entgegen: **"There is a homely strength in our wealth of monosyllables, in which no other European language approaches English" (*Dean Inge*).**

Dieselbe Kürze wird im Satz erreicht durch die Funktionsänderung von Wörtern, durch die oft eine große Einsparung von Wörtern erreicht wird:

to mushroom	wie Pilze aus der Erde schießen
his soldier son	sein in der Armee dienender Sohn

Die Verwendung der nominalen Verbformen (Infinitiv, Partizipien, Gerundium) im Satz führt zu einer sehr beträchtlichen Straffung des Satzbaus.

We did not know what to do.
I prefer people being silent.
You insulted your friend by not coming.

3. Analytic Character — Analytischer Charakter

Das Altenglische war eine synthetische Sprache, d. h. die grammatischen Beziehungen und Verhältnisse wurden durch Endungen zum Ausdruck gebracht. Im Laufe der Sprachentwicklung sind die Flexionsendungen bis auf wenige Reste (die Genitiv-Endung *'s*, das Plural-s, die Personalendung in der 3. Person Singular des Präsens *-(e)s*, die Tempus-Endung *-ed*, die Partizip-Endungen *-ed* und *-ing*) geschwunden. Nach dem Abfall der Endungen wurden die meisten nominalen und verbalen Begriffsbestimmungen (Kasus, Modi, Tempora usw.) durch (analytische) Umschreibungen ausgedrückt. Die Hilfsmittel hierzu sind Präpositionen, die Hilfsverben und die Wortstellung.

Prepositions — Präpositionen

Im Englischen haben die Präpositionen die Kasusendungen fast vollständig verdrängt[1]. Die einzigen Reste sind der "*Possessive Case*" (vgl. 49 ff.) und das unbezeichnete indirekte Objekt (vgl. 213).

I went to the garden,
I went into the garden.
I walked in the garden.

to look after	to look at
to look for	to look on
to look to	to look up

Die Präpositionen bringen eine Beziehung klarer und anschaulicher zum Ausdruck; daher nehmen sie dauernd an Bedeutung zu.
Auch in enger Verbindung mit Verben haben die Präpositionen Verwendung gefunden und zur Bedeutungsänderung geführt.

Auxiliary Verbs — Hilfsverben

Seit dem Verfall der Flexion dienen Hilfsverben zur Bezeichnung der Zeiten, der Handlungs- und Aussageformen. Durch die Verwendung der Hilfsverben verfügt das moderne Englisch über eine größere Zahl von Ausdrucksmöglichkeiten als das Altenglische.

I write,	I am writing,	I am going to write,
I do write,	I can write,	I may write,
I shall write,	I will write,	I am to write.

[1] Vgl. dieselbe Erscheinung im Deutschen: ich schreibe meinem Freund – ich schreibe an meinen Freund; das Haus meines Vaters – das Haus von meinem Vater.

Word Order — Wortstellung

Der Verfall der Flexion hat es weiter zur Folge gehabt, daß das Englische die freie Wortstellung des Altenglischen, in dem die Beziehungen im Satz durch die Endungen eindeutig bestimmt waren, aufgegeben hat und zur festen (gebundenen) Wortstellung übergegangen ist. Subjekt und direktes Objekt können nur durch die Stellung zum Prädikat unterschieden werden (vgl. 226).

4. Nominal Character — Nominaler Charakter

Das Englische hat eine Vorliebe für die nominalen Wortformen (Substantiv, Adjektiv, Pronomen), z. B. *to have breakfast*, *lunch*, *dinner* an Stelle von *to breakfast*, *to lunch*, *to dine*. Weitere Beispiele dieser Art sind:

to have a liking for	to give a welcome	to make arrangements
to have a smoke	to give a scolding	to make mention
to have a bad cold	to give thanks	to take care of
to have a look	to give credit to	to take a walk
to give offence	to make one's appearance	to take a drive
to give a sigh	to make one's escape	

5. Sobriety, Objective Character — Sachlichkeit, Objektiver Charakter

Der Engländer vermeidet es, seine Gefühle zu zeigen, und ist bestrebt, wie in seiner Sprechweise, so auch in seiner Ausdrucksweise sachlich, zurückhaltend und besonnen zu erscheinen. Dieses Maßhalten offenbart auch die Sprache: man sagt lieber zuwenig als zuviel (*understatement*). "*Isn't that fine?*" entspricht dem Deutschen „Oh, wie prachtvoll, wie entzückend!" "*She is rather good-looking,*" ist ein Lob, das im Deutschen „Sie ist bildhübsch" lauten würde. "*That's not so bad*" kommt dem Deutschen „Das ist sehr gut" gleich.

Das amerikanische Englisch[1]

Das Englisch Nordamerikas weicht nicht so wesentlich von dem Englands ab, daß man von einer selbständigen Sprache in den USA reden könnte. Eine „amerikanische Sprache" kann es schon deshalb nicht geben, weil neben der englischen in Nordamerika auch die spanische und andere Sprachen gesprochen werden.

The Historic Background — Der geschichtliche Hintergrund

Am Beginn der Besiedlung des neuen Landes bestand noch eine enge Abhängigkeit vom Mutterland England in jeder Beziehung, auch in geistiger und sprachlicher. Das eigentliche Bewußtsein, eine andere Sprache als die Englands zu sprechen, begann in Amerika erst während und nach der *American Revolution*. Thomas Jefferson wollte dieser Sprache einen anderen Namen als Englisch geben. Viele nationalbewußte Amerikaner nach ihm vertraten ähnliche Meinungen, bis dann Noah Webster[2] dieser Tendenz mit seinem großen und für die weitere Entwicklung des amerikanischen Englisch (AE) sehr bedeutsamen Lebenswerk Ausdruck gab. Man kämpfte nicht nur um die politische Unabhängigkeit von England, sondern ebenso sehr um die geistige Eigenstellung, die sich in dem Bemühen um eine Nationalliteratur, aber auch um eine vom englischen Vorbild unabhängige Sprache niederschlug: "*A national language is a band of national union . . .*", wie Webster sagte.

Drei große Wellen von europäischen Einwanderern sind zu unterscheiden: die erste begann, als 1607 Jamestown gegründet wurde. 1620 landete die Mayflower an der atlantischen Küste. Die ersten Einwanderer waren größtenteils englischer Herkunft: sie stammten vielfach aus der Nähe Londons und gehörten vornehmlich den unteren Bevölkerungsschichten an. Um 1790, mit dem Ende der Kolonialzeit in Nordamerika, kam diese Bewegung zum Abschluß.

Die zweite Besiedlungswelle erstreckte sich bis etwa 1860, also bis zur Ausdehnung der dreizehn alten Kolonialstaaten. Die primär wegen der schlechten Kartoffelernten 1845 bis 1847 nach Amerika ausgewanderten Iren und die wegen der politischen Ereignisse um das Jahr 1848 emigrierten Deutschen bildeten das Hauptkontingent dieser Siedler.

Mit der dritten Einwanderungswelle nach dem amerikanischen Bürgerkrieg (*Civil War*) kamen besonders Südeuropäer und Slawen in die neue Welt. Seit den zwanziger Jahren wurde die Einwanderung staatlich gesteuert.

[1] Nach Broder Carstensen, „Amerikanisches Englisch", in „Amerikakunde", Diesterweg, Frankfurt, 4. neubearb. Auflage 1964.

[2] Noah Webster (1758–1843), amerikanischer Philologe und Journalist; Verfasser des '*American Dictionary*'

Die Westwanderung der neuen Siedler begann, als 1803 das Gebiet westlich des Mississippi von Frankreich an den Präsidenten Jefferson verkauft wurde. Die Ausdehnung nach Westen brachte die große Völkerwanderung der neuen Bewohner des Landes, die bis zur Mitte des 19. Jahrhunderts das ehemals spanische Kolonisationsgebiet erobert hatten. Nevada, Colorado, die Dakotas, Montana usw. wurden später amerikanisch; hier war der Widerstand der Indianer am größten.

Language and History — Sprache und Geschichte

Die Einwanderer der frühen Zeit brachten Elisabethanisches Englisch mit nach Amerika: Shakespeare und seine Zeitgenossen waren auf dem Höhepunkt ihrer Laufbahn, als die englischen und schottisch-irischen Immigranten in Amerika eine neue Heimat suchten. Sie bewahrten anfangs ihre sprachlichen Eigenarten, aber als sie sich dann mit den Gegebenheiten des neuen Landes auseinandersetzen und sich fremder sprachlicher Einflüsse (etwa der Form des Englischen, das die eingewanderten Skandinavier, Holländer, Deutschen usw. unter teilweiser Beibehaltung heimischer Laute und Formen sprachen) erwehren mußten, kam es zu Verschiebungen innerhalb der englischen Sprache. Daß dennoch nur geringfügige Einwirkungen dieser europäischen Sprachen auf das Kommunikationsmittel des neuen Landes zu verzeichnen sind, lag an der großen Zahl der Einwanderer aus dem gesamtbritischen Sprachgebiet.

General Characteristics of American English — Allgemeine Kennzeichen des amerikanischen Englisch

Folgende Grundzüge, die für alle sprachlichen Erscheinungen, besonders aber den Wortschatz, des amerikanischen Englisch gelten, sind deutlich:

1. Der bewahrende Zug. Eine ganze Reihe archaisierender Züge des AE sind bis heute aufgezeigt worden. Das AE bewahrt in reichem Maße ältere Züge des Standard-BE, die z. T. schon von den frühesten Einwanderern mitgebracht worden waren. Das AE *I guess* (für BE *I think*) ist schon in der Sprache Chaucers zu finden und noch im England des 17. Jahrhunderts gang und gäbe. Das AE *fall* für BE *autumn* ist ein altes englisches Wort. *sick* wird heute in Amerika auch prädikativ verwendet, während *to be sick* im BE mit *to vomit* synonym ist. Das AE vertritt auch hier die ältere englische Bedeutung, die im heutigen BE verlorengegangen ist. Als Fazit bleibt, daß das AE oft die ältere Sprachstufe darstellt und manche Erscheinungen bewahrt, die aus dem Standard-BE verschwunden sind. Es darf allerdings nicht übersehen werden, daß das AE neben dieser „altertümelnden“ auch die gegenteilige Tendenz aufweist, die „fortschrittliche“.

2. Das „fortschrittliche" Englisch. Das AE scheint auch in dieser Beziehung besonders produktiv, „fortschrittlich", unbekümmert und spielerisch zu verfahren. Daß das AE mehr Elemente aus fremden Sprachen aufgenommen hat, scheint angesichts der historischen Rolle der USA als Schmelztiegel vieler Nationen nur natürlich. Es ist dabei sehr schwierig, fast unmöglich, zu sagen, was unter „fortschrittlich" zu verstehen ist. Das AE-Wort ist häufig kürzer, ausdrucksvoller, und in manchen Fällen füllt es eine bestehende Lücke aus (vgl. *to debunk* „entlarven" oder *to razz* „ausschimpfen, verhöhnen".

3. Das „kühnere" Englisch. Im Zusammenhang mit der Tendenz, das „fortschrittlichere" Englisch zu sein, verdient eine andere Erscheinung des AE Beachtung: die kühnen, manchmal bizarren und grotesken Bildungen, die z. T. ihren Ursprung in der Zeit der großen Westwanderung der Amerikaner haben und auf literarischem Gebiet in der *tall tale*, der übertreibenden Erzählung, ihre Parallele finden. Heute bedient sich besonders die Reklamesprache dieses Mittels.

Aus der Mitte des vorigen Jahrhunderts stammen solche Wortungetüme wie *rambunctious* „wild, polternd", *caboodle* „Kram, Zeug" und *highfalutin* [ˈhaifəˈluːtin] „bombastisch"; ferner Wendungen wie *to work like a beaver* „tüchtig arbeiten", *to bark up the wrong tree* „an die falsche Adresse geraten, auf dem Holzweg sein" und *to kick the bucket* „sterben". Die Reklamesprache erfand solche bizarren Bildungen wie *fabuluscious* (*fabulous* und *luscious*); ähnlich gebildet sind: *deluscious* und *fantabulastic.*

4. Das einheitlichere Englisch. Dem BE gegenüber fällt die größere Einheitlichkeit des AE auf. Die Dialekte Amerikas sind einander ähnlicher als die z. T. erheblich voneinander abweichenden englischen. Der Unterschied zwischen der Sprache der Gebildeten und den niederen Sprachschichten ist in Amerika geringer. Das Aufsteigen eines *Slang*-Wortes in das *Colloquial* ist in den USA leichter möglich. Die Massenmedien wie Film, Fernsehen und Radio haben erheblich dazu beigetragen, ein engeres sprachliches Band um Amerika zu legen, als das bis zum 20. Jahrhundert der Fall war. (Vgl. 29, *The Pronunciation of American English*)

Verbs with Exceptional Forms

Verben mit besonderen Formen

Die folgende alphabetische Aufzählung der Verben mit besonderen Formen umfaßt
a) alle unregelmäßigen Verben der schwachen Konjugation (durch * gekennzeichnet);
b) alle Verben der starken Konjugation.
Alle kursiv gesetzten Verben kommen nicht sehr häufig vor.
(R) bedeutet: Verbform kann auch mit *-ed* gebildet werden.

Infinitive Present Tense		Past Tense		Past Participle		
(to) abide△	[ai]	*abode* (R)	[əu]	*abode* (R)	[əu]	*bleiben, wohnen*
(to) arise	[ai]	arose	[əu]	arisen	[i]	sich erheben
to awake	[ei]	awoke (R)	[əu]	awoke (R)	[əu]	erwachen
to be	[iː]	was	[ɔ]	been	[iː]	sein
to bear	[ɛə]	bore	[ɔː]	borne (born)	[ɔː]	tragen (born = geboren)
to beat	[iː]	beat	[iː]	beaten	[iː]	schlagen
to become	[ʌ]	became	[ei]	become	[ʌ]	werden
to befall△	[ɔː]	*befell*	[e]	*befallen*	[ɔː]	*widerfahren*
to begin	[i]	began	[æ]	begun	[ʌ]	beginnen
to behold	[əu]	*beheld*	[e]	*beheld*	[e]	*erblicken*
* to bend	[e]	bent	[e]	bent	[e]	biegen, beugen
* *to bereave*	[iː]	*bereaved*	[iː]	*bereaved*	[iː]	*berauben*
		bereft	[e]	*bereft*	[e]	
* *to beseech*	[iː]	*besought*	[ɔː]	*besought*	[ɔː]	*ersuchen*
* *to beset*	[e]	*beset*	[e]	*beset*	[e]	*besetzen, einschließen*
* to bet	[e]	bet, betted	[e]	bet, betted	[e]	wetten
to betake	[ei]	*betook*	[u]	*betaken*	[ei]	*(sich) begeben*
to bethink△	[i]	*bethought*	[ɔː]	*bethought*	[ɔː]	*(sich) besinnen auf*
to bid	[i]	bade, bid	[ei]	bidden, bid	[i]	gebieten, lassen
to bind	[ai]	bound	[au]	bound	[au]	binden
to bite	[ai]	bit	[i]	bitten (bit)	[i]	beißen
* to bleed	[iː]	bled	[e]	bled	[e]	bluten
to blow	[əu]	blew	[uː]	blown	[əu]	wehen, blasen
to break	[ei]	broke	[əu]	broken	[əu]	brechen
* to breed	[iː]	bred	[e]	bred	[e]	züchten, aufziehen
* to bring	[i]	brought	[ɔː]	brought	[ɔː]	bringen
* to broadcast	[ɑː]	broadcast	[ɑː]	broadcast	[ɑː]	durch Rundfunk senden
* to build	[i]	built	[i]	built	[i]	bauen
* to burn	[əː]	burnt (R)	[əː]	burnt (burned)	[əː]	brennen
* to burst	[əː]	burst	[əː]	burst	[əː]	bersten, platzen
* to buy	[ai]	bought	[ɔː]	bought	[ɔː]	kaufen
* to cast	[ɑː]	cast	[ɑː]	cast	[ɑː]	werfen
* to catch	[æ]	caught	[ɔː]	caught	[ɔː]	fangen
to chide△	[ai]	*chided, chid*	[ai] [i]	*chided, chidden, chid*	[ai] [i]	*schelten*

	to choose	[uː]	chose	[əu]	chosen	[əu]	wählen
	to cleave△	[iː]	*clove*	[əu]	*cloven*	[əu]	*spalten*
			cleft	[e]	*cleft*	[e]	
	to cling	[i]	clung	[ʌ]	clung	[ʌ]	festhalten
	to come	[ʌ]	came	[ei]	come	[ʌ]	kommen
*	to cost	[ɔ]	cost	[ɔ]	cost	[ɔ]	kosten
*	to creep	[iː]	crept	[e]	crept	[e]	kriechen
*	to cut	[ʌ]	cut	[ʌ]	cut	[ʌ]	schneiden
*	to deal	[iː]	dealt	[e]	dealt	[e]	handeln
	to dig	[i]	dug	[ʌ]	dug	[ʌ]	graben
	to do	[uː]	did	[i]	done	[ʌ]	tun
	to draw	[ɔː]	drew	[uː]	drawn	[ɔː]	ziehen; zeichnen
*	to dream	[iː]	dreamt (R)	[e]	dreamt (R)	[e]	träumen
	to drink	[i]	drank	[æ]	drunk	[ʌ]	trinken
	to drive	[ai]	drove	[əu]	driven	[i]	treiben, fahren
*	to dwell	[e]	dwelt	[e]	dwelt	[e]	wohnen
	to eat	[iː]	ate	[e]	eaten	[iː]	essen
	to fall	[ɔː]	fell	[e]	fallen	[ɔː]	fallen
*	to feed	[iː]	fed	[e]	fed	[e]	füttern, sich nähren
*	to feel	[iː]	felt	[e]	felt	[e]	(sich) fühlen
	to fight	[ai]	fought	[ɔː]	fought	[ɔː]	kämpfen
	to find	[ai]	found	[au]	found	[au]	finden
*	to flee	[iː]	fled	[e]	fled	[e]	fliehen
	to fling	[i]	flung	[ʌ]	flung	[ʌ]	schleudern, werfen
	to fly	[ai]	flew	[uː]	flown	[əu]	fliegen
	to forbear△	[ɛə]	*forbore*	[ɔː]	*forborne*	[ɔː]	*sich enthalten*
	to forbid	[i]	forbade	[ei]	forbidden	[i]	verbieten
			forbad	[æ]			
*	to forecast	[ɑː]	forecast	[ɑː]	forecast	[ɑː]	(Wetter) voraussagen
	to forget	[e]	forgot	[ɔ]	forgotten	[ɔ]	vergessen
	to forgive	[i]	forgave	[ei]	forgiven	[i]	vergeben
	to forsake	[ei]	*forsook*	[u]	*forsaken*	[ei]	*aufgeben*
	to freeze	[iː]	froze	[əu]	frozen	[əu]	gefrieren
	to get	[e]	got	[ɔ]	got, *AE* gotten	[ɔ]	werden, bekommen
*	*to gild*	[i]	*gilded, gilt*	[i]	*gilded, gilt*	[i]	*vergolden*
*	*to gird*△	[əː]	*girded, girt*	[əː]	*girded, girt*	[əː]	*(um)gürten*
	to give	[i]	gave	[ei]	given	[i]	geben
	to go	[əu]	went	[e]	gone	[ɔ]	gehen
	to grind	[ai]	ground	[au]	ground	[au]	mahlen
	to grow	[əu]	grew	[uː]	grown	[əu]	wachsen, werden
	to hang	[æ]	hung	[ʌ]	hung	[ʌ]	hängen, aufhängen
			hanged		hanged		(er)hängen, henken
*	to have	[æ]	had	[æ]	had	[æ]	haben
*	to hear	[iə]	heard	[əː]	heard	[əː]	hören
	to hide	[ai]	hid	[i]	hidden (hid)	[i]	verbergen
*	to hit	[i]	hit	[i]	hit	[i]	treffen
	to hold	[əu]	held	[e]	held	[e]	halten
*	to hurt	[əː]	hurt	[əː]	hurt	[əː]	verletzen

* to keep	[iː]	kept	[e]	kept	[e]	halten
* to kneel	[iː]	knelt	[e]	knelt	[e]	knien
* to knit	[i]	knitted, knit		knitted, knit		stricken
to know	[əu]	knew	[uː]	known	[əu]	wissen
to lade	[ei]	*laded*	[ei]	*laden, laded*	[ei]	*laden*
* to lay	[ei]	laid	[ei]	laid	[ei]	legen
* to lead	[iː]	led	[e]	led	[e]	führen
* to lean	[iː]	leant (R)	[e]	leant (R)	[e]	lehnen
* to leap	[iː]	leapt (R)	[e]	leapt (R)	[e]	springen
* to learn	[əː]	learnt (R)		learnt (R)	[əː]	lernen
* to leave	[iː]	left	[e]	left	[e]	verlassen
* to lend	[e]	lent	[e]	lent	[e]	leihen
* to let	[e]	let	[e]	let	[e]	(zu)lassen
to lie	[ai]	lay	[ei]	lain	[ei]	liegen
* to light	[ai]	lighted, lit	[ai], [i]	lighted, lit	[ai], [i]	anzünden
* to lose	[uː]	lost	[ɔ]	lost	[ɔ]	verlieren
* to make	[ei]	made	[ei]	made	[ei]	machen
* to mean	[iː]	meant	[e]	meant	[e]	bedeuten, wollen
* to meet	[iː]	met	[e]	met	[e]	treffen, begegnen
to mistake	[ei]	mistook	[u]	mistaken	[ei]	verwechseln, mißverstehen
to mow	[əu]	*mowed*	[əu]	*mown*	[əu]	*mähen*
to overcome	[ʌ]	overcame	[ei]	overcome	[ʌ]	überwältigen
to partake	[ei]	*partook*	[u]	*partaken*	[ei]	*teilnehmen*
* to pay	[ei]	paid	[ei]	paid	[ei]	bezahlen
* to put	[u]	put	[u]	put	[u]	setzen, stellen, legen
* to read	[iː]	read	[e]	read	[e]	lesen
* *to rend*	[e]	*rent*	[e]	*rent*	[e]	*zerreißen*
* *to rid*	[i]	*rid*	[i]	*rid*	[i]	*befreien*
to ride	[ai]	rode	[əu]	ridden	[i]	reiten, fahren
to ring	[i]	rang	[æ]	rung	[ʌ]	läuten
to rise	[ai]	rose	[əu]	risen	[i]	aufstehen, aufgehen (Gestirne)
to run	[ʌ]	ran	[æ]	run	[ʌ]	laufen
to saw	[ɔː]	sawed	[ɔː]	sawn (R)	[ɔː]	sägen
* to say	[ei]	said	[e]	said	[e]	sagen
to see	[iː]	saw	[ɔː]	seen	[iː]	sehen
* to seek	[iː]	sought	[ɔː]	sought	[ɔː]	suchen
* to sell	[e]	sold	[əu]	sold	[əu]	verkaufen
* to send	[e]	sent	[e]	sent	[e]	senden, schicken
* to set	[e]	set	[e]	set	[e]	setzen; untergehen (Gestirne)
to sew	[əu]	sewed	[əu]	sewn (R)	[əu]	nähen
to shake	[ei]	shook	[u]	shaken	[ei]	schütteln
to shear	[iə]	*sheared*	[iə]	*shorn*	[ɔː]	*scheren*
		shore	[ɔː]	*sheared*	[iə]	
* to shed	[e]	shed	[e]	shed	[e]	vergießen
to shine	[ai]	shone	[ɔ]	shone	[ɔ]	scheinen (Sonne)
* *to shoe*	[uː]	*shod*	[ɔ]	*shod*	[ɔ]	*beschuhen, beschlagen*
to shoot	[uː]	shot	[ɔ]	shot	[ɔ]	schießen
to show	[əu]	showed	[əu]	shown (R)	[əu]	zeigen

to shrink	[i]	shrank, shrunk	[æ] [ʌ]	shrunk	[ʌ]	schrumpfen
* to shut	[ʌ]	shut	[ʌ]	shut	[ʌ]	schließen
to sing	[i]	sang	[æ]	sung	[ʌ]	singen
to sink	[i]	sank	[æ]	sunk	[ʌ]	sinken
to sit	[i]	sat	[æ]	sat	[æ]	sitzen
to slay	[ei]	*slew*	[uː]	*slain*	[ei]	*erschlagen*
* to sleep	[iː]	slept	[e]	slept	[e]	schlafen
to slide	[ai]	*slid*	[i]	*slid, slidden*	[i]	*gleiten, schleifen*
to sling	[i]	*slung*	[ʌ]	*slung*	[ʌ]	*schleudern*
to slink	[i]	*slunk*	[ʌ]	*slunk*	[ʌ]	*schleichen*
* to slit	[i]	slit	[i]	slit	[i]	schlitzen
* to smell	[e]	smelt (R)	[e]	smelt (R)	[e]	riechen
to smite△	[ai]	*smote*	[əu]	*smitten*	[i]	*treffen, schlagen*
to sow	[əu]	sowed	[əu]	sown (R)	[əu]	säen
to speak	[iː]	spoke	[əu]	spoken	[əu]	sprechen
* to speed	[iː]	sped (R)	[e]	sped (R)	[e]	eilen, sich sputen
* to spell	[e]	spelt (R)	[e]	spelt (R)	[e]	buchstabieren
* to spend	[e]	spent	[e]	spent	[e]	(Geld) ausgeben; Zeit verbringen
* to spill	[i]	spilt (R)	[i]	spilt (R)	[i]	verschütten
to spin	[i]	spun, span	[ʌ], [æ]	spun	[ʌ]	spinnen
to spit	[i]	spat	[æ]	spat	[æ]	speien
* to split	[i]	split	[i]	split	[i]	spalten
* to spoil	[ɔi]	spoilt (R)	[ɔi]	spoilt (R)	[ɔi]	verderben
* to spread	[e]	spread	[e]	spread	[e]	verbreiten
to spring	[i]	sprang	[æ]	sprung	[ʌ]	springen
to stand	[æ]	stood	[u]	stood	[u]	stehen
to steal	[iː]	stole	[əu]	stolen	[əu]	stehlen
to stick	[i]	stuck	[ʌ]	stuck	[ʌ]	kleben; stecken
to sting	[i]	stung	[ʌ]	stung	[ʌ]	stechen
to stink	[i]	stank stunk	[æ] [ʌ]	stunk	[ʌ]	stinken
to strew	[uː]	strewed	[uː]	strewn (R)	[uː]	streuen
to stride	[ai]	strode	[əu]	stridden	[i]	schreiten
to strike	[ai]	struck	[ʌ]	struck	[ʌ]	schlagen
to string	[i]	*strung*	[ʌ]	*strung*	[ʌ]	*aufreihen*
to strive	[ai]	strove	[əu]	striven	[i]	streben
to swear	[εə]	swore	[ɔː]	sworn	[ɔː]	schwören
* to sweat	[e]	sweat (R)	[e]	sweat (R)	[e]	schwitzen
* to sweep	[iː]	swept	[e]	swept	[e]	fegen
to swell	[e]	swelled	[e]	swollen (R)	[əu]	schwellen
to swim	[i]	swam	[æ]	swum	[ʌ]	schwimmen
to swing	[i]	swung	[ʌ]	swung	[ʌ]	schwingen
to take	[ei]	took	[u]	taken	[ei]	nehmen
* to teach	[iː]	taught	[ɔː]	taught	[ɔː]	lehren
to tear	[εə]	tore	[ɔː]	torn	[ɔː]	zerreißen
* to tell	[e]	told	[əu]	told	[əu]	erzählen
* to think	[i]	thought	[ɔː]	thought	[ɔː]	denken

to thrive	[ai]	throve (R)	[əu]	thriven (R)	[i]	gedeihen
to throw	[əu]	threw	[uː]	thrown	[əu]	werfen
* to thrust	[ʌ]	thrust	[ʌ]	thrust	[ʌ]	stoßen
to tread	[e]	*trod*	[ɔ]	*trodden, trod*	[ɔ]	*treten*
to understand	[æ]	understood	[u]	understood	[u]	verstehen
to wake	[ei]	woke (R)	[əu]	woken (R)	[əu]	wachen
to wear	[εə]	wore	[ɔː]	worn	[ɔː]	(Kleidung) tragen
to weave	[iː]	wove	[əu]	woven	[əu]	weben
* to weep	[iː]	wept	[e]	wept	[e]	weinen
to win	[i]	won	[ʌ]	won	[ʌ]	gewinnen
to wind	[ai]	wound	[au]	wound	[au]	winden
to withdraw	[ɔː]	withdrew	[uː]	withdrawn	[ɔː]	(sich) zurückziehen
to withhold	[əu]	withheld	[e]	withheld	[e]	zurückhalten
to withstand	[æ]	withstood	[u]	withstood	[u]	widerstehen
* *to work*	[əː]	*wrought*	[ɔː]	*wrought*	[ɔː]	*bewirken*, (*geistig*) *ausarbeiten*
to wring	[i]	wrung	[ʌ]	wrung	[ʌ]	(Hände) ringen, (Wäsche) auswringen
to write	[ai]	wrote	[əu]	written	[i]	schreiben

Wort- und Sachregister

Die Zahlen beziehen sich auf die Abschnitte der Grammatik.

Abkürzungen: Not. = Notice K. i. M. = Keep in Mind

A

B

C

D

E

H

I

J

K

N

O

S

W

Y

Z

1/987 654 321